THE LEGACY OF OPHELIA

THE CURSE OF OPHELIA

BOOK FIVE

NICOLE PLATANIA

BOOKS BY NICOLE PLATANIA

The Curse of Ophelia Series

The Curse of Ophelia

The Shards of Ophelia

The Trials of Ophelia

The Breaker of Stars (A novella)

The Myths of Ophelia

The Legacy of Ophelia

The Fatesworn Saga (Book 1 Coming 2026)

The *Legacy* of Ophelia

Nicole Platania

*To those who always give pieces of themselves to others.
You are your own, in every way.*

Author's Note

This book contains depictions of mental/emotional abuse; drug use; grief; loss of a loved one; blood, gore, and violence; discussion of assault; torture; PTSD; and some sexual content. If any of these may be triggering for you, please read carefully or feel free to contact the author for further explanation.

GALLANTIA
AMBRISK
CAPRECION
VALYN
LUMIN LAKE
SPIRIT VOLCANO
TUNDRA
MYSTIQUE TERRITORIES
WILD PLAINS
STARSEARCHERS
TURREN
CASTANI
DAMENAL
SOLISTINE RIVER
PALERMAN
CLIFFS OF BRONTAIN
OUTPOST
XENOVIA
SOULGUIDERS
THE LENDELL HILLS
SOUTHERN PASS
BODYMELDERS
FIREBIRD FIELD
PTHOLE
FRAUGHTEN
THORENTIL
MINDSHAPERS
WAR BORDER
LYTAR TRENCH
GENNIUM FOREST
SEA WATCHERS
RIVER
GAVERAL
SEA WATCHERS
ENGROSSIAN TERRITORIES
BANIX

Pronunciation Guide
Characters who are crossed out were deceased prior to the beginning of The Legacy of Ophelia.

Mystique Warriors

Ophelia Alabath (she/her), Mystique Revered: *Oh-feel-eeya Tuh-vahn-yuh Al-uh-bath*

Malakai Blastwood (he/him): *Mal-uh-kye Uh-gus-tus Blast-wood*

Tolek Vincienzo (he/him): *Tole-ick Vin-chin-zoh*

Cypherion Kastroff (he/him), Mystique Second: *Sci-fear-ee-on Cast-Rahf*

Jezebel Alabath (she/her): *Jez-uh-bell Al-uh-bath*

Akalain Blastwood (she/her): *Ah-kuh-lane Blast-wood*

~~Alvaron (he/him), Master of Coin: *Al-vuh-ron*~~

~~Annellius Alabath, (he/him): *Uh-nell-ee-us Al-uh-bath*~~

~~Bacaran Alabath (he/him), Second to the Revered: *Bah-kuh-ron Al-uh-bath*~~

~~Collins (he/him): *Call-ins*~~

~~Danya (she/her), Master of Weapons & Warfare: *Dawn-yuh*~~

~~Larcen (he/him), Master of Trade: *Lare-sen*~~

~~Lucidius Blastwood (he/him), Revered: *Loo-sid-ee-yus Blast-wood*~~

~~Lyria Vincienzo (she/her), Master of Weapons and
Warfare: *Leer-ee-uh Vin-chin-zoh*~~
Marxian (he/him): *Mark-shen*
Mila Lovall (she/her), Mystique General: *Mee-lah
Love-all*
Missyneth (she/her), Master of Rites: *Mis-sin-ith*
Tavania Alabath (she/her): *Tuh-vahn-yuh Al-uh-
bath*
Willox (he/him): *Will-ox*

Engrossian Warriors

~~Kakias (she/her), Engrossian Queen: *Kuh-kye-yus*~~
Barrett (he/him), Engrossian Prince: *Bair-it*
Dax (he/him), Engrossian General: *Dax*
~~Victious: *Vik-shuss*~~
Nassik Langswoll (he/him), councilman: *Nuh-seek
Lang-swall*
Pelvira (she/her), councilwoman: *Pell-veer-uh*
Elvek (he/him), councilman: *El-vick*
Celissia Langswoll, (she/her), councilwoman: *Sell-
ee-see-uh Lang-swall*

Mindshapers

~~Aird (he/him), Mindshaper Chancellor: *Air-d*~~
Ricordan (he/him): *Rik-kor-din*
Trevaneth (he/him): *Treh-vuh-neh-th*
Sandretta (she/her): *San-drehtt-uh*
Oudry (they/them): *Aw-dree*
Zaina (she/her): *Zay-nuh*

Bodymelders

Brigiet (she/her), Bodymelder Chancellor: *Bri-jeet*
Esmond (he/him), apprentice: *Ez-min-d*
Gatrielle (he/him), allure: *Gah-tree-elle*

Starsearchers

~~Titus Verian (he/him), Starsearcher Chancellor:~~
~~*Tie-tuhs Vair-ee-on*~~
Vale (she/her), apprentice: *Veil*
Cyren (they/them), Starsearcher General: *Sci-ren*
Harlen (he/him): *Har-lin*

Seawatchers

Ezalia Ridgebrook (she/her), Seawatcher Chancel-
lor: *Eh-zale-ee-uh Ridg-brook*
Amara Ridgebrook (she/her), Seawatcher General:
Uh-mar-uh Ridg-brook
~~Andrenas (they/them): *An-dreh-nuss*~~
~~Chorid (he/him): *Core-ihd*~~
Leo (he/him): *Lee-oh*
Seron Ridgebrook (he/him): *Sair-on Ridg-brook*
Seli Ridgebrook (she/her): *Sell-ee Ridg-brook*
Auggie Ridgebrook (he/him): *Aw-ghee Ridg-brook*

Soulguiders

Meridat (she/her), Soulguider Chancellor: *Mare-
ih-daat*
Erista Locke (she/her), apprentice: *Eh-ris-tuh Lock*
Quilian Locke (he/him), Soulguider General:
Quil-ee-en Lock

Non-warrior characters

Santorina Cordelian (she/her), human: *San-tor-ee-
nuh Kor-dee-lee-in*
Aimee (she/her), Storyteller: *Ay-me*
Arenothos (he/him), Fate: *Are-ren-aw-those*
Lancaster (he/him), fae: *Lan-kaster*
Lislee (she/her), Human Commander: *Liss-lee*

Mora (she/her), fae: *Mor-uh*
~~Brystin (he/him), fae: *Brih-stin*~~
~~Ritalia (she/her), Queen of the Fae: *Rih-tall-ee-uh*~~
Rozelyn (she/her), other: *Rawz-lyn*
Salteaire (she/her), other: *Saul-tair*
Meghalle (she/her), other: *Meg-all*
Vaneiare (she/her), other: *Van-air*

Animals and Creatures

Astania, *Uh-ston-ya*
Calista: *Kuh-liss-tuh*
Elektra: *Ill-ectra*
Erini: *Ih-ree-nee*
Hythana: *Hi-thaw-nuh*
Ombratta: *Ahm-brah-tuh*
Sapphire: *Sah-fire*
Rebel: *Reh-bull*
Zanox: *Zaw-nox*
Dynaxtar: *Die-nahx-tar*

Places

Ambrisk: *Am-brisk*
Banix: *Ban-ix*
Brontain: *Brawn-tane*
Caprecion: *Kuh-pree-shun*
Damenal: *Dom-in-all*
Fytar Trench: *Fie-tar Trehn-ch*
Gallantia: *Guh-lawn-shuh*
Gaveral: *Gav-er-all*
Lendelli: *Len-del-ee*
Lumin: *Loo-min*
Palerman: *Powl-er-min*
Pthole: *Tholl*
Thorentil: *Thor-in-till*
Turren: *Tur-in*

Valyn: *Val-in*
Vercuella: *Vair-kwella*
Xenovia: *Zin-oh-vee-yuh*

Angels of the Gallantian Warriors

Bant (he/him), Prime Engrossian Warrior: *Bant*
Damien (he/him), Prime Mystique Warrior: *Day-mee-in*
Gaveny (he/him), Prime Seawatcher: *Gav-in-ee*
Ptholenix (he/him), Prime Bodymelder: *Tholl-en-icks*
Thorn (he/him), Prime Mindshaper: *Thorn*
Valyrie (she/her), Prime Starsearcher: *Val-er-ee*
Xenique (she/her), Prime Soulguider: *Zen-eek*

Gods of Ambrisk's Pantheon

Aoiflyn (she/her), The Fae Goddess: *Eef-lyn*
Artale (she/her), The Goddess of Death: *Are-tall*
Echnid (he/him), The Warrior God: *Eck-nihd*
Gerenth (he/him), The God of Nature: *Gair-inth*
Lynxenon (he/him), The God of Mythical Beasts: *Leen-zih-non*
Moirenna (she/her), The Goddess of Fate & Celestial Movements: *Moy-ren-uh*
Thallia (she/her), The Witch Goddess of Sorcia: *Thall-ee-uh*

PART ONE
PTHOLENIX

Chapter One
Tolek

The needle stung, biting into my flesh.

Not hard enough. It wasn't piercing down to my soul like I wanted it to—it wasn't going deep enough to dig up the grief, to turn it inside out and replace that aching echo of loss with any sort of feeling. I wanted the pain, but I'd settle for emptiness. Which would have been fair considering the vacant space behind my ribs, a hole taking up residence where my heart had been.

The metal worktable was ice cold against my bare chest, but even that didn't bite hard enough.

The rhythmic buzz of the mystlight-fueled needle droned on, my back and shoulders stiffening from hours in this prone position. My muscles cramped, protesting. When that twinging pain wrung my shoulder, I balled my hands at my sides. The needle paused.

"Need a break?" the artist asked.

"No."

"Tolek," Cypherion warned, "maybe you should finish another day."

I lifted my head from the cushion, just enough that I didn't pinch the piece currently being inked into my back. Pale mystlight flashed over CK's face from a half-lit orb dangling in the corner of the parlor. It illuminated the dark circles beneath his eyes, his tight expression as he leaned against the wall, arms crossed.

"No," I repeated.

He contemplated arguing, holding my stare firmly before finally dropping his to the chipped tile floor. The swirling, muddy red and cream pattern swam in my dazed vision.

I turned my cheek back to the cushion, and the needle resumed. Staring at the wall, I relished what little pain rippled through my flesh.

"Stop trying to persuade him. He's going to do what he wants," Jezebel muttered to Cyph, not judgmentally.

"It's unhealthy," CK retorted, voice tired.

Vale's soothing tone was a whisper against the monotonous buzz. "He's suffered a tremendous loss."

"Losses," Jezebel corrected, ice in Baby Alabath's words. She'd suffered, too.

Cypherion grunted in agreement. "How's Mila today?"

"Much the same," Vale answered, her voice coming from further away as she trailed circles around the parlor to appease the rush of magic that had been beneath her skin since the mountains. The Starseacher Angel, Valyrie, had called her a Fatecatcher—whatever that meant. "She's been with Erista and Santorina all day."

Jezebel cleared her throat at the mention of her partner, the betrayal still sinking in that Erista had suspected secrets about Jez's life since they met. At the reminder, resentment in her honor pumped my blood faster, looking for any injustice to latch on to.

Cypherion and Vale switched to hushed whispers about some other diplomatic endeavor they'd been managing since Ophelia and Malakai had been taken.

Taken.

By an Angelsdamned god.

Echnid, the Warrior God who should have never existed, the one Ophelia freed by returning the Angel emblems to their statue in the heart of the mountains and splashing her Angel-cursed blood and magic across it. The god flashed through my mind with a cruel, milky-white smile, and my fists clenched again.

This time, the tattoo artist didn't pause. As the image of the god rooted itself in my memory, I sank into the monotony of the needle and studied the parlor.

In typical Soulguider fashion, the maroon patterned walls were covered with bronze frames inlaid with jewels—probably fake judging by the sparse state of the room and their dull shine—and displaying various artworks patrons could choose from. Most featured crescent moons and skulls, scythes and artistic swords. Legends of the deserts and Goddess of Death along with her demigod daughter and Soulguider Angel, Xenique, were portrayed in a life-size rendition on one wall.

"Her expression is wrong," I muttered.

"What's that?" the tattoo artist asked, pausing briefly to glance at the painting.

"Xenique," I confirmed. "It's wrong."

Cypherion's and Vale's conversation cut off. Jezebel drifted to stand by my head, studying the rendition of the Angel. Her ancestor. This damned demigoddess was Ophelia and Jezebel's ancestor and had birthed Godsblood into their mother's line, suppressing it for millennia to hide her descendants. It had been that Godsblood that caused the Angelcurse to surface in Ophelia.

That Godsblood that resulted in all of our suffering. In us hunting for the emblems.

In my sister being in the mountains the night she fell to the fae queen's knife.

The Angels were at fault for *all of this*. I hated every one of them. If Xenique had kept her Godsblood a secret, what else had she hidden from the warriors?

The artist's curiosity—at who we might be and what answers we may have—tensed between us filled the parlor with a beat of heavy silence.

Every warrior on Gallantia felt the return of their Angel to this realm when Ophelia freed them, but most hadn't figured out what that calamitous shift had been. And those who guessed couldn't know what it meant or that we had been present for it.

This man's stare flicked between us, but he bent down again, not asking anything else. We didn't offer.

But they *had* gotten Xenique's expression wrong. Each Angel of the Gallantian Warriors was burned into my brain: their colossal magic, eclipsing wings, and tangible thirst for freedom, all emboldening and threatening as they gasped down the air of their continent—the air fueled with the ether of their very core—after being imprisoned for millennia; their abundant, burning power after Ophelia replaced the emblems into their statues and bled on them, fulfilling the Angelcurse.

Tilting my chin up, I silently observed CK, who was studying the portrait of Xenique, too. Did he notice how her chin was slightly elongated and eyes much too narrow? That she was shrouded in a black cloak when the true being wore draping skirts as if she was one with her desert-bound warriors?

How did we end up here? How had I ended up anywhere these last three days?

All I could hear over and over again, even now with the needle buzzing, were my sister's dying words to me. The echo of her last breath rattling through her chest. And Ophelia screaming my name as the Warrior God grabbed her. As he pulled her through a veil in the air and *took her* to Spirits knew where.

As I failed both of them.

"Done," the artist said, stretching his hand after the hours we'd been here. He hadn't wanted to finish the piece in one sitting.

I didn't give him an option.

Skin tender, I sat up carefully, ignoring the Soulguider as he recited instructions for the care of the new tattoo. Instead, I crossed to a mirror in the corner while Cypherion and Vale noted the advice and collected the prescribed oils. I angled so the light caught the glimmering ink.

Jezebel stepped to my shoulder, eyes locked on my tattoo in the mirror. "It's beautiful," she claimed, ghosts in her stare.

"It's perfect," I agreed.

An unfurling pair of wings spanned my back, wrapping around my shoulders and ribs. They were incredibly detailed, down to the last feather. And near the top arch, aligned with the curve of the left wing between my shoulder blade and spine, were the words *I love you, baby brother*, the script taken from one of Lyria's letters to me.

Red skin kissed the edges of the gold ink, soreness blistering through my muscles with each flex.

But I relished the hurt.

Finally. Something worn and worthy of how I felt on the inside. Something that woke against the drowning grief and guilt. The pain clawed at my vacant self the way only haunted memories could.

You should have saved them both.

Lyria did not deserve to die.

Ophelia trusted you to scorch the Angels with her.

On the accusations went, until the voices in the back of the parlor pierced through.

"Yes?" I interrupted.

In the mirror, Vale's gaze sliced to mine. "The meeting has begun."

I nodded. "Let's go."

Our Commander of Weapons and Warfare may have been killed, but vengeance for her loss was a map of my next steps. Our Revered may have been taken by a god, but I was promised to her for all the days to come, and I'd dive into the Spirit Volcano before I let her down again.

So, I turned, casting one last look at the wings in the mirror.

And this tattoo, this gold ink that now marked my skin for eternity, it was a symbol. A small piece of the promise of my sister's future taken too soon. Barely five words, but the only ones that mattered. A sign of the healing we'd undergone, the mountains we'd climbed to restore our relationship, and the vow I'd made to carry on her cause.

And the wings sprawling across my body were a promise reaching just as deep. Every line was a stamp of my allegiance to Ophelia—a seraph among warriors and a ruler among Angels—defining a love that would last just as long.

A reminder to anyone who saw it that I would tear every realm to shreds to get her back, gods and Angels be damned.

CHAPTER TWO
OPHELIA

EVERYTHING WAS ON FIRE.

The silk sheets beneath my cheek burned from the inferno my skin had become.

Outside the window, the clouds over the Mystique Mountains flamed with a setting sun. One pane of glass was shattered, but the peaks flickered red in my wavering vision. Where they'd once been my freedom, now, they were the sharpened teeth of a bared jaw threatening to swallow me whole.

The muscles along my back roared.

My wings—the glorious pair of wings that had broken through my flesh, feathers unfurling and bloodstained—sent waves of fire rolling along my body with every slight movement.

"Ophelia?"

Malakai. He had barely left my side since we landed in the Rapture Chamber of the Revered's Palace days ago. At least, I thought it had been days. I couldn't be sure with how I slipped in and out of consciousness. I remembered him tenderly cleaning what blood he could from my wings and back. Each moment had been excruciating, but Malakai had remained attentive.

He crouched before me now, blocking the flame-dancing mountain peaks from sight. Familiar green eyes swam in my vision.

"Are you awake?"

I wanted to answer, but my tongue stuck to the roof of my mouth, throat bone dry.

I wanted to answer, but it hurt.

It all *hurt* down to the very marrow of my bones, every drop of Godsblood and Angel-given-magic incinerating.

The worst pain of all was knowing I'd done this. I'd unleashed this plague on Ambrisk. I'd fallen for the trap the Warrior God and the Angels had laid by fulfilling the Angelcurse. I'd thought I'd been doing good for our warriors, but how could I have been if they'd taken Malakai and me? How could I have been if the Angels had attacked my friends as I left? How could I have been, with those malicious words Echnid had breathed when I asked him what he'd do next?

Now we get vengeance.

It clanged through my mind again and again, the bell a death toll.

And Tolek...he was out there, swimming through the grief of his sister without me. I'd promised her I'd take care of him, and yet within an hour of her death, I'd broken that vow.

My sister, Santorina, Cypherion...they were all facing the aftermath of fulfilling my prophecy. And I was drowning in fire, my spirit a crisped husk.

My body shivered involuntarily, sending my wings twitching. A cry wrenched up my throat at each tremble, fire licked along my flesh, and I thought my bones might crumble. Malakai placed a hand to his chest as if feeling it, too.

Used.

I'd been *so used*, my skin was foreign. My mind tainted.

The Angels, the gods, even the sphinx. They'd all used me to achieve their end. Used the blood I'd been born with and the prophecies I had no control over. Withheld information until the last possible moment. They'd preyed on my desire to restore the Mystiques after the first war against the Engrossians had ravaged our territory.

I'd been going over it in the moments I swam into consciousness, trying to piece it together, and each realization wrung my heart out more. Damien had given me that first prophecy on my twentieth birthday and led me to believe I'd be saving the

Mystiques. Back then, I'd have done anything to see my people return to true power. To reinstate the Undertaking and send our warriors on their rightful paths. To find Malakai.

Was it that determination that made me the perfect toy for the Angels? Or had the Spirits instilled that drive within me because they knew what prophecy would fall on my shoulders? Had the Fates guided me to it, or was it all inevitable?

No matter how it began, I was certain of one thing. The Angels had seen that eagerness—those desperate dreams—and they'd taken advantage of them.

My chest seized, a sob catching in my throat.

Never again.

I would not be their puppet. I would not condemn warriors to bend to the whims of gods who had abandoned us. I would not be weak in the face of their schemes.

"Malakai?" I croaked, fingers curling against the sweat-damp sheets. Angels, it hurt. Tears leaked from the corners of my eyes, and I gritted my teeth against the tremors seizing my muscles.

Malakai's breath shuddered, hands gripping the edge of the mattress. "Yeah, Phel?"

And as fire ravaged my body, as salty tears stained the bed, as a stray, sticky feather brushed my skin and my entire being flinched, I whispered, "I'm going to make them all burn."

Chapter Three
Malakai

"I'm going to make them all burn."

She could barely force the words out, but there was nothing but malice in Ophelia's croaking voice. And I swore Angellight flashed behind her vacant stare. A power so mighty, so Spirits-damned terrifying, it held the potential to incinerate the whole of Ambrisk.

And though Echnid was a god, though seven Angels roamed the halls of this palace under his thumb, there was such conviction in Ophelia's voice that I thought she just might turn them all to ash.

The door creaked open, but in her vengeful, fevered stupor, Ophelia didn't notice. I met a pair of glowing purple eyes through the crack, gold light filtering into the room from his powerful wings.

"Yeah, Ophelia," I agreed, holding Damien's stare over her body. "You fucking are."

"Damien," I whispered, less reverent than I once would have been.

I pulled the door to Ophelia's bedchamber against the frame, not shutting it all the way. She'd quickly fallen back asleep after I forced a few sips of water down her throat, but I wanted to be there when she woke again.

Plus, I didn't trust these fucking Angels to not flash into existence wherever they wanted, including her private quarters. At least the one before me now had the decency to use the door, even if he didn't bother to knock.

"Former heir," Damien greeted me.

I bit back a growl at the name. "What the fuck is happening to her?"

Damien's feathers ruffled, his chest heaving. "I do not know."

"What do—" I cut off my shout, peeking into Ophelia's room to make sure I hadn't woken her. She slept soundly, wings crimson-tinged and splayed on the bed beside her. I'd tried to clean them as best I could when we arrived—in the Revered's Palace of all places—but every touch had her crying out in agony until she'd fallen unconscious.

Tamping down my anger, I faced the Mystique Prime Warrior again. He stood with sandals on the marble floor, a sight that still took me by surprise every time one of these immortal bastards showed up. That they walked as mere warriors did, not always floating or beating those imposing wings through the halls, though, they certainly did that, too.

I took a breath. "What do you mean you don't know what's happening to her?"

"It is...unprecedented." His jaw ticked.

"She has *wings*," I hissed. "Of course, that is *unprecedented*, but what *do* you know?"

"Has the power slipped again?"

Again. Two nights ago, a flash of lightning had shot from Ophelia's body and splintered the window, wild and trying to escape. She hadn't even woken when it happened. If anything, she'd seemed to sleep more peacefully afterward.

"Stop avoiding my fucking questions," I growled, taking a step toward Damien.

"Stop avoiding mine, son of the valiant."

I ignored his twisted, purposeless titles. The Angels were as bad as the fae queen sometimes. "Last night. She had...I don't know, a nightmare or something. The entire room felt like it was on fire. And the light"—sweat beaded on my skin at the memory of the living inferno that had wrapped the walls—"oranges and reds, the very center bright blue."

"The Firebird," Damien muttered of the Bodymelder Angel, Ptholenix.

"I figured as much." I peeked through the crack in the door one more time, but Ophelia was still. Rubbing my hand against my sternum, I asked, "What does it mean?"

"It means she woke something much more powerful than we'd anticipated." His voice was as harsh as the lightning strike Ophelia had conjured, purple eyes darkening. "I believe it's because the blood of the demigoddess occurs naturally within her and mixed with Angelblood organically. Perhaps because the *fel strella mythos* amplifies that magic along with her ability to bring myths to life. Thorn felt it coming and reached into her mind to unlock the final power when we returned. But Ophelia is...well, we will see exactly how this plays out when she finally wakes."

"And how do you plan on getting her stable enough to wake?" She could barely keep water down, couldn't roll over without screaming in agony and tearing open the wounds along her back. My eyes dropped to my hands, the phantom stickiness of her blood coating my skin, though I'd scrubbed it raw.

Damien arched a brow. "That is my job?"

"This entire thing is your fault, Damien! She is your chosen— she only carries that prophecy because of you." I stepped up to the Prime Warrior, his power burning into me. "Do not fucking fail her!"

Damien's chest rose on a harsh breath, wings ruffling. I didn't know what nerve those words struck, but he whispered, "Give me time."

And then, as the Prime Warriors always did, Damien disappeared with no further explanation.

And I cursed the empty air before me, hoping Ophelia had time to give.

～

I only left Ophelia's suite a handful of times in the first five days since we arrived in Damenal, always down to the kitchens to gather provisions then quickly back up. Though I didn't know what one even fed someone who had recently undergone the emergence of a mythical creature within their own self.

I paused before the pantry, picking apart the scant shelves. And fuck me, I didn't know how to make anything with such few ingredients. Cold bread it was. At least I found a few options of jams and a lemon curd Ophelia liked. Maybe that would entice her to eat.

"Where the fuck is the staff?" I grumbled to myself as I climbed the stairs back to Ophelia's room, fresh sheets in a basket on my arm.

Originally, I'd thought Echnid had taken us to a different realm entirely when he ripped that tear in the air in the cavern, but we were absolutely in the mountains. Damenal unraveled beyond the windows, warriors hurrying through the streets beneath the gray clouds. The palace was just fucking *empty*. Every room I'd looked into had a cold hearth and grate no more than ashes, beds half-made and candles down to the wick, as if they'd been left to burn.

When we'd first moved here following my imprisonment, we'd made a point to hire ample staff. To help funnel money back into Damenal's economy. Where had they all gone?

I didn't have time to figure it out, and I shoved down the concern as I rounded the corner to Ophelia's corridor. I needed to focus all of my attention on helping her right now, but—

A gold glow flooded the doorway to Ophelia's bedchamber before I even crossed the foyer.

"By the fucking Angels," I yelled, dumping the tray and fresh sheets on the entry table and rushing inside. Had she woken?

But it wasn't Ophelia emitting the Angellight.

Damien stood at her bedside, purple stare trained on Ophelia's limp form. She was sprawled on her back, her wings beneath her at an unnatural angle and hair splayed across the rumpled sheets. A swirl of powerful light concentrated in Damien's palm as he studied her, the glow bouncing off the closed windows and marble floors.

"What the fuck are you doing?" I yelled, rushing between him and Ophelia.

Damien shoved me aside. "What you asked me to do."

And he blasted that power at Ophelia's chest.

She gasped, her eyes flaring wide briefly as she hovered a few inches off the bed. Her chest rose and fell faster, wings beating animatedly against the sheets. Hair stuck to her neck, her arms and forehead sweat-slicked, and Damien's light poured into her, ravaged her.

"What is it doing?" I asked. My own heart raced, my chest burning. The temperature in the room spiked, as hot as Ophelia's skin had been since we got here.

"Healing her, hopefully," Damien ground out. His face was screwed up in concentration, the scar across one side contorted and pale in the echo of his light.

"Angellight heals," I murmured. In the past, Ophelia had been able to heal her own injuries with the power, and Damien's was vast.

The Prime Warrior grunted, "Yes, and more."

"What do you mean?" My gaze flicked between them as that power fed and fed, her body greedy for it.

"Angellight has healing properties for mortals, but she is more than that now." Sweat beaded along his brow, such a human bodily function it almost shocked me. "She is a seraph."

"That's what you keep saying, but you haven't told me what that means!"

Damien took a breath, the stream of light pausing, the air still. Then, like a roaring wind, it crashed forward again. Gold rushed through the room. It pushed at the windows and heavy curtains, sending me stumbling back. But Ophelia's eyes didn't open again.

"The seraphs were once warriors, former heir," Damien explained over the rush of his power.

I gripped the bed frame as the force of Angellight multiplied. The seraphs were *what?* "No warrior in history had wings or this magic."

"Not warriors as you know them today, but they were another race under the Angel domain. They were our personal defenders, friends, lovers. Much like the warriors, but without the call to guard and guide the powers retained within the Balance as your kind is. Instead, they were *our* guardians when Ambrisk was *our* realm."

Guardians of the Angels. Much like Echnid, that was something our legends never mentioned.

"What happened to them?" I gasped as the wind tunnel of Damien's power burned hotter and poured into Ophelia.

The Angel grimaced. "When we were fooled into Ascending, the seraphs and all magical beings deemed *too powerful* under Echnid were banished, too. Some were locked in adjoining prison realms, some sent to their own entirely. The seraphs...they were slain."

Slain.

My stare locked on Ophelia. An entire species was gone at the hands of the gods? But...what did that mean for her? Would the known gods place a target on her back? Would the Angels demand more of her? I didn't fucking know, but she needed to wake for us to find out and fix it.

Open your eyes, Phel. Fight. I tried to send the plea through our broken Bind.

Hollowness echoed.

"Why?" I swallowed the fear thickening my throat. "Why were they slain?"

"Because seraph magic contained one key factor that set them apart." Damien's wings beat viciously at his back as he called up more and more light to devour Ophelia's limp body. It pushed on the surfaces of the bedchamber, crackling and buzzing. "As our guardians, seraphs could harness an Angel's light, display their power on a muted scale. And Angellight is pure, raw ether, given from the earth."

My eyes widened. "That's why Ophelia can wield Angellight?"

"You misunderstand," Damien said through clenched teeth. "Each seraph was connected to *one* Angel, as the warriors are. They could harness *one* facet of the magic of *one* of us. Ptholenix's fire or Gaveny's rolling tides."

My nails dug into the wood as I remembered the light of seven

Angels whipping around Ophelia, streaked with each signature color of their ether.

"She can access them all," I breathed. Ophelia was not just any seraph; she was one with a power never seen before. Something that had woken thanks to the myth magic she and Jezebel retained combining with the legend of the Angelcurse and Godsblood.

A concoction not even prophecy had foretold.

One not even a god predicted.

And that raised the question: What threat did she pose to them?

Damien's confirmation was a growl as he sent sheets of light wrapping around Ophelia. He called up more and more, the roar in the room deafening. I clung to the bed, forcing myself not to look away.

Ophelia was a seraph, a mythical being who could command and thrive on the power of the Angels. Damien's light would restore her. It had to.

We stood there for what felt like hours, watching her unconscious form. I leaned my elbows on the mattress, stare locked on the girl I used to love, hunting for even a flutter of her wings, a blink of her magenta eyes.

"Come on, Phel," I growled. "*Fight.*" I pushed against the slip of her soul tied to mine in our broken tattoo, begging. Raging. She was at the other end. I could sense her, distantly as it always had been, but she was there.

We waited until even Damien was exhausted—until he'd dug up the depths of his power and fed them into her. Until every fucking beat of my heart was another fruitless tug against the Bind.

And still, she did not wake.

All at once, Damien's light shuttered out, retracting into him with a crack as Ophelia dropped down to the bed. His chest heaved as he watched her. The minutes ticked by like centuries. Color had returned to her cheeks, and her breathing was stronger, but her Spiritsdamned eyes remained closed.

Finally, Damien turned to me. "I am sorry, Malakai."

And he left.

Chapter Four
Ophelia

They were slain.

Wings flapped through my mind. Bloodstained feathers and dying screams.

Open your eyes, Phel. Fight.

Something tugged deep down within me, and I reached for it. I wanted to grab on, but everything hurt so damn much. Every twitch ricocheted through me like a shattering explosion trapped in a cave.

The fire returned to my veins, incinerating from my heart outward. Flames licked along the interior of my muscles, turning everything I was to ash. And in their wake, ice frosted those delicate flakes.

Harness an Angel's light.

Seraphs could harness an Angel's light. Where had that come from?

That incessant tug pulled again, and wings continued to pound with demanding power, striking at my mind like they were beating down a thousand feathered dreams, crushing an army's futile hope and everlasting vows. Light flashed with every pulse, constellations crashing, and my heart racing in time with their drum.

Ophelia can access them all.

And the rhythm inside of me crescendoed on the tails of those words. The heat flamed, and screams elongated, wings fluttered until every feather shed, coating the murky gray plane in dusty white, and my heartbeat sped into one ceaseless beat.

Over it, those words drummed.

Ophelia can access them all.

I could access the might and magic of every Angel. Their power was *mine* to brandish.

Mine to dominate.

Mine to ruin.

And in that fact, determined vengeance inked itself on my heart, sealing a destructive will.

Power flared along my veins, devouring the fire and ice to forge something new. Something hungry and desirous. Something that had been slain many millennia ago.

The power of myths and legends, of seraphs lost and bridges broken.

An instinct sprouted in my gut, endless possibilities sharpening in the shape of ravenous claws and merciless teeth. A cruelty of legends rose within me, one I held at the end of my blade, poised to slice its yearning heart.

Because if I was condemned to this seraph fate—to a threat of the gods on my head and the heaviness of lost legends on my shoulders—I would master it and use it to bend them all to my will.

Power thrummed through me, more unabating than it had ever been, and I peeled my eyes open. The might of the seraph magic beat beneath my skin, the myth alive within me.

And I wanted to *know* it. To control it and use it, as I had been so used and worn.

"Ophelia?" Malakai's voice was hesitant.

I rolled my head to the side, taking in him and the room around us. My suite. We were in *my suite* in the Revered's Palace. We were home, but it wasn't quite home.

Everything was sharper—the green of Malakai's eyes, the angle of the morning sun slicing through the windows, the shattered glass of one pane, and the scratches across another. The breeze rifling the curtains smelled crisper than ever, filtering into my tight lungs and unknotting a drop of the tension stored there.

My mountains. They were still my mountains. The air still smelled of wildflowers and freedom and renewal.

Malakai's heart thudded loud enough to hear as he waited for me to answer. I pulled my attention back to those forest green eyes and curled my fingers into the sheets—even those were softer. Silky, despite my sweat coating them. But Malakai's stare was laden with a concern that pierced me.

"How long?" I croaked.

"Six days."

Six days.

Six days since I unleashed Echnid on the world. Since I fell for the Angels' tricks and manipulation, freeing the Warrior God from his prison, and he uttered that devastating goal: vengeance.

"Are you okay?" Spirits, my throat was achingly dry.

Malakai nodded, helping me prop against the pillows, then he crouched beside the bed and handed me a glass of water. Every inch I moved hurt, but not in the tearing, burning way that made me cry out. This was the satisfied ache of a brutal training session. A soreness that plagued every blink but was a reward of effort. Of clawing back from the brink I'd been on.

Malakai waited until I drained the glass—in slow sips—then answered, "I'm fine. How are you feeling?"

At his question, a flash of seraph power burned through my veins, more potent than the strongest Angellight I'd experienced.

Because it is, a voice in my head said. At the reminder, I pushed myself upright fully. The weight of my wings at my back drew a groan from me as they tugged at the muscles around my shoulder blades. But I forced it down.

I will not be weak again.

I'd always thought myself strong—a Mystique warrior and a proud Alabath daughter. But that day in the theater, after the sphinx revealed the true purpose of the Angelcurse, after fighting Queen Ritalia of the fae and her taking so much from us, I wasn't sure if I had ever been as strong as I thought.

With the power in me now, though, I would claim back that might and then some. I would not permit the Angels or gods to make me anything less than what I was: a legend reborn.

With that determination, I inhaled. As I blew out a breath, I sent a wave of Angellight around the room, burning with ten times the intensity I'd intended.

Malakai swore, ducking below the golden tide as it shimmered across marble surfaces and mystlight chandeliers. Its warmth painted my bedchamber with a conviction that strengthened my spine and soothed the tearing muscles along my back.

The Angellight danced, rising and fading to a steady hum gathered along the ceiling. It cast a glimmer around the room, coloring Malakai's awestruck features. After a few moments, he turned that expression on me.

"I feel okay physically," I said, clinging to the strength of the seraph within me. Emotionally, I was wrecked. Guilty and worried, terrified and so fucking *angry*. The riot of emotions tangled within me, a storm brewing.

Malakai brought his hand to his chest, rubbing his North Star tattoo. My eyes locked on that ink through his thin white tunic, still so stark and angles sharply poised against his scarred skin.

"Are you mad?" he asked, clearing his throat as if the pang of emotion was so potent he actually felt it.

I nodded, gaze dropping to my own tattoo. I brushed my thumb across the four-pointed star, and Malakai's words from another life filtered through my memory. *My North Star. So that we may always come back to each other.*

"We've come so far, Malakai," I muttered.

"A long way from Palerman," he agreed.

"A long way from illegal tattoos beneath the stars," I said, almost to myself. "From looking at the future with wide-eyed hope and eager dreams." Now, we were a product of merciless manipulation and deceit. They had forced us to grow with those things—to become them.

Malakai, still crouched beside the bed, moved so he was in my line of sight. "What do you need, Phel?"

"I need..." I needed my palace to be rid of the god now

commandeering it. I needed this power in my veins to feed on his life and all those who had lied to me. I needed to be back with our family, to know they were okay.

But none of those were what I chose. No, instead I chose the one thing that would encompass them all. "I need to be who they turned me into. And then I need to scorch them all."

Let's make them fucking scorch, Tolek's words burned through me.

Malakai didn't shrink from the ire in my voice as he once would have. He didn't cower or run from the fight. His forest stare hardened like evergreens iced over in winter, and with a straight-lipped nod, Malakai Blastwood, the former heir to the Revered of the Mystique Warriors, the boy who had been ruined by those he trusted, the man who had so much taken from him, gripped my arm just over my North Star Bind.

And he swore, "We're going to do just that."

Something beat beneath the crease of my elbow, an undetermined emotion, but if it was anything like the promise in Malakai's stare, it was a vow. We'd get back to the people we loved even if it killed us.

Angels, despite the unknown danger we were both in with Echnid in this palace, I was grateful Malakai was here with me.

Tenderly, I turned, shifting my legs over the end of the bed and slowly rising to my feet.

"Have you heard from anyone?" I asked. My entire body ached as I tested a step forward, the Angellight slow to heal the extensive damage of the seraph emerging.

"Echnid took all the Mystique ink," Malakai said, helping me take slow steps across the room. "I haven't wanted to leave you more than necessary, but I searched a few offices and didn't find a thing."

My attention sliced up to him, skin prickling. "Why didn't you want to leave?"

"The first time I did, I came back to find Valyrie standing over you."

I froze, eyes flashing to the bed as if I would see her hovering there now. Shaking off the unease, I continued forward, gripping

Malakai's arm like a patient in an infirmary after suffering a grievous battle wound.

"Why was Valyrie here?" I asked.

Her silver-framed, olive-toned face came back to me. Her wafting lilac, star-flecked power and how she'd spoken to Vale. *Fatecatcher*, she'd called her. A word Tolek had found multiple times in the scrolls we'd used to find the Starsearcher's emblem. It was in the one about Valyrie's final reading, but there had been no explanation.

"She seemed harmless in the moment," Malakai said, pulling me back to the present as we continued to shuffle around my bed chamber, "but there's something about her that worries me."

"What do you mean?"

"Valyrie has this edge to her when she speaks. She was only here briefly, but I could feel it. Like I wasn't sure what she'd do next."

I didn't know much about Valyrie, but in the scrolls, we'd learned of her races. How she'd held a tournament, three rounds of challenges resulting in countless dead competitors and twelve remaining as her closest protectors.

Ruthless was certainly how I'd describe her based on her heartlessness over the lives lost.

"I'm not sure what any of them will do," I countered.

"True," Malakai agreed. "Damien seems conflicted. He helped wake you." His voice dropped and he grumbled, "Took some fucking pushing."

"Of course, he did." A whip of betrayal lashed against my heart, and I stopped walking. "Damien killed Annellius, Malakai."

His brow furrowed. "What?"

I nodded. "When the Angels emerged, Vale was hit by readings. Thanks to the combination of blood and Angellight, I saw flickers of them." A wind-whipped mountaintop and blood pouring from my ancestor flashed through my memory, stinging and tainted. "After Annellius found some of the emblems and discovered the purpose for the Angelcurse, something changed his mind. He didn't want to do it anymore, so Damien killed him."

"I thought he died of blood loss."

"He did," I said, the brutality of the death heavy in those words.

Malakai swallowed, understanding. All of the Angels were cruel, savagery multiplying over centuries. Damien may have helped me wake—he may have seemed remorseful—but that only meant it aided *his* cause.

The question remained, what was it?

"Thorn and Bant are who I'm worried about most," Malakai went on when I began walking again. "I tried to only leave when I knew they weren't in the palace."

My heart squeezed at the protectiveness in Malakai's voice. At the attention he paid to my well-being while I was unconscious. Even when we broke up, I never doubted Malakai cared for me— loved me even. Spirits, we loved each other so much, so tightly, that for some time, we were more willing to destroy ourselves than let go. A warm satisfaction spread through my chest at the way we defended each other still. We would until the stars stopped shining.

"Were Thorn and Bant threatening?"

"They always are," Malakai said.

"Thorn is reckless and unpredictable."

"In a different way than Valyrie," he added, and though I'd barely seen the Angels since their return, I understood what he meant. They were each fearsome, ethereal, and exemplary in their own ways.

Thorn had been driven mad before the Ascension, and it seemed it was only amplified by the millennia the Angels had spent locked away. Where Valyrie's ruthlessness seemed to be hard-won, Thorn's was dangerous and reveling in cruelty.

And Bant was...well, Bant was an Engrossian scorned by the Mystique Angel. As Damien's betrayal lashed through me again, I understood what that disdain could drive one to do.

Malakai helped me cross to the table where he'd placed a tray of bread and jams. I looked at the high back seats on either side of the small round setting, my wings aching at just the thought of being crammed against them. Opting to stand and work the muscles in my legs, I took a slice of the bread and spread the strawberry topping on it. My stomach growled at the first taste, as if it had been waiting for me to wake to be ravenous again.

"What about the others?" I asked between bites. "Ptholenix, Gaveny, and Xenique?" My voice tripped over the name of the demigoddess Soulguider. A daughter of the Goddess of Death, Artale—though that fact was her clan's greatest secret. She was my ancestor, too, apparently. The harbinger of Godsblood.

"I haven't seen them much," Malakai said. "I don't know if that's good or bad."

My gut squirmed in agreement. "We need to keep an eye on their movements until we can get out of here." He nodded. At my next thought, the food in my stomach soured. I set down the bread and knife. "Have you seen Echnid?"

Malakai tensed. "I haven't come face to face with him, but I've *felt* him."

My skin chilled. "What do you mean?"

"The god's power is palpable throughout the palace—probably throughout all of Damenal and Gallantia." He ran a hand over the scar on his jaw. "I doubt his return went unnoticed."

I supposed since I woke with so much new, raw power threading through me, I hadn't realized, but I studied my chamber again. How the clink of the chandelier was so much higher as wind danced through the crystal; how the mystlight bouncing between the glass slats rippled and shimmered in more depth; how Malakai's freckles seemed pronounced and my skin more sensitive.

"Warrior power truly was unlocked," I mumbled, my heart tumbling through my chest. "One good thing came of this at least."

"Hopefully," Malakai said. I raised my brows, and he added, "We don't know what's happening out there, Phel. What else woke with Echnid. Let's hope this newfound power is an advantage and not creating greater enemies."

I swallowed the possibility of warring clans and vies for power, of unknown things slinking about the world, and sank against the table, looking back at my rumpled bed. "Let's hope," I agreed.

And as my stare locked on the crimson stains brushed across

the sheets, on my cursed blood painted by feathered fallacies, I whispered, "I need to see him."

Chapter Five
Ophelia

After I washed up as best as I could with my still sore muscles—making Malakai do the same since I learned he'd barely left my side—and searched for a clean pair of leathers in my dressing chamber, slicing a tunic up to tie it behind my neck and back to accommodate wings, we started a slow promenade through the wide halls. The sky beyond the windows was tinged gray as clouds rolled in.

On the surface, there wasn't much disturbed in the palace, but as Malakai cautiously guided me through the halls, I understood what he meant. There was a thick hum to the air, low enough that it took me a while to pick up on, but impossible to ignore once I had.

It draped luxuriously across the walls, as decadent as velvet and threatening as a corded rope around my neck. It permeated the air like a drafty mist, tickling my skin and buzzing around my mind. It was Echnid—

And it had the power to drive me mad.

"You haven't seen anyone?" I asked Malakai as we walked.

"No one."

"Not even any of the council members?" We'd left the Masters of Rites, Coin, and Trade in charge when we left to hunt for the emblems all those months ago.

"They're safe in their homes in the city, according to Damien."

I scoffed. "Who knows if we can trust that information, then."

We fell into silence as we continued, and all the while, that godly essence pulled at me. There was one place I needed to see more than the rest, and my pulse thundered as we climbed the wide staircase toward it.

Every worry vacated my mind when we stepped into the Rapture Chamber and found Echnid standing before the pillared wall.

Tendrils of white mist peeled off his monstrous frame, spilling around the marbled floors and over the edge of the sharp drop. My favorite view in the palace, spoiled by the Warrior God. My hand tightened on Malakai's arm, and tension rippled off him.

This room—where I'd claimed my title and where I'd stood firmly against chancellors; where I'd fought Kakias and she used my blood to begin her journey to immortality; where I'd reveled in the view of my mountains—Echnid had to taint this room, too.

For a moment, Kakias's spirit stood beside Echnid, Ritalia and Lucidius with them, and all heads slowly swiveled toward me. I shivered internally, blinking away the vision until only the Warrior God remained, but I buried my fear deep beneath the power of the seraph thrumming through my blood.

"What are you doing here?" I accused.

Echnid's milky eyes assessed me. In the light, faint gray irises shone in the center. "I sensed this would be the first place you went upon waking."

"Sensed?"

"I know you better than you think, Chosen Child." He scoffed what I thought was supposed to be a laugh. "Are you feeling well?"

"I'd be better if you hadn't commandeered my home and city."

Echnid prowled toward us, each step reverberating through my bones. Spirits, the way he consumed the air made my stomach turn. Malakai was stone beside me.

"Everything on warrior land belonged to me first," the god said.

I bit my tongue to keep myself from snapping that perhaps he should leave it to those he abandoned.

"Will you help heal the land, then?" I asked, much milder than the fire roaring in my veins. Something tapped against my power, sliding along my bones, as if wanting to know what those flames felt like. I scratched at the webbed gray Curse mark on the inside of my wrist as it pulsed.

"If my plans come to fruition, everything that has wronged us shall be healed." The menacing curl of his lips and amusement in his voice did nothing to soothe my nerves.

"What is it you want from us?" I asked Echnid.

He swelled, white mist swirling around him and creeping across the marble floors. "I want to give you everything you dream of, Ophelia Alabath. I want you to bathe the world with the light of the warriors, to raise our people back to their rightful place." He folded his powerful hands behind his back. "*You deserve this*. We could be the most righteous team any realm has ever seen."

His words washed over me, commanding and tempting all at once. They pulled at some facet of me, a root planted so deep, I hadn't known it was there.

And in the mist, I could see that world he spoke of, where warrior power was not suppressed. Where seraphs were never slain, and pegasus and khrysaor conquered the skies.

A small part of me wanted it, an inkling that bubbled slowly to life in my veins.

Echnid leaned closer. "I want you to be my partner as we lavish the warriors and creatures beneath my domain. To rule with me, restore the seraphs, vanquish those who betrayed me, and in turn, see your dreams come true."

I held my breath as he spoke. White mist gathered around my ankles like shackles. I considered running, fleeing, taking Malakai and escaping the palace now, but the allure of Echnid's power promised if I ran, it would find me. It would call me back where I belonged.

See your dreams come true.

What were my dreams? What could Echnid give me?

"How will you do that?" I asked.

Echnid assessed us for a long time, and I fought the urge to scratch at the Curse scar again. Finally, the god admitted, "There is much that has been left out of Ambrisk's history. No truths of the Wars Among Gods that sent worlds to ruin have been told here."

The Wars Among Gods?

"Why are you telling us this?" Malakai asked, his deep voice grounding.

Echnid steepled his fingers and eyed me. The mortal movement was so simple, but what he said next rattled me. "You and I are meant to be a team of fabled proportions, Ophelia. Forget all those beyond these mountains. I ask, what legacy do you want to leave behind?"

A legacy? I'd barely thought beyond today, beyond the battles we'd been fighting. What *did* I want? I'd never hungered for power, but I'd been handed it. And with that power, I wanted to protect those within my rule. But it was so much more complicated than that.

As if Echnid heard my conclusion, he said, "Together, we will restore Ambrisk to the might it was meant to be before that war. We will dismiss the gods who damned me so they have no contact with my warriors, and open the bridges they caused to lock."

Dismiss the gods? Could he do that?

"Won't that only worsen the repercussions felt across all realms, including Ambrisk?" I asked, scratching at my Curse mark. Surely, altering godly magic could destroy worlds. They were in the very fabric of the universe. No one knew where the gods came from, but they had created realms. If their power was no longer tied to warrior magic, surely that would change everything?

But...something within me bubbled up. A morbid curiosity that almost wanted to see the gods suffer.

"Warriors never kept gods beyond me, so why should they be beneath their thumbs? Together, we will wrench this realm from my brother and sister gods for the greater good of all warriors." That was it—what I needed. To help the warriors. Echnid paused as I drew closer to that conclusion. "What is it you desire? Together, we will reach it."

Malakai's hand landed on my elbow, the touch sending a pulse of awareness to my brain that shattered my trance with the god's words, and a voice in the back of my mind cried, *Nothing.*

Echnid could not give me anything because my heart was beyond these walls. It was held in the hands of a man who'd escorted me through the darkness and promised to find me across any realm. It was serenaded not by mysterious, depraved magic but by late night laughter and teasing on moonlit beaches—by child-hood bets and the scratch of a pen against parchment. Citrus and spice and the mountain air and warm amber specks in chocolate-brown eyes.

That love was sealed in the way his voice cracked as he said my name when Echnid pulled me through the rip in the air, and I would do anything to return to him. To benefit the greater good of the warriors with *him* at my side. Those were my dreams—a life with him without any gods or Angels breathing curses into our blood.

I stored all of those vows deep within my spirit, in the place where myth magic had broken free. Beneath the feathers of my seraph wings and every tether to Angel magic, and I gave Echnid a small smile.

"I shall think about it," I said, and Malakai's hand tightened on my elbow.

We dismissed ourselves, and I led Malakai from the Rapture Chamber. As we strolled down the corridor with an unaffected front, the milky eyes of the Warrior God burned into my spine.

It wasn't until we were back in the office in my suite with the door locked that Malakai faced me and asked, "Are you okay?"

"I'm fine," I answered too quickly, mind racing.

"Phel," he said softly.

I wandered to the shelves, scanning the dozens of books I'd amassed in this room since moving here. Most centered on Mystique history and Angel lore, dabbling in various subgenres from folktales to geography to legendary battles.

And not one held an ounce of information as to the weakness of the Warrior God—none even spoke of his *existence*.

"We are entirely blind, Malakai," I whispered.

He sighed, coming to stand beside me and facing the shelves, categorizing the false history we'd been fed in our childhood lessons preparing to rule the Mystique Warriors.

"For centuries, everyone has been playing exactly into his hands," Malakai agreed, not saying Echnid's name. "My father and Kakias amplified clan unrest and planted the idea that we needed to reclaim power we never even knew was ours. The Soulguiders, who didn't know how important Xenique's secrets would be. Past Revereds who handed that spear from one to the next, unaware they were just keeping it warm for the Chosen to find an emblem."

My heart panged at the mention of Angelborn, the memory of Ritalia melting her and Starfire ripping through me.

Malakai went on, "And we had no idea it was all exactly as he wanted, priming us for power and desperation."

"No one but Annellius," I muttered. Only my ancestor, the first chosen, had discovered Echnid's plans. Only he had stood against gods and Angels. "Echnid is trying to sway us to him, for whatever reason. Grand promises and talk of dreams. He needs us on his side."

"And are you?" Malakai asked, almost reluctantly.

I shook my head, studying the books again. So many years of learnings, myths and legends—

A thought tore through me like a lightning bolt. Something the sphinx, Ithinix, had said in the Hall of Wandering Souls when Jezebel and I had found out the purpose of this entire curse. "How do you think Annellius did it?"

Malakai inclined his head, not following my train of thought. Concern seeped into his stare, and he looked me up and down as if checking that Echnid's misty white magic wasn't still tangled around me.

When he found nothing, he said, "He sacrificed his life."

"Yes, but how did he know?" My wings shuffled at my excitement, and Malakai's stare flashed to them, but the pain of the motion barely connected in my brain. Not with the path I was speeding down. "How did Annellius find out if he was not able to speak to the sphinx?"

Malakai brushed a thumb along the scar on his jaw, considering. "Damien's visits?"

"Damien could only say so much because of how the gods locked away knowledge of Echnid." I shook my head. "No, there had to be something Annellius found that didn't blatantly say the answers but pointed him toward it. Something that gave him enough information to not only play the game but win it."

Ithinix had revealed as much. Annellius had found myths, histories, and folktales that didn't align and built the truth out of the gaps between them.

"Yeah, Phel, but we're already too deep in the game." He dropped his voice. "The god is *here*. He's free."

"So, we play differently. We find whatever Annellius knew and use it to our advantage."

"Wouldn't it be best to just try to get safely out of here?" Malakai asked. "To ignite the spark of a rebellion that's bound to flourish as Ambrisk feels Echnid's wrath and let the other gods finish him?"

He wanted to run, and I understood why. Echnid's fury was dangerous, and we didn't know his full goals or motives beyond revenge. This was a war that shouldn't need to be fought among warriors, but that didn't mean it wouldn't be. That didn't mean we shouldn't be a part of a battle being waged for our future.

Besides, I was no mere warrior.

I placed a hand on Malakai's arm. "I am already ahead of Annellius with the wrath of a seraph of all seven Angels running through my veins. We can rewrite the rules here, Malakai."

"How so?"

"I'll play Echnid's game. He wants me here, and he wants me willing. I'll become who he needs me to be in order to cross him."

Malakai contemplated, green eyes searching my expression as he tried to poke holes in the rocky foundations of this plan. But he found none. This territory was uncharted, every path on the map colliding into a tumbleweed of options.

"Okay, I'll go along with this," he conceded, though uncertainty still creased his brow. "But that doesn't answer one thing. Why does he need you?"

"I don't know." I sighed, striding to the window and gazing out; the Northern Quarter was shadowed by a dark gray sky. "There's more we need to uncover. I'm sure he'll show his hand eventually." A chill worked down my spine as Echnid's words wound through my head, the promises he tried to seduce me with. "I imagine there are worse things coming. We need to warn our friends."

"He's taken all the Mystique ink," Malakai reminded me.

I perked up, smiling over my shoulder. "That's not the only way."

Chapter Six
Tolek

I told you I would tear apart every realm to get you back. I meant it, apeagna.

I tossed the scrap of parchment over the nearest mystlight, the pale flame flickering in a brass holder in the center of the breakfast table. But like the last dozen, the paper only burned in the heat. Voices floated through the room, but I tuned them out as the last of the message withered. Until nothing but a charred sliver remained.

With a groan, I dropped my head back against my chair, not caring about any of the fresh fruit or variations of porridge spread across the table. The azure tiles of the mosaic ceiling stared down, mocking me where they swirled in their abstract design. Everything in the Soulguider Chancellor, Meridat's, manor home was bright, lit by the desert sun leaking lazily through high arches. In the afternoons, when the heat laid thick against our skin, the staff lowered wicker shades in every room and walkway, but now, midmorning, they let in the still-cool air.

The dining room was fit for a party of dozens of warriors, with six wide arches lining either side and a grand entrance at one end. It's heavy bronze-and-turquoise-inlaid doors were propped open, Soulguiders drifting back and forth beyond. And while it was extravagant, the light flecking that mosaic ceiling and streaking the amethyst chandeliers was too brilliant for the losses we'd suffered.

Even the airy, soft tunics Meridat had provided weren't heavy enough.

I wanted to fucking *feel*.

It had been a week since those mountains—since I lost them. We'd come here with Erista when we left the theater, accepting an invitation to stay at the Soulguider Chancellor's personal manor in the capital city for as long as we needed. But how was I supposed to focus on something as benign as breakfast conversation when a deranged god had *taken* Ophelia and my sister had died?

Though it was healed, the tattoo across my back burned as if in agreement, the wings wrapping feathered tips around my ribs and shoulders both holding me up and chaining me. How were Ophelia's wings? How long had she bled from those wounds? Did Echnid help her?

I swore to every damn Angel in his domain, I'd slaughter him if he let her suffer.

Scrubbing a hand over my face, I pushed upright and grabbed my pen. I had to keep trying.

But when the next slip of parchment singed to ash, Vale asked softly from across the table, "No luck?"

"Wherever they are, Mystique ink can't reach them." I swallowed that truth I hadn't wanted to admit, because I knew damn well it meant she was further than I hoped.

Cypherion's conversation with Meridat faltered, but attempting to be a proper, attentive ruler, he resumed discussing the Rites of Dusk with the Chancellor. Since Ophelia freed Echnid, the discordant ritual used to restore Soulguider magic hadn't occurred again. Despite the power that flooded Gallantia and the obvious shift in warrior strength and senses, it appeared life went on as normal.

Barrett, Dax, and Celissia had returned to Engrossian territory to address the small sparks of rebellion against Prince Barrett's approaching coronation, and our new potential fae allies were residing in Xenovia with us. Though, they were sequestered to the guest house on Meridat's land, guarded by a Soulguider patrol at all hours.

Yes, it certainly appeared not much had changed.

"Echnid is a god," Jezebel lamented. "He could have taken Ophelia and Malakai *anywhere*." Beside me, she picked morosely at the orange slices on her plate. Even Baby Alabath wasn't eating much.

"He didn't take them just anywhere," Santorina said, striding into the dining room. "They're in Damenal."

Jezebel dropped her fork. Vale, Cypherion, and Meridat all fell silent.

My chair scraped against tile as I shot up. "What do you mean?"

Rina's chiffon skirt swished as she approached the table and dumped a small shell in the center of it. "I was up all night communicating with them. Echnid took them to the Revered's Palace. He's commandeered it. Only the Angels are allowed in or out."

"Why haven't we heard any of this from the Mystique Council?" CK asked, pushing up with his palms braced on the table. I only watched that shell that now held my entire world.

Of course. Santorina and the human training camps were using these Godsblessed Seawatcher shells to communicate basic messages. She'd given one to Ophelia before everything went to hell that night in the mountains. When we'd separated within the Gates of Angeldust to seek out the seventh and final Angel emblem, Ophelia had it in her pocket.

"Echnid is blocking Mystique ink in and out of the city," I guessed, a small bead of hope daring to bloom in my chest.

"That makes sense," Vale agreed. "It links back to the mountains. He can likely prohibit it from working."

Rina nodded, tension framing her shoulders. "He took all the ink from the palace, too."

"Then why can we still write to Barrett?" Cypherion asked in his most commanding Second-to-the-Revered voice.

"Because Echnid does not want to destroy warriors," Meridat said. The Soulguider Chancellor folded her hands on the table, stacks of bracelets clinking against the carved edge. "He wants to empower us. He needs a tight leash on his immediate surroundings, but demolishing our lines of communication would only cause an uproar and, potentially, strife between clans. This is a calculated move to allow us to address the shift we all felt, to see the good he's doing while he keeps those in Damenal under his thumb."

"Why does he need Damenal, though?" Vale asked.

My stare flicked between them all. Was this seriously what they were taking from this? "None of that is what's most important." I turned to Santorina. "How are they? Is Ophelia..."

Hurt? Caged?

Angels, please just let her be safe. Jezebel pushed to her feet beside me, balling her shaking hands into fists.

"She's fine," Rina said. "They both are. I don't have many details since the shells don't allow that much communication, but they're both okay."

A sliver of tension unknotted in my chest. She wasn't being harmed. She was okay.

"We're going to Damenal, then," I said, stepping around my chair and making for the door.

But Rina stopped me with a hand on my chest. "We can't."

"What do you mean *we can't*?" I sneered those last two words.

Grim lines bracketed Rina's mouth as she stood taller, forcing me back a step. "We cannot go to Damenal."

"Why in Damien's name not?" Jezebel lashed out from behind me.

Rina looked between us. "Ophelia said they're staying for now."

Well, that sentence didn't make any sense.

"Staying where?" I growled.

"In Damenal. She and Malakai are staying to figure out what Echnid is up to." Her eyes flitted between mine, as if she was trying to decide if she should keep speaking. I didn't know what she found, but apparently it was desperate and tormented enough to convince her I needed more information. "Echnid wants her, Tolek."

"That's why we have to save her!" I yelled, the tattoo on my back burning, the words ripping through my guilty heart.

I love you, baby brother.

"She doesn't need saving," Rina assured me. "Echnid wants to work with her. I don't know what it means, but he wants her happy."

Still in her seat, Vale scoffed and crossed her arms. "That sounds familiar."

It did sound hauntingly similar to how Titus, the late Starsearcher Chancellor, had proposed their relationship. Santorina gave her a tight-lipped nod. "I thought the same, I assure you. But Ophelia swore this is their choice. They want to learn his plans —to see if he is a threat or an advantage to the warriors."

"She has a point," Cypherion said. Vale and I both swung shocked stares on him. "We don't know what Echnid is going to do. He may *benefit* warriors, but the only way for us to know is to wait. Let Ophelia and Malakai figure him out, then we go in."

So levelheaded. So rational. So Angelsdamned infuriating.

"No," I asserted.

"I'm with Tolek," Jezzie said, planting her hands on her hips.

"Cypherion is right," Rina swore. "We need whatever information they can uncover. This isn't a battle we've ever fought before. This is the *gods*."

"Echnid may truly have the warriors' best interest at heart," CK added, eyeing me carefully.

"Then why did he *kidnap* them?" Jezebel shrieked. She panted, and when no one responded, she sighed. "Forget it." And she tore from the room.

"I'll write to the other clan rulers and update them," Meridat said. That solidified whom she'd sided with. As a chancellor, she was considering the best interest of her people. Not acting *rashly* was her choice.

When she was gone, I glared at CK. "You're really making this decision?" My question was venomous.

Cyph stood his ground, bracing his weight on the table. "I am, Tol. We need to know what we're up against."

"And you agree with this?" I asked Vale. After what she'd gone through, did she truly think Echnid wanted *what was best* for Ophelia?

Her lips rolled together, an icy glare landing on Cypherion that promised they'd be discussing this in private, but she said, "I don't know what to believe. But I want to trust Ophelia that she wouldn't lie if she didn't think she and Malakai were safe."

"Do you *know* Ophelia?" I blurted. "If she thinks it's dangerous for us to get her back, she'd absolutely lie!"

"Not with Malakai there, too," Cypherion said.

Dammit, he had a point. At the very least, Ophelia would tell us to get Malakai out and leave her there.

That acknowledgment siphoned the fire from my voice as I fell into a seat, still avoiding CK's eyes. "I have to get her back," I muttered. "I promised her."

"She has every intention of returning," Rina swore, sinking into the chair Jezebel had vacated and placing a hand on my arm. "She wanted me to tell you that."

Ophelia shouldn't have to fight her way out of there. She should be able to walk out the damn doors. To flood the entire city with Angellight and burn that god to ash.

For a moment, I'd felt so hopeful when Rina had said she'd found them. Damenal. A quick flight from here. I could have had her back in my arms in hours.

Now though, knowing that wasn't what she wanted, I watched the pile of singed parchment I'd tried to send to her, hopelessness rooting in my heart.

I love you, baby brother.

"That's the problem, Santorina," I muttered. "Intentions aren't guarantees."

～

"I SHOULD HAVE KNOWN this was where you went," I said as I walked into the stables and found Jezebel lying on her back in the bank of sand beside the door. Zanox hovered beside her, a wing draped dramatically overhead to keep the sun slanting through the cracked door off her.

She lifted her head as I walked past, letting it thump back down after a beat. "I needed out of that room."

I scoffed. "You don't have to explain it to me."

Scuffing my feet through the sandy aisle, I crossed to Sapphire's stall. Luckily, this stable was old and not as well cared for as some on Meridat's property, the stalls beaten up and partitions broken enough that Sapphire and the khrysaor had enough room for them and their wings.

Dynaxtar currently occupied two combined stalls, sleeping, but Sapphire, Ophelia's pegasus, extended her wings when she saw me.

"Hey, pretty girl," I said as I grabbed her brush.

We kept our warrior horses in a different stable, and I visited Astania every day, but Sapphire was duller since Ophelia had been taken. I'd spent long afternoons at her side, ensuring she was fed and cleaned. Ensuring she got to fly when she wanted and wasn't alone when neither of us could be with her rider.

"How can they expect us just to leave them?" Jezebel said after a long period of only the scrape of Sapphire's brush filling the silence.

"I don't fucking know, Jezzie," I sighed, and Sapphire echoed the sound.

Setting down the brush, I leaned against the wall and sank to the ground, facing Jezebel. Peeking out from beneath Zanox's wing, her eyes were so wide, it struck a chord of terror in my own chest.

"I'm scared, Tolek," she whispered.

"Me, too," I confessed. So fucking afraid of what could happen to Ophelia while in a god's grasp.

"For Ophelia, but also because of this," she said. And the shadows around her flared a silvery-blue with her light. "I still don't know what this magic *is*."

"It's the mythos. The ability to destroy legends."

She laughed. "Oh, is that all?"

I understood her point, but I didn't have any concrete answers for her. We knew the bare minimum of how their magic worked but had no idea what lengths it could go to or the purpose.

"I need Ophelia," Jezebel whispered. "She's the other half. The balance to it. It feels out of sorts without her."

And there was such a fear in Jezebel's voice, I stuffed aside my own wrenching worry. "She's okay," I assured her. "Rina wouldn't lie to us about that."

Angels, I hoped it was true.

Jezebel looked like she was about to say something, but quick, light footsteps fluttered around the corner, halting just inside the door to the stables.

"I'm sorry for interrupting," Erista blurted, glancing between her partner—who notably did not look back—and me. "I heard what happened. I wanted to see if you were okay."

"I'm fine." Jezebel flopped back in the sand, but Zanox removed his wing from where it cocooned her, letting light slip across her face and giving Erista access. Squinting in the sudden sun, Jezebel grumbled, "Meddler."

Zanox huffed, walking across the stable to where three stalls had been converted into one and tucking in his wings to sleep. Jez didn't seem to have enough fight in her to walk away.

Erista nodded gratefully at the khrysaor, her eyes brimming with tears. "How are you, J?"

"Fine," Baby Alabath said again.

Hesitantly, giving Jezebel room to tell her to leave, Erista sat in the sand on the opposite side of the doorway. "I'm sorry about Ophelia and Malakai." She looked at me, too, and I nodded my appreciation.

"Everyone seems to be sorry," Jezebel said.

"Perhaps it's the right—" Jezebel silenced Erista with a glare, and the Soulguider corrected herself, "We're going to get them back."

"What if it's a trick? What if it's not actually them talking to Rina?" Jezebel asked.

I froze, not having considered that. At my sharp inhale, Sapphire's wing draped across my shoulder, damn reassuring in the absence of her rider.

"I've been spending a lot of time researching the gods these past few days," Erista said. There was an urgency in her voice, like she was desperate to help. "Though there's nothing on Echnid since he was wiped from history by Aoiflyn, there's plenty on Artale. I've been looking into the intricacies of her magic that extends to all gods—things like creation properties and how its woven into the realms. How it ties to beings on Ambrisk like Storytellers."

I only vaguely listened as Erista explained to Jezebel how she was visiting the Hall of Wandering Souls in Xenovia's Gates of Angeldust—a place where Soulguiders could sometimes communicate with lingering spirits—and asking the departed if there was any passing wisdom they could share.

As Jezebel lobbied curt responses back, I stroked Sapphire's downy feathers. She continued to prod me with her wing.

At her insistence, I whispered, "What is it?"

Gently, Sapphire beat her wings, and as the breeze she created brushed across my face, I grinned up at this beautiful Angels-damned pegasus.

"Jezzie?" I asked, and the girls fell silent. I held Sapphire's piercing blue stare that said *finally*. "How about we get answers for ourselves?"

~

"YOU WENT *WHERE?*" Cypherion asked during our strategy meeting the next day.

The war room in Meridat's estate—though not being used for war currently—was much like the dining room, with tiled floors and tan walls carved with intricate designs, but here the arches were sealed with heavy wooden doors.

We'd been here for an hour discussing hypothetical scenarios of how Echnid could dismiss the gods thanks to Ophelia's hints to Santorina and Erista's extensive research with fellow Soulguider advisors and apprentices. But Baby Alabath and I had waited until the very end of this meeting to spill our news.

"We flew to Damenal," I repeated. Meridat gaped at us. Vale sat on the edge of her seat. Rina dropped her head into her hands, sensing the coming storm.

Only Mila sat quietly and attentively at the table, stare locked on me. With bags under her eyes and a messy braid, she looked as disheveled as I felt.

"Why in the Angel's cursed name would you do that?" Cypherion roared. "We agreed not to!"

"We had to see for ourselves," I told him. "Had to see the city—see what's happened."

"And did you?" he snapped.

Jezebel asserted, "We did. We saw that nothing has physically changed aside from the gates to the palace being closed, though the streets were empty. And that"—her gaze shuttered—"there seemed to be some sort of invisible barrier keeping us from getting within the city limits."

"God magic," Erista breathed. "It has the power to create—as they did the realms. Echnid must have put up a blockade to keep warriors out."

My teeth ground. We'd hovered up there for hours, Jezebel on Zanox and me on Sapphire. The pegasus had been just as stubborn as us, sensing her rider beyond those bounds, but there hadn't been a way to penetrate the defense.

"Explains why our letters aren't getting in," Rina said.

Fuming, I added, "Even the tunnels in the mountains are blocked."

"You went into the—" Cypherion sighed. As Second, he was trying so hard to hold everything together, and I felt for him, but not enough to *not* try to help Ophelia. "You're going to drive me to the Spirit Realm early." He scraped a hand down his face, and guilt flashed through me at the circles beneath his eyes. But he'd *left* Ophelia there. "Can we at least agree not to do that again now that we know we can't get in?"

"Fine," I conceded, keeping my face wiped of emotion. It wasn't technically a lie. No way in the Spirit Realm would I stop trying to get Ophelia back—no way I'd be as powerless as I'd been in the mountains ever again—but I didn't need to try *that* tactic.

CK squinted at me, likely sensing some sort of loophole, but he said, "We can reconvene tomorrow."

Exhausted, I sank into my chair, glaring at the tray in the center of the table that held Mystique ink, parchment, and a myst-light that was fucking useless to me. The seat beside me scraped back, and Mila dropped into it.

"You didn't see them?" she asked, eyes also on the mystlight.

I shook my head.

Sure, we may have learned something of Echnid's external defenses, but really, we'd failed. I hadn't so much as laid an eye on Ophelia or Malakai. That truth draped over me, thick as the dark clouds rolling through the desert skies beyond Xenovia. Unusual apparently, but then again, everything was nowadays.

Mila sighed, and the breath was as weighted as I felt. I looked at her—at the way her hair hung around her face, eyes dull and skin wan. Mila was the only person who'd lost as much as I did in that mountain theater. I thought she was the only one who felt Lyria's death and Ophelia and Malakai's abduction quite as poignantly as I did, like every breath was a knife driving through my ribs.

"I'm sorry, Mila," I said.

She shrugged. "For what?"

"For not protecting them. For not saving Lyria."

She looked at me, and dammit was that expression haunted by all the ghosts of memories with my sister. We may both have been grieving, but we were mourning different things. Mila had the past, the reminiscing. The solitude their friendship had provided following the first war and through the second.

I was mourning the future. The reparations Lyria and I were striding toward, the gaps we were making up for. All of the things we now would never have.

Both were tremendously fucking awful. Mila's seemed to compress her as she worked through it, but I forced mine to the back of my mind.

"Erista told me what she said," Mila whispered. "That she knew it was coming." Some of Lyria's last words had been just that. An explanation that it was okay because a Soulguider had hinted her end was near. "A piece of me is so mad she didn't tell us."

"Me, too," I agreed. We were robbed of a proper goodbye, instead getting a bloodstained one at the end of the fae queen's dagger. "But I think she was making her own peace with it."

"I think so, too. And she deserved that."

The confusion that accompanied grief clouded between us, and I hated that there was nothing I could say to make it better.

Nothing to absolve either of our pain or speed it along. We'd feel this aching loss for years to come. And how was I supposed to move on when every time I closed my eyes, I saw all the *what if's* playing out in a future we'd never have?

"I'm glad you killed Ritalia," Mila said.

"Highlight of the night," I huffed, happy for the change of conversation.

She laughed softly. "I wish I got to watch it happen."

Mila didn't though. And she didn't get to say goodbye to Lyria. She'd been unconscious the entire time, waking in Meridat's manor two days later to her life being entirely flipped on its head. She hadn't left her room for three days, only Soulguiders going in to try to figure out what happened to her in the Spirit River when she was knocked out by a head wound and the magic entered her bloodstream.

"Did the Soulguiders find anything?" I asked.

"Not yet." She sank into her seat, and every blink, every word, appeared as leaden as I felt. "They're going to take me into the city with them this week. Try some other methods."

"Maybe it really didn't have any lasting effect."

"Maybe." Mila shrugged, her haunted stare drifting back to the useless mystlight flickering in the center of the table. "But when have we been that lucky lately?"

CHAPTER SEVEN
OPHELIA

MALAKAI AND I TRIED TO WORK A DAILY TRAINING session into our schedule. Though *training* was a loose word, given that I was still learning how to balance with the wings pulling at my back. The general soreness of my muscles and constant inferno ravaging my body faded as I adjusted to the magic pushing for a constant release, but the weight made lifting even a training sword an entirely new challenge.

We based our movements on Echnid's. If the god was lingering in a common space, we stayed nearby trying to overhear his conversations. A few times I found myself under the thrall of the god's magic, but Malakai would always whisper something to me or nudge down the Bind, and I'd snap back to myself.

So far, we'd learned nothing of *how* he intended to get his revenge on the known gods or why he needed me to do it. But he was growing impatient. His moments of outrage rippled through the palace. The sky outside turned grayer by the day, and my worries darkened with it.

A few days into our new routine, Malakai was cleaning up from our training session in my bathing chamber—he'd taken to sleeping on the sofa in my suite. With my wet hair trailing down my back, I wandered into my office to go over the books we'd pulled from Lucidius's private collection.

And I stopped in my tracks.

"What are you doing in here?" I spat.

I'd avoided Damien since I woke up. Had avoided all the Angels as much as I could. They were often out gallivanting the cloudy skies or bowing at their beloved god's feet. I hadn't been forced to solely face the Prime Mystique who betrayed me and slew my predecessor since that day in the mountains.

From his spot before the window, Damien cast an uninterested glance over his shoulder, then turned back to the mountainous view. "You forget that it was my home first, little seraph."

"It has not been your home for centuries," I said.

"I have not resided here, but does a home ever truly stop being that which it once was? The halls grow empty, but the heart continues yearning."

A beast roiled inside me, longing to snap and claw at him. Perhaps it was my seraph or maybe just my bruised spirit, but it begged to unleash the fury burning brighter than my Angellight.

Damien scanned the peaks, eyes drifting to the ceiling mural of a warrior dipping his sword in a lake, the blades illuminated a striking blue. And there was such a heavy melancholy to his scarred face, a guilt stiffening his wings, like every twitch rocked through him with the effect of his actions.

Perhaps it was regret for killing Annellius, for lying to me. Perhaps it was something entirely unrelated. Maybe the immortal Angel was simply bored of his existence. But it tugged at the part of me that was his, born of the myth magic that brought my seraph to life.

It was for that part of me—not him—that I softened a touch. "You miss it, don't you? The mountains and the palace."

"That I do. More than words could do justice, little seraph."

I swallowed at that name again, and for the moment, I set aside my grudge with the Angel. More than I needed to be angry with him, I needed answers. "Did you know? All this time, did you know I..." I trailed off, trying my hardest to flutter my wings but wincing.

Maybe they *were* still a little sore. And forget flying. That was something I wasn't sure I'd ever conquer.

"No," Damien admitted, his voice earnest. "No, I never knew

what myth resided in your veins beyond the Angelcurse and the Godsblood. I never knew what you and your sister could do, or"—the Prime Mystique Warrior looked over my limp wings, expression every bit as stony as the statues of his likeness lining these halls—"I may have tried to find a way around it."

"Why?" I balked, stepping closer. My hair dripped water to the floor, the steady *plunk* loud in the silence.

Damien continued to study his mountains, the home he'd built for himself many millennia ago. The one I'd claimed, too. Now taken from us both.

"Because some burdens are too heavy for one person to bear." Before I could ask what he meant, he said, "Come, Ophelia."

With a wave of his hand, he cast a beam of Angellight to shove the balcony doors wide, and I followed him over the threshold. The mountain air was crisp—familiar.

"Can you teach me how to use it like that?" I asked. Damien lifted a brow, and I was certain he knew what I meant, but I elaborated, "The Angellight. I have...I have your power within me."

"You have all of our power within you, Ophelia."

"How?" He'd told Malakai about the seraph magic, but I'd been unconscious. I still didn't understand *how* it was possible.

"He who bore the Angelcurse was always able to create our light with their blood upon the seven."

Tentatively, without an emblem in hand, I held out my palm. In the center, a swirling bud of Angellight bloomed, strands looping and swishing around each other. This was Damien's. If I hadn't known at the core of myself, it would have been clear with the way the light leaned toward him, absorbed his presence.

He studied it for a moment. Then, I closed my fist around it.

"I can do more than just summon Angellight with the emblems."

"You can," Damien confirmed. "And it is because of the seraph myth."

"The seraphs were slain, though," I said. "I heard you tell Malakai."

Damien nodded gravely. "We did not think their return was possible. As some of our strongest subjects, they were a threat. The gods saw to it that that danger was eliminated." Bitterness and mourning mingled in his voice, igniting a fight deep in my gut.

"Do you think there are more out there? In hiding, like me?"

If there were, they didn't deserve to suffer for the wrath of brutal deities.

But Damien shook his head. "I doubt it, and even if a few somehow escaped the slaughter—even if they mated and their lines are alive today—they would not be like you."

"Because I have the power of every Angel." That knowledge sat as heavy in the air as the storm clouds over the mountains.

"Curious, isn't it?" Damien posed the question. "To be the last seraph."

And with that statement, that truth hanging from the tips of the clouds didn't just hover. It compressed, an honorable pressure upon my shoulders. To be the final representative of this race that had been slain, all for the actions of their god.

As it settled within my spirit, a wail bounced off the marble halls, and a shadow crossed over us. Large, sweeping wings beat against the sky, wind whipping my hair into my face as Thorn descended from the highest turret into Damenal.

"Shouldn't you stop him?" I asked, wincing as the Mindshaper's thorny black halo glinted in the light unspooling from his wings. Remembering how his power had dug into my mind and manipulated my own myth magic to unleash the seraph, I shivered.

"He is only here because I allow it. No Angel can enter another's capital city without permission." He paused, but I tucked that interesting restriction away. "Have you ever wondered why the Mindshaper plains are snow-covered?"

I blinked up at Damien. "No, but I have also never wondered why the Soulguiders live in arid deserts or the Engrossian swamps are so humid."

"That is not that same," Damien corrected. "Those regions still experience seasons. But Mindshaper Territory is trapped in an eternal winter."

"What do you mean?"

"There is much to learn from the Angels, Ophelia." He didn't look at me as he said it though, attention shifting inside, trained again on the mural coating the ceiling of the study.

Thorn landed at the foot of the palace gates, his impact with the stone rattling the ground, and he cast a gust of wind to throw the gold bars wide. Even from here, I knew how icy that magic was. How the power of storms ran through his veins—through mine— that cord of Angellight reaching toward him now.

"It was Thorn?" I asked, pulling back the slippery, chilled magic.

"One day, long after that crown graced his brow and stole a piece of him in return, we pushed our brother too far. We tried to tear him from his underground labyrinth." I thought of the winding tunnels beneath Mindshaper Territory that the rebels had adopted as their haven. Ricordan, the man who sheltered us down there when we needed to hide from Kakias, told us Thorn had created the place. That he went mad, digging out the pit we'd eventually found his broken crown in.

Damien went on, "During his answering tantrum, Thorn sent a frostbitten gale across the continent. The rest of us were able to shield our lands, but that only concentrated the extreme might on his territory.

"We are not meant to dispel so much raw power at once, but Thorn...he was long past the rules. Lines had been driven between us hundreds of years prior. We had come back together to try to attend to him."

"A tragedy," I muttered.

"As I said," Damien repeated, this time catching my eye, "there is much to learn from my kind."

Angellight twirled around my hand, dancing up my arms. The warm kind that was a gift of the Angel on the balcony beside me, perhaps touched by a hint of Ptholenix's fire to combat the chill Thorn's sad history left across my skin.

Much to learn, indeed.

There were many things I needed to ask Damien. Why had he killed Annellius? Why had he led me down this path? So many truths that would not change history but might help me make sense of it. In this moment, though, it wasn't what weighed on me the most.

"I refuse to be weak ever again, Damien." I turned to him, and I swore his purple eyes danced with anticipation. "I want to learn to control my magic. And I"—my wings twitched—" want to fly."

~

"WHAT DOES SERAPH MAGIC DO EXACTLY?" I asked Damien as we stood on a secluded mountaintop just outside the Northern Quarter of Damenal the next day. The Revered's Palace sat primly on its peak, overlooking the streets of the capital. Warriors went about their business as usual, but a nervous energy threaded through the city. Furtive glances over shoulders and quicker steps to return home, lest one of the less savory Angels sweep through the cobbled lanes.

Valyrie strolled among the shops, lavender ether swirling from her wings and making her impossible to miss. She'd been frequenting the markets, bringing back tapestries, artworks, clothing, jewelry, and Spirits knew what else.

Malakai had opted not to come with us, remaining in my study with Lucidius's favored tomes to try to piece together false histories. So far, it had been a fruitless search, but we'd thought the same of his journals originally. Splitting from Malakai rooted a vulnerability in my gut that had me squirming—magic itching to be released.

"Seraph magic *is* Angel magic, Ophelia," Damien explained, white panels of fabric draping around his waist. His chest was on display, soaking up what little sun pierced the gray clouds today. "It comes directly from us."

"Does that weaken you?" I asked.

He shook his head, blond curls billowing in the wind. "No. We never felt it. It was nothing more than a connection, like every seraph that guarded me was a link on a chain, and I the manacle at the end."

The metaphor was dismal, but I absorbed every word the

Angel shared. Learning this magic was the first step in understanding what Echnid wanted with me.

"If seraph magic is Angel magic, what are the properties of Angel magic?" I asked, testing my wings at my back as their strength grew.

"As you have seen"—he cast a wide dome of shimmering gold light over us—"it varies between us. But all Angellight is restorative." As he said it, a few withering plants perked up, their leaves tinting a more vibrant green. "All can cure rot and the most deeply planted taints."

A beam of Damien's light burrowed precisely into the earth, ripping up a dead root with such exact movements, the dirt around it wasn't even disturbed. He commanded it with an ease and accuracy that didn't even seem to require a thought.

That. That was what I was here for. What I wanted to learn and why I set aside my grudge.

"Mine is connected to the mountains." The bubble of light solidified then rumbled, the earth quaking. "It can also be its own force. Should anyone try to approach right now, they wouldn't be able to penetrate the space. Should I throw this at an opponent, it would force them back."

"So, it's healing, but it's also defensive."

Damien nodded. "The light itself is raw and endless. It could theoretically have a number of uses and forms. But with my power, I will never be able to command the tides or decipher the stars. There are limits where unique tendencies come into play."

And the only way to truly learn it was to try.

So that was what we did. Daily, Damien and I visited that mountaintop, and he gave me a lengthy routine of exercises that ranged from strength and magic control to physical conditioning. Those typically included *using* magic while I worked out, but the focus was also on balancing my new wings with movements I'd been doing for years. Like a toddler learning to walk. And eventually, hovering off the ground, inching higher in small increments.

With sweat slicking my skin and the mountain breeze tangling through my hair, we went back to the beginning. I conjured light as I had many times before, demonstrating the ways I'd used it, and Damien scolded me for the lack of control.

He pushed me at an impossible pace, and I glowered at him, snapping, "Perhaps if the person that could explain how it worked hadn't abandoned me, I'd know better."

That had a layer of guilt slipping across his scarred features.

"Keep trying," Damien demanded, bottling up any hint of remorse. Why was he so insistent about me learning quickly when I'd been living with this myth secretly inside of me for years and no one knew?

Again and again, he had me create barriers. Bring individual leaves on wilted stalks back to life.

I scrawled shapes and messages in the air with the shimmering threads of his power, commanding very precise control before I was allowed to move to more expansive tasks. One day, Damien even had me practice feeding the power into a dull ring on his middle finger until the stone in the center glowed.

"Is that how you created the emblems?" I asked.

"On a very small scale, yes," was all he said.

After the first week, despite the fact that I was still showing little progress beyond increased accuracy and precision, Damien had Gaveny and Ptholenix, the Seawatcher and Bodymelder Angels, joined us.

Their presence swarmed the mountaintop, thickening the air with their undiluted ether. Ptholenix's wings reflected a burning array of fiery hues, his light licking up his tawny skin like flames. And Gaveny...Gaveny seemed to be made of the tides. When Damien scolded my control and the Seawatcher laughed, it was like a wave crashed around us, mirroring the boom of water against rocky cliffs as I remembered from Brontain.

The first time, I stumbled at the sound, and Ptholenix drawled, "You will get used to it."

"What?" I asked, righting myself.

"Your knees felt rocked on a boat just now, correct?" he clarified, one thick brow arched expectantly. When I nodded, he jerked his chin to where Gaveny and Damien argued about what I should be prioritizing, the Seawatcher grinning to match the latter's frown. He turned his back on me, an intricate tattoo of a rope and anchor decorating his spine.

Ptholenix went on, "We are made of the core of the earth's magic, thanks to how we all came by our power. We were always gifted, but when we truly absorbed that ether, it warped us. It is the most powerful source in the realms, and we began to reflect it in ways that speak to our nature. The Tideshifter"—Gaveny, apparently—"is a living sea, as I am a flame, and Valyrie is comprised of the stars."

It made sense that the Angels, especially the five minor clan Prime Warriors, were comprised of their magic. Now that their Spirits were returned, they ebbed with the heart of that raw source.

"Why is Bodymelder magic demonstrated by flames?" I asked, calling up Ptholenix's thread. Orange Angellight twirled around me, but I focused on shaping it to an actual flickering flame. Something I had yet to achieve.

It sat above my palm in an indeterminable shape.

The Firebird, as Gaveny and Damien called him, watched stoically as I manipulated his magic with my seraph power. "Flames can be more cleansing than water. Where the latter douses, drenches, and drowns, fire can burn away the most poignant curses, allowing us to start fresh as phoenixes are reborn from the ashes. It is similar to how Bodymelders pull at the threads of one's being to heal maladies. They cleanse, like the purest bead of a flame."

Though he spoke proudly, reverently, of the magic, there was a morose tone to his reasoning.

I shouldn't have pried, but the sphere twisting in my hand wilted with the dampened explanation. "Why do you sound upset about that?"

Ptholenix considered me, my brow sweating as I worked to reignite and tame the fiery thread of light. Finally, he said, "We Angels have existed for a very long time. Before the Ascension when we were trapped within stone, this magic lived within us, and I have experienced enough to know that while fire is in fact restorative, sometimes it marks the most dismal moments of our lives. Things can be swallowed in flame, never to be found again. Deaths are often sealed with the burning of bodies to ash."

The light licking along his skin flared at that, illuminating the gold vine tattoo that wrapped around his shoulders from an orchid right between his wings. His light within me pulled to him, wanting to feel connected, but it was clear from the way his voice trailed off that *he*, this legendary being, had lost something very personal to the flames that comprised his spirit. Had sealed a death himself with the ashes.

And that was too intimate to ask about. So, I fanned the fire within me, and we stood in silence as, eventually, a singular, flawless flame danced in my palm.

"Ophelia," Damien barked not long later. I spun toward him, my wings not rocking my body off balance at all, but when I snapped about him being demanding, he summoned a strike of Angellight to crisp the nearest cypher tree. "Restore that."

And we resumed our work, the echoes of a Firebird's sorrow and Damien's urgency igniting even more questions in my mind.

CHAPTER EIGHT
OPHELIA

ECHNID SOUGHT ME OUT THAT NIGHT. MALAKAI WAS reading through a book about Angellight after I told him how pushy Damien had been when the Prime Warrior himself appeared in the study.

"He would like to see you, Ophelia," Damien said through a grimace.

Malakai squinted at the Angel, and my Bind squirmed.

"You'll be okay here?" I asked.

"I will." Malakai patted the stack of books beside him, but his other hand pressed to the hilt of Lucidius's dagger on his hip.

In silence, I followed Damien upstairs, my heart thundering as I guessed where he was leading me.

This is why you stayed, I reminded myself. To get close to Echnid. To learn what his plans were and unravel them from the inside out. So, as we approached the Rapture Chamber, I did so with my wings held aloft and my steps sure.

"Thank you, Damien," Echnid said, dismissing the Angel without another word. Damien didn't look at me as he left, and if I still trusted him as much as I once had, I may have been concerned by that.

Instead, I faced the Warrior God. "You wanted to see me?"

"Yes, Ophelia." Echnid turned away from the drop off into the mountains—the one he always seemed to be staring at. Searching for something. He motioned to the long table where a pitcher of water and small spread of food waited. Including my favorite lemon cookies. "Please, help yourself."

Wariness bolted through me, but I hid the reaction. Damien had explained the Angelglass to me during one of our training sessions. He'd said they'd been able to keep an eye on many of my movements. If Echnid had been watching, he likely knew how mistrusting I was of them all. And I was here to convince him I wanted to help.

So, I strode across the chamber and poured myself a glass of water, eagerly biting into a cookie. Then, locking my trepidation and temper behind my Revered mask, I gave myself up to the god.

This is why you stayed, I reminded myself again as I took a seat.

Echnid poured himself a glass of sparkling wine, sipping as he sat across from me. Neither of us claimed the Revered's chair. Questions bubbled through me, but I reclined, waiting to see what the god wanted.

"I have not always looked like this," Echnid began, and my brows pinched. "Even a year ago, before your Curse took its deepest grasp on Ambrisk, I retained my darker features. But magic changes so much, Chosen Child."

"It appears it does." In emphasis, I fluttered my wings.

Echnid watched that motion with a manic attention in his milky eyes, his mists thickening into tendrils greedily tasting the air. "Ambrisk was created to house the expanse of magic that exists in the universe."

"That is what we are taught." I recited, "The mountains contain magic, the Blackfyre tarpits in Engrossian Territory are the source of its dark counterpart. The Angels created their warriors to protect and guide it after that magic birthed their holy selves. Power is the strongest here, but it fuels every realm and world in existence, too."

"Many, yes," Echnid corrected. "Doesn't it seem odd that Ambrisk is the strongest, yet it is isolated?"

"No," I answered truthfully as the mist swirled closer. "If it's that powerful, I'd say it makes sense."

But a wisp of doubt echoed in my mind. I scratched at my Curse mark as the idea became a steady thrum of life.

It did make sense, right? That's what we'd always been taught.

"Perhaps you make a point." Moonlight splayed across Echnid's pale features as he tilted his head. "But I would caution you to consider that because bridges from Ambrisk to other realms have been sealed, there are a lot of truths left out of this one."

What kind of truths? Endless possibilities raced through my mind, sending my fingers fidgeting around my glass. I ate the cookie with an air of false patience and picked apart every word out of the god's mouth.

"You have learned of the bridges that connect the realms and those who can traverse them," Echnid said.

"The Realmspinners," I breathed. Aimee—the Storyteller Tolek and I had met multiple times on Gallantia now—had told us about them in a pleasure house in Lendelli. She'd been the only Storyteller who knew of the Angelcurse and pointed us toward the Gates of Angeldust.

Had she known about Echnid, too? I wished I could ask her.

"Realmspinners," Echnid confirmed, grimacing, and I pushed aside thoughts of the Storyteller. "They are the only ones with full access to other worlds, though they have not been seen in many, many years."

"Why?" I asked.

"That is a long story for another time," Echnid said as he gazed out over the mountains again.

But I pushed. "Were they killed? Like the seraphs?"

"No," Echnid declared with finality. "The Realmspinners did not see the same fate as your predecessors."

I was going to ask more, but he turned back to the table and continued, "We—my sibling gods and I—are not the only pantheon, but we were the ones who breathed life into Ambrisk and many realms it initially bridged to. And when this source of power grew stronger, we had to break connections with the other worlds. With lower gods and our children who inhabit those realms, and with a number of other creatures and subjects. But they all continue to feel the repercussions of power struggles and events on Ambrisk."

"You and the known gods can no longer access other realms either?" I asked.

"No," Echnid clipped, reclining in his chair and drumming his fingers on the arm. "Not anymore."

Not without Realmspinner magic, apparently. Echnid was stuck on Ambrisk unless he could access that coveted source.

I leaned forward, riveted as my fingers wrapped around my Curse mark, the pulse within mounting. "Where are the known gods, then?"

"They exist in a plane above the realms they created, overseeing and manipulating. If I wish to banish their influence for good, I must first open the way to bring them into this realm." He was so forthcoming with this information, his mist swirling eagerly around the table. It lured me in, tugging at some root deep within me.

"How will you do that if the Realmspinners are lost?"

Echnid considered, and his eyes lit with glee—deranged or exhilarated, I wasn't sure. "There will be a way."

And while chills tried to break across my skin at the words, his mist washed over me and soothed them.

Night after night, Echnid summoned me to the Rapture Chamber—always alone. The meetings went on in much the same fashion as the first. I would arrive and sit at the table where I was settling easier into the wooden chairs. The white mist of his power would creep along the marble floors and over the back of my seat. And the god would speak of his plans.

The days in Damenal started to blur into one endless stream, nothing differentiable, all buried beneath the haze of misty magic and godly demise.

He told me of his goal to lock his brother and sister gods from Ambrisk completely so he could restore the warriors to greatness. Of how for all those years he was trapped in that Stone Realm, he dreamed of a world where our kind was not pushed beneath others simply because he had grown more powerful.

One night, he told me of the horrors he had faced in isolation. And as I sat there, absently brushing a thumb in circles over the Curse mark on my wrist, the part of me that wanted to believe this god grew.

He has the best intentions for our people.

It was that voice that took over when I arrived in the Rapture Chamber one night to find a caged bird chirping between the pillars. When I asked the reason, Echnid told me he wanted to help mentor my magic from the *fel strella mythos* now that we were working together.

That was good. I needed to learn more about the mythos power so I could share it with Jezebel. Perhaps we could help Echnid do away with the gods.

He directed me to stand before the cage and pull up as much of the myth magic as possible. To pour it into the bird within and see how I could transform it.

The shimmering gold spilled out of me, much more controlled now that I was training with Damien. It wrapped around the little bird's feathered frame, and Echnid stood over my shoulder.

My mind was dull, my vision rippling at the edges.

"More," Echnid instructed, his mist gathering closer.

I did as he said.

Until the Rapture Chamber was flooded with light. Until the bird was flapping its small wings uncontrollably, its twittering growing higher pitched.

Until, in a final burst of gold, the night went silent.

And a thud echoed as it fell to the floor of the cage.

My magic snapped back into me, the force ricocheting through my body. And as I watched the bird, horror dawned.

I'd...I'd killed it. My palms grew damp, throat constricting.

No, no, no. It had been too much, too strong. My myth magic had *killed* it.

"Must not have been a good source," was all Echnid said.

Haziness washed over me. The entire chamber turned dull again, and as I scratched at the Curse mark on my wrist, the guilt dissipated.

We sat back at the table, the lack of chirping a deafening

silence, and Echnid continued to tell me of his plans. As if nothing unusual had occurred.

And the meetings went on.

"How will you do it?" I finally asked him one night. "Dismiss the other gods?"

"I am working on that piece, my seraph," he said, grimacing over the words. "I think I have something that will protect us in the meantime." His gaze flicked across me. "How is your training?"

"Good." While the nights with Echnid had become a blur, the time I spent atop the mountains exercising my magic was always clarifying. "I'm much more controlled than I was a few weeks ago."

"Excellent. Now, it is late. Valyrie will escort you back." He rose from his seat and extended a hand toward the door. I hadn't noticed the Starsearcher Angel's entrance.

"Where's Damien?" I asked, but I rose, not truly caring about the answer. If Echnid said Valyrie would lead me to my suite, that was okay with me.

"Damien had some work to complete tonight, so I offered," Valyrie said. The Starsearcher gestured to the hall, sprinkles of silver dripping from her fingertips with the movement. "This way, Ophelia."

I cast one confirming glance at Echnid, and he nodded.

Valyrie's voice was commanding yet gentle. It was easy to see how the warriors in her races could have been bent to her ruthless will so easily. She walked barefoot through the moonlit marble halls of the palace, starlight seeming to follow in her wake. From her hair, her steps.

"Is that your magic?" I asked as silver faded into the floor.

"It is, but not the Angellight you possess," she answered, not pausing her graceful gait.

I hurried to catch up, my wings heavy against my back. Spirits, my whole body was heavy after days of training and rough sleep.

"What magic do you have beyond Angellight?" I asked. "Is it the Fates?"

"You are very clever, Ophelia," she said. "Because of my

connection to the Fates and Moirenna, I often have an excess of power. Its physical form tends to manifest as this." She waved a hand, the silver sprinkles drifting to the floor like fresh snow.

"Will my magic be like that?"

Pulling up the seraph power I'd gotten from the Starsearcher, I sent a beam of star-flecked light ahead of us. It bounced across the marble columns lining the second-floor corridor, harsher than hers.

Valyrie encouraged, "Envision it softer, like the moonlight on our skin. Cool and an essence of the universe rather than a force."

I did as she said, picturing my light morphing into her celestial one, reshaping it as we walked. I spun galaxies in my mind, stars racing through the skies for eons and meteors crashing. Bridges opening among the realms, carving paths between worlds.

And finally, the light softened. The beam became misty, sprinkling the air with a lilac haze and sparkling stars.

"Damien will continue to teach you brute strength," Valyrie commented. "And that is useful in many cases, but it would be beneficial to learn all facets of your seraph."

The storms and seas and souls. The cosmos and cleansing fires. I wanted to conquer them all.

"You have been spending a lot of time in Damenal," I stated as I tried to maintain the power of the light.

"I enjoy the wares," Valyrie explained.

I laughed, and the starlight twinkled with it. "I've noticed. The tapestry you brought back two days ago was so large, I thought you wouldn't be able to fly."

"It had been a while since I'd seen one of such make," Valyrie said sadly. "The story it told of the gryphon armies was one of my favorite tales before..."

Her words trailed off. Before the Ascension. Before the Angels were locked in a Stone Realm. It was unfair that they had suffered for their master—that any of us were dragged into these wars among power hungry gods.

I was about to apologize to her—to an Angel after all they'd put me through—but Valyrie turned her navy galaxy-swirling eyes on me and elaborated, "The gryphons had an affinity for my clan when they roamed Ambrisk, just as the phoenixes did for Ptholenix. Each of us had our favored mythical beasts."

"Why did they all disappear when things like the nemaxese stayed?" I asked.

"A nemaxese may have properties of magic and be woven into their own legends, but they weren't the creatures of the gods."

I yawned as I considered that. Ambrisk, the bridges, the gods. Everything was so much more complicated than we'd been led to believe. But perhaps—perhaps, we were on a path to leaving a legacy worth remembering, if Echnid was right.

"You should get some rest, Seraph Child," Valyrie said. I hadn't realized we were at the door to my suite, blocking out the other rooms in this corridor out of habit.

"Yes," I said with another yawn, my Curse mark tugging. "I think I would like to sleep and speak with Echnid again tomorrow." Part of me wanted to seek him out now, to keep learning.

And as bubbles gathered in my stomach, a haze slipping across my vision, a traitorous part of me thought I might be able to trust him.

"That would be wise," Valyrie encouraged.

She left without another word, but for the first time since waking here, I realized I was content. Maybe I *was* safe.

CHAPTER NINE
MALAKAI

WHEN OPHELIA WASN'T TRAINING WITH THE ANGELS OR being called to meetings with Echnid, she slept a lot. I guessed it was an effect of the magic she was expelling every day. But between that and my own research, I'd barely seen her in the weeks since we arrived in Damenal. Not enough to understand the things she was talking about with the Warrior God. Every time she returned from their discussions, she was contemplative, and she'd even begun insisting the god may have a point.

But until she gave me a firm reason why, I was going to keep researching what Annellius may have uncovered and ways you could banish a god's influence from a realm entirely.

This morning, I woke before Ophelia, and when she started to stir, I made my way down to the kitchens to prepare tea for her. As I waited for the water to boil on the mystlight stove, I stood before the long window above the counter and fought my mind from wandering to the thing that mattered damn more than anything else.

To the person I'd tried not to think about since we got here.

Mila.

My chest rattled, throat tightening.

I braced my hands against the counter, recounting facts.

Lyria was dead.

Mila was hurting.

And I was...here. Trapped.

My nails dug into the marble, and my vision wavered. Iron doors slammed in my memory.

Taunting laughs.

Marks carved into my flesh.

Cracking whips. The scars along my back itched, blood rushing through my ears. I counted my breaths in and out, in and out...

Pictured Mila.

Mila, alive and healthy. My heart rate slowed. Mila, breath against my neck and hands in my hair. My throat loosened. Mila's scars and the way she overcame every damn obstacle so fiercely.

"The girl sleeps often," a silken voice said behind me.

I spun as the kettle started to boil. "Who the fuck are you?" I asked, accusation thick in my tone.

This was no Angel. Moonlight hair cascaded around her frame, a flowing white gown clinging to her curves and slicing low between her breasts. It barely covered any of her skin as she sauntered forward on bare feet, pitch black eyes studying me. Chills pricked my skin, nerves sending my heart pounding.

"She sleeps?" she repeated. A finger stacked with gem-crusted rings traced the silver chain belt around her waist.

I swallowed, trying not to flinch at the links building that chain and how the delicate loops clinked together with each step.

"Who *are* you?" I repeated.

Her gaze roamed over my harried appearance and rumpled clothing. She could have been a warrior—no wings beat at her back nor did pointed ears peek from beneath her hair—but there was something about her that barked in warning. An unsettling aura that raised every alarm in my mind.

"Rozelyn, for short," she answered, as if I should have any fucking clue what that meant.

"And where did you come from, Rozelyn?" I asked, bracing my hands on the counter, one within easy reach of Lucidius's dagger tucked down the waistband of my pants.

With the elaborate onyx handle, it didn't fit comfortably down my boot, so I had to find other methods of concealment. I'd tried to ask Ophelia why she thought all of the weapons save training ones were gone, but she'd insisted it wasn't important.

Echnid's likely having the Angels mend them after years of wear, she'd said.

It doesn't mean anything, she'd insisted.

And the one that had truly set me on edge: *Perhaps Echnid has more of a point than we'd considered.*

"Her exhaustion is curious, don't you think?" Rozelyn asked, pulling me back to the present threat. She tilted her head in a way that I thought was supposed to be alluring.

"Not really," I deadpanned. "She's put under a lot of pressure in training." The sleep didn't seem odd. If anything, it was the weird, distant looks and how she couldn't seem to communicate her full thoughts about Echnid that worried me.

Without answering, Rozelyn assessed me again. Her lips curled into a smile, and with a dramatic exhale, she hummed. "Pity."

Didn't sound like she thought Ophelia's pain was a pity at all.

She took another sauntering step closer.

"Will you tell me why you're here now?" I tried to soften my voice enough to be welcoming. Just to get her to fucking answer.

That smile remained on her lips. "My friends and I have been brought here. To help build a future for the god."

"Build a future?" What in the Angels' fuck did that mean?

But she didn't offer an explanation. Rozelyn's hungry gaze tracked over me once more, and for a sickening moment, I felt like she wanted me to be that future. Then, she turned and floated toward the door, barely there silk dress slithering against the stone in her wake.

As she rounded the corner, the chill that had coated my skin went with her. I stared after her for long, tense minutes, waiting for something to happen, but nothing did. And as I waited, all I could think of was how that shock of white hair had swayed down her back and how it reminded me so much of someone else's, though more void of color where Mila's was as warm as sunlight.

I fell back against the counter, rubbing my temples. Maybe it was lack of sleep and worry driving me crazy. That woman was only an illusion of my tired brain. It was possible, but the gut-tightening nerves her presence had wrought said otherwise.

I took a deep breath, counting on the inhale and exhale as Mila had taught me. I kept up the pattern until the thoughts calmed and the kettle whistled shrilly, then I rolled my shoulders back and prepared the tea, setting everything on the tray.

We were trapped here, but I was okay. And after all we'd been through, my priority had to be making sure Ophelia was, too.

With a furtive look at the door the white-haired apparition had disappeared through, I made sure Lucidius's dagger was secure before leaving the kitchens, and my heart pounded in the back of my throat with every step.

No matter where I looked, I couldn't find Rozelyn over the next few days. I hadn't told Ophelia about her. A part of me really fucking hoped I was hallucinating.

But there was a much larger part of me, the one that was secretly terrified of how much unknown surrounded Echnid right now, that remained on guard.

I swore a humming voice filtered through the air as I walked the second-floor halls. I crept toward the banister and peered into the room.

No one.

There was no fucking one in sight.

Pressed against a pillar, I caught my breath and slid my hand to the waistband of my leathers. The cold handle of Lucidius's dagger pressed into the base of my spine.

Frustration tightened my muscles, but I sighed, scrubbing a hand down my face.

"He is convinced it is hidden in there," a rough whisper spiraled up from below.

Straightening, I checked over the railing, sticking close to the wall. It was still empty. Whoever it was had to be in the entrance to the corridor directly beneath this one.

"And what does he want you to do about it?" a second voice responded, lighter than the other.

"He wants it all taken care of."

A lengthy pause. Heart pounding, I leaned further. Light reflected against the marble floor, gold with a soft orange hue on one end and a hint of blue on the other.

"All of it?" That was Damien, and based on the shades of ether, his companions were likely Ptholenix and Gaveny.

"Yes," the original voice responded. "In three days' time."

I slid to the ground, willing my heart to stop beating so fucking loud so they wouldn't pick up on it. What did *he* order? Was it about Echnid wanting to banish the gods?

Despite all the research I'd done, I hadn't found a fucking hint as to how that would be possible, which was both promising and concerning. There was a chance Echnid hadn't either, but if the hushed conversation below said anything, the god *had* discovered something...

"Three days," I said beneath my breath. I had three days to figure out—

"Xenique?" asked one of the voices below—I thought it was Gaveny.

"Hello," the demigoddess Soulguider Angel greeted them, her voice airy. I pressed closer to the railing, searching again. Xenique stood before the hall the Angellight poured from, her own dark purple ether unspooling lazily around her wings.

"Is everything all right?" Damien asked.

Not answering, Xenique turned, strolling toward the arched windows that looked out over the mountains. Facing west, toward her deserts. Spirits, she was as difficult to communicate with as her warriors when they were receiving a premonition. As sunlight hit her features, I could just make out a small smile that seemed...wistful. Spirits, it was so *mortal*.

"I'm only seeking," she finally answered, as the other three Angels exited the corridor. Their combined ether painted the white marble floors, broad forms and wings imposing.

"What are you searching for?" Ptholenix asked.

"Sometimes, our responsibilities are simply heavy." Xenique's eyes slipped closed, and though her behavior was jarring, the others didn't seem phased, mumbling among themselves about their *three days.*

Finally, Xenique gracefully spun toward them, and I swore for a moment—not even a breath—her gaze flicked up to mine. "Never mind, brothers. Return to your work. You are doing well."

Then, Xenique opened the window and flew off across the mountains, leaving me shivering as I crept quietly back toward Ophelia's suite.

When I entered the office, I buried any residual unease—but I did assess the space before getting too comfortable. Books were strewn across the large dark-wood table, all exactly as I'd left them. Stacks based on categories and their usefulness, volumes tagged with notes.

I tried not to be overwhelmed by the sheer impossibility of what we were facing as I pulled the tome I'd left off on yesterday closer, a book on myths that had been wedged on the highest shelf. I'd found a vague reference to the sisters in the pegasus and khrysaor origin tales and how their magic was its own balance, but hadn't had a chance to show it to Ophelia yet.

Today, I was searching other legends. Anything that pointed toward the gods, their war Echnid had mentioned, or how to *dismiss* them, should Ophelia be wrong, and the Warrior God was in fact as dangerous as I feared.

While wars raged among gods over the Balance Realm, beings of equal measure built their own. On Revarris, the inhabitants fought deities by discovering their fatal flaws and building their armies around the pantheon's weak point. The keen battle strategists planned for years—decades—digging into the core of the world to reach troves and treasures known only to the highest powers who had birthed the realm.

They summoned beings to their side and unearthed blades made of precious ice said to be the downfall of the highest. In the end, it was an arrowhead of the deities' own trove that pierced their heart with a deadly throw. One no mortal archer could have fired, one no founder could have survived.

And the Balance rejoiced.

The Balance rejoiced.

According to this, the Balance of Power didn't want those powerful beings to win. If that was the very force holding magic to responsible standards, it stood to reason that it monitored the gods as well. And the Balance in this myth endorsed the brutal murder.

There had to be a way to slay a god for good.

I blew out a rough breath, leaning against my chair and tipping my head back to study the ceiling.

The gods created Ambrisk. That much we knew. They were responsible for the Angels—or Ambrisk's magic was—thus, the Angels answering to Echnid. Had the gods created worlds before Ambrisk? If so, why was Ambrisk the heart of all magic?

Or were the beings in this Revarris not our gods at all? Perhaps they were Fates or Angels, and that would have made them easier to kill in the myth than a god. There were stories about how to kill those things. But the myth implied these mysterious beings created that realm, which meant they couldn't be Angels or Fates.

Spirits, it was a mess to unravel. How had this fucking book gotten on that shelf in the first place? Clearly, the rest of the volumes were missing, judging by the large number three on the spine signifying this was part of a set. Very few of our books actually spoke of other realms beyond acknowledging that they existed. Why was that?

I'd never questioned it before, but now it seemed odd. Why *had* Ambrisk been silenced after the War Among Gods? If it hadn't, would we have known of Echnid sooner? Would we know a god's weakness?

As the questions ran through my head, I studied the mural on the ceiling. I'd memorized the fucking thing recently, always finding myself in this position. A warrior dipped his sword into a lake, the blade glowing blue for whatever damn reason.

The more I watched it, the more I wanted my own weapons back. Lucidius's dagger burned into my skin as it slid further down my spine.

A chill snaked through the room, the papers on the desk ruffling as I squinted at the mural. I was vulnerable with only this one weapon. So fucking—

A cloth clasped down on my mouth and nose.

I struggled for the knife, but the slim hand was surprisingly forceful as it pulled me back, and my vision spotted.

"Shh," a familiar voice cooed in my ear. "It's all right."

CHAPTER TEN
CYPHERION

"STARGIRL?" I ASKED, PUSHING OPEN THE DOOR TO OUR room on Meridat's estate. The Soulguider Chancellor had been kind enough to loan our group a guest house about a hundred yards east of her manor.

The single-story, six-bedroom building sprawled across the land, sandstone pillars curving around the edge of a serpentine river. This wasn't the spirit-laden source of the clan's magically imbued waterways, though. It wavered harmlessly outside the floor-to-ceiling window of our bedroom, shadowed by tall palm trees on the opposite bank.

And Vale stood before the window, one arm crossed over her stomach and her chin propped on her other fist. The late afternoon sun slanted through the fronds, heating the space. We should have lowered the wicker shade, but Vale was lost in thought.

The only part of her moving was the ripple through her chiffon skirt, the rich maroon fabric trimmed in gold. She'd purchased a few of them from the nearest market when it became clear we were staying here for a while. The style was similar to her clothing from her home in Starsearcher Territory, but with a scarf that wrapped around her torso instead of the tops with long, cascading sleeves and tight bodices she normally favored. She'd seemed to liven a bit with finding the clothing, like it was a part of the new self she was discovering since Titus.

"Vale?" I tried again. The room's thick rug swallowed the thud of my boots against marble as I stopped beside her.

She jumped when I placed a tentative hand to her back. "Oh, sorry." She shook her head. "What did you say?"

Her round olive eyes searched mine, silver tinting the irises. That damn hint of swirling power hadn't gone away since the night she read about the ascension before the Gates of Angeldust, and every time I saw it, a defensive beast rose in my chest.

"Nothing." I took a breath, trying to force away the aggression, but Vale caught it.

"You don't need to protect me from my power, Cypherion." She sighed, exasperated. I was a fucking idiot.

"I know I don't, Stargirl," I said.

She arched a brow. "Then how come every time you meet my eyes, you get a look in yours that says you're about to find a fighting ring to work out the tension?"

"Isn't that a better reaction than trying to kill the Angel who put the magic there?" I joked half-heartedly, but Vale just leveled me her most admonishing look. I rubbed a hand down the back of my neck, over the Bond tattoo that committed me to the mountains. "It's not that I'm angry."

"What is it, then?" Vale asked, turning to face me fully.

"The first time I saw that look in your eyes was in the Valyn Archives." Her expression softened in understanding. "We all know how that night turned out."

"We do," Vale said, casting a glance back over the water. "But I'm a different person now. I'm stronger, and my magic is no longer restrained."

Gripping her chin, I gently turned her gaze back to mine, forcing myself to look into those eyes that held my entire life—my fears, my future, my love—and to see the power within instead of the consequences. It was hard, given that rationale and logic were the two things I'd prided myself on for most of my life and consequence was the natural extension of them, but for Vale, I tried.

Undying strength stared back at me.

"What changed with your magic?" I muttered, cupping her jaw.

"That's what I'm trying to find out." Vale wrapped her arms around my waist and rested her head on my chest. I settled into her heartbeat, and for the first time since Ophelia and Malakai had been taken, I tried to fucking unwind. I'd spent every moment with Meridat's team, studying Artale so maybe we could learn how to combat Echnid.

Honestly, I was drowning beneath the pressure of it all. How did Ophelia accept it so readily?

But for a breath, I just tried to relax.

For the briefest moment, it worked.

But when Vale said, "I can't be protected from fate, Cypherion, and I won't sit by while I may have a way to fight," every muscle in my body stiffened.

She leaned back, looking up at me expectantly. We'd had this conversation repeatedly.

"We need to be smart," I muttered for the hundredth time.

"We can't leave them locked up there."

"If Ophelia is willing to let Malakai stay there with her, the circumstances can't be that bad."

"I was willing to remain with Titus, and that didn't stop you from rescuing me."

Fuck. That was a card she had yet to play, and it was clear from the way the silver in her eyes glinted that she'd been holding onto it for a while.

"Vale." I sighed, stepping back and running a hand through my hair. "Don't use that against me."

"Don't make me," she said calmly. So fucking calm, as we always were when we tried to come to an understanding.

But anger roared beneath my skin. Not at her—never at her—but at the fact that we were in this situation. That she'd experienced such horrendous manipulation that she had this argument to play against me in the first place. That I was drowning.

I propped myself on the edge of the bed, crossing my arms. "I never wanted to be a leader."

Vale softened, sitting beside me. "And yet, you're a terrific one."

I scoffed. "Don't compliment me when I'm trying to argue

with you." Sweeping her hair behind her shoulder, I traced the silver tattoo that had bonded her to Titus, but upon his death, became nothing more than her own personal constellation. "When I made the decision to rescue you, I was only prioritizing *your* safety." Truly couldn't have cared less about the rest of the world. "But now, with Ophelia gone, I'm trying to balance the interests of an entire warrior clan."

"So, use me. Echnid had Valyrie and Damien tell Ophelia not to look too closely at the stars because he didn't want her to see the threats he posed to the world. Didn't want us to know that maybe he shouldn't be free." Her hand landed atop mine. "There has to be more I can find. I can read and try to find a way to rescue them. Then Tolek, Mila, and I will be in and out of Damenal within hours."

I wasn't asking her to stop reading, but I couldn't support a plan that sent her into the Revered's Palace right now. "We can't be sure that even magic as strong as yours will get past Echnid's barrier."

"We have to try!" she cried, pushing up from the bed.

"He's a fucking *god*, Vale!"

"And I have *nine Fate ties*, Cypherion! I can read higher powers! Don't you think if I'm on Ambrisk now, alive and allied with the very people who may be able to change the fate of the world, that's for a reason?"

"The only fate I am certain of, Stargirl, is that you're mine. The rest, I don't know what to believe." Fate was so fickle. I couldn't see it, didn't trust it.

Vale crossed her arms, lips pressing into a pout I wanted to kiss right off her. "If I can't compliment you when we're arguing then you can't say sweet things."

I smirked. "Deal."

Vale stepped between my legs, and I spun her around so she was on my lap, her back pressed to my chest. Gently, I kneaded the spot around her tattoo. "I just don't want to act before we know for certain."

"My certainty comes from the Fates," she swore. "I know their truths in my bones. It's as instinctual as breathing."

I dropped my lips to her shoulder, tracing the edges of that constellation with my mouth, one star to the next. Vale melted against me, the knot of tension between us slipping away momentarily.

"That sort of magic is still new to me," I whispered. "I'm learning to trust it."

I kissed up her neck, and Vale's head rolled to the side. For a long moment, she let me nip and lick her skin—biting that spot just above her tattoo to leave my own imprint on her—and taste the starlight she always reminded me of.

On a breathy whisper, she asked, "Do you trust me?"

She looked at me over her shoulder, lips parted and one hand gripping my thigh, inching upward.

"Of course, I do," I swore, my voice thick.

I slammed my lips to hers, and as my tongue slipped inside her mouth, her answering hum was an agreement to pause the argument for now, on this plateau of trust. I flipped her around so her back hit the feathered comforter, her hair and skin gleaming against the rich jewel-toned bed. Even the silver in her eyes shone.

Working kisses down her neck, I pressed the truth of my statements into her skin. *I trust you. I believe in your power. I'm just so fucking scared.*

The way she pulled me up to her and kissed me said she heard it.

I palmed her breast, pinching her nipple over the fabric, and Vale gasped against my lips, arching into me. "Please, Cypherion," she panted, wrapping her legs around my waist and rocking against me.

"Please, what?" I asked.

But before she could answer, a knock sounded at the door.

"Go away," I grumbled.

"I'm truly sorry," Santorina's stern tone echoed through the wood. "But I can't."

I sighed, cock still hard against Vale's center. "Why the fuck not?"

But it wasn't Rina who answered. Beneath me, Vale gasped—not in lust, but in the way that had me reaching for my scythe. Her eyes were pure silver, a reading forcing itself to the surface without even the aid of incense.

And she whispered, "It's Valyrie."

~

THERE WAS A FUCKING Angel in the manor's meeting chamber.

We'd seen the Angels—all seven of them—and their abundant power swirling in that theater in the mountains. But seeing Valyrie here, her silken silver hair tumbling to her waist, a galaxy of lilac ether undulating around her wings, and a gown that gleamed like the star-speckled sky draping her olive skin, was more striking than before.

When Vale and I entered, Valyrie spun, the train of her gown slithering across the tiled floor—fuck, she really stood on this ground. Walked on Ambrisk. I'd known the Angels were out there, but to see one in a place we'd been spending hours every day was another thing entirely.

And this Angel gave the woman whose hand was twined with mine a smile that was somehow both cruelly cold and warmly welcoming. "Hello, my Fatecatcher."

"Prime Warrior." Vale gave her a nod, dipping into a shallow curtsey.

I stiffened but gave a small bow out of respect. Meridat stood at the head of the long table, flanked by her three advisors, one of each dynastic family that headed their clan as symbols of Xenique's three daughters. Tolek, Mila, Santorina, Jezebel, and Erista all lined one side.

Everyone either had narrowed stares or white knuckled grips, hard jaws and defensive stances. Even those who hadn't been in the mountains knew what threat the Angels posed.

"What's going on here?" I asked as Vale and I took up positions among our friends.

"I will not mince my words, Cypherion Kastroff," Valyrie said, her wings flaring out as she commanded the opposite side of the table. Sprinkles of that celestial magic wafted through the air, her power palpable and swirling against my skin.

I ground my teeth, focusing on Vale's hand in mine and catching the Angel's navy cosmos-filled eyes.

"I take it you know where your Revered and her star tied one are?"

Tolek and Mila stiffened. "Are they okay?" Mila asked.

Valyrie's pause could have been remorseful. "Things at the Revered's Palace are not well."

"What's happening?" I growled, doing my best to rein back the temper that had woken at Vale's silver eyes.

The Angel swallowed, lifting her chin. "My god has descended into desperation, and I fear at this very moment he is preparing to attempt things that will stain his conscience and all of ours for eternity."

"Do Angels and gods even have consciences?" Tolek snapped, his voice a bite of aggression.

Valyrie didn't seemed offended, though. She tilted her head, a subtle iridescent halo of stars shimmering as the light hit it. "It is true that we are less feeling than some. When we were locked away and separated from our Spirits, they took all our emotions with them. We became heartless voids who only wanted to return to our true power and spite the gods who fooled us. Feelings returned in inklings as the Chosen retrieved our emblems and activated them, but when our Spirits returned fully, everything slammed back to living memory."

Her face twisted, lips pursing and cheeks hollowing like she was trying to suck all of those emotions back into herself. Valyrie had a reputation of being ruthless during her life, but those who were the cruelest often had the most damning histories. I tucked that away, squeezing Vale's hand to keeps myself from snapping.

Tolek wasn't as convinced. "Thorn didn't seem to have any remorse when he attacked me."

Cursed Spirits, I'd thought for a moment the Mindshaper Angel was going to behead Tolek with the force of that one slap in the mountains. Time had slowed, and I'd been ready to slaughter Thorn myself.

Valyrie's words were ice. "No, but our Mindshaper brother has suffered in ways that effect his reactions. And the rest of us are adjusting as best we can."

"You fought against us, though!" Tolek roared. "You kept us from following Ophelia and Malakai."

"We did as we had to."

"Glad to know Thorn *had* to strike me," Tol grumbled.

"I would be careful, Tolek Vincienzo." Valyrie's voice rang with the power of twelve Fates. "You do not know what you began with that push against him."

Something akin to a prophetic snow slithered down my spine, and I interjected before Tolek could jump across the table and start another fight with an almighty being. "And now you...what? Changed your mind?"

Valyrie's eyes dropped to my hand locked with Vale's, the soft smile on her lips seeming authentic this time. "I have seen possible futures that have expanded my understanding of our current situations."

My jaw ticked at the vagueness of that statement. This was why I couldn't let myself simply believe the Fates and Angels. I trusted Vale with my entire life but not them.

Sensing my discomfort, Vale took over the conversation. "Have the Fates or Moirenna showed you how Echnid will banish the other gods?"

"My god operates on whims. With his power stored up for millennia, he has considered too many scenarios for even celestial beings to know what course he will take. But he seeks vengeance for ancient acts of war, and many end with repercussions felt across realms."

"What are you saying?" Meridat asked with the cool control of a ruler who held her title for decades. She exchanged looks with her advisors.

"As Gallantian Warriors, you all have a purpose to uphold. Promises to guide and guard precious power on Ambrisk and maintain the Balance," Valyrie asserted. Death bellowed from those words, from her starry stare and the white fire igniting at the ends of her feathered wings. It was an order from an Angel of the Gallantian Warriors, an unspoken command to kill the threat to our kind—the threat to the Balance of Power that weighed all realms on its scales.

To go to war with a god.

Mila hissed, "We've already lived through two wars. And not all of us *lived*." Her eyes shone.

But...fuck. If Valyrie was telling the truth, there was little choice. Echnid may want to raise his warriors above all others, he may be trying to do right by his subjects, but what if it was a blindly righteous cause that shattered the Balance?

Trying to keep us moving, I asked, "How can we be certain of any of this?"

Valyrie took a deep breath and looked at Vale. "Fatecatcher, how are your readings?"

"My readings have been changing for months. From the blockage to the access to the gods to their ever-present humming through my mind."

"But have they faltered recently?"

Vale paused, chewing her lip.

"Have they?" I whispered.

"There was a moment," she muttered, eyes flashing up to mine, still swirling silver. "Yesterday. A stutter, where every Fate cut out."

Valyrie nodded. "Echnid has been seeking ways to sever any warrior ties with the gods beyond his own. That is the first step in his plan to fully seize power."

"Can he do that?" Erista gasped, her frame tense. The Soulguider advisors and Meridat all went equally still, likely considering how that would damage their connection to their spirit tending responsibilities.

"Not easily," Valyrie answered. "And not quickly. That may be your one saving grace."

"But if warriors do not keep the gods, how will them being severed affect things?" Santorina asked, stare bounding between us all.

Meridat explained, "We may not pray to them, but their magic is woven through the world. It could uproot the very nature of all life and power on Ambrisk. Banishing the gods could leave their magic present, but erasing the power all together... That could wipe out the legions of us who do rely on godly magic to uphold our responsibilities, or erase Soulguider demigod bloodlines entirely."

All eyes flocked to Jezebel. And after a beat of silence, she forced out, "Over my dead spirit will Echnid take anything else from me."

"You truly ring with the blood of the demigoddess," Valyrie observed, admiration burning in her tone. And Jezebel stood straighter.

The Angel went on, "You warriors are our living legacy. And if you are what we have left to grace the world with—all hope of the stars running through the veins of magic we have passed down— you mustn't waste it. I suggest you ask what you want *your* legacy to be as well." Her attention landed on me, the pressure of thousands of lives in her stare. "Stand as one or fall as many." Stars whirled through the ether around her wings. "I must go now. My absence will be noticed."

With that, the Starsearcher Angel lifted one of the wicker shades, strode right into the courtyard of Meridat's manor, and beat her powerful wings to take off into the air, stars and lilac ether swirling in her wake. As the echoes of her magic faded from the space, we waited in tense silence.

Finally, I looked to Meridat and declared once and for all, "We need allies."

MY HEAD WAS POUNDING with the plans we'd been making all afternoon when I pushed open the entrance to the guest house and slammed into Santorina.

"Sorry," I said, stepping aside and holding the door for her.

"It's all right." She straightened her dress, the thick leather belt around her waist holding a pristine set of knives. "Actually, I was looking for you."

My shoulders fell. "What's wrong?"

"Nothing exactly." She inclined her head toward the private study off the sitting room, and I followed.

Once the door closed, only the tall, book-and-artifact laden shelves looking down on us, I propped myself on the edge of the desk, sighing. "I'm not sure I can handle more bad news, so tell me quickly."

My mind went to the fae, sequestered in one of the rooms in this very house under Soulguider guard, and Rina's Bounty blood we hadn't deciphered yet.

But she said, "I got a message from Ophelia last night."

"Different than what she sends to you every night?" Using those shells, Ophelia contacted Rina every night to ask that we were okay. And every night, Rina returned the question.

Her lips pressed into a line. "She asked me to ensure Tolek stays away from the palace. That we're looking out for him so he doesn't come for her."

I pulled the leather band from my hair, running my hands through it. "I've tried reasoning with him, but he insists—"

"I know," Rina said, nodding. "But Ophelia is worried. I don't know, maybe we can assign him another task?"

Tolek would never give up on rescuing Ophelia. That much was certain. I knew that, Rina knew that, and Ophelia damn well knew that. He was furious that we weren't staging a rescue attempt for her and Malakai, and every damn day pushed him closer to the point of no return. I wasn't sure what I could do to drag him back without leaning into his anger, but if Ophelia asked...

"I'll figure something out," I told her.

"Thank you," Santorina said. And it was clear a sliver of tension unwound from her spine in sharing this burden with me.

"Are you ready for what you have to do?" I asked as we left the study to find the others for dinner. We'd agreed to venture into Xenovia proper for a last meal before tomorrow was consumed with final preparations. Before the day after, when what remained of our family was divided yet again.

"Ready?" She snorted a laugh. "Certainly not. But I'm going to do it nonetheless."

And those knives lining her waist glimmered in the chandelier's mystlight, giving her the impression of a walking weapon. That's what Santorina had become since the full emergence of her Bounty power: a living, breathing threat.

That's what we all would be to survive the impending storm.

Chapter Eleven
Ophelia

"Ophelia," Damien commanded.

My attention snapped up. "I'm sorry?"

"Have you listened to anything I've said?"

I shook my head, not even attempting to lie. All I could hear through the haze that had claimed my mind was Echnid's stories of gods and Realmspinners, closed bridges and freeing legends.

Echnid has more tales to share, a voice said in my head, and the fog wrapped tighter around my mind. The Curse mark on my wrist pounded as if even the blood pumping through my veins was elated.

The past few meetings, Echnid had me demonstrate how I could wield my Angellight and mythos power. I hadn't woken anything, but the Warrior God watched my precise control with such a keen interest. Pride flowed through me, stronger each night.

But everything in me froze when Damien said, "Today you are going to attempt to fly."

"*What?*" I shrieked.

The Angel nodded, arms locked over his chest, the smug satisfaction on his expression the kind only archaic years could spawn.

"How in the Angel's realm do you expect me to do that?" I asked, crossing my arms to match his.

"We've been strengthening your wings in our trainings for

weeks. Your back muscles are strong, and you've learned to balance your body."

"That doesn't mean I'm going to jump off a mountain," I drawled.

"Did I say to do that?" Damien asked dryly.

I sighed, the fog thickening. "I can barely move my wings."

"You're not trying."

And that accusation snapped something brutal within me. "Don't!" I snarled. Angellight pulsed around us—seraph power of *my* making searing through my fogged mind. Making everything a bit clearer as I pulled myself from recollections of Echnid. "Do *not* tell me I'm not trying. I've done nothing but try for a year—done nothing but work to unravel *your* prophecies and curses."

"This is a part of that, Ophelia. That curse is still alive within you, a tie to the present you are trying to escape, and the magic within you marks it. But just because you found an answer you don't like, does not mean you give up."

His words cloyed in my ears, pressure tightening my chest and shortening my breaths.

"I'm drained!" The confession was hot gravel burning up my throat. "Do you even care?" And the words that had been pushing at me every time I trained with Damien broke free. "You killed Annellius!"

The Angel froze, his stony expression etched from marble.

"Why did you do it?" I barreled on. "Why did you kill him?"

Damien crossed his arms, his expansive wings tucking in like he was uncomfortable, but his tone revealed nothing. "He was throwing away everything we worked for."

"Because he didn't want to free Echnid?"

"Yes," he said through a tight jaw. And his eyes warned me not to ask more—not to taint the air with the question on the tip of my tongue: *What if he shouldn't be free?*

He should be, a voice in the back of my head argued, wrapping the fog back around me like a worn cloak as my light winked out. *Echnid deserves his revenge.*

I nodded, remembering everything the god had told me of his

reasoning for his actions as I scratched my wrist. Though I still didn't know how Echnid planned to achieve his goals, I was beginning to understand him more.

It had been four weeks, and the unnatural phenomenons across Gallantia had calmed. The skies were flooded with rolling gray clouds, but the Rites of Dusk had not occurred, the fires in Bodymelder Territory extinguished, and temperatures across the continent simmered. I didn't know if Echnid himself was responsible, or if it was just magic balancing after his lock snapped, but with him here, things were better.

Damien's light flared, and the fog cleared from my vision. The Prime Mystique's brow creased as he watched me, but I found the trail of our conversation in my memory and asked, "Do you regret it? Killing him? Using me to get here?"

He bit out one syllable that pierced my chest. "No."

"*No?*" I repeated, and my own light snapped around me with a visceral crack. I flinched, my bones jarring.

"This was the purpose of the loophole, to allow us to find—" He cut off his words. "No, I do not regret it."

"You don't regret how you manipulated me into freeing you?" My wings beat in heated aggression at my back, the ache it wrought through my muscles deep and worn and satisfying.

"I did not have a choice," Damien snapped. "This was always meant to happen."

"You are an *Angel*! You have more agency than any warrior, and yet you let fate control you."

"Fate is beyond anyone's control." That was a difference between the gods and Angels, I supposed. The gods wanted to control fate. The Angels bowed to it.

Anger pooled within me, a molten thing that desired answers and repercussions. It boiled through my words as I yelled, "So you just wanted to use your warriors to achieve your own means! Like any entitled ruler—like Kakias led her clan to warfare. That's all any of you do!"

Damien's nostrils flared as the force of my words landed. But he sucked in a breath and said, "I will fly you back to the palace."

"Forget it!" I raged. "You *never* intervene when it matters; don't start now. You are supposed to protect us, Damien. We are your legacy—your cause runs through the Mystique Warriors, through every bloodline alive today. And you killed him."

Damien's jaw tightened, and an emotion I couldn't quite decipher flickered through his purple eyes. I thought it was...shame.

What was the point? Believing in a higher power if they could do nothing to aid you when you needed it most? How many nights had I said prayers to the Angels as a girl, believed in them whole heartedly and was so damn proud to carry the Mystique name?

My wings beat at my back—strong, powerful pumps begging to carry me into that legacy, to write legends and wake myths. Seraph magic pushed at my veins, peeling the fog from my mind.

The Mystique name might have started with Damien, but it had become so much more. It was the boundless courage and determination of the warriors in Damenal and across Gallantia. It was their hearts and families. And for them, I would fight.

"You keep your gods and fate," I said, eyes on the jutting peaks of the mountains beyond the Northern Quarter and the soft grasses that coated the sloping sides, all baring the passion of the clan who guarded them. "I'll take my warriors."

And with the blood of the Mystiques pounding through my body and pushing each stride further, stronger, I took a running start and leapt off the edge of a mountain, allowing my own wings to carry me.

They flared out, pulling at the sore muscles of my back as they caught the wind. I trusted the instincts of the seraph that had been waiting all these years to return to the skies and beat my wings when it seemed I was about to fall, coasting when I could.

I squeezed every muscle in my abdominals and back, my thighs and glutes, activating the ones Damien had been focusing on these recent weeks as he'd had me training with light while also working on control and strength. Training for this, teaching me so that I'd instinctually know what to do when I hit the sky.

It was a wobbly flight, quickly losing altitude I wasn't sure how to gain back, but I breathed in the air from this height. The clouds filtered across the skies, and for a moment, the sun forced its way through, warming every inch of my feathers.

I wanted to soar, to see how far the ends of the world went and what gods and Fates waited there. I held that wish tight to my spirit as I dropped, bracing for impact. It wasn't long before the ground was rushing toward me, and I landed in a sloppy run at the base of the hill Damien had trained me atop of.

With shaking limbs, a racing heart, and an invigorated spirit, I climbed back up to him, and I tried again.

And again.

And again.

~

WHEN DAMIEN finally did fly me back to the palace, we didn't speak. The closer we got to the white stone structure, the more my thoughts melted together, and my anger dissipated.

Echnid has a purpose. He is going to help the warriors. He is going to save us all.

Damien deposited me on the balcony outside my study as he always did. With one lingering glance at the mural on the ceiling—the one of the warrior dipping his glowing swords in a lake—he looked at me. "I do not regret it," he repeated, stoking that betrayed inferno begging to roar within me again.

The fog suppressed it, and exhausted, I allowed it.

Damien continued, words dripping with intention, "But I will not deny, that at times, my decisions have haunted me."

Then, he beat his wings roughly, stirring a wind around the balcony, leaves and flower petals from the planters circling the stone floor. And he flew off, his ominous words leaving me struck silent and my vengeful heart hollow.

~

MALAKAI STILL WASN'T in my suite when I finished bathing and toweling off my wings. The feathers were a nuisance, but with all the dust collected while training, they required thorough washing.

After the fight with Damien, I was feeling both stronger and weaker than ever. His words lingered in my head as I crawled into bed. A haunted warning, some kind of threat, but I didn't know what of.

I had just enough energy to pull out the shell and send a message to Rina—as I did every night.

Okay? I spelled out with the code she'd taught me.

She sent back one pulse for yes. Every night.

I hoped it was the truth, and not something to placate Malakai and me while we were stuck here.

My decisions have haunted me.

Would that be my future, too?

Echnid has a reason. He had to have reasons for everything, and I needed more time to unravel them.

You can trust him, that voice in my head said again, cool mist permeating my concerns and lulling me to lay back against the pillows.

Still, Damien's words echoed as I held the shell in my hand and debated asking Santorina more. About Tolek or how she promised to keep him away from here after I sensed him and Sapphire flying near Damenal recently. But if there really was a threat, they were all safer away from here.

Setting the shell aside, I scratched at my Curse mark.

Sleep, my seraph.

And with that voice in my head, I did.

~

"WAKE UP, OPHELIA," a distant voice commanded.

My body ached from training, but I stirred, slowly blinking my eyes open and relishing in the work I'd put in to strengthen my muscles. As the room swam into clarity, I stretched my wings, beating them gently. They sent a wave of control through my body, steadying me instead of feeling heavy and useless.

"Wake up," that voice said again, and this time, I jolted upright. It wasn't Malakai as I'd expected.

Echnid stood at the foot of my bed, his snow-white hair gleaming and his cheeks tinged pink with...excitement?

"What are you doing?" I asked. The fog across my mind curled in anticipation as I tried to gather my thoughts. Moonlight streaked through the cracked glass in my bedchamber, and I realized that I'd fallen asleep much earlier than normal. "We didn't have our meeting tonight." Sadness twirled through me at the reminder.

Some part of me had come to rely on those meetings with Echnid; perhaps because they were a source of information, but more likely because of the soothing feeling I always left the Rapture Chamber with.

Echnid nodded. "Correct. We did not. I have another task for you."

"What kind of task?" I asked, perking up. Almost subconsciously, my light pushed outward, wanting to dance with the god's mist. Echnid tracked the control with a nod of approval.

He waved a hand, and a gold gown appeared on the back of my door. "Put that on, and meet me in the foyer."

With a dip of his chin, Echnid blinked out of the room, giving me the illusion of privacy. Clutching my robe, I approached the door. The god's power thrummed from the other side as I dragged a finger over the dress, comfort settling around me.

Glittering, light-weight skirts cascaded to the ground—long enough to trail feet behind me, but the bodice...

It was less a dress and more *armor*. My eyes widened as I took it in. Gold sheer fabric wrapped around the torso, but over it, gilded metal plates lined the ribs. They curved upward, forming shoulder caps that flared like feathered wings, and over the breasts, another pair of wings fanned out.

A thick belt cinched the waist above the skirt, and as I slipped the gown over my body, I felt like I was truly stepping into my power.

This was not only a dress, it was a shield and a sword. A facade and my own gleaming weapon, molded after the wings at my back and the light in my veins. This signified all the strength I'd been honing.

"Where are we going?" I asked as we left my suite.

"You shall soon see."

I followed, the fog in my mind giving the marble halls a soft rippling effect around the edges.

"I have heard of the progress of your training," he said. Was it a trick of the light or did the misty ether swirling around him lift in anticipation?

Angellight coiled within me. "It's becoming quite useful," I said, the light drifting ahead of us to prop open the next door.

"That is why I have come to you tonight."

As we came to a stop before a set of high doors in the ballroom, I brushed a thumb across my Curse mark. Echnid's curling smirk seemed so knowing as he placed a hand against the rich wood. It was typically used for Daminius festivities and other formal gatherings, but today, Echnid shoved the door open, and instead of a beaming, jewel-encrusted crowd and billowing gold decor, it revealed Malakai.

On his knees in the center of the room.

Chained to the floor.

My light flared uncontrollably, and I yelled, "What's going on?"

There is a reason for it. Echnid has a reason. That misty voice curled fingers around my mind, compressing my fear into something small and unimportant.

But I rushed to Malakai. "Are you okay?" I gripped his shoulders, looking him over. There wasn't a mark on him besides dark shadows beneath his eyes from lack of sleep.

"I'm fine, Phel." His words were solid, his will still iron despite the shackles around his wrists.

I whirled on Echnid, taking in the room. The Angels were present as well as a group of women I didn't know, but I only looked at the god, barreling toward him.

"What are you *thinking*?" I beseeched. Light pooled in my hands, silver and lilac sparks showering us. "Malakai is an esteemed Mystique Warrior! He is one of the people we are going to uplift."

"The Blastwood and Deneski lines are strong among your people," Echnid agreed, studying me as my light continued to crackle. "That is exactly why we have brought Malakai here."

"What do you mean?" My eyes flicked over the room, landing on Damien. He was stony-faced, his expression etched in marble, but I swore a flash of...pride lit his purple eyes.

No, that couldn't be it. Not for my defiance.

I tore my stare from his, searching for any sort of explanation as the fog tried to push my worries down again. Tried to harden me against this atrocity.

A group of women lined settees at the side of the room. All seven were unnaturally beautiful, with skin that shone like glass in a range of different tones and crisp white dresses that floated like water.

"You have noticed my attendees?" Echnid smiled proudly.

"Who are they?" I snapped, looking between the god and these...mistresses. One rose from her settee and draped herself across Echnid's lap, licking up the column of his throat.

Echnid was a god. He brimmed with power and had the defined body and ethereal beauty to prove it; he was probably skilled at pleasuring partners. But the sight made my stomach turn.

"Rather beautiful are they not? And deadly." The non-answer slithered from his lips.

"They're here to fuck you, then?"

Echnid and the seven *beings* laughed, but the god said, his hand high on the thigh of the white-haired woman on his lap, "Among other things."

A low, rumbling growl echoed from one of the corridors leading off the ballroom. I spun toward the door in time to see—

"Holy fucking Angels," I breathed.

All seven of them rifled their feathers as if insulted by my choice of words, but I truly could not give less of an Angel's wing. Not on a good day given their true nature, and especially not when a massive, three-headed dog was lumbering through the door.

Drool dripped from the tips of its fanged teeth as all three of those sets of eyes scanned the room. Its frame was as large as the khrysaor's, muscled and strong, with short brown fur tight to its body and a skinny tail that whipped as it assessed us.

"That's not possible," I breathed.

"Meet my cerberus, Ophelia," Echnid purred, and though I still couldn't see the answers, it felt like his plans were unraveling around me, and I was caught in his trap. The beast stopped just in front of me, its warm breath pouring over my skin. "She likes you."

She sniffed, lips pulling back into a growl. I wasn't sure Echnid's statement was correct. She looked ready to devour me with one sudden movement. Ready to tear my limbs from my body. But...I had to play the game.

Standing my ground in front of Malakai, I didn't look away from the cerberus. "She is lovely." Hesitantly, but not fearfully, I held a hand out for the creature to sniff. "I'm sure she likes the fresh air after being locked up. Where is she from?"

I had no recollection of waking this beast, but long stretches of my days were blurs. I dared a glance back at Echnid, where the woman was now running her hands over her body in his lap. He only watched me, like he was getting as much sick satisfaction from this sight as she was from him.

"You'll find that in realms beyond Ambrisk, not all myths have been exiled," Echnid said, as vague as ever. "It is unfair, is it not? Perhaps it's a blessing that you and your sister have returned to right that balance."

This time I didn't disagree with Echnid. It *was* unfair that so many creatures suffered. That Sapphire had been denied her true form and the khrysaor were sent to sleep for such long years.

But that only made me think there *must* be a reason. One Echnid was clearly not going to state, because he continued with an adoring stare at the cerberus, "Hythana was the guard of my imprisonment. She was kept outside the bounds of my Stone Realm to ensure no one but the Chosen could free me." His hand tightened on the hip of the woman still writhing atop him as he spoke of the mythical beast. "But I have such a way with wary souls, and my precious here has quite a story. I lulled her with music slowly, over many centuries, before even the Angels

Ascended to me there. We did not meet but through stone until recently."

Were the women of similar origin? From another realm? How?

Hythana, as he called the cerberus, nudged me sharply enough to knock me over. Malakai put a steadying, chained hand to my back, the links clanking against marble.

"Thank you," I muttered.

"You're welcome." His words were intense. Heavy with a message I didn't understand.

"Now, Ophelia," Echnid said. "Let's begin. Or Hythana will be allowed time to play."

My gut tumbled and churned, the power of seven Angels colliding within me, but when I looked back to Echnid, calm swept over my being.

"What is it you brought me here for?" I asked again, the haze creeping tighter across my mind. It dug into my bones and veins, sewing strings to pull like I was some puppet. I could practically see them, and yet I was useless against them. A complete absorption of my independence and command of my autonomy that turned my stomach.

"You said yourself you have been training," Echnid reminded me.

His praise erased my unease in a wash of clouded belief. "I have," I answered obediently, a bird's chirping echoing in my mind.

As if he read my mind, the god said, "Perhaps we had the wrong source."

The Curse mark on my wrist throbbed. The twittering sliced into a deathly silence.

Echnid is here to help us, that voice said as a string pulled.

Listen to him. Another rough tug, and my stomach rolled.

Trust him.

Lifting the woman off his lap, the god floated about the room. The mist dug deeper into my being.

Echnid paused behind Malakai, my attention drifting on the heels of his mist, my mind slipping further away. Malakai's chains scraped against the marble floor, a high sound that reminded me so much of the caged bird's singing Echnid had me silence.

"You alone woke a seraph after they'd been slaughtered, revived the line of Angelic guards wrongfully killed, who shared many traits and magical lines with warriors."

Angellight mounted in my veins with each tug of those strings.

But Echnid smiled spitefully, desperation and hunger bleeding from his every move.

"I want you to turn Malakai into a seraph."

And my light shattered in a high-pitched explosion, searing the fog.

Chapter Twelve
Malakai

THE BLINDING FLASH OF OPHELIA'S LIGHT WAS QUICKLY swallowed by the god's mist. A white wave stronger than any I'd seen him emit so far.

When the magic cleared and Ophelia asked, "What?" there was no inflection to her tone. She tilted her head at him, her fingers not fidgeting at her sides. My blood chilled when I caught those magenta eyes.

It wasn't Ophelia looking back at me. Not entirely.

A haze stole her expression as she observed my chains, my kneeling position in the center of the ballroom. Lucidius's dagger burned at my back as if in warning that something was very fucking wrong. Spirits, I'd barely seen her recently. When had she grown *this* distant?

The Angels watched raptly, lining the side of the ballroom with varying levels of concern or entertainment in their expressions. The sun was just cresting the mountains, pouring gold over their wings.

And Rozelyn, for Spirits' sake, was throwing me smug, knowing glances from her perch on Echnid's chair. At least I knew I hadn't imagined her. She'd been the one that dragged me here. Not that that comforted me at fucking all, now.

"Do we know that he can become a seraph?" Ophelia asked in

that unnaturally calm voice. The same one in which she'd insisted that maybe Echnid had more of a point than we'd considered.

"You woke the myth inside of you," the god replied with cool control.

Ophelia's hand flexed at her sides, the fog in her eyes faltering for a brief moment before she fell still. Mystlight glinted off the wings carving her dress. "And Malakai retains the same power?"

"Seraphs and warriors are wrought of similar compositions," Echnid stated.

"I haven't even completed the Undertaking," I argued, latching on to anything. "Whatever you think will happen won't work."

"Only one way to find out," Echnid said with a shrug.

Ophelia tilted her head again, this time studying me. In her palms, Angellight budded, trying to break free. Her eyes widened, and she shook her head.

"I can't do this," she said, attention whipping to Echnid.

The cerberus growled, and Echnid's power swelled, reminding Ophelia that while she may be the last seraph, he was a fucking god.

"You will." Anguish ripped through his voice. "Unless you'd prefer one of your other friends. Perhaps your sister or that warrior you love."

"I-I—" Ophelia stuttered, shaking her head again as if to clear it. She blinked rapidly, light coming in short bursts in her palms, one color after another. She tried to control it, but each flash only made her shake her head more, that hazy stare warring with her.

"Phel?" I asked, my Bind thudding with streaky confusion.

She clenched her eyes, muttering, "He is trying to help. Trust him."

Ophelia was so distracted, she missed the Warrior God's haunting smile. "Thorn?"

And before I knew what was happening, I was being shredded. A lightning bolt cracked through my mind, pulling apart my memories, emotions, and being. Digging up the pain of my past torture and stuffing it down my damn throat.

I toppled to the side, chains rattling. And rattling. And rattling.

The sounds of my nightmares—of blades being sharpened and irons heated and those damn chains—was unceasing.

A sword slashed my side, a dagger carved my chest.

A whip—it tore and tore and tore at my back.

Someone was screaming. Two someones. One a high, demanding shriek and the other...*me*.

Gold light cracked through the ballroom, bouncing off marble—Ophelia. She'd exploded with it. The magic of all seven Angels swirled around her, stars shooting overhead and orange flickers of flame singeing her skirt.

"Stop! Stop!" Ophelia cried hoarsely, crashing down next to me. The world blurred, but her voice wavered over sobs as Thorn continued to rip my mind apart. Shocking amethyst and bright white lightning shot aimlessly from her as she begged. "Stop, please!"

Echnid snapped his fingers, and with one last wrenching roll of thunder, Thorn's magic retreated. A piece of me sagged in relief as Ophelia met my eyes and worked to wrangle her power back into her body, one strand at a time.

With shaky movements, I pushed myself to my hands and knees, nearly vomiting as I took stock of myself. There was no blood on the floor and no wounds beyond where I'd bitten my cheek and slammed my shoulder into the marble when I fell.

"Look at me, Ophelia," Echnid instructed, desperation piquing his voice.

Stiffly, without another glance in my direction, Ophelia rose and faced the god. Her spine straightened, her wings snapping in tightly.

"What are you going to do?" Echnid asked.

Misty white ether stirred around him, creeping over Ophelia's body. Everywhere it touched, she stiffened, but after a moment the tension uncoiled from her frame. What in the fucking Spirits was he *doing* to her?

"Leave her alone!" I snapped, but they ignored me.

When Ophelia spoke again, it was with that unsettling calm. "I am going to wake a seraph."

"As I thought," Echnid mused, and for the first time, he sounded truly, gleefully evil.

With a nod from the god, she turned toward me, all vibrancy siphoned from her stare again. No Angellight cracked her magenta irises—no life at all. And though I had no fucking clue what was going on, I was certain of one thing.

This... This was not Ophelia.

Whatever she was going to do, it wouldn't work, and it wouldn't be her choice.

Who else would he make her do this to? Which of our friends or family would he drop at her feet?

Panting, my body still ringing with the memory of that torture, I nodded at her, and Ophelia pulled up that glimmering, gold light—one as heated as Angellight, but with a different, unique vibrancy.

Myth magic.

It pooled around her frame, rolling along the hem of her gown as it lapped at the awarded taste of freedom like a damn living creature.

White mist tangled with every gold tendril as if the god was warring with it. Consuming and feeding off it.

"Now, Ophelia," Echnid commanded when she hesitated.

And she shot a beam of myth magic at me.

At first, it poured through my veins and muscles, pumping my blood faster. But after a moment, I knew why Ophelia had screamed so much when the seraph emerged.

Why she'd seemed like a living inferno those first few days.

Her magic felt like it was flaying my skin from my bones, like it was ripping me limb from fucking limb and leaving fire in the wake of its ruin. I bit down on the screams trying to burst from me, knowing she wasn't totally gone. Hearing my agony would only make it harder for her.

But the longer she used the magic, the more awareness returned to her eyes. And she saw the grievances in my tight jaw and the sweat pouring off me. In the way I collapsed to the floor again.

The words and arguments of everyone around me faded together.

For a beat, the magic faltered, like Ophelia had won. But Echnid instructed her to keep going, threatened to have Thorn resume if she quit. She screamed and raged between every breath.

My hair fell before my eyes, sweat-slicked and heavy, but I squinted at the god's eager expression. At the white-gowned women who rose off their settees and flocked to his sides like curious, doting mistresses.

Ophelia's myth magic flashed, and for a delirious moment, Rozelyn's eyes turned a slitted, glowing red and her hair crawled with snakes. In the next agonized blink, they were back to normal, nothing but anticipation gleaming at me.

My back ached, like the magic was trying to rip wings from my being. Trying to create a legend where none hid.

And that was what Echnid didn't understand as he sat there beaming with thirsty malice. Ophelia may have the power to bring myths to fruition, but she couldn't create them. And I was no seraph, didn't hold a bead of life to revive.

"More," he demanded.

"Please, no," Ophelia whimpered, her voice back to its normal tone. "It's not working."

I bit down on my screams until my teeth felt like they'd crack.

"More," Echnid repeated, capturing Ophelia's attention again and sending his mist to caress her skin. Gold light pulled from her, as if the god's magic was siphoning it out of her flesh to bend it to his will.

After a moment, Ophelia dredged up more power. Fed it into me. I wished it would become a blade to plunge into my heart. Wished it would just end me.

But I thought of Mila.

You saved me.

Mila who had survived so much and fought for me every day. Who'd cried when I'd been tortured and worried I wasn't coming back to her. Who I was keeping safe again. I would get all of those tomorrows she and I had promised.

Every single one.

So, I clenched my hands into fists, and I waited until the excruciating pain pulled me into unconsciousness.

Then, I dreamed of Mila, too.

Chapter Thirteen
Ophelia

Echnid made me try to wake a seraph in Malakai for hours.

Until he was an unconscious, sweaty mess on the floor, his body radiating heat from the mythos power burning into him.

Until the sun was setting, the burnished clouds lining the mountains a fiery explosion through my tear-lined eyes.

Until I fell to my knees beside Malakai's limp body, my hand on his chest, trying to feel the off-kilter soul bond in our Bind tattoo. His heart thumped beneath my palm, and I stayed there, tracking that strong beat, until the stars winked to life outside the palace, shining through the tall windows surrounding us.

As the day had progressed, the fog across my mind cleared. Horror took its place. Disgust with myself for what I had agreed to, for thinking there was any way Echnid was right. With my body draped across Malakai's, a tainted feeling settled in my veins.

How had I done this?

Echnid and his group of unsettling cronies left eventually. Those women had an aura about them that ruffled the wings at my back, perking up my Angellight, but I didn't have the energy to ask now.

Later. I'd deal with it later.

Now, I needed to make sure Malakai was okay. That the myth

magic hadn't done irreparable damage. Bracing both hands on his chest, I pulled at all seven strings of my Angellight.

"Come on, Malakai," I said through a steady stream of tears. My vision blurred, but light glowed around my palms, warm and welcoming. It licked across my skin and into Malakai's, searching for a source to heal.

All Angellight is restorative, Damien had said. *All can cure rot and the most deeply planted taints.*

Malakai's body was wrung out beneath my hands, but with the aid of my seraph power, I could restore it quicker. Ease the pain.

I gritted my teeth and poured more into him, until his frame was awash with the golden hue. Until the entire room was bathed in the light fueled by my desperation. His eyes were still closed, his freckles standing out against his pale skin, but his heart pounded ferociously. Alive and well, even if he was still asleep. My wings draped protectively across his body.

"Ophelia."

I whirled at Damien's voice.

"*Get out of here!*" I snarled like a wild beast. Light flared around me, gold streaked with black and white. Damien's, Bant's, and my own seraph power. The Angel studied it.

"Let me help—"

"You let him do this!" My light pulsed. "You let him make me do this!" My voice cracked over the words. Like a looking glass beneath a fist, the knuckles of Damien's betrayal shattered me once again.

As if I'd forgotten after these weeks training and the warnings he'd been giving me. As if I'd thought maybe he was actually trying to help me. Furiously, I wiped my eyes clear of the tears those realizations spawned.

Against my better judgment, a silent part of me buried deep within the strand of Damien's Angellight had believed maybe I could trust him again. That maybe every foundation I'd been raised on wasn't a fucking sham.

"Ophelia, let me take him to your suite."

"Get away!" I roared as Damien took a step closer. A barrier of light rose around Malakai.

"You can't carry him," the Angel said.

My chest rose and fell rapidly, my knees weak from the power I'd expelled and the gross manipulations Echnid had pulled over me. And though I loathed to admit it, Damien was right.

"Fine," I finally conceded, and all my power snapped back into me, buzzing to rest beneath my skin.

Damien picked up Malakai and lumbered from the room, my steps so small and hollow in the wake of the Angel. It wasn't until Malakai was tucked into my bed that my feet carried me elsewhere of their own accord.

I slammed into the room, the door bouncing back against the wall, and raced to the bathing chamber. My knees cracked against tile as I fell and emptied my stomach into the toilet bowl.

Again and again, until I was dry heaving.

What I'd done to Malakai...

The way he'd screamed...

I heaved again.

The heartlessness with which Echnid had watched and commanded me to keep going.

Another heave.

Used. I'd been used once again, was no more than a pawn laced with the facade of power. To them, that's all I was. All I would ever be. But what would happen if my power was not theirs to use but solely mine?

All Angellight is restorative. All can cure rot and the most deeply planted taints.

"I will cure the world of that god," I whispered to myself, before collapsing to the marble.

WHEN I WOKE, I realized I wasn't in my own bathing chamber. With a stiff neck from the hard floor, I pushed upright and rolled my shoulders to work out the knots, blinking at my surroundings. The usual supply of fluffy white towels was dark blue, no combs or cosmetics littered the counter, and the lavender and lemon soap I loved wasn't on the tub ledge. I'd been in such a furious, exhausted stupor, my feet had carried me elsewhere.

A suite I knew as well as my own.

One I'd come to for comfort on numerous occasions but had refused to visit since Echnid brought me back to Damenal. One that had the power to break me, especially now.

Pushing onto shaking legs, I crept toward the door and held my breath as I looked into Tolek's bedchamber. Today of all days, it was the only place I wanted to be.

It still smelled of him. Of citrus and spice. Of home. I crossed to the desk set between tall shelves. Every paper was neatly stacked, the books organized alphabetically by author. A thin layer of dust had settled over it all, but instead of giving the illusion of a time forgotten, it reminded me of something perfectly preserved. Of a room the sun would shine on again, Tolek bounding through the door at any moment. It was only waiting for him.

I pulled a leather-bound volume from the shelf. *Voices of the Lost Steel Age.* It was a tiny sliver of our history, a small dark chunk of decades during the era when metalworking flourished. And this book documented the great poets and artists believed to have lived during that time.

The spine cracked as I opened it, the pages falling flat to one marked by a ribbon. And—

I inhaled sharply.

Tolek's handwriting was crammed in the corners, lines drawn beneath verses, and notes bracketing stanzas. He'd marked every inch of the available space around this piece.

I turned to a page that was folded down to find he'd done the same there. All throughout the book, on the biographical sections and those containing poems. Some were common questions and interpretations, a few only half complete like he'd thought of another note partway through and had to scrawl that down as well. Some were deeper musings about life and love, gratitude and death, dreams and mourning. In a few places, he'd even continued finished poems with his own stanzas, as if he was penning a tale about what happened next.

It was a deeply personal view into his soul, this book, but I couldn't look away. And holding it, touching the pages he'd touched in the room that smelled of him, wrapped a shred of comfort around my bones.

Tucking the book back where it belonged, I quickly flipped through a few others. He'd marked up all of them. Every page. And the stack on his desk was pristine, as if he'd been intending to get to those next.

Angels, I hoped he'd read those one day. I'd ask him to tell me what each one was about. If it was poetry, I'd indulge in the different analyses with him. I'd scrawl my own notes alongside his.

But as much as my heart ached with every inch of space between us, I hoped he was staying away from Damenal. I hoped Santorina and Cypherion were able to keep him away as Rina promised they would, especially after what Echnid made me do to Malakai. The Vincienzo bloodline may not be Blastwood and Deneski, but it was strong. And I didn't think I could bear using the mythos magic on anyone else.

Heart pounding behind my ribs and eyes stinging, I crossed to the bed. The sheets were cold—unnaturally so. The clearest sign that no one had been here for months. I dragged my fingertips across them, fluttered over the pillows and curtains framing the four posts—they were perfectly tied back like he'd left them the day we departed for Brontain.

Beside the bed, a dark wood nightstand held both a half-burned candlestick and a mystlight lantern. I almost laughed at him having both when mystlight was the easier choice, but something about Tolek writing by candlelight made my heart expand in my chest. An empty whiskey glass waited beside it and a journal. All untouched.

I shouldn't have pried, but the tether that connected me to Tolek pulled taut. So, with a shaking hand, I opened the drawer.

"What?" I breathed, brows scrunching at the sight within.

Pieces of parchment, all folded in three, and all with my name scrawled across the front.

Letters.

They were letters, ripped from Tolek's journals if the frayed edges of the pages were any indication.

My heart pounded as I picked one up, and when I opened it—when I saw the first line in Tolek's handwriting and heard his voice reading it to me in my mind—I lost the battle against the stinging in my eyes.

They weren't just letters, they were poems. Poems he'd written for me—*about me*. Things he'd always wanted to say but either couldn't or didn't know how. The deepest, most beautiful thoughts of his heart and soul, captured in black ink on the pages of his many journals.

I fell to my knees, my wings slumping to the ground behind me, and read one after the other. My tears stained the pages, my fingers trembling around them, but I couldn't stop.

He'd marked the date on every single one. Some days he'd written multiple, some went as far back as when we were children. Those were more rudimentary, focusing on rhyming words, and I couldn't help but laugh through my sobs when he talked about how he was never *bored* watching me with my *sword*.

I hurried through them, desperation clawing within me to consume every bit of Tolek's mind that I could, to wear these words like my favorite armor.

Finally, there was only one left. And when I opened it, when I saw that this one began with my name at the top, my heart cracked.

The date—it was my twentieth birthday.

Exactly one year ago today.

The day that Damien had first appeared in my bedroom; the day my life was officially handed to the Angels and gods.

I have a gift for you, he'd said at the party at my parent's manor. *I'll give it to you later.*

This. This was the present he'd always intended. It was a personal note and a poem he'd written. Something small, that could be folded up in my pocket and read repeatedly, always with me for protection—it likely was in his pocket that night. The creases were worn, like it had been opened and studied time and again. But it was the most intimate gift ever intended for me.

Because this wasn't just a poem.

It was a love letter.

He didn't come out and confess his feelings. No, Tolek never would have done that when I was still grieving Malakai. But it was written in every line now that I knew where to look. These words were his way of trying to bring me back to life when I was so ruined. His plea to be strong, to fight through the pain. It was his confession that he cared for me more than he ever would have dared say aloud, and his desperate, hopeless thought that maybe one day I would care for him, too, but if I didn't, he would accept what I could give.

This letter was evidence of the love Tolek showed me every day and a vow to do so for eternity.

I read it again and again—read them all repeatedly until the sun was setting, spending my birthday with Tolek in the only way I could.

No one came to look for me. No one asked me to train or attempt to awake a seraph. No one needed me. So, I sat in solitude with love letters from the man who cradled my broken heart so delicately in the palm of his hands. I wept over the words he'd written for me, and I plotted the day I'd return to him.

Chapter Fourteen
Ophelia

Echnid came to me on the night of my birthday, less than an hour before midnight. He gave me another gold feathered armored gown—this one with lace sleeves that hugged my arms tightly to my wrists and vambraces—and escorted me to the Rapture Chamber, where a decadent feast of fresh fruits and pastries was laid out, wine and liquor in abundance for my choosing.

When I asked why—why the theatrics, why allow me to cry in Tolek's bed all day, why not summon me until the very last minute—he said, "Because you spent the day mourning the life you will no longer know, and now we shall end it looking forward to the future we will live together."

Bile crept up my throat, my jaw trembling with the force of all the words I wanted to spew at the god before me. At the thought of Malakai, still unconscious and recovering in my bed. At the thought of Tolek's letters.

But I sealed those thoughts within me, promises burrowing down to my soul, and pictured chocolate brown eyes and a teasing smirk. Pictured Tolek beside me, godly blood splashed across our faces, while Echnid breathed his last breaths at our feet.

"Yes," I claimed with a savage smile and a sip from my chalice to stifle my dark desires. "We shall."

~

"I'M SORRY," I whispered, as I stood beside my bed hours later and watched Malakai's chest rise and fall. I didn't allow myself to pass out or my subconscious to take me elsewhere when Echnid finally allowed me to leave. I had to stay with Malakai now.

"I'm so sorry." I crawled atop the comforter.

He'd wavered in and out of consciousness when I'd come back from Tolek's room. Shoving down my tears to wipe the sweat from Malakai's brow, I repeated those two words over and over: *I'm sorry*. Now, he rolled his head toward me, eyes fluttering open.

"It's okay, Phel." Malakai grabbed my hand, holding it between us. It was like all those years we spent in our clearing back in Palerman, but it was twisted and warped beyond recognition.

We were.

The pressure upon our shoulders—the weight of the entire world—was so much graver than those two naive children ever thought possible.

"*Why?*" My voice cracked. I wanted to scream the word, but it was trapped. In my heart, in my chest, within these damn walls with a deranged god who was willing to torture his own subjects. "Why is it okay, Malakai?"

"Because," he croaked, voice fading, "if I let him think he can do this to me, he's distracted from whatever his next step is. From whoever else he might hurt."

His muted green eyes slipped closed, his breathing heavy and labored even as he drifted into a restful sleep.

He's distracted.

Malakai was keeping Tolek and Cypherion and Jezebel safe. He was keeping Mila safe. He was keeping every warrior beyond these walls safe because that's what Malakai had always done for us, even if I hadn't understood it. He shielded us, for better or for worse. Put himself in the line of torture time and again, never asking to be a hero but always stepping into the role he hated.

When would it end?

I looked over the scars slashing his body. The rough ax carved into his chest, the small line on his jaw. The thick marks curling around his shoulders from too many damn lashings. What Echnid made me do wouldn't leave scars on the surface. It would leave the memory of the pain scorched into his mind and spirit forever.

For too long now, his defensive nature had meant so much pain for himself. He'd been the back that accepted the blow, curved around the rest of us.

And though that foggy voice still fought to consume my mind, there was no way a god who hurt his people like this had our best interests at heart.

"I'm going to get us out of here." My gaze landed on the Bind inked on his chest, the star perfect and budding with our shared life.

Life...

My eyes flicked up to the star-strewn sky outside the windows, and a hopeful spark of an idea ignited.

"I'm going to get both of us out of here," I swore.

Silent tears spilled down my cheeks as I prayed to no Angels or god for aid, only to whatever power laid in my spirit that the plan beginning to form was good enough.

"I have to figure things out, but I will do it before he makes me hurt you again. I'll take care of you." My tears fell onto Malakai's skin as I leaned my head against his shoulder and his steady breathing filled the room. "I promise, Malakai. Until the stars stop shining."

CHAPTER FIFTEEN
SANTORINA

PRICKLES DANCED UP MY SPINE AND AT THE TIPS OF MY fingers as if I was being stabbed by a thousand needles all at once. The sensation swept through my body every time I came near this door—something I'd been actively avoiding when not necessary. I sighed. This time, unfortunately, it was.

I stopped before the bronze-framed mirror at the end of the hall, potted plants twisting up beside it and pale mystlight cooling my features. The same dark hair was swept back from my face; the same lifted eyes looked back at me. When I raised a hand to touch the inch-long scar beneath my eye that I'd received in the catacombs, the reflection did, too.

It was me, but it wasn't.

Because something had unleashed when the Warrior God and Angels had been freed. Something that allowed me to see every small scuff to the tiled floor in the dim corridor and make out every grumbled complaint behind the door. Something that caused that needle sensation up and down my spine, that pulled my nimble fingers toward the knives strapped to my waist.

I wiped my hands down my navy linen dress, adjusting my belt.

"Ready, miss?" one of the guards beside the door asked.

I laughed, smiling softly at him. "Quilian, I've told you time and again not to call me miss."

"Force of habit." He shrugged one shoulder with a disarmingly charming smirk.

"I stitched up the gash to your side during the war. I think we're past formalities," I argued.

When someone was my patient, it bridged the gap across strangers. I didn't know Erista's elder brother well, but he'd been beloved in the war camp, making fast friends with warriors of every clan in the alliance army. With how he stood easily beside the door, arm resting on his scythe, guard leathers filled out with bulging muscles, a lazy grin on his face, and dark skin crinkling beside his eyes, it was clear why.

Quil's laugh boomed down the hall, and the grumbling behind the door paused. "Santorina, I will always thank you for that. And it didn't hurt that I got to have your hands on me."

A low growl echoed from inside, making my spine tingle, but I ignored it and rolled my eyes. "Shameless flirt, Quilian."

"Always. So, are you ready?"

"No," I admitted, shaking out the prickling that had returned to my hands. "But I suppose it's time.

Quil removed an ornate iron key from his belt and inserted it into the matching lock installed on the door when we arrived here from the mountains. He and the other guard on duty grabbed spears carved from the cypher trees as I opened the door and stepped across the threshold, coming face-to-face with Lancaster. Pointed ears peeked out from his wavy brown hair, canines sharp and predatory.

"Hello, Queen of Bounties." His voice was a low rumble across my skin, and I shivered to remember when he'd first said those words to me. After the Bounty power within my blood had fully woken, when the Angels were free and the final lock within me snapped. When my senses awoke, and all I could smell was the blood-tinged roses that washed off Lancaster's frame, along with something powerful and...

I hadn't addressed that second scent with anyone yet.

"Hello, Hunter," I snapped. Peering around him, I gave his sister a soft smile where she perched in a rocking chair in the corner. "Good morning, Mora."

"Santorina!" she cheered, bounding over to greet me. "How are you today? Are you ready for the journey?"

Where Lancaster was a walking armor of aggression and lethal growls, his sister had embodied sunshine lately. She was just as deadly—just as tricky with her glamour abilities, though they weren't as strong ever since she'd been injured in the emblem hunt—but she'd been friendly. Perhaps exorbitantly so due to how it annoyed her brother.

Her question grated on me, too, though.

"I'm sure it will be a pleasant trek," I said through a tight jaw. I turned to Lancaster and deadpanned, "Have you prepared?"

"I will never be prepared for this," he grumbled, but he brushed past me with a large pack strapped to his back and approached the guards. "Let's go."

Gods, I'd like to stab *him* with a thousand needles all at once.

I turned to follow, but Mora grabbed my wrist. I flinched, my elbow instantly snapping up toward her chin, but she caught it.

"Sorry," I muttered, aggression tightening my chest. My entire body coiled with an energy that wanted to maim, slaughter. I swallowed it, taking a step away from the fae. "I can't control it yet."

"The Bounty instincts are new and likely still waking. I assure you I'm prepared for it." It had happened every time I was near them. One small growl or step too close had my urge to attack snapping beyond my control. It was unpredictable and infuriating, no matter how much I didn't like the fae. "Be patient with him," Mora pleaded, gaze trailing her brother out of the room. "He is still learning how these new stories of the gods change what we've always believed."

"As am I," I answered.

I turned to leave, not needing to defend myself to the fae.

Silently, but for Quil trying to pierce Lancaster's stoic facade with quips, we followed the guards onto the sprawling dunes of Meridat's estate, the river winding through the property a lazy babble in the background.

Almost everyone was already gathered, gray clouds rolling toward Xenovia from the east. Cypherion and Vale stood in the shadows, harshly whispering. From this angle, his frame almost entirely eclipsed hers, but with a sigh, Cypherion tucked Vale beneath his chin, wrapping his arms around her, and muttered against her hair.

Mila and Tolek sat in the sand, both a bit stoic, but Meridat's Soulguider advisors spurred them into comfortable conversation. As we came to a stop, everyone turned, assessing the fae.

"We're ready," I said, slicing through the tension.

"You have your routes planned?" Cypherion double checked as they approached the group.

"Yes." I nodded. "And you will be okay here?" I exchanged a fervent look with Cyph, remembering Ophelia's request. We kept Tolek out of Damenal by whatever means necessary.

Cypherion dipped his head once, grimly telling me he remembered. Then, he stepped forward and handed me a small black bottle. "We should be able to write, given none of us will be in Damenal."

I secured the Mystique ink in my pack and slung it across my back.

"Have you heard from anyone you wrote last night?" I asked him and Meridat.

The Soulguider Chancellor answered, "Ezalia wrote back immediately and said she'll make haste for the desert with a small legion of Seawatchers. She's also going to raise her forces across both halves of her territory to keep a tighter guard on the coasts in case any creatures with godly connections surface."

"We're still waiting on Brigiet and Barrett," Cypherion added.

"And we'll be handling the Starsearchers," Jezebel said, emerging from between two large palm trees. She was dressed head to toe in fitted flying leathers, a sword across her back.

Jezebel pointedly didn't look toward Erista as she stopped beside Vale, Zanox and Dynaxtar flanking her. The Starsearcher was dressed exactly like Jezebel, switching out her usual skirts for the sleek black outfit.

"I didn't realize you were going, too, Jezebel," I said.

"Harlen and Cyren answered our letter," Vale explained. Cypherion's jaw ticked as she spoke. "They think they have exceptional means to help, but we don't want to waste time. Jezebel and the khrysaor are going to fly me there, and I'll use the seeing chambers to search the Fates for everything Valyrie hinted at."

Vale was going back to the place she'd escaped to use the seeing chambers Titus tortured her in to enhance her magic. That explained why Cypherion was so tense.

"Santorina," Tolek said, pushing to his feet. "Are you sure I can't come with you?"

"I'm sure," I answered urgently. "You're needed here. With Cypherion."

Tol locked his hands behind his back, leaning against a palm tree. "I'm not certain I am." He sliced a murderous glare to Lancaster over my shoulder.

The male grunted in response. "You think I want to be doing this any more then you want me to?"

"Then don't?" Tolek argued.

I stepped between them. "I will be fine. Bounty, remember?"

Cyph placed a hand on Tol's shoulder, pulling him back a step. Tolek had been bubbling with pent up aggression since the mountains, but this wasn't the time.

Tolek's expression softened as he whispered to me, "You remember what I asked?"

I nodded. "Of course. I promise."

"Thank you," he said, shoulders falling. "Got the cypher blades?" He'd stayed up with me late last night hastily shaping a few deadly weapons out of branches of the cypher trees as Ophelia had done in the past. It had been nice to have the help, and to know he wasn't flying to Damenal.

"I do," I swore with a grin Tolek returned.

"You two should head out," Cypherion said to me and Lancaster.

Lancaster, who would be my lone traveling companion for the foreseeable future.

Lancaster, who was a Hunter bred to kill me and I him.

Lancaster, with whom I'd been unable to have a single mature conversation in the weeks we'd been forced into each other's company.

Because while my friends focused on rallying our warrior allies,

I was departing for human training camps to recruit those that could fight in our army, and search for any Bounties who may have woken as I did when the Angels and Warrior God were freed.

And who better to seek them out than the very creature meant to destroy them?

What in the Goddesses' names could go wrong?

It is okay, I assured myself when the panicked, second-guessing voice in my head tried to surface. *Ritalia is gone. She cannot wake the Hunter, and I can kill Lancaster if he attacks.*

I did not want to pry any of my friends from their necessary posts for this. Especially not Tolek, when Lancaster and I might have to pass near Damenal while crossing the mountains. I may only be a human, but I could handle this.

As we said our goodbyes, a heaviness settled on my shoulders, like those clouds lining the skies had crashed to the sand. If Valyrie's warning was right and we were truly about to face the echoes of ancient wars among gods, would I ever see my friends again? When all was done, if we defeated Echnid, would we all still stand here?

Tolek, Cypherion, and I exchanged a final glance as I walked away. "Keep yourselves safe," I said, my voice cracking over the emotion I suppressed. "Please."

"Don't worry, my lovely Rina," Tolek said, forcing a bit of his usual humor to the surface and slinging an arm around CK's shoulder. "I'd be willing to wager every bit of wealth in the Vincienzo accounts that we'll win this one."

And everyone knew Tolek Vincienzo never lost a bet.

"YOU CANNOT POSSIBLY THINK this is the best way to travel," Lancaster complained for the tenth time before the sun had even set that evening.

I tightened my hands on the reins, attempting to focus on the dusty horizon and the mountains in the distance. "As I have already said, horses are the fastest means of transportation available to us."

"And as I have said, you are not truly looking at all of our options."

"Please, enlighten me then. Because for all your complaining, you have yet to provide an alternative."

"Because you are too stubborn to listen," he mumbled.

I refrained from answering to demonstrate my keen listening capabilities.

"We run," Lancaster said.

I barked a laugh, looking over at him. "Are you serious, or did all of that grumbling you've been doing mean you suffered a stroke?"

He didn't even flinch at the insult. "I am serious."

"Then I hate to ruin your plans, faerie, but we cannot *run* faster than these horses."

"I can."

I scoffed. "You cannot outrun a horse."

"Have you ever seen the fae? Outside of that battle in the mountains, when we were surrounded by such potent sources of Angel power suppressing us, have you truly seen my kind?"

Aside from him, Mora, and those in Ritalia's court, no. He took my silence as the truth.

"Running would be faster," he repeated as if he'd won.

For him, perhaps. But I, a mere human, snapped, "I regret to remind you that *I* am not in fact fae."

"I promise," Lancaster said, voice low enough that I looked at him. His eyes dragged up my body, from the warrior boots laced at my ankles up my leather-clad legs and the knives at my waist. Landed on the ones whittled from a cypher. "I know precisely what you are."

I gulped past the hatred deepening those words. "Then we cannot run."

Lancaster sighed, mumbling to himself *again*, and stopped his horse. Swinging down in an impossibly smooth dismount, he stalked to my mare.

"What are you doing?" I flinched toward my cypher dagger.

"Relax, Bounty." He lifted his hands but seemed to think

better of it and dropped them to his sides. "I am going to carry you."

I laughed, nudging my mare into motion. "No, you're not."

Lancaster strode alongside us, not faltering. "Yes, I am. We are in somewhat of a hurry, are we not?"

"You can't run all that way."

"Trust me, Bounty, stamina is not a problem for me."

I didn't allow myself to think too deeply on that statement or consider why my skin flushed at the low tone of his voice. "We told the camps it may be weeks before we arrive, depending on travel conditions," I said, refusing to look at him.

"But would it not be better for this potential war brewing if we arrived sooner?"

"You would think in all of those immortal years you'd have learned patience."

"I'm not immortal," he grumbled, as he did every time I threw the term around.

"Living so many centuries next to my pathetic human lifespan is close enough," I said, and a growl wrenched the air.

Lancaster's hand flashed out, gripping the reins and pulling my mare to a stop. His fingers brushed against mine, and even through the leather gloves we both wore, those prickles of awareness needled my palms.

My stare snapped to his, dark eyes burning into me.

Kill, a voice slithered through my head.

Enemy, it roared.

No, I wanted to shout back. No, I would not succumb to that instinct. I would not use the Bounty power against the fae trying to help us, no matter how infuriating he was.

But that instinct kicked up the longer his hand rested against mine, the heavier the scent of ancient, blood-tinged roses settled in the air.

"Lancaster," I breathed.

His eyes turned impossibly dark at the sound of my labored breath. "Yes?" His voice was gravelly, too.

"I do not think you should have your hands on me."

Enemy, the Bounty magic shrieked.

A frown twisted his lips. "I am not afraid of someone trying to kill me."

I swallowed. "Not just someone." Me, who was born from a bloodline that excelled at slaying his kind.

Lancaster's hand did not move, and now it was burning into the side of mine. "I'm not afraid of you either, Bounty."

We were both still, my breaths rushing and my heart pounding as the voice warred in my head. As one half of me instinctually reached for a weapon and the other gripped the reins until my hands ached.

And I hated the way this new instinct wanted to dictate my moves. My entire life, I had been my own control. For years, I'd decided everything for myself, was alone in many ways, though my friends were around me. The only human.

I refused to have some ancient source of blood magic change that. The possibility strangled me, making my breaths tight in my chest and my eyes flare wide.

"We need to move more quickly," Lancaster said in response, voice softer than I'd ever heard it. And there was an understanding unfolding in every word. One that said *I have been there. I have had my control stripped of me.* "I am going to carry you, and we are going to run. We will put the cypher knife in your boot where you cannot reach it without my knowing. If you feel so inclined to pull a regular blade on me, I assure you, I will recover just fine."

The cockiness in that last comment broke my frozen facade. "Fine," I folded, swinging off my horse on the opposite side of him to give the Bounty instinct time to fade. "What about our packs?"

"I will carry them both on my back."

"Of course you will." Unnaturally strong, non-immortal, arrogant prick.

I supposed with that strength, he really would be able to stop me from harming him, Bounty instinct and all. I may be eternally irritated by him, but I did not *want* to kill him. Not if it wasn't my choice, at least. If the day came that I did drive that cypher knife into his heart, I wanted it to be *my choice.*

"Let's hurry up, then."

We scrawled Mystique ink letters to Meridat and sent the

warrior horses she'd loaned us back to her estate. Then, Lancaster took slow steps toward me, his hands open at his sides.

"I am not some wounded animal," I grumbled, closing the distance between us.

"If you do not stop growling, I may not believe you," he retorted.

"It seems your habits are rubbing off on me." I crossed my arms, tipping my chin up to glare at him. He was taller than I remembered, as I'd taken care not to be this close to him.

Holding my eyes, Lancaster's hand grazed my waist; warmth shot through my veins and the scent of bloody roses swarmed me.

He removed the cypher dagger from my side. Instantly, the Bounty voice cried out, feeling defenseless. I bit my lip against it, tightening my fists over the needles shooting to my fingertips, trying to tug them to snatch the weapon back.

Lancaster's sharp, unceasing gaze dropped to my mouth and he sucked in a breath, eyes trailing down to my clenched hands. He noted every straining defense I held, marking them.

Then, he sank to the sand before me. Gently, not moving fast enough to trigger the Bounty, he loosened the laces of my boot enough to slip the blade against my ankle. His nimble fingers tightened it, and he angled his head up at me.

"How is that?" he asked. Was his voice rougher than usual?

I searched his unflinching stare, that understanding tone from before repeating in my mind, rioting with the lethal reflexes and canines peeking against his parted lips. This fae I was born to slaughter—who was bred to slaughter me—was on his knees in the sand before me. He was trying to help me stifle the instincts I loathed. And I didn't know what to make of it.

When I took a moment to answer, Lancaster gripped my ankle, squeezing. I jolted at the shock it sent through my body.

"Good," I answered. "That's good."

He pushed to his feet and slung each of our packs across his back. On most people, it would look uncomfortable, but he was broad enough that he adjusted them easily.

"I'm going to pick you up now," Lancaster said. "Please don't stab me. I'd prefer to at least get to our first stopping point before I need to deal with blood."

A genuine laugh bubbled up my throat at that, and Lancaster didn't smile, but he relaxed at the sound.

One of his hands slipped around my back, fingers curling against my ribs, and the other swept my legs out from under me. He moved so quickly, taking off into the trees, that my arms automatically latched around his neck.

The wind lashed my hair back from my face as he ran. Goddess, it was freeing. The sand and trees whipping around us, the way it all blurred together, yet we ducked and averted every possible collision. It was like flying but close enough to the earth to see its beauty.

It was so magnificent, I was able to ignore the Bounty instinct screeching inside me. To ignore the prickling of heat in my spine and ribs and let my hands rest against Lancaster's shoulders without fear of losing control.

Chapter Sixteen
Tolek

Mila and I walked through the sandy streets of Xenovia, woven tarps stretching across the alleys to keep them shaded in the hot spring sun.

"How did it go?" I asked her as we made our way to the blacksmith.

"Same as always," she responded dully, twisting sideways to avoid a man carrying a crate of jewelry. "The warrior was old, it was his natural time, and he was nearly gone when we arrived. I couldn't guide his spirit home, so I clearly did not absorb Soulguider magic in that river." She sighed, a mix of relief and frustration. "Erista's sister guided him quickly and quietly."

"And you felt nothing?" I asked.

She shook her head. She'd been going on these house calls with Erista and her twin sister for weeks, trying to lure out any power that may have latched onto her when she was under the Spirit River in the Gates of Angeldust.

So far, nothing.

Mila was always frustrated when she returned to Meridat's manor after the tests, so I'd accompanied her today. She'd said it was unnecessary, but Lyria would have done it.

I needed to get out of that manor anyway. I still could barely sit in a room with Cypherion without snapping over him making me

"

stay here or him asking me what I was scheming. Every time I did, Mila suggested we go for a walk.

We'd spent a lot of time wandering the capital aimlessly, theorizing. And I'd needed a distraction, trying not to think of what date yesterday had been.

"I know you don't think—"

"I know what you're going to say, Tolek," Mila interrupted as we turned a corner, the street opening onto a square rimmed by various shops, a fountain sprawling through the center, low and expansive. "But don't. There are lingering..." Her words trailed off.

"Mila?" I asked, hand on my sword. Her attention was honed on a woman across the square, sniffing flowers outside a florist stand. "Do you know that woman?"

Mila tilted her head, lips popping open and eyes blinking rapidly. A haze settled across her vision.

"Mila?" I repeated.

After a moment, she shook her head, pressing her hand to her chest. "Sorry."

I raised my brows at her lack of explanation. "What was that?"

Mila scanned the street, one eye still on the woman, then pulled me to the side. Toying with the gold cuff on her wrist, she whispered, "I've been having these...visions. Every so often and sporadically. There's no connection I can understand of why or what they mean."

"Premonitions? Like when Soulguiders sense a death?" I asked, following her gaze to the woman across the street.

"No, Erista said these are definitely different than hers."

As if sensing our attention, the woman stood up straight, white dress flowing around her brown skin. A short train slithered over the sandstone path as she turned to face us. When her dark eyes locked with Mila's, a grin split her lips.

Mila's mouth barely moved as she admitted, "They are always places I've never been. People and...creatures I haven't seen."

"Creatures?" I muttered, being sure to turn my head enough that the woman across the street wouldn't be able to make out my words.

"Winged human things sometimes. Sometimes what could be warriors riding beasts. It varies."

With a knowing nod, the woman turned away, brown coiled curls bouncing as she sauntered to another shop.

"And you saw *her*?" I guessed.

Goose bumps peppered Mila's arms, and I gripped my sword tighter.

"Just now. With red eyes. I saw her holding a baby in some kind of grove."

Red eyes? What in the everlasting Angel fuck was that about?

Mila shook her head, face pale. "Let's go back to the manor. We'll visit the blacksmith tomorrow."

She didn't mention the visions or the woman in the city again all day, but her memory followed Mila's every step.

CHAPTER SEVENTEEN
CYPHERION

"BRIGIET'S RESPONSE SAID THE BODYMELDERS ARE STILL recovering from the recent fires, but she's sending a legion and a small party to attend our council," Meridat said. In the grand war room of Xenovia's capitol building, she moved a single bronze marker of the Bodymelder sigil to Xenovia, leaving the rest in their territory across the mountains. "They'll likely arrive before Ezalia."

The room was fit for two dozen to sit around the table, with tiered rows of seats lining the perimeter for lower ranking advisors, and there were no windows. Just a bronze chandelier strung with decorative crescent moons and a large portrait of the Angel at the head of the chamber.

In the few days since Valyrie had visited, Meridat's advisors had pinned lists of legions to the walls on one side, and across from them, Erista and Mora were currently building an index of myths and corresponding magic to the gods. Anything that could point to how Echnid would banish them from Ambrisk. The large central table had an elaborate map of all of Ambrisk built into it, points where Artale's magic was known to touch the realm highlighted in bronze.

"Everyone has the same question, though," Mila said from her spot beside Tolek. "How will Echnid sever ties to the gods?"

"That's what we're all asking," I said. And I placed the bronze marker of a dove atop Damenal. "And what will we even be fighting?"

"Hopefully, Ophelia and Malakai will learn more," Meridat said.

"They will," Mila confirmed with a steady nod. Since Valyrie visited, the general seemed to pull herself back to life. Or at least she pretended she had. The sporadic visions were a problem.

Tolek, on the other hand, was still angry. Per Santorina's message from Ophelia, I'd kept him grounded the past two nights with excuses about needing his help on correspondence, which truthfully, he *was* skilled at.

My head pounded just considering what I was going to say to him tonight to get him to stay here.

I rubbed my temples, returning to the map before me. "Right, so until we know—" I paused when a note flared to life above the mystlight in the center of the table. It drifted to the scroll-strewn surface, an onyx sigil of crossed axes glinting on the seal.

"Barrett," I muttered, snatching the letter.

"The Engrossians answered?" Meridat asked, standing at the head of the table.

My stomach soured as I read it. I could barely force a word out. "Uprisings."

Tolek shot to his feet. "What?"

I handed him the note, and Tolek relayed to the group, "There's been uprisings in Banix. Heretics around the tar pits. The pools of dark magic are swarming with warriors who claim under Bant that Barrett is not fit to be king." He swallowed, crumpling the parchment. "Probably that worm Nassik's doing, spreading lies about Barrett's legitimacy. They've had to barricade the palace."

I dragged a hand through my hair. How the fuck did this happen? Neither of the major clan rulers currently held their seats —one due to a god *kidnapping* her, the other due to his people turning against him. And both were trapped in their own homes.

"Are Barrett and Dax all right?" Mila asked.

"For now," Tolek said. "Celissia is with them, as are the staff and the rest of their council."

"They can only survive so long in there," I said.

Meridat took the letter, reading over the less-than-savory details. "He says when his council sent out missives about Echnid to neighboring cities, the messengers were intercepted. Because the crowds were already riled, they think it's propaganda to get them to favor Barrett and are calling on Bant to save them."

"Echnid is a fucking god!" Tolek blurted. "They needed to know."

"One that history doesn't have any recollection of," I reminded him. "Echnid isn't compromising Banix the way he is Damenal. These people only know of the Angels, not the Warrior God, and they want their Prime Warrior to affirm their faith."

"Did Barrett say there's anything we can do?" Mila asked.

Meridat finished reading the letter and set it down. "No. He says he and his people will travel to Xenovia when they are able."

"Maybe..." I trailed off. My gaze landed on Tolek, a loose thread snagging in my mind. "Maybe we need to send our own assistance. As a show of good faith and alliance between the two major clans." I kept my expression as neutral as possible and hoped no one poked through the weak reasoning.

"They'll listen to a Mystique more than they'll listen to their own prince?" Mila asked doubtfully.

"If we show we're willing to set foot in their territory during unrest, it might prove how serious the threat of the Warrior God is."

"Are you out of your damn mind?" Tolek asked me. "They'll put an ax in your skull."

"Not mine," I said.

"You want *me* to go?" he asked incredulously.

No, truthfully, I didn't want him to go. But if he did, he'd be further from Damenal. Further from riding into whatever threat Ophelia believed was mounting in the capital.

And Tolek seemed to read that plan exactly from my mind. Because instead of the confident smirk he usually met every challenge with, he glared at me. "No."

"I'm not asking."

"I'm not going."

"You truly think those Engrossians are going to get a blade on you?" I appealed to the damn cockiness he wore so proudly.

Tolek lifted a brow, scoffing. "Not a chance. You know they wouldn't. But you want me to leave so I won't fly to Damenal." I ground my jaw, trying really damn hard to control my frustration. "I'm not stupid, CK. I know what you've been doing."

But he didn't know why.

"Are you rejecting an order from the Second to the Revered?" I asked, voice tight.

Mila's and Meridat's eyes bounced between us, Erista and Mora pausing their low murmurs in the corner.

Tolek's glare sharpened. Lethal. "Yes, I am."

"You can't keep going there," I declared.

"I will never give up on her."

And I snapped, "Well, she asked you to!"

Fuck.

Tol's answering silence could have incinerated the whole of Ambrisk. "*What?*"

I sighed. I hadn't meant to say that, but now it was out there, and guilt wrung my fucking heart. I did my best to remain calm as I explained, "Ophelia sent a message to Santorina before she left. She wants you to stay away." Tolek's throat worked over a swallow, but he showed no emotion. I pinched the bridge of my nose. "It sounded like there was a threat. Something she didn't want any of us near."

Mila stiffened, but she didn't say anything.

"What kind of threat?" Tol ground out.

I shook my head. "I don't know. But she made us promise to keep you away."

Another swallow from Tolek, his hands fidgeting behind his back. "I'm going after her." And he stormed from the room.

I jolted into motion. "Wait! Tolek, you can't!"

"What do you mean I can't?" he roared, whirling on me in the wide hallway of the capitol, surrounded by artwork and artifacts of another clan. The Soulguiders fell into an observant silence.

I fought to keep my composure in front of them. To maintain the control of a leader. "We're all doing things we don't want to, Tolek. For whatever reason, Ophelia asked you—she asked all of us," I corrected, "to *stay away*. She doesn't want *anyone* to come for her."

Tolek shoved a hand through his hair, leaving it standing on end. "What if something's wrong?"

"We need to trust that she has a plan."

"When has she asked for help, though?" He shook his head, his patience completely frayed. Desperate. "Ophelia doesn't blatantly ask for help. She shows when she needs it, and that's when I step in, but how am I supposed to help her from so far away?" He groaned. "Fucking Angels, CK, it's been a month since I've seen her! How am I supposed to know the signs?"

Spirits, he was broken. He was heartbroken from Lyria's death, and when Echnid took Ophelia his lifeline snapped. Every day without her sharpened the ruined pieces.

Vale had only been gone a couple days, and I was already going crazy, would go to her now if I could. I couldn't blame Tol.

"You and Ophelia—" I sighed. "What you two have built is strong, Tolek. She's coming back to you. She just needs time to figure out what's going on."

He wasn't hearing me, though, too lost to his own grief. "She shouldn't have to! She shouldn't have to be in Damenal with that god. She shouldn't have to be trying to figure a way out of this without me!"

"None of us should have to do any of the things we've done! Malakai shouldn't have had to sign that treaty, you shouldn't have nearly died when a building collapsed, Vale shouldn't have had to go back to Titus—but we're all doing it! We're all doing our damn jobs to try to see the end of this mess, and I need you to do this now." I panted, my words echoing against the tiled floors as Soulguiders hurried about, pretending not to listen.

Cursed Spirits, none of us should be in these positions. Who did I think I was, trying to lead a clan? From another territory, no less? I hadn't been raised to do any of this. My hands fisted at my sides, and I wished my scythe was at my back.

In a whisper, I added, "Ophelia needs you to do this."

Tolek breathed heavily, his head slightly shaking. "Send someone else," he begged.

"You're the only person," I told him. "You and Sapphire. It has to be someone who can fly directly into the palace grounds to speak with Barrett, and Jezebel isn't back from Valyn yet. And it has to be someone that doesn't hold a position of power with the Mystiques, so when you address Engrossians, it doesn't look like you have a hand in our political movements and are there solely as a show of good faith."

"But I'm Ophelia's"—his words cut off, his hand going to his chest where Malakai had the Bind inked—"whatever I am."

Fucking Spirits, those words were heavy. "You're who Ophelia loves, yes. You're who is going to spend the rest of your *fucking* life with her. But you do not have an official title."

It was an awful thing to use against him, and I'd knee Barrett in the groin if we all survived this for putting me in this position, but Tolek had never wanted a title anyway.

For a long silence, Tol fisted his hands at his sides. Then, he straightened and clasped his arms behind his back. "My job is to help Ophelia," he ground out. "That's what I'm here for. That's what I'll do."

"So?" I asked, afraid to state the question.

"Sapphire and I will assist with the heretics in Engrossian Territory however we can."

He strode away, and guilt threatened to drown me. With a groan, I scrubbed a hand over my face and turned back toward the war room.

"That went well," Erista said, following me inside.

"Not the time for jokes," I muttered, falling into my chair and pulling a book on Artale toward me.

"She's right," Mila added, taking the chair beside me. "Tolek and I have both been lost since..." She swallowed, then waved a hand over the table. "At least I know my place here. I think, even if you had to twist some truths, you gave him his."

CHAPTER EIGHTEEN
MALAKAI

My skin was on fire, but there wasn't a scratch on it.

That was my first thought when I finally fully came to after Echnid tried to wake the seraph that didn't fucking exist within me. Gods were so entitled, refusing to acknowledge that maybe they were wrong about one damn thing.

I stretched my arm above my head, and the burn sent a shock through my muscles. Like a fire was truly living in my blood, ravaging down to my fucking spirit.

Rolling my head to the side, even the brush of my hair across my forehead was a lick of flame. Every time something so much as touched my skin it ignited another spark.

Ophelia slept across the bed from me, on top of the covers with Lucidius's fucking dagger clutched in her hand. I almost laughed. As if that would do anything against the Angels or Echnid. Or the cerberus and those women who seemed to want nothing more than to ride Echnid's godly cock in the presence of us all.

She exhaled, legs moving restlessly against the sheets like she was hurrying to get out of this palace. This city.

As I was passing out the last time, she'd sworn she'd get us out of here—until the stars stopped shining—and the way her voice had cracked broke something in me. She'd been so different recently, contaminated by whatever evil Echnid spewed, but this was her. This was the warrior who wanted to fix everyone's problems and build a better future for the Mystiques.

She'd asked why I didn't fight back against Echnid, but I'd thought it was obvious. Ophelia and I were locked in this damn dance of the gods, but no one else had to be. For the same reason she wouldn't let our friends come find us, I took the blows. As if it was some agreement woven in the broken Bind between us.

I'd fought it, but I'd been certain ever since that siren song called to me in the Gates of Angeldust and I retrieved Xenique's emblem that we were trapped together. For long before that, if I was honest. I just hadn't wanted to admit it.

In her sleep, Ophelia shifted, her hand stretching out, and the tattoo inked against the pale skin of her inner elbow was a beacon. Mine heated in response, thudding wildly after all the time we'd spent together these past weeks. Not in a romantic way or even with the strength the soul-bond should have, but with a sense of comfort.

Ophelia and I may be locked here, but if we could distract Echnid, we could keep anyone else from stumbling into the line of fire. No one else would suffer what we were.

Mila.

Mila would not suffer.

My fists clenched at the thought. Fucking Spirits, I needed to see her. Desperation made my chest tight. It shrank the room around me until my breaths were harsh through my throat.

I needed out.

Out of these walls, even if I was trapped in this cage.

Ignoring the fire ripping through me, I grabbed a tunic from the stack I kept in Ophelia's dressing chamber and quietly left the room. Everywhere in the palace was hot, my skin too tight.

Air. I needed cold air and an open sky, not shadows that resembled locked bars.

I stormed through the palace, not bothering to remain quiet. It was our fucking home before the god's. Let him see me. Let him try to trap us even further. We were away from everyone we loved, and I'd survived years in chains at the hands of the man who sired me and was supposed to protect me. A god I never trusted wouldn't sting any more than he did.

I was crossing the corridor that descended down to the kitchens, planning to use the back door into the vegetable gardens, when a flash of light rounding the corner at the other end of the hall caught my attention.

Damien?

The stark gold ether that only he contained spilled across the marble, dancing away as he walked further.

What was the Angel doing down here at this time of night? What was he doing down here at all? As far as I knew, none of them ever came to the lower levels of the palace. All that was down here was the kitchens, the vaults, and—

The cells.

By the Angels, had they captured someone?

On feet that were much too loud given that I hadn't completed the fucking Undertaking, I crept after the Angel. I peered around the corner, but his light was just disappearing down a staircase at the end of this corridor.

I waited against the tapestry lining this stretch of wall. Valyrie had been spending a fortune in the city adding new decor to the palace, and while the entitlement grated on me, at least this piece absorbed some of the sound of my steps. It was an image of a gryphon to guard the treasures and captives beneath the ground or some Angelshit legend.

When Damien's steps faded, I prowled to the top of the stairs. Voices drifted up from the bowels of the palace. Deep rumbling tones and low laughter.

There was little light down there, the reflection of the magic cast off the Angel's wings stark against stone. Gold, and what might have been a hint of blue, faded as they walked further away. Gaveny, most likely. The Angel commanded seas and tides with his magic. I hadn't seen it in action since they were freed, but the torture he alone could inflict on a prisoner had my chest tightening.

I didn't have a weapon, but what good would that do against

an Angel anyway? I had to know who was down there. So, I followed down the stairs, not stopping until I came to a fork in the passageway. But—

What in Damien's name?

They hadn't gone left to the cells.

They went right.

Toward the vaults.

And more low voices were rising now. Male and female, barely more than whispers. I tried to let my steps blend in with them. At least being deep within the mountains abated the fire in my veins, but a sweat broke out for an entirely different reason. My heart thundered, and if they didn't hear my steps, I was certain that damn pounding would give me away.

Pressing my back to the wall, I took a deep breath and told the organ in my chest to shut the fuck up.

The door to the vault was just around this corner, and based on the array of colors playing against dark, craggy stone and the low murmur of voices, all seven Angels and the god himself were down here.

If they saw me, Echnid would certainly torture me until my heart gave out.

"What are we here for, sir?" Damien asked, speaking above the others. His voice boomed against stone, his gold ether shimmering with it.

Not to be outdone, Echnid matched his tone. "The time is up. If we have not yet found it, then it will all be destroyed."

The time?

Three days' time. That was what Ptholenix, Gaveny, and Damien had been discussing when I'd overheard them before Echnid had Rozelyn drug me and bring me to the ballroom. Three days' time, then he wanted them to get rid of...something.

"Are you certain?" Damien asked, voice still projecting, but I almost thought there was a waver of concern in it.

A scrape of metal against stone ricocheted around the passageway.

"Yes," Echnid swore.

The light slowly filtered forward as if the Angels were leaving. I peeked around the corner. The vault door was wide open, and Echnid floated within. Only beams of the Angels' light were visible, cascading to the floor as if they hovered near the high ceilings.

And rows of gold gleamed before them.

Bars of the damn stuff that Lucidius had hoarded for years while his people suffered. Priceless artifacts, weapons that had been dipped in sacred sources of magic or forged in the Spirit Volcano. Paintings and sculptures carved by the hands of renowned artists, from a peaceful age when warriors laid down their swords and indulged in scholarship and art.

The vault stretched deep into the mountains, more wealth than I could count stored down here. I'd only stepped foot in there a handful of times and never explored it all.

What the fuck did Echnid want?

He was a damn god. He didn't need gold to claim power.

I didn't dare breathe too heavily as I watched, trying to figure out what could be in there that Echnid had the Angels searching for.

"Ptholenix," Echnid said, calling the Bodymelder from his perch.

He drifted down with his typical stoic calm, expansive wings reflecting a myriad of oranges and reds as he tucked them in. He landed beside Echnid, neither bothering to look at the other. Their eyes were locked on the glittering treasures before them.

"Melt it," Echnid commanded in deranged glee.

An exclaim of shock slipped from me, but luckily Ptholenix stated louder, "It would be an honor."

And then, flames poured from the Firebird's palms. Orange and red and gold, even the scalding blue hearts. They licked across the first row along the left wall. Gold cascaded to the floor in a waterfall of riches. A destruction of wealth that could promise so much to so many.

Crackles filled the air, heat searing my skin and burning my eyes.

"It will take time," Ptholenix stated calmly, showing no sign of strain despite the force of his magic.

"We have all the time we need," Echnid said.

Holy Angels, I internally shouted.

And as quickly and quietly as possible, I raced back up the stairs.

~

"Ophelia!" I shook her shoulder. "Ophelia, wake up!"

Her eyes shot open, and I gripped her wrist before that dagger landed in my neck. Magenta eyes flicked between my hand and my face, relief loosening her lips.

"Sorry," she panted. She scooted to the center of the bed, crossing her legs and twisting the knife between her hands. "What are you doing awake?"

"I needed air," I answered. Based on her tight swallow and shallow nod, she understood. "But that's not why I'm waking you."

I rushed out the story of what I'd seen in the vault, and Ophelia blinked at me with glee I didn't understand.

"This is our chance!" she gasped, flying from the mattress and dropping to her knees at the edge of the bed.

"What?" I asked.

She dug around and pulled out two packs stuffed to the brim. She tossed me one, and the weight and sharp corners poking the leather told me it was at least partially filled with books.

"What are these for?" I asked.

Ophelia was already slinging her satchel across her body and lacing up her boots. "We're getting out of here, Malakai."

And the glimmer in her eye—it wasn't just hope. It was determination wrought from the magic flooding through her blood. It was shimmering gold seraph power, and it had me grabbing Lucidius's dagger and donning the heavy pack.

Still, I said, "We can't just walk out the door."

Ophelia gripped my wrist and pulled me from the room. "We aren't," she explained as I followed her dizzying steps, trusting her despite the confusion in my gut. "When you were unconscious, I was thinking about something Valyrie said to me. About a legend she loved. And about…other things." She paused. "But I spent the day diving deeper into this myth magic."

"What about it?" I asked. Ophelia led me back through the palace corridors toward the vaults I had come from. "We can't fight them!" I whispered harshly.

"We aren't even going to see them," she comforted me without stopping. "But this is our window of opportunity. You said yourself they'd be in the vault for a while."

Mystlight sprinkled across her wings, beating gently in anticipation. "Phel, I swear to the Angels, if you think you're flying us out of here—"

"Not me," she said, huffing a laugh when we stopped at the top of the staircase heading into the cells and vault passageways. "He is."

She pointed to the tapestry—

"A gryphon?" I blurted. "Where are you going to get one of those?"

But Ophelia was striding in front of me already, pure-gold magic gathered in her palms.

"I'm not going to get one," she purred. "I'm going to raise one."

And like Ptholenix had projected fire across the vaults, Ophelia poured mythos magic over the tapestry. It was the pure shimmering gold of ancient power, not laced with any of the Angels' light.

I squinted against it, removing my dagger and keeping one eye on the stairs. Luckily, Ophelia's magic didn't crackle as loudly as the Firebird's had. It gleamed, stark in the dim passageway, but through the beams, a figure emerged from the wall.

"By the fucking Angels," I muttered.

First came the beaked head of an eagle, talon-tipped feet reaching forward. A lion's lithe body and the grand wings of its aviary counterpart stretching from wall-to-wall. It arched out of the tapestry, landing lightly against stone, like this creature was born for the open air despite its conjured state.

And I stood there breathless as a fucking *gryphon* appeared before us. The tapestry where it had been was now a bare stretch of navy blue, like it was wrenched from the sky.

I'd seen the sphinx Ophelia had woken, but something about actually witnessing the magic in action as it brought a creature of legend to life was altering. Like I hadn't realized just how intense this form of power was. How dangerous it could be if commanded by the wrong hand.

Just what would Echnid make Ophelia bring to life if he had her under his thumb?

"We have to hurry," I said with a glance over my shoulder. Nothing sounded from the vault, but who knew when one of the Angels would drift away.

Ophelia was tending to the gryphon, ensuring not a feather was out of place, but the creature didn't seem riled at all. If anything, it was determined, eyes steely gray and focused on her.

"Come on," I urged.

"Ready?" Ophelia asked the creature.

Unlike the sphinx, this one didn't talk. It snapped its beak with a muted screech, like it was trying to keep quiet.

As we hurried toward it, a gold glow echoed from the stairs. *Damien*.

Ophelia's face paled, her eyes wide. She hastily hopped on the gryphon's back, and I was about to jump up behind her, but she shook her head and flapped her wings.

"Take the lead."

I grumbled, but didn't argue, tucking my knees above the gryphon's wings. Ophelia wrapped her arms around my waist, and I prayed to whatever beings actually cared that she was as steady on a saddleless gryphon as she was on Sapphire. I nudged the beast into motion, and we fled, talons scraping against marble floors. My hands tightened against the creature's thick, feathered neck.

As we rounded the corner, I cast a last glance over my shoulder.

And I met the purple stare of the Prime Mystique Warrior.

Valyrie stood beside him, her star-flecked ether dancing around her lavender gown. *Fuck...*Valyrie. She probably read our escape attempt just now. Damien opened his mouth to say something, but I never heard the words.

We were out of the depths of the palace and tearing through the foyer, down the wide stone entrance and toward the grand staircase to the grounds. Wings flared out on either side of us, and soon, the palace shrank below. The gryphon took flight, soaring off into the night.

"There's one more thing I have to do!" Ophelia called over the rush of wind.

The darkness in her voice sent my stomach spiraling back to the ground.

"What is it?"

I checked behind us, but no Angels were taking to the skies. No cerberus raced along the grounds.

"My Curse mark," Ophelia whispered, speaking of the gray webbed veins that had tattooed her wrist since the first false curse appeared on her. "It's been a connection this entire time, showed up when the Angelcurse first woke. And Echnid has been using it to drug me since he returned."

"I fucking knew it," I grumbled, anger igniting. She'd been catering to the mark since we got here. "I knew something was wrong."

"I don't remember entire days. I swear, Malakai, I-I never would have sided with him. I never would have tortured you, but for some reason this mark allowed his magic access to my thoughts and actions. To control me," Ophelia admitted, words rushed and cracking. "It was always when you weren't around. I think you kept pulling me back, or my subconscious kept coming back to you. Everything was foggy—and there was some voice in my head —and, and—"

Her voice was so fucking broken.

This was it. Ophelia had fought for so long. Against Kakias, for the Angels. She'd been used, but this? This had stolen something from her. Forced her to do things beyond her will.

This was the point at which she'd shattered.

"I know, Phel," I said, holding her arms tighter to me and looking at the black webbing on the inside of her wrist. "I know."

"I need it gone."

"That mark is your veins," I argued gently, thinking about the time she'd made Tolek slice literal dark power from her flesh. "You can't cut it out."

"Not cut," she corrected. "*Scorch*." My skin tingled at the power in her voice. "During training, when I asked about Angel and seraph magic, Damien mentioned it can heal the most deeply planted taints. He repeated it so many times, Malakai, and he specifically mentioned the Curse mark." She shook her head against my back, her words urgent. "I need to try."

She needed to claim her freedom, she meant.

My heart pounded as we soared across Damenal's border. Why weren't the Angels coming after us?

"What do you need me to do?" I asked.

"Just make sure I don't fall."

"Fall?" I repeated, but Ophelia didn't hear me. She was already wrenching up that seraph magic.

A gold aura shrouded us, sparking and cracking with thin beams of light. The gryphon flared his wings in response to it, flying faster and higher. A cloud culminated around Ophelia's arm against my waist, thickened on her Cursed wrist. It coalesced into veiny streaks of their own, lining up with the dark web along her skin.

Then, one golden strand reared back, and like a snake striking, it sank fangs into her wrist.

"What the *fuck*?" I yelled.

Ophelia cried out and clenched my waist tighter. Blood poured from the wound, white mist streaking the crimson. But the seraph magic flared brighter, feeding into her blood. It *burned and burned*, searing through any poison left by the god.

Scorching it away.

"Ophelia?" I shouted, but she didn't answer.

I held her arms tighter, making sure she didn't let go of me as blood and magic poured from her—as it rained across the night sky—and the gryphon carried us further from the clutches of the Warrior God.

The seraph magic burned deeper, gold igniting the night. Ophelia stiffened and whimpered each time, her pain bouncing across the stars.

"It's okay, Phel," I said, knowing there was nothing I could do to fix this. "I've got you."

Because every one of those damn stars still shone, and as long as they did, I'd ensure she was safe.

CHAPTER NINETEEN
OPHELIA

I WAS LOSING SO MUCH BLOOD.

Angellight cascaded from my body.

It was hot; every part of me was burning.

Magic clouded the air with a ghostly gold essence, crimson laced with white mist, streaking into the night.

There was too much.

Too much what? a voice in my head echoed, memory slipping away like water through my fingers.

It was hot. That water would be refreshing.

"Hang on, Ophelia," Malakai whispered, his arms a tight comfort as he held my burning wound. "You're going to be okay. I'm going to get you help."

Help...That's what I was doing. I was helping myself after being manipulated. After a god warped my opinions so I didn't know which were my own. I was taking control back and restoring balance. Balance I was meant to uphold.

I couldn't remember what that meant exactly, but it meant something important. I'd figure it out later. Right now, all I felt was fire. I was consumed by it.

And it felt fucking *good* to burn.

"It's okay, Malakai," I said. "It was my turn to distract him."

And with the magic of Angels—

No. With the magic of *seraphs*, I scorched the Curse mark

from my body, unraveling the connection Echnid had built and burning his drugged control out of my blood.

Even as his claws retracted, his presence lingered. His voice in my mind, his actions in my muscles. The influence remained, trying to pull me back, warring with my seraph magic.

And I feared that while I may steal back my autonomy and get the poison out, I would never be free of him again.

CHAPTER TWENTY
DAMIEN

THEY ESCAPED.

On the back of a gryphon wrenched from the tapestry in the hall above the trove, Ophelia and Malakai flew into the night.

And if the way Echnid screamed said anything, Ophelia had realized she had to burn his poison from her body with the healing properties of the Angellight her seraph gifted her. Despite the tainted control he had taken of her, the words I had repeated in our lessons stuck to her memory.

A cascade of emotions poured through me, still so wild and untamed from the centuries my Spirit was trapped. I maintained a stony expression before Echnid's raging, but deep remorse and exuberant relief collided within my chest.

I met Valyrie's stare as they fled, and her lips tipped up into the cruelest of smiles.

"It is not the chance we expected," she whispered.

"No," I agreed as they faded. "But it is a chance altogether. And we have been waiting so very long."

PART TWO
BANT

Chapter Twenty-One
Vale

"Please, show me where Echnid's fury may lead," I begged the Fate's starfire burning before me.

Though the celestial beings rarely told us precisely what we requested, it wasn't always futile to ask. And I'd been waiting days for this Fate in particular to wake, to stir in my chest and ignite that white fire that indicated a reading was waiting just beyond my bounds.

It had struck this morning, once I was back in Starsearcher Territory. I wasn't sure if that was a coincidence or not. I'd shot out of bed with urgency, lighting a candle and burning incense to fuel the connection.

"Please, share whatever you may," I asked again.

The trail of white fire burning behind the star flickered to life. No bodily shape was determinable, only the blistering celestial form, the outline of a helm upon his head.

And the rumbling voice of Arenothos, Fate of Wrath and Redemption, boomed through the swirling space carved out of the sky, as if from every direction. "The Warrior God is full of my first namesake and hunting the second."

"He wants redemption?" I asked. "But that doesn't make sense. Echnid wants revenge."

"And by enacting that vengeance, he wishes to right his own name in history."

My stomach twisted. Echnid would rewrite the past as we know it. Enforce a world that spoke of him as a victor instead of a conqueror. It was what many wars led to, wasn't it? A wrongful ruler on a throne, legends written in their image. Titus flashed through my memory, and the edges of the vacant tear his death left within me pulsed.

I buried that loss deep down and implored the Fate, "Please, Arenothos, show me the paths that may lead to this foretold future."

Starfire continued to flicker as the Fate sought. I knelt before him, clenching my fists.

I wasn't sure if I was on some sort of Fate plane or envisioning this. Some scholars believed sessions truly transported Starsearchers to a Fate Realm and only our bodies remained in our own, but if I closed my eyes, the marble floor of the room I was reading in chilled my knees. The window was open, and birds sung merrily on the grounds of Harlen's home. My hands were folded upon my thighs, and the various incense I'd lit twined on the air.

I believed that the purpose of the scent was not only to trigger a Fate but to ground us back to that earthly realm, whether we left it or not, and I focused on those bodily sensations as I waited for Arenothos to seek out the *how*.

How Echnid was going to separate godly ties to warriors.

How he was going to banish the gods from Ambrisk.

How.

Starfire swelled, trails stretching up and out. Sparking and sputtering. I squinted against it, searching the white-hot depths as night-bathed heat licked along my skin and sang to my magic.

Wrath and Redemption.

At the nearness of the Fate, the two feelings rose within me, purring to his influence. My blood boiled, teeth grinding, but a desperate hole opened in my chest, as if yearning for vindication. The conflicting desires intensified as he sought. Until, within the heart of the star, an image of Ophelia flickered to life.

As it had every time I tried to seek Echnid.

"I know they are tied together, but what do their entwined fortunes determine?" I asked.

"You have already seen this answer, Fatecatcher," Arenothos said, voice rumbling like a stampeding legion.

"When?"

Arenothos dragged up an image that had haunted me. The future I'd first read of Ophelia. The one Titus had passed off as his own during the Rapture in Damenal, when all I'd seen was darkness, destruction, and her. And Titus had used it to throw Ophelia's rule into question.

"This Fate I once showed you has come to pass," Arenothos declared.

My body iced over. "What?"

"This is the future Ophelia Alabath has condemned the world to in freeing the Warrior God. On the current path, destruction will rain upon Ambrisk, and you will all bow to his mercy."

"*No*," I gasped. Ophelia had only been doing what we all wanted her to do. She'd been doing what the Angels had instructed. "Show me the way to fix it, please."

"I do not have the answer to that," Arenothos said. "You know you cannot change fortune, Fatecatcher."

And before I could scream my fury at the Fate of Wrath and Redemption, I tore myself from the reading. Panting, I landed on all fours in the center of my room.

There had to be some other answer. Perhaps he could only see that future because it surrounded his properties. Theoretically, all Fates could access a number of different scenarios that made up fortune, woven together like the silky strands of a spider's web.

The Fate of Cruelty and Adoration could reach the same conclusions as Wrath and Redemption because cruelty was often born of wrath. The way they presented the paths, though...that was where variations lay. A hundred Starsearchers could see the same reading and interpret it differently due to their Fate's whims at that moment.

But I would take anything they offered to help us out of this.

As I watched the wavering lines of gray in the white marble flooring, I considered my options. Perhaps I'd wait for the Fate of Fertility and Betrayal to speak. We did not have a Fate of Death, but fertility dealt with all manners of lifespans, stretching all the way to endings.

The clock on the mantle let out a loud *ding*, and my head snapped up.

"Oh, Valyrie's tits!" I sprang up and dashed from the room.

~

"Running late as always," Harlen teased when I sped into the foyer where he, Cyren, and Jezebel were waiting. The tall glass doors were thrown open, dull sunshine falling across the dark wooden floors and beams lining the vaulted ceiling. Abstract cerulean stained-glass windows stood on either side of the entry-way, calming the morning light.

"I was never late a day in our young lives, Harls, and you know it." I looked at the grandfather clock to confirm, then at Jezebel, clad in one of her brown-leather Mystique dresses with a sword strapped to her back. "Not flying back?"

She shook her head. "I'm going to stay around for a few days. I'll return to report to Cyph when we feel there's something to share." I didn't remind her that we could simply write to Cypherion should the need arise.

Angels, even thinking his name sent twisting emotions through me. Anger that he wasn't going after Ophelia and Malakai, doubt that he didn't want *me* to, yearning for this distress between us to be relieved, concern that something awful would happen in Xenovia while I was in Valyn.

"Vale?" Harlen asked, piercing that storm cloud. I blinked away the mist in my eyes, and my oldest friend laughed. "Day-dreaming again?"

I sighed. "I wish things were as simple as daydreams."

"Me, too." He squeezed my shoulder. "One day they will be."

That wistfulness thickened my throat, but I swallowed past it. "Let's speak as we walk."

Cyren, the Starsearcher General, led the way down the pale cobblestone path leading from Harlen's home. He'd been assigned it as a member of the council working to instill a new ruler since

Titus's death. There was a row of twelve identical buildings lining the road immediately west of the chancellor's manor. Cyren resided in one of the others.

They took us through the manor's back gates—only two guards stationed here now that there wasn't a chancellor within—and through the orange groves. My chest twisted with memories. Strolling with Titus as a young girl. Picking fruit in the spring.

Thankfully, Cyren sliced through the reverie. "We got Cypherion's request for alliance."

"And?" I asked, voice still a bit shaky as we passed the place where two trees leaned toward each other, and the ache in my chest ripped wider. I used to hide there when I was small.

"You have the Starsearchers at your command," Cyren confirmed. I shook off the lingering pain, forcing myself to focus.

"But we have to know," Harlen whispered, "is it truly a god?"

We rounded a bend in the path, and the manor sprawled before us. My throat constricted, but I tried to keep my eyes on the others as we approached the back porch.

As Cyren climbed the stairs, Jezebel said roughly, "Yes, he is. And he's taken my sister and Malakai captive."

"*What?*" Cyren gasped, frozen on the top step.

"We didn't want to put that bit in writing," I explained, and I told the whole story as we stood outside the manor I grew up in. I even explained the reading I saw when the Angels emerged—or what I could of it, given that so much still didn't make sense to me.

The gods had *been there*. They'd looked at me—Moirenna had spoken to me. *Fatecatcher, we will see you soon.* I hadn't been able to piece together any of it, but I had a sickening feeling the gods were much closer than we'd thought.

Cyren's face paled as we finished explaining Valyrie's recent visit, not even the fearsome leathers and decorated medal on their chest rebuilding their armor. They exchanged a look with Harlen. "We'll have to tell the rest of the council."

"The god's return is no longer a secret," Jezebel said. "Tell whomever you must in order to prepare them."

Cyren breathed in that truth and recovered themself, putting the face of general back on in light of the need for a strategy. "We may have something that can help."

~

The seeing chamber looked nothing like the last time I was here, but still all I saw when I crossed the threshold was Titus's body falling at my feet. Heard the way his bones crumpled.

We entered through the opposite door—the one Malakai and Mila had been escorted through on that fateful night—but that only gave me a perfect view to impose an image of myself slicing a triple blade across my captor's throat.

His blood pouring across me.

A phantom tinge in a bond that no longer existed.

A hand landed on my shoulder, and I jumped.

"Okay?" Harlen asked.

"Yes." I tried to wipe away the memory, but all that did was smear a crimson sheen across it.

"You never were the best liar, Vale."

Narrowing my eyes at him, I shook my head and gestured around us. "What's happening here?"

Because there certainly was something different.

The walls on one half of the chamber were being deconstructed. Warriors with pickaxes and wheelbarrows chipped away at the white marble that shone with an iridescent moonstone sheen.

"We're still testing it," Cyren began as one warrior pushed a wheelbarrow across the chamber to where they'd set up a temporary forge and deposited a pile of white rubble. Cyren led us to the fireside, picking up a triple blade that had recently cooled and holding it out to us. "The walls are imbued with precious resins and minerals from the mountains."

"That's what Titus used to crack open my readings," I muttered, taking the weapon.

Jezebel leaned over it with me, and we turned the blade toward the light. Something glittered within the silver.

"You're pulverizing the rubble?" Jezebel asked.

"And mixing it with the steel in forging," Cyren confirmed. "We don't know how powerful they'll be, but the hope is that with these weapons on their person, Starsearchers in battle will have clearer readings and understand the moves of their opponents with quicker reflexive opportunities."

Harlen grinned beside the general, and he looked like a young boy who'd just found an extra piece of cake.

"These could be very helpful if it comes to a physical fight against Echnid," Jezebel said. "You could make swords, spears, and arrows if you have time. We could arm other clans with them to fuel the entire battlefield with Starsearcher magic."

Cyren smiled. "That was Lyria's idea. After you told everyone about the chamber, Vale."

A thick sadness strung between us, and I was struck with the impact of the dead, lingering not only through memories, but through the missions left behind.

"Can you etch one with her initials?" I asked. "Maybe a single-bladed dagger?"

"That's a great idea," Cyren said.

I turned the triple-blade in my hand, inspecting the sheen the moonstone and other precious minerals gave the steel. My reflection was blurred, but the stained-glass ceiling wavered around it. And within, Titus's blood splashed across a knife. I gasped, the weapon clattering to the ground.

"Are you okay?" Harlen asked, picking up the blade.

I nodded, lips tight and voice stuck in my throat.

But Jezebel squeezed my arm and said, "I have an idea."

~

JEZEBEL LED me to the wide clearing overlooking rows of vineyards where Zanox and Dynaxtar were sunning their wings. Immediately, both khrysaor popped up, tilting their equine heads at us.

Zanox nudged Jezebel, picking through her pockets, but Dynaxtar approached me, giving me a soft, loving tap with her nose. I patted her, studying her slitted eyes, and for a blink, my blood and breath seemed to idle.

"Okay, okay!" Jezebel said through a laugh, batting off Zanox as he nearly knocked her over. He swung his spiked tail around, carefully catching her with the soft underside before she could fall. Jezebel dug into her pocket and pulled out a pear. "This is all I have."

She tossed it in the air, and Zanox didn't seem to mind that it wasn't an apple, snatching it quickly and swallowing in one gulp. Dynaxtar nickered softly, not seeming hungry. The larger, male khrysaor had an insatiable appetite, while his female counterpart was more interested in her time amid the clouds.

"Want to fly?" Jezebel asked me. When I looked at her, she was grinning broadly—the happiest I'd seen her in weeks.

I looked up at Dynaxtar, and that wild, ancient glee gleamed in her gold slitted eyes. It pumped my own blood faster. "Absolutely," I breathed.

Now that all masks were dropped around Echnid and the mythical beasts, we rode Zanox and Dynaxtar freely through the skies, dipping low enough for the citizens of Valyn to see.

The capital unfurled below, all eleven districts and the zones beyond. What secrets did they hold? What histories and legends? The opportunity to discover it all—to truly know the city I'd spent so much time in—made me weightless.

I'd flown to Valyn on Dynaxtar, but that had been the first time solo, and I'd been nervous. She was twice the size of any horse I'd ridden, and though Cypherion insisted, Jezebel had yet to have a saddle made.

Now, though, this close to the home of the Fates and stars, freedom inflated my spirit.

"Let's go over the vineyards," I called to Jezebel and Zanox. She whooped in response, and the beasts soared west.

Warriors roamed the neat rows of grapes, pointing and shouting in curious joy as we passed by, circling above and out over the furthest stretches of the city limits. Jezebel crested the hill leading out of Valyn and stretched her arms up to the sky—

A scream pierced the air, and Zanox roared.

Dynaxtar bucked. I laced my hands through her silver mane to keep seated.

"What's happening?" I shouted.

Jezebel was hunched over Zanox, and crimson streaked the air behind her. I called to her, my heart thundering as loud as Dynaxtar's.

She didn't answer, but silver-blue light flared.

"Get us to safe ground!" I commanded the khrysaor, praying to the Angels she would follow my direction.

She swooped ahead of Zanox, taking point, and as we passed, I gasped at the arrow through Jezebel's arm. One unlike anything I'd seen—gleaming black stone in the head and night dark feathers at the end. Her face was pale, but she was conscious, teeth gritted.

"Who the fuck—" she bit out.

I searched the ground, but no one was beyond the capital limits that I could—

"There!" I shouted, pointing to the sign marking the boundary of the vineyards.

A woman with wine-red hair stood with a bow in her hand and a haughty smile gleaming on her lips. Her stark white dress billowed around her curvy form in the gentle breeze, but even from here she seemed out of place. Ethereal.

"Zanox, turn back!" Jezebel demanded as we soared toward the city center, her words labored. "We need to"—she hissed, and silver-blue light pulsed around her again, untamed and angry—"to get her."

The khrysaor didn't listen. He wouldn't if Jezebel needed a healer.

"Dynaxtar!" I tried, hopeless that she would obey me over her rider.

But she dropped lower, slowing her pace to be even with Zanox. The two shared a silent exchange, and then Dynaxtar was circling.

And my heart stuttered, that idling blood and breath sensation from before returning, making me weightless.

She had *listened to me* over Jezebel. A long-slumbering sense woke, like the khrysaor's decision struck a primal instinct, and I was wound around its cause.

Jezebel swore, that silver-blue light pulsing around her again, but it faded with her voice as Zanox raced to get her to safety. I knotted my hands in Dynaxtar's mane, searching the ground as we circled over the vineyards.

The khrysaor banked, and I nearly shrieked, tightening my knees to stay seated. A black arrow shot past her wing, right in the path of where we'd been a moment ago.

"Good job, girl!"

She preened beneath me and maneuvered through a barrage of a dozen arrows. Dynaxtar was sleeker than Zanox, able to dodge and bank much quicker than his size allowed. She wove in and out of the clouds as if she'd been practicing for this since she woke, and I flowed with each sharp turn and dip.

"There!" I called, spotting the red-headed woman again, her bow loaded—

Dynaxtar tucked in her wings to dive, but a blur shot out of the vineyard, tackling the woman to the dirt. Just before they disappeared from view, I glimpsed cascading dark hair and a willowy form.

But they didn't emerge again. And when we landed, we scoured the neat rows of grapes, but we couldn't find them.

I only shook my head at the empty vineyard, sticking close to Dynaxtar's side as we hurried back to the city and ignored the fact that the woman who had saved us looked eerily familiar.

CHAPTER TWENTY-TWO
MALAKAI

SAND FLEW UP AROUND US AS THE GRYPHON'S TALONED feet slammed into the earth. The sun was just starting to rise, bathing the dunes in a wash of pale gold.

Fucking *gold*. I didn't ever want to see that color again after Ophelia's light scorched whatever connection she had with Echnid from her body. It had flared for nearly the entire flight, until she slumped against my back. The only sign she was alive was her breath brushing against my shoulder.

Shouts echoed around us, and as the sand cleared, weapons were jammed in our faces. Curved scythes glinted in the sun from warriors dressed in lightweight leather vests, linen tunics, and bronze adornments.

Soulguiders.

"State your business!" one demanded, the blade of his scythe jutting closer to the gryphon. The beast snapped its jaw, chomping down on the weapon until it snapped cleanly in two. The warrior jumped back, ripping a hooked sword from his belt.

"Get your weapons away from it!" I growled.

The warrior lifted the pathetic blade. "What is it and how did it get here?"

Two guards crept around the tail of the gryphon's lion body, and I held tighter to Ophelia's arms as she groaned against my spine. Her wings drooped around us, dragging her weight down.

"Just let me fucking dismount, and I'll explain," I said, unlacing Ophelia's hands and twisting to hold her steady while I slipped down.

As soon as my boots hit the sand, someone lunged for me.

"Get off!" I ripped my arm from the Soulguider's grasp, stare intent on Ophelia as I supported her. "Can't you see she's not okay? She needs help."

"What's wrong with her?" the lead guard asked, others shifting carefully around the gryphon where Ophelia slumped along its spine. The creature, seeming to understand who was precariously perched on his back, remained docile.

"She's Ophelia Alabath, the damn Revered of the Mystique Warriors." It wasn't an answer to his question, but I *didn't know* what exactly was wrong with Ophelia. Besides everything Echnid had done to us.

Spirits, he'd *drugged* her. Anger curled cruel and defensive in my chest at the reminder.

"Let us go!" I demanded, roaring as the memory of her admitting that slammed into me.

"How do we know that's true?" the Soulguider challenged. Damien's cock, these fucking guards were persistent. Good for Meridat, I supposed, but dammit, it was annoying.

"She has fucking wings, isn't that proof enough?" Did they know? About Echnid, about Ophelia's seraph?

One brave—idiotic—warrior jabbed his scythe toward the gryphon's flank, and the beast released an angry, threatening squawk. It reared up, slashing its talons at the guard's chest.

"By the fucking Angels," I grumbled, ducking my guard and catching Ophelia as she slipped off its back.

"Malakai?" she mumbled, finally waking. Her feet met the sand, but her knees buckled, hands latching to my tunic. "Where are we?"

I slid an arm beneath her wings, so they fanned out behind both of us and slung one of hers over my shoulder.

"Somewhere in the desert," I guessed.

The guard barked, "You're on the estate of—"

"Stand down!" The command sliced through his sentence, and the warriors shot to attention.

My head whipped toward the voice, shifting Ophelia behind me, but my tense muscles unknotted when I saw the owner.

"Meridat," I sighed.

"Meridat?" Ophelia echoed, stumbling around to see her. She blinked her tired magenta eyes in the bright morning light. Dried blood still coated her arm.

The Soulguider Chancellor approached with a consoling smile, her emerald skirt drifting in the breeze and bronze-plated jewelry catching the dawn. She looked like she'd been awake for hours already, her hair tied in long braids down her back and stare alert as it swept over the gryphon.

"Ophelia. Malakai," Meridat greeted.

I peeked around her, tightening my arm on Ophelia's waist. About fifty yards off, across streams and through a maze of palm trees and cyphers, a sandstone manor waited, its elaborate columns and ornately carved domes and arches barely visible from here. More people were moving across the dunes toward us.

"We're on your estate?" I asked, disbelief racing through me. Thank that fucking gryphon.

The chancellor nodded. "And I would love to hear the story of how you arrived." She eyed the creature behind us, her guards still aiming their scythes at it.

"I have plenty to share," Ophelia muttered with an exhale that was barely a laugh. Every breath from her was so fucking labored.

As I tried to prop her up better, a deep voice cut across the sand, "Is it them?"

"Cypherion?" I called as he raced to a stop beside Meridat, looking us over.

"Thank the fucking Spirits you're okay." Utter relief painted Cypherion's words. He rushed forward, taking Ophelia's bloodied arm and draping it across his shoulder. He eyed the gryphon but only shook his head. "Not sure I want to know."

"It's such a good story," Ophelia joked limply as she patted his chest, but I barely heard the condensed explanation she gave.

My disbelieving heart pounded. Their voices melted together. If Cyph was still here, that meant...

No Spiritsdamned way.

Racing across the grounds was a shock of platinum hair and a lithe, silk-robed body.

"*Mila*," I breathed.

And then, I was running, flying over the damn desert, until I collided with her like two of those shooting stars she loved so much. I caught her, every tensed inch of my body uncoiling, the realm so fucking right again. I sank to my knees in the soft sand with her legs wrapped around my waist, arms tight behind my neck.

"Mila," I whispered into her hair, a sob catching in my throat. My chest unlocked, flooding with a rush of emotion. Every single thing I'd been stuffing aside since the theater broke free as Mila's heart pounded in time with mine. As the weight of her body pressed against my chest and her hands dove into my hair.

Terror at what she could be going through.

Longing to hold her after Lyria's death.

Pain knowing how much she'd hurt.

It all rushed to the surface.

"Malakai," she choked out, and fuck, she really was crying.

I pulled back, keeping her body pressed to mine, and cupped her cheek. Her eyes were glassy, but they were open. Awake and alert, and she was *here*. But grief weighed down every blink, a brokenness, loss, and confusion I hadn't seen before cracking her fortress.

"I'm so fucking sorry, Mila," I whispered, voice shaking as I pressed my lips to her forehead.

"Why?" She pulled back to look at me, and her jaw trembled as she understood. "It's not your fault."

"I never wanted to leave you," I swore, and everything came pouring out, my arms tightening around her. "I wanted to be here for you. To claw my way back to you."

"I know, Malakai." She sighed, tears hot as I kissed the tracks they left down her cheeks. "I know."

She could feel it in each desperate beat of my heart, pounding loud enough for us both to hear. In the promise searing my words. We were two broken people who had been tortured and scarred, but somehow found safety in each other, and something in that shared, fucked up history meant that we found truth in the silence between breaths. Strength in each other's heartbeats, the rhythm a reliable melody when the world was too loud.

"Fucking Angels, I missed you," I breathed. "Rina said you were okay, but a part of me didn't believe it."

"I'm here," she cried, nodding. "I've been—I don't know, but I'm here."

Dropping my forehead to hers, I said, "Tell me later."

And then I kissed her. And Mila's kiss in return was like coming home after too long at war. Every little breath, every inch she clung to me, was her saying *I missed you* in a way words couldn't quite convey.

Sliding my hand to the back of Mila's neck, I tilted her head so I could cement my lips to hers and wipe away the lingering pain of Echnid's torture. Relieve the fear haunting her stare.

Because to me, she was absolution and healing and grace. I'd been broken, but she was the fire that forged me back together. As she trembled against me, I swore I'd mend the agony that rippled off her every move.

Together, we'd fix all of it, even if it killed me.

~

OPHELIA HADN'T GOTTEN another word out before she was unconscious again, but the Soulguiders and Cypherion took her inside, leaving me with Mila.

"That door," she said, pointing to a bronzed archway at the end of the hall in this guest house. Her legs were still wrapped around my waist as I barreled inside and flicked the lock.

I placed her down on the bed and tilted her chin up to me. The room was full of lush jewel tones, bedding in deep emerald and amethysts, gilded decor glittering the walls, but all I truly saw were those ice-blue eyes gazing up at me.

What did you even say after something like this?

Brushing my thumb along her jaw, I settled on, "How are you?"

Mila considered, and for a brief moment, I thought the doors of her fortress were going to snap closed, but she released a trembling sigh weighed down by the last few weeks, and it fucking undid something within me.

I crouched down, pressing my forehead to her thighs. For a few minutes, I breathed her in, this warm and sweet cinnamon and vanilla scent. An aura that had come to mean home and healing and the best damn moments of my recent months. I allowed myself to be my broken form, on my knees before the woman I loved.

"Tell me," Mila whispered, running a hand through my hair.

I tipped my head up, propping my chin on her lap. "Tell you what?"

"Everything." Her hand trailed along my shoulder, stopping where my tunic covered the ends of the lash scars. "Did he..."

"No," I rushed, and relief flickered through her gaze, but her eyes bounced between my own. She could tell there was more. Some sort of fundamental change I'd undergone. It was in the way my skin wrapped around my fucking bones, like a new armor had been forged. "He manipulated Ophelia. Drugged her. Poisoned her. Something." Fire scorched Mila's stare. "And when she was under his influence, he made her try to turn *me* into a seraph."

Her fingers knotted in my hair, her voice like ice. "How?"

"With the myth magic. He thinks she'll be able to turn any warrior into a seraph if she tries hard enough." I left out the details of how it wrenched me apart, burned me from the inside out, and ignited a need to see the god dead. I'd tell her everything eventually —would have to tell the entire group—but right now...

I skimmed my hands up her thighs to her hips. Her skin was warm—alive, unlike the memories I had of her unconscious in the Gates of Angeldust. She felt so good beneath my palms, and every second I spent touching her made me desperate for more. To finally let my guard down after weeks.

"We don't have to talk about it," she said. Her tongue darted out, dragging across her bottom lip, and my entire existence narrowed to that motion. Mourning was thick in her stare, in her voice, deeper than usual, like it had been dragged through nights of tears and grief. "Not yet."

I swallowed the pain flooding those words, understanding she meant she wasn't ready to talk about her weeks either. The fact that I hadn't been here to take care of her after she lost Lyria sealed an already deeply bruised desire for retribution against Echnid. I would take that god to the Spirit Realm.

"Later, I want to know everything that's happened since I've been gone," I clarified, gripping the hem of her silk robe like my life depended on it.

Mila nodded, and then, we both exploded. As if all those weeks I'd been locking away how desperately I both needed to feel her and simply needed her to be okay now overflowed and poured between us.

My lips met hers, and where her kiss in the dunes had said *hello* and *I missed you* this was *I was drowning without you.*

Images of the Gates of Angeldust and her body coming out of that water, limp and weighed down, flashed through my mind, and a groan worked up my throat. I pressed up, not breaking the kiss, and leaned forward until Mila was flat on the bed. Until my hips were pressing between hers and the hard length of my cock ground against her center.

Mila gasped at the contact, her head tilting back. I dragged one hand down her chest, pulling open her robe, and—

"White fucking lace," I said, low and guttural.

Mila laughed. It was her favorite. My favorite, too. I had dreams about that pale fabric against her skin, her scars and body on full display. Mine to worship.

"You chose a good day to return to me, Warrior Prince," she panted as I kneeled and removed the robe so nothing but her and white lace looked up at me. "I was ready for you."

Kissing down her chest and stomach, I cupped between her legs. "Seems like you're always ready for me."

Pushing aside her undergarments, I dragged two fingers up her center, lightly circling her clit. Mila's back arched as she moaned my name, eyes dropping closed and head tipped back. That sound made me ache for her.

She squirmed as I slowly pushed one finger in, having to focus really fucking hard on not letting go too early. Because it wouldn't take much—not with how she looked beneath me—but after these weeks, I was desperate for all of her.

"You're a fucking dream, Mila," I praised as I pumped my fingers faster and circled her clit with my thumb. "All I dreamed of when I was gone. I don't know what I've done in this life to deserve you."

Not only to be gifted her once, but to get to come back to her? To have this safe landing place after so much unimaginable horror? I didn't deserve any of it.

Mila writhed against my hand, begging as I worked her to that ledge and repeated how much I missed her. *Needed her*. If everything I'd been through—the treaty, imprisonment, Titus's torture, and Echnid—was the dark, choking midnight, then Mila was the dawn on the horizon. The one you feared you wouldn't see when the night was thickest but dared to hope for. The one that allowed you to breathe again.

Only after she'd come once on my fingers did I stand and strip off my leathers, peel the white lace down her thighs. Mila watched with lust-drunk eyes and kiss-swollen lips, admiring every inch of me in a way I definitely didn't deserve, but a way I was going to savor all the same.

I crawled over her, fisting my cock and lining it up with her slick entrance. Mila traced my scars and tattoo, her eyes pausing on the North Star.

"Mila," I said, soft and vulnerable. When she looked back up at me, I pushed into her an inch. She gasped, and I swallowed it with a kiss, growling against her lips. "That tattoo is no more than silent ink. You are who I want my soul bound to."

And I sheathed myself inside her. She cried out as my pelvis bottomed out, clinging to me. She was warm and tight and fuck if she wasn't the greatest feeling on Ambrisk. Made just for me, for us to fit together like two fucked up, scarred puzzle pieces whose broken edges couldn't be met with anyone else's.

I pulled my hips back and snapped forward, punctuating my next words. "You and I are meant for every damn tomorrow, Mila

Lovall. I love you, and there is no me without you—not the me I am now or the man I am meant to become. You make me whole in every way."

She paused, those three words I'd never gotten a chance to say sinking in. Then, Mila tightened her legs around my waist, and with a vicious smile, she flipped us. I settled into the overstuffed comforter with a laugh.

A laugh that disappeared into a groan as Mila sank down. She rolled her hips, and with eyes locked on mine, she looked better than any damn Angel.

"You and me. Every sunrise, every midnight, every tomorrow," she said, like she'd taken the words right from my mind. It was a vow, a promise becoming her lifeline after she lost so much. "You make me whole, too, Malakai Blastwood, and I will spend every tomorrow loving you as you deserve to be loved."

I was going to argue, but as if she knew, Mila took that moment to lift herself up and slam down. And this deep, she felt too damn good for full sentences to form.

The soft promises we'd been making melted into desire. I gripped Mila's hips, rocking her, and she threw her head back, one hand kneading her breast, still covered in that white lace. Silky platinum hair tumbled around her, and I watched her claim me as she rode, committing every sight and breath and sound to memory.

"Spirits, I've needed you," she moaned.

"Don't worry," I replied, both of us breathless, "we're going to make up for weeks today."

Mila's eyes snapped to mine, her hands braced on my chest as she swiveled her hips. One palm met my Bind, her nails curving around the edges. I shot upright, holding her in my lap and crushing my lips to hers, sealing every vow as we moved. I dipped my head, catching one of her lace-clad nipples in my mouth, and sucked.

"Angels, Malakai," she purred as the rough fabric rubbed against her, and I could tell she was close.

I pulled that lace down, wanting to see all of her, worship all of her. I teased both of her breasts, until she was panting, then I worked my lips back up her neck. Her chest pressed against mine

—her warm skin against my fucked-up body—and I was ready to explode.

I flipped her back down to the mattress and brought her leg to my shoulder, hooking her ankle behind my head. "Nothing but death can take me from you, General," I swore as I pounded into her. Harsh strokes intent on searing those words into her spirit. "No vengeful god or wrathful Angels."

Mila gasped, her orgasm crashing like a tidal wave, and I followed, spilling into her as I kissed her through it.

Once we caught our breath, Mila climbed out of bed and grabbed her robe, but I snatched it back.

"What are you doing?" she asked.

"What are *you* doing?" I repeated.

She eyed the bathing chamber, then the mess between her legs. But that only solidified my plans, my blood heating and cock hardening again.

Mila's eyes dropped, brows raising. "Already?"

"*Weeks*, Mila. We have *weeks* to make up for."

WE SPENT the day closed in her room—our room now, she reminded me. She told me of every day she'd been wading through her grief over Lyria and how afraid she'd been for me, where all our friends were now. I elaborated on what Echnid was planning and the pieces I'd gathered of other realms. I wasn't sure how they fit together. And when the sun set and the constellations slipped into their formations, Mila opened the tall glass doors leading out to the dunes, and we laid in the sand.

"When this is over, what do you want to do with your first tomorrow?" I asked her as she curled into my side, her head on my chest and my hand propped behind my own.

She hummed in thought, trailing gentle nails over my tattoo. "Maybe have a nice, long drink in a tavern without worrying about our lives being taken the next day."

I laughed. "A tavern? That's your dream for tomorrow?"

"Maybe not a tavern specifically," she mused, shrugging a

shoulder. "I would be happy with a tavern, but truly? I just want ease. I want to relax and turn off our minds for a bit. Maybe focus on work that doesn't involve the stakes of others' lives but simply making them smile." She paused. "What's your first tomorrow dream?"

"I don't know," I confessed, brushing a hand over her arm.

"Have you given more thought to the Undertaking?" Mila asked.

"I don't think I'd want to do it after Echnid. After everything he did to me...I don't want to be tied to the Warrior God or Angels that way. I think I just want to be a normal, non-ascended warrior. And live a long happy life in peace."

"Peace sounds good." Mila considered, then whispered, "Lyria always made people smile. It was one of my favorite things about her."

That fact about her best friend hovered in the night air. It wasn't something she needed a response to. Just a thought to ensure Lyria was remembered every day.

"You could make people smile in a tavern," I offered, squeezing her hip.

Mila flashed me a mischievous grin. "I certainly have."

I teasingly pulled a strand of her hair. "Tell me about them. Those memories with Lyria."

And she recounted some of her favorite nights in taverns across Gallantia, the pair leaving a streak of smiles throughout the darkest corners of the continent. And the thing about Mila was, no matter what she was facing internally, she could make people smile anywhere. And that was her own kind of magic. One that granted me more peace than I ever thought possible.

~

THE SUN HADN'T EVEN RISEN when Ophelia woke up briefly, Cypherion and I at her bedside.

"How do you feel?" Cyph checked.

"Tired," Ophelia barely whispered, voice distant and eyes on her wrist. The blood had been cleaned and the wound wrapped, but I had a feeling that didn't matter. Nerves rolled off Cyph's shoulders as he slipped his hands into his pockets. We both knew what question was coming. "Where's Tolek?"

From the doorway, Mila released a soft, "Oh." I hadn't realized she was here, but the sound made my chest ache.

Cyph swallowed, hesitating, and my heart pounded in the prolonged silence. "He's not here."

Ophelia's unfocused magenta eyes flared with panic, and she appeared ready to find the gryphon once again. "He's not—"

"No," Cyph quickly corrected. "He's not in Damenal, and I've already written to him."

Ophelia blinked up at us, brow creasing as she tried to put it together. My Bind emptied into voided loss as she asked, "Where is he?"

CHAPTER TWENTY-THREE
TOLEK

SAPPHIRE'S HOOVES CLATTERED TO THE STONE TERRACE in the wake of the rising sun cutting through the fog draped across Banix. Neither of us had been able to sleep, so I took her out early.

The swampy Engrossian Territory never appealed to me, but from the back of a pegasus, the crawling deep green trees and layers of thick moss stretched across the land like eager fingers, and something about it was eerily beautiful, like it was welcoming wayward and rotten souls. The pointed onyx spires of the Banix Citadel, their Spirit Temple, and the Valley Palace reached high into the clouds in opposite corners of the city, gleaming black in the morning light.

Sapphire nudged my shoulder after I dismounted, and I ran a hand down her neck, brushing away a fly that settled in her mane. She huffed, turning her face to the sky.

"I know," I agreed. "This isn't where I want to be either." If anyone on Ambrisk loved Ophelia as much as I did, it was the pegasus before me. "Get some rest," I said, patting her and sending her off, though I knew she would be jittery.

I understand that.

As Sapphire left to park herself in the palace stables, and I crossed the terrace into the suite Barrett had assigned me, I could admit the aesthetic of this place wasn't horrible. It was simply a different kind of beauty than Damenal or Xenovia. I was intent on enjoying the view from a bath, but I hadn't expected the prince to be sprawled across my bed at this hour.

I halted. "Let yourself in?"

"Let yourself *out*?" he countered with a pointed look at the terrace and a dramatic crossing of his legs.

I leaned against the doorway, evaluating his boyish smirk for a moment. The one that hid how very distraught he was about... everything. "Shoes off my bed," I said.

"Technically it's my bed." Barrett grinned, but he sat up and threw his feet over the edge of the mattress.

I couldn't argue with that given the entire palace belonged to him, so I strode across the room to the dressing chamber to grab a clean tunic. I'd thrown on a thicker wool one for the flight, but with the adrenaline that barreled through my veins from the skies, I was sweating.

"Couldn't sleep?" Barrett asked, when I walked back out and poured myself a glass of water from the silver pitcher beside the bed. The prince's wolf, Rebel, trotted through the door to my bedchamber, stopping at his owner's feet. Large enough to ride, he turned a wide-eyed stare on me that was as inquisitive as Barrett's.

I swallowed and murmured, "I swear Rebel grows every time I see him." Shaking my head, I added, "No, I didn't sleep a wink."

"Me neither." Barrett squared his feet on the ground and braced his elbows on his knees. "No word from her?"

I clenched the glass so hard it nearly shattered. Setting it down, I took a breath and braced my hands on the nightstand. "No."

"Bant's cock."

Ophelia hadn't written as of when I left Xenovia. Last I'd heard, she'd explicitly told me not to come for her. Despite the uncomfortable tangle of inadequacy that spurned in me, that message alone assured me something was truly wrong. Ophelia knew I'd seek her out in any realm, slaughter any god. For her to urge me away meant...

I refused to consider the worst. *That Echnid had truly gotten his claws in her.*

The tattoo across my back burned like Spirit Fire. But this was where she wanted me to be right now—even if I didn't understand it.

"What time are we meeting?" I asked.

Barrett pushed off the bed. "That's why I came to find you. No one else has been sleeping either. We're ready when you are."

Dramatically, I extended a hand toward the door. "Lead the way, Prince."

⁓

THE ENGROSSIAN VALLEY Palace felt more like it was locked in the morose days of winter than the throes of spring.

"We've been keeping it closed up," Barrett explained when he noted my lingering stare on the heavily locked door and tightly drawn velvet curtains in the main entrance.

"Because of the heretics?" I asked as we turned down a corridor.

"They haven't breeched the walls, but it's a precaution my advisors insisted on." By *his advisors,* I was certain he meant his doting partner. Dax had earned his title as Engrossian General and was protective enough over his prince to prove it.

"The staff?" I asked.

"Haven't seen their families in weeks. Some of them are parents—a few with their partner trapped here, as well. We've assured every child is being cared for, but..."

I cast one last glance to the tall metal door, its iron lock appearing delicate in the fogged beam of light filtering through the lone circular window above, its panes drawing sharp lines in the shadow below.

"But it's not how you want your people to live," I finished.

Barrett nodded, his throat bobbing over a swallow that spoke of torment and fear.

"That's what I'm here to help with," I said, clapping a hand to his shoulder as we rounded the corner. Even though I didn't want to be in Banix, if I could at least provide aid in some way, I would feel more useful than I did sitting on my ass in Xenovia.

"We appreciate it," Barrett said sincerely.

I didn't pause to ask what exactly I was walking into—didn't care since it wouldn't change a single step—but when I followed Barrett into the meeting chamber, I hadn't expected a prisoner to be chained beside the fire.

My brows shot up. "Nassik," I greeted, my voice knife sharp.

"Vincienzo," he retorted. He waved his arm—the wrist ending in a stump from when Barrett had severed his hand during the battle against Ritalia. "We're welcoming enemies in now?"

"He's less of an enemy than you are, Nassik," Barrett drawled as he fell into a chair at the head seat, Rebel plopping beside him. Two strangers sat at the table, along with Dax and Celissia.

"Tolek," the prince's consort welcomed with a nod, holding out his hand. Celissia flitted out of her chair to give me a hug. I hadn't seen either of them when I arrived yesterday.

"Good to see you both," I said, wrapping one arm around her. "Is the ruse still in play, then?" I whispered to Celissia, who had been staging her role as Barrett's queen-to-be to buy him time to win over his people.

My eyes drifted toward Nassik, his head tipped back against the wall and eyes closed. All it took was one seed of doubt to plant an uprising, and roots crawled through the soil.

"Not among the council," Celissia said, nodding to the two Engrossians I didn't know at the table. A squat man with round cheeks and gray hair, and an icy-blonde woman whose eyes seemed to hold a thousand secrets. "My uncle, Elvek, and Pelvira—the two withstanding council members of Prince Barrett's."

"And yourself, Celissia, dear," the prince added as I shook hands with each of his advisors.

She waved him off, drifting back to her seat at the table. "Bare insists I take a place at his table and that I may select my title. But in this room, everyone knows the truth of where we stand."

"We haven't fed the lie to our people anymore, but we're choosing how to reveal the delicate matter," Elvek said. Nerves wavered through his voice as he cast his niece a glance. She squeezed his shoulder in silent response.

"I think it would be prudent to tell them soon," Barrett said.

"Be forthright about it, and position it as what it was: a political strategy, but now love has won out."

Dax leaned against the table beside his prince and crossed his arms, axes glinting at his back. "He has a point. The heretics are already causing a stir. For some, the thought of love will win them to our side. For others, it will fuel their fire."

"Love is the most infallible driving source," I added. It was that very unrequited emotion that carved out my heart for twenty years before I came clean about my feelings for Ophelia. It made every decision for me where she was involved. To hide the truth because she was hurting, to chase after her every time she stormed off, to jump in front of a damn ax aimed for her neck. "It will be difficult, though."

Barrett sat back in his chair, one corner of his lips lifting. "I've never been one to take the easy way out."

I canted my head. I supposed he hadn't. Not when he fled to Damenal and not when he insisted on being present in a war camp where hatred was rife for him.

And me? Well, I'd always loved a challenge. I matched Barrett's smirk.

"Horrid idea," Nassik murmured.

Barrett sliced him a glare, then nodded at Dax, and his consort kicked off the table and crossed to Nassik, slapping him across the face.

"Always so satisfying," the general muttered as he turned back, but his face contorted in pain, his hand pressed to his gut. The air in the room pulled taut, and Barrett was standing in a breath, Celissia at Dax's other side. The pair helped him into a plush velvet chair beside the fire.

"Is that the wound from when Kakias attacked?" I asked, and Celissia nodded grimly. During that last battle, when the late queen's inky magic had been running rampant, it had struck Dax through the gut.

Celissia explained, "I've even tried using more...advanced—"

"Ill-advised," Nassik interrupted through his clenched, still-red jaw. This time it was Barrett who smacked him, the prince's chest heaving as his control came unwound.

"I've been trying more advanced methods from Sorcia resources," Celissia finished. "Though there's little information to go off when it comes to their practice. The means of study are mainly kept within the isles." She traced a finger around the pendant she always wore. "My talisman helps."

"That's Sorcia magic?" I asked.

She nodded, holding the stone pendant up so it's rainbow sheen caught the firelight. "Every sorcerer or sorceress has a talisman, and it helps them channel their magic. This one was a gift passed through my family." Her eyes flitted to Nassik. His were glued to the necklace. "My aunt gave it to me years ago. Talismans are Goddessblessed. Legends speak of some having been forged by Thallia herself and passed down among her children. The ordinary ones—like this—are crafted by Sorcia hands and magic. They're hard to come by and harder to keep on Gallantia, but every sorceress needs one."

Celissia tucked the talisman down the front of her dress. "I've been trying to teach myself how to use it based on research and what scant magic I can access." Her jaw set in determination, fingers curling against the pendant over her dress. "It's been little help."

As they discussed Dax's plaguing scar, it struck me that, aside from Nassik, those in this room were a demonstration of what progress could be made in little time. Only a year ago, the Mystiques thought all Engrossians were our adversaries. Our clan had still been devastated from the first war, and while many families were currently mourning after the second—

My thoughts clogged in my brain, a lump in my throat.

I breathed through it, remembering what my sister would have wanted.

Lyria was in favor of inter-clan alliances and outright loved Barrett and Dax after their time spent at the warfront. She would want me here, despite the pain Engrossians and Mystiques had caused each other. She'd want me to help heal it.

And if I could stand in this room—be welcome in this palace—why couldn't we take these alliances a step further?

"Celissia?" I asked. She tilted her head at the note of fascination in my voice. "Have you spoken with any Sorcia relatives lately?"

Nassik blurted out an argument, but Barrett kicked the former councilman in the stomach. Celissia watched the exchange with a bored mask, then turned back to me.

"No, I haven't. I've never spoken to them, actually."

"Never?"

She shook her head. "It isn't common knowledge that my family descends from them. I don't think it's very much blood, anyway. Diluted over the years, just potent enough to manifest the tiniest sliver of magic."

Well, that could turn this plan to ash. Might as well suggest it anyway. "Could you write to them?"

"And say what?" she pondered.

Standing, I braced my palms on the table, my hair falling into my eyes. "The known gods are responsible for Echnid—*all* of them. And Echnid wants to banish the gods from this realm. This is no longer just a warrior problem. The Sorcia Isles may be interested in sending aid our way."

"That could change things," Pelvira added. "If we had sorceress magic, who knows what it could do."

"Perhaps take down a god," I said with a smirk.

"Just be careful, Celissia," Elvek cautioned. "If they know there's a warrior bloodline with their magic, it could anger them."

The former queen-to-be looked at her uncle with more love than she ever showed her father. "I promise."

"Excellent," Barrett said, clapping his hands with an iota of his usual joy now that a plan had been made. "How—"

Footsteps clattered down the hall, and everyone froze. Hands drifted toward weapons, my fingers curling around my family dagger.

A staff member dressed in a simple, short-sleeved wool tunic and pants raced around the corner, freezing at our defensive positions. Sweat dripped down his pale face, an ax-shaped scar marking his bicep. "I-I'm sorry," he stammered with a bow that had his dark hair flopping in his eyes. "Your Royal Highness."

"That's all right, Allen," Barrett said stepping forward. "What's wrong?"

"It's the pools," he said. "The heretics are organizing some kind of ceremony."

"Bant's shining cock." The prince looked to me. "Looks like our chance for action is coming sooner than we thought."

~

FACING a mob should have been terrifying, but I'd been oscillating between numbness and burning rage for so many weeks, the prospect of feeling someone else's anger sounded like a damn good time.

Barrett and I had Sapphire land a ways from the dark pools nicknamed the Blackfyre, so we wouldn't be seen flying overhead. We ran the final half mile, my fingers curling around the Vincienzo dagger. In silence, we approached the dense tree line that bent and wound around the edges of the tarpits like creeping fingers.

Dax and a troop of guards were following on horseback, but Barrett hadn't wanted to wait to assess—much to Dax's chagrin.

"Looks like a few dozen," I muttered, peeked over a trunk that cut horizontally waist-high across the path. "How long has this been going on?"

"The heretics?" Barrett exhaled. "Centuries. But they usually keep to themselves. It wasn't until news of a Warrior God became kindling to those against my coronation that they started coming into the cities and became a threat to the larger population. Recruiting more to their sycophantic worship of Bant."

Barrett and I crouched low, ducking beneath the branches, and crawled on our stomachs to the edge of the tree line. The mud was thick and swampy beneath my elbows, body dragging through the brush, but every connection with the earth only fueled the Mystique blood pumping through my veins.

As we reached the edge, curtains of moss swaying in the late morning light, voices drifted over, the tones a haunting song.

"It's a bounty prayer to Bant," Barrett whispered as I shimmied forward.

"What for?" I asked.

He shrugged. "A lot of things. The pools are dangerous—even touching the power within can consume you or kill you, especially someone from another clan. But being near enough where you feel an essence and saying prayers to the Angel offers a euphoric strength."

That sort of enthralling power was both threatening and damn attractive.

"Where are the guards for the pools?" I asked, and Barrett leveled me with a reproachful look. Right. "Everybody has a price."

I brushed aside the mossy curtain, and my heart flooded with ice cold rage.

"Fuck, Barrett, there are kids in that crowd. And they're—" I couldn't even quite explain what they were doing. "Oh, fucking Angels."

Four Engrossians stood on the shore of the dark pool, dressed in remnants of armor and torn tunics, the tar ebbing to their toes.

And between them, with her hands bound and feet kicking wildly, a girl, no older than fifteen, was being forced toward the tar.

A strip of fabric was wrapped around her mouth. Long black hair, sweat-drenched and to her waist, flailed in the breeze as she writhed, as she tried to launch her body back away from the edge, but her captors only raised their song and formed a wall behind her.

"They're sacrificing her," I hissed to Barrett.

The prince was on his feet, an ax in each hand. Barrett wasn't a fighter like Dax, but the fury of a king burned through his stare. And dammit, I was desperate for any kind of battle.

"I promised Dax I would wait," Barrett said, his gaze slicing to me. "Don't make me become a liar."

"What are you saying, Prince?"

"These people are fanatics, but most of them are not killers." Barrett's answering smirk was cruel. "Put those pretty words of yours to use and stall, Tolek."

Then Barrett strode out of the tree line into the swampy air, every step radiating the dominance of a king. He was absolutely insane, but I charged after him, sword in hand.

"Engrossians!" Barrett called, voice deep with power. "I ask that you lay down your anger for a moment so that we may discuss this in truth."

The crowd whirled toward us, the four heretics near the pool freezing.

"He will not give us the truth!" one shouted. A halo of woven branches sat upon his head, almost like he was a king. For a moment, I waited for an ax to *swish* through the air, but nothing came.

"I have heard and understand your fears, but today, I wish you to listen to the reason of an ally. Of someone who has no cause to lie to you but begs your understanding of the threats put upon all of our lands." He sighed, dropping a bit of the mask of prince and speaking with sincerity. "Tolek Vincienzo is an esteemed Mystique Warrior, and he has come here out of his own good will to assist in building trust between our people. To answer questions and provide truth."

Truth. A diversion. Whatever he wanted to call it. I just had to talk long enough, which I was damn good at.

Barrett turned to me, eyes flickering with hopelessness, and I scanned the crowd. I had one chance to aid them, one chance to choose the right words and not leave another failed stain on my family name. To save some people here while I couldn't others.

I love you, baby brother.

"Angels spare me," I muttered.

Unsheathing my sword, I handed it to the prince. An awed ripple went through the crowd at the sign of surrender, even the leaders beside the pool stopping to watch.

I strode to where they were gathered on the bank, eyes on a little girl clinging to her mother's leg in the front row. These people wouldn't listen to another *nobleman*. They wouldn't hear my truth from across palace walls. They needed someone they saw as a comrade. Approachable.

I kept well over an arm's length from them—I may be reckless, but I wasn't a complete idiot—and I slid my hands into my pockets.

The crowd retained their threatening stares, but the child

canted her head toward me, half hiding her face in her mother's skirt. The woman propped a toddler on her hip.

Crouching down, I asked the girl, "Is that your brother?"

She nodded but didn't respond.

"I bet he's very lucky to have you as a sister." She watched me warily. The mother placed a hand to her head, and I sat back, making myself comfortable in the dirt. "I had a sister."

"What's her name?" the girl asked, and my chest cracked.

"Her name was Lyria," I said, fighting the tightening in my throat. "She was a *fierce* warrior, but she's not here anymore."

"What happened?" the young girl asked.

I spared her the more gruesome details, but for the first time, I didn't push away the thoughts. Instead of numbness, I let myself truly succumb to the loss. "My sister was the Commander of the Mystique armies. She fought proudly, but in her most recent battle, we lost her."

"Do you miss her?"

"*So* much," I swore, my voice quiet as my vision clouded. "Every day."

I love you, baby brother.

I wiped my eyes and looked to the mother from my spot on the ground. To the Engrossians surrounding her and the fear in their eyes. And with a deep breath, I projected my voice over the crowd. "My sister sacrificed her life for a cause we deeply believed in, and it is not the one you may think. Recently, rumors have surfaced about a Warrior God."

Murmurs broke out, but I raised my voice. "I know it's hard to believe, but I'm here as proof that it's true. That it's true, and my sister lost her life in the process because we didn't trust the warnings given to us. We chose derision instead."

Silently, Barrett sat beside me. A king on the same ground as his people and his rival.

"But that was precisely what the Warrior God *and* the Angels wanted. Now, they pose even greater threats to warrior kind. In order to fight and bring peace to the realm—to avoid the unnecessary loss of life—the Gallantian Warriors *have to* band together."

The stares looking back at me softened, tears rimming eyes.

"That begins with the man beside me." I laughed. "Trust me, when Barrett showed up to aid the Mystiques, I didn't want to trust him. But I learned very quickly that your prince—your *king* —has the best interest of his people at heart. And he was willing to *lay down his life* for it because he loves this clan."

Love is the most infallible driving force.

My eyes fell back to that little girl, her hand now clutched in her brother's. "I love my sister very much. And I am desperately, *hopelessly*, unfathomably in love with the Revered of the Mystique Warriors. I know her heart deeper than my own, and to love her is easier than breathing. I would give my life for hers in a heartbeat, but I do not wish to put any clan in the way of harm. We need to stand together, against the Warrior God, for the sake of love and life."

The words tapered off, but the desperation in my voice when I spoke of Lyria and Ophelia was palpable. I could fucking taste it with every word, see it in the tears clouding the eyes—

An ax flew from the back of the crowd, landing two inches to my left.

"By the fucking Angels," I groaned, jumping up.

So much for *peaceful distractions*.

But a depraved part of my heart lit up. The part that sang for Echnid's head. The part that wanted Angelblood to rain upon Gallantia.

For now, this would have to do.

Barrett tossed me my sword just as a growl ripped through the air and Rebel leapt out of the trees. The wolf soared over fallen logs, jaw snapping closed around the arm of the man who had thrown the ax.

Chaos erupted. Many in the crowd fled, the children who never should have been here bursting into tears.

Dax was in the melee, too. Rebel must have carried him here. They chased down the remaining crowd, angling them toward the path the rest of his soldiers would be charging down.

And the four Engrossians who had been subduing the girl used the madness to their advantage.

Two of them jumped back, grabbing axes from a pile of

tarnished weapons on the ground. The other two surrounded their sacrificial lamb as Barrett and I each faced an oncoming warrior.

I met my opponent strike for strike. My moves were honed as sharp as my anger, and the man fighting me was sloppy. Like his attention was truly distorted by the dark magic.

Perhaps it is, I thought as he swiped lazily to my side. *Maybe that's what affected their minds.*

I parried, swiveling around the Engrossian and ramming my sword in his back. I shoved him to the ground. Barrett hadn't taken out his opponent yet, but he was fighting strongly enough that I wasn't worried about him.

Instead, I whirled toward the Blackfyre's edge.

And I shouted when I met the wide, terrified eyes of the girl as the remaining two Engrossians pushed her into the tar. Their hymn mounted again.

Just before the girl's pale, stricken face sank beneath the surface, she spat out the bind around her mouth, and a cracked and broken scream tore out of her.

"Help!"

But the tar crept up, staining her. Her veins shone against her skin, neck arching as splatters coated her face.

"Over my fucking spirit," I growled and raced forward.

I took out the warrior with his back to me, his glory-seeking stare watching the poor victim sink beneath the surface. One quick swipe down his spinal column, and he crumbled.

"Tolek, don't touch it!" Barrett roared as he felled his own opponent with a growl.

"I'm not leaving her!" I called back, wading into the tar up to my boots.

I searched for a branch, a rope, anything I could throw to the girl fighting to get back to the surface. Angels, I could almost see her limbs struggling, pushing against the flexible black liquid as if it was a solid, gooey barrier.

There was nothing around us, though. Nothing long enough except...

"Damien, I swear on your fucking feathered cock, this better end well," I spat. And then, I flipped my sword in my hands and grabbed the blade.

It sliced into my palms, crimson pouring across my skin as the alluring dark magic reached for me. I stretched forward, grimacing as sweat poured down my face and my blood flowed.

Barrett continued to yell warnings over his fight with the final heretic.

The hilt dipped beneath the Blackfyre, the thick substance pulling at my blade.

I stretched and stretched, leaning so far forward that my abs and thighs burned to hold me back. My blood spilled into the tar, black devouring it, but I reached further, shoving more of my sword beneath the surface.

My sister's lifeless eyes flashed before me, and I leaned forward.

Ophelia's scream wrenched through my memory, and I gritted my teeth.

Tar swallowed the pommel, the entire grip next. It lapped at the cross-guard, and then that was gone, too. And when the shining silver steel met the dark, magic-infused liquid, an eerie blue light erupted.

"Fucking Angels!" I exclaimed, stumbling forward.

Something heavy pulled at the hilt of my sword. The light seared, but I didn't stop to consider what it was. I just dug my heels in and pulled back up the shore with my palms in agony and the weight dragging at the end of my weapon.

And the girl emerged from the pool, black sludge clinging to her skin and silk nightgown. Hair plastered to her body and choking coughs wracking her thin frame.

Barrett gave her his cloak, but I didn't even hear the girl's name. A dying buzz was humming through my sword, a pulse of power and might that ebbed within the steel and into the palm of my hand.

I looked between the blade and the tar, shaking off the shadows that eclipsed my mind.

Chapter Twenty-Four
Santorina

Lancaster and I cut across the mountains—a leg of the trip that should have taken a week—in a matter of days.

"We'll continue through Mystique Territory tomorrow," I said, unfurling my cloak on the ground to set up our makeshift camp for the evening. The sun hadn't set yet, but it was beginning to sink behind the mountains. We were among the rolling hills, the range at our backs with a clean view of the plains littered by clumps of forest near enough to hunt.

"I'll find us food for the evening," Lancaster said, pulling a long, brutal sword from midair using his creation power.

"Couldn't you use that magic to create a tent?" I grumbled, sitting back on my heels and pulling out my canteen. With the long grasses coating the hills, the ground was softer than some, but not entirely comfortable.

"Would you like to share a tent with me, Bounty?" Lancaster asked. There was no hint of suggestion in his voice, and somehow that made the question more of a taunt. Like I was weaker for not being okay with that option.

"Go get me dinner," I demanded, taking a long drink of water to calm the riled sensation flipping through my chest.

Lancaster and I had made peace with the Bounty and Hunter senses over the trip. Or rather, I simply got used to it. It was peaceful to allow my muscles to relax for a moment, the voice inside of me screaming to attack him finally quieting.

I washed up in the stream, splashing water on my face. Then, I ventured into the trees to assess what grew nearby. We hadn't encountered any trouble yet, so the vials of ointments and tonics I brought with me were still fully stocked, but as I wound through the trunks and crouched beside bushes to study the flora, my chest unknotted.

It had been so long since I explored nature simply for the pleasure of curiosity. Lifting the triangular red-tipped leaves of a vine stretching across the ground, I noted the vibrant colors and—

A hand curled around my mouth, yanking me upright.

My heart thundered. I struggled, kicking back and striking the stranger's shin. I ripped a knife from my waist, angling it toward their ribs, but a hand locked around my wrist, pinning it and pressing me closer to a broad, firm chest.

The voice I'd banished raged. *Kill, kill, kill.* The scent of bloodstained roses washed over me.

And I froze.

A husky tone whispered in my ear, "Relax, Bounty, it's me."

In a disjoined rhythm, my heart rate soothed at the rough sound of his voice, but my predator senses tensed. Needles prickled my fingers.

I spun, trying to ask what in the Gods' names Lancaster was doing, but he clamped his hand over my mouth again, placing a finger against his lips to instruct me to be quiet. His hand was solid against me, but his fingers twitched, and I considered briefly how easy it would be for him to kill me right now.

The Hunter was sleeping. He'd promised after Ritalia died that unless someone called upon it using a bargain as the queen had with him, it wouldn't wake. But the threat remained.

With raised brows, Lancaster nodded around the trees to my left. He dropped his hand, fingers curling into fists. Taking careful, impossibly silent steps in that direction, he pressed his back against a thick ash-white cypher trunk, carefully avoiding any splinters.

I did my best to trace his steps. He'd placed his feet where nothing would crunch beneath our boots. With how weightlessly the fae traveled, I was sure he did that as a guide for me. Annoyance rumbled through me. Arrogant immortal.

But I followed his lead, finding a tree to hide behind while I calmed both my rioting heart and the voice still warring for blood. But over both of those, I heard it.

A trilling, high voice.

I whipped my head to Lancaster. *Singing?* I mouthed.

He nodded.

Who is it?

I don't know. He held up a hand. *Stay here.*

Then, he snuck around the tree trunk to follow the voice. Over my dead, fae-killing body would I stand here like prey.

Edging around the trunk, I sank to a crouch and crept along the low brush, searching the paths between the trees.

The voice was growing louder, the words more discernible. It was some folksong, the verses building. I snuck through the undergrowth, checking carefully around every tree, and my heartbeat climbed with it.

"A realm divided,
A sister sacrificed,
And demigods to dance on her grave.
Spinning through veils,
Her wings how they flared,
But then He fell to the blade."

Finally, I reached a clearing rimmed with berry bushes, and in the center, a woman with raven-black hair to her waist picked the feathers from a dead bird. My stomach turned over at the brutal collection of carcasses around her.

Was she hunting? Surely she couldn't need that much food if she was alone. And if she wasn't alone, where were her companions? Why was she cleaning the food here, instead of in a camp?

"The children of his children,
They search for a door.
For a mind child they felt long ago.
When all was lost to them,
And bridges were broken,
And realms did they seek to sew."

Her glimmering white gown shone like fresh fallen snow, revealing in nearly every way it could be, with a swooping neckline and back, slits falling open around her thighs. Somehow, no blood splattered the gown or her light-brown skin from her kills. Only her hands showed the crimson stains.

Unease washed over me, a sense of dread I didn't understand. Like I wanted to go to this woman, but if I did, it would be the worst decision I ever made.

Her back faced me, but partway around the clearing, a slight shuffle caught my eye, my senses perking up. Lancaster crept through the brush, glaring. His gaze snapped between the still-singing woman and me, and he gave his head a subtle shake, sinking back into the trees.

We need to get out of here. That harsh look said.

I retreated, taking care not to step on anything that would crunch. When I found Lancaster back in the foothills, for once the Bounty voice didn't scream. Instead, every tensed part of me eased.

"Who was she?" I whispered, as if she would hear.

He shook his head. "I don't know. But her presence felt wrong." I didn't comment, but I understood what he meant. "We should run a little more before we stop."

I agreed and hurriedly gathered our belongings. "I know where we can go instead."

"By the way," Lancaster said as he picked me up in a way that was becoming familiar, "next time I tell you to stay, obey."

Agitation heated my chest. "Don't tell me what to do, Hunter," I retorted, glaring over the plains.

He only grunted before taking off at a faster pace than usual.

AFTER OUR LAST attempt at camp was interrupted, I wanted a more secure place to stay for the night. A place with quiet streets and familiar voices, even if I wouldn't be speaking to any of them.

"How far into the city is the inn?" Lancaster asked as we crept through sleeping alleys.

"Not far," I answered without looking at him, but his stare

bore into me. Stupid, overly observant fae. "I have to make another stop. I can show you to the place we'll be staying first."

"I'll go with you," he asserted.

Too quickly, I said, "You don't have to."

"I will."

I pursed my lips, well aware that attempting to deter him would only result in him being more insistent. In silence, I led him to the residential stretch of town where the homes sprawled further apart the deeper one ventured.

After a while, Lancaster whispered, "I was thinking about that woman."

"As all males do."

He grumbled something unintelligible, then went on, "I have never seen, read about, or met a being with her presence before."

The singing voice in the forest wrapped around me again, punctuated by the memory of bird carcasses dropping to the ground.

"What do you mean?" I asked as we approached our destination. Shallow pools of mystlight lined the back edge of the manor's wall from lamps hung periodically.

"It is not often I am caught off guard by a creature I do not recognize," Lancaster said pointedly.

Arrogant, non-immortal. But he was right. With all the centuries he'd spent on this world, it *was* rare that he didn't have an idea from his over-inflated sense of self. So, who—or what—was she then?

"I will write to my sister about her when we stop," Lancaster said with finality.

"Good idea," I whispered, turning toward the high stone wall. "Now, help me up."

For a moment, he didn't move. Then, Lancaster's hands met my waist. I suppressed the jolt of heat that shot through me, plucking the string in my chest, and focused instead on not allowing the Bounty instinct to revolt as I pulled myself over the ledge and dropped among the ring of cyphers lining the property, willowing branches opening to a large grassy expanse in the center.

Lancaster grumbled as he scaled the wall behind me, landing clumsily.

"Aren't you supposed to be stealthy thanks to those immortal senses?" I whispered.

"Not immortal," he muttered. "And you didn't say there were rose bushes."

"Well, you already smell like flowers and have plenty of thorns," I said as I crept along the wall, sticking close to the sweeping branches.

"You know what I smell like?" he asked.

My palms prickled. *Kill, kill, kill* echoed in my mind. "I had to borrow your spare cloak as a blanket the other night, did I not?"

He'd conjured clean ones after ours had soaked through in a sudden spring storm. It was inconvenient, though the rain on my skin had been cleansing, bringing out the freshest scents from the surrounding plants. I'd slept well that night.

"Why are we here, anyway?" Lancaster growled quietly as we slipped effortlessly among the trees.

"I told you, you didn't have to come," I sliced over my shoulder. Not stopping to answer his question, I wove through the grove as cyphers cut away from the wall and lined the path toward the manor in the front of the property.

"What else was I going to do?" he muttered to himself.

Luckily, this estate wasn't as large as some of the nearby ones. And given that it was night, the residents were likely to be close to the house.

Lancaster kept to my side, pricking up my Bounty instincts in an infuriating way, but I bit my tongue to keep from exposing our presence. When we reached the edge of the tree line, I peeked between the willowing branches, to where three children no more than eleven played on the wide veranda. The girl—the oldest of them, though only by a few minutes—looked up, scanning the trees as if she heard my ragged breathing.

She didn't, though. It was just those warrior senses I'd never understood as a child. The instincts that alerted you to someone approaching.

My heart clenched. She looked just like her sister.

Lancaster pressed closer behind me, peeling the cypher branch back another inch. His breath prickled the back of my neck as he whispered, "Who are they?" It sounded like he already knew.

"Tolek and Lyria's siblings."

After a beat, Lancaster repeated, "Why are we here?"

"Just looking," I said. Because on that eve before we left Xenovia, when Tolek and I had stayed up whittling cypher weapons for my protection, he'd asked me to come here. He'd told me everything he and Lyria had wanted to do together—that they wanted to protect their siblings from their father's cruel hands—and asked me to check on them. He said he wouldn't drag them into the war we were facing, but he had to know they were okay.

For Lyria.

He'd given me coins to leave scattered in the trees for them to find, claiming his father would never go out there. It wasn't enough to provide for them—we assumed with them now possibly baring the Vincienzo titles, his father would do that—but it was a small token. A little gift to let them know someone was looking out for them.

The three youngest Vincienzos bickered over the marbles they were rolling across the veranda, the stars glimmering down so hopefully on them.

These children were not *fighting* in the war, but they would be touched by it. Warrior and human young ones alike who were so very blameless would feel the repercussions for decades to come—centuries in warrior cases. Wasn't it often the most innocent who carried the worst burdens? Their sister was already gone. Who else would they lose? Who would *we*?

Determination struck truer than ever to do what we could to end this before that outcome came to fruition.

As we watched, the boys teamed up on their sister, but she stood with her chin tilted up and hands on her hips, the same victorious grin Lyria used to wear splitting her round cheeks. My eyes burned at the way she moved so confidently, her long chocolate braid swinging down her back.

She was just like her.

"Come on," I whispered to Lancaster, swallowing past a thick throat. "We've seen them. They're safe. Let's go."

~

"THIS IS WHERE YOU GREW UP," Lancaster said once we were off the Vincienzo property and creeping through a sleeping Palerman.

"It is," I said.

We were only stopping here for the night. Partly to check on Tolek's family and partly because it provided a safe place to rest before the last leg of travel to the human camps. Strolling through the town that had once been nothing but innocent nights—where I'd last lived with my parents and forged fond memories with my friends around every corner—clad in warrior leathers and sharpened blades, with a weapon brewing within me to hunt the male beside me, was an odd difference I couldn't quite reconcile.

But I gritted my teeth and shoved it aside as I led Lancaster down a dim alley. I needed to hold myself together for what came next.

"The bargain between you and Ophelia and Tolek still stands, correct?" I asked, trying to distract myself.

"Indefinitely," Lancaster stated.

"Why couldn't you summon her back from Damenal, then?"

We stopped at the top of a darkened staircase. "It doesn't work like that," he explained. "The boundary around Damenal was created by Echnid to keep magic out. I am powerful for a fae, but even I cannot overcome a God. My bargain would not work across it." His eyes narrowed, flicking between mine as he considered something. "Even someone with Godsblood couldn't overpower it, with the weaknesses of the diluted blood."

"Right," I said lamely, unpacking that final sentence. Lancaster and Mora were powerful, but not enough to use bargain magic across a God's jurisdiction.

For a moment, my mind flickered back to the cavern when my Bounty senses had emerged. I'd sworn there was some different scent among us. Something ancient. Perhaps it had only been Echnid.

I didn't know what it meant that I was vastly more comfortable discussing this with the Hunter in a dark alley than addressing what waited for me inside. With a sigh, I turned toward the stairs, forcing myself to face this problem now.

There was less garbage piled up back here than there used to be. Fewer broken bottles and less shattered glass crunching beneath my boots. It warmed me despite the temperature dropping as we descended the staircase, kept my blood pumping as I broke the lock on the back door.

"No one will be here?" Lancaster double checked as I forced rusty hinges to creak open, the bottom of the wood scraping through a layer of dust. Guilt tightened my chest at the sight.

I cast him a glance over my shoulder and hoped in the dim mystlight filtering down from the alley he couldn't see how torn up it was. "No."

We crept through the storeroom. The walls were still lined with brown bottles and unpacked crates that made my heart ache. When we stepped into the barroom of the Cub's Tavern, and the scratched tables and worn floorboards weren't illuminated by a fire in the hearth, everything in me went cold.

My throat thickened, but I didn't linger, heading straight behind the bar to a door through the little hallway that also led to the kitchen. We hadn't served food in years, but still, every time I looked through that curtain, I saw my mother at the mystlight stove, and the back of my eyes stung. My control was slipping.

I kept going until I hit the end of the hall, a heavy door waiting. Taking a thick-handled knife from my waist, I jammed it into the lock until it splintered, not bothering to save the bolt. Then, I scampered up the stairs, emerging into a small apartment that both wrapped a layer of comfort around my shoulders and threatened to tear down my defenses.

Everything was precisely as I left it a year ago.

Threadbare rug, sofa, and armchairs before the fire, the kitchen perfectly cleaned, though now wrapped in a layer of dust. The hall to the back bedroom free of clutter, but my mother's spare cloaks draped on hooks along the wall. My father's boots beside the door.

It was perfect.

It was home.

It was haunted.

As I busied about the room, dumping my pack and stretching, I said, "We can stay here tonight. We should leave before dawn. People get to work early on this block, and we don't want them to notice us." My voice was thick. "The couch is yours. I'll take the back room."

Before I could even make it there, Lancaster asked, "Who lived here?"

It was a courtesy question. If he hadn't picked up my scent imbedded into the fabrics, he'd see the old schoolbooks with my name lining the shelves beside the fire or the horrible artwork pinned beneath them that I'd drawn and signed when I was a girl. But he gave me the option not to expose that.

So, I said, "No one."

And I went to bed, leaving the fae male standing in my former sitting room, questions and the painful ghosts of memories gathered between us.

CHAPTER TWENTY-FIVE
VALE

JEZEBEL WOVE IN AND OUT OF CONSCIOUSNESS FOR days. She rested in the infirmary nearest Harlen's residence, in a ward closed to any newcomers other than myself, the small group of Bodymelders stationed in Valyn as they were across multiple clans, Harlen, and Cyren, though they typically only stopped by to find me.

"Can you recall how it felt when the arrow struck?" asked the lead Bodymelder, a stiff-toned woman with sharp eyes to match her angular jaw, and warm brown skin.

"Like something very sharp had pierced my arm," Jezebel deadpanned. Sunlight broke through the clouds, pouring through the windows on either side of her bed and illuminating her tawny eyes that had come back to life, the color returning to her cheeks.

"Yes, of course." The Bodymelder's stoic temperament wasn't fazed. "But were there any other effects before you fainted?"

"I—" Jezebel inhaled sharply, her eyes trained on the bandage wrapped tenderly around her wound. "I was dizzy, and then, I think I saw hallucinations."

"Hallucinations?" I asked, stepping closer to the bed.

The healer and Jezebel both nodded, the former taking notes. She was non-reactive, as if that was what she'd expected.

Jezebel went on, "I saw serpents, felt them crawling up my skin." Her cheeks paled with the recollection. "And eyes with red-rimmed pupils. They wanted to snare me, but I was too dizzy to look."

At that description the healer lifted her head. "Interesting. In our inspection of the weapon, we noted that the arrow was coated with something. A shimmering, deep crimson substance that separated from your blood. We've been unable to determine what it is, but if hallucinations were caused, it's likely poison."

"*Poison?*" I gasped.

"And a very strong one at that," the healer added. "From our preliminary tests, it appears to be extremely lethal. It devoured the elthem flowers of a cypher tree and other potent, withstanding plants in a blink."

Jezebel's face was as white as her bedsheets now. "How did I survive then?"

"Perhaps it was a small dose." The healer shrugged, tucking away her ledger. But a flash of silver-blue light burned through my memory. I exchanged a glance with Jezebel—hers so shaken—but I didn't dare speak it aloud yet. "All your tests appear to be normalizing now. I suggest nothing more than rest until your body feels strong enough to return to your duties. Go slowly, get plenty of sleep, food, and water, and you will be as good as new soon."

When the Bodymelder left—her grave undertones with her—I shut the door and turned to Jezebel, leaning against the wood.

"A small dosage, was it?" she asked, as if she knew what I was thinking.

"I do not think that's why you survived." Crossing the room, I perched at the foot of her bed and suggested, "I think your myth magic saved you."

"How, though?" Jezebel asked. "And why? My magic is destructive. It *leashes* myths. Kills them."

"I don't know," I admitted. "But I saw the light, Jezebel. A wild flash of it, like the power acted of its own accord to save you when under attack."

She sighed, leaning into her pillows, and studied the ceiling. The curtains framing the windows on either side of her bed rifled in a near-silent breeze, the hiss against silk seeming to soothe her. I timed my breaths to it myself and set about refreshing the flowers on her bedside with clean water.

"Dynaxtar answered to you," Jezebel said.

I froze for a beat but continued dumping out the vase. "She did."

"She claimed you, Vale."

"What?" I turned toward her. Jezebel still reclined against her pillows, eyes closed.

"I felt a shift, even despite the pain. When Dynaxtar followed your command over mine, that was her claiming you as her rider." She peeked an eye open, and her next words rang like the fulfillment of a prophecy. "Will you have her?"

My fingers curled into the vase, and that same stillness that had taken over my blood and breath with Dynaxtar washed over me now. "I'd be honored."

"Good." She sighed. "She deserves a good rider. And I can think of no one better."

I didn't ask about Erista. She was never Dynaxtar's permanent rider. I didn't ask how it was possible, that the mythical creature chose *me* over everyone else.

It lit me up from the inside out to be tied to her, a constellation given life. To have that connection, to be claimed when for so long, all I'd wanted was a place. I floated about the room with that knowledge.

When I was done with the flowers, I moved to the dresser beside the door. "I brought this," I said, "in case you wanted to see it." From the top drawer I removed the obsidian arrow.

Jezebel sat up straighter. "The Bodymelders didn't take it?"

I shook my head as I approached, holding the lightweight weapon across my palms. "They cleaned it and are studying the poison but returned it. Though, they warned we should be careful. In case the poison is ejected on impact."

"I won't go impaling myself," Jezebel intoned, taking the arrow. "It's airy. But I don't know what material it's made of."

"Me neither," I said. "I was going to give it to Cyren to study, but I wanted to show you first."

Jezebel nodded, handing it back and sinking into her pillows again.

"I'll let you rest," I offered. "If you don't need anything else, I'm going to write to Cypherion and tell him you woke up, then deliver that arrow to Cyren."

That sentence caught her attention. "You told Cyph what happened?"

"I did." He'd written back in a panic. Tolek had just left for Engrossian Territory and Santorina was off on her assignment with Lancaster. I'd worried about how Cypherion would fare with the news without any of his close friends there—he'd certainly blame himself for sending Jezebel here with me—but he deserved to know. And he had his hands full with Ophelia and Malakai back now.

She pursed her lips, feigning disinterest. "Have you heard from Erista?"

A small smile playing around my lips, I crossed back to the dresser and pulled out the other item that I'd stashed in the top drawer. Or more specifically, items.

I dropped the pile of letters onto Jezebel's lap.

She gaped at them. "You said I was only unconscious for a few days."

"You were."

"How many—"

"Fifteen," I interjected. "Erista wrote to me fifteen times to check on you. I swear if Dynaxtar or Zanox were in Xenovia, she'd have flown here herself."

Jezebel worried her lip, staring wide eyed at the pile—a tangible sign of Erista's love.

"Can I offer you some unsolicited advice?" I asked softly, leaving room for her to say no. She only nodded, still gaping at the letters. "We're living in a very tumultuous time right now. Don't turn away someone you love—who loves you with every ounce of their spirit."

Cool blue eyes pierced my mind. The scent of bergamot and sage beneath the night sky. The tension in Cypherion's muscles when we'd fought recently.

Perhaps I was a hypocrite for telling Jezebel this now. Or perhaps it was the advice I needed and hadn't realized.

Jezebel toyed with one of the letters, folding and unfolding the edge repeatedly. "When the truth of mine and Ophelia's Godsblood came out, I was scared that for four years, through all the secret messages and distance, Erista had only been using me. That our relationship was founded on the need for this Godsblood, what status a union could provide her family if the truth was known among her people. And I realize now she couldn't have known it was in *our* line, but I guess I feared that had been a lie, too. That she'd never truly loved me."

I squeezed her hand, and Jezebel finally looked at me. "No one writes that many panicked messages from any place besides true love," I whispered. "Don't push love away out of fear."

Standing, I took the arrow and strode toward the door. "Get some rest." Before I left, I looked over my shoulder. "There's Mystique ink and parchment in the nightstand."

THE SEEING chamber was a maze of construction and chunks of rubble that, truthfully, I'd been avoiding as much as possible. Only a select few of Harlen's and Cyren's crew were allowed access, so at least when I crossed into the space and the press of my readings shrouded my mind, I didn't have to feign stability for too many people.

Harlen spotted me almost immediately. Jogging away from the forge and over to me, he pressed a hand to my back and led me to the shadows of one of the pillars. Its opalescent sheen glimmered in the flickering fire of the forge—a sure abundance of resins and minerals within—but we couldn't knock down the pillars without sacrificing the structural integrity of the room. We were proceeding very cautiously as it was.

I pressed a hand to the column, blinking away the insistent readings.

"Feeling okay?" Harlen asked once I steadied myself.

I nodded. "They're very loud in here."

"All nine of them," Harlen said, huffing a laugh. "I still can't believe that." I raised my brows at him, and he shook his head in a panic. Harlen was so afraid of my anger ever since he'd sold Cypherion and me out to Titus—which was a fear rightfully earned—but he'd also helped rescue me and kept me company during those nightmarish weeks. The slate was clean in my mind.

That didn't mean I didn't love teasing him as if we were still those little kids whose only solace in a horrifying reality was each other.

"I know you can't fathom me being more powerful than you. You always did have to be the loudest."

He snorted. "I was loud because I needed attention." A deep want for approval and protection that led him to the temple in the first place.

"You could have had some of mine," I offered. "I always wanted quiet."

"I can imagine that's hard to come by with the Fates."

I sighed. "You'd be right."

Harlen nodded grimly, wrapping an arm around my shoulder. "I knew you were powerful. I thought two—maybe three. *Nine?*" He shook his head. "And I thought I knew you so well."

He meant it jokingly, but an old sting raced through me. As a girl, I'd wanted to be known, but I was always trapped within these walls.

Before I could get too caught in my own web of emotion, Cyren joined us. "Is that from Jezebel?"

I followed their gaze down to the arrow in my hand. "Oh, yes. The healers confirmed they no longer need it. It's yours for inspection."

The general lifted the arrow just as a Starsearcher in dark leathers prepared for construction approached Harlen. "Interim Chancellor?"

Harlen grimaced but turned to the man with a smile. "Yes?"

"We'd like to run the demolition plan of the east wall by you when you have a moment."

"I'll be right there," Harlen answered. When the man bowed and walked off to join the two others in charge of the project,

Harlen muttered to Cyren and me, "I don't think I'll ever adjust to that title."

"Not looking to make it long term?" I teased. "Chancellor Harlen not quite the ring you're looking for?"

"Not me," Harlen said, shaking his head as he backed away. "I think I'll do something else with my life. I was only ever an apprentice for one reason after all."

To find me. That thought sat heavily on my chest as his steps faded across the room into the commotion of pickaxes and the forge's hammer.

I turned back to Cyren, nodding at the arrow. "Any ideas what it's made of?"

"Upon first instinct, I'd say it's lined with some kind of very thin onyx, but I can't be certain just by looking at it. It may have been imbued with something rather than crafted from it."

My gaze slipped to the hammer against steel, the blacksmith's expert hand crafting blade after blade with minerals and resins. Fates pressed against my mind, stretching out to the precious materials and sanctified power running through the stone.

I shook them away, forcing a smile for Cyren. "Let me know what you discover."

With a sharp nod, the general strode away, their movements crisp in their leathers. I held the hem of my skirt off the dusty floor. Next time I should dress more—

Fatecatcher.

A voice called through my mind. So distinct that I didn't even have a moment of thought before the reading claimed me. My face snapped toward the heavens, and in my mind's eye, starfire burst to life, this time assuming the vague outline of a male's bodily form. It burned with a viscous deep-purple rage.

The Fate of Wrath and Redemption.

"*Fatecatcher,*" Arenothos whispered again, his voice hissing along the white flame. "The god's wrath has piqued," he foretold. "And with it comes falling fortunes."

Then, within the heart of starfire trailing along a concentration of shooting stars, Echnid came to life. He pulled threads as if they were puppets and he their cruel, wrathful master.

Six strings curled around his fist. The god raised a pale hand, equipped with a jewel-encrusted blade that flashed with gold and silver lightning. Without a beat of remorse, he sliced through the threads.

And in my mind, in the heart of the whistling flames, the lives of thousands screamed as ties were severed.

The entire world turned over as they withered, like a backward dreamscape where one walked on oceans and swam through the clouds. Air became ash and fire froze to ice. I stood in the center of a lake that shone with luminescent moonlight, the entire surface swirling with whispers of wishes and nightmares. The water poured over my frame, but I focused on the cries of those puppeted strings.

And a jaw snapped shut around an entire realm, lives silencing.

"When?" I gasped to Arenothos.

"The foretold is racing to the surface," the Fate said.

With a rush of burning starfire and panting breaths, I snapped from the reading. The seeing chamber materialized around me. I stumbled to the alabaster column, resting my forehead against the cool stone.

"Vale?" Harlen exclaimed, rushing over to me.

"I'm fine," I assured him. Physically, I was, if a little dizzy from the sudden reading. But icy horror sluiced through my gut. "We need to write to Xenovia."

"What happened?" Harlen stepped in front of me so the other searchers present wouldn't hear.

"It's Echnid," I whispered, and Harlen's eyes widened in panic that was nowhere near humorous as before. "He's getting closer to an answer. To banishing all the gods and their magic from Ambrisk for good."

My eyes fell to the blades forged and lined with opalescent minerals. And I couldn't help but think their gleam looked like water crafted of moonlight, like tides rich with fortunes, consuming my frozen frame until nothing was left.

And I feared what this future meant for me.

Fatecatcher.

Chapter Twenty-Six
Ophelia

My body is my own.

That was the mantra I repeated to myself as I woke up in Meridat's manor after sleeping off the escape from Damenal for what felt like days.

My mind is my own.

I echoed as I slipped out of bed and found clothing. Not a gilded, armored dress, but a pair of leathers. Lightweight, Soulguider fashion with pants that would hug my thighs in a comforting embrace and a halter top that dipped low on my back and buckled along my spine. Perfect to slip around wings.

As I peeled the sweat-soaked slip Erista had helped me into down my body, I stared at myself in the mirror. At the scars across my midriff and arms—so many marks earned through the sacrifices I'd made for my warriors. I replayed each in my head.

The searing pain of the *lupine daimons* claws slicing into me on the tundra during the Undertaking.

The small nick to my collarbone Lucidius had left after we found out his truth.

The agony of Kakias's poisoned blade tearing up my forearm and the way her dark magic had writhed within me afterward.

I relived the wounds that couldn't be seen—the scars across my spirit from losing my father in an explosion, from Lyria taking a blade in my honor, from Tolek unconscious in an infirmary bed. I memorized the way they felt and how their aching imprints beat in time with my withered heart, the claw marks of those losses and breakings worn deeply into the hollows.

I forced myself to feel every knife and claw and ripping loss because these scars were who I was. Who I fought to be. And as I stood before the mirror, they grounded me. The reasoning behind them—the pride—all reshaped me.

"My body is my own," I whispered, trailing a finger across each visible scar. "My mind is my own."

I was not a puppet to be wielded by Echnid. I was not a funnel for his poison, meant to pour magic at his behest. I had regained my autonomy. Though, after being unaware I'd even lost it in the first place, I wasn't sure I knew what that meant anymore.

The girl in the mirror—the body who had committed atrocious acts at a god's influence—looked the same as she had weeks ago. I knew her. I felt her pain like the roots of my soul.

And yet, I was utterly changed.

And while I feared that old innocence would never return, I looked forward to what crimes she would commit in revenge.

CYPHERION WAS outside when I finally found the strength to dress and leave the room.

"Playing guard?" I asked as I shut the door behind me and took in the hallway. The curtains in my room had been pulled tight, but the wall opposite the door was entirely glass. It overlooked the dunes, the thin veins of spirit-woven water running between them.

It could have been my imagination, but I thought the blood of the Soulguider demigoddess in my own veins beat harder at the sight.

"Just here to see if you needed anything," Cypherion answered, tucking his hands into his pockets. Though he tried not to, his stare bore into my wings. I held them aloft, strong and proud, but I cast him a wary look. Awaited the questions.

My body is my own.
My mind is my own.

Cyph sighed. "Ophelia, I'm sorry."

My brow furrowed. "For what?"

"For sending Tolek away. He should be here with you now, but I did it for his best interest." A shrug. "I *did* think maybe he could assist Barrett, but truthfully, I was mad at him."

So that was why he'd been outside my door. Guilt for sending Tolek to Banix—for the fact that I suffered in Damenal and didn't get to come back to the man I loved—layered his every word. And with it, I recognized the stark pressure of leading a clan you never asked for. Of worrying you were making the wrong choices.

Cypherion had truly been trying to hold us all together this past month.

I tucked my arm through his and flared my wings behind our backs, doing my best to adopt a facade of my normal self.

"Why were you mad at him?" I asked as I followed his steps down the halls.

Everything looked wrong. The walls too bright. Bronze fixtures too shiny. Voices trailing from the distance too unburdened. My chest ached in answer, the slimy sensation of Echnid's influence over me echoing down every bone, but I forced myself to focus.

"Because I told him not to go to Damenal. I asked him to just listen to your messages from Rina and stay fucking put so we could work as a team despite you guys being so far away."

A sharp breath sliced through my chest, my eyes stinging. I'd known he was there. Had felt him more than once. But I hadn't realized they were *all* warning him against it. Fighting over it.

Tolek had come for me despite *everyone's* warnings.

He'd refused to leave me.

And while it was reckless, and I would certainly have to discuss it with him, that knowledge alone was enough to burn away another small sliver of the lingering, tainted echo of Echnid.

"We shouldn't be surprised," I muttered as we turned down another corridor, my gaze trailing over the maze of cactuses in a sprawling stone garden outside the window.

"No," Cypherion agreed. "We shouldn't. I wrote to him as soon as you were in your room, but he hasn't answered yet."

My heart quickened. "Do you think something's wrong?"

Cyph had explained what was happening in Engrossian Territory while I clung to consciousness. Why they'd sent Tolek. Thoughts of heretics and rioting enemies flashed through my mind, of him caught in the center of it. Tol was a strong fighter, but everyone could be outnumbered. What if—

Cypherion stepped in front of me, gripping my shoulders as if my fears were plain on my face.

"He's okay," he comforted, but the way Cyph watched me with such caution confirmed he could tell I was different. Changed. "Letters have been stalled in Banix for weeks. I don't know if it's Echnid's doing or just the magic being stifled with their palace closed up and an influx of correspondence. That's it, though."

I nodded. And I didn't add the *but what if it's not* that raced through my mind. I pulled out the vintage mask of Revered and pretended everything was all right.

"Thank you," I said instead. "For taking care of everything here while I was gone. I know it's not easy—immensely more difficult than usual, I'm sure—but one thing I never worried about when I was trapped there was leadership. I knew with you, everyone would be taken care of."

His shoulders dropped, the harsh lines of his expression softening. "That's my job, Ophelia."

"Reluctantly," I reminded him as we kept walking.

"Reluctantly, yes. And I won't lie and say it's easy—or that I even agree I'm fit for it most days. But it's a challenge I'm honored to take on."

"I'd say it's more of a calling than a job anyway," I teased him, and for a moment, a glimmer of the usual understanding our friendship promised floated between us.

He scoffed, wrapping an arm around my shoulders to guide me forward. "Come on. Breakfast is waiting. And welcome back, Revered."

The next hours were grueling.

My mind is my own, I repeated over and over as I tried to act like my old self. But as I sat in the dining room in Meridat's home, the memory of Echnid's poison in my own Rapture Chamber slithered over me.

Malakai kept eyeing me warily from his spot beside Mila. The general appeared alert, a reassurance compared to how I'd last seen her. Erista and a few Soulguider advisors—whose names I'd been told but had filtered beneath my own mantra—joined us, too.

Even Mora was brought to the table—apparently a new allowance—but it was the fae's eyes I avoided most of all. I didn't know how the injury she'd sustained in the catacombs was recouping, but prior to that, her healing magic had been strong. I didn't want her to try to heal me.

I didn't think there was anything to fix.

I suspected I wasn't broken, simply different.

And I didn't want her to confirm it.

As plates were passed around the table, Meridat reported where all of our allies' forces currently were, but everyone else seemed to already know that information. They'd been having regular meetings, and I guessed the only reason we were at a dining table surrounded by too-bright tile floors and mosaic ceilings instead of in a dimly lit, stiff-chaired war room right now was to make Malakai and me more comfortable as we settled in. I cast him a hesitant glance, the memory of myth magic crashing through me when he met it. The Bind beat once, and he nodded as if to say we were both here together.

My body is my own.

My mind is my own.

I nodded back, taking in every word Meridat said. I could be the Revered I always had been despite Echnid.

No, you can't.

I inhaled sharply at that hissing voice. A memory. Only a memory.

I met Meridat's eyes. "Thank you for taking care of everyone," I said.

"Of course, Ophelia." She folded her hands before her where she stood at the head of the table. "Whatever you need while you're here, it is yours."

"Thank you," I repeated.

"There's something else," Cypherion clipped. His voice was tight enough to send my nerves rocking up again. When I faced him, he slid a piece of parchment across the table. "This is from Vale."

I read it, and my heart stuttered. "Jezebel," I breathed.

"She's okay," Cypherion rushed out, but he was jittery, too. Being apart from Vale was clearly unsettling him.

"She was shot with a fucking arrow! While flying!" I shouted, and a gold wave of seraph power ebbed off my skin with each word. I siphoned it back in when everyone recoiled, but anger roared through my veins. And it was...good. Satisfying ecstasy to give in to this magic.

Finally, something *mine* to feel. To indulge. An emotion I was sure of in this new present.

"She could have died!"

"Zanox saved her, and she's awake now," Cypherion tried to soothe.

My gaze flicked between him and Erista. The Soulguider bit her lips, but she nodded in agreement. "She's okay. She wrote to me herself."

"Angels, what the fuck is happening to us?" I panted, crumbling the paper in my hand without meaning to. I leaned my fists against the table, my knuckles white and chest heaving.

I needed Sapphire. Needed my pegasus so I could fly to my sister and see with my own eyes that she was okay. But Sapphire was with Tolek.

"How did everything go so wrong?" I whispered, breathing through a tight chest.

It was a rhetorical question because I knew where this all began. Everyone did. With an Angelcurse burning through my veins and a solution presented as an option when truly there was no choice. With freeing the Warrior God only to plague the world.

"Who did it?" I asked.

"Vale described the woman, but she didn't recognize her," Cyph said.

My attention dropped to Vale's explanation. *White dress. Otherworldly beauty. Glorified satisfaction.*

My eyes widened, snapping to Malakai's. Angellight sparked in my palms, silver and lilac stars, and he jolted.

"What?" Malakai blurted, pushing upright.

"Have you read this?" I croaked, throat dry.

It couldn't be.

I needed him to say it couldn't be true.

I passed the letter across the table, and Malakai's face paled when he read it. "Echnid's," he muttered.

"It was one of them," I barely whispered.

"How?" Malakai asked. "They were there. They were in the ballroom when you—" His words cut off at my flinch, an apology deepening his green eyes. I shook my head because it wasn't necessary, but also because I had no idea how this was possible.

Mila's hand snaked into Malakai's. He looked down at her, the pained lines in his expression softening ever so slightly.

"Echnid's what?" Erista asked.

Malakai and I explained what we knew of the females who seemed to hold some rich satisfaction from pleasing the god.

"I think I saw one," Mila gasped based on the detailed explanation. "With Tolek." She gave me a tight-lipped smile. "We were in the market one day and there was this woman. Her spirit wound through the streets in a way I'd never felt before, and when I looked at her...that was when I had one of my visions."

The glimpses of strange figures and places she hadn't been able to decipher. Mila and Erista had told me they'd been trying to figure out why it happened and if it was some branch of Soulguider magic the general had absorbed when she was knocked unconscious in the Spirit River.

"What did it look like?" Malakai asked, squeezing Mila's hand.

Her brows pulled together. "I saw her with red eyes and a baby in her arms. I've seen a few similar scenes with babies, actually. I don't know where they were."

"It sounds like the woman my brother wrote about, too,"

Mora added, updating us on a letter Lancaster had sent her about a strange, white-gowned woman singing in the forest. "He couldn't identify what she was."

Erista said, "So the woman who attacked Jezebel, the one Santorina and Lancaster saw, and the woman Mila saw are all brought here by Echnid for—"

"For some purpose we don't know," I finished with a tight-lipped expression. "And they're somehow finding their way all over the continent in the blink of an eye. We need to learn more about them."

"I'll keep looking," Mila affirmed, and Erista nodded, too. "We're working on ways to control the visions."

I nodded my thanks, but my mind was absent.

Angels, was there *any* advantage we still had? My breaths came shorter, my vision blurring. The memory of Echnid in my veins slithered through me.

My body is my own.

My mind is my own.

My fingers curled around the edge of the table, and I dragged in short breaths. I would not be a toy of the gods again—I would not allow it—but everything was slipping, and I was being crushed.

The door at the front of the room groaned, and my head snapped up.

As if in slow motion, the entrance parted, and I swore the whole of Ambrisk could have turned to ash when my eyes met chocolate brown ones, those amber specks so bright even from here.

Tolek froze just inside the door, his stare drinking me in, and something that had withered inside me sprang to life—Echnid's poison burned back another inch.

A smirk lifted one corner of Tolek's lips. "There she is."

I shook, my jaw quivering and knees buckling against the table, but I raced forward anyway.

Raced into the arms of the only man who could hold me together right now. Who always knew how to stitch up my wounds and my broken heart. Who made every day lighter just by breathing and flashing me those perfect smirks he wielded like a blade.

Who could see the scars I'd always had, and Angels willing, love the new ones I carried.

I collided with the scent of citrus and spice and that alone peeled back more of Echnid's grasp on me. Like Tolek's light solely seared away the mist. His arm banded around my back, expertly tucked beneath my wings, his other hand cradling my head to his neck as I trembled.

"Shh," he soothed. "It's okay, *apeagna*. It's okay. I'm here."

"Thank the fucking Spirits," I blubbered, and I kissed him.

He groaned in approval, dipping me back so my wings brushed the ground and stroking his tongue against my own. Every sweep of his lips was another reminder, another pull back into myself, away from everything I'd gone through in the past weeks. Everything I'd done and become.

And something in my chest fully cracked open then, a tearing sensation behind my sternum, like it was finally okay to stop trying to hold it together because every one of his heartbeats was building this new cavern of safety for me to crawl into. For me to break within.

He was *it*, grounding me in a way no one and nothing else could, and even as I shattered in his arms, I was more shielded than ever. I couldn't get lost again.

I bit down on his bottom lip, needing to be even closer, wanting to fuse us together so we'd never be parted again. And if the way his hands grappled to pull me closer said anything, Tolek wanted that, too.

He broke the kiss, cupping my cheeks and searching my eyes. It was only then that I realized his hands were shaking, too.

I counted the amber specks in his irises while I waited. I didn't know what he found, but he brushed his thumbs across my cheeks, catching the remnants of tears wrought of a god's torture and a heart reborn, and something heated in his own stare.

"I think whatever you're all doing here can wait?" Tolek said, not even bothering to look at the table or get an answer.

And though I was the one who bore Angellight, as he scooped

me up and tossed me over a shoulder, he carried me out of the dark.

Chapter Twenty-Seven
Tolek

I stormed into my room with Ophelia hauled over my shoulder and paused. The bed was mussed, the scent of lemon and jasmine heavy in the air.

"You slept in here?" I asked.

"For days. It's my room, isn't it?" She grabbed my waist, her wings curving around her to beat against my shoulders. Those fucking *wings*. My memory didn't do them justice. The gold woven through the downy soft feathers mesmerized me.

Ducking, I flipped Ophelia back over my shoulder and slid her down my body, planting her on her feet close enough that every breath she took pressed her into me.

"Actually, love," I corrected, smirking, "it's my room."

She quirked a brow, and her eyes dropped to my lips, the air between us thinning. "This is where Cypherion put me," she said on an exhale.

Fucking Spirits, the sound of her voice, already so breathy, went straight to my cock. I needed her so desperately, it was the only thing making my heart beat. To feel her breath against my lips, see the flutter of her pulse in her neck—she was alive and real and here, and the realm was more right for it.

I gripped her chin, tilting her head up, and whispered, "Right where I want you."

Then, I sealed my lips to hers where they belonged. I'd almost lost it when she kissed me in the meeting chamber. Was ready to lay her down on the table, glorious wings splayed around her, and tell everyone to get the fuck out.

But we had things to talk about first, and more than anything, I just needed to *feel* her.

I held her tightly—was never letting go of her again—as I broke the kiss and searched those magenta eyes. Her irises glowed gold around the edges, like the power of her Angellight and seraph magic and whatever else she contained was bursting to get out of her.

But there was also a haunting emptiness behind her powerful stare that was so foreign, it clawed through my chest like a riled beast, dragging up unpleasant realities that we had to address.

"You told me not to come for you," I rasped.

Ophelia's eyes widened at the tone of my voice, then her brow set in determination, and ribbons of gold light twirled around her hands where they pressed to my chest. "You didn't listen," she challenged. The magic flared. Oh, we were both fucking angry.

Good. We weren't burying anything.

"Damn right, I didn't."

"Vincienzo—"

I gripped her jaw. "No, Alabath."

Slowly, I walked her back toward the bed as her ribbons of light curled up and over my shoulders, waking sparks of heat and pleasure every damn place they touched. "I don't care what the risks are. I don't care if a god is going to flay me alive. When you are in trouble, I will come for you."

"And I don't care how positively reckless you attempt to be," she spat back at me, hands gripping my hips to steady herself, nails digging into my leathers, and on Damien's fucking grave, I wanted to anchor her to me. Wanted her light to brand me. "If there is a way for me to protect you from harm, I am going to do it."

"That's the problem with your logic, Alabath." Her brows rose skeptically, light still coiling around me. "The only thing that will truly harm me is something happening to *you*. Because you hold my entire heart and spirit in those hands of yours—wield them like they're your damn blades—but I am *nothing without you*."

Her thighs met the mattress, and I pushed her down on it. Her wings fanned around her, and I crawled on top of her, settling myself in the cradle of her hips as that Angellight burned brighter.

"You are *everything to me*, though," she argued, light flaring with a medley of colors.

I dropped my forehead to hers. "And you're everything to me," I repeated, my throat thickening. "I need you, *apeagna*."

I needed her here. Needed her safe. Needed her by my side while we got our fucking earned retribution together.

"I need you, too," Ophelia admitted. She exhaled slowly, eyes falling closed. Her magic slowly spooled back into her, trickling across my skin. For a long moment, we breathed each other in. The numbness shrouding my chest peeled back, and something warm seeped through. Not the heated anger that had me lashing out recently, but relief, pure and soothing from that light.

I could fucking *breathe* again.

"Do they hurt?" I checked, dragging a hand down the edge of her velvety wing.

Ophelia shivered beneath me. "No," she panted, that voice sending a different kind of warmth through my body. Angels, I needed her this way, too. "Not anymore. That feels good."

Noted.

I kissed her, one hand toying with the feathers until she was squirming and insatiable. I licked and nipped down the column of her throat, sinking my teeth into her collarbone.

"Tolek," she begged, ribbons of light uncoiling from her hands and reaching for me. The control was astounding, so in tune with her every breath.

Brushing a hand up the inside of her thigh, I pressed against her center over her leathers and worked my lips back up her neck. When I got to her ear, I whispered, "Never tell me to leave you again."

She angled her hips up to meet my hand in an insistent pattern. When our eyes met, there was nothing but promise searing back at me. For now, that was enough.

"Please, Tolek," she whimpered.

There was a brokenness in her voice that had me pausing. It

wasn't her, frenzied, begging for me. It was haunted and *needing* this damn connection to ground her. It was the result of true torment, and my anger reignited.

"What did he do to you?" I growled. She fidgeted, like this was something she hadn't been wanting to tell me. "Alabath," I whispered, my head falling to her shoulder. "Tell me. Please, tell me so I can take it away."

Let me take the pain. Let me hold her anger, cradle it like she did every secret of my fucked-up childhood. Her fear was so vibrant, I could taste it. It weighed down the air, seeped from her skin. I lifted my head, meeting those magenta eyes again, and cupped her cheek.

Then, she shattered my entire world.

"He...poisoned me."

Sharp, slicing fury. The heated steel of a freshly forged weapon. That was all I knew.

"He *what*?" I seethed.

Ophelia took a breath that tugged on my own lungs. "He used his magic like a drug, through my Curse scar, so I was under his influence—addicted to his presence—agreeable and malleable. Then, he made me..."

I froze, leaning up. Horror dripped icily through my veins. "Did he touch you in any way? *Did he hurt you?*"

"Not physically," she confirmed. "He made me hurt Malakai."

Tears formed along her lashes. Not the wracking sobs I'd heard from her before. These were slow and steady, leaking from her eyes one languid drop at a time, like it was something she'd cried over— been sick over—so often now that she didn't have the energy left to spend.

"Echnid wants more seraphs." Her wings shifted beneath her, light continuing to slowly undulate in a soft ebb, like her magic was trying to soothe her. "He tried to make me use my myth power to wake one within Malakai, but it didn't work. And he just made me try and try, burning him over and over again until we were both unconscious. And I barely realized what I was doing because I was in such a haze from his poison, a part of me thought it was the right choice."

It was unsettling how calmly she stated it all, but anger roared inside of me.

"Angels, *apeagna*," I breathed, kissing her forehead and sitting up to cradle her to me. "I'm so sorry. I am going to slice that fucking god's head from his body."

Ophelia gripped my hand, kissing it. "We'll do it together."

Fucking Angels, I liked the sound of that.

Together. Again. Infinitely.

"By the damn Spirits," I promised, "we will."

And at that vow, a fire simmered within us both. One that devoured the pain we'd felt while we were apart. Forged a new promise together. She slammed her lips to mine, and I was ready to ravage that agony, to let it fuel our revenge.

Ophelia's legs wrapped around my waist, her hand diving into my hair, and her ribbons of light tangled back around me. The touch of her magic against my skin was some sort of bliss, the heat and intimacy a pure rapture I could happily die in.

I laid her on the bed and kissed down her neck, untying her top and peeling it down her body. She writhed against me as I gripped one breast, rolling my thumb across her peaked nipple. I scraped my teeth across the other and she arched up.

"Tolek," she breathed, and one ribbon of light dragged around my waist.

"Say it again," I said as I nimbly unhooked the clasps at her lower back and pulled off her top entirely. "My name. Say it again."

"Tolek," she repeated, hips lifting for me to shimmy her leathers down as I kissed her stomach.

"Please, never tell me not to follow you again," I begged, searing the words into the skin beneath her navel. "When you say my name like that in our bed—like it is the last word you're going to breathe as you go to the Spirit Realm—don't tell me to leave you in danger. Because we fucking need each other," I finished as my mouth landed between her legs.

She cried out, light flaring as I flicked my tongue against her, tasting her like she was the first meal I'd had in weeks. It felt like it, with how numb I'd been.

"I fucking missed this," I said, lavishing her.

"Angels," she swore, her spine arching, heels digging into my back, right over the tattoo she hadn't seen yet.

I devoured her, two fingers pumping into her, but with my other hand, I stroked the edge of her wing, and Ophelia fell apart, coming on my tongue with the most satisfying moan I'd ever heard and a burst of shimmering Angellight that rattled the chandelier above.

When she was done, I rose from my knees and went to the window, pulling the curtains open. Ophelia tilted her head back, breasts rising and falling in a beautiful sight. Her brow creased, and light curled in lazy tendrils from her.

"What are you doing?" she asked.

I crossed back to her, undressing as I did. Gripping her waist, I flipped her to her stomach, then pulled her onto her hands and knees. I pressed slow kisses from her tailbone to the base of her neck, and she rewarded me with small moans, grinding back against my aching cock.

Brushing aside her hair, I whispered in her ear. "What lies in that direction, *apeagna*? Beyond the deserts?"

She lifted her head, dazed. "Mountains?"

"Mm-hmm," I hummed, dragging my length through her center. "What mountains?"

"The Mystique Mountains," Ophelia said, her head tipping back as she arched her spine.

"And who do those mountains belong to?" I lined myself up with her entrance.

Ophelia cast a curious glance over her shoulder, her lips swollen and cheeks pink.

"You," I commanded, and I slammed forward to the hilt.

Her wings flared out, catching the glittering gold light she burned with, and it only encouraged me to pull back and plunge into her again and again. Listening to how I made her feel, seeing the physical reaction of her rocking against me and gripping the sheets. I wanted those nails digging into *my skin* instead. Leaving crescent moons among my scars.

Wrapping an arm around her waist, I pulled her up. Her wings were soft against my chest, and they were sensitive to her, but holy fucking Spirits, the velvet of them against my bare skin nearly undid me, too.

She wrapped a hand around my neck as if she heard my thoughts, digging her nails into the Bond tattoo inked there. A ribbon of light snaked out from where her hand met my neck, wrapping around my throat and trailing down my body. Her body. Exploring every damn inch of the two of us together, teasing around where I sank into her. Seeing her take that control after what had happened to her, combined with how she felt, drove me wild.

"Those are your mountains, Ophelia," I growled, trying to remember what I was saying as I moved inside of her, hitting so fucking deep from this angle. Her eyes were trained perfectly on the distance, hungry and desiring. "That's my girl," I murmured, kissing her neck. "One day, I'm going to fuck you atop those mountains so you can scream my name to them because *you* own them just as you do me. The power within them, the beauty. It's all yours. No god can take it."

I gripped her hip and ran my other hand down the place where her wings met her skin. Her entire body clenched and uncoiled with the touch.

"Fuck, *apeagna*," I ground out. "Is that where they're most sensitive?"

"I-I think so," she panted.

"Interesting," I said, and I pressed her forward again so I had better access to her wings, climbing onto the bed to kneel behind her.

I pushed into her, timing every thrust with a brush of my fingers over the joint of her wings or a kiss across the place they met her back. She was a mess beneath me, telling me what felt best but barely able to form the words, just little moans and breaths and my name amid gold light streaked with colors I couldn't even decipher.

I pressed my hand into her spine between her shoulder blades, palm flat, and leaned over her. "Ophelia," I whispered in her ear.

She hummed in acknowledgment.

"When I touch your wings next, I want you to come."

"Please," she begged, and while I wanted to string this out, to continue to have her beg, I couldn't wait.

I reached one hand around her hips to rub tight circles between her thighs, and with my other hand I matched the pace against her wings. And Ophelia imploded, her light hitting every sensitive spot on my body, too. With a groan, I went right with her until I had nothing left to give.

And fuck if everything on Ambrisk didn't feel right again for that one dragged out moment of us falling apart together. Our shattered pieces forged into one in the heat of her Angellight, and if being broken meant I got to be sealed to her, I'd break myself for eternity.

After we caught our breath, I flipped Ophelia onto her back again and kissed her senseless.

"The things you do to me," I muttered, dropping my head against her neck. "I think I like this new seraph magic. And the wings."

She laughed, dragging her nails up my arm, but froze. "Tolek," she said, "what's this?"

When I lifted my head, her eyes were on the ink curling over my shoulder, gold shimmering in the Angellight.

"That's my new tattoo," I told her simply.

"A new tattoo?"

She pushed me off her so we could sit up, and I turned around. Ophelia's breath caught. We were both silent, her eyes burning into my back, peeling apart every inch of the golden wings unfurling there.

"You got this...for me?" she asked, doubt turning her voice to a whisper.

"Of course." My heart pounded in the silence. She traced the ink, her nails dancing lightly over the details and raising goose bumps along my skin.

"It's beautiful," Ophelia breathed. Her hand stopped at the top of the left side, and from the slow, barely-there touch, I knew what she was reading. "Lyria."

I dared a glance over my shoulder, heart splintering at the tears slowly tracking down her cheeks. I pulled Ophelia to me, laying back against the pillows with her wing draped across my chest and the other spread along the bed, her body flush against mine.

"How have you been coping?" she asked. It was such a damn personal question, but from her, it cracked the ice numbing my heart. Or maybe her light had burned it away.

And in its place, a flood of feeling soared through me. Grief, guilt, despair.

"I haven't been," I admitted. "I've just been trying to figure out a way out of this mess because I couldn't even come to terms with what happened."

"Do you want to talk about it now?"

I considered, dragging my fingertips up her spine. "I want to understand. Lyria told me—" I paused, my sister's final moments a bruise I was afraid to press. But the floodgates opened. "Lyria knew it was coming. A Soulguider hinted something cryptic, and she figured it out, so I'm grateful she seemed to be at peace with it, but I'm just so fucking lost as to *how* this could happen to her. How is it fair? How did she deserve such a short life?"

"She didn't," Ophelia responded quickly. "She deserved so much more than what she was given. Death isn't fair, and that's why we're fighting. For Lyria and all the Lyria's of the world."

"Death isn't fair," I repeated, resting my head atop Ophelia's. "That's such a fucking painful truth, Alabath."

She brushed her fingers over my ribs absentmindedly. "When my father died, I questioned it for months. I still do. I don't know why the Spirits give us these people to love so fiercely only to have them taken from us too soon. But the only comfort I can come up with is that some people—those like Lyria, like my father—are full of so much love that they leave the same impact in a short lifetime that others leave in centuries. They deserved to have those centuries regardless, and it will never be fair, but their Spirits will forever echo with their impact. Through those of us they loved and left behind."

Ophelia had lived with her father over her shoulder at every turn since he left. I'd do that for Lyria now. I didn't know when I'd grow to understand what happened to her—how it could happen —but I'd take it one step at a time. Grief was slow, healing was slower. But every damn thing I did from now until Echnid was gone from this realm would be for the commander who loved so fiercely, she gave a lifetime's worth in a few decades.

"I love you, Ophelia Alabath," I whispered. "Since I was a boy and infinitely."

"I love you, too, Tolek Vincienzo," she answered, fingers dancing over the edge of my tattoo. "I am so relieved to be back."

She rested her head on my chest then, her tears still warm and flowing, but a different sort of peace sealed between us as we gazed out in the direction of the Mystique Mountains, a little closer to healing now that we were together.

Chapter Twenty-Eight
Ophelia

THAT FIRST AFTERNOON BACK, TOLEK TOLD ME OF THE numbness he'd slipped into after Lyria's death. Of how he didn't feel like it was her time and had been wrestling with how to accept that. Of how he was trying to find a steady place between burning anger and echoing emptiness.

And I told him every little detail of Echnid and how I feared what the god was trying to turn me into.

Tol showered me with affection to erase the stains left on my soul. His hands along my skin, gripping to the point of bruises blooming, erased the Warrior God's poison lingering in my veins. The small purple spots across my ribs were works of art dotting my scars. Visible markers for the tainted soul within.

And as he stroked gentle fingers up my arm beneath the sheets, I whispered to him, "My body is my own. My mind is my own." It was safe, to be held by him.

"No one else's," he assured me, lips against my shoulder, life brimming in his hungry eyes.

My body is my own.

My mind is my own.

And that night, when he kissed down my stomach and lowered himself between my legs, a part of me thought, *My body is his.* And he was the only one I wanted to give it to.

Chapter Twenty-Nine
Damien

Bant and I stood atop the mountain peaks facing southwest, his eyes locked on the horizon.

"You know there are others out there—the friends of the girl—who have somehow retained more magic than they were meant to," my companion, once my sworn enemy, said. Somehow, despite the missteps we both made in delivering us to this spot, we had become allies. We disagreed on every process but desired the same results.

"They have, but that may work in our advantage based on what the prophecies require," I reminded him. "It may be a scheme of the Fates, orchestrating an opportunity."

"You know the Fates do not interfere in that way. Their purpose is guidance and maintaining fortunes, not changing them."

"I know that is what Valyrie has always said," I muttered, squinting into the distance, where our sister swooped back onto palace grounds, her arms laden with purchases, "but I do not always believe it."

The Fates were not so different from us, rife with a power often overlooked.

"Either way," I continued, turning from Bant and striding to the opposite edge of the cliff, looking over my city, "the pieces are falling into place." A breeze ruffled my feathers, blowing my hair across my face. I inhaled the mountain air I had yearned for so long. "Remember, she was never supposed to be as she is either, but she is a promise we did not count on. Perhaps others will be, too."

With a grunt of agreement, Bant added, "Valyrie has spoken wishfully of the Starsearcher."

"She has." I glanced at him over my shoulder, raising a brow. "And your own warriors?"

Bant kept his hands folded behind his back, his unkempt black hair trailing around his shoulders. The two great lashing scars on his wings caught the light between his feathers. Without turning, he answered, "The one with the wound intrigues me. When the queen impaled him with my magic, it...lingered."

"Has he become blessed?" I asked.

Bant contemplated, still staring in that same direction. "I will have to get closer to truly see."

"Bide your time," I advised. "Especially after what happened in the dark pools recently."

"That was unexpected," Bant agreed, wings ruffling. "Echnid believes that power will be his key, so he is watching it closely. Do you think they will figure out the truth before him?"

"If they are as smart as the warriors we once knew, they may," I grunted.

If all went as we hoped, we could orchestrate a glorious downfall and earn back the might we truly deserved. A sensation I had not felt since before the death of the last Chosen inflated my chest. Pride. It was unfamiliar and brightened my ether, sending a golden glow tumbling down the cliffside.

"We will need to be careful of Thorn," Bant said, piercing that bliss.

"Yes," I agreed. Our fallen brother was the wildest of cards in this plot.

His move in unlatching the final lock within Ophelia's mind that woke the seraph was risky, but it gave Echnid something to focus on. A mission to distract him while the seven of us worked toward our own goal—goals. We had many priorities after so many centuries being stifled.

And it allowed Ophelia to command the full might of a seraph, which would be necessary.

Beneath his breath, so low I could barely hear it, Bant muttered, "He is only steps away from his solution."

"I know," I exhaled the words, fearful in a way I was unused to. "I know."

But now that the Alabath sisters had this myth magic, we may be able to achieve everything much more easily than we initially thought. After centuries, we would stop at nothing—would see whatever crumbled reigns and bloodshed that it took.

And I doubted something as humane as remorse would drown out our victory.

Chapter Thirty
Santorina

THE HUMAN SETTLEMENT ALONG THE WILD PLAINS north of Palerman had been turned into a training camp a few months ago. It had expanded since I first visited, but the same charming cottages dotted the paths, laundry strung along the fences. Training circuits bordered by hay bales were jammed in the clearings between cypher patches, and the market was busy as usual. It was quaint despite the quick growth resulting in temporary tents sprung up in yards while lodgings were decided.

At the start of the year, Jezebel had flown me to visit a few of the camps, along with Erista and Ezalia, and the welcome was incredibly warm. But as Lancaster and I knocked on the door of the cottage belonging to the lieutenant of the Mystique armies who manned this camp, my stomach twisted.

Jittery, I scanned the pink rose bushes lining the walkway. "Ugh, roses," I muttered.

"You have a vendetta against flowers?" Lancaster drawled, an emotion I couldn't identify tightening his words.

"Only the ones that smell like your bloodstained soul," I answered dryly.

Lancaster blinked at me, and despite his usual quick wit, I had a feeling he didn't know if I was joking this time. The fae all smelled like iron-tinged florals to me, and after him carrying me all night as we traveled here, I couldn't get the scent out of my damn nose.

He was about to comment when the door swung open. A kind-faced man, eyes glinting over his high, dark-skinned cheekbones, gripped the knob in a steel fist. He was still in a light tunic and pants, not yet dressed in leathers for the day.

"Willox!" I greeted. "It's so nice to see you again."

"Santorina," Willox answered, his stare flitting to Lancaster and instantly hardening. "We hadn't expected you for a few weeks at least."

"Yes, well," I said, biting my lip as I glanced at the male beside me, "my traveling companion has a knack for speed."

"I see."

He knows he's fae.

Perhaps I should have written and given Willox and the human commander a warning, but I'd been worried what they'd say. And we didn't have a choice. If we wanted to prepare humans for the coming war *and* discover any more Bounties, Lancaster was the best option.

I assumed the authority I'd seen Ophelia don as Revered numerous times, attempting to strike a balance between friendly and stern. "Many things have changed since I was last here. I'd love to explain everything." I lowered my chin, pointedly adding, "Inside."

Willox chewed over those words for a moment then inclined his head, the long braids piled atop it shifting. "My partner and our children are still sleeping. Wait in the kitchen, and I'll send a quick missive to Commander Lislee to let her know you're here."

Relief washed through me. "Thank you." I exhaled.

As Lancaster and I traipsed down a narrow hall lined with paintings clearly illustrated by tiny hands, I cast him a warning glare. *Do not say anything until I tell you.*

He squinted at me but didn't argue.

We each took a seat at the small round table that occupied the majority of the open floor in the cramped kitchen. With Lancaster's inhuman presence swarming the air—and that damn scent of roses—I was grateful for the window propped open above the sink.

"She'll be here in a minute," Willox said when he entered only a few moments later. I supposed humans were comfortable with Mystique ink if Lislee had already written back. Or at least the leaders of the camp were. "Can I get you anything?"

"Tea would be lovely, thank you," I said just as Lancaster commented, "No, thank you."

I shot him a sharp look.

"We'll both have tea," I told Willox without looking away from Lancaster.

The male's dark eyes tunneled into me, and for a brief moment, I was captivated. The soft scent of musk and florals coated my mind, forming a barrier around us. Something in my chest hummed, like a harp's string being plucked. Lancaster's jaw ticked as if in pain, and my attention zeroed in on the slight motion.

But I blinked away the distraction and gave him a look that said, *It's polite. Drink the damn tea.*

I don't like tea, his glare said back, and he seemed rattled.

I don't care what you like, I shot at him, my thoughts humming like that string.

And I swore one corner of his lips twitched up in amusement, as if he truly heard those words and felt the ire burning in them. At least, I hoped it was ire.

"Here you are," Willox said, setting a tray between us with four cups. I gave Lancaster a smug grin.

The back door opened, and Lislee rushed in, her angular brown eyes as bright as the morning sun. She appeared to be in her early forties, and I was almost taken aback at the difference between a human and a warrior of that age. I'd spent so much time with the latter lately, I forgot how early my own kind began getting fine lines around our eyes and streaks of gray in our hair.

Unlike Willox, she'd dressed in a casual leather vest over her tunic, complete with a thick weapons belt, boots, and pants. Armor for a human making their way in the warrior world.

"Sorry, it took me a moment to get out the door," she said. "The kids were just waking."

"Not a problem," I answered, rising to shake her hand. "I'm Santorina Cordelian. We only met briefly last time I was here. I believe it was the week you arrived."

"Yes, Miss Cordelian." She claimed the last seat at the table, her sharp black hair swaying around her chin. "You were here with Jezebel Alabath and a few others, correct?"

Lislee showed no visible reaction to Lancaster, so I assumed she was not a Bounty. Nerves twisted through me at the stark reminder of how difficult it was going to be to seek out any—if they even existed. I hadn't even fully acknowledged the sense within myself until Echnid returned, and an entire host of magic washed over our land.

I nodded. "And it's on business concerning them—concerning all of us—that I've returned."

"Is this an explanation for those ominous letters last week?" Lislee asked, a note of disapproval for the lack of explanation staining her tone. She was direct—I liked her.

"It is," I said, and reluctantly turned to Willox. "Lieutenant, did you or your warriors feel any sort of power surge last month? It would have been early in the morning; many might have slept through it."

I paused as recollection dawned on the warrior.

"Yes," he said clearly. "A ripple went through the land. Woke my children up and my partner, Michale. Is this about that?"

I sighed. Lancaster stiffened. A part of me had been hoping maybe they hadn't felt it. That maybe the Soulguiders in Xenovia only had because of their proximity to where the theater was in the mountains—that Echnid wasn't strong enough for it to echo across the land.

What a foolish wish that had been.

"It is. I'm aware the news I have to share is going to sound impossible, but please, let me finish."

And I told them the astounding tale of a god being released from his stone prison, of a vendetta he held against his peers, and a threat he now posed to us all.

"Having another god—one who respects human lives—is not

a bad thing," Lislee argued. "I would think you'd be happy with this development, Miss Cordelian."

"One would think," I repeated. "But Echnid only *thinks* he is going to benefit his subjects. In truth, I believe his plans will cause the downfall of Ambrisk's very nature."

"What do you mean?" Lislee asked.

"Echnid seeks revenge against the gods who locked him away. We have on good authority that he is searching for a way to sever the ties between the gods and the warriors for good." I paused. "Likely locking the gods from Ambrisk entirely. From all of their subjects."

Lislee's face paled, and the gravity of what I'd said hung in the air.

"Whose authority is this information on?" Willox asked, eyes narrowed on me.

I couldn't tell him Valyrie. If she truly was on our side, providing aid, we couldn't have that getting out for risk of what Echnid would do to her.

"Someone currently within Damenal. The Warrior God has closed off the city to messages and newcomers, but our source found a way to contact us. And we have a powerful Starsearcher on our team who has confirmed he's getting closer to figuring it out."

Willox's eyes widened, his gaze flicking down the hall. "We have cousins in Damenal."

"They're likely fine," I assured him. "But they wouldn't have been able to contact you."

The lieutenant's jaw ticked, hand fisting atop the table.

"We heard rumblings," Lislee said, exchanging a glance with her warrior counterpart, "of something of this legendary sort taking place recently. I dismissed it as camp rumors."

"I wish it were," I said. A blanket of solidarity surrounded us, stitched tight with fear of the unknown.

"What I still don't understand," Willox said after a pause lightened only by the birds chirping outside, "is why Ophelia Alabath would have done this."

Malice dripped on those words, and dammit, how was I meant to answer that? Ophelia didn't have a choice, for a number of reasons. But those who didn't see her torn in that cavern, who didn't feel the pain wrenching her apart...they wouldn't understand.

But Lancaster's deep voice grumbled beside me, "She was manipulated."

All shocked eyes, my own included, swiveled toward him. "Manipulated?" Lislee asked.

"Tricked by a number of parties," Lancaster went on. "The Queen of the Fae, a sphinx who only wanted her Angelic mistress to return, your Angels themselves, and a curse that would destroy those she loves. Take your pick of which you would like explained first. We can sit here all day."

I squeezed my eyes tight. Lancaster was certainly not honoring the *polite* request I'd made of him.

But Lislee only said, voice piquing a notch. "He's fae?"

My eyes peeled open, and I nodded. Goddesses, this was not going how I'd hoped. I'd jam my cypher dagger somewhere nonlethal on Lancaster later for interfering.

"And he's here why?" Lislee clarified.

Lancaster began, "With all due respect—"

"Oh, Gods," I muttered, looking to the ceiling.

"—this predicament was not brought about by Ophelia Alabath." He canted his head as he continued, "She was handed an impossible task by higher powers who are twisting the lives of their subjects as if we are nothing to them. Ophelia is the only chance everyone on Ambrisk has of surviving."

"I am no warrior, but neither am I a threat to your humans." Sincerity deepened those words, a tone I'd never heard from the male before. "And I have come here to aid in the unique way that I may because this is a problem for all of us. It was caused by Aoiflyn and Thallia as much as Echnid. By Moirenna and Lynxenon, Artale and Gerenth."

"Aoiflyn may be the fae goddess," I said in defense of Lancaster, though Goddesses knew why I felt the need to, "but she and her people sacrificed as much as everyone else. We may not worship her for those fae abilities, but we do honor her heritage— the fertility and bounty she blesses Ambrisk with. It is an unlikely alliance, and I understand it is difficult to allow Lancaster to remain here, but the nature of all alliances in the world are reforming."

Lislee and Willox seemed to consider for a moment. They were not entirely swayed, but they shifted. Closer and closer, they shifted.

Willox exhaled a rough breath. "You said some of the Revered's councilmen were there when this happened? What about Commander Vincienzo? Where does she stand in this?"

My heart stuttered.

"The commander died fighting to defend Ophelia Alabath," I choked out. Willox's eyes turned glassy as he blinked at me in shock.

"The commander died," he echoed hollowly.

My nod in confirmation was the most soul-crushing motion I'd ever committed. "Some of her last words were telling Ophelia to free the God because she thought it was in the warriors' best interest, and she did not want the Alabath line to remain plagued by this curse forever, nor did she want Ambrisk's magic to suffer."

And that—that was what was needed to sway Willox to ally with a known enemy. The intentions of his commander and the final wishes her brave spirit imparted on us all.

"How did she die?" the lieutenant asked, probably thinking of the soldiers he'd have to notify. Gods, Lyria had just led them to victory in a *war*. She seemed indestructible, but her death was felt across Gallantia.

I dared a peek at Lancaster, and before I could respond, he admitted, "My queen killed her. And Lyria's brother got revenge for that blow."

Lislee gasped, leaning forward. "The Queen of the Fae is dead?"

Lancaster and I both nodded.

"And you are still here freely?" Willox asked him. Another terse nod from the fae. "Why?"

His jaw tensed, and I was about to intervene, but Lancaster said, "Because I have lived a very long time at the whims of others.

Now it is my choice to be here. To atone for things I have been forced to do."

He is still learning what this new world means, Mora had claimed of her brother. For the first time in centuries—in nearly his entire life—he was not solely the Hunter. How would that affect him? Who would he become beyond who he was forced to be?

As if reading the direction of my thoughts, Lancaster nodded softly to me. I began, "There was an ancient line of humans called Bounties who were born with an instinct to hunt and kill fae. It was the original reason the fae became predators to our kind." I met Lislee's wide eyes. "Before her death, Ritalia revealed that I am the last of a direct line to the Queen of the Bounties." I took a deep breath before adding, "Lancaster was bred to hunt us. Only at Ritalia's command. Now that she is gone, he has free reign over the impulse, but he can still detect us among mortals and warriors."

"What is it exactly that you want of our camp?" Willox asked, tone dutiful but wary.

"Are you asking us to go to war against a god?" Lislee added.

Those words clamped around my heart. "I truly hope it does not come to that, but we need strong defenders. We need humans who have learned to fight, and we need—" Another glance at Lancaster, and his nod of encouragement had my own chin lifting, a steel brace of confidence stacking my spine. "We need Lancaster to see if there are any other Bounties among your ranks who may excel with fighting stronger opponents."

They exchanged a glance, a silent form of communication sealing between them.

"We'll need to discuss this today," Lislee decided. "There's a cottage on the lot behind our homes that is unoccupied that you can stay in until tomorrow. Single room—sorry about that." She didn't appear very sorry.

I hid my wince, looking up at Lancaster. Every muscle in his body pulled taut.

"And we'll place a guard rotation at your door," Willox added with a not-so-subtle glare at Lancaster, now only seeing him as *the Hunter*. Annoyance speared through me.

"Trust me," Lancaster said, inclining his head toward me, "she is the only guard I require."

~

THE COTTAGE WAS in fact single occupancy. With one bed perched beneath the window in the back corner and not so much as a sofa or settee. The front half was barely a kitchen with a dining nook, and a door along the back wall led to a bathing chamber.

"They certainly don't go for opulence here," Lancaster grumbled, glaring at the bed.

I sighed, crossing my arms. "Can't you simply create another one?"

Dramatic as all Spirits, Lancaster slowly looked around the room. "And where exactly would you like me to put it, Santorina?"

The way he said my name trickled along my spine, sending goose bumps down my arms. He rarely called me anything other than *Bounty* or *human* or sometimes a colorful creation like *you fragile mortal*.

I wasn't sure how I felt about him choosing now, within these tightly pressed walls, to let those syllables roll along his tongue in time with the hum in my chest. He waited for my response, his lips parted on a breath, and for a brief moment of insanity, I wanted him to say it again.

Damn not-immortal fae, probably distracting me with some sort of magic I'd never heard of.

Regardless, I shook off the fascination and blinked sweetly up at him. "You can put it outside?"

Lancaster raised a brow. "You want me to sleep on the porch?"

"Or I can." I shrugged.

"No," he answered instantly, those dark eyes burning into me with some primal instinct I didn't understand. "I will sleep out there, Bounty."

Back to that one now. Good.

"Watch out for violent creatures." I hummed as I busied myself with our packs and searched for food. "You never know who may try to harm you."

He mumbled something beneath his breath that sounded an awful lot like, "I think the most dangerous thing to me is within these walls."

And for some reason, it stung. We may have been natural enemies, meant to hunt one another down to our baser instincts—and he may have been the most arrogant and insufferable prick I'd ever met—but I'd thought we'd come to an understanding.

Attempting to smooth over our situation—because we *were* stuck together in here whether we liked it or not—I said, "Thank you for what you said in there. For admitting Ritalia's involvement and stating your true purpose here."

"You did good today," he said.

"Thank you." For some reason, that praise mattered.

"And I meant what I said in there." Lancaster swallowed, his hair wavering around his sharp-featured face. "I am tired of being controlled by her. My entire family has been."

His family? "Mora?"

"Mora." He paused. "My mother."

Those dark eyes snared mine, my feet rooted to the wooden boards. "What happened to your mother?" I whispered.

The silence stretching between us was desperate and somber. For some reason, I needed to know. Needed to understand how Lancaster had become the Hunter and who birthed him to be so. He was severely subdued, a wave of sadness pressing upon him at just the thought.

"I'm sorry—"

But he cut me off. "My mother was a great female, but no one cared about that." He appeared to be choosing his words carefully. "They cared about her for the same reasons they care about me. About Mora."

"Power," I breathed. I could taste the word on the air. Taste the ugliness it derived in the world.

"And blood," Lancaster added.

I didn't know what he meant by that exactly, but fae power was honed in their bloodlines, and magic as strong as his and Mora's meant that their mother must have been unearthly powerful.

I wanted to ask more, to put together the pieces of this adversary because maybe then I could understand.

But Lancaster averted his stare, and the spell between us broke. He moved about the cottage, arm brushing mine and sending unwanted tingles through my skin at the connection. It had to be the Bounty instinct. The scent of iron and flowers was nearly unbearable, and my chest was humming.

I searched the room for something to say. Opening the top dresser drawer, I found a collection of children's storybooks and games.

"At least we have entertainment," I commented.

Lancaster only grunted.

We spent the day in tense silence inside the cottage, the windows thrown wide and books and cards at our disposal. When night fell and Lancaster retreated to the porch, I lifted the curtain to peek out the window.

He laid on his back on a small bed roll, blanket pulled down to his hips and all of his proud scars on display. My eyes snagged on the one from the catacombs, when he'd been impaled with a cypher stake, and I'd spent hours removing the splinters. Even all these months later, I remembered how warm his skin felt beneath my bloodied hands. How his muscles had flexed, and his low voice grated against my memory. He'd seemed in such pain over the way Ritalia controlled him and his sister.

He is still learning what this new world means.

And as I watched this male study the stars in a territory of his enemies, I thought perhaps, if we fought our way out, it wouldn't be such a bad new world after all.

CHAPTER THIRTY-ONE
MALAKAI

Mila and I rode through the dunes surrounding Xenovia at top speed.

Well, as fast as Ombratta and Luna would deign to go in the sand. Spirits, I'd missed my horse. And even if the sand wasn't her preference, being out here now, beneath the afternoon sun, was the kind of freedom I'd craved while in Damenal. No chains, no threats, just Mila's pealing laughter and the way it rolled along my bones.

Each day, I was healing a little more. I'd pulled myself back from the dead before; the physical and soul-level pain of the myth magic was nothing in comparison.

Thick gray clouds rolled across the desert beyond the city, but the sun beat down on the Soulguider capital. As we tore around the borders between cyphers and cacti, Ombratta seemed to flourish, too.

"Come on, Warrior Prince! I have something to show you," Mila called, voice trailing on the wind with her braid. And for a beat, I forgot about war and gods and realms, and I just followed the girl I loved with my shadow horse.

~

WE STOPPED where a network of thin streams converged among stony fields of cacti, shimmering waters lacing through the desert like they were woven by some ancient, monstrous hand. Like Artale herself had painted them when her demigoddess daughter became the Angel.

"The Spirit streams?" I asked Mila as we dismounted and approached the central point of this cluster of waterways.

"Mm-hmm, I found this patch recently," Mila hummed, crouching beside the water. "All leading back to the Gates of Angeldust."

"Have you visited the one in Xenovia?" I asked, sitting beside her.

She was quiet for a moment, then she shook her head. "I was afraid of what I'd find."

All Gates of Angeldust had a heart, a well of deep magic flooded with the power of the Spirit Rivers. It came from beneath the ground, a source connected to the Mystique Mountains, but the rivers gushing through the Gates branched out into streams all across the deserts. It was these networks the Soulguiders used to escort spirits home. This magic Mila succumbed to when she was swept under the current and knocked unconscious.

I scooted closer, wrapping an arm around her shoulders. "Do you feel anything?"

I sure as shit didn't, but my stare flicked between her and the streams, studying both. It was just a misty layer of water to me, the sand dark at the bottom. Mila's gaze shifted about the slow tide, searching for something.

"The visions are more concrete around the waters," she admitted. "I can't summon them at will, but I'm able to see more."

"How'd you figure that?"

"The few times they've been the most vibrant have been when I was near fountains that were fed from the Spirit Rivers as opposed to other sources of water." She blinked a few times as she trailed a delicate hand through the very edge of the stream. "And—"

A voice sliced over the dunes, hauntingly high and otherworldly. "Mistress of myths beyond the walls…"

Mila and I both shot to our feet, the streams forgotten. In the distance, a woman floated about the desert, her pristine white dress flowing around her and making my heart race. My skin burned with the memory of myth magic.

She was wandering away from us, away from Xenovia. Like she'd just left the capital. From here, we were partially shielded by the cacti jutting six feet into the air.

"Is that..." Mila began.

"Yes," I answered, swallowing the riot of fear in my fucking throat. "One of Echnid's. Is that who you and Tolek saw?"

"I think so." Mila dared a step forward, peering around the plants. Then she gasped, and her eyes became glassy.

"Fucking realms," I muttered. Those visions had the best fucking timing. Cupping her cheek, I shuffled us toward the horses and turned her to face me. "Can you hear me?"

"Yes," she said, voice haunted. "But I can see other things." She squeezed her eyes shut, like she was trying to fight through it.

"What things?" I held her closer, pressing her palm to my chest, letting my heart beat against her so she knew I was here. We were still here.

"Winged things...like Ophelia. Armies of them. And"—another gasp—another tightening of her eyes and her hands on my leathers—"Malakai, it's her. That woman."

"Tell me about her," I urged. She needed to keep talking to me. Needed to stay present. Memories of the Gates of Angeldust tightened my throat.

"She has *wings*." Mila shook her head, and when her horror-stricken eyes met mine, my heart pounded faster.

"Wings?" I echoed, forcing my voice to be calm. "Like a seraph?"

"No. Hers are leathery. And her eyes..." Mila shuddered, horror lacing her tone. "Spirits, she's closer. But I don't think she can see me. She keeps walking right by. Pacing back and forth with a child in her arms."

A child this time, too. Why did they always have children when Mila saw them?

"What about her eyes?" I asked as I situated us on Ombratta,

Mila tucked in front of me, and snapped the reins. Luna galloped behind us.

"They're bright red," Mila whispered, voice smaller than ever. "And she has fangs; there's blood dripping from them."

The fangs were new, too. I cradled Mila tighter to my chest as we raced back toward the city, the woman long gone now.

"I think this is another realm." She breathed faster. "I think this is wherever they came from, and I think I'm seeing...what they want to do."

"What is that?"

"They're studying a map with markings of their targets, and... it's us, Malakai. All of us. Echnid is sending them after Ophelia's closest confidants."

"He's making sure she's not raising anymore seraphs without his knowledge. Or maybe he wants her to so he can gather us..." Why did the god want seraphs anyway?

"Yes, and," she said, and I clung to her every word as we sped through the city gates, needing them to keep coming, "the children. He wants children."

Fucking Spirits.

Echnid wanted demigods.

CHAPTER THIRTY-TWO
SANTORINA

THE HUMAN TRAINEES WANTED NOTHING TO DO WITH Lancaster. Or me by association.

Last time I visited, I'd floated among the ranks and conveyed the very helpful instruction my warrior friends had taught me. Today at the training circuit, I was only met with wary glances and averted smiles.

"At least they're being polite when they refuse me," I huffed, striding to where Lancaster had perched on the hay bale border of the ring. "It certainly is the nicest rejection I've ever received."

"Do you receive many rejections, Santorina?" Lancaster drawled without looking my way, an innuendo dragging out his words.

There he was again, using my full name in a way that sent a tingle down my spine and plucked the string in my chest. He'd done it this morning, too, when he made tea while I was readying myself in the cabin's bathing chamber.

For you, Santorina.

It had been made precisely the way I liked it, with a single spoon of honey stirred in as soon as the water was poured. I supposed he had endless room to fill in his non-immortal memory; observing my habits was simply a piece of his Hunter instincts.

For no reason I could decipher beyond his insufferable studying of me, I wanted to challenge the male beside me. "I'm not normally the one making advances to get rejected. So, I would say no."

Lancaster looked me over, gaze lingering on the weapons belt accentuating my waist. "With knives as sharp as those, I would think men and women would be afraid to approach."

His eyes were on that one dagger—deadly to no one in this camp other than him—and I wondered if a part of him *did* fear it. Fear what I was capable of with a cypher weapon. If I would choose to use it on him.

"Only the ones who aren't worth my time," I answered, voice lower than I realized. I leaned back against the hay bale beside him, a few inches between where our hands hung casually.

Lancaster's stare flicked back to the sparring ring, whatever snare had formed between us shattering. The heat I hadn't realized was crawling across my skin dissipated.

"Are any of these fools worth your time?" he asked, and it almost sounded like he was suppressing a growl.

"When it comes to training, everyone with the courage to wield a blade is worth my time."

It wasn't what he meant, and based on his dismissive grunt, we both knew it.

"You could be kinder to them, you know?" I supplied, crossing my arms. "Attempt to show them they can trust you."

"They are not kind to me."

"So be the bigger man. Male," I quickly corrected.

Lancaster surveyed the ring as the humans paired up for a new round. Finally, he said, "I have never gone out of my way to be kind to others."

"You've been kind to Ophelia and my friends," I corrected.

"I have owed them debts."

That was true, I supposed. Outside of the bargains between Ophelia, Tolek, and Lancaster that none of them had touched since the theater, he'd also owed us all for assisting his sister after the catacombs. Though the wound still plagued her, we'd kept her alive this long.

Still, with how he'd betrayed his queen to keep Tolek alive

while Ophelia went against Ritalia's wishes to fulfill the Angelcurse...

"I think many of us would consider those debts paid," I said.

Lancaster angled his body toward mine, the sharp lines of his face appearing to question me. As if he thought perhaps I was kidding. With the shift, his pinky brushed mine, and a pulse of fire went through my body. His jaw ground at precisely the same moment—stare latching on to me with a planetary force—the overwhelming scent of roses filtering through the air. No blood this time.

I blinked rapidly as my heart rate returned to normal, but the heat lingered *everywhere*. In places I especially did not want to feel it.

Clearing his throat, entirely unaffected and probably bemoaning my weird human reactions, Lancaster turned back to the ring. For a while, we observed the training in silence, my muscles utterly at ease after a morning of tense interactions attempting to crack the stubborn ice.

The humans kept a wide berth around the bales we sat on, and each time they passed by, my fingers clenched into a fist. Lancaster noticed, gaze silently dropping every instance.

Those were my people out there. My fragile, short-lived, humankind, and yet around them, I was shaken. But I was entirely comfortable sitting quietly on a stack of hay with a predator beside me.

I tried not to look too deeply into that.

"Do you sense anything in them?" I asked Lancaster after a while. Were any Bounties among us?

He shook his head, but he asked a question I didn't expect. "You aren't from Palerman originally, correct?"

His words were business-like, but his dark eyes were softer than I expected. Like he was remembering the small apartment with the threadbare rug and how I'd shut myself in the back bedroom without an explanation.

Shaking away the painful memories, I pushed off the hay and wiped my hands down my leathers, ready to force myself to make another attempt with the humans.

"No, I'm from a northern city. Why?" I took a step forward, nodding for Lancaster to accompany me. He didn't, so I rolled my eyes and carried on, but my toe caught on something, and I stumbled.

Instantly, though I was far from hitting the ground, a broad hand wrapped around my waist, fingers splayed against my stomach.

Heat sizzled through my body again, roses surrounding me and my chest thrumming. My gaze snapped over my shoulder, meeting his.

"You shouldn't have done that," I whispered.

Lancaster's eyes widened for a fraction of a second before setting in a steady frown. "No. I should not have."

His pupils were dilated, and I had a feeling mine were, too. These Bounty and Hunter instincts were running rampant. Carefully, he removed a stalk of hay that had gotten tangled in my ponytail, flicking it away as if it was the most distasteful thing he'd ever seen.

I only blinked at him for a moment, inhaling the heavy scent of roses before I snapped myself out of the reverie. Pushing the male's hand away—absolutely not mourning the heat of his palm—I stood upright.

"Why did you ask about Palerman?"

Lancaster took a moment to reply, but finally answered, "If you're the last direct descendant of the queen, maybe we should be searching for Bounties where—"

An agonized screech rang through the training camp, drowning his theory.

It cut off in a gargle that could only mean one thing.

My gaze sliced to Lancaster's, and I whispered, "*Death.*"

Without a word, we sprinted in the direction of the scream. The training ring turned into madness, humans rushing every which way, their senses not as attune as a fae or Bounty to decipher precisely where the cry had come from.

"Lower ranks, fall back!" I hadn't realized Lislee, the human commander, was on our heels, but she was shouting orders to her trainees, instructing only those who were confident to charge.

"It sounded like the western ring," Lancaster growled to me, without a hint of breathlessness despite the running. He whipped branches out of the way without any care as to splinters. There were multiple training circuits built into clearings in the camp, separated by patches of cyphers.

Another ragged scream pierced the air, this one dragged out. Lancaster kept pace beside me.

"Run faster!" I yelled. His stare swept over me without missing a step, reluctance heavy in his gaze. But I ordered, "Go, or this cypher dagger will find a new home when more lives are lost unnecessarily!"

Lancaster swallowed any response to my threat. He reached out and created that same long sword I'd seen before as effortlessly as if he'd been doing it for centuries.

"Be careful," he commanded, making me meet his eye.

I ducked sweeping cypher branches. "You, too, Hunter."

And he was gone, leaving only me, Lislee, and a handful of Mystiques and humans to charge the ring from the southern edge.

The screams mounted as we arrived, bursting through the trees and leaping the hay bale border. Blood splattered the scene, and in the center—

"Oh my Gods," I panted, stuttering to a halt.

Three bodies piled up, hearts wrenched from their chests. And standing in the center of them, head tipped back on a gleeful, crackling song and a beating organ still in her palm, was the same woman I'd seen plucking feathers from the carcasses of birds in the forest.

Only this time, it was *humans* lifeless before her.

She cooed that same folktale, her dress somehow immaculate despite the gore on her skin and the earth beneath her bare feet.

"Oh my Gods," I repeated.

Behind me, someone retched. At the sound, the woman's head snapped in our direction, and she paused. Stepping directly over the bodies, she glided toward us.

I pulled a dagger in each hand, allowing the steel to stifle the horror thrumming through me.

How was she here? *Who* was she? Did she really kill those humans with her bare hands as the blood to her elbows suggested?

And where in the fucking realms was Lancaster?

"Ah, it is you." She posed the statement like a part of her song, but her eyes never left my face.

At my back, Lislee and the few remaining soldiers fanned out around me.

With one hand and without breaking eye contact, the woman snapped out a wrist. And it went directly through a fleeing human's chest.

Bile stung the back of my throat, but I forced it down. I didn't allow my knees to shake or my grip to falter.

"Who are *you*?" I snapped.

A haughty smile split her lips. "I am Vaneiare," she sang.

"Perhaps I should have phrased that differently. *What* are you?"

The burning stares of my backup pleaded with me not to provoke her, but there was an unfamiliar power rippling off her. Her otherworldly beauty only magnified with each step she took, luring each of us to put our hearts within reach.

"Oh, but you'd love to know," she purred. "I know who you are, though."

"Do you?" I asked, grip tightening.

Vaneiare gestured to the bodies around her. "I found them first. Had to check they weren't who I sought." Her eyes swept up my frame, pausing over my shoulders. "That nothing has been done. Then, I was allowed to have my fun."

What did any of that mean? *What* had not been done?

She floated closer. I only needed one good throw to disarm her.

Before I could take it, the man to my right lunged. A blade sailed past the woman's torso as if it had been aimed for her gut, but she shifted imperceptibly at the last minute. In response, she only smiled, and the knife clattered to the earth behind her.

Then, she snapped a hand out.

"No!" I screamed.

But it was too late.

His heart was in her hand, like she'd tricked him into stepping just an inch too close with that throw.

"Lislee, go!" I demanded.

"No," the commander swore.

"You," the woman cooed as if nothing had just happened, "are the human friend of the seraph girl."

She prowled forward. Morbid curiosity burned in her stare, and I was forced to step back, back, back, until my heel met the border of hay.

I have seven blades on my person.

She prowled closer. "We have been tracking you all."

I will not go down until each is coated with her blood.

"All the seraph's little followers," she added, and though it unsettled me, I showed no sign of weakness. "We remember who was there. Who she may try to turn."

She was almost within arm's reach now. Instead of lobbing a knife at her, I lunged, slicing down.

The surprise worked in my favor, but I only scratched across her collarbone before she tossed me aside. I rolled across blood-stained dirt, biting my lip at the impact. Iron coated my mouth.

The woman pressed down on me. As I crawled backward toward the center of the ring, I kicked out, the heel of my boot striking her shin. She grimaced but stalked closer.

I crouched, keeping my knives up and my stare on her hands. Flicking my wrist, I sent one at her. She didn't move quickly enough this time. It sank squarely into her palm, piercing right through the flesh.

But it didn't stop her. The blood pooling around the blade only seemed to be an encouragement.

My heart thundered in my ears, nearly drowning out her words. "They will be thrilled to hear—"

But the taunt ended in a growl as a broad hand wrapped around her face, fingers curving into her jaw. The woman roared, her teeth shifting into points. They sliced into the palm of the male holding her, but his grip did not relent.

With her bloodied hand, she gripped his face, her own blood smearing across his lips, flesh slicing further on his canines.

And with strength unlike anything I'd ever seen—unlike anything I'd thought possible even of the Hunter himself—he ripped the woman's head from her body before she could kill me. A chord was struck in my chest, like my lungs were a harp being played.

The woman's songs faded in the wind, and Lancaster tossed her body aside like a used doll, the white of her gown finally staining red.

"Santorina," he said, almost sounding relieved as he knelt beside me. "I am sorry it took me so long. There were children trying to get away."

The annoyance in his voice nearly made me laugh.

"I'm fine," I assured him, sitting upright. I dusted off my hands, taking stock of my body to assure I wasn't in shock and neglecting any wounds.

When everything seemed okay, I lifted my gaze to Lancaster's.

There was something burning behind his endless eyes, but before I could question it, they slipped closed.

And the string humming in my chest went still as Lancaster toppled to the dirt.

CHAPTER THIRTY-THREE
OPHELIA

"Damien said seraphs, like Angels now that they have their spirits back, feel every emotion to an extreme," I explained as Tolek and I prepared to meet with everyone.

Tol tilted his head at me, fascination igniting his chocolate eyes. "How do you feel right now?"

Setting down the letter I'd been rereading from Jezebel assuring me she was okay, I rose off the bed, slid a leather halter top over my head, and lifted my eyes to his—

Molten need was splashed across his features as he studied me —as he studied my wings, ruffling at my back. Even just his stare tracing across the rounded feather tops had my core heating. Seraph magic budded in my palms, whirling and excited.

Desire dried out my throat, tightening my voice and every inch of my body with it. The spot between my legs throbbed, and I released a shaky breath.

Tolek laughed. "Oh, I think I like enhanced emotions on you, Alabath."

He strode across the room, so put together in his deep indigo tunic—the ties purposefully unlaced—leather pants, and boots. His gleaming silver sword was strapped across his back, and the Vincienzo dagger was slung on his belt.

But the most dangerous weapon Tolek wore was his sinful smirk as he gripped my hips and spun me around. In the weeks we'd been apart, Tolek had changed. This rage-fueled, grief-stricken part of him came undone, and it unleashed a raw, pure strength in every step. One that could cleave apart the world with barely a blink if he so wished.

And I *hungered* for it.

It sang to the power within me, the two stirring and melding.

Tolek had always been his own kind of magic. So open, so giving. It was like it left room within his spirit to absorb whatever overwhelming emotions and power clung to the air around us. Where I created Angellight, he channeled every last drop. And together, we could scorch.

Deftly, his fingers clasped the buckles of my top, and every brush of his skin against mine was so poignant. Tol dropped a single kiss to the curve of my wing—as I had traced the glorious golden pair inked across his back all night—and heat pooled within me.

Tol's hand skated around my waist to cup between my legs, and he murmured, "This is going to be fun."

Then, he stepped back, leaving every inch of me empty and cold, and frustration roared up in its place.

"You forget that the bad emotions are amplified, too," I growled, storming to the door.

He gripped my wrist before I could leave.

"One more thing," he said seriously, turning me to face him and digging in his pocket. He removed a gold chain with—

My breath caught in my throat.

"Angelborn?" I whispered. The shard from my spear shone in the light—the one that had been Damien's emblem, used to free him from the Stone Realm. "How did you get it?"

"On one of my flights to the mountains, I made a detour." Tolek clasped it around my neck, his fingers tracing the cool chip of metal where it fell against my chest. Then, he opened the drawer in the nightstand. "I got these as well."

A glimmering blue jewel and scrap of leather that was once part of a grip sat in the palm of his hand. The only pieces of Starfire that survived Ritalia. My heart splintered at the sight, at the fact that this man had gone back to that place—back to where his sister had died—to retrieve these for me.

"Happy birthday, Ophelia," he whispered, bending to kiss me softly. "I'm sorry it's late."

"Thank you," I barely forced out.

I didn't mention the letters I'd found in his suite in Damenal, but even from afar, Tolek was the reason I survived that place. Survived the venom of a god. *Thank you* would never be enough for him, but before I could find the words, he opened the door and nudged me into the hall.

His guidance confirmed there was no need to say more.

Sunlight streaked the tiled floors through the wall of windows, thick clouds forming along the horizon. Those were Echnid's clouds, I was certain of it. His presence was everywhere, unspooling across Gallantia and spilling that slime-coated sensation in my veins. I scratched at the Curse mark on my wrist—the one Echnid had rooted his influence in. It was empty now. No more than an ordinary scar. But it still reminded me of him.

As if understanding, Tolek switched to my other side, blocking the windows from view.

"If the Angels feel everything so extremely, why did they never react to any of the harm they did?" Tol asked.

"Their Spirits were separated from their angelic forms when they were trapped in that Stone Realm," I explained. "Damien didn't feel *anything*—not fully—until they were freed."

How did that change them? To exist so long like an empty vessel, only recollections of memories like drifting breezes against your skin.

"That makes me feel a little bad for the fuckers," Tolek said.

"Me, too," I sighed. "Despite my better judgment after all they've taken from us."

He only exhaled, nodding, and when I looked up, his eyes were wandering. It was clear he was trying not to think of it, but his silence bit at my spirit.

I pulled him to a stop to face me. "Lyria will always be with us," I swore to him, taking both of his hands within my own. "She is here every day, just as my father is, and she is so proud of who you are becoming, Tolek."

His forehead dropped to mine. "I know, *apeagna*," he sighed, brushing my hair behind my ear. His voice was gravelly as he added, "But I'm not done getting my revenge."

"Good," I agreed with a smirk. "Because neither am I. Now, let's go start."

~

THE MEETING CHAMBER in Xenovia's capitol building was ready for war as we filed in. Tolek and me, Cypherion, Erista, Meridat, and a number of Soulguider advisors, including Erista's twin, older brother, and father. We were only waiting for Malakai, Mila, and Mora.

"The necklace from our trove turned out to be exemplary, didn't it?" Erista's father asked smugly when we got to speaking of how the final emblem had been found within the Gates of Angeldust.

"Father." Erista sighed, rubbing her forehead as if to alleviate an ache sprouting there. Her brother—the Soulguider general, Quilian—shook his head, exchanging a glance with the twins.

"I only think it's extraordinary!" their father gushed, his short, black beard bristling with his surprise. "We kept it safe all these years."

From what Erista had mentioned over the months, her father was a very proud man with a specific interest in wealth and their family trove. That much was obvious from the elaborate jewels adorning his body. But he seemed harmless beyond that.

"Yes, we are certainly grateful that piece called to Erista," I said. "It was meant to be." I gripped my own necklace, the shard of Angelborn lifeless now that the Angelcurse was fulfilled. A part of me preferred it that way.

Shaking my head, I leaned forward in my chair. Meridat had given me one with low arms and a narrow back to accommodate my wings, and the sensitive feathers shivered as they brushed the velvet lining.

"We have more important things to discuss now, though," I said, and every head turned toward me, a respectful silence falling over the room. I nodded at Meridat.

"This letter arrived from Santorina." The chancellor placed the wrinkled parchment on the table. I'd already read it, my heart sinking to my stomach. "She describes an attack on the human camp this morning that left Lancaster injured."

A harsh breeze swept through the room as Mora sped in. "Is he all right?" she asked, frenzied and taking the note from the chancellor. There wasn't a hint of the controlled female she typically displayed. Her long brown curls were a mess, dark circles beneath her eyes.

Malakai and Mila came tearing through the door a moment later. "Fucking Spirits, you're quick," Malakai panted.

"I heard my brother's name," Mora muttered, her face ashen as she handed them the letter.

"Where have you guys been?" Cypherion asked. He'd been jittery all day, Tol and I having to repeat things a few times to get his attention.

"And have you slept at all?" Tolek added, looking over their rumpled clothing and tired eyes.

"Are Rina and Lancaster okay?" Erista demanded, gesturing at the letter. The energy in the room rippled with everyone's assorted anxiety.

"Let's all sit down," I directed as the tightness overwhelmed my chest. These damn seraph emotions. Light pushed at my skin in frustration, and I directed the seraph power to concentrate around my wings as I'd seen the Angels do. Gold shimmered across the feathers, peeling off the heightened energy little by little so I could focus.

I held my hand out to take the note back from Malakai as he, Mila, and Mora found seats, a thick book in his hand.

"Lancaster is injured, and Rina is taking care of him," I said, handing the note to Tol who had yet to read it. I held Mora's stare, trying to reassure her as concern for her brother bled across the table between us. "Between her care and his internal healing magic, he should be just fine. That's not necessarily the concerning part, though."

"This was another one of those mistresses of the fucking god, wasn't it?" Tolek growled, doing his best not to crumble Rina's letter.

"I believe so," I said, blowing out a defeated breath and turning to Malakai. "Right?"

His eyes weren't flooded with the panic I expected, though. No, the forest green shone as he said, "We've figured something out about them."

Tolek leaned forward. "Don't hold back, brother."

"Yesterday," Mila began, "Malakai and I were near the streams out beyond Xenovia, and we saw one of those women."

"Where exactly?" Meridat asked, her warriors tensing.

"She wasn't near the city when we saw her, but she was coming from that direction," Malakai explained. "She was roaming, speaking to herself, but we lost her when..."

He looked at Mila, and the general swallowed. "One of my visions showed her to me, with leather wings, fangs, and red eyes. And another child at her breast." The air in the room went taut. "We know that Echnid brought them here, and I think I was seeing them in their original realm, but the purpose"—she exchanged a glance with Malakai, who nodded in encouragement—"has to do with you creating seraphs."

My stomach turned over at just the thought. I braced my hands against the table as my magic riled, shaking my head. Tolek's palm brushed down my spine. "That makes sense," I forced out. "Rina said the one that attacked them was looking for her specifically to make sure something had or *hadn't* been done."

So, Echnid thought I'd continue his experiments once I escaped. Why?

"There's more," Malakai said.

"There always is," Tolek muttered, eyes locked on me.

"Based on what Mila saw of them in whatever fucking realm that was, we think Echnid wants to procreate with them." Silence crashed through the room at Malakai's words. "He wants an army of demigods."

"What?" I gasped. "But...why?"

"It means a few things," Mora spoke up, recovering her previous panic now that we were discussing her myths. "First, I believe we know what happened to Mila in the Spirit River." She faced Meridat. "Have you ever met a Reflector of a Realm, Chancellor?"

Meridat's full lips parted, her head shaking. "No. I thought their lines died out long ago."

"What are they?" Tolek asked.

Erista leaned across the table. "They were similar to Storytellers, but a branch touched by Artale's magic, whereas Storytellers are of Thallia and Moirenna. Instead of speaking historical facts, they saw visions of other realms. Legends say it was a connection built through the waters in the Spirit River, a gift from the Goddess of Death to view windows to Spirits, since it is believed there is only one Spirit Realm between all worlds."

The power of that had my jaw dropping open. Mila was not a Storyteller, though I wouldn't mind the chance to speak to Aimee right now. She was not a Realmspinner, either, able to open the bridges between worlds, but she could detect creatures made of different ones—see them in their own worlds. A Reflector of a Realm.

"And when I absorbed that water, I somehow became one," Mila said confidently. Malakai's arm wrapped protectively around her, and I had a feeling the general was pretending to be much more comfortable with this news than she truly was. "I saw the realm the women came from, saw their true forms and their threats. It's why I kept seeing them baring children."

"Fucking Spirits," Tolek cursed.

"That's what I said," Malakai agreed, face solemn. Behind the table, Cypherion paced the room as we took this in, his strides agitating my own magic.

Mora was not as shocked as the rest of us. She held a hand out for Malakai to give her the book and turned to a marked page with the very creature Mila described portrayed in faded ink. "The women trailing after the god are gorgons."

"Gorgons?" I echoed, reading the notes scrawled around the

painting. Spirits, I'd never even heard of these things, in any story or legend.

"Yes," Mora went on. "Gorgons are creatures that have not been seen in this realm for a very, *very* long time. Much longer than even I have been alive, but like the pegasus and khrysaor, there are still mentions of them in the legends if you know where to look."

"And how do you know?" Erista's father asked.

"I am very old. I've had plenty of time to read," Mora said flatly. When no one argued she continued, "Gorgons have two forms—their beautiful humanoid form, and their demonic one. The second is excessively dangerous because they are able to turn someone to stone with a single glance and their blood is poisonous —lethal in that form, but merely venomous in their human one." Her lips pressed into a line. She cleared her throat. "Based on Santorina's account, that venom is what my brother ingested. He should be fine in a few days, once his body purges it. He's fortunate nothing worse happened. But these women are known for their fertility rituals and beliefs. There are countless tales of higher powers mating with them to produce powerful offspring who can take form as full-grown adults if the right magic is employed."

Spirits, it was all there once we knew where to look. I sat back in my chair, absorbing everything she'd said. The sense of a looming tidal wave hovered over me—like it was slowly curling up, ready to crack.

A vengeful god, seven ruthless Angels, and now a growing army of foot soldiers with poisonous blood and no remorse.

"Thank the Spirits Lancaster killed it," Tolek said, breaking the silence.

"He did?" Mora blinked wide eyed, flipping through her book again. "How? They are typically *very* difficult to slay, according to legends. Their weapons are made of a metal they're infallible against, but that will slay their enemies on impact." That explains the poisonous arrow shot at Jezebel. "And the gorgons themselves only have a few weaknesses—none of which I'm sure we can find in this realm."

"Your brother found the most natural way," Cypherion commented absently as he paced.

"Rina said he ripped the woman's head from her body when it attacked her," Tolek embellished, nodding at a second letter from Rina we'd received with more detail. He dragged a hand through his hair. "It sounds impressive."

"He...interesting," Mora commented with a smug smirk, but she didn't elaborate.

My mind was still stuck on one thought. One that hardened into a lump of guilt in my stomach more by the second and my light fading into my skin. It made my limbs heavy and chest impossible to breathe through as Meridat's advisors continued to lobby questions at the fae female, and the chancellor sent a few of them off to set up a patrol around Xenovia. These creatures—gorgons—were *myths*. Not supposed to exist in this world, and yet...

"Did I—" I swallowed, the room falling silent at the waver in my voice. "Are they here because I somehow raised them?"

"I do not believe so. Not exactly," Mora clarified, and the guilt dissipated a touch. "In legendary battles, gorgons were sometimes described as serpentine beasts of prey that countered the Guardians."

"Seraphs," I breathed, my wings tensing.

Mora nodded. "My theory is that the Balance allowed Echnid to bring them from another realm because a seraph has returned—a seraph with the power of seven Angels—despite the fact that Ambrisk is meant to be cut off from most bridges."

The Balance. The loopholes that ensured equilibrium among Ambrisk and all other realms. Spirits, where was it now to save us? My palms tingled with Angellight—seraph magic—and the tattoo beneath my arm beat.

"Xenique's library in the city center has been helpful. That's where Malakai, Mila, and I have been all night," Mora explained, curling up the corners of the pages. "The demigoddess seemed to have an affinity for her kind, and since gorgons are known to procreate with gods, we were able to dig. They are seen as a weapon of female power." She added that last part with an almost pleased tone.

I shook my head, staring down at the faded drawing. The light streaming through the wicker shades cut it at an odd angle that emphasized the snakes atop her head, making her hauntingly beautiful. "Yes, well we have powerful enough females in this realm. We have no need of them."

Cypherion, finally stilling, crossed his arms. Agitation unlike anything I'd seen since we got Vale back rippled off him. "So, these things are just *traipsing* around Gallantia? In every territory?"

"It appears so," I muttered, and I knew precisely who Cyph was worrying about when he huffed and resumed his pacing.

"I saw their demon forms when we were in the ballroom," Malakai said to me. When Echnid made me burn him. I swallowed, and Tol gripped my knee. "They were almost shifting. I thought I was hallucinating." A mix of relief that he wasn't and fear of the truth sank over his frame as he leaned back against his chair, brushing his thumb over the scar on his jaw.

"They lure in their prey with their beauty then shift," Mora said without looking up. "They were likely prepared to feed off your pain and strike if Echnid allowed it."

The cruelty of that threat turned the air to lead. They'd been so close, and we'd been so vulnerable.

I intervened, "There are six more out there that we know of, and they may have powers beyond what Mora has found. We have to remain vigilant, and we should write to city leaders and assure they know."

Meridat's advisor raced to the writing desk at the back wall to do just that.

Tolek exhaled, sinking back in his chair. "Did Valyrie return when I was gone?"

"Valyrie was here?" I asked, exchanging a glance with Malakai.

They recounted the Starsearcher Angel's initial visit. Her plea for action.

"If Valyrie is trustworthy, then Xenique must be, too," I muttered.

Meridat asked, "How are you certain?"

"Something Damien said. The Angels all have protection over their capital. One can't enter without the blessing of the Prime. If Valyrie was able to visit you here..."

"Then at least two Angels are secretly working *against*

Echnid's wishes," Meridat finished, beaming at the confirmation of her own Angel's loyalties.

It made sense if Valyrie and Xenique were partnered against the Warrior God. Their clans both had ties to their own deities. If Echnid succeeded in his plan to dismiss the gods, they would suffer.

"The question is," I began, "which others can we trust?"

"And what are their true motives?" Tolek added.

We spent the remainder of the meeting discussing gorgons, Echnid's in particular, and how we could combat them. Mila and Malakai agreed to take point with Mora on that front. Malakai's forest eyes shone with determination when we finally adjourned the meeting, a need for revenge for all that was done to him burning there.

Before Mora could sneak out, I grabbed her hand. "He'll be okay," I assured her. "Jezebel was."

Though I hated to think about Jezzie fighting off a gorgon, she had survived, and if she could, I was sure Lancaster would as well. But that didn't alleviate the desperate worry Mora was certainly feeling right now. There was a responsibility we felt toward our siblings. If they hurt, we hurt for them.

The female nodded, her brown eyes warm with gratitude and a spark I didn't understand. "Based on Santorina's letters, I believe he will be." She squeezed my hand. "Thank you, Revered."

As everyone left, Tolek whispered, "It's so fucking good to see you here again." I slumped back against the chair. He leaned over, one hand on either arm, caging me in. "To see you ruling."

I was beginning to feel more myself, too. I wasn't broken, but I was different, and I was settling into the new wounds on my spirit.

Tolek kissed my shoulder, my wings ruffling, and he laughed against my collarbone.

A throat cleared behind him, and as Tol groaned, I leaned around him, laughing. But all humor faded when I saw Cypherion's tight expression. "Cyph?"

"I need to talk to you."

Chapter Thirty-Four
Vale

"How many do we have now?" I asked, fingering the triple blade's impeccable steel, it's opalescent sheen glinting in the sun filtering through the skylight. The sharp peal of pickaxes against the eastern wall filled the seeing chamber. We were almost through what we were able to salvage in this room.

"Hundreds. And swords, spears, and arrows as you suggested," Harlen confirmed with a boyish grin. It reminded me so much of long summer nights spent on a balcony in the Lumin temple, playing games and counting stars long after curfew because that was the time we were unwatched.

Two children, unburdened by warfare, blissfully unaware of the pain in their futures as they fought the torment of their present. Little hands that had never held real weapons—weren't trained to be them ourselves, yet.

I set the blade down, rolling my shoulders back at the hint of melancholy the memories dragged up.

"Send them south with the foot soldiers heading to Xenovia," I said. "When will they leave?"

Cyren answered, "They'll be ready in a day or two. The final counts of imbued weaponry is the last thing they're waiting on to move the first legion."

"I'll fly back tonight now that the healers cleared me," Jezebel added. "I've written what's safe to share to Erista and Ophelia, but I'll deliver the full report once I return."

The thought of her soaring over open land again lodged a knot of worry in my throat, but Jezebel was eager to get back to the desert. I guessed it had something to do with the way her eyes lit with yearning every time Erista was mentioned—recent events having given her a new perspective—and the fact that her sister had returned.

"You'll fly high?" I asked, and Jezebel nodded.

"That should keep her out of range of an attack, should that woman return," Cyren confirmed. Then, from within the fold of their midnight-blue cloak, the general pulled out the onyx arrow that had sliced through Jezebel's arm. "Though, it will be important to remain vigilant. If the letter we received from Ophelia yesterday is right and one of them attacked Santorina, they clearly have little care for life."

They hadn't given us specifics about the monstrous women in case letters fell into the wrong hands, but the message was clear. *Be careful*. Nerves curled in my stomach.

"It would make sense why my magic reacted," Jezebel said, scowling at the arrow. "The thing and it's poison was a myth."

As we discussed it further, a clatter of hurried footsteps pounded through the manor outside the chamber. I whirled, reaching for a blade, but my favorite person on Ambrisk sped through the door.

"*Cypherion?*" I gasped, rushing toward him.

He caught me, arms banded tight around my waist and face buried in my hair as he spun me around. The warmth of his body seeped into me, unknotting the tension of weapon counts and marching armies and unsettled gods that had riled my bones. Bergamot and sage sank into their place, lacing through me and pulling tight to stitch my will back together.

"Hey, Stargirl." He sighed against my shoulder, pressing a kiss gently to the spot where my silver tattoo glimmered.

Cypherion set me on my feet, and I cupped his cheek, studying him. His hair was wind swept and cheeks pink as if he'd flown here.

Fates, I'd missed him. We'd written every day and had discussed our disagreement over rescuing Ophelia and Malakai, but despite the letters, a piece of me worried I wouldn't see him again to officially resolve the differences that—in the grand scheme of looming threats—were inconsequential.

"What are you doing here?" I asked.

Cypherion kissed my palm. "I had to see you." His deep blue eyes searched me frantically, ensuring I was all right. "The woman that attacked you—the gorgons—they're all over the continent. Going after those close to Ophelia. After Santorina and Jezebel...I need to be where you are."

My chest squeezed to the point of bursting at the love bubbling beneath that frenzy. "But you're Ophelia's Second," I said.

Even if we disagreed, I was endlessly proud of him for the work he was doing to protect his clan. I'd never ask him to sacrifice it simply because I felt more comfortable with him by my side.

"Ophelia is back and feeling up to meetings. I can help from here." He brushed a thumb across my cheekbone, catching a tear I hadn't realized was falling. The utter relief that splintered through me to see him, to breathe him in, took over. "I'm doing that job because I accepted it, and maybe some days I like it, but I never cared about the title. *You* are what matters, Vale. You will *always* come first."

Pressing onto my toes, I leaned in and kissed him. With his lips against mine, those splinters cracked the surface of all my worries.

A throat cleared behind us, and Cypherion looked up, eyes flaring wide. Then, with one hand locked in mine like he'd never let go, he strode to Jezebel.

He sighed as he hugged her. "You really scared us."

Jezebel waved him off. "I'm clearly fine. But more importantly, what are gorgons?"

"I'd like to know that, too," Harlen said, giving Cypherion a nod as the Starsearcher slipped his hands into his pockets and our group moved out of the way of the crew tearing down the walls.

Cypherion dropped his voice below the construction noise and explained everything they'd discovered back in Xenovia. The entire time he spoke, he kept his fingers wound through mine, his thumb brushing over my knuckles. And while terror at the details of Echnid's schemes turned my blood to ice, I couldn't deny the warmth his touch speared through me.

"While I'm here," Cypherion said, turning to me with a squeeze of my hand, "I'd like to make this official."

My brows lifted with a disbelieving laugh. "Are we not already?"

"Official in *every* way, Stargirl."

His step toward me thundered through my bones with the force of the hammers ringing on steel in this very chamber—and my body heated like the forge.

"What do you mean?" I asked.

Cypherion brushed my hair over my shoulder, gently massaging the place my silver tattoo was inked no longer bonding me to Titus. He watched it as he said, "The Bind Vale. If this turns into an all-out war among gods, I want to face it knowing I have every claim to you I can—at every soul bound level. You're my future, Vale, and I want even the gods to know that."

I inhaled sharply, and his eyes locked on mine.

"We can start with the Starsearcher ceremony and vows while we're here," he explained. "Then, when we return to Mystique Territory, we can receive the Bind, too."

"We don't even know—"

"I've looked it up," he assured me, eyes gleaming eagerly. "We can receive both clans' promises. Children will have to choose allegiance to one when they receive their Fate ties or attempt the Undertaking, but we are able to bond under both."

"Children?" I asked mockingly, my throat thick.

Cypherion's eyes heated. "I plan to have many with you, Stargirl." He dropped his voice. "We'll have a good time making them, too."

I laughed, my core aching at the rough tone to his words—at the implications and promises.

Cypherion came all this way during a looming threat of godly warfare because he wanted to bind himself to my soul. To seek approval of the Fates and Angels to be *mine*, and make me his in return, so we may face the god's threat as unified as possible.

When I still didn't have the words to answer, he said, "If you don't want the Bind, that's okay. But I'd like to take the Starsearcher vows with you. Here. A fresh start in Valyn after everything you went through." He paused, then rushed to add, "If you aren't comfortable, though, we can do this *anywhere* else. I just want all of Ambrisk—the Angels, Spirits, Fates, gods...everyone—I want them all to know we belong to each other. If that's what you want, too."

If it's what I want.

For months now, I'd longed to truly explore Valyn. My entire life, I'd yearned to feel known. Now, a man who saw me down to my spirit stood here, asking me to be his in the highest way possible, but also offering me the option to claim him however *I'd* like. To weave our love into the magic of this city, a way to seal it as mine.

I bit my lip, the echoes of clanging metal still ringing around us like nothing had interrupted. But my heart fluttered under Cypherion's patient stare. I turned to Harlen and Cyren, their whispers with Jezebel immediately slicing off.

"How long would it take to arrange a bonding ceremony?"

CHAPTER THIRTY-FIVE
CYPHERION

Apparently, Harlen and Cyren were able to use their significant connections to arrange said ceremony in only a few hours. We were in a small, secluded temple in Valyn's Ninth District. I still didn't know the purpose of the different districts, but I'd specifically pulled Harlen aside to ensure the ceremony wouldn't take place in the temple above the archives.

"I don't really care what I wear, Jezebel, and I don't think Vale will either," I said as she fluttered around me, straightening the silver-lined lapels of my jacket.

"I care, and I was shot with a poisoned arrow, so appease me," she retorted.

My attention dropped to the puckered scar on her arm, visible since she'd changed into a flowing lavender gown with a thin silver cape pinned to the dainty straps on her shoulders. The wound was healed—she was fine—but it had my fist's clenching with the stark reminder of the threats mounting beyond these walls. Of why I'd raced here in the first place, urging Sapphire to fly at her fastest pace.

"Fine," I agreed. "But are the cuff links necessary?" I grumbled as she fastened on tiny diamond clusters that looked like a constellation. In the candlelight flickering from every available surface around the small alter at the rounded front of the temple, they sparkled.

"What a ridiculous question," Jezebel mocked, shaking her head. "Cuff links are always necessary. They tie together the entire night."

I shrugged, not knowing what she meant by that.

With the glinting accessory unnecessarily in place, Jezebel stepped back to admire her work. "Perfect!" She beamed, scurrying around me to grab my scythe.

When I'd arrived, Cyren and the priestess who would conduct the ceremony had explained it was tradition to carry weapons in the Starsearcher commitment ceremony. I was grateful they allowed me to keep my weapon of choice rather than donning a Starsearcher one. It was comfortable, and I was entirely out of my depth here. Not with Vale—cursed Spirits, I was sure of her. But with the finery. The life vows beneath celestial beings. I'd never witnessed anything like it.

As she helped me lay my scythe perfectly across my back, Jezebel said, "I think this ritual is a wonderful idea, but have you considered that some people may be a bit sad they aren't here?"

I only grunted in response. The guilt *had* been weighing on me, but Vale was my priority. She was all I'd been able to think about—even more so than usual. Like every thought in my mind was wiped clean except for those about her, demanding more and more attention as the day wore on and the stars came to life.

Like they were calling me to her.

"Tolek is going to be furious," Jezebel added, flicking a speck of dust from my shoulder.

"He'll get over it," I said.

Jezebel leveled me with a stare.

"I'll allow him to throw us a party once this is all over," I conceded, and her eyes lit up at that, too. *"Fucking Spirits."* They were going to be way too extravagant. A part of me hated it, but a larger part refused to crush their joy. A party would be fine.

I let it go, drifting to the head of the aisle to study the mural of Fates entwined, two white and silver blurs of starfire tangled around each other above where the priestess and Cyren muttered quietly. But then the door to the temple creaked open. And when I turned, I forgot how to breathe, my heart ringing in my ears.

"Holy cursed Spirits," I whispered.

"You won't complain about my outfit choices now," Jezebel teased as she took her position behind me.

"I certainly won't," I agreed, still breathless as Vale walked down the aisle toward me.

And my Stargirl looked like one of those Fates herself. The dress hugged every inch of her body but still moved like moonlit water, flaring over her hips and trailing beyond her. The sleeves wrapped tightly to her wrists, the material sheer along her arms and toward the bottom of the skirt.

With glittering gems crusting it, it almost reminded me of the dress Titus had forced Vale to wear the night I left her in Valyn. But it was different—sharper and more lethal with its design. Cut for the woman she'd forged and the strength she'd honed.

And complete with Harlen escorting her to me, it was almost as if she was saying goodbye to a girl who used to be and crossing the threshold into who she was meant to become. A Fatecatcher, whatever fortune that may be, and the woman cementing my future with every step.

When she met me, I laced my fingers through hers. "You look..." I shook my head, chest physically aching at how beautiful she was. "There aren't words, Vale. But you look like everything I want to see every day for the rest of my life."

Everything I would die for, everything I needed. The stars kept pushing me toward her.

Vale ducked her head, cheeks flushing, and the pins holding back the front pieces of her hair glittered. They were tiny constellations, twins to my cuff links.

I cast Jezebel an appreciative nod, catching the tears glimmering in her eyes. Pride shone among them.

The priestess took her place before us, Cyren and Harlen standing behind Vale as witnesses, but I barely even heard a word anyone said. All I could focus on was Vale. My heart beat in the damn rhythm of her name as moonlight dripped through the open skylight, a beacon over her.

As the priestess finished the opening rite and turned away, her navy robes swishing against the ground, she explained, "Now we'll light lavender for love, protection, and happiness. Lemon verbena for unity, and sage for wisdom in the long life the Fates will give you together."

With each explanation, the priestess ignited a stick of incense, the mingling scents filling the air with aromatic clouds. Quickly, they turned dense, obscuring the rest of the room until it was only Vale and me beneath the moon and star light. Each added scent pulled at something within me, my chest pounding, and it took every ounce of strength I had not to kiss Vale.

I didn't know the Fates, but it felt like they were telling me to.

"Please recite the Warrior's Words," the priestess instructed, her voice melodic through the haze. We both did, echoing the promise members of any clan made when they swore their lives to another. "And now your personal vows," she said as she continued to light candles in a ceremonious order I didn't know.

Vows.

I'd made Vale so many promises in the near year we'd known each other. Some to hate her forever that were now blown to dust, some to protect and cherish her. And I'd keep all of those last ones, but what I said tonight—these were different.

I wanted to speak to her spirit in a way no one else could.

"Vale," I began. Fuck, my palms were sweaty. No way I was letting hers go, though. I cleared my throat, listening to that urge to take a step closer. Something in my blood calmed as I did, and I was able to speak. "You've fought for me in so many ways—a lot of ways I didn't deserve—and I promise to always fight for you. To never cage you, but to encourage you to soar in any way you can. To be a home when you were robbed of one for so long, and to follow you wherever you need that reassurance." Tears shone along her lashes, and even my voice was thick, but I had to force out the rest. "I vow to be the blade at your back when you turn toward the stars, your partner in every way. And I promise on the Fates to take you to your hot springs every year so you can see the constellations in your favorite place."

She laughed softly at that last part, but starfire burned in her eyes, and I knew she heard the intimate promise beneath those words. The memory of how we'd reunited in that place and the oath to never allow that passion to die.

"Cypherion," she began. Always my full name. Spirits, I loved it. "I promise when we are apart to always look for you in the stars, and when we are together to be your home. I promise to support you when you need to believe in yourself and to fight the Fates for you every day. To chart our path with love and warmth, with beauty and fortune. I love you, Cypherion Kastroff, and I vow to make sure you feel it every day."

"I love you, Stargirl," I answered, squeezing her hands. "Us against the Fates."

Every word on her lips was tempting. Kissing her was no longer a want—it was a need. A desperation to taste what she spoke and seal the promises in the way we did best.

Something nudged me a step closer, my blood thrumming under the press of magic in the room.

"Now is when a joint reading would typically be done," the priestess explained, "but with unions across clans, the Starsearcher conducts the session for the two of you, asking a blessing of the Fate they are tied to."

Lifting our entwined hands, I kissed the back of Vale's to tell her to go on. Spirits, she was so beautiful as she closed her eyes and slipped into her reading, that dress cinching to her body like it was painted on, her lashes dark against her cheeks, and her lips parted.

The scent of lemon turned heavier on the air. *Lemon verbena for unity*, the priestess had explained. To bring me closer to Vale as she conducted the most sacred piece of this ritual.

Vale squeezed my hands, her brow furrowing, and I squeezed back.

And then, something flashed in the haze around us, and my pulse pounded.

"What was that?" I gasped.

"Shh," Vale cooed.

I focused again, willing it to return because I swore—

"Holy cursed Spirits," I barely breathed.

It was hints of her vision. There and gone in a blink, but a glimpse at whatever fortune the Fates were bestowing on her.

For us.

A flash of an auburn-haired little girl smiling up at us. A night beneath the hot springs with snow covering the rocks. A montage of holidays and storytelling beside fires with plenty of family and *pure joy* radiating through every breath.

I didn't have a childhood like that, but fucking Spirits, I wanted that life. Desperately. I clung tighter to Vale's hands as if it would pull that future into existence. She was magnificent, power radiating off her with a palpable thrum. I could have stood like that forever, watching Vale dive into her magic, searching for hints of it around us. I was so enthralled, I didn't realize at first how everything shifted to a silver glow.

Vale gasped, her shoulders hiking up and eyes roving beneath her lids. Panic ratcheted up, vines lacing between my ribs.

"What's happening?" I asked, stepping closer.

Overhead, the stars shone brighter, a spotlight burning down on us.

Beyond the star-streaked fog, Harlen muttered, "I don't believe it."

"What?" I growled. Vale still wasn't answering, but a calm had softened her features. A tear streaked down her cheek, the path carving right into my heart.

But it was Harlen who answered with awe, "You're Fatesworn."

"What?" Jezebel asked.

Vale's voice flashed back to me as I gripped her hands tighter. From a small room above an apothecary shop in this very city, when she'd first explained the Starsearcher commitment ceremony to me.

"We exchange vows in a ceremony," she said. "Incense is burned, a joint reading done. Then, and only if the Fates deem it appropriate, some searchers receive commitment tattoos. Become Fatesworn. But I've never seen it done."

"The Fates have to give permission?"

"They don't choose whom you end up with—except in rare legends—and if they don't approve, you do not have to heed their

warnings for the first part of the ritual, but you can't receive any tattoos without that recognition."

"The Bind is all about choice, not permission."

She shrugged. "They're both beautiful in their own way. One about freedom, one about a promise of the stars."

"It means," I said, my chest tight—with nerves and anticipation and pure, undiluted disbelief, "the Fates chose us for one another."

Eons ago, when Ambrisk wasn't even formed and gods were building realms, the stars had promised my spirit to Vale's. That urge that had been pushing me toward her intensified, and I finally understood what it was. My soul was stretching out, encouraged by the Fates, searching for a link to hers. A bond that would be irreversibly and irrevocably sealed. A link welded so permanently, no flame was hot enough to melt it.

Heat spread across my shoulder, skin tingling like needles pressed into it. And as Vale's eyes snapped open, shining with tear-streaked wonder, that was it. If I hadn't already put my entire fucking soul into her hands, I would have with that one look. The Fatesworn bond snapped between us.

She was it. She was mine. My Stargirl.

CHAPTER THIRTY-SIX
VALE

STARLIGHT TUNNELED THROUGH MY VEINS AS Cypherion hurried me into the cozy office off the temple, the sound of his heart pounding heating every inch of my skin from head to toe. The power of becoming Fatesworn and the soul-binding tattoo appearing from the stars amplified my own magic. It cascaded through my body, alighting every sense and nerve. And as Cypherion towered over me, blue eyes deep and hungry, an insatiable need burned between us.

He'd looked at me like that the entire time we'd rushed through the end of the ceremony. Like he wanted to devour me.

And I'd looked at him like I'd let him.

I kicked my shoes off, feet sinking into the soft blue carpet as he backed me toward a worn dark-wood desk. Stars filtered in through the high windows, and every breath in the small space was consumed by him. His scent, merging with mine. His heartbeat, calling to my own. And his soul, dancing along with mine as our new Fatesworn bond burned between us.

Cypherion approached slowly, brushing my hair behind my shoulder.

"Let me see it." His voice was husky and commanding, rolling along my bones and down to my very core. I wanted to strip my clothes off—strip his, too—but I listened, turning, and pulling down one shoulder of my dress.

His fingers brushed across the fresh tattoo, the skin tender beneath his touch. Goose bumps spread across my arms at the contact, every inch of my skin hypersensitive.

Ducking, Cypherion blew a soft breath across my shoulder. I gasped, shuddering as that sensation traveled between my legs. I ached for him, but he moved so reverently, like he wanted to carve every second of tonight into memory.

Magic pulsed incessantly through my veins, only surging stronger now that he and I were bonded. He blew another breath across my skin.

"Cypherion," I whimpered, squeezing my thighs together.

"It's beautiful, Stargirl," he said, tugging me a few feet to the left so I could see our distorted reflection in the window. He spun me, gathering my hair over my shoulder so the tattoo was visible, and every brush of his fingers against my skin set me aflame with starfire.

"*You're* beautiful," he whispered, ducking his head and kissing gently along the fresh silvered ink.

The new tattoo had appeared as the bond was given. Inked by the Fates, it incorporated my old one, a unique array of stars swirling around it. Some large and almost winking, some no more than glittering specks.

"Our own constellation," I muttered, brushing my fingers atop his. "Like our own Fate."

"Rewriting the old one," he agreed, attention lingering on the part of the tattoo that had once held me a captive. This new fortune was rooted in heartbreak and love. Forged with fortitude. The story of a woman used for her magic and the man who showed her freedom. Of their friends and family and future.

Turning away from the window, I looked back up at Cypherion. And with barely a breath, his lips were on mine.

There had always been passion between us. Something burning hot and fierce enough to shatter all that we were, but as Cypherion touched me now, as his hands worked my dress down to my waist and he cupped my breast, tweaking my nipple in a way that made me gasp, we were a blazing inferno. One that could drive me to climax with nothing more than the heat of his hands against my skin and the press of his body as he bore down on me.

"Fates," I gasped as he moved his lips down my neck.

Cypherion groaned, spinning me back toward the window and undoing the rest of the buttons down my back. My dress pooled around my feet, and he guided my attention toward the glass.

"So beautiful," he whispered again, but this time, his other hand traced my jaw. The column of my throat. My collarbone. And he kept my attention on us as that hand traveled lower. As he circled my breasts, lavishing each, then kept going.

"Cypherion," I begged, squirming back against him. His cock was hard against my back, and the need to feel him coursed through me, clawing at my control. This new bond between us *needed* to be satisfied by it.

"Look at us, Vale," he said as he dipped his fingers beneath the waist of my undergarments and teased me. "Look at how good we look together." Lips against my shoulder, he added softly, "Forever."

"Forever—" My words cut off in a gasp as two fingers slipped inside me.

I ground against his hand, one arm flying to his neck to tug his lips to mine.

But Cypherion kept my jaw steady, facing ahead. "I want you to watch," he commanded. "See why I love this so much."

I knotted my fingers in his hair but did as he said. My eyes were glued to the movements of his hand, intensifying the way every little shift felt within me. Glued to the way his body curved around mine, eclipsing and protecting. To the way his stare drank me in, utterly captivated.

At every stroke, the Fatesworn bond burned brighter, as if it liked the slow teasing, too. Cypherion plastered kisses to my neck, my shoulder, the tattoo—and the combination of his mouth, the way his fingers toyed with me, and the sight of *us* in that reflection had me crashing into oblivion.

And I swore, through my ecstasy-driven gaze, pure starfire flamed in the air around us.

My climax roared through me with an utter euphoria unlike

anything I'd ever experienced. It pounded to the beat of Cypherion's heart. The bond sang, a flash of the brightest white and silver completely igniting along the string of tethered souls. Forging into something stronger than iron as it sealed.

Angels, she's fucking beautiful.

I gasped as those words echoed in my mind. *His words* through the threads of our bond. And my magic rioted at it, starfire bursting through me.

As soon as I came down, I turned and jumped on Cypherion, latching my arms and legs around him. He caught me, hands gripping tightly to my ass, and pulled me close.

"Spirits, Stargirl," he panted. "I don't want the first time I fuck you with this bond to be on someone else's desk."

"I don't care," I said as I kissed his neck and unfastened the remaining buttons of his shirt.

When he didn't respond, I ground my hips against him, my center barely brushing the head of his cock, stiff beneath his pants. Cypherion groaned at the slight contact, and the ledge he was close to jumping off of was evident in our burning bond, insistent magic coursing through us both. As I rolled my hips again and shoved his shirt back to lick along his collarbone, nipping gently, I pushed the flood of my Starsearcher magic down the bond so he could feel how desperate it was.

Cypherion's hands tightened on me, and with a hiss, he ground out, "*Fuck it.*"

Then, he was spinning, dropping me on the desk, and ripping off the rest of his clothes. The new silver tattoo, twin to mine, glinted around his shoulder.

Cypherion tugged my soaked undergarments down my legs and tossed them aside, grabbing my hips. In one thrust, I was gasping and begging him for more. My legs locked around his waist, his hands bruisingly tight. Angels, I loved when he was rough. When he knew I could handle every mark on my skin because they were his. When he left them there to remind me who created them, that no one else owned me.

I gripped him tighter to me as I rolled my hips in time to his.

"Kiss me," he said, and I did, but what he should have said was *devour me* because that was what every thrust and stroke felt like.

Harder, I said in my head, aiming for that bond, and Cypherion stiffened for a moment. His eyes widened, and I bit my lip waiting for a response.

Then, as understanding settled, he unleashed himself. He pulled his hips back and snapped forward with merciless effort, hitting so deep inside me I thought we'd morph together as one. With our souls connected, I supposed we were.

How's that, Stargirl? he asked hesitantly, testing the bond.

In response, I bit down on his bottom lip, sucking. *Good.*

Tell me what you want, rang through my mind, and I climbed closer to my climax at the sound of those words, the most intimate thing I'd ever experienced.

More, I begged mentally. "Everything," I said aloud.

"It's yours," he answered both aloud and down the bond. Dropping one hand from my waist, he rubbed tight circles at the apex of my thighs.

I threw my head back as I cried out, feeling like pure starfire, and his chuckle rumbled down our soul bond. He kept up his pace, pushing me closer and closer to the edge. He was almost there, too, his movements more erratic and his cock impossibly hard within me.

A ball of glowing euphoria was building in my chest, heat undulating around my hips and spine.

"Kiss me," I demanded this time. His lips slammed to mine, as rough as his hand on my waist and as delicious as every inch of him.

We came together for the first time since our Fatesworn bond woke, and the ecstasy that crashed through me was brighter than starfire and sweeter than fresh wine. It seared me, Cypherion's slip of soul dancing against mine. The two tangled, sealing with this connection, and I swore I came again just from that caress.

Damaged soul against damaged soul.

Sweat-slicked skin against sweat-slicked skin.

Pounding heart against pounding heart.

I soared through that burst of bliss, and starfire continued to flash, but it didn't stop as I came down.

No, the burning, searing white only glowed brighter and brighter, this new height of power opening the way for something else. And then, thanks to all the magic unlocked and tumbling through my body tonight, a powerful reading slammed into me.

My euphoria was replaced with one that was tainted and rotten. An image solidified within the trails of white fire, so quick I couldn't be sure which Fate was sending them. Long pale hair and a horrifying mist.

Echnid.

He was glowing with a terrible glee, the power ebbing around him in excited pulses. I could practically feel the joy rolling off him.

Along with something else—a beat of desperation from someone I couldn't see, but whom I thought I knew in the back of my mind.

Battles filtered through the light. Tolek and Malakai, swords pointed at each other. Ophelia and Jezebel amid cracking lightning. Cypherion facing down a being with huge powerful wings. Santorina drenched in blood.

Echnid wavered back into view. He was talking, but I couldn't hear him. There was an elation in his expression and a successful gleam in his eye that turned my stomach over.

"*No,*" I gasped.

Because from the images playing out now, it was clear what this reading was warning of. And based on the sharpness of them, it was close to occurring. And then, I was ripped from the session, the white fire incinerating in a burst of shooting stars.

"Stargirl?" a panicked voice asked.

Arms wrapped around me, holding me tight to a sweaty chest. Bergamot and sage. Heated skin. A heartbeat that mirrored my own.

"Breathe with me," Cypherion said, and I mimicked his inhales until I could speak.

"He knows," I forced out, panting. "Echnid knows how to banish the gods. He's about to act."

"WHERE EXACTLY ARE WE GOING?" TOLEK ASKED AS I dragged him through the stone garden behind the guest house, the dunes sprawling beyond. The sun was just setting, the sky a dusky purple and air crisp with promises of the night.

"I had an idea."

Tol's eyes lit up. "My favorite sentence."

He followed me from the walkway around the side of the house, and a pair of wide white wings greeted us.

"Back already, Sapphire?" Tol asked, brows raised.

"Cypherion sent her back as soon as he landed. Said he'd stay and fly back with Vale on Dynaxtar." I brushed a hand down my pegasus's side and pressed my forehead to hers, breathing her in for a moment, feeling for that thing inside of me that had always connected us. "Are those wings up for another flight?"

She nudged my shoulder as if to say *what are you waiting for?* And the tie between us flared in my heart. Seraph magic lit up my bones, my palm ebbing with gold light where I patted Sapphire's nose.

"We can't walk where we're going?" Tolek ran his fingers through Sapphire's mane exactly the way she liked, and she leaned into him. The way they'd bonded when I was gone had a soothing warmth spreading behind my ribs.

"Not tonight," I said, clearing my throat and circling Sapphire to hop onto her back.

It was still a bit awkward, getting used to holding my own wings in a comfortable position to fly with my pegasus, but I wouldn't trade it. Though I spent today with Tolek watching me attempt to fly from the balconies of the manor while manipulating Angellight—and I was doing fairly well—there was something different about flying *with* Sapphire. Something my myth-born blood hungered for.

Tolek placed a hand on my knee, pulling me from that thought. "Where exactly are we going, Alabath?"

"The Lendelli Hills," I said without a beat.

He tilted his head curiously. "A bit reckless to go alone, no?"

He didn't even need to know my entire theory about what was in the Lendelli Hills, he only wanted to ensure I was safe. Angels, I loved him. My chest was crowded to the point of bursting with it, and gold light shimmered along my wings, his eyes tracing every drop.

But while he had a point—perhaps it wasn't the wisest option for the two of us to head out on our own—I was tired of making decisions based on Echnid. The fullness in my chest punctured at the reminder of the god, chills spreading along my veins. It solidified my determination, though. Perhaps a bit reckless and indulgent, but fury and guilt and a medley of other emotions flooded me.

"Only two of us can fly on Sapphire. And besides, that's why we're going at night," I declared, waving a hand at the fading sky and avoiding Tol's eyes as I tried to wrangle the emotions coursing through me.

But Tolek Vincienzo never allowed me to win that game. He gripped my chin, turning it toward him and searching my expression. And the depths of his chocolate eyes burned with such devotion and concern, my heart splintered beneath the weight of it.

"What is it?" he asked, and that heavy sincerity—such simple words laden with silent understanding—forced those fissures to spread out, threatening the foundation I'd been working to rebuild.

My body is my own. My mind is my own.

"Nothing," I swore.

His thumb stroked along my jaw, and my lips trembled.

"I still feel him, Tolek," I barely whispered, but the words burned in ire. "In my blood. My mind. I *need* to do something against him. This is all my fault, and I *need* to take him down."

And it was enough of an explanation for him. Echnid's taint may be gone, but I would not wait for him to return. I'd been forced into positions too many times; I needed to *act*.

"None of this is your fault, *apeagna*." But Tolek nodded, pulling me down to kiss him and whispering against my lips, "But I vow to you, we will see that god's blood rain across Ambrisk."

Those words floated over my skin, not abating the rage burning through me but tempering it. Only temporarily, but enough to take the next step.

"Now scoot up," Tolek added, placing a hand to my back to nudge me forward.

I didn't move. "You have to sit in front."

"Not a chance," he said.

"Wings, remember?" I lifted them, ruffling my feathers with the kind of command that sent an arrow of pride through my heart.

Tol studied them for a moment. "We'll make it work."

Without another word, he shifted me forward on Sapphire and swung up behind me, positioning himself so my wings hung gently on either side of his thighs and his arms drooped low around my waist.

"See?" he said, pressing a kiss to the side of my neck. "Now I can do that, too."

The heat of his lips sank through my body, sending a shock to my very core. Angels, I wanted him even more desperately now than ever—had spent every spare moment since he returned tangled up in him. I was half tempted to abandon this plan and drag him back inside.

Instead, I leaned against his chest, allowing my wings to absorb the familiar, citrus-and-spice warmth, and squeezed Sapphire with my knees. She took flight, and despite the fact that our safe haven was sinking away beneath us, I relaxed.

~

"Why do you think Echnid hasn't come for me himself?" I finally voiced when Xenovia was far behind us. "Why has he only sent his gorgons?"

"I don't know." Tolek sighed, frustration deepening the breath. "Perhaps because he's busy working out how to banish the gods?"

"Mm-hmm. That doesn't make me feel better."

"Me neither," Tol admitted. But he kissed my neck and said, "Can you show me the light again?"

Dismissing concerns of the god, I spent the rest of the flight going over my plan and attempting to not give in to Tolek's taunts as his hands slid absentmindedly along my skin. Hidden up in the clouds, I practiced small, controlled displays of each of the seven types of Angellight, explaining to Tolek how they varied.

By the time we landed on the roof of the pleasure house in Lendelli, it was the middle of the night.

The city was still, but a hum radiated from the building beneath my boots.

"Keep watch, girl," I said to Sapphire as Tolek scaled the ladder down.

I followed, jumping right into the air and testing my wings to float myself to the foot of the stone steps below. It was a choppy descent—a large portion of it more of a fall than anything—but I kept myself aloft and landed with barely a stumble.

"Progress," Tolek said, kissing my temple.

I flexed my feathers. "Do you think if the gorgons can banish their wings into another form, I can, too?" I asked as we climbed the stairs to the ornately carved front door.

Tol grabbed the handle, pausing. "Do you want to?"

"It could make it more comfortable for us on Sapphire." Truthfully, though, the wings were beginning to sync with my muscles in ways I hadn't expected. The flow of communication from my mind to the new appendages was instinct, their weight a welcome presence.

Tol observed the feathers peeking over my shoulders, and he

smirked. "I like them. They're beautiful, legendary, and strong like you are. And you know I love a challenge."

Wings beat through my chest, but without another word, Tol tugged the door open and gestured for me to step inside. I didn't even have a moment to respond before the alluring thrum of the brothel stretched out to us, wrapping around my being and enticing me in.

We crossed the threshold into the dimly lit foyer, the rich finishes and scarf-covered mystlight exactly as it had been last time we were here. The pull was even stronger, though, and I wasn't sure if it was because of my seraph or the fact that it was even later in the night now. More hours for the proclivities within to sink into the stone, for the air to become heavy with temptation.

Doing my best to shove the lust to the back of my mind, I approached the desk across the foyer, arches rimming the space and beckoning us into their shadows.

The madame was exactly as I recalled. Hair pulled back and accentuating her sharp cheekbones, lifting her eyes. Dark fabric wrapped her body tightly to her chin, and a pipe hung between her lips.

"Welcome back," she hummed.

I quirked a brow. "You remember us?"

She blew a ring of sweetly scented smoke in her air, eyes glimmering. "I remember everyone who enters my hall." There was a threat in there, a twist of her tone that implied she knew more than she let on. But she continued, "You two had a very fun night in the public rooms last time you were here."

Last time we were here. When Brystin, one of Queen Ritalia's fae guards, had snuck in and gravely attacked a Storyteller, leaving my sister panicking because her myth magic ripped the woman's spirit from her body, finishing the kill.

But before that...

Flashes of Tolek's hands grasping my body. Of his breath hot against my skin and his clear desire jutting against my back. Of his threats to take me, to claim me right where everyone could see, and how desperately I'd wanted that. The spot between my legs throbbed at only the recollection, and I glanced up at Tolek. He gave me a knowing smirk, stepping closer and sliding an arm around my waist. I shivered at the touch.

Spirits, this place did things to me.

Swallowing, I matched the madame's glinting stare. "We certainly did."

"You have new...additions?" the madame asked with a purely curious glance at my wings.

Tolek dragged a finger down the feathers. "She does," he stated, voice sultry, and I had to release a slow breath to stay focused. "And they make the games even more fun."

The madame grinned, holding out a hand for the coins we owed to enter. We paid despite the fact that we wouldn't be using any of her rooms or staff. Allowed her to think we were.

"Enjoy yourselves," she said as she waved us through one of the archways.

"You're certain about this?" Tolek checked once we were well out of earshot, his hand roaming up and down my spine leisurely.

Over the moans echoing from behind closed doors, I met his gaze, trying my best not to give in to the hunger in my bones and focus only on him. "If we're looking for truths about the seraphs, gorgons, or gods, Aimee will be the one to know. She was the only Storyteller who knew anything about the Angelcurse."

Malakai and Mila had explicitly asked a different Storyteller about it, and she'd claimed there was no record of an Angelcurse. Yet Aimee had given us clues. It had bothered me ever since; there had to be a reason.

"After learning more about Mila's Reflector magic, I got thinking about godly powers and how they lingered on Ambrisk today through things like Storytellers," I elaborated in a low whisper that had Tolek leaning in. "I was talking to Erista about Xenique's demigoddess abilities, too, and how they connect to Artale. The Goddess gave her extra protections and blessings. Knowing more about those could help us figure out how to combat whatever demigods Echnid and the gorgons throw at us."

Not to mention that I'd been desperate to speak with Aimee ever since I'd woken up in Damenal over a month ago. That need squirmed within me as we got closer.

Tol nodded, scanning my body and taking a step toward me. With a desire-drenched stare, he skimmed my neck with his fingertips. Goose bumps erupted as he whispered, "Let's find ourselves a Storyteller, Alabath."

And then he turned down the hall, leaving me with a frustrating craving burning through me.

I groaned, Tolek laughed, and we wound our way through the labyrinthine corridors, not stopping as we had last time. Not until we were once again in the Storyteller nest, plush divans, ornate chandeliers, and rich silks adorning the wide space.

No writhing bodies pleasured themselves in here. Only clusters of shawl-wrapped Storytellers and those who listened to their tales. My heart thudded in my chest as we scanned the group, Tolek's hand firm in mine.

Last we were here, Aimee had hinted us toward the Gates of Angeldust. And if I was correct, she'd seemed apprehensive. I hadn't understood at the time, but perhaps she'd known what I'd unleash by going there.

Perhaps she feared it.

The possibility had been nagging at me more the further I got from Echnid's influence. The more I tried to unravel a way to slay the heart of his schemes. Aimee had to be the answer.

"Do you see her?" I muttered to Tolek.

My heart rate increased with each unfamiliar face I searched. Each creased brow or wide-eyed stare that met mine.

"I don't," Tol said, stretching out the words like he was reluctant to say them. Like the distress clawing at my chest was seeping off me with the ether that tumbled around my wings.

"She has to be here." My voice piqued, anticipation pinching my lungs. I pulled Tol deeper into the room, our boots scuffing over the silks trailing the floor. "She has to."

Something tugged at my hand, and I spun to a stop.

"Breathe, *apeagna*," Tol said, cupping my cheeks. I hadn't realized I was panting. "We'll find her."

He was so calm, the counter to my harried panic. My gaze flicked between his eyes, searching his expression as he pressed my hand to his heart and let the beat restore my own.

A gold tendril peeked above the collar of his leathers, and I focused on it. On the tattoo he'd gotten for me—one that may not be imbued ink and may not bind our souls but sealed a promise between us.

With that thought, my pounding heart slowed.

I looked around the room with fresh eyes and met the intrigued stare of a sandy-haired male Storyteller leaning beside the door, arms crossed and heat in that piercing look.

"There," I muttered, tugging Tolek after me.

"I remember you two," he greeted as we approached. His gaze draped across us, lingering on Tol. I curved my wing behind him, pulling him a step closer.

"We're looking for someone," I snapped.

The man lifted his brows, amused. "Who?"

"Aimee. She's a Storyteller here."

The man tilted his head. "There's no one here by that name."

I groaned. *Of course,* she wasn't here. "Will she be returning soon?"

The man straightened, hands slipping into his pockets. "You misunderstand. There is no Storyteller here by the name of Aimee. There never has been."

Chapter Thirty-Eight
Ophelia

THERE NEVER HAS BEEN.

"What?" I gasped. Angellight burned in my palms at the shock. Fiery red like Ptholenix's.

"We spoke to her," Tolek added sternly, his hand squeezing mine despite the flame, as if he felt the frustration and crushing defeat slipping off me and needed to carry the burden with me. "We had a conversation—you saw us here."

"I did not see you with a Storyteller," the man corrected. Of course not. He saw us in the other rooms, hands and lips all over each other.

"But she talked to us. Told us things only a Storyteller could know," I swore, my voice rising. Angellight curled around Tolek's wrist now, too, spreading from me to him and lacing with inky black as it traveled up his arm. "And I'd seen her before! In an inn. She was sharing legends about the Angels."

The man shrugged, lips dipping into a frown. "I do not know of whom you speak. There is no Aimee at this nest, nor has there ever been, darling." His hungry stare returned to Tolek. "But if you two would like to make use of the rooms, I could find one of the madame's people to join us."

Jealous growls rumbled from both me and Tolek, seraph magic flaring brighter. The Storyteller laughed, but he left us.

And as we swept through the room asking more Storytellers

for confirmation, my frustration only mounted. Until coils of light spun around me, slithering in the wake of my footsteps.

No one here had any recollection of the woman we'd spoken to. It was as if she never existed.

~

"How does no one know her?" I asked as Tolek and I flew closer to Xenovia.

The sun was nearly risen, pale gold bathing the desert, piercing the morning haze. We'd been discussing it on a loop since we left Lendelli, but no theories seemed plausible enough. Everything was a stretch, an impossible explanation for a senseless experience.

"We talked to her—we'd both seen her *before*," I said, fingers tangling in Sapphire's mane to ground me. Soft purple Angellight had been trailing behind us the entire flight—Xenique's. I'd chosen the Soulguider's amethyst because it seemed to blend into the night the most, but I needed to expel the frustrated energy and the guilt that wanted to strangle me.

I knew Aimee was the same woman I saw in the Wayward Inn last year when I'd rescued Tolek from Mindshaper Territory. And both he and Aimee had recalled their passing in Bodymelder land.

So how had she *never* existed?

"Maybe she uses different names?" Tolek suggested, but his words were thick with doubt. We'd described her to a number of Storytellers in vivid detail, and still there was nothing.

"She was Aimee in the Wayward Inn when I first saw her, too," I reminded him.

"I know," he conceded. His arms tightened around my waist, and I tried to sink into the comfort. "Fuck, I don't understand it either, Alabath. They could have been lying to us..."

"But why," I finished for him, and he nodded.

Xenovia was breaking through the haze in the distance, bronze minarets atop glass domes stretching high from the capital's most prominent buildings. A chill wrapped through the air, and some-thing crept along my skin. Sapphire shook her head, mist tumbling over her namesake blue mane.

Mist.

I sat up, a bolt of awareness striking through my body as my Angellight snapped back into me. That mist wasn't the normal haze of early morning. It was denser and snow white.

"Tolek," I gasped. The icy feeling that had starred in my nightmares sluiced through my veins. His voice in my memory. "Tol, I think—"

But my words were buried beneath a high-pitched wail as a shadow masked us from above. My head snapped up, Tolek's arms loosening to grab a blade right as Thorn swooped from the clouds.

CHAPTER THIRTY-NINE
TOLEK

THORN'S MASSIVE FUCKING WINGS ECLIPSED THE morning light as he charged right for us. All I could see was the cavern in the mountains when I'd tried to get to Ophelia and the Angel had thrown me back.

I'd been numb to the impact of it then, mind staked on one thing only, but it rang through my bones now. All I heard was Ophelia screaming my name—screaming for help as Echnid took her. Her distress echoed in my memory as I wrenched my family dagger from my waist and threw it at the Angel.

It tumbled end over end. He was distracted by the Angellight building in Ophelia's palms, around her wings, crackling with bolts of the Mindshaper's stormy power. And the blade swiped against the underside of his wing.

But it glided through his feathers without leaving a scratch.

"*Fuck,*" I grumbled, tightening my legs around Sapphire to stay seated as she dipped.

Not even a fucking mark.

I wrapped one arm back around Ophelia's waist as I thought. I *had* hurt the Angel weeks ago. That scar stretching from his shoulder and across his torso like a jagged lightning bolt was blatant on his bare chest, the fur cloak floating around him not obscuring it. Thorn had *bled* when I attacked him with Cypherion's scythe in the theater.

The Angel looped through the sky, his wings pounding and clouds rumbling around him. Dense dark-gray masses crackled, lighting streaking across the desert. Manic onyx eyes met mine, and that slicing stare confirmed he remembered exactly what I did to him.

"Hello again." His cooing words purred along my bones in an unnatural, disgraceful way. Ghostly fingers clawed at my brain, tearing into the matter and trying to pry up my memories. Emotions. Thoughts.

I gripped those hands at the wrists and twisted. Fought. Tried to shove them off despite the panic gripping my chest at the familiarity of this fucking sensation.

My vision flashed between the skies above the deserts and a dimly lit tent.

Between Thorn and Aird.

My heart pounded, and my skin was clammy. Ophelia. She was so fucking warm and alive in front of me. She'd come for me then, despite my failure; she'd returned to me when I wasn't able to save her, and she was here now.

Fighting off the Angel.

Fuck me to the Spirit Realm if I wasn't going to fight by her side. To seal that vengeance together. Pulling my sword from my back, I gripped the cool hilt tightly, a surge of power rumbling from the steel into my arm.

And I prepared to take down an Angel.

Ophelia's seraph power burned so brightly, I swore it tunneled into me, fueling my own movements and pushing back Thorn's clawing Mindshaper magic enough that I could focus. Lightning sparked along my blade, the steel glinting and illuminating the gray skies.

Ophelia shot ropes of Angellight toward Thorn. The Angel twirled his hand through the air, lashing back with a roaring wind. A wall of scorching light flickered to life between us and Thorn to block the gale. Ophelia groaned as her magic strained, her wings tensing.

"Alabath!" I called over the wind. "We need to surprise him. Get on the offensive. He's too wild to strategize and will just keep blasting us with power." I tightened my grip on my sword as another pulse of power radiated up my arm.

"Any ideas how?" she panted.

As I considered, my gaze dropped to the sand thirty feet below.

"Oh, Damien's fucking cock," I forced out.

Echnid's gorgons had arrived. Six of them, with bows pointed up at us, lethal black metal tips as dark as the tar pits in Banix's valleys. Ophelia spotted them just as the first fired. Maintaining her shield against Thorn's raging wind, she sent a single whip of light toward the sand, knocking the arrow off its path.

Dammit, I wished I had my own fucking bow and arrow. My sword would do nothing from here, and my dagger was in the sand below.

Thorn's magic kept clawing at my mind, more as Ophelia's light was stretched thin, less of a barrier around us.

When we were in the pleasure house and her power had reacted with her frustration, the light pulsed into me when I gripped her hand. Like I could relieve her of the pressure of it and channel it—

Channel it.

I flipped my sword in my hand, relishing the hum of power shooting through the steel—the same as in the tar pits.

Thorn cackled again, thunder rumbling down my spine as those hands pried me apart. It took everything in me to fight him off as I formed a plan. To cling to Ophelia's light and body before me.

"I have an idea!" I called. Black-tipped arrows rained around us, the gorgons wild in their shots and Sapphire dodging them skillfully.

"Tell me what to do," Ophelia gritted out as she sent another whip of seraph power at the gorgons. One hissed, jumping back as it struck her foot. Her hair was beginning to shift into venomous serpents.

"Keep Thorn distracted, and when I jump, drop the shield and shoot a bolt of his own light directly at my blade, okay, *apeagna*?"

"When you *what*?" she screamed, but I didn't answer.

I lunged off Sapphire's back, hurtling toward the Angel.

Ophelia shrieked and light exploded from her in every direction. The power of the Blackfyre ebbed through my blade, and a sharp bolt of lightning—of Ophelia's Mindshaper ability—struck the steel perfectly as I swung down.

That's my fucking girl.

Thorn's eyes widened, rage and madness swirling to the surface as the impossible blow *landed*. As a mortal weapon actually injured an Angel.

My sword cleaved part of the joint between feathers and flesh. And a gleam of silver light sparked as Angelblood coated steel.

Gold blood—gold now that the Angels' Spirits were reunited with their bodies.

"Holy blasphemous Spirits," I exhaled over the burn in my arms.

Thorn wailed, and I fell. Plummeted to the sand below.

And it was so fucking worth it to see him bleed.

Chapter Forty

Ophelia

"TOLEK!" I SCREECHED AS HIS WEIGHT LEFT SAPPHIRE'S back behind me and my pegasus dipped. Gold Angelblood spilled through the air, my light crackling with my terror. The stormy skies illuminated with each explosion, puffs of gray clouds becoming gold-streaked shadows around our winged forms. An image torn from a book of legends.

"Catch him!" I screamed to Sapphire, pulling my feet onto her back and pushing upright.

My own wings flared, narrowly dodging another poisonous black arrow. The sand loomed thirty feet below—I wasn't strong enough for this height, but I didn't give an Angel's feathers. I leapt off my pegasus's back and beat, beat, beat as she fell away. As she plunged after Tolek.

Thorn raced toward him as I glided down, my wings catching the Angel's wind to soften my fall.

Sand scraped my knees and the heels of my palms as I stumbled to the dunes, boots struggling to find purchase.

I sprang to my feet, willing light to heal the small cuts. The gorgons closed in. Still in their human forms, they formed a wall, isolating me from Sapphire and Tolek. Stormy clouds pressed around us, obscuring my warrior horse and the man I loved entirely.

My heart leapt into my throat at the crushing familiarity,

exactly like the theater when the Angels had separated me from my friends. When they handed me over to a vicious god to be used.

But I had escaped that tainted place, and I would not return.

Two of the ethereally beautiful women held their bows aloft, arrows aimed at my heart. I avoided the one who was partially shifted, staying out of reach and not meeting her eyes to avoid the poison in both blood and stare.

"What is a poor little seraph to do?" one taunted, a sheet of black hair drifting around her dainty frame. She was shorter than I was, but she radiated wicked power. Red-rimmed eyes studied me with sheer joy.

"All alone out here. None of her kind to help," another said, releasing an arrow. I dropped my wing, and the piercing point only ruffled my feathers. The red-headed shooter growled.

"It doesn't matter if I'm alone," I argued, leaning forward on my toes, ready to spring at them. Angellight crackled in my palms, up my arms, the colors of all seven Angels whirling and melding beneath an overpowering white gold that was *mine*. "There is a reason Echnid wants me much more desperately than he wants you. I don't know if it's only this." A whip of light struck the sand at their feet. "Or if it's something else. Whatever it is, he wants you to give him an army, but me? I am more valuable to him than the six of you combined."

Grimaces smeared across their beautiful faces, ranging from rage to distaste to repulsion. And the seraph inside of me rose, wanting, no, *needing* to defend against this natural enemy.

The four gorgons who hadn't spoken fanned out around us, either out of arrows or never having had them in the first place. I didn't turn to track them, but I noted every shift of the sand beneath their bare feet. Every slither of a gown across the ground.

Spirits, I didn't even have a sword—hadn't replaced Starfire since Ritalia melted her. I had a number of small daggers strapped to me that I'd borrowed from Erista's family's trove. That was it in terms of steel. But...

My palms warmed.

Beyond blades, I wasn't defenseless.

Before they could react, I coiled a whip of Angellight in one hand and latched it around the throat of the nearest gorgon, the small one. It tightened and tightened as I willed it, the control as razor-sharp and masterful as if I was slicing her skin open with Starfire.

In my other hand, I pictured that blade, and I honed my magic as Damien had taught me all those weeks in Damenal. Willed the light to take solid form, to become a freshly whetted edge and hilt and grip. To mold to my palm as only one other weapon had in my life.

And in my hand, buzzing with the might of all the slain seraphs, my light forged a sword to end a thousand enemies.

With a grunt, I tugged the gorgon by her neck. She stumbled forward, breath faltering, and I jammed the sword of seraph power into her chest.

Mora said we didn't know how to kill these demons, but this was the answer.

Me.

The power of a purely woken seraph, the scorching effervescence that only my myth-born magic could conjure. And the counter to the demonic being before me. I twisted the blade, relishing every small give between bone and muscle.

Too late, the red-headed gorgon released another two arrows. They whizzed toward me, but my attention was so intensely focused, I dodged without even a glance up. Instead, I watched the poisoned blood of the gorgon seep across my hand. The light fade from her red-rimmed eyes.

Wrath poured through my body, every drop of Angelblood and Godsblood burning with it. Seraph power fanning those hungry flames.

My frustration and confusion from not finding Aimee collided with the fear for Tolek and betrayal of the Angels—with my hatred for Echnid for what he'd done to Malakai and the torrent of guilt at releasing the god upon the realms. The emotions strung together, becoming the ballad my blood beat to as I reveled in the power of the last seraph.

And I twisted the blade of light deeper in the gorgon's chest before shoving her to the ground.

Without a glance, I sent another whip at the gorgons circling me, forcing them back. My magic acted as a sixth sense, feeling where I couldn't reach and defending where I couldn't see.

The red-headed woman in front of me was unfazed by the death of her comrade, the brutal, heartless demon snapping out a pair of fangs with a gleaming smile. She dug them into her wrist, two perfect circles of blood forming along her pale skin.

And she flashed that crimson-pointed grin at me. "Care to try?"

Mist gathered around the edges of our circle, my nerves spiking.

"No, thank you," I said sweetly, despite the seraph turning feral within me. "I prefer living. And though I'm certain my magic could overpower yours, it would be such a tragic waste of a day."

Challenge flared in her stare, the red hue deepening. "I promise it will be rich," she said with a saccharine smile, extending her arm. "The sweetest thing you've ever tasted, and with your beauty, it will only make you more...desirable."

The others released low laughs at her attempt to prey on the mortal need to feel alluring as lore claimed the gorgons often did.

Around us, white mist pressed closer. It chilled me to my bones, biting at my resolve. Coaxing it to bend and wither. *He is trying to protect us.*

I shook my head.

No, no, no.

Echnid was getting closer. He was stretching out that influence, seeking what might still linger in my veins, what torment I hadn't yet overcome.

I'd hoped he sent the gorgons and Thorn on this attack, but it was a fool's wish. The god was desperate to accomplish his revenge, and for whatever reason, that included me.

With an anguished lash of power, I burst out five beams of razor-sharp Angellight, striking each of the women surrounding me. They hissed and cried, stumbling back, scorch marks marring their flawless skin.

"It's your future," the red-headed gorgon tutted.

Then, before my eyes, her hair shifted. The long, fiery strands became whipping heads of snakes. *Hisses* poured across the sand, slithering and writhing until it felt like the ghostly tails of their masters were twisting up my legs.

I couldn't lift a foot—bend a knee. I was summoned by their blood-red eyes.

Don't look at them, I reminded myself as I fought to flex my fingers. Death laid in those eyes when she shifted to her non-human form, and her skin was paling by the second, leathery wings extending behind her.

Digging within myself, I blasted as much Angellight as I could muster at the gorgon, wrapped her in a typhoon of my own making. The woman screeched, snake hair hissing violently. Her skin sizzled and blistered beneath my light.

Seraph magic heals, I repeated Damien's words as I gritted my teeth and dug my boots into the sand. It seeks to restore and balance under the hands of the gods—

And it was boiling her gorgon blood.

Her poisoned blood.

Attempting to purge the taint from the inside out. Another weakness for our artillery.

I wrapped the entire pocket of mist with light, targeting each of the gorgons. As my power mounted, their shrieks ripped through the air. They clawed at my magic.

I didn't kill them all—I needed to conserve some power for finding Tolek—and with every passing second, the god's familiar, repulsive presence crawled along my blood. I couldn't see him, but *fucking Angels*, he was all I could feel.

Nausea swooped through me, and my vision dimmed. Black spots swarmed the air, dunes rushing up toward me.

Ophelia, echoed through my mind.

"*No, no, no.*" My hands clamped against my ears as my light recoiled, shuttering back into me. Hiding from the god.

He was everywhere. Mist gathered closer, dissolving my Angellight.

It wrenched my head back, my mouth open.

And with utter consumption, in the most violating way, the

Warrior God's power shoved itself down my throat. I choked and flailed, my neck straining, but my body was locked in his grasp.

"Ophelia," Echnid purred, appearing out of a swirling mass of power. One step closer, and those phantom snakes held my limbs in their coiled grasp. I was forced to bow further backward as the magic kept pouring into me. "You should not have run."

I will always run from you, I wanted to say. To scream and rage and roar. I would never be his. In whatever way he wanted me—power, mind, body—he could not have me. *My mind is my own. My body is my own.*

Echnid's milky eyes shone as he leaned over me. He caught my chin in his grasp, forcing my watery stare up. I forced myself not to cough and splutter.

"You are under my domain, Ophelia," Echnid hummed. "You are already mine. You will rule with me, and I will give you all the power you dream of."

And that was the flaw in the logic of ancient gods. I didn't dream of power. I dreamed of peace.

Of a life where I was not used by them.

Of mornings where fear did not crowd my chest.

Of not having to choose between being selfish or being sacrificed.

Of a home with Tolek where boots lined the entryway and little feet pattered on bare wood.

Tolek.

I dreamed of Tolek as mist fought to consume me. I thought of his hands on my skin and his breath in my ear.

My body is my own. My mind is my own.

Echnid laughed morbidly, like he saw all those trivial dreams and could banish them with a flick of his fingers. But beyond the god, the mist parted, and—

I choked on the power as a scream tried to wrench up my throat. Sapphire glided through the air, her wings and hooves coated in golden Angelblood, and Tolek sat atop her. Sword in hand, every bit alive and fighting.

The pure heart of a warrior gleamed in my pegasus's eyes as she looped around Thorn, and it fueled my own determination. Tolek raised his blade, and with the dregs of magic I could pull up over Echnid's torture, I sent another bolt of Angellight to channel into the steel.

I didn't know which Angel it stemmed from or if it was purely mine, but just as Tolek whipped his head around and found me on my knees before the god, choking on his power, Echnid sealed the wall of mist between us.

NO! I wanted to scream—tried to—but it was no more than a jagged thought.

Terror flooded every facet of my body. It clawed at my heart and pierced my lungs like a living beast.

Heat—it was the fire of the Spirit Volcano laced with vitriolic thoughts.

Burning—it was hungry and raw and riled.

Effervescent—it was the hope and will of an entire species slain before their time.

And light burst from my skin. Shining and endless, it shot toward Echnid, toward the gorgons. It blasted through the mist for Tolek, seeking to reassure and feel and touch. Seeking a beating heart and pumping blood, a laugh that healed my own spirit and eyes that glimmered with mischief.

"Behave, my seraph!" Echnid roared, desperate mist tunneling against my light. Where golden beams blazed, his power turned denser. It swallowed and masked the world until it was all I could see, all I knew. The chilling, vengeful dreams crawled beneath my skin and tried to devour me.

Desire radiated through the god's power. He wanted me. Wanted me in his command, under his hand. Wanted my blood laced with his venom and his poison spewing from my lips. It was a sick fascination but also a need—Echnid was *desperate* for me.

I am not yours! I roared internally, and from the way the god bared down, from the way our powers battled, I thought he heard it.

But right when Echnid opened his mouth to respond, two flying forms broke the horizon beyond the mist. Dark armored scales reflected the sunlight, born for battle.

Khrysaor.

Chapter Forty-One
Cypherion

"Got a read on them, Stargirl?" I called through the wind as Dynaxtar sped over the desert on Zanox's heels. The khrysaors' scaled wings were practically blurs.

A white mist was gathered less than one hundred yards ahead, too dense to see through. We speared toward it, as fast as they could fly. Wind whipped around us, stinging my eyes, but my blood pounded.

Vale's gaze was narrowed, flicking between silver galaxies and olive green, but her voice never faded. As if her readings were controlled enough to be present in both worlds at once.

"Positive," Vale said, and then she gasped. Her nails dug into my arm. "He's there now!" she yelled. "Echnid—he has Ophelia!"

"On the fucking Angels' graves!" Jezebel roared, and Zanox sped up.

I growled, locking my legs tighter around Dynaxtar. The khrysaor had chosen Vale, my Fatesworn, so I was putting all my trust in her as I sank into that place I went to before a fight. The one that clocked my opponent's every flinch, every shift to calculate how to beat them. The one that had my fists aching. The one that had won time and again in the ring and on a battlefield.

With my focus honed in, I bellowed, "Stay true!"

And we plunged into the mist.

The khrysaor roared a monstrous sound I'd never heard as they spiraled down, flying in opposing circles and wrapping round and round the god. We cleared the perimeter of the mist, and—

"Holy cursed Spirits," I swore, my scythe burning across my back.

Echnid had Ophelia on her knees before him, bowed backward and arms stretched out on either side of her like some sick devout ritual. Mist poured down her fucking throat, choking her and holding her captive. Women clad in flowing white silk surrounded them. *The gorgons.*

A bright spark of silver-blue light ignited the white fog, and a bolt of Jezebel's myth magic shot straight for the heart of the circle. Spearing toward one of the gorgons, she barely had time to gasp before it struck her through the chest.

And she crumpled to the ground. Dead.

Echnid roared, attention whipping to Jezebel, but his magic continued to push at Ophelia. Spirits, it was going to suffocate her. Tears streaked from her eyes into the misty wind.

With a wave of his hand, Echnid ripped a veil in the air like the one he pulled Ophelia and Malakai through in the mountains. The gorgons were swept into it, including the two lifeless bodies.

Then, the god turned. And as his mist relinquished Ophelia, all of his focus landed on Jezebel.

"Cypherion!" Ophelia choked out, struggling to her feet shakily but as quickly as she could.

"Drop me, Stargirl!"

Vale nudged Dynaxtar, and the khrysaor swooped low enough that I could jump to the sand, catching Ophelia as she stumbled over to me.

"Are you okay?" I asked, holding her with one arm and pulling my scythe with the other.

She shook her head, panting. Panic and pain scratched her voice as she croaked, "We need to find Tolek. Thorn is here."

Zanox and Dynaxtar were still swooping circles around Echnid, Jezebel conjuring a barrier of myth magic to push back against the god.

Tolek, I tried to say down the Fatesworn bond, and it must have worked because Vale and Dynaxtar dove to the side. The khrysaor's wings parted the mist, carving a tunnel.

"Come on," I said, pulling Ophelia along. She dug her heels in, eyes flicking between her sister and the narrowing path the khrysaor had created. "You need to find Sapphire," I urged. "You may have wings but you're not ready for that sort of flight, Ophelia."

Her brow pinched, face still pale from what Echnid had done to her, but Angellight flared in her palms.

"Let's go," she said, and we charged after Dynaxtar, something beating relentlessly within me.

Tolek and Sapphire were both covered in some glimmering gold substance. The same thing leaked from a slice to Thorn's back as he carved circles through the air, giggling and rioting, storms rumbling around him.

"By the fucking Spirits," I breathed as that beating drum kept up in my head. How had they managed to do that?

In a flash, a sword of Angellight burst to life in Ophelia's hand, and she was running for Tolek. He and Sapphire were trying and failing to find a way through the mist Echnid hounded them with. It was so much thicker, like the god wanted to make a damn point to Ophelia that he could touch anyone she cared about.

But he couldn't.

Because as she ran, Ophelia sliced through the haze with that glowing sword. Beams shot from her other hand, light obliterating the god's power. Tolek and Sapphire both saw her, the pegasus landing and galloping for her rider. I kept one eye on the Angel soaring above, my scythe in hand.

Right as Ophelia swung up onto Sapphire's back in front of Tolek, Dynaxtar landed, sand flying up around her. That agitated, relentless pounding went quiet within me when I saw Vale, and I realized it had been the new Fatesworn bond. Spirits, it was going to take a while to get used to this thing.

I took one single step toward Vale, but her eyes widened. She inhaled sharply, sliding off Dynaxtar and stumbling toward me.

"What's wrong, Stargirl?" I asked as I caught her.

Her face tipped toward the heavens as Echnid's mists parted. And in the distance, a blurry figure illuminated the desert with a burst of white light and silver smoke.

And one word fell from Vale's lips—

"*Moirenna*."

CHAPTER FORTY-TWO
OPHELIA

THE GODDESS OF FATE AND CELESTIAL MOVEMENTS was starlight incarnate in the midst of Echnid's fogged magic.

She emerged from the depths of the mists, a pulsing white glow and silver smoke puncturing the wicked, tainted power of the Warrior God. His tendrils fell to the sand, and Jezebel and Zanox came soaring toward the rest of us, landing with an earth-rocking thud. I looked over my sister to ensure she was okay, but we didn't have time for more than that.

A layer of Echnid's fog hovered across the sand, wrapping carelessly around our ankles as if tasting us, coaxing us closer. Sapphire and the khrysaor pranced in place. But the god only had eyes for Moirenna.

The goddess stood before him, sister versus brother, immortal enemies facing down ancient blood feuds.

Battles I was exhausted of being held accountable for.

Rage curled through me at seeing the two gods together, their power so effortless and mighty, yet they'd strung their squabbles upon those weaker than them simply because they could.

Seraph magic gathered around me, everything taking on a gold sheen.

"Easy," Tolek whispered in my ear, soothing me before I shot it rashly. "Wait for your chance."

He was right. I'd get one opportunity to hit Echnid. I couldn't waste it.

As gold light purred around us, the air shifted. The threads of emblem power originating in me coiled tighter, and my attention snapped toward the skies. The Angels emerged out of nowhere. All six who hadn't bothered to fight moments ago.

My eyes locked with Damien's as he swooped nearest us, below Thorn, still prowling overhead with focus homed on Echnid. The Prime Mystique shook his head, expression stony, but I swore there was something in those purple eyes. Be it warning or anger, I couldn't peel them apart in the wake of my own fury.

He'd betrayed me. He'd fed me to Echnid's poison when he'd promised to protect me, and then he contributed to trapping me there. So, despite what was in that beseeching stare, I turned away.

Ether dripped from each Angel's wings. All seven of them directed their attention to the showdown of the gods.

"Brother," Moirenna called out, and I rocked back on my heels at the sound of her voice. So much power ebbed through those two syllables. Like with only one word she could command fortunes, create worlds, and rearrange heavens. The khrysaor, Jezebel, and Sapphire all shivered at it. Vale pressed forward on her toes, like pure will was the only thing keeping her from floating to the goddess who reigned over fates.

Echnid sneered at Moirenna. "You sacrificed your right to call me such when you locked me in that realm."

"You will always be my brother regardless of our feuds," Moirenna said, almost laughing at Echnid's refusal.

As if in demonstration, she lifted her hands, smoky silver mist shimmering off her. It was similar to Echnid's, but where the Warrior God's was a dense white fog, Moirenna's was stardust ripped from the depths of the heavens, glimmering and twinkling. It was what you'd find lurking among the cosmos, and I almost felt as if it would purify anything that touched it.

Valyrie's Angellight within me stretched out to the goddess, but I tugged against its leash to tame the star-flecked magic.

"We are derived of the same sources," Moirenna continued,

power peeling off her ivory skin. "We are born of the mist's willfully gifted hands."

"Willfully gifted," Echnid scoffed, the sound so mortal. If he existed on this world for long enough, would his power amplify to match Moirenna's? Would it surpass it as it once had, so close to the heart of all magic?

I grimaced, Tolek's arm tightening around my waist. His touch steadied me, helping me assess the situation closer. We could not allow Echnid to get as powerful as the known gods. Could not allow Thorn to roam free after today.

Sliding off Sapphire onto silent feet, I pulled a dagger from my thigh and gathered what remained of my Angellight in my other hand. I was drained from Echnid's intrusive magic. It still swirled through my blood, but I forced it down. I *had* to.

My body is my own.

My mind is my own.

And my fucking power is my own.

Jezebel and Vale came to stand on either side of me, Cypherion, Tolek, and the mythical creatures behind us.

"Do you deny who created you?" Moirenna asked. Her head tilted, porcelain expression remaining calm and pristine. "You seek to destroy the very Balance of all realms."

"I do not seek to ruin. I seek to right," Echnid answered, and cruelty warped every word, tight enough to kill. "And I have found the way."

I have found the way.

Echnid knew. He knew how to sever ties of the gods to the warriors. To Ambrisk.

Moirenna nodded, and it was clear she was already aware. She'd come here because she'd seen in the celestial movements that Echnid had this piece of information.

And he was prepared to wield it.

"You think this is the wisest choice?" Moirenna asked. She was frustratingly calm. Was that something she'd learned over the centuries? Had she seen the possible outcomes and was navigating them silently before us?

I searched the row of Angels above, curved around their master. Always with him—imperative to whatever he planned.

My hand tightened on my knife. Valyrie was at the end of the row, wings tilting toward the Goddess of Fate and Celestial Movements, like the tide was pulled by the moon.

All seven of them were preoccupied, swarming toward their god, and I pulled up all seven facets of their powers. Let it gather beneath my skin as Echnid said to Moirenna, "I fear that is where we disagree. See, you believe I am making a choice when we both know I am fulfilling a destiny."

And for a moment that sent my heart plunging to my stomach, Moirenna's eyes widened. The Warrior God had caught her in her own game of Fates.

Echnid started speaking, uttering words in a language I had never heard. One I didn't think even Tolek had studied. A glance over my shoulder confirmed it when he shook his head.

This was it—this was how Echnid had discovered to banish the gods. And that meant it was our one shot.

I summoned all of the power within me, and without another thought, I tore my arm back, and sent my dagger launching toward the Angels and their cruel master.

I chased the blade with every bit of magic I could drag up—the might of myths and seraphs and Angels—of every drop of Godsblood and Angelblood that had been steeping in my veins for years.

"Ophelia, no!" And that voice shocked me. *Damien.*

His stare seized mine, and that was fear widening his purple eyes. Terror cracking the facade he worked so hard to maintain.

But I only sent more and more magic after the blade, pushing it forward—hoping for any impact against a god.

Every Angel whirled toward us, including Thorn, a wild glee fueling the Mindshaper's beating wings.

Silver streaked through the air, Jezebel urging the dagger on with her own power. As my magic collided with my sister's in the air, the two wrapped around the small knife, surging it forward.

But right before it landed—right as the steel pulsed with spine-tingling magic—the god gave me a victorious smirk.

The light consuming the air was siphoned into Echnid's waiting palms where his mists gathered and swallowed it whole.

My stomach flipped, a wrench twisting in a way that dragged me back to the ballroom, when Echnid had convinced me to try to turn Malakai into a seraph.

"STOP!" I screamed, time seeming to slow.

In the god's hand, my magic pressed and condensed, crackling and booming. Morphing until nothing but a solid white meteor hovered before him, silver and gold lights woven through it. The Warrior God extended his arms out, palms splayed, and with a deafening force, he clapped his hands.

That ball of power shot forward.

Beside me, Jezzie pummeled Echnid's back with bolts of silver magic, but it did nothing to derail him. Gods were beyond myths. They were the foundations of entire universes.

Moirenna's eyes slipped closed, her chin lifting high as if in acceptance, and the meteor collided with her chest.

The blow rang through the desert. It sank the dunes and bent the skies. Stars—the constellations I could restore—screamed. The goddess hung suspended as victory smeared across Echnid's rotten features.

"Take care, my Fatecatcher," Moirenna's melodic voice echoed along the air.

Then, the goddess—the only one who had come to our aid, to try to dissuade her brother of this very thing—she wasn't just banished from the realm.

Moirenna died in a burst of flaming white light that resembled two stars colliding in the sky. The remnants rained down to the sand, coalescing around Vale.

Power exhausted, Echnid fled through another veiled rip in the air, the Angels following. Before he sealed the gate, Echnid gave me one last glare that promised this wasn't over. There was a haunted ownership in that stare, a threat compounded by his victory.

But he was gone, and the desert roared to a stillness.

Aside from a slight sizzle and crackle of starfire.

And like vipers following a rhythmic song, the silver beads that had showered the earth in the wake of Moirenna's death trailed around our Starsearcher. They gathered at her feet, then across her body, and sank into her skin one drop at a time.

Vale's eyes flared the brightest silver.

And in a moment that had my wings shivering, the magic of the Fates became the Fatecatcher's.

PART THREE
DAMIEN

Chapter Forty-Three
Damien

We had not seen an Angel fall ill in the millennia since we walked Ambrisk. In much longer than that, truly, since our power kept us strong. But when the Goddess was slain, Valyrie crumbled in the skies.

"The transfer of power is likely taking its toll on her, as well," Ptholenix explained to me in a hushed whisper outside the room we had been monitoring our sister in.

"She will wake?" I asked.

"Oh, I am certain she will wake." The orchid tattoo between the Firebird's wings caught the light as he peeked back around the curtain at Valyrie. Turning back to me, he explained, "Now more than ever, the Balance will need powerful Starsearchers to retain the Fates' magic."

That thought settled on my Spirit. My teeth ground together. "This will have deeply stretching repercussions."

Ptholenix nodded in grim agreement. In all the time we had existed, nothing of this magnitude had occurred. The War Among Gods that locked Ambrisk from other realms happened so long ago, we had been young at the time, still indulging in the proclivities of our immortality. Not present for the worst of the battles.

And any other godly disputes...well, they had not been within our realm.

But the murder of the Goddess of Fate and Celestial Movements would not go lightly. And Valyrie would feel the weight of it strongest. Her Starsearchers would be in question.

"Once she wakes, we will have to ask after the Starsearcher who was with the Chosen Child in the mountains," I said, quickly quieting when a sweep of power pushed at the walls.

But Xenique fluttered around the corner, and my hesitation subsided at the recognition of her amethyst ether.

"How is she?" our Soulguider sister asked.

"The same," Ptholenix confirmed.

Xenique seemed to be satisfied with that explanation. She dropped her voice. "We must be prepared for an accelerated timeline now that he has discovered how to slay them."

"We have to find—"

She cut me off. "He is more motivated now than ever. He is close to opening a temporary veil."

"How close?" I clipped, agitation at her speaking over me crowding my chest. I did not take kindly to the way these emotions flooded in and out of me so blatantly after so many centuries of them being suppressed.

"With the bounds he's recently passed, I would wager any day now," Xenique said. "The one Moirenna opened to get here has sealed tightly again."

"Can you stand in his way?" Ptholenix asked, giving Xenique a very pointed stare.

"I may have something." She traced the blade of the hooked sword at her waist, etched with crescent moons as an ode to her mother. "It is no guarantee, but it is a precaution many years in the making."

"We must buy as much time as possible," I asserted.

Xenique nodded. "When the time strikes, we will have only moments, so the girl will need to be ready. Have you spoken to her?"

"No."

She leveled me with a glare. "Can you?"

"I will when the time is right." My tone quieted both her and Ptholenix for a long moment.

Then, the Firebird muttered, "We need to tell Bant the time to push them has arrived."

"And they all must believe it is their idea," I reminded.

Ptholenix's eyes narrowed on the window. "I will assist him in that."

Studying his stoic features, I nodded. "Fear not. I think these warriors are much more determined to exact their revenge than those we once knew."

Which meant—for my fellow Angels and myself—they were either much more significant allies than we ever partnered with or much grander threats than we were prepared to face.

CHAPTER FORTY-FOUR
VALE

STARFIRE CRASHED BEHIND MY EYES, THE VOICES OF eleven Fates screaming in collective anger. Or was it terror? Perhaps some were even...gleeful? Their hands stretched through the gauzy curtains of their realm, trying to grasp me, to claim me.

The *Fatecatcher*.

They showed me all manners of futures, some my very own paths, some of those I loved, and even strangers across Ambrisk. Across realms.

Cypherion with a constellation Fatesworn tattoo around one shoulder.

Ophelia with wings burning at her back.

A girl I thought I recognized but wasn't quite sure.

Leagues of winged beings, those with skin that swirled like galaxies, and others who carried themselves with the might of a god, rings on their hands and chains around their necks.

Bridges wove tapestries across starry skies.

A realm bedecked in darkness, another crackling with lost lightning.

And this realm—Ambrisk—was soaked in shining crimson blood, the mist of the Warrior God cleansing and tainting as it swept across Gallantia. Among the wreckage lay the bodies of my friends. Of our alliance armies and mythical beasts—gryphons and sphinxes and pegasus alike. Fates, even a pair of severed feathered wings.

And Echnid reclaimed an empty world, set to repopulate it with subjects bowing to him. He ripped a tear between realms—a bridge reopened—and they flocked through.

I gasped, eyes snapping open.

But I wasn't in my room back in Xenovia. I knelt upon a glimmering marble floor, pristine white and shimmering with silver. The smallest speckles of deep sapphires and amethysts littered the solid slab beneath my knees, the same shades in billowing curtains draping across the windows.

And before me stood two women I'd revered all my life: Moirenna, the Goddess of Fate and Celestial Movements, and Valyrie, the Starsearcher Prime Warrior. I bowed before the Angel, waiting to speak until she commanded me to rise.

When she did, I angled my chin up to her companion. "How are you here?" I asked the goddess. The now-dead goddess. "Did Echnid truly..."

Moirenna nodded gently, an amethyst amulet around her neck dipping with the movement. It caught the starfire burning in sconces around us but didn't glimmer, like it winked out as her existence had.

Needing a moment to gather the weight of a god being slain, I searched the space we were in. I couldn't see beyond the thin curtains, but power tugged at my skin. It hummed, much louder than my nine Fate ties.

"I thought he was only going to banish you, not...How is this even possible?" I muttered, still watching those curtains waver. No glass lined the floor to ceiling windows they covered. From the glimpses between the pillars, it was empty air. Like a world had been swallowed whole beyond these bounds.

My attention snapped to Moirenna again, the Angel hovering quietly at her side.

"What will happen to Ambrisk now? To the Fates?" I asked.

Moirenna lowered herself to the ground, kneeling before me as if we were equals. "Child, the Fates are imperative to realms beyond your own. Everything I sacrificed matters beyond Ambrisk. And it was a choice I proudly made."

"A choice...you knew this would happen?"

Of course, she did. She was not a mere Starsearcher, seeing the fortunes the Fates passed. She was the one who commanded them, who wrote them into star maps in the inky sky. While legends said Valyrie controlled the Fates, the goddess penned their messages. Or, she had.

"I knew that eventually, I would fall to my brother's hand. I did not know which brother or when, but it was always where my path led." There wasn't an ounce of regret in her voice. "There may be a way for me to weigh the other possibilities, other realms I will dance in. Forms I can take. But for now, this is my end."

I shook my head, my hands clasped tightly in my lap, and my voice was barely a whisper. "How did he do it?"

"There is magic alive on Ambrisk that has not been seen in..." A heavy pause. "Since the stars were forged. It brings once impossible feats to life."

"What will happen now?" I whispered.

"The Fates persist," Moirenna confirmed. "As does your Angel to rule over your warrior clan." My gaze flickered to Valyrie, lilac ether unspooling around her wings as powerful as ever. "But you, my sweet girl"—Moirenna cupped my cheek, and I jumped at the contact—"are so much more now."

"Wh-what?" I stuttered, the goddess's touch chilling my skin. My magic pulled toward her. The Fates grew even more insistent, humming through my mind.

My palms tingled with it, and when my gaze slipped down, I lurched back. Starlight glistened at the tips of my fingers, burning white and fiery.

Moirenna kept her palm on my cheek, directing my attention back up. In a motherly gesture I hadn't felt in over twenty years, she swept a thumb across my cheekbone. "Sweet girl, do not be afraid," she soothed.

"What's happening?" I asked.

"You are the Fatecatcher," she whispered. "I was able to sacrifice myself against Echnid unlike my brothers and sisters because I had you to uphold my power. You are born to wield the Fates upon the death of the goddess. Your future has been foretold—for eons. As long as I have existed."

"I saw it in my final reading," Valyrie confirmed. My harried eyes met her calm navy ones, and I remembered—the scrolls. Titus had given us a scroll that recorded the Angel's final reading. We'd assumed it had been about the Angel's death, but it was *Moirenna's*. And it had used the term *Fatecatcher*, though we hadn't known what it meant. We'd glossed right over it.

When the Angel dipped her chin, it was such a human movement that I steadied my breathing, collecting my thoughts.

"Why am I the Fatecatcher? Why not Valyrie?"

Moirenna explained, "Power beyond the bounds you warriors understand exists in the Angels." The goddess cast Valyrie a harsh glance that the Angel returned. "She cannot hold the weight of Fatecatcher in addition to all her other magics and responsibilities. It would upset the Balance of power too greatly."

"Then what am I to do? Am I—Do I become the Goddess of Celestial Movements now?"

"No, sweet thing." Another delicate brush against my cheek, her fingers tucking hair behind my ear. I felt like a child again, four years old and being cared for by my mother. "You are not the one meant to replace me. You are born of great strength and a well of hidden magic, but that is not your fortune. I will waft among realms, and she will come to surface, but you—you are more similar to a conduit."

"A conduit?"

"A *Conduice*—it is a word of another realm. One that has no meaning here." Valyrie's wings shifted at the mention, but Moirenna only kept her concerned eyes on me. Worry *for me*, I realized, despite her fading existence. "In that realm, the *Conduice* seek and distribute magic. Here, you will harness what I am leaving behind in death. You will carry it so it can exist beyond me, and it will be passed to Starsearchers and Fates as it has since the world began. But you are not intended to create fortunes, only maintain the magic."

As she spoke, it was almost as if that hole I'd ripped in my spirit when I killed Titus was flooded with power. The one Cypherion's love had solidified the edges of while I forged myself into something new.

Now, I was not only some*thing* new. I was some*one* powerful.

"What lies in Ambrisk's future then? Will Echnid...destroy it? Wage another war of gods?"

"He will try," Moirenna confirmed gravely, sitting back and crossing her legs. It was almost easy to convince myself she was not a goddess, that we were truly equals. With the power expanding within me by the moment, with the way my blood churned with the stars, I could believe it.

She gestured to Valyrie, and the Angel did not think twice before she settled down beside us, the goddess, the Prime Warrior, and the Fatecatcher sitting in a circle in this unearth-bound palace.

"There are ways to stop him," Valyrie answered. "I cannot dictate Fate, and I do not know the answers, but the only true way to stop him lies in the heart of the seraph with her volatile power. Help her, Fatecatcher." Valyrie took my hand, begging. "Push the bounds of that magic. Your friends may be the answer we lacked so very long ago. Ophelia can confirm a finality to the Balance."

I studied her for a moment. Her wide navy eyes softly swirling with galaxies. Her posture almost identical to mine, hands folded in her lap and leaning forward earnestly.

"You are truly on our side?" I asked softly, not daring to hope.

Valyrie nodded. "I am doing everything I can from beneath his thumb."

Some of the others in my group carried disdain for the Angels, and I understood why. Thorn had tried to kill Tolek for sport, Damien had betrayed us, the whole lot of them had used Ophelia for their nefarious needs. But the one before me now seemed so genuine, and the Fates whispering through my body—the power I now held as the Fatecatcher—screamed to believe her.

Daringly, I placed my other starlit hand atop her own, our silver-ring-clad fingers twisting together. "And we will do everything we can. Please, be careful, Valyrie."

The Angel nodded.

I turned my attention back to Moirenna. "Why am I the Fate-catcher?"

"Because you have earned this honor," the goddess answered.

"Honor?" The power grasping my spirit and soothing its edges reared its head at the word, and though it was natural, it sparked a hint of worry. Was it an honor, or was it a pressure? Another weight after Titus used my magic for so long? Another thing to control me?

"You have never failed to embrace your magic. You have loved the Fate ties as they are intended to be, and you have flourished *with* them—not in spite of them. Many who are given the gifts you have been given crumble beneath the weight, but you own them. They *are you*."

Her words landed, but I didn't understand them at first. My magic was simply who I was. I neither chose to embrace it nor push it aside, I simply lived with it.

A smile spread across the goddess's beautiful face as if she heard that reasoning, and I supposed that bone-deep assurance was exactly what she'd meant.

I breathed in that truth now—that fate. I had always been meant for more than a chancellor's grasp. I'd been meant to break free of those chains, to live beyond them. Now, I would do so with the power of a goddess flooding my veins.

"Now that Echnid has"—I chewed my next words carefully—"gotten rid of you, do you know what his next move will be? Now that he's won…"

"He has not won," Moirenna reminded me. "As long as there are warriors on Ambrisk to stand against him, the god has not won. No matter how dark the nights seem."

Valyrie's eyes gleamed with the goddess's assessment. We could still end him. There was a chance—we only had to find it.

Moirenna went on, "I do not know precisely what magic he used to kill me—it did not happen as any of the times I had seen it play out—but I allowed that fortune to pass because in finally doing so, he exposed something pivotal."

"What?" I asked.

The goddess and Angel both grinned, and these were not the comforting, soft smiles they'd given me before. These were ruthless and cunning. Female deities who had survived for millennia on their own sheer will, daring to do what others would cower against. Daring to fight.

And Moirenna said, "Even gods can die."

CHAPTER FORTY-FIVE
OPHELIA

JEZEBEL LEANED HER HEAD ON MY SHOULDER IN THE doorway of her room in the guest house, the desert quiet in the night. The doors to the dunes were thrown wide, the moon speckling the ground, but despite the calm night, panic had gripped my chest all day since we fought Echnid.

"Why do you think he left?" Jezebel whispered as she dragged her fingertips through the sand gathered along the entrance.

"I don't know," I admitted. "Maybe it has to do with how the Angels can't enter the capitol. Or perhaps Echnid used too much magic against Moirenna."

Both ideas felt like the beginnings of a puzzle. The frayed threads that would contribute to a tapestry, but...we were missing something vital.

Jezebel sighed, watching the khrysaor and Sapphire frolic through the sky. "I'm so relieved you're back."

Kissing the top of her head, I asked, "How are things with Erista?"

"Good." Jez smiled and bit her lip, blushing softly. "We talked earlier, and she promises she didn't know anything about our Godsblood. She said she doesn't care about it, and even if her father tried to use it to their political advantage, she'd stand against him."

"You believe her, right?" I checked. She'd been so hurt when

323

that revelation had come out in the Hall of Wandering Souls, and while *I* thought Erista was telling the truth—especially after seeing how little she seemed to share her father's love for splendor—it only mattered that Jezebel was confident in that, too.

"I would have stood against him on my own to defend my blood," Jez began. "But it's nice to know she would stand by me."

My heart inflated at that, tears stinging my eyes. "You're feeling okay after the gorgons?"

She scoffed, turning fiery tawny eyes up to me. "Everyone seemed to freak out about it."

"You *were* shot with a poisoned arrow," I reminded her.

"My myth magic took care of it." She shrugged, faltering.

"What's wrong?" I asked.

"I just...wish I understood it better. I'm grateful for the power, don't misunderstand, but I wish I knew *why* we had it."

We had Godsblood, sure, but so did everyone in our mother's line. Why had the myth chosen us? Why now? What did we contain that those before us lacked? Was it as simple as the Angelblood in the Alabath line mixing with the Godsblood as it had to wake my Curse, or was it a hand dealt by the Fates?

"I don't know," I agreed, shaking my head. "All I know is that I'm thrilled it took care of whatever poison the gorgon laced her arrow with."

"All in a day's work," Jezebel said, flicking her hair over her shoulder.

"That's a horrifying thought."

"It's sort of fitting for the horrifying reality we're facing then, isn't it?"

Something inside of me went cold at the words, the panic in my chest digging in sharpened claws. "Yes, the horrifying reality..." I mused, light flaring in my vision.

Jezebel sat up straighter. "Don't do that."

"What?" I blinked away the power budding beneath my skin.

"Act like it's all on you."

I sighed, biting back a rush of magic, my heart pounding over my words. "Jez, I—"

"You what?" she challenged, and seraph power pushed at the

surface of my skin. Grasped for a release. "You suffered for us all? You were tormented and drugged by a deranged god? You take all of this so that we don't have to?"

With each question, my magic thrashed.

"I deserve it!" I exploded, and light burst from me, all seven shades of Angellight plus my own shimmering gold shot six feet around us. A column tunneled up to the sky, trapping me. Jezebel stumbled back. "*I deserve it*!" I screamed over the roar of my magic. "It is *my fault*. My fault, Jez, don't you understand?"

My sister pressed a hand to the medley of light separating us and yelled, "No! Under no circumstance do you carry this blame alone."

"But I did it!" With every panting breath, the wall of seraph power solidified, like a glass barrier keeping me from her.

Protecting us both, maybe.

But Jezebel—my courageous, devoted sister—pounded on the barricade. "You may have freed the god, but you did *not* do this!" Her voice rose, silver light crackling against mine, veins shooting through the gold. "You are not responsible for the actions of a deity or for the prophecies they've assigned to you."

Then why am I the one who must bear it?

There had to be some level of responsibility if I was the one carrying the burden, didn't there?

If you join Echnid, none of this will matter anymore.

No. I shuddered, wings flaring wide as if to shield me.

No, not that voice again. It echoed through me, grasping for me with such dominance.

"*Get out, get out, get out!*" I screamed. The taint of his mist poured down my throat, and I crashed to my knees, whimpering, "Echnid wants *me*. He wants me."

He had pulled at my magic today—he had taken it. I'd denied it until my shattering thoughts allowed the truth to push past my barrage of Angellight. Somehow, in the desert, Echnid had pulled my own magic from the air today. Had seemed to command it.

This fearsome, beautiful thing I'd come to claim—the power of myths and seraphs that I alone had woken—the god had used it as his own.

I'd thought he'd done it once before, when he was forcing me to hurt Malakai. But then, I'd had even less agency over the magic. I'd convinced myself it wasn't possible.

But he had.

The wall of power rippled around me in time with my shaking body, the light burning brighter.

"Ophelia!" Silver-blue bolts shot through my seraph power. "*Ophelia!*" Jezebel shrieked and shrieked.

Partner with the god, and all of these worries will be absolved, the voice slithered through me.

No—I couldn't. I wouldn't.

The phantom sensation of Echnid's misty power streamed into me, consuming me. I shuddered, choking on it. Clasped sand in my palms. The grains slid between my fingers—as so many things in life were. All of these little opportunities stolen and warped by a curse that was mine to bare.

But I tightened my grip. This curse was mine to bear, but it did not have to be mine to fall under.

My body is my own.

My mind is my own.

And with that thought, I screamed.

Echnid wanted me to become his puppet, his weapon. But I would become something else entirely.

The column of light exploded across the dunes, power tunneling out of me and wiping away the mist trying to claw out a home in my body. It dug up the roots of the taint and melted them until nothing but ash remained.

I'd burn the whole realm if that was what it took.

I didn't know how long I yelled, how long seraph magic illuminated the night. But I kept going until my throat was raw and there was nothing left of me to give.

And when the light winked out, all of that endless power snapping back into my body, I collapsed forward onto my hands and knees, my trembling wings draped around me.

"*Apeagna?*" Tolek stood before me, taking a step closer as worry-laced chocolate eyes met mine.

I shook my head. He shouldn't come near me. No one should,

not after the things I'd done beneath the god's hand. Anger and guilt and desperation coursed through me, each pounding in time with my pulse. My own war drum that had my wings beating along with it, soft thuds against the sand.

But Tolek dropped to the ground before me, not hesitating to pull me into his lap. Not hesitating to press soft kisses to my temple, my cheek, as furious golden tears dripped from my eyes, falling to the sand in gleaming puddles.

Because in all our years, Tolek Vincienzo had never let me break alone.

"I'm sorry, *apeagna*," Tol whispered again and again. "I'm here for you. None of us are going anywhere."

And it wasn't until he said that last sentence that I lifted my head and glanced beyond him. Jezebel had crouched next to us, brushing my hair back from my face, but...everyone was here. Malakai and Cypherion. Mila, Vale, and Erista. Even Mora, the fae's eyes dim with a brutal sympathy that said she understood to some extent how I was feeling.

I met Malakai's stare as I scanned them all, and a staggered beat of comfort echoed in the hollow Bind. I tried to send gratitude back, followed by a wave of sworn vengeance. He rubbed his chest, nodding as if he felt it.

A sob cracked up my ravaged throat, and I folded myself back into Tolek's embrace.

And there, with my family protecting me, I let myself shatter beneath the weight of everything I'd been forced to do and become.

Then, with Tol whispering sweet promises of revenge against my skin, I sealed those fissures with seraph magic and forged the person Echnid wanted to turn me into.

But instead of standing by his side, I would make the god bow at *my* feet.

Chapter Forty-Six
Santorina

The worry knotting my fingers in my apron was becoming more aggravating by the minute.

Lancaster slept off and on for a couple days after the attack on the human camp, only waking to retch occasionally and take small sips of water. His fae body was dispelling the toxins quickly, but it didn't escape me that in order for him to be struck so badly—leaving his skin pale and sticky with sweat from fever—it had to be powerful poison.

The male had told me once that fae didn't experience common illnesses. Their bodies were too powerful, healing too instant.

Why then was he now...like this?

I swore, pushing up from my chair beside his bed and crossing to the small kitchenette to organize my already-clean supplies. My eyes were dry and heavy, exhaustion begging me to settle for even an hour, but I couldn't. Every time I tried, the shredding sensation of a head being ripped from a body tore through me. The warm splatter of blood splashed across my features.

Lancaster's low groan as he collapsed before me echoed, and something in my chest rioted in alarm.

It was annoying, the thrumming instinct becoming a kicking, pounding against my ribcage again like a prisoner's fists trying to break through the bars. It rattled my thoughts, made the jars before me shake and blur, and a part of me wondered—

A groan reverberated behind me, and I spun, a bin in my hand before I even realized I was grabbing it. I sank beside the bed, but Lancaster didn't retch. He blinked his eyes open slowly this time, dark irises alert despite the shadows framing them. When that deep, searching stare landed on me, he sighed.

"Bounty."

I couldn't tell if it was relief or vexation in that tone. Perhaps the two were entwined, and he was happy to be able to speak but irritated that I was the one helping him yet again.

"How do you feel?" I asked hesitantly, setting the basin aside and sitting back in my chair. The scratchy material was warm from the hours I'd been planted here. Watching over him, sorting supplies, writing to Ophelia.

I pulled the seat closer, brushing a hand across his brow. Lancaster inhaled at the touch, his throat working over a swallow. His skin glistened with sweat, muscles taut in his bare shoulders, and his stare snagged mine. Goddess, I couldn't read those emotions.

"I am better," he announced, but the words were still tired. I jolted at his voice, removing my hand from his forehead.

"Your fever feels like it's gone," I agreed, clearing my throat.

"I have never had a fever before," he said almost curiously.

I laughed. "I think it was the thing's blood that did it."

"I figured as much," Lancaster said solemnly. His blinks were heavy, but he held my stare despite the clear need to rest, as if refusing to look away. And those words seemed very intentional. How could he know that? He'd been asleep while I passed letters back and forth with Ophelia. He didn't know what she'd explained to me about gorgons and their wretched, poisonous blood.

"What do you mean?" My jittering stilled now that he was awake and speaking. I leaned back in my chair.

Lancaster contemplated me for a moment. "My kind—fae— our magic is blood based, regardless of the class. Even my creation bound powers derive from the blood, which means we are extra sensitive to tainted sources. When the leaching power spread so quickly through my body, I assumed it was a result of the blood that creature forced into my stream."

"The gorgon," I corrected. "One of Echnid's personal mistresses from another realm, or something of the sort."

"Gorgon," he repeated. "I am sure my sister is having a field day with those legends."

"She *has* been working closely on investigating them, apparently." I handed Lancaster the letter in which Ophelia had explained what they suspected thus far about gorgons and Echnid's goal of raising a demigod force. It was the last one I'd received. Only silence had sustained since.

As Lancaster took the parchment, his fingers brushed mine. The tangled scents of flowers washed over me, less roses and more something unique that I couldn't name. Something new and bountiful. The soft hum vibrated in my chest.

The male's eyes darkened, but he carried on. I shook away the sensation as he read, and by the time he was nodding in understanding of the horror that had attacked us, I'd collected myself.

"What did you mean your kind is *sensitive* to blood?" I asked.

Once, he wouldn't have answered. He would have stormed away in a huff, making a joke about my lack of knowledge as a short-lived mortal.

Now, Lancaster pushed himself up straighter, shirtless muscles tensing as he reclined against the headboard. His features open and much more relaxed than I'd expected upon his waking.

"I should not share this." There it was. Secrets of the fae. But he went on, and I tried to hide my surprise. "Fae magic is more complex than we lead our enemies to believe. There are a number of unique facets. One of which—the most useful if you ask me—is the ability to absorb power from the blood of another."

Absorb another's power? "Does that mean..."

"If we drink one's blood or consume it in any way, a fae temporarily engages their power."

I blinked, unable to hide my shock this time. "*Any* power?"

"Any power, Bounty." He nodded. "It is one of the best kept secrets of our kind. Blood exchanges are closely monitored among fae. They are only meant to be used in extreme cases."

That was dangerous. A way to outsmart any enemy if you could simply get your hands on their blood, like when the gorgon forced her sliced wrist against his lips. And with those sharpened canines peeking out as Lancaster spoke, it couldn't be hard to do.

"Ritalia did it," Lancaster said. Was that derision in his voice? "That night in the mountains when she burned Ophelia's weapons. That was not her magic. I do not know which soldier she took it from—she hid our powers as much as possible—but it was not hers."

A form of summoning magic. Or perhaps a contrast to Lancaster's, where he created, she destroyed. A balance, as our entire world and every realm in existence was built on.

"Do you think you absorbed the gorgon's power when it fed you its blood?" I asked.

He toyed with the sheet as he thought. "If I hadn't fainted, I think I would have absorbed it. But it appears whatever poison she carried was stronger than the absorbing power. I'd wager other facets of my magic battled the toxins off enough to keep me alive."

"Healing magic?" I asked, my eyes dropping to my hands. Suddenly, my own healing capabilities felt so useless. I'd stirred tonics, applied compresses to his skin, and cleaned his wounds, but that was truly all I could have done against this.

For the first time, incapability curved my shoulders in.

Unexpectedly, a finger was beneath my chin, tilting my eyes up. "Healing magic, yes. But also other things. Things no healer—no matter their strength, intelligence, or origins—could have provided."

Gods, how had he known that thought was going through my mind? He saw straight through me, to the wounds I kept hidden. The belief I rarely indulged that because I was human, I was smaller. It did not lift its head often, but when it did, the thought struck deep. As if because it was neglected, it gathered power for the times I unintentionally set it free.

Lancaster's skin burned into mine, his eyes searching as he ensured I heard his words—ensured I felt them deep to those hidden parts of myself. Why? Why was he being...*kind*? I was a Bounty; he was a Hunter. Natural-born enemies, divided by the instincts to kill one another.

And yet he looked at me with a softness I'd only seen him

direct at his sister. Perhaps it was gratitude for keeping him comfortable while his body healed. But I owed him after he saved my life.

"How did you do it?" I forced out, voice as small as I'd felt a moment ago.

"Do what, Santorina?" His skin still burned into mine, that unfamiliar floral scent ladening the air. And the way he said my name…I'd never heard him say anyone's name like that.

"How did you rip off the gorgon's head with your bare hands? They're supposed to be difficult to kill."

Lancaster's jaw ticked, and he dropped his arm. A cold settled across my skin as he sat back against the pillows. "I was…angry."

"Why?"

Those dark eyes pierced me, the florals wrapping tighter between us. That hum in my chest beat fists against my ribs. I swore I could hear the pounding in the silence.

Lancaster sighed. "I never wanted this life. I never wanted to be…the Hunter." Malice twisted through those words.

Mora had told me as much. She'd implied on more than one occasion that there was more to her brother, and I'd spent countless nights wondering how he became this creature bred to slaughter me. Digging up old texts on the fae that now crowded my room back in Xenovia.

I scooted to the edge of my seat, keenly hoping he was going to show me now.

"This may be a surprise to you, Bounty, but it does not please me to kill those who have no power over their instincts. Who may even be unaware of the instincts within them. But I do it because it was a promise I made."

"A promise?" I asked, but he was too focused on his story, eyes on me, mind in the past.

"When I was eighteen, I was summoned to the capital with my mother. I was her youngest child, and since I'd been born, we'd resided in the country." A soft laugh. "I should have known there was something wrong. My mother, much like my sister, was born to be in the bustling city. They were both invigorated by the life of it all.

"Mora was already there. In Ritalia's employ for her glamour magic." He grimaced as if the tie of his family to the late queen pained him physically. "She wanted me, too. I was promised to her by my mother in exchange for keeping her secrets."

"What secrets?"

That time, he seemed to hear my question. His eyes flicked back and forth between mine. My chest pounded.

"My mother's blood is very powerful."

"And Ritalia could scent bloodlines," I finished for him. It was how the queen had kept her enemies and allies under her thumb—that very rare type of magic.

"She discovered what was within my mother the moment they met by happenstance when they were both young. And she kept traces on her and all her children over the centuries."

I'd asked before, and he'd never answered. First while stitching him up and plucking cypher splinters from his wound, and countless times since. Once he couldn't say it, and after he'd refused. But when I asked this time, something told me he was going to give me an answer.

"What is in your blood that she wanted?"

And with no preamble, Lancaster said, "My mother was the daughter of a demigoddess." Those words clanged through me. "Her mother was the daughter of Aoiflyn and a fae male of inconsequential power. Some would refer to my mother as a Deige. A child with Godsblood and blood of magic. Some simply refer to her as a demigoddess. Either way, the blood of the Fae Goddess, Aoiflyn, flows through our line."

It was a conversation we'd had before.

"Why is your magic—and your sister's—so much more powerful than a typical fae?"

He dragged his tongue over his teeth. Ground his jaw. And—

"Why aren't you answering, Lancaster?"

Nothing beyond his nostrils flaring as I said his name and hatred pooling in his dark eyes.

"It's related to the Gods and Goddesses you're blocked from speaking of."

Gods, I'd known then that there was some sort of connection, but I hadn't dared to consider it might be the actual blood of a Goddess herself within the fae siblings. It was unprecedented. Until Ophelia and Jezebel, I'd believed Godsblood was so far removed from the present day, it wasn't possible more than a drop flowed in the veins of the descendants. Not enough to make them powerful, surely.

How recently had the Gods walked the realm?

"Is that why you never spoke of it?" I asked. "Did Ritalia bind you from sharing this lineage?"

Lancaster nodded. "When she died, that bargain snapped, but it was natural to keep secrets that did not seem prudent."

"To protect your mother," I whispered. And Gods, I wished my chest didn't crack at that statement. If my mother was still here, I'd have done anything to guard her secrets.

Lancaster's expression shattered just as my heart did. "I wish it was for the reason you're thinking, Bounty." It was the most distress I'd ever seen bleeding across his sharp features. Lips down-turned and eyes burning with centuries of pain. "Ritalia first manipulated my mother, then her children. When I went to the capital, my mother moved with me. She wanted to oversee my Hunter training, and that was when I first observed the dynamic between her and the queen."

His words tightened as he went on. "It became clear Ritalia was making her into a tool. She used her for her body, to produce powerful children to line the queen's guard and man posts across Vercuella over the centuries." Lancaster fisted the sheets, shaking his head. "Then, when she had the Hunter she'd been waiting for —when my mother's blood mixed with the right male for me to appear and be forced at Ritalia's whim—she stopped protecting my mother."

He sat forward, the sheet falling low around his hips, his elbows braced on his knees.

"All it took was one person to learn who she was—one thief to break in while she was unguarded, and one powerfully poisoned cup of faerie wine with no cupbearer to taste—and even my mother's demigoddess blood couldn't save her life. The male who did it never even looked her in the eye as he robbed her, took vials of her

Godsblood from her vein, and murdered her. And I promised then I would protect those this world tried to beat and cheat the power out of."

Thieves are dishonest.

That night, before we went to the Gates of Angeldust and retrieved the final Angel emblem, before the mountain theater and Ritalia and Echnid and everything—those were the words he'd spat at Brystin, the fae sent to break into Ophelia's room and steal the emblems.

Thieves are dishonest.

It hadn't only been because of the pure fact that fae cannot lie. It was a deeper wound scratched open when a male snuck into someone's room in the dead of night. Had he seen his mother in Ophelia's place, as I did every battle my friends ran in to?

"I'm sorry, Lancaster," I said softly, holding his gaze. "I'm sorry you've been used that way, and I'm sorry you lost her."

The ache behind my ribs stretched deeper, like I was feeling his pain, too. But for the first time since the gorgon attacked, the pounding in my chest quieted.

"I killed the male brutally," he admitted.

I smiled softly. "Good."

He huffed a small laugh. "I have spent centuries being angry about the cowardly way my mother was taken. And when that gorgon attacked you, all the anger pooling within me erupted. Something within me *needed* to slaughter her—the Hunter needed to protect you more than it did hurt you."

Those words rang through my body like a pulse, a string plucked. That low hum pulled me toward him, leaning forward in my chair just as he did on the bed. That thing in my chest was unavoidable and insistent, needing to attend to the vulnerability in his words.

"I'm okay, Lancaster," I assured him. "You saved me."

Goddesses, I hated that that was true. But I couldn't deny it. And it was that gratitude that had me ripping open my own wounds to show him he was not alone.

"I understand that pain," I went on. "I lost my parents in the first Engrossian-Mystique War. Before Malakai signed the treaty, they died. For a battle that wasn't theirs. It was unjust and cruel that their lives were cut short like that. But what keeps me moving forward is the reminder that every day I wake up—every day we survivors go on—we are doing so in their image, with their dreams and hopes and visions of a brighter future shining in our every step."

"I did not know how they died," he muttered. "I am sorry." There were more words beneath his stare, but he held them in. Like he was still figuring out how to phrase them.

"You should rest," I finally said after a long silence of being picked apart by those intense irises.

Lancaster's eyes drooped over me, then around my shoulder. "Where will you sleep?"

I patted the arms of the chair, leaning back. "Right where I have been." I hadn't slept, but there was an odd concern in his voice that made me not want to admit that.

The fae looked at the bed he had yet to move from. "I would not mind if you wanted to sleep here."

"Where?" I asked, hands tightening on the arms of my chair.

Lancaster gestured to the bed. "Here."

"Where will you sleep?" I asked.

"Also here."

My brows rose.

"This bed is large enough for two. Though I would suggest changing the sheets as I seem to have sweat with the fever." A disgusted crease formed between his brows, and I laughed at the reminder that Lancaster had never experienced a fever before. He didn't know the symptoms.

I did as he suggested, letting him rinse off in the attached bathing chamber as I switched out the clean linens Lislee had provided. The humans seemed to have come around on the fae since he defended them and their children.

Then, I changed into a softer, short-sleeved tunic, and we settled down side-by-side in the bed. And while it was technically large enough for two, it was swarmed by the presence of the not-immortal fae.

Our arms brushed as I shifted.

"Sorry," I said, looking up at the ceiling in the dark.

"It is all right," he clipped. Gone was the vulnerability in his tone. The tightness had returned.

The air was thick, and with us both in this bed, the floral scent drowned me. I forced away all the things I thought it might mean, refusing to acknowledge them until I had proof. Instead, I stared out the window, pretending it was that fresh night air I was drinking in.

Lancaster dozed off beside me, his fae blood likely still burning away the poison. The moonlight accentuated the sharp lines of his face as the secrets we'd exchanged filled the space between us.

My mind wandered in the silence, but it kept returning to one question. How would Echnid banishing the known Gods from Ambrisk affect Lancaster and Mora? And would their Godsblood make them a target? A pawn, as Ophelia and Jezebel had become?

The blood of a Goddess in their veins.

It was threats of the Warrior God that painted my dreams that night, making me restless, my chest pounding and humming abrasively until a calm *finally* stole me.

When I woke in the morning, an arm was draped possessively across my waist, as if guarding me from fitful sleep.

CHAPTER FORTY-SEVEN
MALAKAI

AFTER ECHNID'S ATTACK, MILA AND I STAYED WITHIN the city while testing her Reflector powers. Thin streams of Spirit-blessed water carved through a portion of Meridat's land, and we'd found a tangle of them in one corner, near the edge of the property. Mila sat at the center, drawing lazily in the sand as she studied the water.

"Can you see anything?" I asked, arms crossed.

Mila shook her head. "Nothing."

Sinking to the sand, I rubbed her shoulder. "You've been trying this for a while, Mila. Maybe we should take a break."

We were all exhausted. Vale had been overwhelmed with her power when they all returned, and she and Cyph had barely left their room all day. Jezebel had been nearly vibrating with her myth magic after dragging up so much of it to fight Echnid, and Ophelia...

The image of her in the sand, light pummeling the dunes and her so tormented, haunted me. What I'd gone through with Echnid had left scars, but what Ophelia went through had been a different level of violation, and I was damn tired of seeing it happen.

Echnid's recent attack and killing of a goddess had tightened shackles around our damn wrists, but it had also ignited the need to fight within us all. The moment Mila heard a recount of the battle, she jumped into action. The general strategizing for war. And the first step she wanted to take was turning this new power of hers into a weapon aimed at the Warrior God.

The lack of results was clearly aggravating her, making me desperate in turn. She dug her hands deeper in the sand surrounding the streams.

"There's wavers." Her teeth ground. "It's a thin film over what I'm seeing, but I don't think I'll be able to actually see into realms unless one of those creatures is nearby."

My heart beat uncomfortably fast with that implication. "Let's think about it," I said around the fear tightening my chest. "Figure out the best way to make it happen without risking anything."

"I should have been there when Echnid attacked." Her hands fisted, and in a broken whisper, she added, "Lyria would have been there."

"Mila," I sighed, massaging the back of her neck as I sat beside her. "Lyria might have been there. Or she might not have been. None of us could have predicted that."

Her silky white braid slipped over my hand as she looked up at me, silver lining her ice blue eyes. "I want to see her. Since we figured out what I can do—what I've become—I think a small part of me has been hoping I would see her, in whatever realm she's in."

Hoping for a chance to see her best friend one more time. Across realms, sure, but just to get that moment of closure. We'd talked a lot about Lyria since I came back from Damenal—she and Tolek had, too, and there was one thing Mila continually wrestled with: She wanted to live centuries in her best friend's honor, but she didn't know how.

She hadn't mentioned leaving the army since Lyria died, but following the last war, she'd wanted to. A part of me wondered if that would be an easier place to heal, but I couldn't decide that for her. And I wouldn't force her into it. Spirits knew Mila let me heal from a fucking mess. She just held my hand and reminded me that I wasn't alone.

I didn't know what it felt like to lose someone who was practically a sister—I hoped I never did—but I sure as Spirits experienced loss. All I could do was be at her side, even though I didn't have a single fucking answer.

"We're going to keep trying." It was a lame response, but it was all I could think to say. Time and effort. A path forward that looked like it may never end.

Mila's gaze dropped to the streams again. "I wish I could have said goodbye."

"Perhaps it is not goodbye," Mora said, and Mila and I both shifted our attention to the fae female, lounging in the shade of a palm tree and flipping through her books on demigods. "Just because you have not figured out an answer yet, does not mean you never will. Your life is only beginning, Mila Lovall. True solutions, the lasting and impactful kind, often take time. That does not mean they won't come or that you will carry this pain in your heart forever. And even if it is not through your Reflector powers, you will see signs of her across the world. You must simply look for them."

"It's not goodbye," Mila repeated, a light dawning in her eyes that I hadn't seen in weeks. She turned back to me, vitality renewed.

"Now, I would like to try something," Mora said. Closing her book and standing, she disappeared through the trees. When she returned, the khrysaor and Sapphire followed her.

"How long have you had them waiting?" I asked.

"As long as we've been out here," she stated as if it was common sense.

Mila pushed to her feet, turning her back on the streams. "And why?"

"These creatures are of this realm, technically, but legends say they are not solely from here. They were born of the constellations, which traverse multiple worlds. I'd like to see if your Reflector powers respond."

"It's worth a try," Mila said with a sigh that sounded both wary and determined.

Taking another deep breath, she faced the khrysaor and pegasus, the three creatures staring back at her with equal resolve. I swore they seemed to thrum with power after their recent battle.

Like facing off against Echnid had fueled them. Each of them stood docilely, though, blinking at Mila with clear understanding and probably the same desire for a fight that was now rolling off my general.

"I don't quite know what activates it," Mila said, not tearing her eyes from the animals.

"If it is like other magic sources, you will have to reach inside yourself," Mora taught patiently. "When you went into that river, the magic embedded itself in your soul. It became a part of you. Remember, Reflectors come from Artale. They are touched by a Goddess."

I ignored the panic grating through my chest, tried not to remember Mila limp in my arms. As if she felt it, she reached a hand back to me. I slipped mine into her waiting palm, squeezing once.

We were all silent for a few moments, Mora continuing to coach Mila through distinguishing the power within her. She gave Mila a small dish of water from the streams to dip her fingers in, trying to channel the magic. Dynaxtar canted her head, her silver mane shimmering while Zanox stood unnaturally still, intimidatingly so, and Sapphire's tail swished behind her.

After long minutes where I fought the nerves making me jittery, Mila gasped.

"What is it?" I asked.

"It's—they're flying. Hordes of them."

"The khrysaor and pegasus?" I asked, and Mila nodded.

"It's some kind of battle."

"Is it the same place you saw the gorgons last time?" I just wanted to keep her talking so she didn't slip into this vision completely. Spirits, how did Cyph deal with this happening to Vale all the time with her readings? No wonder he became such a grumpy ass over her protection.

"I can't be sure." Mila shook her head, voice entirely lucid.

"Keep digging," Mora instructed.

Mila did. She relayed the formations of the armies and the khrysaor flying above. Then—

"It's changing," she whispered.

"What do you mean?" I asked.

"There's only one person now. And she's—" Her explanation cut off as the reflection was playing out before her eyes. I gripped my sword just to make myself feel less useless. My chest ached, and I rubbed the heel of my palm down it.

Finally, Mila blinked back to awareness. The khrysaor and Sapphire jolted into movement, too, grazing along the sparse tree line.

Mila whirled toward the fae, and even Mora's eyes widened. "It was you," she gasped.

"What did you see?" Mora asked, clearly as caught off guard as I was.

"Not you precisely, but I saw someone who looked like you." Mila tilted her head, trying to put the pieces together.

"A glamour?" I asked.

"I don't think so. There were enough differences that it *was* someone else."

Mora's gentle, ever-present curiosity flamed to something brighter. "Was she older, perhaps? Her skin fairer and eyes green?"

Mila nodded, taking a step forward. "You know her."

"I believe it was...my mother." Tears lined the fae's eyes, some deep emotion I didn't understand, but she didn't seem like she was going to offer up any more information.

Not wanting to pry too deeply into that, I tried to keep us on track. "Was your mother from another realm?" I asked hesitantly.

Mora shook her head. "No, but she had very special blood."

"A Realmspinner?" I asked.

"No," Mora answered, again not offering more details.

"She was fighting," Mila explained, picking up on the female's evasiveness. "She was jumping between places. Infiltrating enemy camps with her glamour."

"With her glamour..." Mora's words trailed off, and she turned her face toward the heavens, muttering. A prayer, maybe. When she was done, she looked back at us, grinning mischievously. "That gives me an idea."

CHAPTER FORTY-EIGHT
OPHELIA

THE DAYS FOLLOWING ECHNID'S AMBUSH WERE SPENT either shut in the capitol meeting chambers with representatives of various clans, strategizing how to take down a god, or we were training. Unable to rest for fear of the god striking, I practiced with seraph magic and flying. Turning my light into a number of physical weapons and mastering the winds. What the god had done to me, and what Thorn had tried to do to Tolek, lit a renewed fire in my Spirit, and it burned between us all.

Following Moirenna's death, Vale was almost always tucked away communicating with the Fates to try to read what the god had done, and Cypherion planned for the incoming Starsearcher forces and imbued weaponry to stand among our own. Soulguiders continued to gather historical accounts of godly magic, led by Erista. Malakai and Mila explored Reflector powers with Mora, and Bodymelders were working on a mass triage strategy in case this war did bloom. Xenovia was flooded with warriors of almost every clan, and the tense threat of a god wrapped the city's borders.

"I don't think we need to fear him infiltrating the city," Erista proposed as she entered the war room where Meridat and I worked. Steaming cups of tea sat between the chancellor and myself, the herbal aroma doing nothing to soothe me.

"Why not?" I asked.

Erista flipped open a book on Artale. Faded ink stretched

across the top of the page, barely legible despite the bronze myst-light chandelier overhead. "This legend claims Artale provided extra protections to the city named for her daughter. That no god may enter."

Reluctant to feel too relieved, I scanned the page, ether softly unspooling around my wings. "That would explain why he didn't follow us here," I murmured, searching for a loophole in the text.

"If that's true," Meridat began with a reassuring smile, "then theoretically, Xenovia would be the safest place for us all to be gathering."

"Or the biggest target," I countered as gold light shimmered faster along my wings.

"A good point," Meridat agreed with a nod.

Before we could discuss it any further, Jezebel burst into the room, cheeks flushed and a beaming smile on her face. "You have to see what's just arrived!"

We raced after her, past the delicate mosaics, elegantly carved arches, and detailed frescos adorning the halls, calling a number of questions, but they all died on the breeze when we exited the building and saw who—and what—waited before the massive sculpture of Xenique that marked the heart of Xenovia.

"Ezalia!" I called, rushing down the steps and across the square as the Seawatcher Chancellor came into view. "How in the name of the Angels did you get a *cannon* here?"

"I don't care how," Tolek said, eyes glowing as he emerged from the crowd with Cypherion. "I only care what we're going to *do* with it." He placed a quick kiss to the chancellor's cheek before scurrying to the weapon, which was on a wheeled cart. Spirits, the thing must have weighed tons. No wonder their progress was slow.

"Just what he needed," Cypherion muttered, fighting the first small smirk I'd seen him flash since the ambush. "Good to see you again, Ezalia."

"And you," the chancellor said, nodding at Cyph and hugging me to her.

"CK! Mali! Come look!" Tol yelled, as excited as a child given his first sword. Malakai, Mila, and Mora had just arrived, the three admiring the weapon. Cypherion excused himself, leaving me with the chancellor.

"Thank you for coming," I said, relief unwinding in my chest. Ezalia had not only become a political ally since I assumed my title as Revered, but she was a friend. A hugely comforting presence in the wake of my father's death, too.

"From what your letters said, this is every warrior's battle." Ezalia nodded, her sharp features set in determination. She stepped back against the fencing of a tailor's shop, the city center crowded with onlookers as the Seawatchers branched off to find their assigned lodgings. "Tell me everything," she added.

And there was something in her firm authority that made me comfortable enough to expose how truly frightened I'd been while Echnid held me down. While he'd drugged me in Damenal. It was the same sort of assurance Meridat provided, the two women having ruled peacefully for decades with reigns I hoped to emulate.

If I couldn't have my father for guidance, I was grateful for them.

By the time I finished, Ezalia's face had paled slightly, but her sea glass eyes were sharp as daggers.

"I don't know how a god can be killed," she said as we climbed the steps back into the capitol building. "But I've seen unheard of magic before. We will find a way."

And as we filed into our seats with the others following, a tempest of fury roared in her stare.

Erista and Jezebel sent quick Mystique ink notes to the other clan leaders currently in Xenovia, notifying them of Ezalia's arrival and the meeting about to be held.

"While we wait..." Cypherion cleared his throat when Vale arrived. "We have something we need to share."

All eyes swiveled their way. They exchanged a look, seeming to communicate silently.

The Starsearcher nodded, folding herself into Cyph's side. Her hair slipped behind her shoulder, and I swore the angle made her tattoo appear larger.

Cypherion continued, "While we were in Valyn, we became Fatesworn."

The following silence echoed so loud, you'd hear the beat of a pegasus's wings leagues off.

Then, Tolek slammed his hand down on the table and blurted, "On Damien's fucking grave!"

"I told you he'd take it well," Jezebel muttered to Cypherion.

"By the Spirits," Cyph grumbled.

"*Take it well?*" Tolek snapped. "One of my best friends became promised to the woman he loves in an unbreakable bond, and I *missed it?*"

"It wasn't a large ceremony, and we're going to receive the Bind anyway," Cypherion explained. Vale only snickered and tried to cover her smile with her hand.

"Large ceremony or not, I should have been included!" Tolek demanded.

"I'm your cousin! I should have been a witness," Malakai added, stifling his amusement as he joined Tolek's argument, clearly more to rile him up than anything.

"You, too?" Cypherion dragged a hand down his face.

"Did you say the vows? The tattoos?" Tolek insisted. How he knew so much about the Fatesworn ceremony, I didn't know, but he was a romantic at heart.

"Yes," Cypherion gritted out.

"You got a tattoo without telling us?" Malakai pushed.

At his grin Cyph threw out a hand. "It just appeared! Not like I had a say over it." Vale scoffed, mockingly offended, and Cyph ducked his head. "Of course, I would have chosen it if I did." Then, he looked back at Malakai. "You don't even care! You're only trying to encourage him."

"I care very much!" Malakai insisted. Mila elbowed him, but she was laughing, too. And Spirits, it was such a relief to see everyone joking in this odd moment hovering between godly threats; for a moment, I reveled in it.

Tolek fell into a seat at the table taking up the majority of the room beneath the bronze chandelier. I stepped beside him, rubbing a hand across the back of his neck and shoulders, his winged tattoo peeking over the collar of his tunic.

"We're all thrilled for you," I said to Cypherion and Vale.

"Both of you. Vale, I always suspected you'd fit in with our family. I'm pleased you made it official."

"Thank you, Revered." Vale leaned further into Cypherion, and the full expanse of her new tattoo caught the mystlight. A veritable galaxy was inked in silver upon her skin, absorbing the old binding mark Titus had placed on her. Together, it was like she and Cypherion had remapped the stars.

Tol's fingers wrapped around mine on his shoulder, but when I looked down, his eyes were on my Bind. And instead of a promise, the North Star was a brand. As long as I had it, there'd be no receiving a second. No way for Tolek and me to link our souls as mine and Malakai's should have been.

Clearing my throat, I straightened and pressed a kiss to Tol's temple. He tilted his head, catching my eyes, and he understood the reassurance I was offering. We may not have a soul bond, but we had this instinctual connection we'd nurtured unknowingly for years. One no god or Angel could steal from us or weaponize.

Finally, the remaining council members filed into the room, and I redirected the conversation. "Now, lifelong bonds aside, we need to make a plan for Echnid. The cannons could be helpful with the god based on how he caused Moirenna to..."

"Implode?" Cypherion offered dryly.

A shiver went out across the table. It certainly did look like that when the goddess faded from existence, but there had been a grace about it, too. Based on what Vale said about communicating with her in a recent session, I wondered if the gods had spirits that could continue to live elsewhere.

With that troubling thought in mind, I said, "We need to make sure whatever we do to him, it's final. Not even a hint of him can remain. Not like Moirenna."

"The goddess insisted it can be done," Vale said, her voice taking on a power I'd never heard from her before. "Valyrie said she's read that it's with you, Ophelia. Finality in the Balance."

Jezebel's feet slipped from where they were propped on the arm of Erista's chair. She leaned forward. "Does she know how?"

Vale shook her head.

"As cryptic as ever," I mentioned as images of my magic illuminating the desert pounded through my mind, Jezebel's silver flickering through it.

Tolek scrawled notes, saying, "That's only the god. We have to be able to battle any forces he brings. We can't rely on only Ophelia and Jezebel to be able to kill the gorgons or demigods."

"And the cerberus," Malakai reminded us. I met his hard stare, and I knew we were both recalling the beast that prowled in Echnid's defenses, the one whose affection he'd won through a stone wall. We hadn't seen her since Damenal.

"I can try to raise more aerial forces of gryphons and sphinxes," I suggested. "But that won't help us on the ground. And I can't seem to do it with just any source."

"What do you mean?" Cypherion asked.

"I've been trying with other renditions of sphinxes around the city," I explained. "It has to be a true myth frozen in time. Like the ones in the Gates of Angeldust." Unfortunately, Ithinix was last spotted loitering near the mountains, likely waiting for Xenique.

"What about the gryphon? You pulled that thing from a tapestry," Malakai suggested.

Vale said, her eyes swirling silver, "That was Valyrie."

I met the Starsearcher's eyes and nodded. "I'd suspected that for a while. Valyrie was very busy shopping in Damenal. I think she knew we'd need an escape route Echnid wouldn't suspect. She placed a tapestry that trapped the mythical beast in our path, covered it up with her other expensive purchases around the palace, and told me about the legends of gryphons to point me toward it."

"We really can trust her," Jezebel muttered.

Ezalia's lips pursed as she massaged the back of her neck. "That makes one."

"Two," Meridat added, speaking of her own Angel.

"Two," I agreed. The reminder was a slight relief.

"So, the cerberus," Malakai said, bracing his elbows on the table, scanning the map. "We need something that could challenge a creature of that size. Especially if he could possibly bring more."

Mila gasped, gripping Malakai's arm. "You know who had mounts that could rival a cerberus?"

Malakai searched her gaze, and it almost felt as if they were communicating just as Cypherion and Vale had. Then, his eyes widened. "Mindshapers." His attention snapped to Tolek and me. "They had them during the final battle. Wolves. Rode them into the mountains."

"Like Rebel?" I asked.

"Even larger," Malakai said.

For a brief moment, my heart inflated, but Meridat asked, "Do we have a Mindshaper contact?" and I deflated.

"A contact, but not anything near an alliance." We'd written to the Mindshapers to alert them of the current threats, but we'd given them only necessary facts, not knowing who was receiving the letters or assuming leadership.

Spirits, I was wary of anything to do with that clan since Tolek had been kidnapped last year and we'd learned the true depths of their magic. It was the most manipulative and dangerous of any, in my opinion. Had that power grown with Thorn's influence and Echnid's return?

"We don't have an *official* alliance," Tolek added, voice harsh. "But we do have a debt we could call in."

I sighed. "That's one I'll have to go in person for."

"You can't," Erista reminded me. "If Echnid truly can't enter Xenovia, you can't leave the city."

At her partner's side, Jezebel nodded vigorously. Angels, she looked so scared, tawny eyes wide and lips pressed firm. So young and worried about me breaking, like when she'd first found the Curse on my wrist and insisted I would not face it alone.

Jezebel wasn't that girl anymore. No, the warrior who swooped in on the back of a khrysaor to save me from a deranged god was not young and inexperienced. She was capable of conquering the realms, and still the thought of something happening to me rattled her defenses. My chest tightened.

"She's right, Ophelia." Meridat nodded grimly. "Echnid seems to want *you* specifically."

They were correct, but with the might of a god breathing down our necks, it would take all seven clans united to stand against him.

We'd been here before, attempting to rally a united front against Kakias. But this was so much bigger than a broken-spirited queen. This was the fate of Ambrisk's Balance and the fabric of the realms woven around us. And a clock ticked over our heads, counting down to a god's domination.

"I know it's risky, but we have to figure out a way," I said as that time beat on in my mind, making my magic ripple over my skin. "Even with all seven clans, we might not stand a chance against Echnid. His force may very well blow through whoever stands against him, but our best attempt at survival is together. There's been division among the Gallantian Warriors for too long." I looked at every person in the room, imploring, "Is that the world we want to build? To leave behind? Do we want the legends to say we stepped aside, or do we want our legacies to be that we fought with the beating heart of this world?"

Because there was a very real chance many of us would be leaving legacies behind in the coming battles, no more than stories on a page for our ancestors. What messages did we want them to learn?

As my words rang through the chamber, Mora, who had been silent the entire meeting, flashed her pointed smile and said, "I believe I have a plan."

Chapter Forty-Nine

SANTORINA

"YOU'RE CERTAIN?" I ASKED LANCASTER, NOT DARING to release the excitement budding in my bones. Anticipation tangled with that sensation still humming through my chest.

It hadn't relented the entire trip north as we traveled to the next training camp. And with it, nerves swept through me. We were near Caprecion now. My first home. I had so few memories of it, having moved to Palerman when I was only eight, but they were full of my parents.

"The scent is impossible to miss," Lancaster said, breaking me from those reveries. He studied me carefully, like he felt the yearning in my heart when I looked north.

He'd been doing that often since the gorgon attack. I wasn't sure if he was watching me to ensure nothing else came for me while we were working together or for some other reason. Perhaps to ensure I wasn't shifting toward my cypher dagger.

But I couldn't worry about it now. Not with the excitement from his response.

I continued gathering my things in the tent we'd been given in this camp. We were, once again, forced to share a small space, but I hadn't minded sleeping next to the male's steady breathing last night. Something in it was soothing, almost like my own personal lullaby. Everything Lancaster did had a rhythmic grace to it—apparently even his breathing.

The hours I'd spent caring for him after the attack seemed to have created a reliance on that consistency. If the lack of complaint was any indication, Lancaster was accepting it, too.

It was that comfort that made me ask, "What do I say as the queen's descendent?"

"That is up to you." Lancaster shrugged. "It needn't be anything more than a statement of ancestry if you don't want it to be. You could be a leader, or you could simply be one of them. I doubt any of them will expect you to outright be their queen, but they may turn to you for validation and guidance given that we are the ones exposing this bloodline."

Validation and guidance, like when I dealt a patient a difficult diagnosis. Hopefully, the Bounties would be welcoming to the idea, and I—as the last known descendent of the ancient Queen of Bounties—could help them figure out what it all meant, even if I didn't yet know.

Ducking beneath the tent flap, I picked up my boots only for the sole of one to flop down from the heel, the leather shredded.

"Fucking Goddesses," I cursed. I'd forgotten it had worn through last night when we'd arrived. I'd been too tired from the travel to care.

"What happened?" Lancaster asked, following me outside. Tents sat in orderly rows of six, stretching west toward the mountains. This camp wasn't as developed as some of them, still needing to establish proper housing for long term residents.

With a huff, I handed the fae my boot. "It broke last night."

"You've been wearing these for months?" he asked, inspecting them, bending the leather backward and forward as easily as if it was parchment.

"They've sufficed!" I declared. "They've gotten me through an entire war and many an emblem trial, might I add."

"I would wager that is why they look like this." Lancaster flipped the boot over so the heel flopped like a dead fish.

I turned my nose up. "Give it back. I'll find someone to fix it. We have to get to the training arena."

He shook his head. "There's no fixing this. You'll need a new pair."

"Then I will find a new one. Hand it over." Gods, he was *aggravating*. Right as I thought we were slipping into an easy partnership.

But of course, Lancaster did not do as I demanded—typical arrogant fae. Instead, he tossed the poor mangled boot into the nearest bushes.

"What was that for?" I yelled, making to run after it—with only one shoe on.

But a steel arm banded around my waist, the scent of flowers overwhelming me. Swallowing, I lifted my chin. Lancaster's dark irises were so close, his face angled down toward me with...was that amusement twinkling in his eye?

The string in my chest hummed with a deep, resonant note as the fae studied me. Once, being close enough to see the tips of his canines when his lips parted would have sent a bolt of fear through me. It certainly woke the Bounty instinct enough to make me want to lunge at him, but it did something else, too.

It sent a wave of fire crashing through my blood. It had me gripping his arm around my waist and reveling in the corded muscle, in the heat pouring off his skin. In the bob of his throat when he swallowed and the way his pupils dilated. Gods, I might fall right into that dark stare.

"What are you doing?" I breathed, with a deep swallow of the floral coated air.

Lancaster didn't speak—something told me he couldn't, that he didn't feel in control. Instead, he reached to the side, and from midair, pulled out a pair of boots.

Not just any pair. An exact replica of the ones I'd been wearing for weeks.

"You remembered what they looked like that easily?" I asked.

"I have a very good memory."

That sentence said too much. Had he been studying me as an adversary? A Hunter and his prey. The Bounty who was now in his grasp, his teeth close enough to dig into the skin of my neck—

I straightened at the thought, stepping back. "Thank you," I said as he extended the boots.

And when I slipped them on, abandoning the one remaining

from my old pair, I had to hold back a gasp. Lancaster had not simply created a pair of boots for me—they were worn in the exact places I needed so my feet wouldn't blister when I broke them in.

I dismissed the odd rush of emotion that thought wrought, the string in my chest being plucked again, and we resumed packing and strapping weapons to our bodies.

"What do Bounties smell like?" I asked, returning to our earlier conversation.

"It's smoky, like an earthy sort of ash," Lancaster said, sheathing a sword down his back. He didn't typically carry his weapons where they were visible, storing them wherever his magic allowed him to and pulling them out as needed, but today, he clearly wanted to intimidate.

"That doesn't sound pleasant," I said.

And Goddesses be damned—Lancaster laughed. It shocked me enough that I dropped my dagger to the dirt.

Picking it up, Lancaster extended it to me. "The scent is not meant to be appealing," he said, my fingers brushing his. "But I'm finding I like it."

Hum. Hum. Hum.

I had to tell that instinct in my chest to shut up. The sensation was drowning my thoughts.

"I smell roses," I blurted, my voice much more breathless than I intended.

Lancaster stiffened, and my cheeks heated. He was quiet for a long moment, sharp jaw ticking. Then, he said, "Let's go find the Bounties we're recruiting so we do not have to stay here another night."

He stalked off, his shoulders tight and steps precise down the dirt lane.

I watched him go, wondering what in the Gods' realms had just happened. But my worries were overshadowed when something ruffled behind me, and a Mystique ink letter flared to life over the lantern just inside the tent.

Scooping it up, I recognized Cypherion's handwriting.

"Well, I suppose it's good Lancaster doesn't want to stay," I muttered to myself.

We had to leave today.

CHAPTER FIFTY
CYPHERION

THIS COULD BE A CATASTROPHIC IDEA. BUT THEN AGAIN, when it came to the gods, there weren't many good ideas, were there?

I supposed if I wanted to figure out how we'd ended up here, I'd have to go back to when I was twelve years old and met my friends. I wouldn't trade that for the world, though. Them, and the Starsearcher before me with a serene, unworried expression on her face as her eyes swirled silver. Those were the things that mattered.

But this extremely reckless idea put everyone at risk.

It put *her* at risk, and that made the Fatesworn tattoo burn. Made my stomach tighten and my hands ache with the need to fight.

I opened my mouth to comment, but even with the stars in her eyes, Vale tutted. "Don't say it."

"Stargirl," I groaned.

"You've made your argument a dozen times, Cypherion."

"Then, once more won't hurt," I muttered, the bond riling even though the rational side of my brain knew she was capable of this.

Vale withdrew from her reading entirely at the tone of my voice, taking strides across the sandy space toward me. We were in a desolate area of the desert, far enough away from any city or even small settlements that no one would get hurt.

One where, if Erista was correct in her theory that Echnid couldn't enter Xenovia, the god *could* reach us. And hopefully he would. If Valyrie's plan with Vale succeeded, Echnid would take our bait and show up here, where we were prepared to distract him.

Dynaxtar drank from the small oasis, palm trees rimming the space to provide shade and cacti jutting up between them. As Vale approached and braced her hands on my chest, I eyed the khrysaor over her shoulder. Dynaxtar lifted her head, slitted eyes finding me like she felt my attention.

We protect her, I thought her stare said, and something in the Fatesworn bond relaxed in agreement. With a hand on my cheek, Vale pulled my gaze back to her. I had to admit, the worry eased for a minute.

"This will work," she assured me.

"And if he realizes he's been tricked, you read, and I fight," I repeated for what felt like the hundredth time, though anxiety still scratched through the bond.

Typically, I would work out a number of contingency plans for all of these vague situations—ones that allowed me to stop being so damn worried. I'd been trying to for the past few days of planning and travel, barely fucking sleeping.

But I'd come up empty beyond using Vale's stronger Fate connections to instruct me down the Fatesworn bond.

Spirits, I was the Mystique Second, but I'd been feeling less and less like a capable ruler lately.

My scythe was heavy against my back. That, the khrysaor, the adrenaline coursing through my veins, and the pure amount of power Vale contained, would have to be enough.

"I'm with Cypherion," Malakai called from where he leaned against a tree, arms crossed.

"Why does that not surprise me?" Mila joked, but she slid an arm around his waist, muttering something I couldn't hear.

"He doesn't know exactly what I am," Vale reminded me. "I've seen it. I'm as unprecedented as a seraph returning. He's curious—everyone is."

Ophelia's haunted stare when she first returned from Damenal flashed through my mind. "That's not as comforting as you think," I mumbled, pressing my lips to her forehead.

A shadow drooped over us, making the world colder.

"Dynaxtar," Vale said with a small laugh. She pulled back and patted the khrysaor's mane affectionately, but that slitted eye met mine again, and her promise repeated.

We protect her.

I nodded, and an alliance sealed between me and the beast. One centered on the incredible Starsearcher in our midst, the Fatecatcher of the goddess.

"Don't worry, Cyph," Jezebel added, emerging from the tree line atop Zanox, "we have a few hidden tricks, too."

My gaze flicked over her shoulder, but before I could comment, Vale gasped.

Her eyes were pure silver again, power practically rippling off her as it did the gods and Angels as the Fatecatcher channeled an abundance of readings. And that unsettling, misty voice that sounded so much like Moirenna's floated from her.

"It's almost time," she said with a proud grin. The Fatesworn bond between us hummed with awe. I could have wondered over it for days if the air ahead of us hadn't begun to waver.

"All right," I conceded, fists clenching. "Let's hurry."

Dynaxtar dropped a wing, and I boosted Vale up, following her onto the creature's broad back. I angled my scythe so it laid against her flank. It wasn't ideal, but with that protective look she'd given, I knew the khrysaor was okay with the weapon.

"Come on, Dynaxtar," Vale instructed, still reading.

Jezebel and Zanox marched steadily beside us, Malakai and Mila between the khrysaor as they purposefully crossed the dunes. White mist seeped through that rippling spot in the air ahead, swirling in a thin layer around the khrysaor's legs. Their clawed feet sank into the sand, but the beasts strode forward with the steadiness demanded of war with a god.

"I'm watching Valyrie's decisions," Vale whispered to me.

"She's been orchestrating specific moves all day so they would be tied to Echnid—wait..."

Her words trailed off.

I stiffened, hands tightening on her waist. "What is it?"

"Change of plans," Vale muttered, voice stony.

I exchanged a glance with Malakai, he and Mila pulling their swords. Jezebel tightened her grip on Zanox.

"What kind of change?" Malakai growled.

But in a blink, a tear ripped through the undulating air across the dunes.

And instead of the Warrior God, his gorgons poured through.

The Fatesworn bond shuddered as they eyed Vale. My hands tightened on her waist, but I stifled every instinct to tell Dynaxtar to fly. My tattoo pounded, pulling on the fierce need to protect her.

Guard up, Stargirl, I sent down the bond.

Because even with Valyrie's aid, the god was one step ahead of us. As fucking always.

Chapter Fifty-One
Malakai

"Of fucking course," I breathed as Rozelyn led the other gorgons through the veil, the air sealing up behind them. Her sharp eyes locked on me, white hair flowing around her.

"It appears it's my lucky day," she purred as her stare dragged up my body.

"And my unfathomably unlucky one," I grumbled back, hand flexing around my sword.

A second gorgon stepped up beside Rozelyn. When her eyes landed on the khrysaor, her long blonde hair shifted, the heads of venomous snakes whipping around her shoulders with violent hisses that skittered across my fucking skin.

What were they doing here? Where was Echnid?

Vale's eyes were entirely silver, and I'd bet every weapon on my body she was reading that exact question.

"Not yet, Salteaire," Rozelyn commanded, and while the blonde one—Salteaire—didn't respond, the serpents drooped to gently writhe against her shoulders, their hisses a dull hum that rose the hair on the back of my neck.

A third and final gorgon joined them—the one Mila and I had seen outside Xenovia. Only three, though. There was at least one more still alive somewhere on Gallantia.

Cypherion was muttering to Vale as she read, and I tried to pull the gorgons' attention away from them.

"Where's your friend?" I demanded.

Rozelyn smiled sweetly. "Occupied. I can show you if you'd like?" And from the sultry tone in her voice, I guessed what that meant.

"No thanks," I responded, remembering the way these women were frantically infatuated with Echnid.

Beside me, Mila went utterly still at Rozelyn's suggestion. I stepped closer, a growl rumbling in my chest when the gorgon tracked the movement with a smug smirk.

"Anything?" I whispered to Mila.

She was silent for a beat, reaching through those Reflector powers, but she shook her head.

"Where's the seraph?" Rozelyn asked. So Valyrie had told Echnid she'd seen Ophelia here. That part of the plan went right, at least. Then, where was the god?

Our entire group tensed, but from behind us, a calm, collected voice called out, "I'm here."

And Ophelia emerged from the palm trees, Sapphire carrying her across the sand. They stopped beside Jezebel and Zanox, an assessing glare sharpening Ophelia's features.

Mora's features, glamoured to look like Ophelia.

The fae had thought of it after Mila saw her mother glamouring herself as enemy soldiers to infiltrate their camps and take them down from the inside.

And that was a common horse beneath her disguised as Sapphire. The wings on both were a dead giveaway, neither strong enough to actually fly, but we just needed the gorgons to believe the illusion. Needed them to report back to their master that Ophelia was truly here with us. That she had been while we travelled far enough from Xenovia that no one would be caught in the crossfires.

Rozelyn smiled as she studied the false Ophelia, the upturn of her lips satisfied. Yet jealousy lurked in her stare. "He will be so happy we found you."

"Unfortunate for you," Mora answered as Ophelia. Her voice wasn't quite right, but aside from that, the slightly off-shade eyes, and the fact that she'd had to hide throughout the day to refresh her magic, the glamour was pretty damn good.

Good enough, hopefully.

Vale was muttering more urgently to Cypherion now, and from the corner of my eye, I caught the slight motion of his hand toward his scythe.

The gorgons did, too, the ones behind Rozelyn studying him closely. And their eyes lit up. The air between us all turned heavy, a thick sludge as my attention flicked between then.

"What does Echnid want with me?" Mora asked, bringing the gorgons' focus back to her.

"He has told you, seraph," Rozelyn sneered. "Our god wishes to work together."

Cyph had his scythe braced now. Vale's and Jezebel's fingers were curling tightly into their khrysaors' manes.

Mora tilted her head. She may have looked like Ophelia, but her movements were still as graceful as the fae. "Again...unfortunate."

Then, the tension bubbling in the air cracked like a fucking dam. Vale yelled to Jezebel, and the khrysaor reared up, spearing the gorgons. Wings ripped from the demons' back, and Cypherion crashed to the sand.

Mora raced off into the trees, because if she fought it would be too obvious that she wasn't Ophelia.

The khrysaor roared as they kicked into flight, and thick white mist poured out from another rip in the air. Echnid's magic permeated the space though he didn't deign to show himself.

"Are you okay?" I asked Cyph as I hauled him up.

Fury burned across his features as he watched Vale and Dynaxtar race into the mist, Jezebel and Zanox on their tail.

"Fine." But his stare was icy. "Fine," he repeated, as if convincing himself. Then, he shook his head, grabbing his scythe. "Echnid made this switch too last minute—Vale couldn't see why. But she said Valyrie is taking care of it, and he still thinks Ophelia is here."

Every word out of his mouth had a bite of annoyance—likely

from being caught off guard—but he shoved it all down when a piercing giggle echoed behind us.

Rozelyn advanced—when she'd gotten around us, I didn't fucking know—and Salteaire.

Fuck.

Salteaire was stalking toward Mila where she dove in front of Mora's escape route. She had her twin short swords in hand, but her eyes were fighting to glaze over, succumbing to the god-given Reflector powers.

With infantilizing condescension, Salteaire whimpered at Mila. "Are the glimpses into our home too much to handle?"

"Not too much at all," Mila spat. "Though I think you all may want to return soon. Things are going to get very bloody here."

Salteaire's fangs descended, and she flashed a pointed grin, her serpents thrashing. "My preference."

"Of course," Mila spat. And the two lunged for each other, Mila's sword slicing through three of the serpents waving around the gorgon's head.

Salteaire screamed, and it only intensified the vitriol radiating off Mila.

I hadn't seen her like this before. I'd seen her fight, had seen her shaken, but something in the claims of the gorgon was driving her absolutely wild. Channeling all of the frustration and aggression that had been bubbling in her since the Gates of Angeldust and losing Lyria.

And I fucking loved it.

Baited, another of Salteaire's serpents reared back, its fangs flashing for Mila as it sank forward. Mila dodged, and impossibly quickly, Salteaire sped around her.

After Mora.

"GO!" I shouted, and Mila was gone.

Sword in hand, Cyph and I tore after her, but Rozelyn caught me with an arm against my throat, shoving me back with impossible strength. One of her snakes snapped at Cyph, but it only latched onto the sleeve of his leathers.

I choked over the pressure against my windpipe, cursing the

gorgon in wheezing breaths. Collecting myself, I gritted my teeth, but she smiled haughtily. And her eyes were shifting red.

With barely a blink to spare before she was fully transformed into her demonic form that would turn me to stone with one head-on glance, I ducked.

Cypherion was at my back, swinging his scythe between us. The blade whistled as it came down, barely missing the gorgon's paling skin.

"Interesting weapon," Rozelyn purred to Cyph, eyes glinting as she studied his scythe.

Lunging, he slashed at her. The gorgon deftly rolled away, but—

Fear flashed through her reddening eyes at Cypherion's pursuit. *Fear* as she took in the curved arc of his blade.

It was gone in a breath, and Rozelyn turned, disappearing into the thickening mist after the khrysaor.

As a bolt of silver-blue light tinted the wall of white, I caught Cypherion's glance, canting my head as if to ask if he noticed the gorgon's strange reaction. His lips pressed into a line, and he nodded. Then, we raced after her.

"Vale!" he bellowed, desperately slashing through the thickening mist.

Silver light flashed, parting the way, and we chased after it. Another tear was opening in the sky, leading a way for the gorgons to return to their master. Before it, wings flaring and sharpened claws ready to kill, Jezebel and Vale battled two airborne gorgons.

"Shouldn't you all be busy spreading your legs for the god? Producing heirs, or whatever you want to call it?" I spat at Rozelyn as she swooped toward me.

A haughty laugh left her lips. "So naive to how our bodies and magic work, sweet warrior prince."

"Don't call me that," I growled, lunging and avoiding her eyes. Only Mila—and occasionally Barrett—were allowed to utter that name.

Cypherion herded Rozelyn back, and Vale and Dynaxtar soared low enough for her to tell me, "Valyrie is holding off Echnid, but I don't know how."

"What do you mean?" I asked as feral growls ripped from the gorgons, and Zanox answered with his own.

Vale shook her head, keeping her voice low enough that no one would hear. "Her decision was to give him information to distract him. Something he's been asking her to read for."

"Fuck, that could be anything," I ground out. And it could be *bad*. Something Echnid wanted bad enough to skip a chance to get Ophelia...

Worry wavered in Vale's eyes as she nodded, then she and Dynaxtar shot into the skies, circling high enough to search for Mila and Mora. I turned back to the battle.

Rozelyn's fangs descended, and I joined Cyph against her. Dodging her next strike, I pulled my ax from my belt. The khrysaor spat blue fucking fire through the air, one blast catching the wing of the other gorgon.

"Meghalle!" Rozelyn shouted as she crashed to the dunes with a shriek.

Zanox spiraled down after her. Sand flew up around his winged form as his claws dug in. He released a bellowing roar, his head lowering—

And his jaw opened, preparing to snap her neck.

"STOP!" the shout sliced through the space.

Whirling, I found Salteaire shoving Mila to the ground, a blade in her calf.

And everything within me crashed to a roaring silence.

Another scar on her fucking body, thanks to these demonic women.

I wasn't sure when Mila and Salteaire had burst back into the bubble of swirling white mist, but the gorgon was bleeding poisoned blood over Mila's crumpled form.

Anguish tore through me, and without thinking, I ripped a dagger from my waist and launched it at Salteaire. The blade pierced her leathery wing, and her echo of agony spurred me into action. My heart pounded against my ribs as I ran, Dynaxtar's fire heating the air within the mists as she and Vale landed, too.

Mila. Mila. Mila.

Fury raged through the general's eyes, the ferocity she bore in Lyria's wake.

Salteaire wrenched my dagger from her wing, her poisoned blood dripping to the sand. But before she let it fly, Mila shoved herself up on her good leg and swung her short sword in a graceful, fury-born arc.

The blade drove into the gorgon's side as she screamed, and Mila let out a gasp.

"Eyes, Mila!" I roared, as the gorgon spun toward her. Mila collapsed back to the ground, closing her eyes as she rolled away from the fountain of poisoned blood and the lethal red stare.

"Salteaire. Meghalle," Rozelyn barked, and I saw it then. The poisoned arrow she'd aimed at Mila when the general took that extra second to attack Salteaire. But instead of striking, Rozelyn directed her comrades, "Retreat."

"What?" Salteaire gasped over the wound in her side, her hands clasping it and red gushing between her fingers.

"Now," Rozelyn demanded, her gaze landing on Jezebel, Zanox's jaw prepared to clamp tighter on the gorgon's neck. "Release Meghalle, and we will leave you all for another day."

Jezebel hesitated.

"Jez," I said softly. And when she looked at me, I nodded at Mila. She was so close to the gorgons' grasp. It would be so easy for them to hurt her.

Understanding deepening her stare, Jezebel patted her khrysaor, and the beast's maw snapped open. Shallow puncture wounds formed a ring around Meghalle's neck. She scrambled to Salteaire's side, and the two supported each other as they escaped through the veil.

Rushing to Mila, I let them go.

"I'm fine," she gritted through a labored breath. Her calf was still bleeding as was a shallow slice above her eyebrow. "It's going to heal just fine. Listen, Malakai, when I cut her just now, I saw something with her blood. The demigods they birth with Echnid—they're creatures of shadow and fire. He injects the magic of the Spirit Volcano into them to attune them to this world."

"What in the—" I shuddered at just the thought but kissed her forehead. "Okay." I didn't know what any of that meant, but at least it was a drop of information. And right now, all that mattered was making sure she was okay.

Death pounding through my veins, my stare snapped to Rozelyn's retreating form. But she didn't notice.

No, the gorgon was too busy casting one last lingering, narrowed glance at Cypherion's scythe, her entire body flinching. Then, she dove back through the veil, too.

And I hoped we'd bought enough fucking time.

CHAPTER FIFTY-TWO
OPHELIA

ANGELS, EVEN WITH THE SERAPH MAGIC PUMPING through my blood, Mindshaper Territory was cold. I'd forgotten how much the chill bit at you, consumed you. Perhaps, like the way my emotions now came in crushing tidal waves, I was feeling the physical sensations more, too.

"Is it freezing to you?" I asked Tolek, testing the theory.

"Not any worse than when we were here before," he said.

I nodded, rubbing my hands down my arms. With a small laugh, Tolek slung off his cloak and wrapped it around me, doing his best to drape it around my wings.

"It's like an ice palace in here," I complained, nuzzling into the body heat lingering on the wool.

"I don't think the ruins of a manor qualify as an ice palace," Tolek challenged, a playful smile on his lips.

At the sight, relief washed through me. I'd tried to persuade him not to come with me on this mission, but with everyone else distracting Echnid, he'd insisted.

Memories of his wrenching nightmares after he was captured by this clan and how he'd thrashed trying to escape ignited a kernel of worry in my gut, but I watched his smirk and told myself it was okay.

He was okay.

And truthfully, that fact alone kept me upright most days lately. Still, concern for our friends warred within me.

"I never thought we'd be back here," I said to Tolek as we stood in what had once been the open courtyard of an ivy-coated, abandoned manor.

Now, no more than rubble piled up around the space, one run down end hiding what was once an entrance to the sitting room. Much of the original structure still stood, but this ruin was the result of discordant magic and a khrysaor crashing through the ceiling. Wind whipped through the gaping holes in the walls.

"I wish we weren't," Tolek admitted. The hard line of his lips told me he was remembering when I'd swallowed that magic. How he'd held my body while some part of me disappeared to the bridge between realms.

Linking my fingers through his, I squeezed to tell him *I'm here.* Tol kissed the back of my hand, warmth threading along my skin, and turned his attention to the view beyond the courtyard.

"I didn't expect it to be quite so snowy in the spring," he commented.

"Always is," I drawled, studying the pure white lawn around the manor. In the distance, feathered birds swooped low, hunting among the tall grasses that somehow persisted through the endless winter.

"I know it's a cold climate, but I didn't realize how drastic." His observant stare picked apart the perimeter, and I knew he was searching for more. For a hint of a god uncovering our plan.

"Damien said it's because of Thorn," I recalled. For a moment, I was back beside the Angel, looking over my city from the Revered's Palace. "When Thorn went mad, he coated the entire territory in an eternal winter. The other Angels were able to shield their lands from it, but not him."

"He was distressed enough to cause *this*?"

I nodded. "Raw Angel power."

Tolek contemplated that for a moment, his thumb sweeping across the back of my hand. "That actually makes me feel bad for the bastard."

"I suppose even immortal beings act on the whims of their emotions."

We both considered that as we continued to watch the wildlife enjoy their winter abode in the height of spring, beneath a sky thick with rolling gray clouds. My seraph power buzzed just beneath my skin, gold undulating around my wings, ready for a fight if it came to it.

"When will he be here?" Tolek asked.

Just as I opened my mouth to answer, boots echoed beyond the collapsed walls.

"Right now, I suppose."

But it wasn't the Mindshaper we were waiting for that climbed over the wreckage and jumped down into the courtyard.

"*Santorina*?" I blurted, rushing toward her and pulling her into a crushing hug. Spirits, it had been so long since I'd seen her. I cupped her cheeks in my hands and looked her over. She was in one piece, face bright with the cold, and she seemed whole. Strong as ever, thank the Angels. I pulled her to me again. "What are you *doing* here?"

Lancaster scaled the rubble after her as Rina said, "Cypherion wrote to update us about the ongoing plans. He mentioned where you'd be, and we thought you may need assistance."

Releasing her, I said, "Cyph didn't mention you were coming."

"He didn't know. We weren't sure we'd make it."

"Not that we're not thrilled to see you," Tolek said, pulling Rina out of my arms and hugging her himself, "but assistance, how?"

Santorina looked up at Lancaster, and I could have been mistaken, but it seemed there was a bit less ire in her expression than usual.

"When I was traveling your continent before we made our bargains, I established contacts within this clan," Lancaster explained. "I have come to see if any of those will be beneficial in your discussions."

We'd known Lancaster had spent time in Mindshaper Territory given that it was where I met him at the Wayward Inn and that he'd been the one to tell Tolek where the Labyrinth was after discovering the rebel faction. I hadn't realized any of that information had evolved into relationships we could use in an alliance.

"Thank you," I said, blinking at him with a hint of shock. "But how did you get here so fast? Weren't you in Mystique Territory?"

"We cut through the mountains," Rina explained.

Tolek said quizzically, "But that would still take—"

"My kind runs very quickly," Lancaster answered plainly.

"Runs?" I repeated, and he nodded. I looked to Santorina. "And you…"

"He carried me."

"He carried you?"

"That parroting trick is amusing, Alabath," Tolek said, wrapping an arm around my waist and squeezing me to his side. "Want to try something original now? Or I can think of some very colorful phrases for you to repeat. How about—"

"Not necessary!" I burst out, but I couldn't help my laugh. "I was just surprised."

Last I saw Santorina and Lancaster, they'd been snapping at each other incessantly, the Bounty and the Hunter. But something seemed to have changed. Even the way Rina stood beside him, her posture entirely at ease, was different. Like they weren't ancient enemies but…equals.

"As was I," Rina said. "But how are you?" She looked beyond me warily, eyeing my wings.

"I'm g—" The word stalled on my tongue. Was I good? I was better. I was healing from what Echnid had done, but good? "I'm happy to be back."

Rina nodded, her lips pressing into a line. "I'm happy you're back, too."

Her words were nearly as quiet as mine had been, but there was a supportive understanding in them that I'd missed. Everyone had been so accommodating since I'd escaped Damenal, their love the true thing keeping me sane, but there was an underscore to Rina's presence that I'd needed, too. One that provided her own brand of gentle anger and forged strength. I needed all of them to be whole myself.

"The wings are wonderful," Tolek said, throwing an arm over my shoulders. "I love them."

"I wouldn't expect anything less when it came to Ophelia," Santorina said, and Tol nodded proudly. "When will they be—"

Lancaster held up a hand. He tilted his head softly to the left, and Rina knowingly followed. The male whispered, "They're here."

Straining my ears, I heard it, too. Warrior senses had increased when Echnid returned, our eyesight sharpening and hearing perking up at more distant sounds. We were all still learning to trust it, but there *was* a distant crunching, and when I spun toward the opposite wall, a small group was crossing the icy yard toward us.

Four Mindshapers led by Ricordan, the older warrior who had aided us in the underground labyrinth when I hunted Thorn's emblem. They were coming from the edge of the property where smoke spiraled into the sky. There must have been a smaller home out there, one they were occupying while repairing the manor we'd wrecked.

"Here we go," Tolek said as they marched closer. He dropped his arm from my shoulders and removed the extra cloak, flanking me on the left with his hand casually on his sword. Rina stood on my right, and Lancaster was on her other side. I shook my wings, letting the feathers fan out, and gold ether tumbled over them.

As Ricordan crossed through that gaping hole in the wall, his jaw tightened, eyes assessing the damage once more. His council—if that's what they were—spread out on either side of him, and the man nodded. I recognized the woman to his left, her red-gold hair braided back and eyes much more alert than when I'd last seen her under Kakias's enchantments of the broken crown.

"Revered," Ricordan said. "Welcome back to Mindshaper Territory." His words weren't unkind, but they were wary. Last we'd seen each other, I was sending his newly reunited family away from the Mystique Mountains after confirming that his son, Trevaneth, had written to Kakias to reveal our plan to catch her in this very manor, causing her and her troops to move on our armies earlier than planned.

It had almost cost us the war, but the boy was young, and he'd been tricked by the queen just as warriors ten times his age had. He'd only wanted his mother back, his family whole again.

"Thank you," I said, infusing my voice with as much genuine gratitude as possible. "I didn't think we'd return so soon. I am happy to see your family reunited." I nodded at his wife, and she returned it, but her eyes traced the wings at my back uncertainly.

"Thank you," he said, slipping his hand into hers, stance relaxing. The casualness with which he stood was less a ruler receiving a potential political adversary and more a man trying to represent his people. "Tolek, Santorina, Lancaster. It is great to see you all again, though I will admit we are surprised to see you...together."

His stare flashed to the fae, who said, "We are as surprised as you, but it appears we have a common enemy."

"Ah, not many things bond quicker than that."

"Very true, Ric. Thank you for meeting with us," Tolek said. "And we're sorry about the redecorating we did the last time we were here."

Ricordan shook his head, frowning. "We didn't want to return to this place after she'd used it."

If they still held grudges against Kakias, even in death, that was a good sign for us. The muscles holding my wings so high eased slightly.

"I'd like to introduce my companions, here. First, my wife." Ricordan held out a hand, and she stepped forward. "Sandretta. And our friends, Oudry and Zaina." He said each of their names with warm affection.

"You were in the labyrinth," I said to the latter, the warrior with her dark hair shaved close to her head.

She nodded. "I was stationed near the pit."

"You showed us to the prisoner we interrogated," Rina said, the memory dawning as her eyes widened. Spirits, that had been a brutal moment. The warrior from Kakias's army had been crazed by the queen manipulating half of Thorn's broken crown. He'd been shouting at me, things about my father and magic being alive.

I was glad I'd killed him.

"And Oudry was stationed at the entrance nearest Bodymelder Territory," Ricordan said of the broad umber-skinned warrior whose belt was strung with jagged knives. "They'd been traveling when you all arrived."

"They're who told me where to find the place," Lancaster added to our party.

So, these may be friends of Ricordan's, but they also appeared to be chosen strategically based on their previous interactions with us. That was good. The Mindshapers were calculating, and that made me more comfortable allying with them.

"Great to meet you," I said to Oudry.

"If you don't mind me asking," Sandretta said. "You have wings?" Tolek laughed, and her eyes widened. "I'm sorry, there was likely a much more tactful way to ask that, but I've never met anyone with wings before."

"Don't apologize," I said, smiling. "I hadn't either—well, besides Damien." If possible, her eyes widened further at the casual mention of the Angel. "But he doesn't count. It's a long story, though, and truly one I am still learning the end of."

Worry twisted through me at the acknowledgment that I didn't have total control of the situation, but Ricordan said, "We have time," inviting me to continue.

I told them what had happened with the emblems and how not only had the Angels been released, but Echnid had, too. How we'd hoped he was back to redeem the warriors and restore Ambrisk to its natural balance, but it appeared he was set on revenge. How he had killed a god, and we were worried how the Balance of Power would react if he slew the rest.

I left out the bits about Tolek attacking Thorn and vice versa, but he tensed beside me when I got to that point. I brushed my wing against his shoulder silently—Sandretta tracking the movement—and finished.

"We have come for an alliance with the Mindshapers. As many soldiers as you can offer, but we need something else, too."

"Which is?" Ricordan asked.

"Wolves," I said, nerves making my fingers itch to tie knots or scratch at something. "Echnid has a cerberus—"

"Impossible," Zaina breathed.

I ruffled my wings. "You'll find we've stopped saying anything is impossible." I looked back to Ricordan. "We don't know what else Echnid will bring if this comes to a battle. A warrior horse is no match for that beast."

The thought of Sapphire or one of my friends' mares going against Hythana made my stomach turn.

"We were told the Mindshaper legions in Kakias's army rode wolves into the final battle," Tolek added, implying it was no use hiding that fact. And I was willing to bet they'd only grown stronger in the wake of the power shifts on Ambrisk.

"They did," Oudry confirmed, arms crossed.

"Have you gathered other allies?" Ricordan asked before I could respond.

"We have. Everyone is gathering in Xenovia as it's the only known city the god can't enter."

"How?" Zaina asked.

"It's protected by Artale."

"We're off topic," Oudry said. "Alliances." They were a warrior of few words, but heavy observation.

I kept my voice as firm as possible and my stance strong. "Soulguiders, Starsearchers, Seawatchers, and Bodymelders are joining Mystique forces."

"Bodymelders?" Oudry raised their brows, the brawny warrior impressed.

"They have sent forces our way. What they can afford to spare right now."

"No Engrossians?"

Tolek interjected this time, "We are working closely with the prince. He is addressing problems within his own capital at the moment."

He left it at that. Truthfully, we didn't know when or if Barrett would be able to rally a host to our side. Both Malakai and Tolek had been exchanging letters with him since Tol returned to Xenovia, but messages in and out of Banix were slow.

"And fae?" Oudry asked, directing the question at Lancaster.

"Unfortunately, it would take weeks to get fae forces here. And with our queen dead, we do not have a current sitting ruler," the male explained. Spirits, I hadn't even considered the mess taking place on Vercuella right now. "My sister and I stand with the warriors in this battle, though. As devout worshippers of the goddess, we will do anything we can to protect her."

Santorina shifted at that final sentence, but I didn't quite understand why.

Oudry nodded, seeming encouraged by Lancaster's answer.

"I think there is an important question no one has asked," Zaina interjected, and her stare landed on me. "Even if a force is assembled to challenge Echnid, how will you kill a god?"

It was the question that had the power to sweep the world out from under me.

I didn't have an answer. Not a good one. All I knew was the desperation in my gut to destroy Echnid for what he'd done to me and what he wanted to do to the world.

My throat scratched with the uncomfortable sensation of power pouring down it. His taint roared through my body, dulling all my senses.

My body is my own. My mind is my own.

"I do not know how yet," I admitted, my voice burning with conviction that could melt the snow beyond these walls. "But I will do it with my bare hands if I have to."

The vow settled into the stone around us like it was becoming one with the magic laced in the earth. For a moment, I wished it could. Wished I could wrench up every drop of ether in Ambrisk's core and drown the god with that promise.

My body is my own. My mind is my own.

Interjecting to buy me time to collect myself as the memory of Echnid washed over me, Tolek asked, "I'd like to know where the wolves even come from?"

"Clan secrets," Sandretta said with a sly wink.

Wrapping his arm around his wife, Ricordan elaborated, "There are many legends surrounding them. Some say they originated in another realm, banished here for their sins against the gods. Some say they are blessed by Thorn. Some say they simply grew stronger than normal wolves based on the food in their home region." He shrugged as if to say, *who knows.*

Clearing my throat, I said, "Sounds like they would be a perfect match for a vengeful god's beasts."

The older warrior smiled at the comment, and it was such a fatherly expression, grief twisted through me.

"Let us confer," Ricordan said.

"Of course," I nodded.

The Mindshapers gathered out in the snow, speaking far enough away that none of us could hear—not even Lancaster. Nerves fluttered through my body as we waited, my wings flapping softly at my back and Angellight curling in abstract shapes through the air. Tolek asked Santorina and Lancaster about where they'd been so far, and they updated him on the small group of Bounties they'd found who were now also traveling to Xenovia.

It was working; we *were* winning allies, building an army. But they were all foot soldiers. Regardless of the ferocity in their hearts and righteousness of their cause, none of them would be a match for a gorgon, cerberus, or demigod, let alone the god himself. We needed *more*.

And I was afraid to admit how slim the chances of finding it were feeling.

Zaina's question echoed. *How will you kill a god?*

I was still stewing over the question when the Mindshapers returned a short while later, and I wasn't sure if that was a good sign or an obvious rejection.

"We can't force any legions into another war," Ricordan said. "Not only would I refuse to do so, but none of us have that power. When Kakias took over the armies, she slew our commanders to bring everyone under her reign, and we still have not appointed a new chancellor." My heart sank. The Mindshapers didn't even have a functioning force.

"However," Ricordan went on, "we owe you a debt for sparing our son any sort of punishment in the war. With your permission, I will spread your story among the heads of the legions who do remain, and I will do my best to argue your case. The choice will be left up to each of them individually if they want to join. And I will tell them the wolves were requested as well."

A bit of life beat back into my chest as something rustled on the ground beside Tolek. "Thank you," I said, voice wrung out with gratitude and desperation. "Every body on a field makes a difference."

"Alabath," Tol said, and the gravity of his tone had me whipping around, prepared to find white mist creeping across the grounds.

Instead, he held a letter out to me. Vale's dainty handwriting in Mystique ink.

Plans changed. Valyrie seeing to him. Return as soon as possible.

My heart leapt into my throat. "Thank you for meeting with us," I said again to Ricordan and his warriors. "But we must go."

Ricordan promised to write in three days' time, and while I wanted to hope that united, we may stand a chance, the entire hurried flight back to Xenovia with Sapphire and Tolek, Zaina's question pulsed in my mind: *How will you kill a god?*

And as I scanned the deserts for any hint of attack, I feared I didn't know.

CHAPTER FIFTY-THREE
CYPHERION

BACK IN OUR ROOM IN XENOVIA, UNSCATHED BUT emotions warring through the bond, Vale looked out the window with one arm crossed over her stomach, her other elbow propped against it and her chin in her hand.

And silence stretched with a deafening roar.

"Vale," I said softly from my spot on the edge of the bed.

"Mm-hmm." In her reflection in the glass, her eyes swirled a dim silver. Down the Fatesworn bond, worries flickered back and forth, but I couldn't understand a fucking thing. They were too jumbled, my own tangling with them.

I sighed, exhaustion weighing down every inch of my damn body. "Can you tell me why you did it?"

"Did what?" she asked, voice distant.

Pushing up and ignoring the soreness radiating down my muscles, I approached Vale and braced a hand on the window over her head. "Can you try to stop reading for a minute and look at me?" I asked softly. It wasn't her fault, but we'd been sitting here for hours.

She shook her head, snapping out of it as if she hadn't even realized what she'd been doing. Those fucking Fates. I'd found this Fatecatcher business damn impressive at first, but it was consuming her. I couldn't help the worry.

"Sorry," she muttered, looking at me over her shoulder. "What's wrong?"

"Why did you do it?" I asked again.

"Do what?"

"Why did you push me off the khrysaor?"

Vale stiffened, turning all the way around and looking up at me with those damn stunning olive-green eyes. Thank the cursed Spirits.

But there was a guard in her voice when she said, "The gorgons were preparing to attack."

I scoffed, as if that was a fucking explanation. "I was aware. They sprouted wings, and you shoved me to the sand like I was some defenseless child."

"I didn't do it because I thought you were defenseless," she said, confusion creasing her brow.

"Then why?" The terror that had lashed through me at that moment clung to my heart now, scratching against my ribcage. When she flew off without me, when she disappeared in the mist...

I'd yelled down our Fatesworn bond.

And she'd ignored it.

I cleared my throat, straightening. "Vale, when you did that, and then I couldn't see you, it fucking terrified me."

"I was fine, Cypherion," she said calmly. "I was able to read the movements coming for me quickly enough that I could easily dodge them. Dynaxtar has claimed me as her rider, so between the two of us, we've got a connection that makes us faster. More agile. On the same page."

On the same page.

On the same page as a fucking khrysaor and not me, apparently. I paced the distance between the bed and the floor-to-ceiling windows, the setting sun streaking through heating the room, testing me as I tried to keep my temper down and have a rational conversation. Dammit, when it came to her, it was so hard to be rational.

"You can't just shove me away, though," I said.

"So, you get to keep me out of harm's way, but I don't get to do that for you?" she asked, the tiniest bit of snap in her voice.

"What do you mean?"

"Damenal," she recounted, crossing her arms and standing her ground. Her cheeks flushed. "When you wouldn't let me help Tolek try to rescue Ophelia and Malakai."

Spirits, this discussion again. Not argument. We weren't fighting—nothing was worth fighting with her—but we did keep coming back to this topic.

"At least when that happened you knew why I made that decision. When you shoved me off Dynaxtar, I was entirely in the dark. You didn't even give me a warning, and I may have a bond to you, but I don't have Fate ties or Fatecatcher magic. I can't see what's coming like you can, and it blindsides me," I admitted, pausing my pacing and cupping her cheeks. "And that feeling of not having a fucking clue what's going on? When you're at risk, Stargirl? That's my worst fucking nightmare."

She heaved a deep breath. "I didn't have time to tell you. I thought you'd trust me."

Those five words ripped me fucking open. "I do," I murmured, pressing a kiss to her forehead and tucking her beneath my chin. "I trust you so much."

"Then when I shove you to the sand from the back of a flying mythological creature, know I have a good reason," she muttered, voice muffled in my chest.

I laughed as her arms wrapped around my waist, her touch soothing the panic in my chest. Enough for me to say, "I grew up without a lot of security. Before my mother went through whatever changed her"—my father's death—"she'd been a damn good mother." I stroked the back of her hair as Vale tightened her grip, knowing what came next in this story. "Then, one day, she was different. I just don't want to lose anyone else overnight like that. You're everything I want in every lifetime, Vale. Those things we saw during the Fatesworn ceremony? The future...the children and festivals? I want it all. And I'm just so damn scared of something ripping us apart again—of me losing you."

And death was a lot more permanent.

"Nothing is going to take me from you, Cypherion," she said softly, tipping her chin up to look at me. "You are never going to lose me. I already knew it months ago, but the Fates have named it so, too." And some kind of enlightenment spread across her features, shooting down the Fatesworn bond. "You don't fully understand it, do you?"

"What?" I asked.

"The Bind—it's so different than this." Warmth down the bond again. "Of course, you're still learning it."

"But you haven't had a Fatesworn bond before, either."

"No, but I grew up hearing stories of them. The rare, aspirational romances."

"I *am* happy for it," I said. "I do want you this way. Every way I can have you."

"I know. But you can want it without fully understanding it. Being Fatesworn carries a substantial weight to the Starsearchers. To me this bond means that in any life—in any realm—our spirits were meant to be together, Cypherion Kastroff. It goes beyond the bounds of love and desire. But because of that, it's going to cause us to do wild things for the other, especially now as it takes root."

"So that's why I'm feeling extra defensive," I said. In theory, I knew the purpose of the Fatesworn bond, but I hadn't been prepared for how it could feel.

"And why I *had* to get you away from Echnid," she confirmed. "It's just a difference in our cultures and upbringing that we're going to have to continue to work through. I'm sure your Bind will feel different to me when we receive it, but it'll be a blending of Mystique and Starsearcher customs unique to us."

Unique to us. I liked that.

"I'm trying, Stargirl. I promise I'm trying to remember that." I cupped her cheek, dragging my thumb across her bottom lip. "Just keep talking to me about it, and my stubborn skull might let it through."

She laughed. "No one is more stubborn than the Fates."

I exhaled, kissing her again.

"I do trust you," I said as I pulled back. "So next time you shove me from the back of a flying mythological creature, I'll try not to panic." I didn't have any argument against her asking me to trust her. Because I did. More than I allowed myself to trust anyone outside of the tight circle of friends I'd known for a decade. "But only if you attempt to give me a warning before you do it."

"Deal," she agreed, tilting her chin up. Those olive eyes searched my expression. "And I promise, Cypherion, you will never lose me the way you lost her. I won't leave you."

That vow tightened my throat.

I love you, Stargirl, I said down the bond.

I love you, too, Cypherion Kastroff. Or Deneski. Or whoever you choose to be.

I laughed, letting the fears melt away as I tilted her head back and my thumbs swept along her jaw. I dropped my lips to hers. When I pulled away, Vale's eyes were still green.

She searched my expression. "The gorgons were interested in your scythe."

"I know," I exhaled and rested my forehead against hers.

"That's part of why I pushed you," she admitted. "Echnid was focusing on it in my readings, too, and I wanted to lead them away from you."

"Echnid was?" I repeated, and Vale nodded. "Why do you think he didn't show up himself? He didn't go after the real Ophelia either."

She and Tolek heeded Vale's letter and raced back to Xenovia as quickly as possible, Rina and Lancaster not far behind.

"Whatever information Valyrie offered him must have been a large enough deterrent." She traced my palm, the calluses from my scythe seeming like beacons calling for her attention. "I haven't seen what it was."

"She hasn't shown you directly?"

Vale shook her head. Fuck, what was the Starsearcher Angel doing?

Massaging her shoulders, I asked, "Do you think they're interested in my scythe because it injured Thorn in the mountains?"

"Perhaps," Vale said. "Normal blades aren't capable of harming an Angel." Perhaps Valyrie had been feeding Echnid information about the weapon and that's why Vale kept seeing it.

"What the fuck could he want with it?" I asked, sighing. "Have you been able to read anything?"

"Now you like the readings," Vale chided with an arched brow, but the tension between us had dissipated.

I just wanted to hold on to her while everything was...a fucking mess. So, I merely grunted in acknowledgment of her mocking, sent a wave of a laugh down the Fatesworn bond that I was pretty sure I did correctly since her cheeks flushed, and I nodded for her to continue.

"I haven't seen anything other than Soulguider symbols and Xenique—which makes sense since it's her clan's weapon—but you can bet on Valyrie's wings that I'll keep looking," she swore. "No matter what it is, though, we need to find out more. And that means we need answers about why that weapon was given. We know it was gifted to your father by a chancellor or someone else of high status. Maybe there's more to it."

I nodded slowly, reluctantly. "And that means I'll have to find out about my father."

CHAPTER FIFTY-FOUR
TOLEK

THE SHOCK OF POWER THAT ROCKED THROUGH MY BODY when I'd fought Thorn in the desert followed my every step, even days later. It sharpened my senses as I hunted for Ophelia in the sculpture garden outside the guest house the day after we returned from Mindshaper Territory. But a different voice called for me, and Vale came rushing up.

"I was looking for you," she said, one hand behind her back.

I quirked a brow, stifling that unnamed energy. "I think CK was looking for *you*. I had to drag him to our meeting this morning." He'd grumbled about leaving her side the entire walk there, and as soon as we were done, he'd been off again.

Vale's cheeks flushed, one hand fiddling with her skirt. "He found me right as Harlen was arriving with the Starsearcher cavalry, so I told him I'd meet him shortly."

"I'm sure he was thrilled," I said with a laugh.

"He'll be fine." Vale waved me off. "I wanted to give you this."

She pulled a dagger from behind her back and held it out to me. The weapon was delicate, the blade pristinely crafted, etched with an elegant constellation along one edge, and the handle—

My heart stuttered. "*L.V.?*"

"For Lyria," Vale whispered. "The constellation is tied to an ancient story of a female warrior born of music. It was said she was fierce on a battlefield and with her voice."

I ran my finger along the sharpened edge, memorizing the grooves of each etched star. It was perfect for my sister who sang with her blades but also maintained a dreamer's soul.

"Harlen just gave it to me," Vale explained. "It was Lyria's idea to imbue weapons with the resins comprising Titus's seeing chamber. We now have hundreds of blades that will aid sessions while fighting, thanks to her."

My throat was thick, and when I met Vale's gaze, her eyes were glassy.

"Thank you for this, Vale," I whispered. "It means a lot to know this battlefield will be lined with a piece of her."

"Her heart and memory are fueling this fight as much as anything," Vale agreed. "Now I really should go find Cypherion. I left him to help Harlen settle in, and I have a feeling that's going swimmingly."

As she disappeared, I hung the blade on my belt beside the Vincienzo family dagger. The weight was right. Like a piece I'd been missing was returned.

And it gave me the strength to face something else I'd been avoiding.

Attempting to gather myself, I leaned against the statue of a giant coiled snake, its exposed fangs the size of my forearm. The thing was frightening, and I hoped Ophelia would keep her myth magic far away from it in case it was some legendary beast turned to stone.

Shivering and shuffling aside, I shifted my gaze to the path. Low clusters of cacti and stones carved walkways across the sand. In the heart of the labyrinth, the Alabath sisters exercised their magic. Jezebel rolled her eyes, and Ophelia tipped her head back, laughing. The faint trickle that reached me made me smile.

Fucking Angels, what I wouldn't do for that sound. When she was gone, my heart felt like it had been ripped right out of my chest. Now, the damn thing beat faster at just the sight of her.

She'd been hollow and tortured when she returned, but seeing her with her sister, actually *smiling*...it ripped me apart. Because for a moment, she was carefree, and all I wanted in this life was for her to be happy.

But also because so many threats hung on her shoulders. On all of ours, but specifically on hers.

Echnid wanted her.

No, he didn't just *want* her. He seemed to *rely* on her coming under his thumb. And that sort of motivation almost felt worse. It led to his desperate, depraved actions before, and if he tried to touch her again...

"Ophelia!" Jezebel called, laughing.

"I didn't think it was going to work." Ophelia's amusement was clear from here, and curiosity had me sheathing my vitriol—burying all of those crushing emotions as deep as I possibly could—and jogging up the path to them.

"What's going—*Damien's shining cock*," I spat, skidding to a stop. Ophelia and Jezebel turned to face me, smiling brightly. "Did you do that, Alabath?"

"Not intentionally," Ophelia said with a shrug, turning back around to face the massive gryphon perched among the still-stone statues. The beast tipped its beak toward the sky and snapped at the air, eyes hazy as if it had truly just woken up. It was oddly adorable, which was never how I thought I'd refer to a creature I didn't think fucking existed.

I strode forward, draping an arm around Ophelia's shoulders. "You're damn impressive, you know that, *apeagna*?"

Ophelia rolled her eyes, but her cheeks flushed, magenta irises bright with wonder as she gazed at the gryphon. It stood, spreading its wings and testing the wind. Then, it took a few earth-shaking strides and leapt into the air.

As it soared off, I mumbled, "I guess that's one more myth woken." The gryphon faded into the distance, heading north to Spirits knew where. As it went, the weight of the magic Ophelia wielded mystified me.

"Santorina isn't with you?" I asked, having overheard them all talking about researching the mythos magic earlier.

Ophelia shook her head. "She had books about the gods pulled from the archives in the city." A curious crease formed between her brows. Shrugging it off, she added, "What are you doing here, anyway? I thought you were busy with Malakai and Cypherion this morning."

"I was, but Mali wanted to return to dote on Mila," I explained.

"Didn't Mila specifically tell him to go so he would stop doing that?" Jezebel asked, stuffing her feet back into her boots and lacing them up.

"I believe her exact words were, 'if you don't go with Tolek I'm going to strangle you with the bandages you keep trying to change,'" I said as Ophelia snickered.

Mila's injury had healed quickly thanks to the healers in Xenovia. But when Mali started saying he should check on her, CK insisted he had to see Vale, too. I wasn't sure if it was their new Fatesworn bond dragging him back or something else, but he'd been contemplative all morning. He'd even gone so far as to pick up a bouquet of desert marigolds on the way back to Meridat's manor.

"So, why'd you come out here?" Ophelia asked as Jezebel disappeared back up the path. Her gaze dropped to the new dagger at my waist, her brow creasing briefly as she read the initials. Her eyes widened and flicked back to me.

I brushed a strand of hair behind her ear, toying with the end as nerves thickened in my throat. "I need your help with something."

The Gates of Angeldust in Xenovia were similar to the Lendelli Hills location. Large gleaming bars lined the entrance, topped with wings and sphinx busts looking down on us, and somewhere inside, springs babbled with spirit-laced water.

"Are you sure?" she asked softly, squeezing my hand when we approached the end of the pathway to the gallery.

I tried to say yes, but my voice stuck in my throat. Instead, I pressed my lips into a grim line and nodded once. Briefly taking my eyes off the doors, I lifted Ophelia's hand and kissed it. Thank the fucking Angels she was here. I'd thought about doing this weeks ago, but I couldn't get myself to without her.

"Let's go, then," she said. Sadness layered both her voice and her eyes, but she led me silently up the steps.

My body was numb as the doors opened, the grief of recent months slamming into me all at once.

I love you, baby brother, echoed through my empty mind and the weight of her lifeless body pressed against my chest, my arms. My skin heated with the memory of her blood as we crossed the foyer.

The statue in the center was Xenique, seated on a tall throne, her palms held out on either side of her and opened toward the sky. A sphinx reclined leisurely at her feet and a pool surrounded their forms.

We bowed, dipping our fingers in the cool water and anointing our palms as Erista had explained. It was something about honoring the Soulguider mission to escort spirits home, but truthfully I hadn't absorbed a word she said. I'd been too wracked with nerves to really hear.

Ophelia pulled me to my feet and led me toward the center of the room. We waited for a few minutes, my thumb brushing across the back of her hand in anxious circles. She stood beside me, letting me steal strength like the greedy man I was when it came to her.

But the longer the silence stretched, the more my chest tightened.

After what felt like endless minutes, I started, "Maybe—"

But an echoing groan stifled the words. It fucking rippled down my bones, uncomfortable but familiar. I wasn't sure if that was the force of the stone grating against the marble floors or if it was the magnified power of what was revealed as the Hall of Wandering Souls slid into view.

Legends claimed there was one in every Gates of Angeldust, but they only exposed themselves when need be. When they appeared, those with Soulguider blood were meant to travel into the hall, for reasons unknown. With Ophelia and Jezebel, it had been to meet the sphinx and learn the truth of the Angelcurse and Warrior God.

Tonight, though, no one would be going within.

Tonight, the hall opened for an entirely different reason.

And I nearly fell to my knees as my sister appeared in the swirling mist.

"Ria," I gasped, rushing to the newly revealed archway.

Ophelia pulled me to a stop, hands tight on my arm so I didn't charge straight into that sacred space. I was grateful; a part of me knew if I tried to hug my sister, she wouldn't be corporeal.

No, this was Lyria's spirit smiling before me. And if she slipped through my hands, it might crush the resolve I'd been very carefully building for weeks to come here.

Lyria looked every bit as real as I remembered, though. She hadn't taken on the misty form of the Spirits from the Undertaking yet. Her cheeks were even a touch rosy, and her dark flowing gown was made of rich black velvet. It was exactly something she would have worn when she was...alive.

"Ria," I repeated, my voice cracking. Heart thundering.

"Hello, baby brother," she said, a ghostly echo hanging on the tips of each word.

"Hi," I muttered, frozen. Ophelia squeezed my arm again. "Ria, fuck. I miss you so much. I'm so sorry."

"Don't be sorry, Tolek," she said.

"But you shouldn't have—it wasn't time yet!" And it all bubbled through my chest. The grief, the confusion, the anger. Every feeling I'd been suppressing, masking. Everything I hadn't been ready to face. "It wasn't time!"

"It was," she assured me. "I was meant to fall that way. To a blade and for a cause much larger than any of us. Than all of Ambrisk."

"But not this soon. Fuck, I *need* you, Ria." Every time I said her name, my heart bled further.

"You don't," she said. "You have everything you need beside you." She nodded at Ophelia who had silent tears streaming down her face. I hadn't realized my eyes were wet, too.

"We were going to do so much," I whispered.

"We were. And for that—and for the time we won't have in this life—I will always hold regrets. But *you* will still accomplish amazing feats, baby brother. And do not think for one moment that I won't be watching each of them."

"You're watching?" I barely muttered.

"Every day, Tolek. I saw the Blackfyre when you saved that girl. Saw you fight Thorn, and you better believe I roared my fury to all the spirits around me at what that fucking Angel did to you." Her voice was just as passionate as I'd remembered, as alive as ever.

I laughed, sniffling. "Spirits, Ria. Any tips on how to kill the fucker?"

Her eyes dropped to my sword, then the dagger carved with her initials, and finally Ophelia's hand locked in mine. "I don't know, but like I said, I have a feeling you already have everything you need. Don't look past *all* the weapons at your friends' disposal." She put an odd inflection on that sentence, but her expression sobered, and I tucked away the note for later. "But Tolek, I want you to heal. I want you to cope with my death because I know you haven't. It is okay. You don't need to carry guilt for still walking your realm."

Your realm. No longer hers.

That ripped me open. "How am I supposed to do that, Ria? How—how do I just move on from something I don't understand?"

"You take it one day at a time—one breath at a time if you have to—and you search for a light in every one of them. Sometimes it will be hard to find, sometimes it will feel impossible, but that is when you turn to the shoulders beside you, and you hold one another up." Lyria lifted a hand as if to reach for me, then seemingly remembered she couldn't and dropped it back to her side. "Please, baby brother. For me. I want you to heal. Remember the good moments, but don't carry the bad."

Those words delivered a weighted assurance I hadn't realized I needed. Unknotted my grip from the dagger I'd been purposely driving into my chest each day, not allowing the wound to heal.

Holding onto the rotten guilt and anger rather than remembering the moments we were gifted and honoring her spirit.

Swallowing, I dropped the weight and said, "Okay, Ria. For you, I'll try. I love you so much. And I just had to see you. To know that you're—you're okay."

Lyria smiled softly at me. Her eyes were bright, her hair in full waves around her shoulders, everything about her looking so healthy and vibrant.

"I am okay, Tolek."

It was a stupid fucking statement. She wasn't okay. She was taken from Ambrisk far too soon due to a fight I dragged her into. But she was smiling, and she seemed...at peace. And knowing that she'd found some relief in death's embrace—that she wasn't suffering—well, that soothed a bit of the bruise that had formed across my heart as she bled out in my arms.

And that gave me the confidence to ask the one question that had burdened me at her appearance. "Why haven't you left yet?"

Though I was grateful to be able to speak with her, a part of my heart broke to know she was lingering here. That she hadn't gone to the Spirit Realm.

But Lyria's answering shrug was peaceful. "I accepted my death before it happened, but I wasn't entirely ready to vacate Gallantia."

"Did you have unfinished business?"

"Not of that sort," she assured me, a devious glint in her eye. And I had a feeling Lyria Vincienzo was just as scheming as a spirit as she had been as Commander. But she didn't elaborate beyond, "Soulguider magic is very intriguing. This war hasn't seen the last of me, baby brother."

"You'll stay?" I whispered.

She nodded. "For a while. I'm content, and it means I'm closer to you. I promise, Tolek, I won't leave for good without saying goodbye."

Goodbye. It was one of the sourest parts of death—the fact that we lost so many without getting that chance to say goodbye. I'd gotten those horrible final moments with my sister while I held her in the theater, and that exceeded what many received, but I was fucking relieved to have a few more.

More time, more moments, more guidance when I needed her so badly.

Then, Lyria turned to Ophelia and said words I thought could break her. "I've seen him, you know."

"What?" Ophelia barely breathed, hand tightening in mine. My own body tensed.

"He was the first to seek me out in this in between. He's fully passed on to the Spirit Realm, but he's so very proud of both of you, and he wants you to continue to be strong, to fight these injustices as the warrior sisters legends spoke of. He asked me to tell you he loves you."

Ophelia suppressed a sob, but her entire frame shuddered. I pulled her closer.

Her father.

Lyria had spoken to her father. Not only that, but he'd been the first to find her, to comfort her when she was probably fucking terrified. And out of all the messages he could have sent to his daughter, he chose the simplest but most powerful: pride, strength, and love.

Ophelia's lips trembled as she fought to maintain that strength now. "Thank you."

Lyria nodded, smiling softly. Peacefully.

"Can you...can you tell me what it's been like?" I asked. "What you've seen and how it feels?"

For whatever reason, I thought it might help ease that bruise on my heart further.

"I'll tell you everything I can, baby brother," Lyria said.

I swung my sword off my back and sank to the ground, the marble cool through my leathers, and pulled Ophelia down with me, wrapping an arm around her.

"By the way," my sister added to the woman beside me, "I love the wings."

We both laughed, Ophelia wiping her eyes as she said, "Thank you. I think I do, too."

Lyria matched our pose, sitting on the floor with her legs crossed and black velvet fanned out around her. And for hours, we remained there, listening to my sister's stories of the afterlife in the Hall of Wandering Souls.

And as she spoke, I thought all three of us found a bit of healing.

CHAPTER FIFTY-FIVE
OPHELIA

IT WAS LATE WHEN TOLEK AND I TOOK THE LONG ROUTE back through Xenovia to Meridat's manor. The Gates of Angeldust were on the opposite edge of the city, backed up to the border where the well of Soulguider magic within would pour easily into the open desert beneath the ground and beyond. I didn't mind the slow walk, and I didn't think Tolek did either as he contemplated everything Lyria had said.

"How do you feel?" I asked as we passed a rowdy tavern. A small cluster of Seawatchers placed bets on a card game against Soulguiders; Starsearchers exchanging incense and rolled herbs with Bodymelders. The alliance forces were thriving, the city crowded as we wove through the streets, but even this small moment of levity couldn't eclipse the ache in my heart at seeing Lyria again. At hearing her message from my father.

It ignited another flame of rebellion against Echnid. A warm assurance that we were on the right path. The tears were still thick in my throat as I committed my father's message to memory, allowing it to erase more of Echnid's words that had tainted my mind.

"Relieved," Tolek admitted after a few moments, though his tone was flat.

I nodded, clinging tighter to his hand. "She seemed...okay," I coaxed. Though I chose my words carefully, it wasn't a lie.

"She didn't just seem okay," Tolek said. "She was free. Lighter."

A hollow bead bloomed in my chest at the words, my eyes stinging. "She did," I agreed.

Lyria had seemed unburdened in a way I hadn't seen in years. And though her absence was an insistent, desperate ache among us all, it was healing to speak with her.

"Are you going to tell Mila?" I asked softly as we exited the part of the city where the night thrived and strolled down a desolate street, the chirping dune crickets accenting the voids between our words.

Tolek's swallow was loud in the night, and I stopped walking, turning to face him. His sharp jaw, coated in a thin layer of stubble, was gilded in the moonlight, his throat working on a second swallow as he thought. His eyes tracked his fingers entwined with mine, and he toyed with the bargain ring he still wore from Lancaster.

"I was worried Ria wouldn't be there," he admitted. "That she'd moved on already. Part of me hoped for it, but the much larger selfish part of me would have been fucking devastated if she had. And Mila never got to say goodbye in the first place. I would have felt so fucking guilty dragging her there—giving her hope—if it hadn't worked."

There was something so intimate about the chance to converse with those we'd lost. Such a rare phenomenon, occasionally seen in rituals like the Undertaking, but it was a beautiful second chance, an experience to treasure.

I cupped his jaw, bringing his eyes to mine. "I love you, Tolek Vincienzo. Your beautiful spirit and your heart. You aren't selfish for wanting more moments. It just means that heart of yours is so big, even death can't sever how deeply it loves."

Tolek leaned down, pressing his lips to mine in one of the gentlest, but somehow the most meaningful, kisses he'd ever given me. It was tender and passionate but layered with a soft desperation. Not nipping and groaning, but grateful.

For my words, for my support. For my love.

Angels, he could have it all. Anything I could do to ease his hurt, I would.

When he pulled back, he folded me into his side, and we continued on to the manor. And the one thing that radiated off him was this immense sense of closure. Tolek would miss Lyria for every day of his long life, wishing her footsteps shadowed his, but he would not wonder. And that was a gift of the Angels.

As we crossed through the gates to Meridat's property and neared the main house, a commotion sounded from the grand entrance in front of the manor where the resplendent fountain of Xenique and her three daughters bubbled.

"What now?" I muttered as voices mounted.

Tol cocked his head to listen, grinning. "Come on."

"Barrett?" I blurted when Tolek dragged me closer. The Engrossian Prince spun, mystlight pouring from the open doors of Meridat's manor and highlighting his messy curls and mischievous smile.

His wolf, Rebel, bounded around his legs, weaving between him, Malakai, Dax, and Celissia with excited yips. He may have been nearly horse-sized by now, but he was still a pup.

"There's our Revered!" Barrett gushed, rushing forward and scooping me into a hug. When he set me down, he turned to Tolek. "And my favorite new inter-clan advisor."

"Excuse me?" Malakai called, his arms crossed and a brow raised.

"I love you dearly, brother. Don't worry," Barrett said, striding back to his side.

"Cypherion is my favorite blood relative now," Malakai retorted, and Barrett released an affronted gasp.

"What's going on?" I asked after I greeted both Celissia and Dax, the two eyeing their prince a bit warily.

"How are things in Banix?" Tolek added, his words tight for an entirely different reason than seeing his sister. The unrest he'd told me about in the Engrossian capital was severe.

"Things have changed," Barrett explained, still with that untamable glee, bordering on manic.

"What happened?" Malakai asked, stepping closer to his brother.

But it was Dax who answered, "Bant paid us a visit last week."

"He *what*?" I gasped, fear flaring bright within me.

"He showed up in the valleys." Barrett's hands curling at his sides were the only thing giving away his anger.

Dax scoffed, growling, "Attacked them is more like it."

"There aren't many accounts of what actually happened," Celissia explained, her face pale. *Most firsthand viewers died*, she didn't need to add, and my breath froze in my lungs. Many of those present had not escaped Bant's attack. "But he did something to the pools. Whether he was using the dark magic within or tampering with the Blackfyre somehow, we don't know."

"Why are we just hearing of this now?" Malakai asked.

"All of our stores of Mystique ink went up in flame," Barrett said coolly. "As did any we tried to procure on the ride here."

"Flame?" Ptholenix's thread of fiery magic curled in my gut, orange Angellight flickering in my palms. Barrett nodded solemnly, as if to say he had the same suspicion, and the air around the six of us prickled with anticipation.

What were the Angels up to?

Barrett went on, "The heretics were pleased to offer themselves. They dove right into the tar pits, sacrificed for Bant's favor. The few who made it away—*carrying the weight of the message forward*—" he added, fingers curling into quotations in the air, "went on a rampage through the capital. Pillaging in the name of the Angel."

"And Bant didn't *stop* them?" Malakai grumbled.

"Why would he?" I suggested as the fear dripping through me coalesced into burning wrath. "Whatever this was, it was likely on Echnid's demand. And the god has made it clear that while he wants to uplift his warriors, he doesn't mind who dies to do it."

Even if it left him with fewer subjects.

"Surprisingly," Barrett said, his smile grim as he dragged a ringed hand through his hair, "this worked in our favor."

"With everyone enraged over the Angel, more are now supporting Barrett's claim," Dax elaborated, wrapping an arm around his prince's waist.

Barrett's eyes turned glassy. "And thanks to Bant, the vast majority of dissenters support a Mystique alliance."

I closed my eyes against the sting. Against the tangle of relief and hope that dared to well in the back of my throat. "An actual Engrossian-Mystique alliance."

The first true one in...Spirits, I didn't even know how long. It was caused by the despicable actions of the very Angels we were meant to honor—the ones whose ancient feuds pitted us against each other in the first place. And now, we would stand against them.

Tol's hand slid across my shoulders, massaging above my wings. With a crooked smirk, he asked, "Celissia, have you heard anything from the sorcia?"

Tolek told me he'd suggested she write to her sorceress relatives for aid. They were as involved in this godly war as anyone. Their goddess, Thallia, had been the one to forge Echnid's lock in the Stone Realm.

But Celissia's lips set in a frown. "They sent an outright rejection. Claimed no part in this war."

"By the fucking Angels," Tolek swore.

It was a different sting of betrayal than Bant's vehement actions. One from people who lived on Ambrisk, who would suffer the wrath of the Warrior God as we all would, and yet chose to do nothing simply because this war was not on their doorstep.

But even if we didn't have the sorcia, thanks to Bant, we had all seven Gallantian Warrior clans to stand against a god.

And that *had* to mean something.

"And while we're on the topic of partnerships..." Barrett said. "When I declared to my people that we would be supporting the greater alliance, I told them I would do so with the man I love by my side."

"Does that mean..." I began, eyes flicking between him and the other Engrossians. Based on Celissia's and Dax's wary glances, this was the part of Barrett's behavior that had been troubling them.

But the prince positively grinned. "If there's time before a god tries to kill us all, we have a bonding ceremony to plan."

Tolek whooped and immediately said he'd speak with Jezebel and Erista to see what could be done, muttering about how at least one person let them plan a proper ceremony, but Malakai whispered to his brother, "You're sure this is a good idea right now?"

Dax jumped on the argument, as if hoping someone might suggest it. "He has a point. I love you, Barrett, but you only *just* secured a loyal clan. It's volatile still, and I don't come from a noble house."

With a gentle hand on his arm, Celissia added, "Let's just consider it, Bare. We can end our ruse without jumping so quickly."

"Dax never will hold a title, though," Barrett argued, then looked to his consort. "You and I will always be the prince and general who ran off to aid the enemy." His desperate tone pulled at my heart. "The fact of your lineage is never going to change, and if that is what the people want of me—if either of those things upset them—I'd rather them know now what they're getting. Rather be truthful and show them their ruler than build a reign on the premise of lies."

"I'm not saying never," Dax clarified. "I'm just proposing that this may not be the most prudent time to perpetuate unrest. We can wait as long as is needed."

But Barrett shook his head, proudly declaring, "Love is precisely what the world needs right now. And I am fucking tired of letting everyone else decide who I get to be as king."

Worry warred across Dax's features. Worry for the man he loved, for their people. He looked to Malakai, who shook his head as if to say *he's a stubborn ass, but you're the one who loves him.*

I stepped between them, looping one arm through Barrett's and another through Dax's as I dragged them toward the manor, Tolek escorting Celissia ahead. Conceding, Malakai followed.

"I think Barrett is right," I agreed. "We don't know what the coming days will bring, but if we can control even a fraction of happiness, I think we have to. Now, Dax, tell us what soldiers you brought, because I know you wouldn't come all this way without support."

Resigned, Dax sighed. "We brought as many troops as we had ready to mobilize while still leaving enough to defend Banix."

My chest inflated as Malakai added, "Cypherion, Mila, and Meridat are already working on lodgings. The city is crowded."

"Excellent," I said as satisfied whirls of gold seraph magic curled over my wings. "It's safest here, and that gives us a perfect opportunity to prepare for the expanding threats." I forced out a slow breath, calling my light under control as the large front doors closed behind us with a thud. "I don't know what the Angels are after, but they're raising the stakes every day. I don't think we have much time left to uncover Echnid's weaknesses."

And if we couldn't, what fate would that leave Ambrisk to?

Beyond the god, for some unknown reason, the Angels were out for warrior blood, and the question remained: How far would they go to claim it?

Chapter Fifty-Six
Malakai

I slammed back against the door, my life flashing before my eyes as I panted. "By the Spirits, I think he's going to kill me." I gripped Lucidius's dagger at my waist just to let the metal cool me down.

"Not enjoying the ceremony planning?" Tolek teased from the armchair he lounged in before the unlit hearth in Cypherion's room, a glass of liquor in one hand and a weaponry book in the other.

"Not to the extent Barrett is," I said, crossing to the sideboard and pouring myself a measure of the citrus whiskey Tol must have brought. I knocked it back fast, pouring another. "He just arrived yesterday, yet he managed to gather six different outfit options and made me help him choose."

"What did you pick?" Cyph asked, striding shirtless out of the dressing chamber off the main room with a tunic in hand. His silver Fatesworn tattoo shone in the bright mystlight, practically swirling.

"I don't even know." I pinched the bridge of my nose. "They all looked the same. Thank the Angels this ceremony is tonight."

Tolek laughed loudly, Cypherion shaking his head as if I was the ridiculous one in this situation and not my half-brother who was attempting to plan an elaborate bonding ceremony in the midst of a godly war.

"I think it's exciting," Tolek said, taking another sip of his drink and flipping a page. "We need a good festival after Cypherion cheated us out of hosting a Fatesworn celebration."

"*Cheated*?" Cyph gasped, tugging on his tunic. "You're never going to let it go, are you?"

"Never," Tolek said with a sharp glare.

Cypherion turned questioning eyes on me. "I'm with him. I wanted to be there," I said flatly, falling into the chair opposite Tol's.

Cyph tipped his head back as if praying to the Spirits for strength. Then, he poured a drink and propped himself on the foot of the bed. "You two are aware that this bond with Vale wasn't planned, right?"

"Yes, but the ceremony was! You flew there for it," Tolek argued.

"I flew there because I couldn't fucking stand her being away anymore," Cypherion corrected bracing his elbows on his knees. His half-full glass hung from his fingertips. "The ceremony was a mid-flight decision, and you both had your hands full here."

Neither of us could argue with that. If it had been our girls, we'd have done nothing different. Absently, I rubbed the heel of my hand over my chest where the Bind was inked and avoided Tolek's eye as he tracked the movement.

Fuck, were we ever going to be able to get rid of this tattoo? Maybe Vale could read a way how.

But I was reluctant to ask her after her own fucking binding tattoo had severed with Titus's death. The way she'd screamed... even though I was being tortured at the time, I'd never forget the sound. It ripped at my very soul.

Still, despite the obvious pain, I'd do it. If there was a way other than death to remove my Bind to Ophelia so I could receive one with Mila—and Ophelia with Tolek—I would. We didn't need the damn thing.

A part of me was afraid to find out what it would be like without this North Star tattoo. If the first Bind I'd received never worked correctly, would a second? I didn't think I could stand that, and I didn't want to see the broken look in Mila's eyes if that happened.

I was almost certain the reason Ophelia's and my Bind never worked correctly was because I'd had so many secrets when we'd received them. I'd signed the treaty and had been planning to disappear. But there was a part of me that feared it was some twisted piece within me that truly ruined it. Something that would damage any ritual or bond I received my entire life.

I shoved the fear aside for now. It was useless unless we actually found a way to sever a Bind.

"We're happy for you," I told Cypherion.

Tolek sat up straighter. "We are. We just want a chance to celebrate the union and officially welcome Vale into the family."

Cyph looked between us, eyes narrowed, but he relaxed. "Thank you. This new bond has been making it hard to focus."

"How?" Tolek asked, head cocked.

"I've been extra defensive of Vale but domineering." He shook his head. "I need to get a grip on it."

He had been a bit more surly than usual when Vale wasn't around, and she'd been more assertive, but I'd assumed it was just her Fatecatcher powers settling in. Apparently it was their emotions tugging back and forth on the bond, attempting to regulate after being stitched together by the hands of the Fates.

Was Cyph providing that newfound strength for her? And was it the new risks of this magic driving him to be more protective? Cypherion thrived on order and control, so I understood why that would disrupt his normal behavior.

Spirits, is that what I should have felt with the Bind? I didn't fucking know. Didn't fucking know if I wanted to either. Because if it was, something was clearly wrong with me.

"You'll adjust to it, CK," Tolek assured him confidently, tracing the hilt of his sword where it leaned against his chair as he went back to his book.

"What is that you're reading, anyway?" I asked, leaning forward to glimpse the cover. "Not your usual type of book."

Tolek shut the volume, tossing it on the table between us. "Something Lyria said last night got me thinking." When he and

Ophelia saw her spirit. That's where Mila was now. I offered to go with her, but she'd wanted to go alone and insisted I help Barrett.

Tolek pressed the heels of his hands into his eyes as he thought. "She said something about using all the weapons at our disposal." Sitting back, he dragged a hand through his hair. "Maybe she wasn't being literal, but the way she emphasized it...I don't know. It felt important."

"You think she knows of some secret weapon we have?" Cypherion asked dubiously.

Tol studied his sword, shaking his head. "If she did, she'd tell us. But Lyria was smart—she came up with the idea to imbue the Starsearcher weapons. Maybe she had other ideas that hadn't fully formed. And she's been watching *everything*." He sighed and took a sip of his drink. "The theory feels like it's right there, and I just can't grab it."

Trying to help, I asked, "Any thoughts on what happened with Bant?"

"When I went to the Blackfyre, the heretics were already out of their right minds. They were forcing that girl beneath the tar without an ounce of remorse. I don't know if it was the allure of the power or simply losing touch with their civilized warrior selves, but they were gone." Tolek traced his palm, a faint scar slicing diagonally across each. He studied them, muttering, "It was fucking atrocious."

"It's a far jump from worshipping the pools to pillaging the capital," Cyph said.

Tolek nodded. "But that power...it's consuming. And it's the source of dark, corrupted magic for all worlds. I've *felt* it's strength..." His eyes landed on his sword, the steel catching the mystlight flicking in the chandelier above. "Actually"—Tol placed his drink on the table and pushed upright, grabbing his weapon and balancing it across his palms—"I still feel it."

"What do you mean?" I eyed him, leaning forward. Cyph straightened, coming to stand between our chairs.

"I never looked into it further," Tolek said, eyes sweeping over the blade. "I was distracted by saving that girl, and then I got the letter that Ophelia was back."

"What happened?" Cypherion asked, pulling Tolek back on track.

He shook his head, a crease forming between his brows as he studied the weapon like the memory played out along the steel. "When my sword dipped in the pool, it flashed with light. It was bright—searing—but not like Ophelia's Angellight." Tolek shrugged, looking up finally. "I haven't seen it since, but it was empowering. It radiated through the blade and into *me*."

"Into you?" I echoed.

"It was like a pulse of power through my veins. It's lingered. I felt it when I used my sword against Thorn in the desert, too."

Cyph inclined his head. "When you injured him, you mean?"

"Had that sword been blessed in any sort of forging ceremony?" I asked. Precious Mystique weapons were forged in the fire of the Spirit Volcano, and each clan had similar rituals and superstitions. The blades were highly coveted, rumored as able to sever the richest life forces and anoint sacred ceremonies.

Tolek shrugged. "Not that I'm aware. It's just a normal weapon. I've had it for years."

"It could've been blessed centuries ago in your family," Cypherion suggested, but Tolek laughed.

"You think my father would have a sacred sword and *not* brag about it?" Tol sheathed the weapon, gesturing to the ornate silver dagger at his hip. "If anything, I'd bet my family dagger was the one blessed, but this sword? It couldn't be."

"Did dipping it in the pools somehow do it, then?" I asked.

"As in, I'd blessed the blade myself?" Tolek questioned, tilting his head curiously.

"I don't know how that would be possible." Cypherion dragged a hand over his jaw. "Those rituals are pretty guarded, performed by priestesses, Angels, the like."

Something nagged at my mind, and when my eyes caught on the portrait of a desert oasis above the fireplace, the memory snapped to the surface. "There were murals in the Revered's Palace of blades being imbued in a stream."

I recounted the ones I could recall, all the while something pounded in my chest.

"Damien painted those," Tolek said. "Ophelia told me."

Energy buzzed through the room with each passing second. The three of us exchanged wary looks, as if not daring to say what would come next, but we were all wondering it.

Cypherion added, "When we fought the gorgons, they were focused on my scythe—a weapon that has *also* injured an Angel. Vale read that Echnid is interested in it."

"And Echnid likely was the reason Bant blasted through the tar pits a few nights ago," Tolek suggested, nodding slowly as he rose from his seat.

"Echnid burned the trove," I breathed in awe. The memory of the Firebird's flames seared my skin. My attention snapped up to meet Tolek's and Cypherion's. "Every piece of gold and artwork beneath the Revered's Palace. When Ophelia and I escaped, it was because Echnid was having Ptholenix melt down the trove—full of weapons."

There was no way. No way this answer had been before us so blatantly, that we'd been seeing it again and again but hadn't realized Echnid's plain fear.

"You think there was something in there he didn't want us to get our hands on," Cypherion said hesitantly.

"I think it's very likely there was something in there that could bring about his downfall."

The trove, Cyph's scythe, Tolek's sword. Bant *wrecked* the tar pits...

"And with the Blackfyre possibly imbuing weapons..." Tolek began.

I stood now, too. "Do you think there's a chance that Damien painted those murals intentionally?" I asked, heart fucking stampeding behind my ribs. "That maybe he knew we'd need this information one day."

"That would mean he's on our side..." Cypherion added.

"By the fucking Angels," Tolek said, throwing back the rest of his drink and sliding his weapons belt around his waist. "We have to find Ophelia."

CHAPTER FIFTY-SEVEN
OPHELIA

ERISTA AND I WERE IN THE WAR ROOM REVIEWING MORE godly texts, desperately trying to find anything ahead of Barrett and Dax's ceremony.

"None of these speak of traveling between realms?" I asked. "Realmspinner magic?"

"Not that I've found." Erista frowned, tucking a curl behind her ear. "The gods probably didn't want records kept of that fallible magic, if opening bridges was one of the few things they were unable to do on their own."

"You'd think they would have found a way, though. Created some way to do it." I drummed my fingers on the table. "What about killing the gods?"

Erista pulled over another heavy book. "It sounds like Echnid would have had to use magic not born on this realm, since the gods are"—she flipped the page—"*unable to fall to that which they created.*"

A sour sensation curled through my stomach at how quickly time was passing. Echnid was probably growing closer to his goals each day, especially now that he'd killed one god. It was only a matter of time until he had the others.

Before the worry could fully form, three excited men burst through the door. Tolek, Malakai, and Cypherion stumbled to a halt across the table from us, eager grins on their faces.

"I don't like those smiles," I muttered.

Shutting her book, Erista disagreed, "I'm a bit curious."

"We figured something out," Tolek said, the three of them looking among one another. Spirits, why did this feel so similar to the time when we were fifteen and they'd schemed up a plan to sneak bottles from my parents' liquor supply?

"What is it?" I asked.

And they launched into details, each interjecting over the other. About Tolek's sword in Banix and Cypherion's scythe. About Bant's attack and injuring Thorn and the trove and murals Damien had painted in the Revered's Palace—

"He pointed those out to me," I said, recalling the Angel's words. "Many times. He'd always seemed a bit...sad over them."

All three of them nodded, Cypherion saying, "What if he wasn't sad, but eager for you to figure it out?"

"Eager?" Erista echoed, engrossed in their theory now.

"Trying to hint to you," Malakai added.

"Because he didn't *want* Echnid to be free," Tolek suggested. "What if he was worried, and that was why he kept pointing you toward those murals?"

"What are you saying?" I asked warily. Damien's betrayals still stung so fresh, a wound that not only struck me but dug itself into the Mystiques as a whole. I wouldn't forgive it easily. Not with my people at risk.

Tolek read that unease and stepped around the table, sinking into the seat beside mine. "What if there *is* a way for a mortal warrior to kill a god, *apeagna*? With a blade imbued by a sacred source of power from Gallantia?"

I looked to Erista. "*Unable to fall to that which they created,*" I repeated.

"Theoretically," she answered, pursing her lips, "the combination of that much ether could be greater than anything made on this world."

"When I was researching in Damenal," Malakai said, "I found a book that spoke of a godly war on another world. Of how the people had killed the tyrant with a particular weapon that exposed its fatal flaw, one from the god's own trove."

My jaw popped open, and Erista gasped. "How did you even find that book?" She waved a hand over the table. "I've been having to piece together small tidbits about the gods from the books here."

"Maybe someone put it there," Malakai said pointedly.

"But imbuing weapons at that level is a rare practice," Erista challenged. "The stories always say that it's highly regulated and the *true* blades—not just ones dipped in your Spirit Volcano or forged with resins but those containing raw, powerful magic—are difficult to come by."

"All the more reason this could be it," Tolek said.

The words sank into my spirit, some wild, desperate tangle of hope and fear emerging. I didn't want to allow myself to imagine it was true, but Angels, if it was? The chance this could provide.

In my mind, I plunged a blade into Echnid's heart.

His godly blood spilled across my hands, and I relished the heat of it.

I watched existence fade from his eyes, his form wither to nothing but mist.

The poison he'd plied me with sang within my own veins at even the mere consideration. The revenge I sought for him using me, the safety I wanted to instill across the continent. This could be the way to all of it.

But—

"It still sounds too simple," I admitted. "And Damien..."

Tolek smiled softly, as if understanding why that possibility frightened me so much. He cupped my cheeks, and a sharp vengeance bit through his words. "None of this has been simple, *apeagna*. Perhaps it's time we finally started studying Echnid's fears to turn this game on him."

My spirit warmed at how he always saw the light when I was shrouded by the darkness around us. I longed to share that way of thinking, but I hesitated.

My eyes flashed to Malakai. "You think it's true?"

He shrugged. "I think it's worth investigating. That book wasn't there on accident."

And because Malakai had lived through Echnid's torture with

me, his encouragement meant as much as Tolek's. Sighing, I leaned forward, pressing my head against Tol's chest and allowing his embrace to soothe me.

"Vale said Echnid is focused on my scythe, and the gorgons seemed worried about it," Cypherion added. "Meridat has people searching their records to see if there's any chance it was imbued. So far, we just know it was given to my father after he performed a great act of bravery in Soulguider Territory."

Cyph's scythe and Tolek's sword...There had to be a reason behind them, something we were meant to learn. When it came to fate, coincidences didn't exist.

"If Echnid burned the trove because there was a weapon in there he was afraid of, then we're going to have to make our own. We need to figure out *what* sort of imbued weapon can kill a god," I muttered, scratching at my Curse scar as my thoughts bound from one possibility to the next. There were wells of power within the Gates of Angeldust. We could start—

But Malakai interrupted my thoughts. "We had a theory on that, too."

Cypherion added, "We're going to need to find Cyren."

"You think it's *me*?" I asked incredulously.

"We think it's possible," Cypherion corrected as Tolek walked around the war room, turning up the mystlight lanterns. The maps and briefs that normally littered the table had been moved to the smaller surfaces framing the room.

While they'd explained their theory to me, Erista and Malakai had left to find those we needed. They returned now with Cyren, the Starsearcher General, in tow as well as our Bodymelder friends, Esmond and Gatrielle, who had arrived in Xenovia a week ago with healers from their clan and had been assisting in triage plans.

When I raised my brows after greeting them, Malakai said, "Gatrielle is Angelblessed." He'd told us before that the Bodymelder was a rare *allure*, one of their clan who were deemed blessed by the Angels, giving him access to sacred sites across the continent, like Firebird's Field.

Or places to bless weapons.

Gatrielle's brown curls bobbed as he nodded. "When I studied to pass my Angelblessed exams, we had to memorize the process and production of the rituals that forge sacred weapons."

"Can we see your sword, Tolek?" Esmond asked.

Tol unsheathed the blade and handed it to them. The Bodymelders examined it, muttering softly to one another as strands of gold magic spun overhead in anticipation.

Finally, Gatrielle said, "This sword doesn't have any of the markings of one forged in your Spirit Volcano, for example. But it does *feel* like it."

"What do you mean?" I asked, pivoting to his side.

"Here, Revered." He held out the hilt.

When I grabbed it, a hum shot up my arm. I gasped at the contact, wide eyes swinging to Tol. "I don't remember your sword ever feeling this way."

Tolek nodded in agreement. "You probably feel it even more than I do with your magic—but I know what you mean."

"I still wish we'd been able to speak with Aimee," I mumbled, frustration at the Storyteller who never existed mounting within me again. "She *has* to have answers to all of this."

How could she never have existed?

"I know, but think about it, *apeagna*. Echnid wants *you*." Tolek's hands curled into fists until his knuckles turned white. He cleared his throat. "The god can suck my cock if he thinks he's getting you," he added as he came to stand behind me at the head of the table.

"Threats aside," Malakai continued for his friend, "what if part of why Echnid wants you so close and part of why he drugged you was because he doesn't want you to figure out that *you* can destroy him?"

I'd wanted to send the god to ruin from within—I'd wondered if I made a mistake by getting out before I'd learned all of his secrets—but perhaps breaking free of his hold was the answer.

Owning my mind once again, regaining the strength I'd always burned with, would spell his downfall.

"So, you think seraph magic can imbue a blade?" I asked, and all three of the boys nodded vigorously.

"You've said yourself that Angel magic is raw power," Tolek said. "The seraphs are no longer of this realm, and that magic is akin to the power of Angels, right? All seven of them? Safe to say that power rivals a god when combined. Probably the next most powerful thing on Ambrisk. It's something that hasn't been seen in living history in this realm, and as Erista said, blades imbued with this level of magic are rare."

That thought settled between my wings, making me stand taller. *I* was that next most powerful thing on Ambrisk.

I flared my feathers wide, asking Gatrielle, "Think it will work?"

He shrugged, claiming one of the seats at the table among Erista, Cyren, and Esmond, who leaned forward to continue discussing his theories about what kinds of steel absorbed magic best.

Gatrielle said, "I don't know much about seraphs given that you're the first we ever knew existed. But I think most new discoveries begin like this. With an innovative idea and someone insisting it's worth a try."

"We're worth a fucking try," I said, and Tolek brushed a hand down my wing in encouragement, making me shiver. I shot him a scolding glare over my shoulder, but he only smiled with mock apology, knowing exactly how to work me up with these damn things.

"What weapon are we using?" I asked, turning back to the table. Malakai and Cypherion stood on either side now. "I still haven't replaced mine..."

My voice trailed off at the memories of Starfire and Angelborn being melted down.

"We thought of that," Tolek said, and he pulled his family blade from his hip, extending it toward me.

I whirled, blinking up at him. "That's the Vincienzo dagger."

"It is," he said. "And I can't think of a single greater honor for it."

"Tolek, no—"

But Tol stepped forward. My wings rose behind me, giving us a semblance of privacy. The heated look in his eyes told me whatever he said next was meant for my ears only.

"Ophelia Alabath," he whispered, and the way he said my name had my throat drying out and my heart running rampant. He cupped my face, thumb brushing my cheekbone. "This weapon has been in my family line for generations. It's been passed from parent to child, has seen countless battles, and has innumerable stories etched in it. But from the moment I stole it from my father's armory when I was sixteen, I knew I wanted to give it to someone else. That I wanted to do *more* with it. To let it mean something beyond Vincienzo."

Because Tolek had already loved me so fiercely at such a young age. He may not have dared to dream I would be the one he gave the dagger to when he stole it, but he knew how powerful those feelings were—how strong they could be for someone—and he knew he'd want to show his love this way. To rewrite a history of how his father had treated him and carve out his own path with this very blade.

By handing over his legacy when it mattered most in order to build a new one together. A greater story that could outshine the gods.

Spirits, if *my* legacy was nothing more than being loved by him, I'd be the luckiest warrior to ever grace Ambrisk.

"This dagger is meant for the family," Tolek reminded me. "You have always been my family. And I've known for a while now that I wanted it to be yours until the day we have a child to pass it down to."

My heart squeezed so tightly at the thought of that future with him. If someone dug through my spirit at that very moment, they'd find Tolek Vincienzo's signature all over it. He was mine, and I was his, and this blade being handed to me with promises of legacies rewritten only carved him even deeper into my fate.

Taking the dagger from him, I pushed onto my toes and kissed him. My hand holding the weapon laid flat against his chest, both of our hearts pounding against it. "I love you, Vincienzo. And I know this is so much more than a blade you're offering me now. I know it is every bit of your present and future. And I don't care if we don't have a tattoo promising it, I gladly claim you."

"Infinitely," he swore. Then, his eyes turned hungry. "Now let's make them scorch."

As I spun back around, reinvigorated, the others' conversations broke off. I placed the dagger on the table and stepped back until my wings brushed Tolek's chest.

"How do I do this?" I asked Cyren, the Starsearcher General having been in charge of the project to imbue weapons with precious resins and oils with the goal of making their readings more powerful on a battlefield.

"We've been imbuing ours in the forging, so I would imagine the heat of your Angellight would need to weaken the metal. Make it more malleable so it can truly absorb the properties of the magic." They steepled their fingers on the table, resting their chin atop them and waited with an eager look in their eye.

Let's make them scorch.

I took a deep breath, thinking of every warrior who gave their life for this cause. Thinking of Lyria, who had supplied the offhand idea of forging weapons with the power of the seeing chambers and of Damien who may have guided us here.

On the exhale, I poured seraph power forward. A storm of gold light crashed through the room, flickering with the signatures of every Angel. Fiery reds and tempests of blue waves, stormy skies and glittering lilac constellations. The amethyst of encroaching death, the inky black of the dark pools, and the vibrant effervescence of Mystique magic. But shrouding it all, containing it, was the pure, white gold shimmer that tugged at the deepest parts of me. That *was* me. My own personal brand of power.

The *whoosh* of light flooded the room, drowning out the theories of my friends and their shocked gasps at the sheer intensity of the heat. I poured and poured that magic forth, willing it to sink into the steel—

No.

To bend the steel to its will as I would the might of the Angels and gods who stood against us.

I found the individual raw magic of every one of those Prime Warriors—the power only I had ever wielded all at once—and I forged the Vincienzo blade into something new and more deadly with it.

I gave until the strings stretched to their very fibers, and then, I dug deeper still, imbuing and bending and wielding. Until I was panting and collapsed forward, sweaty hands catching me against the table as my ears rang.

Tolek came up behind me, wrapping an arm around my waist. "Anything?" he asked Gatrielle and Cyren.

They assessed it, the Angelblessed Bodymelder tilting the blade toward the light. "It's heavy, like it absorbed the power, but there are no physical signs."

"That isn't surprising," Cyren added, "given that you weren't attempting to carve new designs."

Gatrielle nodded in agreement, hissing when he touched the blade. "It's hotter than Ptholenix's fire, that's certain." He shook out his blistered finger. "This isn't a typical sacred source, so I'm not positive what to look for."

As they studied the weapon that held all my hopes, the clock hanging at one end of the room chimed six times.

"Damien's cock," Tolek grumbled.

"Come on," Erista said, "we need to get ready for the bonding ceremony. If we're late, Barrett will never let us hear the end of it." The Bodymelders and Cyren followed her from the room with promises to keep thinking about ways to ensure this worked.

Malakai was on their heels, grumbling about Barrett's preparations as he cast me a worried glance. Cypherion comforted him with a reminder that he'd get hours to dance with Mila regardless of what the prince made him wear.

"Come on, *apeagna*," Tolek said, dropping a kiss to my temple. "We aren't giving up yet."

"Not a chance in any realm," I swore, grabbing the dagger he'd gifted me and sheathing it beside the other at my thigh, relishing in the way the metal nearly blistered my skin.

~

I WASHED and dressed quickly for the ceremony, bustling out of my room in the guest house with my waves trailing between my wings and heels echoing on tile. Tolek had gone ahead to escort Meridat at my insistence since I was almost late, but when I rounded the corner toward the foyer, I collided with Malakai.

"Oh," I gasped. "I'm sorry."

"It's all right," he said.

I stepped back, taking in his finely woven tunic. "You look very nice, Malakai. I'm sure Barrett will be pleased."

"He better be. He made me try on more outfits than I could count," Malakai grumbled. He rubbed his chest sheepishly. "Thanks, though. I was actually coming to find you."

"Me?" I asked.

"You were running late, and you tried what you did with the blade earlier...I just thought..."

The memory of seraph and myth magic clashed through my mind. Malakai's shaking form crumbled beneath it. I heaved as poison warped my blood.

My body is my own.

My mind is my own.

"I'm okay," I promised, scratching at the empty Curse mark with shaking fingers. "I'm as okay as I can be."

Malakai eyed me. "Are you sure?" He didn't have to elaborate. Even those few words from Malakai after what we'd been through together were comforting.

"I'm sure," I promised.

I *was* okay. At least, as okay as I had been this morning, which I thought might have been a little more okay than the morning before. By regular standards, I supposed I wasn't okay, but attempting to imbue the blade hadn't triggered any of those memories from Damenal and it hadn't woken the lingering effects of Echnid's tainted poison I was still trying to forget.

"Are *you* okay?" I asked in return.

Malakai blew out a breath, offering me his arm. "Would it be bad to say I wasn't?"

"Never." I squeezed his wrist as we walked briskly through the front door and toward the gates of Meridat's estate, the maroon fabric of my skirt dancing on the gentle breeze.

"I'm worried about Mila and this Reflector power. About what it means for her and the threats it could put over her head if Echnid decides he wants that, too."

"Mila's strong," I assured him. "She's been through a lot, but she's going to keep fighting."

"Should she truly *have* to keep fighting, though? She's fought enough." He let out a humorless laugh. "Spirits, Phel, you've fought more than enough, too."

My heart clenched at his words. "We all have."

"I'm tired of us fighting," Malakai admitted. "Someday it has to stop."

"It will," I promised, the words quiet among the revelrous streets of Xenovia, flooded with warriors of all clans making their way to the city center. "That's why we can't stop now. We need to grasp that future for the sake of"—he waved a hand across the crowds of jubilant faces—"all of them."

Malakai was quiet as we walked. But just as we reached the building, he swore, "It's going to end. Whatever it takes, we're going to get that future where no one has to fight battles of the gods and Angels ever again."

And I hoped to the Spirits he was right.

Chapter Fifty-Eight
Malakai

I scratched at the collar of my tunic, the heavy embroidery framing the hem rough against my skin. But it was *elegant* as Barrett and Jezebel took no hesitation in reminding me every time I grumbled about it. A dark mossy-green fabric that was truthfully pretty soft, but with thick silver patterns swirling along the collar and cuffs.

Engrossian colors as Barrett had requested. He may not have been in his home territory for the ceremony, but he was still damn proud of the people he was leading and wanted everyone here to know it.

Dax was dressed in a fresh pair of deep-black leathers, and he'd carry his axes at his back, gleaming to perfection.

Though it was last minute, Meridat had spared no expense, and as I watched my brother fuss over his hair in the mirror for the hundredth time, I was grateful to the chancellor who had no obligation to take us under her wing but did. She was a fucking good leader, and when I'd told her so earlier, she'd said all she wanted was a chance for her people—for all of us—to experience a little bit of joy before the looming threats.

"How are you feeling?" I asked Barrett in one of the back rooms of the city center's capitol building, Rebel lying at our feet.

"Like this one curl needs to lie flat," Barrett muttered, aggravated, but I couldn't even tell which it was. His hair looked fine.

I chuckled, striding to stand beside him and tucking my hands in my pockets. "And about the ceremony? Are you nervous?"

"Not in the slightest," Barrett said.

"Really?" I asked, brows shooting up.

The prince straightened, eyeing me in the mirror. "I couldn't be nervous when it comes to Dax. He is…" He faced me head on. "For years, he was everything good in my life, and now, he is the light that reminds me of the good when I am unable to see it."

"What do you mean?" I asked.

"These months have been challenging," my brother said. "I know you're all aware of that. But if I didn't have Dax…" He shook his head. "He's the one that continues to push me. The one I look at and remember why I'm fighting. He's reminded me nightly of the people that are counting on me, and while my love for him stretches deeper than the valleys, he has also reminded me of all of you."

"Of us?"

"Dax is everything I've ever wanted, but there are other reasons to keep going. These alliances…none of you are just allies to us, Malakai."

His words knocked on that open cage within my chest, like he'd let a damn bird loose inside and its eager wings rattled the bars.

That's what love and hope and dreams were, I supposed. The reasons we fought when the battle seemed so brutal. For a day when we could simply say *I love you* without the threat of it being our last breath.

"You're not an ally, Barrett," I said, clapping him on the shoulder. "You're my brother."

His face lit up. He'd never stop reacting like that—and I didn't want him to, despite my complaints. Barrett felt his emotions so deeply and showed them in their entirety. Every damn one. And while those expressions had grated on me initially, I was starting to see them as brighter points of my days.

Like the warmth I felt with Tolek and Cypherion.

Like a pair of ice blue eyes that squinted in laughter.

Barrett was my brother, and I didn't want him to live in a world where he had to dampen his true self.

"I'm not nervous," Barrett affirmed, turning back toward the mirror and straightening his tunic, tucking it into a thick black belt with a shiny silver buckle. Rebel sat up beside him, studying his reflection as the prince went on, "Dax reminds me every day. When I'm feeling drastic, he tempers me. He is as much a king as I am—probably a better one some days—and always prioritizes my wants and needs. In declaring our love and stepping into this bonding ceremony, I'm putting him first. Making sure everyone knows where he stands. And hopefully setting an example for all of Gallantia that when things are bleak, we have to choose our happiness."

Those damn ice blue eyes flashed in my memory again, and the tattoo on my chest ached. Not emotion from the person at the other frayed end of it, just my crippling longing for my own general. For her to know where she stood, to be sure she was the happiness I was choosing every damn day, despite the ink I was forever marked with.

I cleared my throat. "Beautifully said, King Barrett."

Then, I smoothed down that supposedly stubborn lock he was wrangling and handed him the thin, dark silver crown he wore as prince. He placed the circlet upon his head, its small onyx spikes poking through his curls. Before I could say anything else, Jezebel peeked around the door in a gown of flowing rose silk.

"We're ready," she said, grinning, and Barrett nearly squealed in excitement. Rebel trotted over to Jezebel, and she scratched between his ears as they left.

"You have what you promised?" Barrett checked with me.

I grabbed the satchel by the door, swinging it over my shoulder and patting it. "Let's seal your bond."

⌇

IN THE WEEKS we'd been in Xenovia, I'd never seen the city center so packed. It was as if every warrior, of every clan present, had shown up to watch the future Engrossian King finally claim the man he loved as his bonded partner.

Candles lined the wide steps up to the capitol building, the crowds fanning out around the base of the stairs. Children sat on shoulders, climbed statues, but everyone fell into a silence humming with anticipation as the prince and his consort exited the building from opposite doorways at the top of the platform and walked toward each other in the center.

Though *walked* was a loose term since Barrett was nearly running to Dax, Rebel on his heels. Spirits, I'd never seen anyone so excited. Dax, in turn, crossed in a calm manner, but even he couldn't hide his fucking grin.

Once they were there, hands clasped, a priestess of Xenique climbed the steps to stand before them. Her flowing amethyst robes slithered over the stones as she turned to face the crowd, a large amulet set against her chest and halo arching over the crown of her head.

"Good evening, warriors. I am conducting tonight's ceremony on the blessing of Bant's priestesses in the capital of Banix," she announced, voice carrying over the city. "The branch of the Angelic Sisterhood has extended their confirmation of this holy union, and it is with their favor that we bond Prince Barrett and his consort, General Dax Goverick."

A reverent applause rang out across the desert, stretching deep into the city. Mystlights wavered over the street as the sun set, giving the entire crowd and Xenovia that anticipation of nightfall. The one that made you feel like anything was possible.

The loudest cheers echoed from our friends where they lined the steps ascending to where Barrett and Dax stood. All of them, from every clan. Even the Bodymelders, Harlen and Cyren, Erista and her siblings. They were all present and celebrating the bonding of the Engrossian Prince.

"Who witnesses the ceremony?" the priestess went on.

I stepped to Barrett's side as he'd instructed at least a dozen times, his eager eyes swiveling toward me. "I do," I declared. "Malakai Augustus Blastwood, brother of the prince and a quarter Engrossian descent."

Apparently that lineage piece was important for the ceremony to be valid.

"And I do." From Dax's side, Celissia's voice rang out with sheer reverence and appreciation for the symbolic ceremony. "Celissia Langswoll, daughter of the noble House of Langswoll of Engrossian descent."

The priestess nodded to each of us in turn. "We are grateful for your overseeing of this momentous occasion." She held her hands out to Barrett and Dax. "I invite you to recite the Warrior's Words and your vows under the blessing of Xenique and Bant."

She placed her hands atop theirs, bowing her head and muttering a ritualistic prayer as they each repeated the words that every clan adopted for their sacred ceremonies. My eyes flitted to Ophelia briefly, my skin itching as I remembered a time—over five years ago—when I'd said those words to her in the privacy of our clearing. Surrounded by honeysuckle and jasmine, I'd thought they'd be forever. But fate intervened.

Ophelia leaned back into Tolek, his head bowing between her wings to whisper something in her ear, and I couldn't find it in me to regret my promise to her or to wish it had stuck. No piece of my fucking wrecked spirit wanted things to be different. Instead, my attention shifted.

And when I met Mila's eyes, glassy with joy for my brother and his future, that itching along my spine faded. Nothing but damn desire took its place. Her, in that form fitting ivory dress I wanted to disappear under. Her, wearing bronze Soulguider bangles I wanted to peel off. Her, smiling so fucking proudly at me as the Warrior's Words faded.

Perhaps fate hadn't intervened with Ophelia and me. Perhaps it had been us, trying to prematurely force a future that had never been intended to survive in the first place. We were meant to be in each other's lives, but not that way.

Mila winked, and I smiled, turning back to my brother.

"Dax." He began his personal vows. "My love for you stretches deeper than the valleys, and it was born of something just as dark. Yet somehow, you manage to turn every day into light. You are the beacon in the night that keeps me moving forward, and I vow to love you as clearly and wholly for the rest of our days, with you as a king by my side."

A rumble of shock rolled across the crowd. Dax stared wide eyed at his prince.

"Bare—"

"No," Barrett cut him off, squeezing his hands. "You are worthy of this, Dax. I will see you take a crown beside me. You can be a Warrior King to lead our armies, but I will not sit on a throne without you on an equal one by my side."

Barrett nodded at me, and I removed the silver crown from the satchel he'd given me. The one he'd had fashioned after his own months ago and brought from Banix.

Handing it to Barrett, I stepped back, and the prince faced his consort—his king. "Kneel, Dax Goverick."

Dax swallowed, clearly struggling at the sentiment ringing through Barrett's words and the weight of this action. A palpable excitement buzzed through the air—not a single warrior speaking out about how this should not be done.

The general knelt, and with a steady but reverent movement that was as symbolic as the rest of the evening, Barrett placed the crown upon his head. Neither of them were technically kings yet—those oaths would come at their coronation—but it didn't matter. Tears shone in both of their eyes.

"Barrett," Dax said, his words softer. "You are such an impulsive person at times, but it's because you love with your entire heart. And it is that big-hearted prince that caught my attention years ago in a dark palace corridor. And it is that prince I fell in love with." He took a deep breath. "With your capacity to love others, and your capacity to drive me absolutely wild. I want nothing more than to nurture those things, and I vow to you that I always will. Whether from a throne or a battlefield, you have my heart and my ax, King Barrett."

Everyone in the crowd was shifting now, eager and bubbling with excitement. My attention flitted to Mila every other second, tracing the low-cut gown and the lace peeking above the neckline, but also thinking of all the promises I wanted to make to her.

"The scarring," the priestess said.

Celissia stepped forward, removing a black-bladed knife from the waist of her moss-green gown. A ceremonial weapon, I'd learned earlier. When Barrett left Banix, he made sure to have that in his pack, as well.

Dax took the weapon first, and Barrett held up his hand. This was the more brutal part of an Engrossian bonding ceremony, where the participants each inflicted a mark on the other and their blood mixed over a blessing. It was meant to represent the combination of responsibility and magic woven into the assignment to guard the dark pools.

I didn't know what symbol they'd selected, but each of them cut the other's palm, and they clasped their hands together.

"By the valors of the Engrossian Prime Warrior," the priestess said, and Barrett and Dax echoed the words, blood dripping between their linked palms, "and by the magic of his Angelic self, I swear myself to thee."

Something snapped between the two men with their hands entwined, like the Angels heard those promises and sealed their souls together. It was almost a tangible force, a band tethering them.

Looking around, it was clear everyone felt it. Cypherion hugged Vale tighter, Jezebel leaned her head on Erista's shoulder, and Mila pulled my attention to hers. I was barely cognizant of the anointing of Barrett's and Dax's wounds with the ointment that would scar them for eternity. I was barely present at all when I looked at her.

And as the future king kissed the man he loved, the entire crowd of Gallantian Warriors roared.

～

I ONLY LASTED a second before my hands were all over Mila. In her hair, tugging up that fucking sinful dress, gripping her thigh as it wrapped around my waist. She was everything, my heart beating out her name, and I needed to feel every inch of her.

"Shouldn't we get back to the ballroom?" she gasped against my lips as I carried her in the opposite direction of the crowd, down the mosaic-lined halls of the capitol.

"Is that really where you want to be right now?" I murmured into her neck as I searched for any sort of open door.

"Barrett and Dax are about to make their entrance," she forced out as her head rolled back.

"Don't care."

There.

Up ahead, a tall, willowy figure had just exited a room, leaving the door open wide behind her. A storage closet probably.

As I sped toward it, the woman cast an amused glance over her shoulder. Her dark hair cascaded around her, and I briefly thought I recognized her, but Mila was slipping a hand beneath my collar, and all recollections left my mind.

I slipped into the room and kicked the door closed, not bothering to take in our surroundings beyond a small skylight overhead, plants lining one wall, and a fountain trickling away in the corner.

Mila worked her lips down my jaw as the cheering from the ballroom carried down the hall outside. "Sounds like the festivities have begun," she hummed as her hips rolled against mine.

"Then I guess we better make this quick, General."

And though the union we'd witnessed tonight was blessed by the Angels, there was nothing holy in the smile Mila returned. "I won't be quiet."

"Good."

I spun her around, pressing her against the nearest wall between two potted ferns, and I pulled down the delicate straps of her dress.

"Of fucking course," I grumbled at the layer of white lace beneath it. It had peeked above the scooping neckline, but I hadn't dared to think what she really wore for the sake of my sanity. The bodice was entirely sheer and so fucking tempting, her nipples hard and begging for me beneath it.

Mila's legs gripped tight to my waist as I ducked my head, flicking my tongue over the fabric covering one breast, then the next. She writhed against me, tossing her head back on a moan when I bit down.

We hadn't made it far from the crowded ballroom, and there was a very good chance of someone walking down this hall, but I didn't fucking care. Not as I hiked up her skirt and pulled aside her undergarments. I swept two fingers down her center, finding her so ready, and plunged into her. She cried out my name, not expecting me already, and I continued to drive her crazy.

"Fuck," she panted as her hips angled up.

"Tell me what you want, Mila," I growled, nipping at her shoulder, her breasts, everywhere I could fucking touch. Spirits, I was hungry for her.

Desperate.

"I want," Mila breathed as her hand worked my belt, all our movements frenzied. "I want you, Malakai."

"You have me," I swore.

Her hand froze, coming to my chest, right over the Bind. "I know," she muttered, and I froze, too, removing my hand from between her legs. "But I want you that way, too. Like Barrett and Dax. I want all of you."

My head fell to her shoulder, guilt wringing my heart. "I'm sorry," I whispered.

"I don't want you to be sorry," she said, still pressed against the wall.

But I was. I'd potentially fucked up our entire future by insisting on this Bind when I was only seventeen. I'd thought it was the right thing back then, but damn, what a stupid kid I'd been.

"I promise, Mila. I am going to fix this." I kissed her to seal that vow, and then whether it was the genuineness of my words or my tongue stroking hers, she was moaning into my mouth again. Her hips ground against me as she pulled me closer.

"For now," she panted, "show me."

"Spirits, I love you," I said as she undid my belt, pulling my cock out. Her legs were still tight around my waist as she brushed a thumb over the tip, and I shivered, slamming a hand to the wall above her head.

"Fuck," I said. "Are you trying to kill me?"

Mila laughed, lining me up with her entrance. I wasn't sure there was a better sight on Ambrisk than that. Her hand around me, her ready to take me.

"What a way it would be to die," she said sinfully.

Not taking my eyes off where we were joined, I sank forward slowly, catching every gasp and moan that rolled off her lips. And as we both gave ourselves over to wrecking the other, every touch and every kiss promised I would fix this. I was eternally hers, every damaged part of me, and she was *mine* in return.

Fuck. *Mine.*

I growled, pounding into her with enough force that she cried out again. I didn't know I could love a word as much as I did *mine.*

"I promise," I swore to her on a husky whisper. "I promise I am all yours. Now, tell me, Mila." She knew that this time I wasn't only asking what she wanted.

"All of my tomorrows, Warrior Prince. They're all—" She gasped as I picked up my pace. "They're all yours."

"That's fucking right, General."

I didn't know what had been in the air, if it was just the effect of witnessing a bond being struck or something deeper, but I felt like I'd die if I lost Mila. Like this desire ringing deep in my bones was my life force and she was the only thing that kept it pumping.

I kissed her, needing to taste her, and she clenched tighter around me.

"Please," she begged, hands grappling against my tunic as she pulled it up over my head and pressed her lips to my chest.

"Angels, Mila," I breathed as I rubbed tight circles against her clit. And we fell into absolute fucking ruins together, the water in the fountain not nearly drowning out the noise. Her hand pressed against my Bind, and I thought that touch alone would burn the thing away.

I held her against the wall as she stopped shaking and blood returned to my brain. Then, I set her on her feet, the moon through the skylight casting her features in a pale glow.

"So fucking beautiful," I whispered, ducking to kiss her again, but Mila's attention was over my shoulder.

"What is that?" she asked.

Still holding her chin, I followed her gaze.

"A mural?" I asked. Like the many throughout the city and capitol, the artwork portrayed Xenique, her powerful frame taking up much of the wall. With the fountain that was clearly supposed to be for making offerings to the Angel, I guessed I should have felt a little bad about fucking Mila in a sacred space, but I didn't.

Mila ducked around me to approach it, and as I followed, I realized there was something different about this depiction.

"Where are her wings?" I asked.

Mila strayed closer, her fingers drifting over the artwork. It was a mosaic, I realized, crafted of the smallest, almost imperceptible chips of colored tile. "It's not Xenique," she whispered. "It's Artale."

A chill traveled down my spine.

"The Goddess of Death," I breathed. Smaller figures knelt at her feet, one winged. "That must be Xenique, then," I said, pointing to the clear Angel.

The rest, I wasn't sure. An array of beings. Some might have been spirits, some skeletal and emaciated. And some...some were casting ripples of what I could only guess was magic up toward the goddess. Toward a weapon her demigoddess daughter was placing in her hands.

"Malakai," Mila breathed, "does that scythe look familiar to you?"

My answering *yes* was drowned out by a door in the wall cracking open, a tunnel exposed.

And as we peered into the dim hallway, mystlight barely illuminating the space with shallow pools, my mind went back to the woman leaving this room earlier.

And I wondered if we hadn't chosen this door at random after all.

CHAPTER FIFTY-NINE
SANTORINA

THE BALLROOM SWIRLED WITH BRIGHTLY COLORED gowns, from rich emeralds to deep amethysts to cursed blood reds. Women's dresses floated around them as their partners lifted, dipped, and twirled them. My own skirt clung loosely to my frame before trailing out behind me, the silk fading from lavender to deep plum around the hem. It almost looked like a fading dusk sky, the matching top tied loosely in a knot at my neck, leaving a few inches of my stomach bare and a gold chain belt slung across my waist.

Where Jezebel and Erista had found it, I wasn't sure, but as I watched the dancers from the edge of the floor, the outfit made me feel somehow mysterious, alluring, and powerful all at once.

"You can't keep avoiding me, Santorina Cordelian," Ophelia chided as she strolled up to me, the thin maroon fabric of her dress billowing around her.

"Avoiding?" I asked as I scanned the room with a very convincing air of nonchalance.

Directly across the floor, Lancaster and Mora were discussing something in what appeared to be aggressive tones, their heads bowed and many warriors giving them a wide berth. As I watched, brows creasing, the male's head snapped up. When our gazes collided, that feeling in my chest hummed, the string plucked.

Between the dancers, Lancaster's eyes flicked over me, his sister still speaking animatedly at his side. His jaw set, anger radiating off him even from here.

"Yes, avoiding," Ophelia said, calling my attention back to her.

Forcing my gaze away from the fae, I argued, "I haven't been *avoiding* you. I've been busy."

"Busy shut up in your room with books on the gods? What have you been searching for?"

My stare flitted back to the fae male across the room, but I quickly averted it. "Information about Echnid."

"Mm-hmm."

I knew she wasn't convinced at all, but despite the fact that she was practically a sister to me, I wasn't ready to discuss exactly what subjects the books I collected focused on. Especially not—

A shadow dropped over us, my attention snapping up as the string in my chest sang. *Imposing, demanding, and arrogant non-immortal.*

"Can I help you?" I seethed.

Lancaster's jaw ticked. I thought the tension in it might have intensified since he'd crossed the room. In the stewing silence, Ophelia watched me with an expectant, self-satisfied smirk.

"Do they not teach you manners in your long lives?" I snapped at Lancaster.

"Where have you been?" was all he asked in response.

I squinted up at him. "What?"

"You have frequently been missing since we returned."

"As I said," Ophelia whispered beneath her breath.

I ignored her, saying to Lancaster, "You don't know every piece of work I conduct."

"Have you been with that Bodymelder?"

I blinked up at him in confusion. "Esmond?" When he bobbed his head in a single nod, my chin pulled back. "He's my friend. We've worked closely together in the past year." At the war front and before that in Damenal, Esmond had tutored my healing practice. It had been a welcome surprise to see him in Xenovia.

"Worked closely," Lancaster echoed.

"Well, if they don't teach you manners, at least they teach you to listen," I grumbled, draining the rest of my drink.

"Did working closely entail intimate matters?"

The wine I'd just swallowed nearly came back up as I choked, and Ophelia hissed, patting my back.

"*Excuse me?*" I sneered.

"Were you—"

I cut him off with a hand to his chest, dumping my empty glass on a nearby table. I ignored the way my palm buzzed to the same melody as my chest when I touched him. "I did not mean you to clarify," I sputtered. "Under no circumstances is that *your* business."

There went that ticking jaw again. "It is much more my business than you understand."

His voice was so low and harsh, it rolled against my skin. And under no circumstance did I enjoy it. That wasn't something low within my core clenching tight or heat gathering between my legs. It wasn't me shuffling forward a step, pressing onto my toes.

"In no realm, under no God or Angel rule, is that true," I hissed. Could he hear how breathy my voice had become? It was the burning anger. That was all.

Lancaster's hand cupped mine where it was still pressed to his chest, an impossible fire searing the air. When his skin brushed mine, *everything* within me hummed.

And as if he felt it, too, and that string was pulling his voice tight, his next words were barely audible. "If only you were correct."

This damn Bounty instinct was dragging me toward him. *Kill. Slaughter. Enemy.* That's what was happening. The instinct wanted to unravel the Hunter, to become his prey if only to strike when his defenses were down. It was messing with my senses, layering his last five words with...

Fire.

Fire that was suddenly tearing through me. I jolted back, trying to wrench my hand from his chest, but Lancaster held it tighter.

"Dance with me," he said.

"Wh-what?" I blinked up at him. All annoyance drained from my tone, shock emptying out my chest. Not even the string hummed.

"Dance with me, Queen of Bounties," Lancaster repeated, holding my stare.

"Are you asking me to dance or demanding it?" was all I could think to say.

"It is an option," he said, finally dropping my hand. My palm tingled, but instead of the Bounty sense, this time it was a rush of emptiness. "But I would prefer one outcome over the other."

"In all of your non-immortal years, you haven't learned of a better way to ask a woman to dance than that?" I challenged.

Lancaster squinted at me. "I am not normally attempting to win over women such as yourself."

"What does that mean?" I stiffened, defensiveness instantly rearing up with him.

Ophelia muttered beneath her breath, "You're not very good at this, fae."

Lancaster barely glanced at her, focus on me. "Dance with me, and I will explain myself."

"That's still not a question." Gods, this *insufferable* male. "But fine," I bit out.

And he...smiled? It was soft, genuine, and I thought maybe a bit insecure. I didn't understand, but at the sight, the humming in my heart mounted again.

Slipping his hand into the cool emptiness of my still-tingling palm, Lancaster pulled me onto the dance floor. I ignored Ophelia's pointed looks as one hand held mine, the other curling around my back to hold me close to him. The scent of iron-tinged roses fell around us like a curtain, shrouding the rest of the warriors spinning through the room.

"Now you have me here," I said after a moment, trying to ignore the heat of Lancaster's palm pressing against my spine. "Explain."

He sighed, and it sounded like a weight pressed firmly on his chest. "Must you always assume the worst of me?"

"You have given me plenty of reasons to," I retorted.

Lancaster lowered his head, and his lips...Gods, his breath was so warm against my neck. I shivered, arching closer to him as he spun me around time and again.

I was so distracted, I almost missed his next words.

"I have also given you plenty of reasons not to."

"Not willingly," I gasped out.

"That is even better in my opinion," he said. I tilted my head, my hair swinging down my back so my neck was now fully exposed. What would it feel like for him to drag those canines across my skin? To sink those fangs in and *take* all I had to offer.

I wasn't offering.

He went on, "Sometimes the person one becomes when they are not trying is the truest version of oneself, wouldn't you agree?"

Those words pressed into my flesh, ready to burrow to my bones.

"I suppose there is a certain truth in freedom," I replied, swallowing thickly.

"Freedom." The word was almost a scoff, but one that got stuck in his throat, like he was as affected by his skin against mine as I was.

Lancaster's palm pressed closer to my spine, curving around my waist. His thumb dragged along my ribs absently, like he didn't even realize he was doing it, and his eyes...

Gods. They were trained on my wildly thrumming pulse.

"What did you mean? When you said you don't usually attempt to win over women such as me?" I pushed because if I didn't say something, the humming in my chest was going to cause me to make foolish, reprehensible decisions. And I never allowed myself to be foolish.

Perhaps I should.

No.

"I meant that you are very different than females I have known before." For an inexplicable reason, my chest pulled tight at those words. "You are much more fearless and straightforward, especially for—"

"For a human?" I finished, the bubble his words had been inflating in my chest popping. I dropped my gaze. That was why I never allowed foolishness. I was a breakable, weak human. I had to be careful to frame my existence in this world of warriors and fae.

"No," Lancaster said, his hand still entwined with mine

lifting my chin. "For someone who has been taught her entire life that she is weaker than those around her, but who has proven to them all that a human heart can devour the realm with fervor."

Those words were practically plucked straight from my spirit. What had I been fighting for these recent months? To be seen as more than simply a human. My friends always said I had a warrior heart, and I loved them for that, but I did not want it to mask the very human, vulnerable parts of me. And with one sentence, Lancaster encompassed that want. Displayed who I fought to become so simply, like it was impossible not to see.

There was a warmth in those words. One I thought I could crawl into and build a very comfortable, sheltered, yet exploratory haven.

When his thumb stroked my ribs again, dangerously close to the underside of my breast, I pressed forward, and this time, it might have been voluntarily.

Certainly not entirely.

But there was a chance a little bit of it was.

"What were you fighting with your sister over?" I asked.

"When?" Lancaster asked.

"Just before you asked me to dance."

"Did I ask?" And I froze because he actually *joked*.

Recovering myself, I gave him an admonishing look. "*Told* me to dance. Do not change the subject." The song was mounting, the warriors around us speeding with it, but he held me so steadily, I didn't even notice the tempo increasing.

Lancaster smirked at my tone, but his next words came out with a grimace. "She finally revealed the extent of how her magic changed after the bite in the catacombs. It appears she's hidden some grave details from me."

"Like?"

His eyes flicked between mine, his thumb still steadily grazing my ribs. "Like the fact that whatever Angel magic was woven into the enchantment that kept the corpses awake was transferred to her when the one bit her. And how"—he dropped his voice—"since much of our magic is Goddess-given from our mothers line, and there were ancient spells within that bite, many facets of hers are not working."

Ancient Angel magic often warred with Godly magic. Nerves for Mora—and for Lancaster, too—had me fidgeting.

"Is she all right?" I asked.

"She is vulnerable, especially facing a God and creatures of another realm. She insists she was fine against the gorgons despite the fact that her glamours aren't as infallible as they once were, but I told her she should return to Vercuella tonight before a Godly war strikes. She refuses."

My gaze flicked to Mora where she was speaking amicably with a group of Seawatchers. On the surface, she appeared fine, but—

There.

A slight roll of her shoulders and a barely perceptible wince. If the physical wound still pained her, I could only imagine how it was tampering with her magic.

"I'm guessing she's choosing to stay here?" I asked as we spun about the room.

Lancaster's jaw tightened. "Vehemently."

"She loves you. She wouldn't want to leave you behind." Just as I couldn't fathom abandoning my friends amid these unknown battles. Funny how whether you were human, warrior, or fae, love manifested all the same.

"And it is because I love her that I need her to go," Lancaster swore, voice low. His fingers curled into my back as if he was trying to grab on to me. To root himself. And he sounded so utterly vulnerable when he admitted that weakness.

It was difficult to reconcile these pieces of the male with the one I'd thought I'd known. The one I'd judged based on the history of his people—a people who only hunted mine because we were bred to do the same.

But there was more to Lancaster than I'd originally known, and I'd slowly been gathering these new facets of him. Like a diamond under the light, each angle refracted a new color.

And I thought I might like every shade.

Beneath the burly surface, there was a male who cared deeply for his family and who wanted nothing more than a taste of freedom his Hunter instincts had denied him. It was as alluring as this dress made me feel, the hum in my chest crescendoing just as the music did. My heart thundered, my whole body vibrating with the need to say something to him. To tell him—something— anything—to get these thoughts and unexpected admirations out of my mind and hopefully appease the insistent thrum my chest had become.

But the music ended. And Lancaster took a step back, effectively ending those sacred moments of vulnerability. My entire body chilled, the string in my chest crying out as if looking for something to latch on to.

Entirely unaffected, he nodded, turning away.

And desperate, I called after him, "Why did you want to dance with me?"

Lancaster looked over his shoulder, searching my expression. By the Gods, did I wish I knew what he was looking for. In that moment, if it was at all within my power, I would have found it just to absolve this unfamiliar, needy feeling within me and heal the vulnerability he'd withered beneath moments ago.

But his expression faltered. "I supposed I missed your company."

And then, he left.

Chapter Sixty

Ophelia

"Finally," Esmond said as he joined me at the edge of the dance floor where I was still watching Santorina and Lancaster.

"I think he's a bit jealous of your friendship with Rina," I told the Bodymelder.

He chuckled, tucking his hands into his pockets. "Good. Santorina deserves someone who is willing to fight for her."

And with the way Santorina's and Lancaster's frames unknowingly melted into one another, with the flush of her cheeks and his stare locked on hers, I knew he would. Even if neither of them would admit it yet.

"Magic and attraction can do wondrous things," Esmond muttered.

My attention snapped to him. "You think there's magic involved?"

"Possibly," he said as the music ended. Lancaster stepped back from the dance, his jaw ticking over something Rina had said. "But that possibility aside, *that* is *pure* attraction."

Santorina stared after the fae for a moment, then she picked up her skirts and turned away. She nodded in our direction, an emotion I couldn't quite name stealing her expression.

Ignoring the curiosity that interaction spun within me, I said,

"Thank you for your help with the weapons earlier. Tell Gatrielle how much I appreciate the insight, will you?"

"Of course, Ophelia," Esmond answered seriously, crossing his arms. "We're here to assist you however we can. I only wish it had been more successful."

"Yes." I sighed. But I dispelled the sensation of a shadow at my back, a threat closing in. My gaze dropped to Esmond's knuckles where the *KLP* Bodymelder tattoo was inked. Knowledge, logic, precision.

"I met Ptholenix when I was in Damenal," I said.

Esmond's brows rose. "You did?"

I nodded. "More than simply met him. He assisted Damien in training me."

I tried not to focus on how that statement lodged a knot of confusion in my mind. Why had they trained me if they wanted to trap me there? Was it only so I'd be more powerful when Echnid used my magic? Or was there more to their motives?

"What was he like?" Esmond asked, a bit mystified.

In my memory, the heat of Ptholenix's presence sizzled down my spine. Ropes of fiery magic licked across his brown skin, his orchid tattoo stark against his defined muscles, unspooling between his wings.

"All of the Angels have larger than life presences," I explained. "But Ptholenix's was different. With Gaveny, you almost can't avoid him because his very voice feels like a booming tide. Damien and Bant are all-encompassing. But Ptholenix...he was the heart of a fire. As unexpected, silent, and quickly moving as a freshly burning flame, hungry to consume whatever lay in his path, but with the power to send the world to ash sitting just beneath his skin."

Esmond's fingers flexed against his arm. "Was he helpful with your magic?"

"Very. He acted like it was mine to command, where Damien always seemed to have a bit too much of a personal edge involved." The Mystique Angel always made me feel like if I failed, he failed. "Ptholenix also left me with some thoughts to ponder."

"Such as?"

"Like explaining that fire is more cleansing than water."

Esmond ran a hand over his hair. "Interesting that he'd say that," he mused. "Have you ever heard the legend of the Firebird and the Fox?"

"No." But I perked up, the ancient seraph magic within my veins snapping to attention.

"It's a folktale among Bodymelders, and it's not told about Ptholenix specifically, but it's long been a rumor that the original story was about him."

"About his life?" I asked. That fiery thread of power from the Bodymelder Angel whipped within me.

"A part of it," Esmond told me. "It's either a romance or a tragedy depending on how you view it. Really, I think it's either about the lengths one will go to fight for a love not meant for them or claiming a love above all else, no matter which version you hear. They've all been altered over time."

As all legends were. My gaze landed on Jezebel as she and Erista danced to the slow melody seeping across the ballroom. We were sisters born of myth, to raise and slay constellations and legends, and even we didn't know what that legacy meant. What we were meant to do with this magic and why the Balance of Power had decided it was needed *now*.

"He said that while fire is cleansing, it also marks the darkest moments of life," I commented.

Esmond's lips pulled into a line as if unsurprised by that. "The tragic version of the story claims the Firebird—assuming that means Ptholenix—fell in love with the fox."

"The fox?" I echoed. "And that was tragic because?"

"No one knows who she was. Some say a thief, some even say a fae female who could glamour her appearance into the furry creature itself, and some say she was no more than a common warrior with tattoos that reminded him of foxes. But she caught the attention of the firebird somehow."

My seraph magic heated, purring in recognition of Esmond's tale, but there was a resolute sadness beneath it. All three of those accounts would have ended in forbidden loves in one way or another. All would have been ripped away from the Firebird and his fox.

And all could have instilled the heavy regret in Ptholenix's tone when he'd spoken atop the mountain.

"How does the story end?" I asked as a romantic ballad swept through the room.

"In fire," Esmond confirmed. "Sometimes with the death of the fox, sacrificed into ashes as the whims of the Firebird's power grew too strong for him. Sometimes with a burning village and no bodies recovered. But always in fire."

Fire, a property both cleansing and ruinous.

It reared its untamed head within me now, and my heart clenched. How far would one go for a love deemed unsuitable? Was it purely hopeful to think that with love in our hearts, we could outrun the flames, or did their might stretch to the ends of the realm? Did it outlast the realms?

What would one sacrifice to fire in order to save another thing they loved? And if the realms burned to ash, what would be left behind?

"There's one question that has always bothered me about the folktale, though," Esmond said, appearing to be thinking out loud more than to me. "The tragic versions end in ashes, but there are the more romantic views. Either way, we know Ptholenix Ascended. But if the more hopeful ending is to be believed, and the fox did not die...where did she go?"

Chapter Sixty-One
Vale

THERE WAS BLOOD EVERYWHERE. EVERY GRAIN OF SAND in the desert was drenched crimson, every body laying lifeless and wrenching a deep sorrow in my gut. How did this happen? How did we get here?

If I could unveil the path, perhaps we could alter it—

No. Fates could not be altered. That was not the purpose of this magic. My hands fisted in frustration, nails digging crescents into my palms until the skin sliced open.

Readings were given to Starsearchers to map the paths that would get us to their ends, and then choices could be made, but we could never know how one small decision would shift the entire future. Horror turned my bones to ice as I dug through more star-given paths. Every one ended here.

Unavoidable.

One of the most feared words to a purveyor of fortunes because it was so permanent. My breaths came shorter as more bodies fell. As white mist crept forward in shrouding tendrils, and I raged to the Fates. Begged for a way to combat it.

As I dropped to my knees atop crimson sand and screamed for someone to show me a way; as blood seeped through my skirt, sticking to my skin; as I pleaded and cried.

No one answered.

Not a single of my nine Fate ties had anything else to share.

The gravity sank a rock in my chest, my breathing turned short and panicked. The celestial-born Fatesworn bond riled feverishly within me.

Pressure. There was pressure on my hands. My arms. Tugging me across realms.

Vale.

I snapped from the reading.

"Cypherion?" I asked without turning away from the balcony view, the starlit dunes still in the night beyond the revelrous city. Pristinely moonlit, not a drop of red in sight.

"What's wrong?"

I blinked up at him. "What?"

"I could read you pretty easily before, but now..." He tapped my Fatesworn tattoo. "I can feel something is wrong." His deep blue eyes searched the view as if he'd find the culprit.

In reassurance to myself after what I'd seen, to prove he was here, soul tied to mine, I sent a beat of love down that starlight-threaded connection.

"Stargirl," Cypherion sighed when it reached him, and my tension unraveled at that word on his lips.

He tilted my chin up, and between the riled magic and the bond, the kiss was consuming. It seared down to my very core. I ached for him, for his touch across my skin, his lips against my body.

His hand threading through my hair sent a shockwave of pleasure through me, the other pressing me tightly enough to him that every line of hard muscle was evident. The bond craved him, sweeping every other thought from my head as the spot between my legs throbbed.

But Cypherion pulled back, stare dazed and voice husky as he asked, "How is the Fatecatcher power feeling?"

"It's a bit overwhelming," I downplayed, struggling to catch my breath. Truly, it was an immense well in my chest waiting to burst. "I don't know if it's because there are so many warriors here tonight. Maybe because the Starsearcher legions brought so many of those imbued weapons, so the resins are pulling at the depths of my readings, but the Fates have been exceedingly loud."

"What are they speaking of?"

I swallowed, turning in his arms so my back pressed to his chest. "War."

It was much worse than that. Bloodied bodies across sandy dunes, unseeing eyes still open as if waiting for absolution. Bones singed to nothing more than ash, and gold-tinged feathers raining down from storm-clouded skies.

It was carnage and ruin. It was an upset balance and hungry gods leaving us to fight their battles.

It was our future, but no clear path to it, only certainty that it would come one day. But because of the unknowns and how I knew Cypherion's worries were coiled tightly within his muscles already, I didn't elaborate on the gruesome details.

"I think that's an unavoidable future for us," Cypherion muttered, holding me closer.

That word again. *Unavoidable.*

"It's confusing," I confessed, changing the subject but leaning my head against his chest. "I've been gifted this new array of power —a direct link to a dead goddess and the Starsearcher Angel— because I'd always been so in touch with and accepting of my magic. But now, I feel like I could drown in it."

It wouldn't be the same soft sinking beneath a wave as Cypherion's arms were around me. It would be a total eclipse of myself. Guilt twisted my chest at the disjointed feelings.

Loving my magic all my life. Fearing it could crush me now.

I sighed, and Cypherion's hand skimmed across my collarbone with the sound.

"Do you wish you didn't have it?" he asked, his chest stilling as if he held his breath.

"No," I said adamantly, and he exhaled. I almost laughed at the notion that he'd been worried I had a problem he couldn't fix. Spirits, I loved him.

I went on, tipping my head back against his shoulder, "I've cherished my magic all my life because for so long, it was all I had. Even if it isolated me from others, it was comforting." I considered that sentence. "Maybe that's a twisted way to view it, since it was the reason I was kept so alone."

"You clung to it because it was all you knew, but there's nothing wrong with that. I'd even wager that since it's rooted in you—not Titus or a temple or whoever tried to take advantage of it—that power is the most natural source of comfort you could have found."

"Thank you." I exhaled. "I don't wish I didn't have this new Fatecatcher power. I'm honored to have been chosen, not burdened by it. I only wish I understood it better."

"We'll figure it out together, Stargirl," he promised, kissing my temple. Alleviating all my worries in that effortless way only Cypherion Kastroff seemed to have the power to do. "We always do."

And that assurance gave me the strength to settle. I had conquered my own prison, Cypherion had come back for me, and he had helped me find the light again after my soul bond broke. We may be fighting the unknowns of fate, but we were together.

"Should we find the others?" Cypherion asked, his arms squeezing around me.

I nodded. "I'd told Harlen I owed him a dance before the night ended, and last I saw, he was cornered by a pair of much older Soulguiders that looked like they were about to have their way with him."

Cypherion's answering chuckle rumbled through my back. "Maybe we shouldn't find him then."

I rolled my eyes but pulled him toward the door. "He looked like a field mouse about to be swallowed whole by a nemaxese. Come along."

We found him quickly, and—emphatically grateful—Harlen whirled me away into a very informal dance, him never having learned proper routines after growing up an orphan in the temple.

"Stop stepping on my toes!" he mocked when it happened for the fifth time.

"Perhaps if you led correctly," I teased.

Harlen gripped my waist and lifted me, spinning with my hands on his shoulders. "Problem solved," he said. Setting me back down, we continued twirling among the other couples. "My steps are much more fun than the *correct* ones, anyway."

"They make it rather difficult when you're the only one who *knows* them," I challenged.

"Well perhaps others should take a bit of a lesson from me, Interim Chancellor and all."

I couldn't help the laughter that bubbled out of me. "I'm happy you're here, Harls," I told him as the music came to a close.

"Me, too," he said, spinning me one final time.

"It feels right," I emphasized as he draped an arm over my shoulder and surveyed the room. "We can't thank you enough for coming to our aid. And for everything with Titus." I shivered, and Harlen wrapped his arm tighter around me. Not in a romantic way, but as a protective sibling might. As Cypherion would for Ophelia or Santorina. It almost shocked me to realize that I had a similar bond with Harlen, even if our past looked different.

I brushed away the emotion that welled within me at the thought. "I don't think I could have survived what the chancellor put me through without you."

"You don't owe me any thanks," Harlen said, tone entirely serious. "It was partially my fault you were there."

In a sense yes, but he'd also been the one that knocked on my door each morning to ensure I got out of bed. He'd sat with me when it took me hours to eat a single meal. He'd helped me clean up after the sessions became so intense I vomited on myself, let alone the beatings he took when I couldn't read anymore.

So, without a doubt, I was grateful Harlen had chosen my friendship over a chancellor's lies.

"I think Titus would have gotten me there no matter what," I confessed.

Briefly, Harlen pulled me back into a dancing position and dipped me once, saying with utter gravity, "Don't worry about him. We're free now."

And Fates be damned, truer words hadn't been spoken.

"To freedom," I said, as I took Cypherion's hand next, and Jezebel placed hers in Harlen's.

As the night wore on, we all truly celebrated. Ophelia and Tolek, Santorina—though she seemed agitated and distracted every time Tolek or Cypherion dragged her onto the floor—Jezebel and

Erista, Barrett and Dax, Harlen and Ezalia, and every warrior who had been a stranger not that long ago but was now a dear friend. The only ones missing were Malakai and Mila, but they'd appeared ready to tear each other's clothes off at the ceremony. I imagined they were otherwise engaged.

As we reveled, I couldn't help but consider that perhaps everything I'd suffered through my entire life was to bring me here. To the strangers that would become family, to the man that would become home.

And when Cypherion pulled me into one final dance, I closed my eyes, rested my cheek against his chest, and for the rest of the evening, I purposefully shut the window in my mind to the Fates' messages of warfare and blood and death.

And I simply breathed in the freedom.

CHAPTER SIXTY-TWO
SANTORINA

MY HEELS ECHOED AGAINST THE TILE FLOORS IN MY room, that thrum in my chest intensifying with each step I paced before the glass doors overlooking the dunes, books forgotten on the small table before the fireplace.

I suppose I missed your company.

The scent is not meant to be appealing, but I'm finding I like it.

Anger roared through me as Lancaster's words from both tonight and weeks ago replayed in my mind. They shadowed every interaction—from my Bounty instincts screaming to jam a cypher dagger between his ribs, to the gentle way he'd crafted new boots fit perfectly to me, down to the burning, *claiming* grip of his hands on my skin while we'd danced.

Something within me pulled taut with each memory.

I would not mind if you wanted to sleep here.

His body heat warming a bed. My heart rate timing to his steady, slumbering breath. His arm slung possessively across my body.

I had no idea what to make of him, but if the books I'd scoured since returning to Xenovia were correct, I was beginning to suspect one very, *very* dangerous fact. One that warred with my Bounty instincts and threatened the Goddess blood churning through his veins. One that was in no way human.

Groaning, I stormed toward the door, following the hum in my chest as I wrenched it open.

Only to find those intense, dark eyes glowering down at me.

"You are agitated," Lancaster stated.

"How did you know that?" I asked, fear spiking my voice.

No, no, no. This could not be true.

Lancaster's jaw ticked as he considered me. Goddess, if he'd only answered a question for every feather of that damn muscle, maybe I wouldn't be so lost now.

"I could hear your storming," he said, gripping the doorway with one hand, his arm effectively caging me in.

I scoffed, certain that was not the truth. Unless he'd already been waiting in the hall.

"Why did you shut down when I said I smelled roses?" I blurted out.

Lancaster's characteristic scowl twisted his lips. "What?"

"Back in the training camps, you claimed the Bounty scent was appealing. When I said I smelled roses, it was like a gate slammed up between us." Gods, until tonight, I hadn't allowed myself to admit what that had done to me. Not until those words.

I suppose I missed your company.

Because I had, too. Lancaster had become a reliable presence. Perhaps not a comfort. He was too steely for that. But the constant bickering was a spark of loathing, and it scorched a path through the brush of every prickled branch between us, leaving nothing but ashes in its wake. It made room for a seed of truth to sprout, one illuminating more day by day. A new beginning from the ashes.

It was reliable, and I wanted to *burn* in it after such turmoil and in the face of more loss.

When he remained silent, I swallowed past the lump in my throat, suddenly very aware of the fact that this was a ridiculous claim. I was drawing conclusions on very little evidence, but that string plucked wildly in my chest as Lancaster's eyes held mine.

"You don't know what you're asking." His voice was rough, like he felt that same thickness in his throat as I did.

His hand tightened on the door frame, emboldening me to step closer. My steps were loud, but my words were a slicing, accusatory whisper. "I might know more than you think."

"Bounty," he sighed, his head dropping under the weight of whatever this truth was. His knuckles turned white.

"Tell me," I pleaded. Gods, I hated how vulnerable my cracking voice was. And in front of *him*. "I have lived my entire life not knowing the truth of my heritage. Do not keep me in the dark anymore, Hunter."

At the name, Lancaster's attention snapped up. "Do not call me that. Not you."

His eyes darkened, tongue flicking out across his lips in a hungry movement. I leaned closer, the humming in my chest begging us both to say it. To confirm what it knew and give in.

"Then do not call me Bounty."

"I thought you'd accepted your heritage," he growled.

"As much as you have yours it seems," I shot back, tilting my face up to his. Though he towered over me, he was closer than ever. "Tell me, Hunter, what else have you been working to accept?"

"I am not—"

"Your magic won't allow you to spin the lie," I said victoriously.

His scowl deepened, but I swore he pressed closer. The hand not braced on the door hovered over my hip, fingers fisting in the air like he was restraining himself. The string hummed wilder than ever.

"What is it you think you know?" Lancaster asked.

"I think there is something in your blood that calls to mine."

"The Bounty—"

"Beyond our twisted instincts to kill one another. Beyond the prophecies and the Goddesses. There is something..." I pressed my hand to my chest, stealing courage from the thrumming energy. "Tell me what the roses meant to you."

Lancaster chewed over that demand. "What do they symbolize to humans?"

"It varies," I began, brows pulling together. "Beauty, mourning, passion."

"Keep going," Lancaster commanded.

"Royalty," I said, nearly panting as he stepped closer. "They are a fae symbol in that nature, too." All of the queen's regalia had been adorned with the flowers. "And love…"

At the word, Lancaster gripped my hip. I gasped at the utter relief that thrummed through my chest, the need to have his hands on me such a tangible thing I thought I'd drown in it.

"Roses symbolize love," I barely forced out over the heat rushing through me.

Lancaster's thumb traced the waist of my skirt. "On Vercuella, there is a specific type of rose that never dies. To my people, they symbolize an eternal promise."

He stepped forward, releasing the doorway, his other hand coming to my waist as well. I took a step back to match, but I wasn't sure who was guiding whom.

"To my people," Lancaster continued, "that rose is a powerful symbol of the Goddess and the vows she wove through bloodlines. Of one vow in particular that is chosen by the Gods and Fates and all other deities plotting out the fortunes of the realms."

"What vow is that?" I gasped as he cleared the doorway, the lock clicking shut behind him. He continued to guide me backward.

"It is one which removes all choice from you. It is one you were never supposed to be aware of, Bounty. One that I would never force on anyone, let alone you."

My spine stiffened, his hands freezing on my skin. "Why not me? Because I'm human? Because I'm so low—"

"Because you, Santorina Cordelian, have a fire in your soul that no Goddess deserves to control. Your flames burn so brightly, I did not wish to indulge my own selfish suspicions when you already had so much taken from you at the hands of others—their pursuits and vengeance was never yours to bear." A smirk morphed his scowl, and fucking Goddess, it was alluring. Not at all what I'd expected right now—not with the twisted ire in his words. "You are not lower than anyone, Bounty. You have showed me these months that while your life may be shorter, your mortal blood magicless, humans retain a strength that my people have never had to know. A determination and courage that is more admirable than any Goddess-given power."

His words—the praise beneath them—it didn't make sense. Did he mean he admired *me*? Surely not. Lancaster hated me. Hated humans.

But the string in my chest twisted painfully at the thought. His brow creased as if he felt it.

"Then what is the vow?" I repeated. "What are the roses?"

"Roses mean eternity. They mean promise when you find that scent." Lancaster dropped his lips to my ear, his breath tickling my neck. "They mean *claiming*, and I did not know until that day that you sensed it as well. I did not think it possible."

"Sensed *what*?" The words came out as a shiver.

Lancaster pulled back, his eyes flicking between mine. He scanned my room quickly, noting the books stacked on the table. The ones on Goddessblessed bonds I'd been studying since we returned.

The ones I was begging to prove me wrong.

"You already figured it out." When I didn't answer, he added in a growl, "Say what you think I am to you."

My throat was dry, senses drowning in roses and musk and *him*. "I am—" I gasped as he brought his hand to my throat, and his thumb stroked across my pulse. "We are…"

"I need you to say it, Santorina." His voice was so gravelly over my name, the sound poured through my blood, so desperate it forced the words out of my mouth.

"We are, as the fae would say, *mates*."

He laughed, low and guttural. "It is more than that. The ancient tongues called it *aequelis*. It means we are equals, in every way. Carved for each other since the days the realms were formed."

"*Aequelis*," I repeated, breathily. Lancaster's eyes darkened when I said the word.

"Equals," he panted. "And resisting such a Goddess-given instinct woven through my blood—knowing it was there and that your soul deserves so much better—has been tormenting me in every cursed sense of the word."

Tormenting him. Just as his hands on my body now were the purest, most delectable form of torture. And I wanted it all, every bloody moment of that sweet torment. I wanted to suffer with this

Hunter, to taste him and feel him, to be the equal to my natural born enemy.

But I also wanted the choices I was denied my entire life as a human. I craved the agency of deciding precisely what my future held, not having it dictated by a bond the Goddess wrote into existence eons before I was born.

How was that fair, to have my future dictated when I had barely lived?

"It is only a physical need," I choked out.

A soft, vicious laugh. "That is what you think?"

Words caught in my throat, and I nodded.

Lancaster's endless eyes searched mine, the blacks molten. "Lie to yourself, then, Santorina, but you cannot lie to the Gods." One hand skimmed up my ribs.

My back arched. "It is...a physical need," I sighed. "One derived of torture and burning fortunes and everything wrong in the realms." I wouldn't let it be more than that. Wouldn't admit anything beyond desiring the torment of his touch.

My thundering heart filled the silence, but with one final stroke of his thumb across my pulse, he growled, "Damn us both, then."

His restraint snapped, and when his lips crashed into mine, the string in my chest sang—an unbreakable vow of the Gods weaving us together through blood and magic. Lancaster kissed me unlike anything I'd ever experienced before. One hand gripped my waist, pulling my body flush against his with raw demand, and my fingers dove into his hair. It was a release of the need pulling between us that I hadn't understood, and I gasped at the pure pleasure coursing through me.

"Nothing more," I reiterated against his lips. This was nothing more than the pent-up aggression.

"Whatever lies you must tell," he murmured, and his mouth took mine again.

"How?" I was barely able to get the word out. Gods, I may deny this bond, but it was useless to fight how badly I wanted to devour him. To let him devour me. To feed this thing that had been living inside of us both, pulling us toward each other all these weeks.

"I don't know, Bounty." When he said the name this time, it was layered with the adoration of everything he'd confessed, not the hatred I'd come to search for beneath his words, and my traitorous heart certainly didn't soften at that.

But Lancaster had seen every side of me. The one who hungered for revenge, the one haunted by loss, and the one who feared she wasn't as strong as the world around her. And behind them all, he found the fierce heart and fire within. He found someone he did not hate as he should have, but someone he wanted to worship.

When his lips dragged back to mine, that devotion shone through every stroke of his tongue. I stumbled back at the shock of it, Lancaster's firm grip guiding me carefully, though he continued to ravish me.

"I don't know how it's possible," he continued when the back of my legs met the bed. He paused, his voice tight as he fought to find words, his hands drifting up and around my ribs, my hips, my spine. Sending a wild humming through every spot he touched. "I've never heard of an *aequelis* bond between a human and a fae before."

"I'm not a human," I gasped as his thumb skated across the underside of my breast.

"Finally admitting it?" A smile nearly showed on his lips. Lips swollen from kissing *me*. Lips I wanted to feel on every part of my body, following the fire scorching below my navel.

I arched forward, hands tangling behind his head. "I think I am starting to love being powerful."

"Santorina Cordelian," Lancaster breathed, hands dragging up my spine, "I believe you may have more power over me than I have ever allowed."

Goddess, that statement had my toes curling beyond my better judgment. "And how do you feel about that?"

"I know that while I may have fought this, I was made to bow to you, if you will have me."

The intention of those words was not lost on me. Lancaster

didn't only *feel* it or *think* it. He *knew*. He was confident that this bond wasn't something he wanted to run from.

And what did I want?

I'd sworn this draw to each other was nothing. A reliance of companionship after our time traveling together. But perhaps I'd been lying. Why else would I have spent days pouring over books on fae bonds and bargains, trying to find some explanation for the pull toward this male before me?

"Everything in my life has changed so vastly lately," I said, still close enough to Lancaster that his heart thundered against my chest. "From moving to Damenal, to hunting the emblems, to becoming a Bounty. None of this is the quiet, tavern-running life I thought myself chained to." His jaw ticked as he waited for what he feared I'd say next, but I went on, "But there is a part of me that always knew my life was meant to be experienced beyond the bounds of the Cub's Tavern. I will always have the home to return to, but I knew I was meant for more."

Lancaster barely moved, his fae senses holding him impossibly still.

"Ask me, Lancaster. Ask me what I want for that life."

He swallowed. "What is it that you want, Santorina?"

"I want *fire*." My chest hummed, and he grunted as if he felt it, too. "I want *passion*." My lips hovered over his. "I want someone whose very presence lights me up, and I don't want it dictated by the Gods. I want to choose it every day of my mortal lifespan."

Lancaster looked about to argue, but I forged on, "And though this may only be a physical need, in this moment, I choose you."

I didn't wait for his answer. I kissed him, and Lancaster groaned into my mouth, the most desire-laced sound I'd ever heard. He pressed closer so my back bowed over the bed. His mouth worked across my jaw, down my neck, and his canines scraped over my skin. I gasped at the pleasure that coiled through my body, and his hips pressed against mine, his length thick and hard against me.

Goddess, I wanted him. All of him, and as reluctant as I was to admit it, it was likely not only due to the bond.

I'd seen other sides of him in our travels—the young man

who'd loved his mother, the one who staked his morals off her tragedy. The male who would rip a predator to shreds for me and who wished to aid the defenseless, even if they did not want him. The fae who would use his magic to provide me comfort but who believed in my strength to do so on my own, too.

The reasons that I was enraptured with him beyond a bond flooded through my mind as he pressed me down into the bed. His teeth dragged over my collarbone, back up my neck. And while those fangs were close enough to rip out my throat, I had never felt safer and more cherished in my entire life.

"Santorina," he breathed, one hand brushing my hair from where it had fallen over my chest. "Please, can I touch you?" His voice trembled, like he'd fall apart if I didn't give him this.

Instead of answering, I sat up. He followed the movements, staying close enough that his breath fanned across my skin. I untied the knot behind my neck, and my top fell forward. Lancaster's gaze dropped to my breasts, nipples peaked and begging for him.

"Please, Hunter," I breathed. "Please touch me."

His lips slammed back to mine, consuming me as he wrapped one arm around my waist and laid me back against the pillows. My legs bracketed either side of his waist, his hips hovering just enough over mine that I couldn't feel him, but I *ached* for him.

Lancaster broke the kiss, pressing his forehead to mine as he watched his hand circle my breast. My breathing turned more ragged by the moment, but he was clearly taking this as slowly as only a non-immortal could.

"Please," I begged, arching up so I pressed into his hand.

He groaned as he kneaded, his head dropping to my other breast and taking my nipple between his teeth. Every sensation was *more*. More intense than any I'd ever experienced, more exhilarating, more euphoric. I was burning from the inside out, squirming beneath him.

I may have said it could only be a physical bond, but it was the most exquisite form of torture.

And Lancaster took his time as executioner. Slowly, he kissed down the plane of my stomach, fangs scraping along the chained belt around my waist, pressing it into my skin. The cool metal was a contrast to the scorching heat his tongue left behind. He gathered the chiffon panels of my skirt, dragging slow fingers up my legs and leaving goose bumps in his wake.

"Santorina," he exhaled against my skin. "Goddess, I never thought I wanted a bond with anyone." Higher, those fingers went, dancing along the trim of my undergarments. "Never imagined how badly I could need someone. But this feels like it will shred me apart."

He pressed slow circles over the sensitive spot between my thighs, and I couldn't even tell him I felt that need, too. That I wanted him as badly. Words were utterly lost to me as he added more pressure.

"Can I taste you?" he asked.

"Goddess," I finally forced out, my back arching as he teased me. "Stop asking and do it."

He laughed, the sound alone making my toes curl against the comforter, my heels somehow gone though I'd barely noticed. "Always with such an attitude, Bounty."

Lancaster peeled my undergarments down my legs, tossing them aside. Then, he knelt before me. A Hunter on his knees for a Bounty.

He moved aside my skirt, the slits to the thigh making it easy, and he bared me to him. Spreading my legs wider, I was entirely vulnerable, but as he looked at me, there was nothing but worship in his eyes. Something that pulled at my chest and tried to tear apart my rationale of this being purely physical.

He kissed up my legs, sweeping two fingers up my center. My breathing quickened.

"Goddess be damned," Lancaster muttered as his mouth landed between my thighs. "I'm going to enjoy this much more than I should."

And then, he lavished me. His fingers pumped into me, his tongue flicking against my clit and—Goddess, those sharp canines dragged over the sensitive spot as he worked up a rhythm that sent the string in my chest humming. All of my blood *buzzing*.

Lancaster growled as if he felt it too, the sensation vibrating through me and making me gasp. He gripped my hips, pulling me even closer.

My hand shot up, gripping the headboard because if I didn't have something to hold on to I feared I would slip right away from this realm, and I was nowhere near done with the Hunter yet.

"I can't tell you how long I've been dreaming of this," Lancaster muttered, pressing another kiss to the inside of my thigh as his fingers continued to work. "When I carried you across the mountains, when you slept beside me in that bed. Every time your damn scent wrapped around me, I almost snapped. *Almost claimed you.*"

"Claimed?" I asked, voice shaking as my legs did over his shoulders.

"Claimed," he repeated, fingers hooking inside of me and hitting a spot no one had before.

"Fucking Goddess," I blurted as heat poured through my bones and the bond snapped within my chest. "It's only physical. No claiming."

He laughed at my insistence. "Of course, Bounty."

His tongue and fingers picked up their rhythm as he drove me to total and utter ruin. And I didn't know what claiming meant, but I knew—though I'd never admit it—that in that moment, a piece of my soul was sewn to his. Promised by the Gods, for all eternity.

The Bounty, claimed by the Hunter.

Chapter Sixty-Three
Damien

Fear.

Fury.

Injustice.

Betrayal.

As I watched Echnid prepare to commit his heinous crimes from my palace atop the mountains, they all flooded me. Growing every day since I left that deficient Stone Realm, where depravity lurked beyond the scope of the walls.

I shoved them down, fear coiling at the knowledge of what would happen if Echnid sensed it. With how entwined our power was with the realm, he was capable of it.

His attention was honed elsewhere now, though, as it had been since Valyrie had given him the knowledge he needed to break the long-standing protection of the Goddess. His distraction was our saving grace at the hands of the mist's legacy.

But that unrepentant mistress was a ruthless bride of the realms, bending everything to her will, and her will was the mother of the gods. The one who birthed them to such almighty powers. And now, Echnid had his final pieces. His henchmen reaped in shadow and fire, the prophetic sacrifice to allow him access to a city long sealed, and finally, the understanding of the key that could carve open a bridge to deliver him those he sought to slay.

If he could only get it.

Echnid stood at the edge of the Rapture Chamber where my brothers and sisters and I gathered, and he prepared to tilt the world into travesty and chaos.

"You all know your orders?" Echnid repeated.

My cold heart withered at his tone, as we all echoed, "Yes."

"Xenique?" Echnid asked.

"I am certain that is the blade." My gaze flashed to my sister, concern lashing through me, tangling with the fury. I had not thought she would truly allow this tragedy of sacrifices.

Xenique exchanged a quick glance with Valyrie, and my concern morphed to curiosity. I was not accustomed to so many emotions changing so rapidly. It had my wings ruffling behind me.

Gaveny cast me a look, but there was no hint of his lingering mortal self in his expression tonight. The Tideshifter had sealed it all away on the cusp of what we were about to do—the crimes we were about to commit that would alter our existences permanently, but hopefully help us win steps toward what we had so long worked for.

Bant had played his part beautifully in the tarpits, driven the warriors to seize control and stumble into our path, but we had no certainty of what had occurred since. If now would be the right time. It appeared we had no choice.

"Fly now," Echnid said, taking his throne before the pillars overlooking the mountains. His shadow fell across the view, a starry sky outlining his godly frame. One of his remaining gorgons slithered across his lap, her legs falling open as his hand dropped between them absently. "I will follow when the time is most opportune."

One by one, we stepped to the ledge of the Rapture Chamber. And with a reluctant beating of wings, we plunged to the drop below. Thorn's laughter pealed into the dark sky, cracking off the stars.

I looked over my city—a reminder of why I must stick to this plan. Dread clouded my chest as I took flight, my golden ether spilling among a medley of colors and infiltrating the night.

And as Damenal was left in the distance, I clung to that desperate, ruthless but confident look my sisters had exchanged. And I wondered how deeply they'd woven their web around the god's greed.

Chapter Sixty-Four

Ophelia

Tolek had led me back to our room, a roguish smile across his lips the entire time. He'd run a hot bath full of jasmine-scented soap, and helped me into it, slowly massaging my shoulders, my neck.

His mouth had followed his hands until I was the purest form of relaxed. Then, he'd spun me around and I'd straddled his lap, riding him in a combination of gentle kisses and burning desire, seraph magic shimmering across the tiled bathing chamber the entire time.

When we were clean, he'd toweled off my hair, slipped a robe over my frame, and disappeared back into the bedchamber. I'd followed, leaning against the doorframe as he threw the curtains wide.

"Dance with me?" he'd asked, crossing the moonlit room to where I stood.

I laughed. "There's no music."

Tol shrugged as he took slow steps backward, pulling me with him. "We'll make our own."

And as I'd settled into his arms, the syncing beats of our hearts and the rhythmic sway of our steps did just that. The stories we'd written through our past and the legends we'd spin in the future became the tune we moved to. That was our song, the lives we'd build, tales yet to be written.

After a few dances, I pulled him back to the bed where he continued to lavish my body and whisper words of sweet adoration in my ear. When he was done, I used my seraph magic to form unbreakable binds around his wrists, pinning him to the headboard as I kissed down his body. I showed him exactly how grateful I was for the care he'd shown me every day since I'd escaped Echnid.

Those hours, as Tol held me in the silence and made me laugh until my cheeks hurt, I thought of the Firebird and the Fox. And I knew with every fiber of my cursed being and every drop of Angel and Godsblood within me that even come fire and ashes, I would go to the ends of the realm for this love.

We were not purely built on hope but fate as well. And together, the two burned brighter than any flames, unbound and utterly unquenchable.

And if this looming battle really did take us, I would have wanted to go just like that, with Tolek imprinted on my skin and my light burning the realm to ash.

DESPITE THE UTTER bliss making my limbs weak, I couldn't sleep. My heart raced uncomfortably, but I didn't want to wake Tolek, so I dragged on my leathers, strapped the Vincienzo dagger to my thigh, and crept out of the guest house and down the long drive leading to Meridat's manor. The night was so dark, a near-starless sky above, only orbs of mystlight set in bronze lamp posts illuminating the way.

There were still celebrations carrying on in the city, their gentle hum seeping through the night. I turned down the nearest path from Meridat's home, nearly jumping to find a shadowed figure wandering ahead of me. She passed under a lantern hanging above a door, her brown hair gleaming.

"Ezalia?" I asked.

The Seawatcher Chancellor turned. "Couldn't sleep either?"

I sped up to match her stride. "No. I think it's all the excitement from the day mixed with the anticipation of...whatever's coming."

The air prickled as I said it, rippling over my skin, and my heart pounded harder. My fingers brushed the Vincienzo dagger as if seeking a gentle reassurance that it was there.

"I've had plenty of sleepless nights for the same reason," Ezalia admitted.

"I'm sorry," I said.

She raised a perfectly arched brow. "For?"

"That you're here—that we all are. The gods' wars only surfaced because I freed Echnid." Guilt wrapped around my throat, threatening to suffocate me. "If I hadn't done it, no one would be suffering this threat."

"But we *would* be suffering," Ezalia reminded me. "The Balance was unraveling in other ways, we just didn't realize it. Alpheous attacks on the coasts were growing worse by the day. My warriors could barely complete one expedition without their ships being wrecked. So, I don't think not acting would have equaled no suffering. It would have only been a quieter kind. Sometimes we have to be loud and face conflict head on in order to reach solutions."

That's what we'd been doing for months now, wasn't it? Starting with the day Damien first appeared in my room. I hadn't once run from the threats; I'd charged into them with my head held high and my heart prepared to scream and bleed for our cause. And while I dreamed of a day where that wouldn't be necessary, not fighting now wouldn't derive peace.

"I hope I can be a fraction of the ruler you are one day, Ezalia."

She patted my shoulder, squeezing gently. "You already are."

Mystlight haloed her features as we turned another corner onto an open square. The gems lining her ears shimmered in their pale blues and greens and corals, and a tattoo down her spine peeked over her leathers.

A cluster of warriors of various clans gathered around the fountain in the center, more spilling out of a tavern where music slipped over the night. I inclined my head toward the benches rimming the space, but we'd barely taken a few steps when the air shifted. A ripple shivered along my skin again, and seraph magic pressed to the surface. Everyone in the square seemed to slow, to pause.

"Do you feel that?" I whispered, placing a hand on Ezalia's arm.

"I do—"

But her words choked off, and she stumbled forward.

"*Ezalia?*" I gasped as I caught her.

She fell heavily, warmth pouring over my skin. Heart pounding, I rolled her over.

"*No.*" Nausea swept through me, a cold and piercing numbness dulling all sound around us.

Crimson spread across Ezalia's chest, a fast-blooming bud beginning where an arrow jutted directly through her heart.

"Ezalia!" I shrieked again, crashing to my knees with her in my arms.

I cupped her cheek, turning her to me. "Ophelia," she wheezed. Blood stained her lips.

"Ezalia, hang on." I looked around, voice tearing as I screamed, "*HELP!*"

But even as Bodymelders rushed up and I tried to force Angellight into her wound, life slipped from the Seawatcher Chancellor's sea glass eyes. The same ones her young daughter had, her son. The ones that would never look at the man she loved again.

"Oh-phelia," she sputtered.

"I'm here, Ezalia," I choked. "I'm here. I've got you."

She took a ragged breath, her eyes flaring wide as a shadow swooped over us. And my attention snapped up right as Gaveny dropped to the street before me.

PART FOUR
ECHNID

CHAPTER SIXTY-FIVE
OPHELIA

"GAVENY?" I GASPED.

The street was a mess of rushing warriors—of screams for weapons and loved ones.

But all I could focus on was the weight of the chancellor in my arms—my friend who did not deserve this, who'd been such a caring, genuine guidance—and the Angel before me whose might rippled like a roaring tide, blue ether peeling off his wings. His bow lowering after loosing that silencing shot.

No—no, he couldn't have.

Ezalia was his Seawatcher. The ruler of *his* clan, and Gaveny had always seemed so amicable while training. A bit unpredictable, like the force of his seas thrashed beneath his skin, but he'd seemed well-intentioned and *helpful*.

Yet his eyes locked on the place his arrow pierced Ezalia's chest, and while there was maybe a hint of remorse, there was no grief. Only solitude and acceptance.

"G-Gav..." Ezalia choked out. Her eyes flared wide, and I realized this was the first time she was seeing an Angel in the flesh, the first time most warriors now frantically tearing through the night around us were.

And what a twisted irony that he'd put an arrow through her heart.

"I hoped it wouldn't happen this way," Gaveny told Ezalia. I didn't know what he meant, but the look they exchanged seemed like some private conversation of clan secrets.

"What are you doing here?" I growled at the Angel, holding Ezalia closer to shield her from him.

"Little seraph," Gaveny greeted, taking a step toward us.

"*Get away*." My words were feral, animalistic. Tears poured down my cheeks, their warmth fueling me to stand against him.

"If only it were that easy," Gaveny answered.

Before I could respond, he shot into the air, leaving a wash of ether eddying across the plaza as cool as a tide. Hunching over Ezalia's body, I tracked his flight.

"*No*."

Six more winged forms crisscrossed through the sky, leaving trails of magic in their wake. Weapons were strapped to their bodies, plates of armor glinting in the night.

Thorn and Ptholenix. Xenique and Bant. Valyrie and Damien.

They were all here, all within the city walls, which meant Xenique—Xenique whom we had trusted—had granted them permission to enter. To ravage her capital.

Gaveny flew in circles, using his influence over seas to command the water in fountains and streams. It shot through the air in spiraling torrents, bending bodies to the ground and forcing warriors to retreat behind closed doors.

The other six Angels soared through the skies, gazes intent on *something* below. Something I couldn't see.

Screams of warriors pierced my shock, and I jumped into motion.

"Ezalia?" I asked.

"Ophelia," she barely forced out. She clung to me like I was her last breath, one hand grappling against mine.

"I'm so sorry, Ezalia," I muttered. On my knees in the center of Xenovia, I wished I could pray to any deity for safety. What an utter devastation that they were the ones killing us in the first place.

Ezalia took a ragged breath, and every shutter seized my own lungs.

"Ophelia," she breathed. "You are...good leader." She squeezed my wrist with a fluttering grasp. "Your father. Proud."

"Thank you," I whispered, my lips trembling. "Thank you for everything."

For believing in me back when I barely had a title to claim, for escorting me through the uncertain days of early leadership, for being a resolute, dependable ally in the wake of so many threats.

"Tell my daughter...I'm sorry."

Seli's bright disposition and radiant enthusiasm flashed through my memory. Seli, who would no longer have her mother to guide her.

"For what?" I asked urgently. The light was rapidly fading from her sea glass eyes, her words no more than breaths.

Ezalia tried to shake her head, only managing one jerk. "She will know one day." Her hair was matted to the mess of blood on her chest, her body so frail as she inhaled. "I love them."

Tell them I love them, she meant. Her family—the twins and her partner, Seron—who had given so much for this Angelcurse already.

"I will," I muttered. "I promise."

I would not die tonight. Not with this vow in my heart. I looked to the skies, tracking the Angel forms. No, I would not face the Spirit Realm tonight—but they would.

For abandoning us.

For threatening us.

For turning us into a god's tragedy, another chapter in a war that was not ours.

Standing, I hefted Ezalia's limp form into my arms.

"Bring her in here!" a woman called from the nearest alley.

Without even considering, I raced after her and toward a doorway propped open halfway down the street. More warriors were flooding the alleys now, shouting directives from their generals, assembling into the uniform legions we'd prepared for weeks, ready for what we were born to do. Defend Ambrisk.

The door closed behind me, sealing out the chaos for a moment. The tiny establishment was a back room in some sort of shop—an office with boxes taking up the rest of the available space, a desk in one corner and a low settee in another. Gently, I laid

Ezalia on the cushions, careful not to jostle her, though her chest had already stopped rising.

"Fucking Angels," I said to myself, a sob lodged in my throat. "The arrow." It still protruded from her heart, her blood cooling across her chest. "I should take it out. I shouldn't—shouldn't leave her like that."

A gentle hand touched my shoulder, and I jumped, Angellight flaring to life in one palm, the other reaching for the Vincienzo dagger at my thigh. The woman who owned the place gave me wide eyes, stepping back.

"I'm sorry," I breathed, siphoning the magic back in. "I forgot..."

Forgot she was here. In her own office.

She gave me a sympathetic smile, toying with the dark braid trailing over her shoulder. "I understand, Revered. I can care for the chancellor. I believe you are needed elsewhere."

A *boom* echoed from the square outside.

Elsewhere. Where a battle was raging.

Ezalia was only one of many fatalities we'd see tonight, but if I was fast enough—strong enough to conquer the Angels and their god—maybe we could limit the rest.

"You'll clean her up?" I asked, swallowing down the tears.

"And guide her home with reverent care."

Some part of me was so reluctant to leave her, though I had to face this battle. This war brought upon my people and our allies by my own Godsblood and the curses it wrought.

But I was scared. Scared of what would come and scared of whom else we might say goodbye to. If I was sure of anything, though, it was that deep down, I knew there was no room for being afraid. Fear would slow my movements. It would dull the dagger-sharp edge I needed against vengeful Angels.

And right now, as I stared down at my friend whose body was much too still and the echoes of screams tore through the night beyond these walls, that anger morphed into an unremorseful, unrepentant fire.

It ripped through me, seraph magic raging to be unleashed against its Angelic sources.

Wiping my tears with a staunch finality, I looked at the Soul-guider who had opened her shop to care for Ezalia. "Thank you."

Then, I barreled through the back door and straight into a war of gods and Angels.

~

The city had descended into madness.

"The manor," I panted as I ran, my boots scraping over stone and sand.

I needed to get back to Meridat's manor. Spirits, I hoped my friends hadn't left yet. Had any of the Angels gone straight there? Fear sent my arms and legs pumping faster, sent me leaping over fallen piles of rubble as I tore down residential streets, beating my wings to clear pillars and broken beams as warriors around me rushed to defend their city.

I rose into the air, assessing. All inhabitants of this area were either hurrying to their lines or hunkering down with the defenseless. Using all the strength I'd practiced, I flew above the two-story buildings, and—

I gasped, nearly crashing back to the ground. The Angels shot beams of light from the clouds, collapsing walkways and paths out of the city to keep us centralized.

No one would be leaving Xenovia tonight.

In the distance, bronze minarets and domes reflected cracking magic. The gray clouds that had rumbled around the border of the city for weeks crowded the skies overhead, glowing in an array of colors with each bolt of Angellight. Bright purple streaked down, crumbling a stone statue of Xenique only blocks away.

Heart racing, I dropped back to the ground and continued ducking beneath awnings and shadows to get to the manor. I didn't know what the Angels were doing, but I could guarantee one of their goals: *me*. And I had to find my friends and the leaders of the other armies before I could let that happen.

Gaveny had a chance, and he'd flown off. My breath sawed through my lungs, the Vincienzo dagger burning in my palm as I tried to make sense of it all. But as the dust of a city being sacked spiraled into the air above me, I didn't give an Angel's wrath. I only tore around corners and down alleys, blasting seraph magic at anything in my way until I hit the wide cobbled street the manor stood at the end of.

"Ophelia!" a shout broke above the rest.

"JEZ!"

I collided with my sister before the open gates to Meridat's home. Zanox was behind her, his leather wings coated in razor-sharp scales, and Erista talked quickly with a group of Soulguiders, their chancellor commanding her advisors along with Esmond, Cyren, and Dax.

"What's happening?" Jezebel asked, panting. Mystlight from the sconces lining the street flickered across her terror-stricken face. "Everything is so loud—the spirits."

Fucking realms, she was hearing all of it. I'd kill every Angel responsible for the pain clawing through her voice.

"The Angels are here," I explained. "I don't know how or why, but—"

The air shuddered, a ripple going all throughout Xenovia. We froze, gripping each other tightly. My sister's eyes squeezed shut. I brushed her hair behind her ear, wishing to every Spirit that she didn't have to suffer this power.

"Can you do this, Jez?" I whispered. "Can you fight? If it will be too painful—distract you—flee now. Get on Zanox and go somewhere safe."

Her eyes snapped open, and with the burning stare she gave me, I'd have thought *she* was the sister who commanded Angel-light. "Absolutely not. I've fought in a war before, and I will do so again, sister."

The fire in her voice was the steel will of a Mystique Warrior.

"I'm so proud of you," I said, pulling her to me.

Over her shoulder, a blue and white blur dove from beyond the manor walls. Sapphire's hooves clattered to the stone, and Tolek hopped off her back.

"Alabath!" he shouted as he sped over. His arms curled around me, and for a moment the fear returned. It crashed over us like one of Gaveny's tidal waves.

"Tol," I breathed as heartache bloomed fiercely, pulling back to meet his eyes. "Ezalia. Gaveny—he killed her."

"He *what*?" he growled.

Vale and Cypherion were just behind him on Dynaxtar, the latter sliding off the khrysaor and hurrying to Meridat while the Fatecatcher stayed mounted. Lancaster, Santorina, and Mora raced into view next, the male carrying Rina until he stopped before us.

I nodded, taking stock of them all. "I don't know why. He said *I hoped it wouldn't be this way*. And the rest of the Angels are here. They're effectively locking down the city."

"They don't want anyone to find a way out..." I could tell from the tone of Tol's voice that he was trying to work it out as quickly as I was. And from the way his arms tightened around me, he came to the one answer I had, too. "If they're here for you, they won't get you. We've fought them off before, we will again."

A sick feeling in my gut told me he was wrong, but I didn't voice it. We couldn't lead an army with fear or fear would win.

"Cypherion!" I called, and my Second was there in an instant. "You and Mila will lead the Mystique forces?" When he nodded, I ran my hands through my hair and took a deep breath. "If you can find any gap through the city walls, get as many people out as possible. There is *no* shame in warriors not wanting to be trapped in here."

They may have been willing to give their lives on a battlefield for this cause, but they did not volunteer to be carrion picked off one by one within closed borders. The commanders may have had a plan in case of siege, but no one anticipated this level of destruction and betrayal.

"Will do, Revered," Cypherion said, turning back to Meridat.

"Where the fuck *are* Mila and Malakai?" Tolek asked. I gripped my Bind absently, the North Star as dull as ever.

"They're fine. They're somewhere." With the noise mounting through the city shielding my words, I whispered, "Tol..."

But he gave me a smirk, one hungry for an Angel's blood on his blade. "I know where I'm needed."

If there was one thing I was certain of right now, it was the way our hearts sang to the tune of revenge.

And I matched his depraved smile as I muttered, "There he is."

Before he could leave, he cupped my cheeks and pressed his lips to mine. It was one of those kisses that traveled through my entire body, that made my chest ache and my stomach flip, sent a shiver across my wings to the tips of every soft feather. It was a kiss that said more than words could in the face of certain death, one that latched on to my heart, my spirit, my very bones, and promised to see me at the end of this.

"I love you, *apeagna*," he whispered when he pulled back, stroking his thumb across my cheek. "Make those fuckers scorch for ever thinking they could manipulate you." He kissed my forehead one more time. "I don't want to find you in any realm but this one, though, so be sure to be here at the end of this battle."

And that was the thing that might have finally undone me. The reminder that we'd already lost so much and we may stand to lose more tonight. For this was a war greater than any we'd fought, and how many times could one truly beat the odds?

"I love you, too, Vincienzo. I'll see you over a god's corpse."

With one last hungry, torturous smirk, Tolek left. The fae and Rina prepared to dispatch behind him to aid the foot soldiers. I hugged my Bounty friend as tightly as possible before they disappeared.

"You are capable of such greatness, Santorina Cordelian. And you deserve all the love in the world." My eyes landed on Lancaster where he waited, irritated. "Go show the Angels and warriors what a human can do."

"And you remind them of the legacy of seraphs the world dared to forget," she whispered back, tears cracking her voice. Then, they were off.

Sapphire pranced over to me, nudging my shoulder with an impatient whinny.

"Ready?" Jez asked, nodding to Vale behind her, Dynaxtar's and Zanox's slitted eyes bright.

I hopped onto my pegasus and flared my wings as she did hers. "Let's get to the skies."

CHAPTER SIXTY-SIX
MALAKAI

"WHAT IN THE NAME OF THE SPIRITS IS GOING ON OUT there?" Mila asked, rising from where she'd reclined against the wall, a book in hand.

The tunnel that revealed itself had been short, leading to a small, cramped room stacked with dusty volumes. An altar with lit candles sat beneath an image of Xenique, and I was trying really hard not to be unsettled by any of this.

"Probably the festivities getting rowdy," I commented, but Mila crept back up the corridor into the room with the mosaic of Artale, that ivory gown clinging to her every step.

I didn't follow, my attention locked on the book in my hands. We'd been here for hours, and I knew I should have gone to find Ophelia and the others, but we were still trying to make sense of all the information here and the sort of fated luck that opened the door in the first place. And we wanted to wait until Barrett and Dax had left so we didn't take over their night.

But what we'd found—the records on weapons and the pure sources of magic they were imbued in—it was inconceivable.

The fucking Angels, always scheming. Each page I turned, I thought more and more that those damn winged beings were perhaps even more clever than the gods. That while the gods had fought wars among themselves and their realms, the Angels were planning for a larger overhaul. One that could stretch beyond the bounds of Ambrisk.

I flipped to a new page as another roar echoed from outside.

"Fucking Spirits," I breathed, pushing to my feet. The weapon recorded in this book looked like—

"Malakai!" Mila said, running back into the room. She was braiding her hair, a band held between her teeth. "We have to go."

"What's wrong?" I rushed out, abandoning the papers. She appeared fine beyond a distant echo of fear in her eyes.

"Something's happening in the city." She tied off the braid. "Come on."

Mila grabbed my hand, and I barely spared another glance at the information I'd just found. The information that changed everything.

~

"HOLY FUCKING ANGELS," I breathed as Mila and I stood on the steps of the capitol building where just hours ago, Barrett and Dax had sworn their vows. Their blood from the scarring still stained the stone just beneath my boots.

Only now, crimson bathed the rest of the city, too. Rubble coated alleys and sand blew in great gusts through the squares. Soldiers marched down streets, attempting to fortify any walls and borders they could.

"What's happening?" Mila asked.

A burst of light laced with inky black lashed down from the sky, illuminating the city in an eerie glow, and a feathered silhouette burst through the clouds.

"Fuck," I answered as roofs and statues warped beneath the dark tendrils of power. "Bant."

The Engrossian Angel dove from the sky with a grandiose ax in hand. His long black hair trailed on the breeze, dark ether shimmering and highlighting the sinister smile on his face. He plummeted for a group of warriors defending the square, weapon launching from his hand.

"NO!" I shouted.

Bant's ax landed in the chest of a warrior commanding a small unit to clear an alley, and a ripple of power shuddered through Xenovia.

Behind me, Barrett echoed my scream as he and Dax raced from the capitol building.

"Was that one of yours?" I asked.

Dax's jaw ticked. "Yes. One of our advisors."

"What in the fucking Angels," I breathed. Bant had just killed one of *his own* warriors. And he'd smiled as he did it.

Barrett tried to leap down the stairs, but Dax caught him with a grimace, pulling him back into his chest.

"Let me go!" Barrett roared.

"No," Dax commanded. "I finally got you. I'm not losing you yet." The general ripped an ax from his back and shoved it into Barrett's hands. "Be smart."

Once Barrett collected himself, Dax released him, removing his other ax and assessing the square below.

The prince's outcry had captured Bant's attention. Pulling his weapon from the warrior's chest, the Angel flared his wings wide. And with one more gut-churning smile and a nod that seemed like a promise, Bant shot into the air.

More soldiers poured into the space, crossing to their designated zones. Soulguiders and Bodymelders carried away what injured they could, and a cluster of Starsearchers stood behind a Mystique line, reading for any hint of what forces would be deployed next and shouting commands ahead.

Still hovering over the square, Bant drifted in high circles, sending down another whip of tar-streaked light. He wrapped it around a chimney of a shop bordering the square, crushing it with a flick of his hand. The entire wall crumbled across a wide street leading away from the plaza, and warriors rushed to clear the debris.

It was quickly morphing into carnage.

"Malakai," Mila said, gripping my arm, voice laced with fury.

I followed her stare to the center of the square where, perched atop the bronzed statue of Xenique, an all too familiar white-haired woman sat, leather wings exposed at her back.

"*Rozelyn*," I growled.

The gorgons were here, too.

Their leader watched the mess unfold below, eyes locked on Bant's recent kill. Horror knotted my chest as those eyes shifted to red. A warrior kneeling beside the one Bant had slain looked up as if summoned.

"Don't!" I yelled, making to run down the stairs, but Mila caught my hand.

"You won't make it!"

Bile crawled up my throat as the man's eyes locked with the gorgon's, ensnared in her trap, and he turned to stone.

"Bant's gleaming cock," Barrett swore.

"Don't make eye contact," I instructed. "There should be three more somewhere around the city." It was a guess, but I didn't imagine Echnid would send his Angels and only *one* gorgon here tonight. No, this felt like an all-out force. A final stand. And Spirits save us to find out what else he had planned.

The cerberus's lumbering gait and snapping jaws came to mind. The Mindshaper forces hadn't arrived yet. We were alone on that front.

"They all wear those white dresses," Mila added. "They might have the leather wings out or serpentine hair if they're not in their human form."

Barrett shivered. Dax nodded gravely. And I slammed the cage within my chest shut as I looked over the two of them and Mila. I couldn't afford to consider losing any of them or the rest of my friends that were no doubt out in that city right now.

"We need to find weapons and leathers or armor," I said to Mila, ripping Lucidius's dagger from my waist—the only one we had between us—and holding it out to her.

"You keep that," she insisted, pulling her hand back as I tried to place it in her palm.

"You need—"

She raced back into the hall and grabbed a hooked sword from where it was displayed on the wall beneath a mystlight lantern, slashing the sharpened blade through the air.

"I've always wanted to try one of these," she said with a grin. "Now is as good a time as any."

I smiled at the gleam in her eye, the way her stare shifted to icy resolve, and she prowled to the edge of the steps, looking over the city descending into ruin. Wind whipped her braid around her face, loose pieces framing her cheeks, but her stare was honed intensity when I joined her.

"Leathers or armor if we can find it. Head to a nearby weaponry or Meridat's, whichever we can get to first," I repeated the earlier thought. "And we need to find Cypherion."

"Cypherion?" Mila echoed.

"I'll explain as we run," I said tightening my grip on my dagger. "And General?"

"Yes?" Mila's fortress dropped momentarily as I stepped up to her. I searched those ice-blue eyes as the rumble of another wall being hit by Angellight shrouded the city. Smoke spiraled high, the shouts of warriors mounted, but I only looked at her.

At this woman who had found me when I was broken but didn't turn away. Who saw the collapsed ruin within me and the potential to rebuild from the rubble. To piece me back together one stubborn, crumbled brick at a time.

I'd been wrecked just as this city was being razed now, but I was not a lost cause. Neither was Xenovia. We wouldn't relent.

When I met Mila, I may have been looking over the edge of a cliff, but she pulled me back from the jump. Showed me how fucking bright the stars could be if I dared to look up.

Sliding my hand around her waist, I pulled her flush against me and kissed her until she was panting.

Then, I dropped my forehead to hers. "You promised me every tomorrow. Don't break that promise tonight."

"Not a fucking chance, Warrior Prince."

And we dove into battle.

CHAPTER SIXTY-SEVEN
VALE

Go on, Stargirl, Cypherion had said to me before he joined the others in battle. *Go show the gods how you command the Fates.*

I'd kissed him once, told him I loved him fiercer than any Fate tie, and Dynaxtar took to the sky. She was normally such a gentle creature, content to weave among the clouds and feel the mist along her leathery wings, but as she rose over a rubble-strewn Xenovia, dust clouding the mystlights and giving the entire bronze-domed city a hazy hue, she flew with the ferocity of a beast ready for battle. With precision and sharp turns.

Zanox was beside us, Jezebel leaning low against his back as she called orders to him. They were creatures who had carved out their names in legends, born to bear fierce warriors, and they showed no hint of mercy now.

I tightened my knees around Dynaxtar's sturdy body, hands tangling in her luminescent silver mane. "Let's see what we find in the stars."

Taking the directive, Dynaxtar peeled away from Zanox as he and Jezebel continued their loop around the outer perimeter. Ophelia and Sapphire had disappeared as soon as we'd left the ground, soaring off on their own pursuit. My khrysaor speared higher, wings out and razor-sharp scales gleaming as we sliced through cloud coverage.

I cast a glance over my shoulder, but no Angels followed us.

"You're on watch," I commanded Dynaxtar, patting her neck, and she whinnied in agreement.

Then, I opened up the channels of Fate I'd closed earlier tonight, the effects of the imbued blades below pulling hundreds of fortunes to the surface. Starfire burst behind my vision as they slammed into me. I gritted my teeth, hunching lower over Dynaxtar. I focused on her body beneath mine and the soft strands of her mane to keep myself grounded amid the flaring fortunes.

Shooting stars whirled, whites blindingly bright. Magic tunneled through my veins into the Starsearchers below. I hissed against the pain of so many readings crowding my chest, head spinning.

"*Fatecatcher!*"

"Arenothos?" I shouted back, unsure if I was yelling on Ambrisk or in that other place within my mind.

"We have been calling you for *hours*," the Fate of Wrath and Redemption growled, voice as much a threat as his name.

"Who has?"

"All nine of your ties." Fire burned in those words.

No, no, no. My palms turned sweaty, slipping on Dynaxtar. They couldn't have been trying to get to me.

"You shut us out," Arenothos spat. "No one is meant to do that. Look at the ruin that has transpired."

Readings rushed by, forcing a cry up my throat as wind whipped at my cheeks. Images of Echnid's gleeful grin and him commanding all seven Angels. They stood in a chamber over-looking the mountains. The Revered's Palace. It was recognizable, but slightly warped. The god's misty magic dulled the view and statues of Angels, the floors a dull white as opposed to pristine marble.

One by one, the Prime Warriors flared their wings. Arrays of colorful ether shimmered off white feathers, the only facet of the reading not dimmed by Echnid's influence. Each Prime Warrior grabbed the weapons of their clan, some donning elaborate plates of armor or vambraces. None covered their entire body in true defense. They were for one thing: intimidation. The impression of wealth and power.

Then, each of the seven Angels took to the skies with remorseful grimaces or haunted smiles, anticipation bouncing along a spectrum of causation.

"What's happened?" I asked Arenothos as the reading faded into pure white starfire again.

The Fate's silhouette shimmered within, swelling with anger. "We tried to warn you, but you missed the chance to adjust the paths against this."

No. Horror dripped through me.

"Unfortunately, yes. First the Goddess, and now the Balance Realm will succumb. More Gods will rise in his stead."

And though Arenothos was the Fate of Wrath, he did not sound pleased. His legends spoke of warfare, of bloodthirsty battles where he bathed in the life source of his enemies. Some said he drank it like the sweetest wine and adorned his suspected palace in the Fate Realm with their bones.

But the fates were so much more complex than legends painted. Where Arenothos was born of Wrath and fueled by bloodshed, he was also enraged by injustices that he did not deem worth the life. He wanted extremes—the worst of rage and fury, the righteousness of redeeming faults. He wanted blood on a battlefield, not innocent lives spilled in the deserts.

Fates were fickle and hard to unravel, but I'd spent more time with my nine Fate ties than I had any living warriors. Arenothos's rage rolled along my spine; it pumped my blood faster.

"The Goddess of Fates and Celestial Movements was a tragic loss," I growled. Tears tore down my cheeks as Dynaxtar climbed higher in the sky, and I rooted myself in both planes. "But she was a martyr for a greater cause, and now *I* am the Fatecatcher. I will not let her death be in vain."

"It is too—"

But Arenothos's words were swallowed by another barrage of fortunes. Of a different tie, raising hope against wrath.

"Unless you bear a solution, stay out of my way, Arenothos," I spat.

Then I shoved the Fate from my mind, and planted myself firmly in the realm of the living. Unmoving stars rippled back into vision in a navy sky, the moon full and bright, watching us. My Fatesworn bond beat alive and vicious as Cypherion fought in the city below. My tie to Dynaxtar burned, seeking out an enemy for my sweet girl to devour after she'd been caged for so long.

She and I were the same. Both pushed to the edge of our fury, both with sugared countenances burying the beasts within. Now, together, we shed those skins and let them roar.

"Let's claim the freedom we've earned, Dynaxtar," I called.

And then, the khrysaor tipped her head back. She opened her jaw, and blue flames shot from the back of her throat, burning like the stars she was forged of. They torched a path through the clouds, and before I could marvel over that power, a winged figure came into sight in that window.

"Valyrie!" I yelled.

The Angel's silver hair wound around her frame, lilac ether spilling through the sky. A scalloped silver plate covered her breasts, matching chains crossing over her stomach and décolletage. What appeared to be gloves covered her arms, but as Dynaxtar soared closer, I realized they were chain mail, looped delicately around each finger. And on her waist, just above her flowing silver skirt, a line of triple-bladed daggers were strung.

This was the Prime Warrior, made for battle in the heavens and on earth.

But the familiar understanding haunted her eyes. The one that had come to warn us of Echnid's motives. The one that had spoken with me and Moirenna in that foreign realm.

"Valyrie?" I pleaded, trying to bridge the two. "What's happening?"

"I am sorry, Fatecatcher." The deep regret burdening those words twisted the strand of hope I'd been clinging to. "But we did not have a choice."

My throat was dry. "What did you tell Echnid when he sent his gorgons after us?"

She only shook her head. Beneath me, Dynaxtar riled, as if feeding off my agitation.

The Angel repeated, "I am so sorry."

"Valy—"

But she dropped through the clouds, plummeting to the ground at an impossibly fast rate.

"*Valyrie!*" My voice tore on the scream, and Dynaxtar was diving, too. Wind and smoke stung my eyes, my hair whipping out behind us as I leaned low against my khrysaor.

Xenovia came back into view in a blur. Fires roared across the desert capital, orange and gold flames flickering off the bronzed arches, spires, and onion-shaped domes. Weapons clashed as—

My breath caught in my throat. There were other things crawling through the streets. The gorgons and a cerberus, but beasts bedecked in shadows, too.

But I couldn't worry about them now. Valyrie was plunging toward the city, and fear ratcheted up within me every second. Her wings tucked in as she dove, Dynaxtar hot on the trail of her ether.

"Please, Valyrie!" I shrieked. "Help us!"

My next scream was louder, more ragged than ever. It rang through my ears, and the Fatesworn bond tugged violently as Cypherion reacted, but I couldn't answer. Valyrie plummeted toward a target, intent on one warrior in the throng of battle.

And Harlen didn't even see her coming as she landed behind him and scooped him up with a leash made of stars. As she used the will of her Angellight to bind his wrists behind his back and force him against the nearest wall.

"NO!" I screamed again as the Angel pulled a triple blade from her waist.

"It is him or you," Valyrie called back over her shoulder as my oldest friend struggled against her. Dynaxtar landed with a boom I barely heard, and I dove from her back.

Valyrie's ether shoved at me, light erecting a wall between us. I beat with fists and feet, screamed and clawed and raged with all the fury of the Fate of Wrath.

"What are you *talking about*?" Harlen yelled still ripping at the Angellight pinning him. His eyes flicked between me—desperate and sobbing—and the Angel.

Valyrie turned to him and repeated, "It is her or you."

"*WHY?*" I shrieked, the word so broken. "Harlen!"

My friend only met my eyes. And as I saw the resolution dawn, I crumbled. My heart tore from my chest, a deep, slicing pain. Every moment of our childhood poured from the wound. Summer nights on balconies, healing cuts and bruises after punishments in the temple, crying on each other's shoulders as we realized the horrors we faced weren't ending. How he'd held me through Titus's recent torment, every ministration he'd taken to protect me, and the smiles he'd forced out of me when I thought there was no hope left.

"*Harlen!*" I screeched again. I ripped my short sword from my waist and slashed at the Angellight, lilac only reflecting along the blade. Dynaxtar bellowed her own blue flames at the wall. Readings slammed into me from the onslaught of power in our foot soldiers' weapons, searching for another fortune. Any other fortune.

But nothing helped.

Nothing could stop what the Fates had already decided.

Harlen held my stare. "I love you, Vale," he said. "You are the sister I never thought I deserved, but the one I will go to the Spirit Realm to protect." Then, he looked at Valyrie, and there wasn't a hint of a tremor in his voice as he said, "It is me."

And the Angel opened his throat with an unremorseful swipe of her triple blade. Her Angellight flared along the weapon, and Harlen collapsed to the floor.

I crumbled with him, sobs wracking my body and palms flattened against the Angellight wall.

Valerie turned to me, but I didn't look away from the friend who'd given his life for mine as the Angel said, "He felt no pain."

Then, she was airborne, the wall dissolving before me. I tumbled forward scrambling to Harlen.

"There has to be—He isn't—"

But he was. His lungs didn't search for final breaths, and his eyes were peacefully closed. The wound was no longer bloody, like that last flare of Angellight had killed him, healed it, and cleansed the slice all in one.

"Harlen," I sobbed again, my entire body quaking.

An arm wrapped around my waist, and I didn't even try to fight the person off. My broken soul knew who it was.

"Stargirl," Cypherion soothed. His hands held firm to my body as mine searched Harlen for any sign that this could be undone. That he hadn't been taken from me just as we both found a freedom we'd deserved all our lives.

I collapsed back against Cypherion, the battle raging in the square behind this small alley. At least we had that—this one moment of peace that should have been a lifetime.

"Why did she do this?" I cried into Cypherion's chest.

"I don't know," he said.

And as he held me when I said goodbye to my only childhood friend, something extinguished within me—and something entirely new woke.

A star blinking to life.

I looked around Cypherion to Dynaxtar and saw the same burning in her slitted eyes. A white-hot rage birthed by the tearing sensation through my chest, the well of Fatecatcher magic bubbling up, ripping a way for something to come through.

Undiluted fury and the promise of revenge, sealed by the Fates.

Chapter Sixty-Eight
Ophelia

Sapphire and I flew above Xenovia, ducking around columns of dust puffing up from the debris of the fallen walls and barricades. Below, a mystlight lamp crashed to the ground in the market, and a fire flared up in its place, latching onto the drapery that covered the stalls bordering the street. Screams echoed—the cries of warriors who *weren't* active soldiers, who were supposed to be as safe as possible in this city, guarded by Artale's magic.

Spirits, what was happening? Where in the damn Angels was the Goddess of Death now to protect the warrior clan her daughter ruled? Where was Xenique?

Jezebel and Zanox were on our tail, my sister and I shooting whips of gold and silver light down to clear pathways when we could. As we circled, the fire spread through the market.

"We're flying lower! Check the rest of the city, and track the Angels if you can!" I shouted to Jezebel. She nodded, Zanox taking off across the sky as Sapphire dove into the melee.

Warriors were trapped in the market stalls. We flew for the center, and as we passed over the fountain marking the heart of the square, I pulled at Gaveny's light. A wave of blue ether dug into the water in the basin and sent it cascading over the nearest stretch of flames surrounding a candle stall.

It was a cheating way to command the water—not pure

control—but it worked. A small section of flickering orange was doused before it could reach the wicks of their wares. Feet pounded as those who had been stuck behind it ran free.

As Sapphire looped back around, I honed my seraph magic into a shimmering wall, tossing it up to hold the smoke back so a group of warriors who'd been crouching beneath a stone shelter could flee, coughing and heads bent against the searing heat.

It was a barrage of power as we tried to evacuate the market, one stall and one threat at a time, and still the flames crept higher. The smoke filled the sky and tents. As if in answer, the Angellight of the Firebird woke within me, purring at how near the fire was, wanting to play.

"Fly higher," I breathed to Sapphire, my eyes stinging as I tried to find anyone else who needed help. Her hooves skimmed the tops of the still-intact tents, and catching my breath, I reached down into the depths of my power, picking apart the strands. Then, I sent a coil of orange-tinted seraph light licking across the ground, tapping into the Bodymelder affiliation with living beings to sense any beating hearts below.

"There!" I pointed, leaning closer to Sapphire's body, and my warrior horse charged, her wings tucking in as she got closer to the stall. Once a fruit stand, now ashes and crumbling wooden beams trapping four warriors within.

A creaking filled the air, and Sapphire flared her wings out, screeching to a halt that nearly unseated me as one of those beams crashed across our path.

Craning my neck around the debris, I called, "Are you injured?"

They all shook their heads, three eagerly crowding the front while the fourth lingered in the shadows. Wrenching up a wave of power, just as I'd seen the Angels do, I sent a crackle of seraph magic against a nearby stone wall, some building I didn't know nor care the purpose of right now. The surface crumbled, but as stone lined the path, it didn't burn.

No, it formed a barrier through the lower flames, providing a bridge of sorts. Three of the warriors raced to their safety, but the fourth lingered, fear morphing her features as she studied the fire and shook her head.

"You have to run!" I yelled, but she'd waited too long.

The fire rose higher, devouring that escape route and locking her within. Running would send her straight into turmoil.

"Never mind," I coughed out. "You're going to have to jump!"

The woman flashed me wide, fear-stricken eyes, but she assessed Sapphire. And finally, she nodded, long, teardrop earrings swaying against her olive skin. Her dark hair was knotted on her head, silver bangles reflecting the fire surrounding her and casting flames and shadow against her skin, giving her an ethereal appearance. Like she was from another realm entirely.

She gathered her flowing black dress, tucking the end of the skirt into the belt around her waist. Then, she scaled the half-wall.

"Watch your left foot!" I yelled, voice buried in the crackling flames. Her eyes lifted and I gestured to the portion of the wooden barrier that was crumbling, right where she'd been about to step.

Biting her lips, she nodded again.

Flames licked across the ground between where Sapphire hovered, and the fruit stand burned. We could fly closer, but we'd only have one second. It would have to be timed precisely, and maybe...

I pulled on the threads of seraph power within me that sparked like fire. A cleansing and an awakening, ash turned to ruined promise. I channeled every poetic thought of flames as Ptholenix had taught me and studied the wavering streaks.

They're no more powerful than I am, I told myself. *I am fire and storms, tempests and fates. I command the might of seven Angels as one, and they all bow to me.*

The flames were strong, tugging back against my magic, and I had a sick feeling the Firebird himself was responsible for these, based on their durability. So, I latched onto the piece of him that existed in me and let it meet its source.

As I exhaled, I envisioned light folding as a flame danced. Reds and oranges fading to ash. I fed seraph power into Ptholenix's particular brand of magic within me, but his fire was strong—

unbelievably so. Much more powerful than I'd ever thought of the Angels. It pushed back against me, wanting to roar.

I gritted my teeth, sweat rolling down my temples. The fire took out more structures, wooden beams splintering and collapsing around us. Soot swirled.

And with a ferocious burst, I directed my seraph power to wrap around the Bodymelder Prime Warrior's magic. To dance with his flames and command them.

Why is Bodymelder magic demonstrated by flames?

It is similar to how Bodymelders pull at the threads of one's being to heal maladies, the Angel had explained.

It was more than simple fire. It was a web of intricate power. And slowly, I coiled mine around it. I claimed control of each drop and peeled it back. Siphoned the strength of those flames into the heart of my magic. Heat melted across my skin, soot coating me, my pegasus, and the woman waiting for us.

Just before where she clung to a post, the wall of fire parted.

The woman's eyes met mine, and I nodded. I gripped Sapphire's mane, legs squeezing tight. And with a preternatural grace, the woman leapt.

Sapphire swept by, the tips of her white feathered wings grazing the curling edges of the flames, oranges and scarlets reflecting against the snowy surface. The woman's weight landed squarely behind me on my pegasus as we climbed higher in the sky, leaving the burning market behind.

But right as I gasped down clean air, a hand latched around my throat, and a cruel, otherworldly voice whispered in my ear, "You will not fly away this time, little seraph."

A sharp pain sliced through the top of my wing. My scream was lost to the battles, and warmth poured over the feathers. Sapphire whinnied with my agony, her flight speeding up as she tried to get us to safety.

The woman's face came into my peripheral view, and her smile —she had lost all of the hesitant mask she'd donned below. Now, her face gleamed with triumph. And there was something else in her eyes—something that told me this was no warrior I'd just saved.

"Who—" I gasped over the shooting bolt that ricocheted along my wing. She'd *stabbed* me. "Who—are you?"

My head was heavy, limbs leaden.

"Your downfall," she simpered.

"You're not a gorgon," I choked out. No, this woman had not been in Echnid's lap back in Damenal, nor did she wear one of those pristine white gowns that marked them.

"Born of one" was all she said.

"*Demigods*," I wheezed.

And with a smug smirk, she threw herself backward off Sapphire.

"NO!" I screamed, every ounce of the agony shooting through my wing poured into that word.

The woman flipped through the air and landed perfectly on the balls of her feet in the height of madness in Xenovia. Then, she ran, disappearing into a cloud of smoke.

"Fucking Angels," I cursed.

Grimacing, I ripped the blade from my wing. Blood slicked my skin and feathers, making everything...sticky...and it was all... slower. I looked at the blade in my hand, taking a moment to realize it was that same black onyx as the gorgon arrows.

Poison.

By the Spirits. It crawled through my blood, slithering serpents sinking their teeth in one pierce at a time. Gorgon poison, wrought of the seraph's natural-born enemy. Lethal.

No. No I could not go down like this. Could not become such an easy target for Echnid to grasp. Not while a battle staked on *me* raged below. Not with the Angels and gorgons and whatever else wreaking havoc.

But I was no mere seraph. I reached into the depths of myself, beyond my bruised spirit and into the magic birthed by my Gods-blood and myth.

I channeled every drop of healing power toward the serpentine venom crawling through me, to leach out the tainted substance this woman had planted in my body. This poison may have been lethal to a single seraph, but I was *of every Angel*, a rival of the gods.

As Sapphire continued to circle, climbing higher to keep me

out of the fight, I found those vipers in my blood and choked them one by one with leashes of shining seraph power.

With fire and the brimstone it bore, I scorched them. Drowned them with a raging sea and called on my own Godsblood to seal the death of the poison until the world swam back into its ruinous view.

I'd slumped against Sapphire's neck, her wings keeping us perfectly balanced so I didn't slip.

"Thank you, girl," I said, sitting up. Pure appreciation for this magnificent creature burned through me as bright as Angellight.

Looking over my shoulder, a gash shone in my wing. Not healing. It was no longer bleeding, but dark drops of poison seemed to ooze from the wound. A rock sank in my gut. Not even my Angellight would mend it right now.

I wouldn't be able to fly without Sapphire tonight. My myth born horse would be with me until the end, or I'd fight on foot beside my warriors. And despite the terror at what waited, pride bubbled within me. Pride to stand against the gods and Angels.

As if summoned, the pair of wings I'd been searching for flared up in front of us. Sapphire was speeding through the skies so quickly, she looped around the Angel, stopping on the other side of him, her back to the open desert rather than the city beneath.

"Damien!" I called, and there was no bite of pain in my tone. No hint that I'd sustained a wound to my hyper-sensitive wing or that I was expending precious magic by the minute to staunch it.

No, my voice was utter rage.

"Ophelia," Damien greeted, not even beating his wings to stay aloft. He was held by that raw power I was beginning to suspect ran deeper than any of us knew.

"What are you all doing? Is it me you're here for?"

"Yes and no," Damien explained. "You know Echnid has been working on his plans."

"And I know you have been helping him do it!" My hands fisted against Sapphire's back.

"You truly still believe the worst."

I threw a hand out, encompassing the city. "I have fair proof!"

"I have helped you learn your magic."

"Only for it to be manipulated!"

He remained frustratingly calm, gold light tumbling from him and wings still perfectly clean, like he hadn't visited the battle raging below. The scar along his face glowed eerily in the night like a crack to the surface of a frozen lake.

And that shattering ricocheted deep in my bones as Damien said, "We have been waiting for our chance for much longer than you have, Ophelia. We may all be on the same side."

"I cannot believe after all of this, you expect me to believe that! You expect me to take your word for it that you are truly trying to help the warriors?" Ezalia's weight pressed against my memory. "I saw what Gaveny did—what the others are doing. When will it end?"

As those four words that had been strangling me squeezed out, I looked over my shoulder, across the desert. And my heart stuttered to a stop. A hazy white mist seeped across the dunes, pressing closer and closer to the city borders.

Damien followed my horrified stare, and his jaw tightened. "I have to find my sacrifice. I promise, Chosen Child, that answer is coming." Then, he left, dipping down into the city, and Sapphire turned about to face the mist.

The Angel's words echoed in his wake, both a threat and a vow. Something I couldn't peel apart—couldn't tell if it meant to choke off my life right here or fuel my anger into battle.

Perhaps that was what they wanted. Us feeling small and lost, unsure whom to trust. Those who were afraid were easier targets. But I took that fear and sharpened it to a point. Everything Echnid had done to us heated the forge. The lives snuffed out too early were the coals, the feuds Damien and Bant had passed down to their warriors were the molten steel hungry to be shaped, and the memories of Echnid stealing my autonomy were the hammer.

My body was my own. My mind was my own. And I was the weapon he never meant to make.

And now, with the imbued Vincienzo dagger burning into my thigh, I faced the god—poised to kill.

CHAPTER SIXTY-NINE
CYPHERION

VALE WAS MADE OF WRATH AS WE RODE DYNAXTAR HIGH over the city.

My Fatesworn bond had gone wild, and for a moment I'd feared it was being torn in a way only death could sever. But it had thrashed and thrashed, and as I followed that instinctual sign in my soul to find the woman at the other end, I'd known it wasn't Vale suffering. Not physically.

That was pure despair echoing from her side.

I'd had a selfish rush of relief, then terror when I burst around the corner to see Vale crashing to her knees behind the wall of Valyrie's light—Harlen dead at the Angel's feet. Then, that slicing pain was my own, too. Harlen hadn't deserved this, no one falling through the capital did. Harlen had done nothing but atone for his unintentional betrayal, and he'd been such a dependable ally since, leading the Starsearchers and calling their troops to our side. Organizing the preparation of the imbued blades our forces were fighting with below.

Spirits, I'd been so damn certain Valyrie was on our side.

We'd hidden Harlen's body, then hopped on the khrysaor. As I searched over the khrysaor's wing, Starsearchers shouted results of their readings to other clans, telling them where to head to help evacuate the city, where the gorgons were going next.

Vale shook before me, her tears dried but their tracks a

constant reminder as she gritted her teeth and said, "The Angels will pay."

A collision echoed high in the sky, a shower of silver-blue flames and gold sparks. Ophelia and Jezebel. No Angellight followed in response, and I prayed to every cursed Spirit that was a good sign.

"They sure will, Stargirl," I swore along with her.

What I couldn't figure out was *why* the Angels were killing their warriors. Gaveny had shot Ezalia. Valyrie, Harlen. And I'd witnessed Thorn and Ptholenix take out members of their own clans before I found Vale. I hadn't seen any of them amid the foot soldiers since.

You or her. Vale said Valyrie gave Harlen the option. And Gaveny had claimed he didn't want it to be this way. They weren't just taking out their people, they were each targeting one specific warrior.

Why? My jaw ticked over the question as I searched the ground.

"There!" I shouted, pointing to where Malakai fought a pair of gorgons, Mila, Barrett, and Dax with him. Thank the fucking Spirits they all appeared okay, even if the triangular wedge between low storage buildings was strewn with fallen pillars. One entire wall had crumbled, blocking the way back to the plaza at the heart of the city where light flashed animatedly.

Dynaxtar dove, landing in the center of the battle and roaring a column of blue fire that had the gorgons scampering back long enough for Vale and me to dismount. I pulled her after me, not wanting to let go of her hand after what she just went through.

"Cyph!" Malakai called, racing to me as the others backed the gorgons to the edge of the courtyard.

"Are you guys okay?" I asked. "We were all wondering where you'd been." Despite the dust and grime covering him, he seemed in one piece. He'd found weapons at least—a sword, and he still had Lucidius's dagger.

"We're fine." He waved me off, guiding Vale and me into a shadowed corner. "We were still in the capitol building when we heard the first attack. But listen, Cyph, I need to talk to you."

His words were rushed, urgency causing him to fidget. His eyes flicked between me and where Mila was attempting to corner the blonde gorgon, Dynaxtar guarding her back and breathing a ring of that blue fire around the demon. This small pocket boasted no shelter but had solid corners. They'd lured the gorgons here to try to keep them contained and away from commoners and the fighting lines.

"About what?" I asked. A *boom* sounded, not a collision above this time, but somewhere in the city. I focused on Malakai, though.

"When Mila and I snuck off tonight, we ended up in a room with this mural of Artale. And Xenique was handing her—Duck!" He shoved me down, an arrow embedding in the wall above our heads.

"Fucking Spirits," I cursed, casting a glance over my shoulder to find yet another gorgon.

Two men trailed her, both radiating with that same kind of unnatural beauty and grace. Their dark hair was styled pristinely, black jackets and pants cut perfectly to their lean frames. Nearly identical, they marched with easy steps behind the woman in a flowing white gown with the same dark hair and olive skin. And while they appeared otherworldly, they also seemed to blend perfectly into the night, like they were carved from Ambrisk itself.

Moving ahead of Vale, I pulled my scythe, and Malakai took up a spot beside me. Fuck, they caught us with our back to the wall. We couldn't pivot, but at least that meant they couldn't sneak up on us.

Malakai continued, "Xenique was handing her mother a scythe, Cypherion. One that looked an awful lot like yours."

"What?" I tightened my grip on the weapon.

"And then a secret tunnel opened—by the grace of the goddess, I don't know—and the room it led to was full of *weapons records*. But not just any weapons."

"Weapons forged in sacred sources?" I guessed, blocking a second arrow—this one flaming—with the blade of my scythe. The curved metal glinted sharply in the mystlight lanterns hanging overhead.

"Yes," Malakai confirmed as the gorgon raised her bow again.

The men behind her kept their hands in their pockets, amused, hungry smirks on their faces as we dodged two more arrows. "And one specifically that was crafted during Xenique's time within the Gates of Angeldust. It was claimed the Angel herself had it laced with unknown powers and gifted it to a warrior who saved one of her daughter's lives."

"Makes sense. Nothing was more precious to Xenique than her daughters." The entire capital was adorned in portraits and statues of the trio. The three dynastic families that ruled beneath the chancellor and acted as advisors were modeled after them. Some even claimed to be direct descendants.

Another flaming arrow whizzed past, and I sliced my scythe through its path, knocking it off course. The fire extinguished as the head clattered to the ground at my boots, the shaft disappearing.

The same onyx as the one that shot Jezebel back in Valyn gleamed up at me. I exchanged a look with Vale over my shoulder. Her nod said she'd noticed, too.

"The file I found traced the weapon through history," Malakai said, getting us back on track. He ripped a small knife from a vambrace at his wrist and launched it at one of the men behind the gorgon. I did the same from the band of knives across my chest, but they waved them away with a flick of their fingers, steel disappearing into shadow. "It was passed down among that warrior's descendants. His grandson ended up *marrying into* a different dynastic family, and then the weapon was passed among them, sitting in their trove untouched because no one knew what power it held."

More arrows. More knives spiraling through the air from Malakai and me as we backed around the space, the shadows seeming to creep out to us. Vale murmured beneath her breath behind us as she read.

"And one day, a *Mystique Warrior* came along," Malakai said. "He served that family as he was commanded *by his Revered*, ended up on a quest that took many weeks across the continent, and he nearly gave his life to save a member of that dynastic family."

"Mali," I said, "are you saying..."

"I'm saying *that* is where your scythe comes from, Cypherion. It was created by the Angel herself—that's why it has the three markings that signify it's from the highest honors—and it was given to your father." A thunderous crack echoed through the city, almost like the shattering of a giant glass dome. Overhead, Angel-light of seven different colors spiraled high into the sky, colliding into a barrage of sparks.

That couldn't be good.

Malakai finished, eyes still locked on the gorgon, "The names were never mentioned, but the stories line up perfectly. I doubt Riolan ever knew what power it retained. He was just leaving it to his son."

His son. The words shot through me, as right as holding this weapon had always felt.

"The mural even showed it being fed those unknown powers," Malakai added.

"But why the fuck would Xenique create a weapon that could hurt the Angels?" I grunted as I dodged another arrow. The gorgon's quiver was nearly empty now. "This scarred Thorn, remember?"

"Because," Vale answered behind me, arrowheads in her hands, "the Angels had abandoned her. Ophelia learned as much from the sphinx when she was in the Hall of Wandering Souls. Xenique wanted community, companionship. She was *lonely*, and for many centuries, even her closest comrades did not answer her pleas."

So, she created a way to destroy them, and left it among her lineage. Spirits, what unknown magic *did* this thing contain?

Clearly trying not to say too much more about our theories in front of the gorgon, Malakai said, "Remember the murals."

The murals we'd thought Damien may have been pointing to. That led us—among other hints—to try to forge a dagger that could kill a god.

And now...

I tossed the scythe from one hand to another.

Now, I possessed a way to kill Angels. My gaze lifted. Possibly a way to kill *any* creatures of other realms.

I stepped forward as the gorgon put together what we'd realized. Her black hair swished around her as she cast a look over her shoulder at the two men stalking after her. "Children, flee," she commanded.

"I knew it," I muttered.

The demigods obeyed, drifting into the shadows faster than I could track them, simply vanishing. But the gorgon's desire to save them caused her one grave mistake—one fatal second. I swung my scythe back, swiping down across her neck before her eyes even widened fully.

Echnid was right to be wary of this weapon. Perhaps it wasn't the one that could kill him, but it was powerful enough to take out his followers. If you removed the armies building up a corrupt regime, you could topple the entire Spiritsdamned rule itself.

And as the gorgon's head was severed from her body, hair grue-somely mid-shift into serpentine coils, a confident purpose ripped through my muscles. Here I was, a man who'd once been a boy with nothing—not even a strong warrior name—ready to help lead an army against a god.

"I need to go find Mila," Malakai said, rushing toward the alley she and her gorgon had disappeared down. Barrett and Dax were still fighting theirs, her wings out and eyes red.

"Be careful, cousin," I called to Malakai as he left, to which Barrett let out a dramatic scoff and shouted something about how I should love him as a cousin, too.

I actually laughed as Dynaxtar landed loudly between us.

"Okay, Vale," I said, cupping her face in my hands. "I'm needed down here. I have to go find Meridat and ensure any evacu-ations are taken care of, plus apparently I need to try to kill these gorgons, but you go high. Dynaxtar will protect you while you read, and when you have a chance, get any fucking Angel or gorgon close enough to me to take them out."

She nodded, jaw set but pain staunchly darkening her olive eyes. Silver ebbed around the irises. "I'll look for you in the stars, warrior. Don't start losing fights now."

I cracked a smile. "Never, Stargirl."

CHAPTER SEVENTY
TOLEK

ANGELS, OPHELIA AND SAPPHIRE WERE FUCKING magnificent flying over the battle, blasting beams of Angellight down to clear debris. It had crackled with every color, burning through rubble and tumbling down streets like a storm.

I hadn't seen them in a while, though, and I ignored the wave of Spiritsdamned nausea that swept through me at the fact. At the very real possibility that Echnid was waiting beyond the walls.

But while I'd wanted to jump onto Sapphire's back right behind Ophelia and take to the skies so I knew she was okay, I had another job tonight. And I'd raced toward it as fast as my damn legs would go after I said goodbye to Ophelia.

Now, I assessed the monstrous creation before me, wheeled up to the roof of the capitol building a few days ago. Its rusted iron barrel gave it the allure of a weapon that had seen centuries worth of battles. That had taken as many lives in defending its coasts.

I dragged a finger up the body, and power radiated through me at the touch.

Finally. A cannon.

Placing a hand on my sword, I spun to face the Seawatchers behind me. Only a handful had been assigned to this roof, the rest stationed at battlements along the city walls or high lookout points in the tallest buildings.

Ezalia had planned for everything—every point to be

502

covered. Every scenario that could befall us. She'd taken me under her wing to head the cannon operations, as if a part of her had an inkling she may not survive the war Echnid brought our way.

"Is the powder loaded?" I asked the Seawatchers.

There was no need for a fancy speech. These were her most finely trained warriors. They knew what was at stake and had seen their chancellor fall. The only thing they needed to know was my determination matched the steel glint in their eyes, carrying out the mission she died for. So, I kept my voice firm and actions decided. The dagger carved with my sister's initials hung at my waist, giving me strength.

"Enough for a half dozen shots," one broad warrior said. The bow slung across his back was over half the size of my body.

"And how much do we have after that?" I asked.

The man grinned something savage, stepping aside. Entire *crates* were piled behind him, full of the pulverized, magic-imbued rock mined from the Mystique Mountains to fuel the weapons.

"We can go all night, sir." His thick brown beard rippled with his proud exhale.

"Excellent," I said, spinning back toward the weapon and positioning myself behind it. "And what's your name?"

"Seviren, Sir."

"Seviren," I said, as I searched the skies beyond the scope of the roof, trying to ignore the chaos happening in the streets below. "Call me Tolek. We're going to be here a while; we may as well be comfortable."

The Seawatchers manned their posts along the building's edge, Seviren baring closest in case I needed something. Ezalia had spent her final days teaching me the precision of the cannon, instilling her confidence in me to command this post and weave it with the military strategies that had been planned and replanned for weeks in the building below.

And as I stood behind the carriage now, one hand on the lever, the pressure of her reliance inflated my body. It buzzed along my muscles, a sense of accomplishment and capability in every move, tangling with that weird thrum of power my sword had instilled in me. The one that wanted to claw to the surface, unleash on the enemies before us.

The tattoo across my back heated, Lyria's words echoing through my mind. *You already have everything you need.*

Fucking Angels, I did.

My eyes locked on a bolt of lightning-streaked magic rumbling behind a cloud, and the shadow of wings flashed within it. I lined up the shot with the Angel's path and yelled, "FIRE!"

And we launched a cannonball directly at Thorn as he emerged.

The concentrated power exploded toward the Mindshaper, and for a moment, my heart fucking sang. My mind emptied out as if the torture I'd suffered at the hands of his clan was dying with this blast, and that beating energy reared inside me. But Thorn's eyes locked on mine.

At the last moment, he turned so the perfect shot narrowly grazed his wing.

I swore, turning back to the cannon. "Reload!"

The warriors along the building's edge fired a barrage of arrows. A number of them struck true along the foot soldiers, and the warriors fired at anyone that appeared to be fighting the alliance army—though I wasn't sure what that made them—but none touched Thorn. Seviren helped me swing the cannon around, trying to follow the Angel's path.

"Where did he go?" Seviren breathed, wiping sweat from his brow.

Thorn had vanished. Right among his own storm cloud light, he'd been swallowed up by the night.

A buzz hummed through the air, my pulse spiking. And then, lightning struck the roof beneath our feet. It caught the crates of pulverized rock and sent a barrage of cobalt flames igniting around us.

"What's the order?" Seviren yelled. Seawatchers rushed to stamp out the fires in a losing battle.

"GO!" I commanded. Another crate exploded, the heat searing. "Get to the other lookout points and man the borders."

They fled as I swiveled the cannon around, the strain nothing.

I pulled the lever, lining up another shot and preparing to ignite the powder at a moment's notice.

"Where are you, you fucking eternal bastard?" I muttered to myself. Flames burned higher on the roof. I only had minutes before the thing caved in, the bronze adornments melting in the heat of the pulverized magic.

But a cruel, cackling voice dripped down my spine from behind me. "Here."

And magic plunged into my brain with the force of a thousand damn lightning bolts, every tortured emotion that built me roaring to life. The darkness that had consumed me at my sister's death mounted, the buzzing power from the Blackfyre surging it on.

Hastily, I tried to shove every thought and feeling and thing I cherished deep down, locked away where no one could touch them. Where the Mindshaper couldn't taint them.

But he took the rest.

Chapter Seventy-One
Malakai

Mila dove out of the way of a poisoned arrow and my heart fucking crashed around the cage in my chest. Angels, I would fucking *kill* Echnid.

I ripped a blade from my vambrace and threw it at Rozelyn, the white-haired gorgon who'd been my own personal fucking *plague* since Damenal. Like she had a sick fascination in knowing my whereabouts at all times and trying to lure me in. It made my stomach curl.

The tip of the knife dragged across her cheek, leaving a stark red line against her blue-tinged skin, entirely shifted to her demonic form now. I avoided her eyes, dropping to help Mila up.

"Nice throw, Warrior Prince," she said, brushing dirt from her bare hands. We couldn't find any gloves her size or a full set of leathers, so she'd slipped into a pair of tight pants and torn the skirt off her dress, strapping a slightly loose breast plate over her chest.

Alongside the tunic I still wore from Barrett and Dax's ceremony, vambraces and weapon's belt secured over it, it was the best we could muster up.

"Thanks, but now she's bleeding," I pointed out. We'd have to be careful to avoid that. In her fully shifted gorgon form, we'd die from any of that poison making it into our bloodstreams.

Mila nodded grimly, scanning the area for the blonde gorgon who had threatened her. "Where are the others?"

"Barrett and Dax have Salteaire," I said, keeping my attention on Rozelyn. I tracked her steps, hands, anywhere that blood may be dripping from her body without looking at her face. "Cypherion killed another."

We backed down the ally and emerged into an empty square. As long as we kept the gorgons away from the general public we were doing well.

The space was wrecked, a fountain in the center in ruins and shooting water straight into the air, like a blast of power had shattered the stone. Rubble sprinkled the courtyard, rolling beneath my boots, but the buildings rimming the square—apartments by the looks of it—were either empty or the inhabitants knew to hide, thank the fucking Spirits.

"And we're here," a voice answered Mila. And from the shadows of the courtyard stepped those two males, dressed head to toe in black, suit jackets buttoned immaculately and shoes unscuffed.

"*Demigods*," I growled, pulling my sword as Rozelyn emerged with a lethal grin. Children of a god and the demonic challengers to the seraphs. What kind of powers would they hold?

Barrett and Dax charged into the courtyard, herding Salteaire as Mila searched the males. It was clear from her dazed eyes that she was seeing through a veil, using those Reflector powers to identify them. "They were born in this realm. The ones Echnid formed from shadow and fire."

That explained the weapons Cypherion and I threw at them disappearing in midair. Swallowed by shadows. And that sense of ownership in their steps—they were born of the Spirit Volcano, of Ambrisk itself.

Mila added in a murmur, "The gorgons can fall to Ophelia's and Jezebel's powers and Cypherion's scythe, but what are your weaknesses..."

"Rare," one of the fucking creepy demigods stated. His hands rested too casually in his pockets. "And our father will gift us Gallantia after this."

Gallantia? But what about the Angels? They were fucking sending their warriors to ruins, and for what? If Echnid wasn't even going to give them their land back, what was the fucking point?

Perhaps what I'd suspected after finding the papers about Cyph's scythe was right. The Angels had a bigger plan here.

"He can't do that," I challenged.

"He will if we earn it," the other demigod stated with a cruel smile.

"That's why he used the Spirit Volcano," I breathed. "So, they'd have a direct tie to the realm."

"How will you earn it?" Mila spat.

All the demigods did was grin, chilling me to my bones. Before I could ask, lightning flared, and they stepped back, fading into shadows again. This time, Rozelyn and Salteaire went with them, but both flashed Mila lethal smiles before they did—one of pure jealousy and another of unfettered revenge.

"Malakai," Mila said, spinning toward me as her eyes cleared, either oblivious or ignoring the gorgons' expressions. "I have something I need to do. I'll be back, okay?"

I gripped her wrist. "Where are you going?"

"Echnid is using the Spirit Volcano. I think it's time we get our own help from another realm."

She pressed onto her toes and kissed my cheek before I could respond. Then, she was fleeing in the direction the demigods had disappeared in. I tried to run after her, but footsteps pounded down the alley behind me, and the back of my neck prickled.

Spinning, I lifted my sword, but quickly relaxed. "Tolek?"

He halted, his eyes whirling with some frazzled emotion I couldn't quite name. Dax and Barrett prowled the edge of the courtyard, searching behind every open door and in each corner for the threats who'd just slipped away.

Atop one of the buildings rimming the courtyard, a winged figure loomed. I couldn't tell who, but they didn't move. Only watched.

It didn't matter which Angel it was—all of them had betrayed us. Fucking unreliable bastards leaving us for a slaughter centuries in the making. My eyes flicked between the Angel's hovering form and Tolek explaining in an almost detached voice why he wasn't atop the capitol with the cannons.

"Tol," I began, gripping my sword tighter. "Are you okay?"

"Yes," he said, once again his voice slightly off. Void of emotion.

Barrett cast me a wary look as he came closer, but the shadow of an Angel raised a hand. Tolek's raised with it.

And then, Barrett was screaming.

Dax shouted, rushing for him, but the prince dropped to the ground, writhing beneath some beast we couldn't see. Angellight cracked through the clouds, my attention snapping up. The form on the roof illuminated—

Thorn.

He was tormenting Barrett's mind.

Tolek grinned down at the prince, an evil look twisting his expression.

I charged, shoving him back against the wall. "What's happening to him?" I yelled both to Tolek and Thorn.

"No—no!" Barrett screamed, his voice alternating between a ragged whisper and a sharp, bone-shattering shout. "Don't touch him! I just want to help!" Dax crouched over him, but I kept my eyes on Tolek.

But it wasn't Tol—it wasn't my best friend of two decades— who looked back at me as he said, "What all warriors who let their emotions rule them deserve."

Then, Tolek was pushing me back. He and Thorn both raised their hands again, and those invisible bolts of power lashed at me. They zapped Dax, but neither of us went down the way Barrett had.

"Curious," the Angel's voice echoed from the rooftop. "I seem to have found some of those we need. They'll be coming for you." Magic prickled along my skin again, my North Star tattoo heating. "In the meantime, I will take these two."

With a shrug and a beat of his powerful wings, Thorn launched into the air, a mad cackle following him. Tolek casually strolled after the Angel, ignoring the rubble of the courtyard and the sputtering fountain. And Barrett—

Barrett ceased his quaking, rising to his feet. Dull, lifeless eyes looked at us, nothing recognizable in that stare.

And he turned to follow Tolek.

Chapter Seventy-Two
Santorina

There were creatures moving through the shadows. They jumped from patch of darkness to patch of darkness, disappearing and reappearing as if they were made of nothing more than air. Each time they vanished and popped back up behind a warrior, great talons or teeth the length of my hand ripped into their next victim.

"What are they?" I whispered to Lancaster.

I'd stayed with him and Mora because each time I tried to follow a new threat, the damn string in my chest rioted violently. Now, we stood back-to-back in the center of Xenovia's art district, sculptures towering on either side of the wide streets. We kept out of reach of their shadows. I gripped a dagger in each hand, and Lancaster wielded his impossibly large sword.

"Demons of some kind," Lancaster whispered.

I inhaled sharply. "Demons?"

"That's the only word I have for it." Warriors gathered around us in the wide street, all avoiding the edges where awnings drew pools of shadows for the creatures to pounce in. Many of them didn't have weapons on hand when the attack struck, having been painting or drinking in the galleries. Everyone leaned toward Lancaster as he spoke. "They're likely from another realm. I do not know their names, but in Vercuella, we consider beasts that roam in darkness to be demons."

"I do not think that is exactly what we're seeing, brother," Mora chimed in, her voice low but eager. "These do not have the marked characteristics of those. Demons are meant to counter angelic figures—as the gorgons do seraphs—but these seem to be more animalistic. Shadows but not demons."

I tracked the one that prowled the perimeter of the galleries and storefronts that were now locked tight. Demon or not, it was clearly calculating its moves, a predator. Each slow step of its large clawed feet—no. Paws. Those massive paws were precisely placed, agile yet commanding. A long tail swished lazily behind it, dusting the edge of the shadowed circumference, and bright-red eyes studied us.

"It looks a bit like a nemaxese," I breathed. With black sinewy skin instead of fur but the same body shape as the biggest feline on Ambrisk—and paws that looked powerful enough to crack a skull —it was a darker, more malicious version of the creatures that belonged to the God of Mythical Beasts.

Mora exhaled in agreement. "Perhaps they are their brothers in another realm."

Warriors around us muttered, shifting as the creature circled.

"I do not care what they are or where they are from," Lancaster grumbled. "I want them dead."

Without warning, he lunged. The creature released a wild screech, rearing up as Lancaster sprung into the shadows. He brought his sword down on its neck, but the clang reverberated through the night like a blade against a shield.

"What in Aioflyn's—"

"Under its throat!" I called as the weaponless warriors around us took the chance to escape the alley.

This creature wasn't only similar to a nemaxese—it was precisely that. Some relative of it at the very least. And Ophelia had told me of how she'd fought off contaminated felines before. Their flesh was impenetrable with a weapon, but they *did* have a weakness.

The beast swept a claw at Lancaster's leg, but he dodged it. My heart pounded in my throat, that string of a bond between us pulling taut with every inch closer those threatening teeth snapped.

"The throat is impenetrable," Lancaster panted.

"Aim *beneath* its jaw!" My grip tightened on my daggers.

The shadow creature tackled Lancaster, rolling through the dark with him. They vanished, reappearing with a crash behind us. They cracked a window, sending glass shattering and slicing across Lancaster's cheek.

And those sharpened feline teeth snapped, a hair's breadth from Lancaster's neck. Ripping open again, they closed over his shoulder and the beast shook its head.

Lancaster yelled—I yelled—and as they tumbled, fae blood flying, Lancaster fell beneath the beast. That jaw snapped wide, releasing him to aim for his throat, and the hum in my chest became a roar.

He was *mine*.

My mate, my bonded, *mine*.

And no one would make him bleed but me.

Ripping my arm back, I launched a dagger at the beast's back end. It bounced against its armor-like flesh, skittering across the ground, but I was already running. I leapt over its lashing tail, swiping my knife up off the ground as I landed in a squat.

The creature rounded on me, forgetting Lancaster.

I ducked another vicious swipe of its paw, ignoring the fae as he chastised me for rushing into this fight. The shadow beast pressed me back into the wall, and I allowed it, needing to be close to get my dagger beneath its chin.

It snapped its jaw, spit flying and red eyes glowing bright. I was numb to the pounding of my heart, to the way the bond with Lancaster riled in my chest. Jumping into his path seemed to awaken the need to defend him. To claim him as mine.

Because dammit it wasn't only physical, this need for him. The damn arrogant fae had wrapped himself around my soul.

"Bounty!" Lancaster roared as he rushed to heal his wounds, the pure distress in his voice breaking through that numbness in my heart.

"Santorina!" Mora called, but I wasn't fleeing as the beast pressed closer.

I had spent so long feeling weak, not being able to defend myself or those I'd cared about. Until Lancaster came into my life and held that dagger to my neck, I hadn't felt the call to be able to guard myself. He'd woken that instinct within me, and I'd spent months honing it to protect not only myself but also those I loved.

I wouldn't let it fail me now. I wouldn't sit by and let him fight my battles just because I was human.

So, when the beast lunged at me, I didn't shrink away.

I charged right back.

Lancaster screamed in agony. Mora was running now, too.

I met the eyes of my mate and tried to send a message of adoration and gratitude down this bond written by the gods, then I shut it down. Because I didn't want him to feel what came next. Didn't want him to feel the pain as the shadowed nemaxese sank a claw between my ribs.

But I did let him feel the satisfaction as my blade stabbed clean into the underside of its throat.

And right as the beast fell, as my vision blurred against the white-hot slice to my side, and a wave of white mist laced with gold tackled the city, I let him feel the drowning pride.

CHAPTER SEVENTY-THREE
OPHELIA

THE BARRIER ARTALE HAD PUT AROUND XENOVIA ALL those years ago fell like a collision of planets in the sky. Cataclysmic and life-altering, the magic of the Goddess shattered, and Echnid's white mist pummeled the Soulguider capital stronger than any sandstorm.

It stung my eyes and scratched at my skin, purring along my being like a familiar mythical creature itself, whispering *hello* and *goodbye* and *we are here for you* all at once. I clung to Sapphire, cupping my wings around us to fend off the might of the god's magic, and my warrior horse clung to the skies where she belonged.

Magic ravaged the city and the desert with the force of torrential winds. The one place we were supposed to be fortified from this threat. The loss was the twist of a knife in my heart.

But instead of blood, *fury* erupted.

A blast of shimmering gold seraph magic—pure and not streaked with the colors of any Angel—exploded around Sapphire and me. It expanded and compounded, soaring out over the desert, tangling with and devouring Echnid's magic.

I pushed back, back, back, forcing away the mist—the mist that went on for miles into the night.

How long had Echnid been saving this explosion of power? How far did it reach?

My seraph and myth magic tangled among his as I roared and

dug up power from the depths of my soul. Gold cascaded around us, spanning to the furthest reaches, stretching my entire spirit and sense of self until I was wrung out and exhausted.

And through it all, as I panted over the force of the magic, I found the milky eyes of the Warrior God. He stood in the dunes just beyond Xenovia, his white robe and hair billowing around his sturdy frame.

Power ebbed off him. It shoved through my own magic, the two warring in the skies above the desert and washing over the city below. White mist pried at my being, trying to reinstate his influence over me.

My body is my own.

My mind is my own.

He could have no part of me ever again.

As if he heard those declarations, a creeping smiled curled over Echnid's lips. At the sight, I channeled more seraph and myth power to devour his, to stretch beyond the god's reach and swallow it whole, just as it had with Ptholenix's fire.

I am the last seraph, I repeated to myself as magic tugged at my being and sweat rolled along my skin. I was a threat the known gods felt the need to banish, and my power would not be leashed.

A huge *crack* echoed over the desert as I broke through his force, showers of gold sparks and white mists raining to the sand, the latter reeling in the god's magic where it pummeled the city. I panted as Sapphire rose and fell in the sky, whinnying her battle cry.

"Stay true, girl," I gritted out, rage bubbling beneath every word.

And she dove to the dunes, ready to face a god.

As she landed, sand flying up around us, I pulled the Vincienzo dagger from its sheath and held it flat against my thigh. It warmed in my palm, the blade hungry to take a god's life, as I had—Spirits willing—imbued it to do when forging it with the power of all seven Angels.

"Echnid," I said, sitting tall atop Sapphire.

"Ophelia," he greeted, both of our wells of power carving out a space as the barrage slowed. "Have you finally decided to join me?"

I scoffed. "If you truly still believe I will do that, you're more delusional than I thought."

"Delusions and dreams are not that different," he said, hands folded before him, infuriatingly calm as mist rolled off his shoulders.

"Spoken as someone truly in his own world."

"You understand the idea," he purred.

"Is that the plan?" I asked. Sapphire slowly rotated around him as I spoke, moving imperceptibly closer with each step. "To consume Ambrisk once you take out the gods?"

"The plan is to first harness your power because you will be the ultimate asset. Then, I will dispose of my siblings, absorbing their strength in the meantime."

I blanched at the concept of him consuming all of the known gods' power.

"You didn't absorb Moirenna's." No, Moirenna had the Fate-catcher to account for.

Echnid hummed. "All of that will be remedied in time."

Vale flashed through my mind, and a defensive instinct roared up. He would not lay a hand on any member of my family.

"And what?" I spat. "You command Ambrisk, then? You allow your Angels and gorgons free reign over the realm?" He'd mentioned once he wanted to open bridges, to restore the truths that have been lost to this realm and attend to *others*. But he'd been drugging me at the time, and those days all blurred together.

"Ambrisk is the Balance Realm, Ophelia. It is the heart of magic of every realm. He who controls Ambrisk, controls all."

"So, this all goes back to control, then? Control and revenge?" The oldest motives known to warrior kind. To command that which does not belong to you, to outlaw all those who would speak against you. It was a violation of the very nature of Balance we were woven by.

And yet, the ego of a god saw it as earned. He could not *earn* our respect in title alone, though.

How sad must that have been, to spend your entire existence thinking your legacy expounded that of others, simply by nature? To think you knew better, enough to force them to bow to you?

Sapphire was closer now, Echnid turning slow circles around himself to watch us. A satisfied smile played along his lips.

"First, it will be revenge against my siblings. Then, against all others. Pantheons that have built their own empires. Those who have kept us out. I will open the locked bridges, let my children rule Ambrisk as they wish, and I will conquer other paths."

My blood chilled. "How did you do it? Break down Artale's barrier?"

"On the whim of sacrifice, Ophelia." Cruelty radiated from that proud smile and the straight set of his shoulders. "The Goddess of Death wove her magic against me with the blood of her own daughter, and the warriors beneath her. One significant offering from each Angel was all it took to unravel an enchantment so densely cast."

I have to find my sacrifice, Damien had claimed. Gaveny and Ezalia. Spirits, my gut sank as I understood they were offering us up, blood drawn at their own hands, the loss that would impact each clan.

I shouldn't have been surprised, yet my stomach turned with the truth. "Why make the Angels offer such a thing when they are loyal to you?"

The mist thickened the closer Sapphire and I got. And in it, I saw something I recognized: Betrayal.

"It's a punishment," I choked out. "You were never going to give this land back to the Angels, were you?"

Echnid nodded in approval. "They failed once. They do not get a second chance."

I'd assumed that had been the deal. The Angels help Echnid enact his revenge, they return to their strength on Gallantia. But if Echnid was to be believed, he never planned to give warrior land back to them.

That was why he needed the demigods as generals and wanted me to raise seraphs as his guardians. So, when he did away with the Angels, he would not be standing alone.

Then what were the Angels doing supporting and empowering him?

If this was only the god's steppingstone, I feared for all the realms. He'd send this one to ruin in his wars. Like the cleansing of a Firebird, it would be no more than ash.

"Those Angels have been loyal to you," I growled, and fucking Spirits, I couldn't believe I was defending them. But we were the same, if on different ends of the line. They were used by Echnid as I was used by them. "They are fighting and killing for you right now."

Sapphire was so close, Echnid's power pressed on me. Swarmed me, like I was caught beneath a wave and being tumbled around.

My body is my own.

My mind is my own.

"They are attempting to redeem themselves," Echnid said. "They deserve to struggle."

I tightened my grip on the Vincienzo dagger.

"No," I gritted out over my fury. "No one deserves what is being done tonight." I paused, tilting my head in mock consideration. Sapphire stilled as I tapped my finger three times along her back. "Except you, I suppose."

And my pegasus reared up, her hoof striking sharply against Echnid's skull. I swung to the side and plunged the dagger into his neck.

Gold magic rippled off the weapon, through his flesh, and he hissed in pain. I twisted the dagger, pouring more seraph power into the blade, imbuing it with the pure ether of every Angel, so much stronger than I'd ever imagined.

I sent all seven threads into the god, attempting to shred his very heart and self.

And then, I ripped the dagger out just as viciously.

Sapphire took to the air, looping around, and I watched Echnid with bated breath, searching for the satisfaction of a god withering, dying.

But—

No.

The wound was sealing over as if my magic and the power of an imbued blade meant *nothing*.

Echnid gave us a malicious smile. "You thought that was all it would take?" He laughed. "You thought you could kill a god so easily?"

And I truly felt like a fool because I had. Or at the very least, I'd hoped it would be enough. That I'd been given these seraph powers for a purpose some other god or Angel or Fate was aware of, even if I was still figuring it out.

Gods *could* die. I'd seen it happen only weeks ago. Seen this vengeful Warrior God slay his own sister...but what had sealed it?

The desert flashed through my memory as I picked it apart. My magic launched a dagger through the air, and Echnid siphoned it into himself, compressing gold and silver—

Silver.

Silver bolts had shot through that condensed magic, too. Jezebel had been trying to assist me, but her myth magic...

One to raise myths, one to hold their leashes.

I looked down at the dagger in my palm, at the blade sharpened to a lethal point, humming with life.

It wasn't only life we needed. Not the power of a seraph or the Angels after all.

Tightening my knees around Sapphire, I sent out one mighty wave of Angellight against Echnid, using all the power of Angels within me to light up the god's magic and burn straight through its haze. Then, my pegasus took off into the night, speeding toward the stars as Echnid roared in fury.

And I prayed to any deity listening that this theory was right. Because I may be the last seraph, balancing the powers of all seven Angels in one being, but I was only *half* of one myth.

I needed my balance.

I needed my sister.

CHAPTER SEVENTY-FOUR
OPHELIA

I HAD TO ALLOW ECHNID TO GET CLOSER TO XENOVIA AS I found Jezebel, but Spirits, it felt so fucking wrong as he crossed through the city gates while I circled above. Like I was handing over the keys to everything I held most precious. And all those innocent warriors...I was supposed to protect them, and I was letting in the enemy.

It was for a good reason, I told myself. Because if I was right, Jezebel and I could truly end him. Together.

"Ophelia?" Jez and Zanox sped to a stop beside me in the skies. "What's happening? Are you hurt?"

"No," I told her, despite the very clear gash still open in my wing. "I need your help."

"What?" Her gaze flashed between me and the Warrior God marching through the gates below.

"Jez, remember when Echnid killed Moirenna? He seemed to absorb my power."

"Yeah, he siphoned it off—"

"Malakai, Tolek, and Cypherion thought Damien was trying to tell me to imbue a weapon with seraph magic. They thought *that* is what Echnid was afraid of because it's the might of all seven Angels and hasn't been seen on Ambrisk before—why he wants me."

"Because the power of seven Angels combined can overcome

the god," she said, her hair whipping in the wind as Zanox beat his scaled wings.

"It can't, though," I explained. "I just stabbed Echnid with the Vincienzo dagger, and…" I gestured to the city below, and her face paled when she saw him walking among the ruin, bleeding warriors at his feet. "I think it's the myth magic, Jez, not the seraph power. That's what we need to imbue the blade with. Echnid took *both* of our power that day in that desert. Yours was chasing mine, remember?"

"But how? Your magic gives life, and mine can't kill a god. Even together, they can't do that."

"Think about it, though. We keep asking why," I reminded her. "Why now, why us? The gods, the Fates, the Angels—whoever reincarnated the myth of the warrior sisters in us knew it would be needed *now*."

To balance each other—to balance the entire realm—we had to try.

Echnid was now strolling through the city. His cerberus had joined him, his mist pouring around him and making it look like he was floating across the rubble. They passed warriors battling feline-like creatures without care.

I turned back to Jezebel. "We have to be quick."

"Okay," she rushed out. "Of course. What do we do?"

And the way she accepted it so easily had me taking a breath. My sister was unflinching, even when she was scared. Facing every problem head on because it was the way through the challenge.

She'd been dealt a power that would cripple older warriors, but Jezebel had grown up with it. Her spirit speaking and death magic were part of her. Though the strength frightened her at times, it was as natural as breathing. And now, as we called on that power for a feat neither of us imagined, she did so without quaking.

"I'm going to toss the dagger up—get it far enough away from both of us—then, we shoot. Don't relent until I say so."

Jezebel nodded, and I met her eyes, letting the battle below fall away. We had to trust everyone else to defend the city now, hope the Angels foresaw Echnid's betrayal and that they may grant us one act of grace in exchange for their cruelty.

The Vincienzo dagger was cool against my palm, humming slightly like it was excited to accept such powerful magic. With a breath, I threw it as high in the air as I could manage, watching the legacy of Tolek's family flip end over blade.

When it reached its peak, I shouted, "*Now!*"

And gold and silver erupted, colliding in the night sky with enough force to rattle Xenovia below. Light flashed, cracking and searing. I squeezed my eyes closed against it as I poured forth all the life-giving myth magic I could muster, and when I opened them—

"Holy fucking Spirits," I breathed.

"What's happening?" Jezebel called, her voice pure steel.

"I don't know," I shouted as magic crackled against my skin. "Keep going!"

We were on a familiar murky plane, our pegasus and khrysaor still beating their wings as if entirely unfazed. It was like the first time we'd traveled to that bridge, after I'd ingested the power from Kakias during the final battle of the war and our myth magic had fully manifested.

Only this time...

This time, it didn't seem like one bridge.

No, under the clashing powers of gold and silver lights was a giant intersection of them. At least five spanned off into the universe. At this end, Ambrisk upheld the beating heart of all magic. The Balance Realm. But at the others...Winged creatures among endless cliffs and weeping stars in eternal slumber. Towering, glass-made buildings and crumbling statues that reached to mountainous heights. Fiery realms shrouded in stone, forms locked behind glimmering iron bars, and shadows that spiraled higher than the heavens.

I couldn't keep them straight. Not as my magic twined and snapped with Jezebel's, the air around us cracking with silver and gold lightning. Not as they flooded the entire junction, and Ambrisk's strength pulsed incessantly at our backs, a heart of magic begging to break free, to seep through these veins into other worlds.

This. This was what Echnid wanted. What he was going to open. All of these bridges to other realms, powers mingling and raising curious heads. And Ambrisk was fighting to open that gate. Her magic pushed against my skin, trying to shatter the bars of isolation our realm had been trapped in for so long.

The mountains across the bridges quaked. The stars blinked rapidly as the edges of windows to other realms started to curl and wither.

And I could see what would happen if the veil was permanently peeled back. The worlds would crumble. That was the might of the Balance Realm. Why it was locked.

If given free reign, the magic of Ambrisk would *devour* the realms.

Echnid couldn't be allowed to do that.

Jezebel and I continued to flood mythos power into the Vincienzo dagger, and I gritted my teeth against the fear of realms falling. It fueled my steel will. My vendetta against Echnid no longer only my own.

"I'm running low," Jezebel panted, her hair whipping across her face in the roaring wind tunnel of the bridges.

"When I say *now*, we let go, okay?"

Jez nodded, lips pressed tight and profile bathed in silver as she held on for these final seconds. As we gave everything we could over to this blade that was our last hope in slaying a god.

And with the final burst of magic, a crippling wave of gratitude shuddered over me with the torrent of gold and silver light burning in the sky.

I met my sister's eye. "I love you, Jezzie!" I shouted, voice lost among the roar of magic.

Beyond words, I loved her.

From the moment the false Curse appeared on me, Jezebel had stood by my side. She'd pushed me when I was most stubborn, shook me awake when I was fading beneath my own sadness, and suffered losses, hand-in-hand by my side. We may have been the warrior sisters born of myth, a legacy returning to Ambrisk when they were needed most, reincarnated between lifetimes, but strip away all those legends, and I was simply grateful for *her*.

She mouthed, *I love you, too*.

And then, I shouted, "Now!"

Our magic whirled through the air, snapping back to our bodies with the force of a hurricane as the desert rematerialized below. Gold flooded the air around me, and I pressed up on Sapphire, reaching for the Vincienzo dagger as it fell.

And as my fingers latched around the handle and I landed back atop my pegasus, the ravenous power ebbing up the blade thrummed through my blood, ready to end a god.

Chapter Seventy-Five
Tolek

There was power within me. In every step I took, in every look I cast at a passing warrior fleeing the city or charging into battle with such an innocuous fury that didn't make sense with the calm in my mind.

Calm and emptiness. No pain, though deep, deep down it was there, lifting its head with stifled aggravation. And bolts of vibrant light kept knocking on that door.

They were all fools to run. Didn't they understand they'd lost? By letting things like love command their actions, defend their hearts, they'd built their own pyres. By relying on anything other than themselves and the vast ether of Ambrisk, they'd opened the gates.

The power stemming through me reached out to the most vulnerable around me. The ones who were built of the most fallible instincts. The prince was useful, too—someone with influence. Someone who would deliver both territory and soldiers. Minds to feed on. Those who gave into something as feeble as *love*.

And the touch of darkness within this mind made it so much easier.

I turned down a street packed with warriors battling Echnid's demons, a demigod at the head of it. Those despicable creatures were not right for this realm. They'd be gone when we were done. When only the Angels remained to extend their rule and become the gods they always should have been, and they could finally uncover secrets long lost to seal revenge. A cackle split through me at the thought.

Tendrils of magic flickered across the ground like living lightning bolts. And one by one, the weakest of warriors clutched their heads.

They sank to the ground, curling over their knees. Screams wrenched from their throats. Thoughts pounded against their inner minds. All the worst fears they'd ever had brought to life.

A flash of gold light poured across the skies—a blast rivaling any I'd ever seen.

Familiar. Warm and good. My chest went wild as memories stuffed deep down flooded upward.

Another flash of gold, and I was hungry. Driven and insatiable. I wanted it.

I shoved those instincts down until I was calm and empty once again.

Light exploded, shimmering like...like something I couldn't recall but something that could right every wrong, heal every bruise I'd suffered. I turned toward it as the warriors writhed on the city street. A blur of white and blue shot across the night, that pure gold in its wake.

This time, I didn't just want it. I needed it. Something twisted in my chest, clawing up from the depths of my being.

That place all feelings were locked away shook, bolts of gold light hammering against it.

And turning toward the light, I went after it, ready to unleash this power thrumming through me on it. Until it was mine.

Chapter Seventy-Six
Santorina

"Bounty!" Lancaster gingerly wiped hair from my face.

I was in his arms. How had I gotten here? How long had it been? The sky above swam, the stars hazy, whether due to smoke from Xenovia or the blood loss from my wound, I couldn't tell. I didn't care.

His body was warm, his arms holding me firmly as he applied pressure to my wound. Pressure was good. Pressure stopped bleeding.

If I hadn't lost too much already. Which was entirely possible.

"How...is...the wound?" I choked out. I was certain the battle was still raging somewhere, but I couldn't separate the dull hums of noise.

"It's deep," he gritted out. Lancaster's shadow shifted across me as he bent closer, his healing magic a numbing tingle along my side.

"Did...you...disinfect?" I studied the dirt and blood smeared across his cheeks to give me something to focus on. The slice to his face was healed, his high cheekbones and firm jawline dusted with drops of crimson, like tears.

And the look in his eyes—it was the same crazed concern as when he'd killed the gorgon for me. As if he'd already known then that I'd belonged to him, and that stare meant ownership. Possession.

Lancaster huffed, the sweaty strands of hair framing his face lifting with the exhale. "That's what you're asking? If I'm healing it properly?"

"Never know...with your"—I hissed as fire flared along my ribs, biting sharply through the numbness—"immortality."

"I assure you, I can handle it."

A feline screech and a shattering of glass echoed from somewhere nearby.

"Lancaster." That wasn't Mora. I turned my head as much as I could manage. Long dark hair, innocent round eyes, and pale features swam into vision. Celissia. When had she arrived? She was discussing something with Lancaster, their harsh words washing together as I tried to focus.

"I cannot move her," Lancaster spat, his cheeks flushing with the rage in his voice.

"This entire alley is going to be in shadow soon," Celissia pointed out. She still wore her gown from the bonding ceremony, but huge gashes ripped through the skirt. She gripped the talisman hanging around her neck, the stone giving off a rainbow aura in the hazy mystlights.

"The wound is taking longer than usual because she's a Bounty," Lancaster said, fierce protection sharpening every word. "If I move her, I'll undo whatever good has been done. She could bleed out before we get somewhere safe."

"That sounds unpleasant." I exhaled, rolling my head against his chest where it was warm and comforting.

"Santorina," Lancaster whispered, turning his attention down to me. Something soft brushed against my cheek. "Keep your eyes on me."

But I'm so tired.

"I know, Bounty," he whispered. I hadn't realized I'd spoken aloud. "I know you're tired, but we need to close the wound first."

Right. Falling asleep now would not be wise. I was smarter and stronger than that. I pried my eyes open, meeting his endless ones, trying to ignore the worry deepening them.

"Good girl," Lancaster said, pressing a soft kiss to my lips that made the string in my chest hum. His breath caught as if he felt it, too.

"She isn't safe here," Celissia repeated as if that exchange hadn't occurred. I tipped my gaze over Lancaster's shoulder, counting the wind chimes framing the nearest gallery's door. Shaped like small doves, they pinged together with every gentle breeze and thunderous roar.

The fact of my safety had Lancaster stiffening. His eyes burned into me as he asked Celissia, "What do you want me to do? Your sorcia healing isn't speeding it up either."

But Mora answered, "You know there is one more option."

"No," Lancaster growled, that demanding, arrogant tone I'd heard so often.

"It is a good option," Mora pushed as she approached, blocking the wind chimes from view. "She already—"

"*No*," Lancaster repeated.

"What is it?" I slurred as Mora's features came into focus. Huge swipes of blood painted the front of her leathers. She must've disposed of the shadow beast.

The female assessed me, her full lips thinning before she said, "He can claim you."

Claiming. Where had I heard that before?

Every time your damn scent wrapped around me, I almost snapped. Claimed you.

Earlier tonight, Lancaster had said he'd almost done it numerous times, but I'd been too lost to pleasure and denial to ask what it meant.

"I won't do it," Lancaster swore, and my heart splintered.

"Because," I hissed on an inhale, "I'm human?"

Lancaster's eyes swam with grief as he took me in, his palm cupping my cheek. "Because I do not deserve to claim you, and it is not a choice you can make in this moment."

"Explain" was the only word I could force out.

"This is wasting time—"

"Claiming is when an *aequelis* bond is fully sealed," Mora interrupted, and Celissia gasped, clearly recognizing the Goddess-given bond for what it meant. "It means you become each other's in every way, more so than you are even now. In theory, claiming is not necessary. This bond is real and active no matter what."

I wheezed a laugh. I'd denied the bond to Lancaster's face, but when I saw that beast lunging for his throat...

Mora continued, "Claiming solidifies. And you have each saved the other from mortal danger, which sets the process in motion."

When Lancaster saved me from the gorgon, he'd begun it. He'd been so different after that, closer. Was that why? He'd felt the claiming ignite. And I had saved him tonight, unknowingly answering that call.

"Claiming has added benefits that my *stubborn brother* is refusing to see."

Lancaster's hand flinched against my side. He was still pouring healing magic into me, but my Bounty blood rejected it too rapidly. The tingling sensation faded compared to the fire of the wound's rough edges.

"Benefits?" I asked. The sky was getting darker. Their forms wavering.

"His magic would work much faster on you than on anyone. You may even adopt some of the properties over time."

"I would absorb his magic?" I would no longer be human. Not just a Bounty with an instinct to hunt fae, but I would truly have power.

And I wasn't sure how I felt about that.

"She's uncertain," Lancaster argued, reading those emotions straight through our open bond. "We are not doing it."

"It will also link your lives," Mora added. "Your lifespan, your magic, your bargains. All would be tethered."

"It would chain you to a fate you never wanted or chose," Lancaster added, and it was clear in the tightness of his voice that he was replaying all of my rejections from earlier.

"It would save her life," Mora challenged.

The siblings continued to bicker, but the pain in my side shifted beyond fire. It was icy numbness. My entire body was. The air no longer felt warm or cool, it just brushed against my skin. I was slipping away.

And the humming string in my chest was growing quieter, a dim melody that hadn't even gotten its chance to flourish.

I should have been upset that this claiming had been set in motion without my knowing—that I had confirmed it unintentionally, without all the facts. But isn't that what made it so worthy? That I'd saved Lancaster out of pure desire to—out of my own form of claiming—without knowing about the Goddess's magic?

In that act alone, I'd given myself the only answer I truly needed, right as death reached for me.

These weeks, I'd been growing closer to Lancaster, though I denied it. And right when I finally gave in, it was being taken? From both of us?

And Lancaster...he had suffered so much pain in his long life. From the loss of his mother to being at the queen's beck and call. I wouldn't take another thing from him if I had a choice.

A choice that really was no choice at all but a gift of fate.

Maybe I would have to sacrifice some small pieces of my human self in order to claim and be claimed by this fae. It would not take my heart, nor would it take my strength or my kindness. It wouldn't change who I was down to my soul.

"I want it," I choked out.

Lancaster's attention snapped down to me. "Bounty—"

"No," I wheezed. "You are not forcing this on me. I choose it. I choose to live with you. I *claim* you, Hunter. For as long as the Goddess blesses us."

Which I prayed would be years beyond this night.

His eyes flicked between mine, a lock of thick brown hair falling into them, and I forced myself to hang on to reality, to not let my eyes slip closed again despite the darkness pulling at me. To not let myself shiver at the roars of battle pounding among the city or the mist pressing through the alleys.

"You're certain?" Lancaster asked after a long minute.

I nodded, grimacing.

His eyes narrowed shrewdly. "You fought it earlier."

"I lied," I wheezed, and despite the state of my voice, he *almost* smiled at my confession. "What do I do?"

"You have to drink my blood," Lancaster stated baldly, as if he was hoping that would change my mind about giving up this piece of myself to him.

It did make the pain in my side disappear for a moment. "What?"

"Many fae customs and magical rituals are derived from our ancestors who thrived on blood," Mora chirped. "It is why our magic is tied so deeply to the life source."

"Okay," I said, truly not caring how inhumane the custom would have sounded at another time. I wanted to claim Lancaster, and if this was how it must be done, I would do it.

Something pinched in my chest, and I realized it was Lancaster's internal war with this decision. My limbs were heavy, but I stretched up, brushing the back of my fingers across his cheek.

"I claim you, Hunter," I repeated.

He swallowed, the column of his sturdy throat wavering so fearfully. "I didn't want you to have to do it like this." Not when I was bleeding out, not when there was no other choice.

"And that is precisely why I am." Because Lancaster had goodness within him, despite my initial thoughts. He would kill anyone for harming me and still give me the choice to control my own future. And I was.

Nodding, Lancaster shifted so he held me with one arm. He lifted his other wrist to his mouth and sliced into the vein with a sharpened canine. Then, slowly, as if giving me time to back out, he pressed that incision to my lips.

Warmth flowed across my tongue, sweet and musky and heady. It was the richest wine, drowning me in pure pleasure as it flooded into my bloodstream. I moaned against his wrist, and a growl rumbled in Lancaster's chest at the sound. My eyes locked to his, nothing but the blackest fire looking back at me.

As his blood melded with mine and I claimed him, ecstasy shot through my body. If we hadn't been in the middle of a battle of the gods, I would have claimed him in every way possible.

Lancaster bowed against me, his scent awakening a curling instinct below my belly. His pupils were blown wide, and his fingers curled into my hair, gripping my jaw forcefully. That touchpoint became the center of all the realms.

I drank until my limbs were strong again, until my heartbeat pounded a steady, healthy rhythm and the string in my chest was thrumming louder than ever. Until Lancaster was able to easily heal the wound in my side and it was nothing more than a scar that looked days old.

Then, Lancaster pulled his arm from my grip and brushed a thumb across the corner of my mouth, wiping away a lingering bead. My eyes locked on the wet outline of crimson lips against his wrist. A bloody kiss that sealed our fate.

Chapter Seventy-Seven
Cypherion

I charged through the barrage of mist with a small but strong Soulguider and Mystique ensemble.

Meridat led her soldiers beside me, the chancellor looking formidable as any warrior with bronze-plated armor adorning her body and a scythe in hand. Blood dripped steadily from a nasty hit she'd taken to the head when Echnid's magic forced through our last barrier, a storm of wooden planks and blocks exploding, but her stare was focused and steps pounding steadily against tile floors as she led us through an abandoned building, offering a reprieve from the magic. With wide corridors draped in various sigils of bronze and deep amethyst and rooms of desks on either side, it was a safe bet this was one of the boarding academies.

"We need to open a path through the eastern gate," she shouted to me as we tore around another corner and into a grand hall lined with three long dining tables. "The slums border that end of the city. They'll be the most defenseless and the least likely to evacuate on their own."

Fuck, they wouldn't even have proper weaponry in that part of Xenovia, and there weren't many easy paths to flee.

The chancellor exploded out the back door of the dining hall, flying across the academy's stone garden.

"How far are we?" I scanned around every turn for any hint of a gorgon, demigod, or Angel.

"It's over the next bridge. The Spirit River through this part of the city marks the boundary."

As she explained, the bronze pillars framing the bridge came into view, each topped with a carving of a sphinx, wings flung wide and jaw snapping open. Where were the damn mythological creatures now?

We tore across the bridge, the feet of a dozen warriors pounding and the Spirit River thrashing gray and murky below. As we raced into the slums to a chorus of pained cries, I cast a final glance back at the churning water, and the knowledge that spirits whirled within—that more were sinking into those depths to find their way to the Spirit Realm—was ice through my veins.

Meridat shouted orders to her citizens as we cut up and down alleys, helping the injured to stand and flee or knocking on doors. Some called back that they were staying to guide the dead home, others eagerly took our help. We only had minutes though, and my throat fucking tightened with every one we spent here. With every person who did not want to abandon their home or clung to the few belongings they had.

I passed an abandon textile shop, freezing at the mystlight that flickered through the small windows into the basement.

"Fucking Spirits," I growled, charging inside and crashing down the stairs.

"You all need to evacuate!" I called to the maybe two dozen warriors who came into view as my eyes adjusted to the dim light. Storage shelves lined the walls, their sparse contents tipped over and unfolded along the floor. "We need to get you beyond the city bounds."

"This is our home!" a man called from the corner. I couldn't even see his face.

The building shook, Echnid's power battering it from the outside. Children cowered against their parents and grandparents. Spirits, it was an unstable structure. Footsteps pounded the streets above as my warriors and the Soulguider soldiers brought more and more citizens to the eastern gate.

"We will defend your city," I swore. "We won't let it fall to the

Warrior God, but we need to get you all to safety first if you're unable to fight or guide the dead."

"The Angels are fighting against us, though," the first man called. "I saw Xenique—she killed a Soulguider apprentice before my own eyes."

My heart stopped at that. *Erista?*

No. It couldn't be. I swore to myself it wasn't as I racked my mind for a way to convince these people. Unfortunately, they wouldn't listen to logic. Their hearts and legacies were entwined with these buildings.

Legacies. The word rang through me.

I had one chance.

Swinging my scythe from my back, I said, "This weapon is of your people." Many of the group shifted, leaning closer to view the weapon better. "It was blessed by a sacred source in this very capital many centuries ago. It was passed down my family line, left to me by my father."

I rotated the weapon, the blade catching the dimmest drop of mystlight and shining pristinely. As powerful as I felt wielding it, the steel was capable of so much more than the average blade.

"I bear this weapon to defend myself, yes, and the people I love —the family who is out there fighting this very battle right now. But I also do so because this scythe was *meant* to be mine. It passed fairly into my hands as an honor from your people, and I carry it with pride." Silent awe met me, the room buzzing. "I hope to do so through the night, but I refuse to leave you all behind."

Hesitant murmurs echoed my words, my pounding heart scratching against my chest. Then, a small child, no more than eight, marched over to me. She extended her hand, looking up without a hint of concern. So damn confident.

I slipped my fingers around hers and assessed the rest of the room, raising my brows as if to say, *You're going to let a child be the bravest of you?*

They were on their feet in a heartbeat, and with my blood pumping faster, I stepped aside to let them race up the steps. We emerged onto the street as the building swayed again.

"Get to the east gate!" I roared.

I waited for them all to get out the front door then did another sweep. Only when I was sure the building was empty did I run.

The east gate wasn't far. The exit was burrowed between a bend in the river and the high wall surrounding the city. But when I reached it my heart sank.

"What the fuck happened?" I screamed.

Meridat was there with a horde of warriors. "Most have gotten out, but the arch collapsed."

The entire exit—the only one we could reach without taking the Soulguiders across the river and into the heart of the battle—was gone.

"We have to get back," I said anyway, searching for some outlet. "Back to your manor. They can hide there until this is over."

"We won't make it," someone said. It was the same man who spoke in the basement. The one I hadn't been able to see before. Now, his wrinkled expression came into view. Tarnished earrings adorned either ear, and a light cloak fell off his shoulders. His expression was stony. Proud. "We will defend our home from here."

Before I could answer, a winged figure dropped to the ground beside us. Many screamed, stumbling back in shock. I spun with my scythe raised to meet Xenique, and she gave the weapon an affectionate smile.

The Angel raised a hand, amethyst Angellight rippling in her palm. I braced for impact, but she shot it at the arch, blasting straight through the debris.

Meridat and I gaped at Xenique for a moment, but the Angel gave a pointed look at the now-cleared escape, and we jumped into action, herding warriors through the exit.

"Sorry about that," Xenique whispered to Meridat. "I had to ensure you did not get out before I found him."

I stiffened as Meridat asked, "Him?"

Xenique inclined her head to me. The chancellor cast me a wary glance, but I told her to go.

She turned to escort warriors out, stopping at the last moment. "Thank you, Cypherion."

"For?" I asked.

"For fighting for the weakest of my people. The ones with the biggest hearts. You're a good ally." She gave me a look that promised she'd be back to battle beside us, and she left, shouting to her Soulguiders to move quickly into the desert.

When they were gone, I raised a brow at Xenique. "You're helping us?"

The Angel watched my scythe.

"When I made it, I hoped it might see this battle one day," she said, and chills broke across my skin. "I never knew it would fall to the hands of a Mystique, though." The demigoddess held out a hand. "May I see it?"

I gripped the weapon tighter. Xenique waited, eyes burrowing into me.

"Why?" I asked.

The Prime Soulguider's expression softened, promise deepening her words. "Because it is a key. One that unlocks a way to end this."

My stare flicked between her and the exit she'd just cleared— the lives she'd just saved, and the hope that ebbed through that sentence. Spirits, we *needed* to end this.

"Is it for Echnid?" I checked.

"He believes it is."

She didn't offer any more explanation, but reluctantly, I handed my weapon to her. My fists clenched and unclenched at my sides as I waited.

"This will be over soon." She said it like a vow as she studied the weapon she'd forged so long ago.

"How?" I asked.

"My mother will see to it."

"Your mother?" The Goddess of Fucking Death? Perhaps I made the wrong decision handing her my scythe.

Xenique didn't answer. Her eyes closed, muttered words slipping between her barely parted lips and hands locked tight around my weapon. Overhead, dark clouds churned.

The Angel's wings beat gently, a soft wind stirring up at her feet, amethyst ether spinning faster. One hand extended skyward, my scythe clenched in her fist, as if offering it up.

And from the darkest, most dense part of the night sky, a storm erupted.

Purple lightning cracked through black clouds. In the heart, shadows of humanoid forms seemed to shimmer, illuminating with each violet streak.

A bolt shot down, striking the curved blade of my scythe, and I stumbled back, squinting against the sheen. The lightning didn't disappear with a single zap—it locked on to the weapon. Power fed along that connection, humming back and forth from storm to scythe.

The whole alley was bathed in a purple glow. Xenique's features were carved with it, like the statues in her likeness now littering the city.

Above, the clouds tumbled quicker as if reeling something up from my blade.

Then, with an ear-splitting crack and a blinding flare, the connection with the lightning extinguished.

"Excuse me." Xenique extended my scythe like nothing had happened. I jolted, taking it back, and the Angel added, "I have somewhere I need to be."

Chapter Seventy-Eight
Ophelia

Zanox roared, blue fire pouring from his jaw as we broke through the clouds. Sapphire's entire body emitted a gold glow that roiled in time to my pounding heart. These newly unleashed powers of theirs burned brighter than ever.

And that only made me certain. We *had* to be right. The myth was brought back now for this reason.

"Get to the perimeter," I yelled as Sapphire wheeled around toward the city. "See if that fire can burn through the gorgons and demigods."

Jezebel nodded, leaning lower over her mount. Just before they flew off, she said, "Be careful."

"I promise," I swore.

Then, we split. And I prayed to the Spirits I would see my little sister when the sun rose.

As Sapphire dove back into Xenovia, I didn't let myself worry for my friends or Tolek. Didn't let myself fear where they might be —whom or what they might be fighting. There was no room for that fear to seep into my actions.

There was only room for the fury and valor pumping through my blood, the instincts that would sing as Echnid fell to a myth-woven blade and the realms were freed from a tyrant's grasp.

When she landed, I slipped from my pegasus's back, needing to maneuver through the narrow streets much more nimbly than her wings would allow. As my boots hit Ambrisk's earth, a sense of rightness rang through me. Before I ran, though, I turned to my warrior horse and pressed my forehead to hers.

"I love you so much, girl," I whispered, brushing a hand down her cheek. "Thank you for everything."

She nickered softly, and then, Sapphire was in the air once again. And I was gone. Sprinting through the tangled streets of the desert capitol, leaping over fallen beams and rubble, heading toward the city center where I'd seen Echnid from above.

My boots skidded over sand as I turned a sharp corner, nearly sliding out from under me. I pressed my hands to the ground to catch myself, shooting up before I even noticed the stinging scrapes on my palms. I willed Angellight into them to staunch any bleeding, not stopping my breakneck stride.

Warriors raced around me. Some—weaponless—heading toward the perimeter of the city. A few—with swords and scythes and axes at the ready, steel determination in their eyes—in the direction I headed. Starsearchers shouted readings to their comrades, and Soulguiders and Bodymelders raced to assist the fallen.

Leaping over a toppled, cracked bronze bust of one of Xenique's three daughters, I emerged into the square that had been packed with reveling warriors at the bonding ceremony just hours ago, and I halted.

It was a massacre now.

A battlefield that was never meant to be, shining sculptures painted red and stone crumbling from buildings, dug up from walkways. The Spirit River that wound through the desert city churned maroon with blood beyond the capitol building.

And Echnid stood in the center of it all, on top of the dais leading to the enormous statue of Xenique that marked the city center, behind rows of warriors.

Hundreds, from every clan, dressed in all manners of garments and baring an array of weapons, stood with their backs to the god and their eyes trained on me. Eyes that swirled with a distant, unnatural vision.

Deep purple lightning crackled through the sky, the power sending my heart rioting and magic tugging at my skin.

"What have you done?" I yelled over the heads of the warriors. Their stillness breathed a haunting chill down my spine.

"You seem to think you can end my rule, Ophelia Alabath, but you will be a grand part of it. And these subjects"—the god raised a hand, his mist so dense around it—"have joined us."

The ranks parted, and from within, the woman who stabbed my wing emerged, bangles of fire wreathing her wrists. The demigoddess, daughter of a god and a gorgon. On either side of her stood a male, all three dressed in the same stark onyx, all pristinely polished.

But I couldn't even begin to question them because from behind the demigods stepped two familiar forms that stopped my heart.

Tolek and Barrett, unrecognizable masks of cruelty on both of their faces. The rest of the city went silent as I met Tol's eyes.

"Vincienzo?" I gasped. The sky swirled a deep amethyst, purple lightning crackling again and sending my blood pounding faster. The Vincienzo dagger nearly slipped from my fingers, but I caught it, the silver warming against my palm.

Tolek tracked the motion without a hint of recognition. That gaze that had poured over me like molten lava so many times roved from my head to my toes, but there was no familiarity. No warmth in his chocolate irises.

As if he didn't know me at all.

Beside him, Barrett had the same detached expression across his princely face. No—not detached exactly. But removed, the usual emotive, boyish charm replaced with distaste.

"Tol," I said softer, a voice I only ever let him hear. "Tol, what's going on?"

Behind me, warriors shuffled, but I couldn't break his stare to look at them.

Tolek picked me apart, and I swore his eyes flashed with something warm. Only for a beat, but long enough for me to piece together that *this* was not Tolek, not even pretending. It wasn't some scheme he and Barrett had concocted or some conniving alliance they'd discreetly secured with the demigods.

Something had gone very wrong.

Wings beat overhead, and seven Angels crashed to the ground behind the warrior ranks. Lightning skittered through the air, and rumbling rattled my bones. My attention landed on Thorn, and ire burned through me as I understood.

"*What have you done to them?*" I hollered, all sense of decorum in this face off lost.

"Ophelia…" Damien warned.

"No!" I sliced through his protest. "Why, Thorn? Why have you done this?"

Thorn had worked his way into Tol's and Barrett's minds. He'd corrupted them and taken advantage of their worst nightmares in order to wrest control of their physical forms, as he likely had the rest of the warriors now standing before Echnid. They were all tortured spirits, and the Angel with the power to influence emotions and minds pulled their strings.

It was despicable. Broken rage splintered through my gut, and in response, I gathered a storm cloud of my own, light snapping and whirling around me.

And I let it fly at Thorn.

It crackled more fiercely than the Angel's magic, fueled by the injustice of everything we'd suffered. Of stealing the autonomy of people I loved and was sworn to protect, of the years I'd spent being lied to and betrayed.

I shoved every bit of fury the Angels had wrought within me into the sparking clouds and burning light—calling down that purple lightning painting the skies to streak through it—and slammed the power into Thorn's chest, right across the mark he bore from Tolek's attack in the mountains.

The scar lit up, Thorn's answering laugh and chilling glee singing as he soared all the way back to the capitol building. He crashed into the facade, stone rumbling, right as the army of indentured foot soldiers he'd amassed roared to life.

And they charged straight at me.

I lifted my hands, Angellight of swirling colors gathering, the purple lightning glinting. Seraph magic roared to life around me, but before I shot, a wave of soldiers surged from behind, meeting the opposing forces with clashes of steel and cries of war.

Malakai and Dax. Santorina and Lancaster and Mora. Celissia and Erista. And hundreds of warriors for each of them. They charged into the collision without a hint of fear, taking on their own in order to clear a path for me to get to Echnid.

Vale and Jezebel swept overhead on their khrysaor, blue fire spitting from the creatures' jaws, *burning* demigods, gorgons, and the beasts the god brought. Sapphire soared among them a trail of shimmering gold falling from her wings and helping Bodymelders quickly mend the injured.

And my heart sang with the song of the Gallantian Warriors.

"Ophelia!" Cypherion panted, racing up behind me. Relief forced a breath from my lungs at seeing him whole and in control of himself. He looked to the sky where purple lightning still flickered. "What's happening? Is it Xenique?"

"Xenique? No, it's Thorn." Erecting a shield of Angellight around us, I rushed out the explanation, and a sob launched in my throat. What if we never got them back?

No. That was a future I refused to accept. Tolek would find me across any realm, and I was the last fucking seraph. I'd fix this even if it used every ounce of my power.

"Why did you think it was Xenique?" I asked as more warriors rushed around us.

He pointed toward the sky. "Because she did that. Using this." He held his scythe between us, the steel reflecting the flashing purple lightning. "Said it's a way to finally end all of this. Something about her mother and Echnid thinking it would help him."

"Unexpected," I muttered, trying to decipher what the Angel could have meant. But a body slammed into the wall of seraph magic around us, and I shook my head. "We don't have time."

Cypherion's jaw hardened as his quick-thinking gaze assessed the melee raging around us. He glanced to my hand, where the Vincienzo dagger was tightly gripped. Waiting.

"You need to get to Echnid," he said, tightening his hold on his scythe. "Leave Thorn to me."

"Thank you," I said, throwing my arms around him before

dropping the shield and dashing into the heart of the battle, my Second unleashed with his scythe at my side. And for that brief moment, I allowed the gratitude for Cypherion's skill—for the fact that he'd had a plan and had been so quick to communicate it so I could breathe for a single moment—to flood through me.

The Vincienzo dagger burned in one hand. I summoned bolts of Angellight, splintering the cobblestones beneath the feet of contaminated warriors to trip them up for our forces. Dodging duels breaking out, I leapt over fresh pools of blood, slid across debris.

And as I ran, light flared to life in my empty hand. I honed it into the shape of a brutally beautiful sword, gold and shimmering with the light of the Angels and feathered wings carving the hilt. I avoided any killing blows but used the heated blade to swipe through opponents' defenses and kept my eyes on the gleaming bronze statue in the center of the city.

I was halfway to Echnid when a feminine form crashed to the stone before me with a force of power larger than life. I dug in my heels, holding my glowing sword aloft. Her delicately flowing gown unraveled around her, brown skin bathed in moonlight rather than the bloodshed currently unspooling across her city.

"Xenique," I growled.

My distant ancestor, the one who had passed blood of the Goddess of Death down my mother's line. Who had given me the agent that activated the fucking Angelcurse in the first place. Who had been completely absent ever since.

"Daughter," the Angel said. Purple lightning flashed overhead again, illuminating the amethyst skies and their swirling black heart.

"What—"

"When you strike," she interrupted, lifting her massive wings higher, "strike true, for the sake of us all."

I blanched, my sword dropping a few inches. She wanted me to believe she was on my side.

"You left us to *ruin* these months," I growled.

"We have always had a plan," Xenique admitted. "We have not been able to show it until now. I am sorry for what it entailed, for

how selfish we have been, and for how it has used you. But this"—
she gazed around the capital, the massacre turning her gaze cold—
"was never what we wanted. Not I, at least."

Her curls blew across her face as each of the Angels swooped
overhead, but Xenique kept her stare intent on me. Her heart-
shaped lips and deep-set eyes gave nothing away, but the pure focus
alone rattled me. The fact that she'd risked telling me this when—
if the Angels truly did have their own agenda—it could expose
them to Echnid.

It meant they expected this to end tonight. One way or
another, they really were standing against the god.

And the time had come for them to use me to finish their final
battle.

I lowered my sword, shoving my shoulders back and taking a
deep, steadying breath. "Where?"

The light flashing above shadowed Xenique's expression, and
for a moment I feared what deaths she was seeing. What warriors'
spirits were falling.

"The heart." She swallowed. "His weakness."

I nearly laughed at the prospect of Echnid having a heart. "If
you speak true, Xenique, you need to get me to him."

"That is why I am here now." She nodded, fear still in her eyes,
but her gaze turned skyward. "To help open the way to right this."

Following her attention, I paused. The power churning within
those lightning-streaked clouds was jaw-dropping. A dense heart,
pulsing as if life breathed just beyond. A giant beast ready to
devour what waited below. It rivaled even what I'd seen Echnid
blast across the desert.

And it was that amassed magic that truly made me understand.
The Angels had been waiting millennia for this singular chance—
whatever their reason—to bring Echnid down. They'd been
waiting to show that final hand.

It was all or nothing for them tonight. Though I could not
care less about their motives, perhaps we could work together.

"Thank you," I said.

And then, I ducked around her and ran.

I'd only taken steps when the sky ruptured. Purple lightning streaked down, catching the seraph sword in my palm, and an arch exploded around me. Blinding and rushing. Walls of sparkling Angellight slammed up, forming a perfect tunnel. At first, they were the deepest purples, but then, constellations broke out within the light, shimmering silver and whirling with—

Oceans.

Gaveny joined the ranks of Valyrie and Xenique, carving out a path through the city for me. My eyes stung, and I gasped over breaths.

Fires roared along the base of the walls, lapping at the ground and scorching any debris that stood in my way. Inky tendrils of black and pure gold joined in. Ptholenix, Bant, and Damien. And finally, prickling clouds rolled through.

Thorn.

Even Thorn, whose mind was too far gone to reason with his crimes.

All the Angels who had betrayed and used me for their own means now sent gusts of light at my back. My seraph magic purred in acceptance, and I raced faster toward the god, flying over rubble and ruin.

Alone, the god's form shadowed the end of the tunnel, growing larger by the second.

I moved so quickly he didn't understand what the explosion of light surrounding him had been. Hadn't realized the Angels he turned his back on were prepared to drive in the blade.

The whites of his eyes became clear, and Echnid threw up a wall of mist.

But it was too late.

I swept out my sword and sliced cleanly through his power, as though the god's magic was nothing more than steam.

And as my blow came down, I drew back the Vincienzo dagger.

And with the most satisfying give, the blade imbued with the power to raise and slay myths sank into Echnid's chest, splintering bone and piercing a heart I hadn't believed he had.

Godsblood poured across my skin, and I relished the warmth of it as I stared into the Warrior God's eyes. As I watched dark irises part the milky white. As I twisted the blade and refused to break his gaze.

The light of all seven Angels roared around us, the tunnel becoming a howl of rainbow wind, the effervescent heart of a tornado.

Echnid gasped, his frail grip latching on my wrist, but I forced in the blade.

"I hope you die seeing nothing but my rage," I whispered. My own seraph magic erupted, crackling through the rumbling orb surrounding us. Fire and lightning and stars, I was made of the universes the gods built, and as the hilt pressed flat against his chest, I ripped the masterpieces to shreds.

But his skin...his skin on the hand gripping mine was not paling. It was darkening to a healthy hue. As were his eyes and hair.

"My seraph," he wheezed, the sound so cold and cruel that my heart stuttered, "I am not dead yet."

And he shoved the blade from his heart, sending me crashing back against the wall of light.

Chapter Seventy-Nine
Ophelia

Echnid's chest bled, the mist around him withering until it laid lifeless on the ground. I watched in horror as his features shifted and form shrank. His brows and eyes darkened to a rich black, skin pulling in a lively flush instead of his ghastly white.

But he was not dead.

The light shattered around me like a wall of pure glass as I slammed into it. I ducked as shards rained over me, but strong hands gripped beneath my arms, wrenching me into the air.

Terror-stricken, I couldn't even kick or fight, eyes on Echnid as I watched the god *who didn't die.*

Something changed within him. The mist hounding the city shrank in on itself until it vanished altogether, the god's form withering with it, but his cruel smile was intent on me. I was carried higher in the air, away from his reach, until my feet finally met the roof of a nearby building, looking down on the battle raging below.

No one had stopped when I stabbed the god. They hadn't let the shattering tunnel of Angellight deter their mission, warriors refusing to lay down their swords until the bloody end.

"Ophelia," someone behind me said, and I whirled. Damien. It was Damien who had lifted me out of the god's grasp at that moment, taken me to this rooftop away from the fight.

"What are we doing up here?" I panted, and my sword sprang back to life in my palm. The luminescent blade distorted the air, casting dancing light across Damien's stoic features.

"I needed to get you away from him. To speak with you."

I looked around the rooftop, searching for anything to latch on to as I reeled with what went on below. There was nothing up here but smokeless chimneys and stray bottles likely from teenagers drinking without their parents' notice. It was so mundane compared to the conflict below. A monotony I was trying to get us back to, when people weren't losing their lives. Their loved ones.

"I don't understand!" I yelled at Damien, my Angellight blade beating brighter. The Vincienzo dagger was cool in my other hand. "I killed him! I sank the blade into his heart, and he bled—struck true as Xenique said. I saw the life leave his eyes."

"There is more to it," Damien claimed, hands fisting at his sides. The gold plates around his shoulders and matching vambraces twitched as if his muscles violently tensed beneath. "A god cannot be killed with a single blade, no matter how it is forged."

Fury boiled in my gut. "There is always more to it! *Always* one more thing I must do, one more emblem I must find or enemy I must face. When does it *end*, Damien?"

The words clawed up my throat, broken and raw, and I turned away from the Angel, gazing out over the battle below. Tolek. Where was he? Was he okay? Was Thorn's magic ravaging his mind?

Memories of his nightmare-inflicted screams tore through me. I had to find him. Had to help him.

"It is not only a blade that is needed to sever Echnid's life from this world," Damien added as if I hadn't said anything.

I whirled on the Prime Mystique, my voice as sharp as the dagger in my hand. "But he burned the trove! You pointed me in the direction of these infallible weapons, capable of severing the strongest life sources. Malakai read about them in other realms. Everything you pointed us toward implied that *this* was Echnid's weakness. This was what it took to get rid of him for good."

"Yes, I did. And Echnid did have Ptholenix burn the trove,"

Damien clarified, raising his voice over the shouts in the streets. "He did because he *does* fear blades—one specific weapon in particular, and he believed it was within the vaults of the Revered's Palace. It was a weapon beyond warrior-made steel, one that could do more than kill his godly self. It had been traced back to the Mystique Revered's trove until we lost track of the history. To be safe, he had the entire thing burned to avoid it falling into anyone's hands. That's why I pointed you toward forging new weapons."

We'd been right. Through the murals, Damien *had* been trying to tell us to imbue a new blade because the Angels couldn't risk exposing that they were working against the god. That assurance calmed me enough to ask, "What do you mean *more than kill his godly self?*"

"While a single strike would not seal his death, with that dagger, he could be made mortal, and from there..."

From there, he could be killed. By stabbing Echnid with a blade fashioned after the one he feared, I had turned him mortal.

My heart pounded. I extinguished my Angellight sword, crossing my arms and fixing Damien with a hard stare. "Explain."

"In order to truly kill a god, the god must be made mortal first."

"But Moirenna—"

"That is what Echnid had been doing in Damenal. He was trying to figure out how to turn his siblings mortal so he could finally kill them. He read about the *fel strella mythos* after you escaped and learned more about the warrior sisters' powers in the books we'd left for Malakai to find." His throat bobbed, his scar twitching with guilt. "He learned it required the combined magic to *slay* and *raise* a myth. He used your power that day he killed Moirenna."

He *had* absorbed our power in the desert that day. I'd suspected it with mine, but I hadn't realized Jezebel's had been pulled within his orbit, too.

My head raced. It was the Angels' fault he'd found that answer. Their fault because they hadn't been willing to outright offer their help and reveal their own plans.

"If Jezebel could kill his godly side, why couldn't we use her magic to end him completely?" I asked.

"Because it takes the power of both sisters. A perfect balance to restore the Balance Realm to its true self. Have you not wondered why this myth woke *now*?"

I was quiet. We had been asking exactly that.

"Your mother's line had the blood of the Goddess since Xenique walked Ambrisk, Ophelia. But the sister legend did not wake until it was time. Until you and Jezebel were both needed as equal forces. One to kill the immortal, one to *lock him* in mortality."

It was not a coincidence that the Angelblood and Godsblood had brought a myth back to life now. Not while they woke the Angelcurse and seraph within one being. There were few coincidences where fate was involved, and even less with the Balance of Power.

Echnid was no longer a god.

"How do I kill him, then?" I asked as resignation crashed over me. "He won't forever haunt Ambrisk as a mortal, right?"

No. That couldn't be the end. We didn't come all this way to still be shadowed by his eternal presence. I wouldn't stand for the god that manipulated and abused me to walk this world.

"Chosen Child," Damien said, so softly, my spine prickled. "You know the answer to that already."

I know the...

And the truth, as miserable as it was, solidified in my mind like some unavoidable force. Like a key I had always carried forcing itself into a lock I'd been reluctant to see.

The Balance of Power. It always came back to that.

"No." I shook my head, lips trembling as the truth sank through my bones like lead. "No, Damien. I can't—I—I have fought too damn hard for that to be the end."

"You know it must be."

Exhaustion crashed over me. I was tired of seeing people I loved suffer, of godly figures using us for their ancient feuds, and I was so fucking tired of constantly being the answer to everything.

Because *I* was the loophole. I was the way to ensure Echnid truly died. Spirits, it made so much sense now. Somehow, in the tangle of prophecies and blessed blood and emerging seraphs, my life became the tether that balanced Echnid's.

"Wh-why?" I stuttered. My limbs fell slack at my sides.

And Damien's shuttered stare truly appeared sad now. "I wish there was another way."

I walked to the edge of the roof, staring out over the battle raging below. Warrior against warrior, an unnatural opposition that would only anger the Balance further. Angels against demigods, gorgons waiting for a seraph to challenge them, and beasts prowling the shadows.

There was no other way to end it. I supposed a part of me had always known, been preparing for this. It was why I'd fought so desperately to cling to the things I loved in life. First Malakai and my warrior training, and more recently, my family and autonomy.

It was why Echnid made such a grand display of positioning us as a *team*. Why he posed as wanting me by his side, an equal.

I had been the key to Kakias's immortality, the only life standing in the way of achieving a scheme centuries in the making. But that had all been child's play, a warm-up for what I was truly meant to be used for.

Perhaps it had been my first lesson. A test of the Fates to see how I would react so I would be poised to accept it when the time that mattered truly came about. There were no coincidences after all.

"How?" I asked, voice dull.

"You will need an Angelblessed warrior of every clan."

I spun toward Damien. "I won't kill—"

"Willing blood after a sacrifice," he interrupted, and my rage subsided back to numbness. "We have done enough of the latter. Now, you need a union. Angel kissed of each clan and those touched by other godly hands."

"How do I find them?" I had to do it fast. Tonight. This fight would not see the dawn.

"We are taking care of that," Damien explained slowly, like he was giving me time to understand. As if there was not a war storming through the city below.

"Are you truly on our side, then?" I asked Damien.

"We are on our own side," he answered.

I nodded despite the tightness in my throat.

The Angel went on, "We did not go willingly into the Stone Realm all those centuries ago. My kind—we are quite literally *made* of the ether, Ophelia. We are meant to be as powerful as a god, not bow to one. We had always hated being beneath the Warrior God's thumb—sought ways out for centuries following their war—but once we were tricked into sacrificing our power and trapped with him, we quickly learned that the best way out was to kneel. To work from the shadows to undermine his progress."

Was that not precisely what I'd intended to do with Echnid? If only I had known of the Angels motives earlier, perhaps we could have been a team.

For now, their goals aligned with the warriors. They truly had been trying to get us here tonight—wanted to see us victorious. Everything they'd done had been for their cause.

Bant attacking Banix was to push the Engrossians to aid the Mystiques. Whoever left that book for Malakai wanted us to know of other realms. Even Valyrie's frivolous shopping in Damenal—buying the tapestry woven with magic and telling me of the legend of the gryphons it was made to honor—had been a hint.

Thorn distracted Echnid tonight by forming an army to stand before him, though it was through horrendous means, but his mind was too far gone to know the difference beyond meeting his Angelic cause.

They'd ravaged the city to disguise their true motives until the time was right.

And Xenique had dropped the barrier to allow them all here tonight. To begin the process when the timing was most advantageous.

They'd orchestrated it all. Had been the masterminds pulling the strings for centuries.

It had never just been about who Echnid wanted me to become. It was about the sacrifice the Angels needed me to pose, as well.

"Damien," I whispered as a tear streaked down my cheek. He

moved to my side, looking out over the melee. "I think I hate you all for letting me hope there was a way out."

"I know," he said.

"But I am happy we are on the same side tonight."

A soft silence. "I am, too, Chosen Child."

A sob lodged in my throat. "When you gather the others, do not tell them," I said, one final request for the being that had ruined my life. He nodded in acceptance. "And make sure you bring the fae male."

Another nod. And I didn't let myself harp on the fact that if Damien was telling me the truth of their motives and agreeing to my requests, it meant it really was the end.

Finally, everything made sense. If Echnid kept me beside him, I was safe. He didn't only long for my power—he longed to keep me alive.

Because now that he was mortal, as the harbinger of the Angel-curse and the restoration of the Balance, if I died, he died, too.

I thought when I escaped him I was done being used. I thought I was free. As I'd found Tolek again and he held me in his comforting, safe embrace, I'd thought we'd beaten the god's claim over me. That it was me and him, infinitely.

My body is my own.

My mind is my own.

But my life...my life had never been my own.

And I had to bargain that life for a god's death.

Chapter Eighty
Vale

Fury over Harlen's death clung to my spirit just as his blood clung to my skin, hardening into the armor I now bore vengefully. Like Moirenna, Harlen would not die in vain. If I ensured one thing tonight, it would be that.

His sacrifice fueled every beat of Dynaxtar's wings as we hovered above the battle. We landed silently on a rooftop, the flat surface allowing my khrysaor to rest for a moment.

After light had exploded in the heart of the plaza, Ophelia and Echnid at its center, the battle had stuttered for a moment, the mist receding, but Dynaxtar flew on, roaring blue flames over the beasts that crawled through the shadows of Xenovia until they were crisped. It wasn't enough to soothe the rage in my spirit, though. Neither was the onslaught of readings that continued to tunnel through my veins. I needed more.

As we watched, Thorn landed in the center of a crowd below us and aimed his storm cloud Angellight at another group of healthy warriors.

"Dynaxtar!" I shouted over the roar of battle. "*Burn.*"

I didn't know if she knew what the word meant—if the khrysaor and pegasus truly understood us—but Dynaxtar opened her mouth, and those flames poured forth, blue hearted and silver around the edges. They eclipsed Thorn's winged body, falling around him and bouncing off the stone pathway. A solid wall of swirling gray light shot up, the fire and storms ricocheting off either side.

It wasn't enough to kill him, to kill any Angel, or Valyrie would be dead before me already, but the khrysaor's fire was more powerful than regular flame. It was born of myth, ripped from the stars with her constellation, a reason I thought we were a chosen pair. Fatecatcher and a beast born of the stars.

The flames forced Thorn back, the warriors he'd been after taking the opportunity to flee, and the Angel slowly turned his attention toward the rooftop. His eyes flicked over Dynaxtar with an unhinged curiosity.

And they landed on me.

And with all the wrath burning through me, I grinned viciously down at the Mindshaper.

Dynaxtar let us stand there for a moment, studying each other. Then, without a word of instruction, she leaped into the skies.

I didn't have to look to know Thorn followed. His deep-gray ether swirled on our heels like the heart of a storm. We had to get him within reach of Cypherion's scythe to truly harm him.

Angellight blasted toward us, but Dynaxtar was a creature born of legends—she dipped and dodged, flying in jagged paths to avoid the Angel's sloppy attacks.

Thorn's magic wasn't precise. It was as wily as the Angel who bore it, like the winds of a hurricane and the lashing rain that drenched it. My hair and clothes clung to my skin under the force as if my khrysaor really was tearing through a storm.

She was working to loop around him. To catch him off guard and breathe that fire again.

And with the creature I trusted implicitly guarding me, I allowed my Fate ties to open. I pushed through the mass of fortunes I bore as the Fatecatcher, their magic stronger than ever as it channeled through me and to the Starsearchers below, fighting with their imbued weapons. Up here, at least, I wasn't swarmed to a crippling point.

I searched through the readings for my ties, my own Fates screaming their fortunes at me. Arenothos was blessedly quiet, chastised after our last interaction, but others roared.

Cruelty and Adoration.

Prophecy and Demise.

Foolish—

No. The previous one blasted forward with a burst that rivaled a star exploding. *Prophecy and Demise*, brandishing a tale of a chosen one from start to finish. It was either the blink of an eye or an eon as the story unfolded. Sisters once born with the powers of constellations, ripping stars from the sky to breathe life into them and banish them again.

They rode into battle atop their loyal creatures, legions of flying beasts at their backs. They challenged the known gods, and Fates, they scorched others from this very world. Compressed them, made them smaller.

A massacre that, in turn, sent the sisters to an untimely grave— but a temporary one. Bodily, they rested for eternity, but their spirits...

Their spirits rose again with the force of a god's blood. With the fury derived from an Angel's grave, a Fate's death, sworn to one end. In that god's blood, a root grew. A leash that wrapped itself around one sister.

One sister who not only bore the myth but enraptured the Angels with her own magic. She became the tether. The key to a god's downfall.

Faces I knew too well faded in and out of the reading. Ophelia, Jezebel, Tolek. Dax and Celissia. Lancaster, Gatrielle, and a few I hardly recognized. In a flash, they all blinked out, nothing but bright starfire illuminating my mind.

Then, magenta eyes flared through the unending white. A determined blade in her fist and resolve gritted between her teeth.

"*No*," I gasped as the reading shattered into a thousand falling stars, and I wrenched myself back to this realm. Thorn was still on our heels, but we'd have to deal with that later.

"Dynaxtar!" I called, leaning forward. "Find the others!"

CHAPTER EIGHTY-ONE
MALAKAI

Spirits, Tolek was fucking mad.

He was gone, his mind overrun by Thorn. The Angel had disappeared once that tunnel of light Ophelia was in exploded, but Cypherion and I lured Tol away from the heart of the battle, away from where he could hurt himself or anyone else. We backed him toward a corner, between a glass blowing boutique and an imported liquor store, moss clinging to the damp niche in the buildings.

Tolek's stare was manic. And it wasn't the whirl of shining excitement my oldest friend often had. This was darker—it belonged to someone else.

"Tol," Cypherion pleaded, holding his scythe stiffly. "Snap out of this."

"Snap out of what?" Tolek stomped on a glass bauble that had spilled through the broken window, tilting his head curiously at it. I'd seen him make that same motion so many fucking times, but this had malice at the edge. It curled through my stomach, making me sick.

Dax had cornered Barrett similarly in a different area of the square, getting him and Tolek away from each other. Rebel paced circles around them, whining. The Engrossian general had to be suffering the same pain we were. The same fucking desperation to get them back and kill Thorn in exchange.

"You're stronger than him, Tol," I said. Both Cypherion and I held our weapons up reluctantly. Tolek had his sword angled at the floor, dragging through the shattered glass, one hand in his pocket as if we were casually talking. "Don't let him do this to you."

"I am not letting him do anything," Tolek responded with a rough chuckle.

"You are," Cypherion countered. "But this isn't you. Don't let heartlessness win. Don't become the man your father wanted to make you."

Backing Tolek further into the shadows of the mossy corner, I added, "Don't let this fucking Angel control you and force that future on you. You've fought too damn hard to get out of that."

"I am nothing," Tolek spat, sneering.

"That's not true!" I argued. "You're our best friend. You're one of the smartest people I know—one of the fucking bravest. You don't let any challenge stop you, so why are you letting him now?"

Tolek had always been shadowed by his father's cruel words and greedy intentions for their family, but he'd been strong enough to shine through. Now, as Thorn drove Tolek's true self away and wielded his worst emotions, he was shoving him back into a place he'd clawed his way out of.

"He's right," Cypherion added. "You don't live with cruelty, Tol. You're the opposite. One of the warmest people we know. The one we go to when we need advice or a laugh."

"You're our brother!" Desperation cracked my fucking voice.

"That may be true, but I am useless unless I am *this*. I am—" His words cut off, his head tilting again as he listened to something I couldn't hear. His attention swiveled to the right, gaze lifting. "Her."

I followed his sightline.

"That's Ophelia," I blurted out, hope inflating foolishly in my chest.

She stood atop a roof, scanning the battle below. There was something wrong with one of her wings, and a glowing sword made of light simmered in one hand, but her gaze was pure fire as she studied the city, then she whirled away from the ledge, toward whoever was up there with her.

"Ophelia," Tolek repeated. And for a fucking second, it was his voice again.

But just as quickly, hostility overtook his expression, his brows pinching in and his normally smirking lips turning down. Tolek tossed his sword in the air, flipping it and tightening his grip.

Lifting the weapon as if he'd cut his way through his closest friends, he growled, "I *want her.*"

Before the horror of those twisted, spiteful words fully sank through my bones, Tolek lunged.

His sword cleaved the air between Cypherion and me. We dodged, raising our weapons to catch his next blows as he swiveled around us. His fighting was shockingly sloppy under Thorn's control. Cypherion and I exchanged a glance, and ducking low, we charged. We each slammed into one of Tolek's shoulders, pivoting to shove him back into the corner. His head snapped against the wall, and he hissed.

I wrestled his sword from his hand, tossing it aside. The metal clanged against the wooden crates full of empty liquor bottles as I slammed his wrist beside his head.

"You don't want her," Cypherion corrected. He pinched Tolek's cheeks in one hand, forcing his attention toward him. Cyph's knuckles were split open as if he'd thrown a number of punches tonight, but I knew from the iron grip he had on Tol that he was trying not to make our friend the recipient of the next one. "You don't want her like that."

"You love her," I said.

Cypherion added, "You love her, and she loves you."

"Almost disgustingly so," I finished.

Tolek shook his head, kicking out. "*I want her,*" he swore, more viciously this time. His hair stood on end, his eyes wide and wild.

"I know you do," I gave in. "You always fucking will, but later."

Later, once we got out of this battle and fixed his mind. Then he could have her.

The ground shuddered, and I glanced over my shoulder as Vale slid off Dynaxtar's back, but I kept my hold on Tolek.

"Malakai!" Vale called, and if I hadn't been surprised enough that she was saying my name and not Cypherion's, the frenzy wavering in her tone would have done it.

"What's wrong, Stargirl?" Cyph asked.

"It's Ophelia," Vale panted, skidding to a stop before me, her long silk skirt shredding on the broken glass. Her eyes swirled with the silver haze of a powerful session, her wavy hair frizzy and dust covered. "She's going to do something horrible."

"Ophelia," Tolek echoed, but Cypherion shoved him harder against the wall, kicking weakly at his shin to distract him.

"What's she doing?" I asked, trying to ignore them despite the panic rattling my chest.

Vale looked nervously between me and Tolek, and I had a sick feeling she'd seen this very moment written out by the Fates, even if she hadn't known what it meant then.

She shook away whatever fortune was clouding her memory. "I'll tell you on the way."

"Go," Cypherion said, jerking his head toward Tolek. "I'll take care of him."

With only a nod and a final look at Tolek's enraged, *wrong* stare, I tightened my grip on my sword, and I ran after the Fate-catcher.

CHAPTER EIGHTY-TWO
SANTORINA

SHADOWED BEASTS PROWLED AROUND XENOVIA, pouncing on unaware warriors as they stumbled into the dark patches before buildings and beneath awnings. They didn't differentiate from our allies or Thorn's foot soldiers, tackling anyone that stepped in their path.

"Santorina, behind you!" Celissia called.

I spun, striking out with my dagger on instinct. It sank into the exposed throat of another dark nemaxese as it lunged for me. Lancaster grabbed the creature from behind, tearing it to bits in a way that I'd hate if he wasn't doing it for me.

I faced the battle again. My friends. Where were they? Damien flew off with Ophelia. Jezebel and Vale had been soaring above, the khrysaor chasing someone through the smoke, but I had to find the rest of them. To make sure they weren't hurt—or worse.

The thought took root, and I charged for the heart of the melee. Echnid's cerberus was stomping through the city, a chorus of barks echoing into the smoky night. I wasn't sure what was worse—the three-headed creature or the shadow beasts.

"You're okay, Bounty?" Lancaster checked as he sped up beside me.

"Doing just fine, Hunter."

Blood stained us both, splattered head to Godsdamned toe,

but the wound in my side was entirely healed, nothing more than a raw pink scar peeking through the torn fabric.

Since Lancaster's blood melded into my bloodstream, I'd been energized more than ever before. Was this what it felt like to be near-immortal? This strong, this fast? Goddess, it was exhilarating as we raced through the battling crowds of warriors, leaving non-fatal injuries behind to slow them down.

But there were so many of them—too many of them. More of our side was falling back, trying to recoup their injured while they could.

The remaining gorgons were shifted into their full form, flying above and dropping down before defenseless warriors, the head-on sight of their bright red eyes turning the warriors to stone. So many of our own had been frozen that way, an entire corner of the square a statuesque graveyard.

But Sapphire swooped low over them, emitting what resembled Ophelia's myth magic, and—

Gods. Some of the stone warriors were waking.

Celissia and Mora fought fiercely at our backs, the Engrossian keeping up better than expected even if we slowed our pace for her at times. She used her hatchet to disarm opponents, but there were too many rimming this outer courtyard. And killing them would not end this fight.

"We should get to the center!" I yelled. "There's no way Ophelia isn't going after Echnid, and she may need—"

A high-pitched shriek cut me off.

Lancaster, Celissia, and I turned toward it.

"*No,*" I gasped as a shadowed nemaxese sank its teeth into Mora's gut.

Terror flooded my chest. Not just my terror, I realized. It was too all-consuming and life-altering to just be mine. This was Lancaster's horror I was feeling as he raced toward the beast, his fury as he watched it drop his sister to the ground, the female's blood running too fast for her to—

My throat was tight. Too constricted to breathe.

In heaping gulps, I forced air down over my mate's terror as I helped Celissia move Mora to the side of the square. A shattered orb of mystlight turned the blood streaking the ground into a glimmering smear of death. I dropped to the stone, cutting off my sleeve and putting pressure on the wound.

I swallowed again over my tight throat.

No, that was Lancaster's panic as he struck the beast in the chest with his bare hands, sending it stumbling into darkness, and he fell to his knees beside his sister. Celissia propped her up, searching for a way to heal her without any supplies and such weak sorcia magic. She uttered words I couldn't hear over her talisman, ducking closer to Mora.

"Why isn't it healing?" Lancaster asked as he held his sister.

"Her magic is too weak," Celissia answered. "It's been deteriorating for months."

Ever since that corpse bit her in the catacombs, ever since Ritalia's bargain tied her to life, her magic had been depleting.

"Mines not working on it either," Lancaster griped.

Mora was fading, her stuttered words barely audible.

"It's her body," Celissia said. "It's rejecting both of our healing now that her own magic has faded so far. It doesn't want it."

"What can we do?" Lancaster forced out, voice hollow. It was the first time I'd ever heard him sound truly lost. My chest was flooded with his heartache and desperation.

"Please, Celissia," I muttered as I applied pressure to the wound. "Is there anything?"

Celissia chewed her lip, flinching as the nearest building shuddered, glass shattering. "There's not..."

Defeat washed over her features. One I understood as a healer. It was our mission to save lives, and when we failed, it was such a personal loss. To see a spirit leave this world when we'd taken life on as our vow was salt in the wound of a death.

Lancaster held his sister's hand as they knelt in a pool of mystlight. He pumped wave after wave of healing magic into her, but it didn't matter. The frenzy down the bond grew more riled as every desperate moment ticked by. As she slipped away.

Mora gaped up at us, not able to speak over the pain through her abdomen. But some sort of understanding passed between the brother and sister who, for centuries, only had each other.

And when Mora's eyes landed on me, the trust in them was like she was handing her brother into my care.

Gingerly, Lancaster scooped Mora off the ground and kicked open the nearest shop. A bookstore, it appeared. Fitting given how much Mora loved books. Hopefully they would comfort her.

Mystlight flooded the aisles as Lancaster laid her on the front counter. He bent to whisper something in his sister's ear, and I gave them a moment, but just as her eyes slipped closed and Mora's chest stilled, a snarl sounded right outside.

Celissia and I whirled toward the door, determined to guard Lancaster while he finished his goodbyes, but something white hot burned along the string in my chest.

"Goodbye, sister," Lancaster whispered behind us. "And thank you. Go be with Mother now." Then, Lancaster bolted past us, and the heat in the bond roared.

Vengeance.

His wrenching desire to tear through the beast that took his sister from him. He had all other emotions shut down, ready to commit whatever brutality this war took—no matter who it hurt.

No remorse and no conceding.

And I was on his heels, following the thrumming string in my chest.

We slammed the door into the bookshop, and Lancaster piled crates and broken tables and chairs before it. Anything he could grab, tossing the furniture around as if it weighed nothing. Celissia and I shoved a fallen bust of the Angel his way.

A second snarl had us all turning. I stumbled back into Lancaster's chest, and he dragged me a step behind him, resolve blatant in his grasp.

Two shadowed beasts bore down on us, teeth the length of my hand gnashing together. Crimson shone along the tips.

Mora's blood.

That was *Mora's* blood flying with each deadly snap. The blood of the fae Goddess coating this otherworldly beast.

Lancaster curled his arm tighter around me, his fingers digging into my hip as he pressed back, like every point of contact was a reassurance that I was here and okay. Celissia was a step behind us, too.

"Do not worry," he swore, but it was obvious from that rumbling tone that even he was searching.

Searching for a way out.

For a Godsdamned reason this had happened.

Because as I looked beyond the nemaxese, it was evident we were losing.

All across the square, warriors fell.

"I'm getting you out of here," Lancaster said. "I promise—"

But his words drowned to a chorus of howls, and then, a second beast was flying at the ones before us.

Not just any beast.

A wolf. A mountainous wolf.

Furry limbs tangled with sinewy ones as it sank its teeth into a shadow creature's throat. Dozens of them jumped from roofs and alleys, warriors in thick furs atop their backs, launching jagged daggers at the shadowed nemaxese. Taking on the cerberus with a vengeance.

A sob cracked through my chest as I clutched Lancaster.

"Mindshapers," I gasped out, my hand tightening on the fae's arm. The last of the Gallantian Warrior clans to accept our alliance —the legions that hadn't made it here in time. They parted the crowds of dueling warriors in the square, rallying our forces amid snarls and howls.

And from the skies, breaking the horizon over the tallest minarets of the capital, wings of fire ignited the night.

Phoenixes.

A flock of them swooped around the city, leaving burning trails of flame in their wake. Their glorious wings were spread wide, feathered infernos dropping sparks among the crowds.

To the north, a cluster of something else soared. Some with bodies like lions but front legs and heads of eagles, and a small few with the heads of female women. *Gryphons and sphinxes.*

"Ophelia," I breathed, gripping tighter to Lancaster as chills danced along my skin. "That blast of power we felt when Echnid breeched the city. It was her mythos magic."

"She woke them," Lancaster breathed.

The myths had all come to life in that consuming burst of magic she'd sent across the world, stretching far and wide enough to touch legends long buried.

And Gods, wherever Ophelia was in this mess, I hoped she saw them. Saw that the risk she'd taken in going to Mindshaper Territory had been worth it. That her words combined with Lancaster's influence had been enough to get this final ally to join her cause. That her power was so mighty, it returned a horde of sleeping myths to Gallantia, and no God could compare.

I hope she knew that she'd done it. She'd given us a fighting chance.

"Those aren't just Mindshapers," Lancaster added, placing me on my feet in front of him, his hands still glued to my waist.

And I felt it then, too. A sense I hadn't had before—not until I'd taken his blood and our powers merged. An earthy scent clung to the air, and I gasped.

I barely dared to say it, my eyes watering. "Bounties?"

Lancaster's canines flashed. "And the entire league of human forces."

They were atop the backs of the wolves with the Mindshapers, ducking between the legs of the furry beasts and grabbing opponents from behind so the stronger, faster warriors could detain them. Engaging in their own fights with swords and spears and not a drop of fear.

Humans.

Not only had the warriors and the Bounties made it to our side, but my magicless people had rallied with them. They may have been humans—the weakest among Ambrisk—but they became the heart of the battle.

"I can't believe it," I whispered.

"How, though?" Celissia asked.

I breathed in awe. "Because of us."

With a sob, I threw my arms around Lancaster's neck and pressed my lips to his. Without him, they wouldn't be here. He was the one who got me to those camps, who spoke up against his own late queen in favor of the warriors. He was the one who reminded me just how strong a human could be.

Lancaster held me tighter, moving his lips to my ear. "What do you say, Bounty?" His voice was still laced with agony over his sister and that brutal edge that needed to see her death avenged. He pulled back, holding one of the daggers from his own belt out to me. "Do you want to be their queen?"

He'd told me the choice was mine, how I wanted to claim this title. I could simply be one of them, or I could guide them.

The Bounties and humans had shown up tonight because of us. And I would not leave them to fend for themselves when the dawn broke. I may not have known what it took to be a Queen of Bounties, but I understood what it meant to stand together.

Wrapping my fingers around the handle of Lancaster's dagger, I whispered against his lips, "There'd be no greater honor."

"Actually," a voice said, a shadow dropping over the debris. All three of us spun, my eyes popping wide when they met Damien's. "Ophelia has need of you."

CHAPTER EIGHTY-THREE
TOLEK

I WANT HER.

Her.

Her.

Ophelia.

Something in the back of my mind ticked with each syllable of that name as I watched the aggravated warrior and the petite woman disappear amid all the other soldiers. Why was it so familiar? And why did an instinct deep within me shake and rattle at the thought?

The auburn-haired man before me pressed me further into the corner, droning on and on about something I didn't care to listen to.

I didn't truly care about any part of this battle raging right now. Didn't care about anything but the power at the ends of my fingertips and how I could master it. How I could fuel it.

A burst of gold exploded in the sky.

Her.

That was right, she was the one I needed—

A sharp sting rang across my cheek.

He had slapped me. This warrior with his arm banded across my shoulders had *slapped* me. Judging by his size, it wasn't as powerful as it could have been, but I laughed anyway.

Pathetic, all of them.

"You need to fight back, Tolek!" he urged. "Fight back for infinity or whatever in the fucking Angels it is you're always whispering to Ophelia!"

Ophelia. Infinity.

No. That was wrong.

The top of my scalp prickled, like sharp points digging in. The rattling deep in my spirit mounted, and bolts of lightning zapped through my blood.

Infinity.

No. Not infinity. *Infinitely.*

"Ophelia?" I choked out. My chest ached at her name, desperation clawing up my throat, partnered with a sliver of pure bliss only she gave me.

"Yes!" the warrior before me chanted. "Ophelia—she needs you, Tolek! She needs you to fight him."

The prickles dug in deeper around my scalp, a crown of thorns doing its damn best to steal my mind, but it was too late. Every feeling I'd shoved deep into myself when Thorn attacked forced its way free.

And they screamed through me to the tune of one name: *Ophelia*.

The Mindshaper Angel dropped to the ground behind Cypherion, and his eyes locked on mine. Lightning skittered over my skin, that power digging deeper into my skull, but I held tight to everything that was good in my life. To every memory of her that chased away the nightmares because as long as I had Ophelia then I couldn't be trapped in that damn darkness again.

And in my mind, I grabbed on to the Angel's sharp bolts of lightning. Their power that tunneled through my body became one with me like my blood flowed through my veins. I absorbed and warped it, consumed every last drop of storm-drenched magic as my sword had, the Blackfyre, blade and wielder conduits.

Then, I turned them right back on him.

Until the splintering bolts were forcing their way beneath *his* skin.

Until he was screaming with the agony that haunted my nightmares.

And with a clawing, tearing sensation, I ripped my mind from the Angel's grasp.

"Get the *fuck* out of my head!" I roared as lightning crackled between us.

Thorn's eyes widened, and I swore the everlasting bastard stumbled back a step.

Cypherion released me, cheering as he realized I'd wrenched control back from the Angel. Pivoting around me, he tossed me my sword.

I took up the position at my friend's side, and together, immune to the Angel's fucking twisted manipulation, we charged.

Thorn sent the ground rumbling like thunder beneath our feet, a gust of deadly wind blasting at us. I gritted my teeth and kept my head down against the torrent, the power of the Blackfyre in my sword tunneling through my body. Cypherion and I attacked from opposite sides, in perfect balance.

Thorn cooed, "Your dreams are so very sweet."

"Stay the fuck away!" I roared as loud as his wind.

"You are a weakling, plagued by human emotion."

Cypherion swung his scythe for the Angel's leg, and Thorn's attention pivoted to him. The flat of my blade caught the Mind-shaper in the ribs, the strike to his statuesque figure reverberating up my arms.

"I'm not fucking weak!" I said as my bones rattled. As power thrummed through me.

I twisted my grip, and the steel imbued with the dark promises of the tar pools sliced across his side, another scar from me added to the eternal bastard. Gold blood poured over my sword once again, splashing across my face and leathers.

A ghastly grin split Thorn's features. Lightning bounced between his fingers.

"Not enough," he said, as the wound stitched up. "You are foolish."

I quirked a brow, my laugh crackling like Thorn's gleeful one. "Maybe, but I am so much smarter than you."

CK had been waiting for my diversion. And right as Thorn's

lighting bolted for me, Cypherion struck with that scythe. The blade carved through the air, gleaming with the glow of the amethyst lights flooding in the sky, and it cleaved his wings from the Mindshaper Angel's forsaken back.

The Prime Warrior's cry echoed with the force of torrential storms and brutal torment. The power I'd wrenched from him roared inside of me. A piece of the Mindshaper *I* now controlled, after being tortured by his twisted magic.

And in the haze of pain, just as Cypherion's scythe completed the blow, a veil ripped open behind Thorn, a bridge stretching to nowhere.

The Angel stumbled back, him and his severed wings swallowed up in a mess of gold-blooded feathers.

The roaring storm went silent, the clashes of battle returning around us.

Cypherion and I only looked at each other and his scythe, utterly lost, as Valyrie dropped before me. Wide eyed, she looked at where Thorn had disappeared, her expression paling.

But she shook it off.

"Tolek Vincienzo," she said in her most commanding tone. "We have need of you." Her attention cut to Cyph. "And where is the Fatecatcher?"

He scoffed. "After you killed Harlen, you want her help?"

My stomach soured at that piece of information.

"It had to be done," Valyrie explained without a hint of emotion. "It had to be a sacrifice the clan would feel. Be happy it wasn't her."

Cypherion lifted his scythe as if he'd repeat what we'd just done to Thorn, but before he moved, a battle cry echoed from the city. And over the tops of the buildings, a mass of white, misty bodies charged.

Spirits.

Literal spirits, broken from the Hall of Wandering Souls. Headed by—

Fucking Angels.

"Lyria," I choked out as I gripped the dagger carved with my sister's initials.

She led the front line of an army of spirits, Mila on the ground ahead of her. The ghostly white forms fell among the battle, targeting those Thorn had claimed and seeming to wrench their minds back to their bodies. But my sister and Mila...together, they raced to me.

Lyria floated down, her form outside of the Hall now the same as the Spirits I'd seen during my Undertaking a year ago. White and misty, a clear differentiation from the living.

"How are you here?" I whispered.

"I told you I was working on a way to help. I couldn't let you have all the fun," my sister teased. That same dress as before hugged her form, no armor or weapons in sight. "We can't stay long, but we bought a little time."

"To win," I said, matching her taunting tone, though my eyes fucking stung.

"Damn right, baby brother. I'd been trying to find a way for the spirits caught in between to return for short periods since I was trapped there." Her expression softened. "There was always something stopping us, and I was afraid to tell you in case I couldn't solve it, but then Mila visited..."

"As soon as I saw Lyria, my Reflector powers reacted," Mila finished. "It showed me another realm where devout worshippers of a deity could use spells to place themselves into a temporary sleep in place of the spirits."

And now, with their precarious place on the cusp of life and death, the Spirits could help pull our warriors back to their own sanity. They could sever Thorn's hold on them.

I'd always known Lyria was supposed to be here still. I hadn't realized perhaps she *could* be in this battle from beyond the realm.

"Xenique helped," Lyria said, and *that* shocked me. "With her priestesses in the city."

"That's amazing," Cypherion said, still scanning the skies for Vale.

"Damn spectacular. Thank you," I added, hugging Mila as tightly as I could. Dammit, we really were all here. Making a final stand together. "Let's go—"

"Stop!" Valyrie demanded as we turned toward the heart of the city. I'd forgotten the damn Angel.

"*What* do you want?" I growled in frustration.

"Ophelia needs you."

CHAPTER EIGHTY-FOUR
OPHELIA

MYTHICAL CREATURES POURED ACROSS THE SKIES IN perfect formations, like they'd been trained to fight battles of legends, and tears blurred my vision as I watched them. The myth power I'd shot against Echnid—I'd hoped it might find a few, but it had done this. It had woken an army and called them to our cause in one last desperate defense, to the aid of the known gods they answered to.

My chest tightened as the phoenixes dipped low, wings igniting the shadowed beasts attacking our forces. A gryphon sank its talons into the chest of a demigod and flew the male into Zanox's path, the khrysaor spewing blue fire over its godly body. He writhed and screamed as smoke spiraled into the air, the scent of charred flesh thickening in the night.

And I nearly fell to my knees as a wolf bound before me, Ricordan atop its back.

Nodding, the Mindshaper said, "Revered."

"Thank you, Ric." My voice cracked over the words.

They'd come. They'd all come to stand or fall beside us.

And among them, spirits soared. Not just any spirits. Lyria and...*Annellius Alabath*.

My ancestor, the original Angelcursed who had condemned us to face this battle, came back to help. He flew with his cohorts,

577

dropping to help wrench victims from Thorn's grasp in a way living warriors couldn't.

The fact that he hadn't abandoned us for good stirred emotion in my chest that I didn't have time to indulge now. Not as I stood at the bottom of the stairs leading up to the capitol building with the caved-in roof. Fire roared through the broken windows, sparking over the ruined edges of the ceiling and licking up Xenovia's banners, deep purple velvet falling apart in singed clumps.

And alone, Echnid waited in the center of the steps.

I stuffed down the wrenching gratitude and agony of what I was about to do and turned my back on the battle to challenge the mortal man glaring down at me. If I was meant to die tonight, I would face that death with a fearless smile.

Echnid showed no care for the fire burning in his wake. He wasn't ready to run, but he appeared ready to talk. With that malicious, manipulative grin on his face, he was still trying to win me to his side.

But I knew...I knew how this had to end.

Finally, thanks to my willingness, I was a step ahead.

Exhausted, heart leaden, and breaths heaving, I pulled the Vincienzo dagger from the sheathe at my thigh, my hand sagging with the monumental weight. Echnid tracked the motion. When his no-longer-milky stare narrowed, all sound around us dulled.

He hadn't known I had it—he'd thought he destroyed any weapon capable of severing his life when he burned the trove. He hadn't known any blade on Ambrisk was able to drain his immortal life.

Once again, my opponent had underestimated me.

For a beat, concern flashed across his face. Worry that I had more secrets up my sleeve. That I was willing to give more to guarantee his downfall. And over the agony, over the tears fighting to break free, I smiled wickedly.

"Ophelia!" Tolek's voice cut through the night.

Shoving the pain clawing through my chest deep down inside me, I wiped my eyes and turned to face him. He raced up to me, hands cupping my cheeks. Gold was splattered across his skin and leathers.

"*Apeagna*," he said with utter relief.

"You're back." My voice cracked.

"I wouldn't leave you," he said, brushing a thumb across my cheekbone.

But I am.

No. I told the voice in my head to quiet. I was not leaving Tolek by choice. I couldn't. He was a part of me. Bind or not, he was woven deep within my bones, and even though I had to go now, it would be with his soul wrapped around mine. Our bodies parted, but our beings forever entwined as our spirits traveled across realms.

I would wait for him there. Wherever I went next, I would wait for Tolek to find me.

And those thoughts must have shown on my face because Tolek asked, "What's wrong?"

I have to leave you.

"I have to end him," I said through gritted teeth.

He nodded as if he understood, but he didn't. And I couldn't explain it if I wanted to hold on to what strength I had left.

"Valyrie told me there's something you need my help with." Tol brushed a strand of hair behind my ear, and it was such a tender movement, a touch I ingrained in my memory forever. I could take that with me when I went, at least.

I peered around his shoulder. They were all almost here now. Assembled between the steps I stood on and the battle through the city center.

As Tol's hands warmed my fear-chilled skin, I thought of the legend of the Firebird and his fox that Esmond had told me earlier tonight. Was it truly such delusion to hope that with love in our hearts, we could outrun the flames of any fire?

Tol and I had been born of loss and hardship. We'd fought to get to this very battlefield, fought for each other and beside each other. He'd held my broken shards in the palm of his hand through so many trials, had pieced them back together so I could forge myself into the weapon that stood before him today.

Through all of that—after all that strife and in the face of a brighter tomorrow—were we meant to burn to nothing more than ash?

Perhaps, but Ambrisk was a realm worth saving.

And if that was true, in order to be that sacrifice, I had to believe that the love I was willing to die for—the love for this man, for our family, and for this entire realm—was the most powerful flame of all.

That if everything went to ruin, something beautiful would be born of the ashes.

Fire was cleansing after all, as Ptholenix had told me. And as the flames of this fate devoured everything in its path, I had to hope Tolek could be that fox, living in this world, persisting as a legend of hope through the devastation.

And it was with that resolve that I swallowed any hint of despair as I squeezed Tol's hands. "I need you to stand back with them and listen to Damien."

Tolek's brow creased. "Okay, *apeagna*. Okay."

He kissed me softly, and for one last time, I memorized the feel of his lips against mine. Of his hands on my body and his heart beating so fiercely—his heart I was about to break to save the realms.

I laced the spell of Tolek into my soul as he backed toward my sister.

Jezebel, with the blood of the Soulguider Angel and the Goddess Artale flowing through her, and the khrysaor she sat astride, representing the God of Mythical Beasts. Beside her was Gatrielle, the Angelblessed Bodymelder, then Dax, with a wound still laced with Bant's magic.

Ezalia's cousin and general, with a connection to the Seawatcher Angel that I didn't understand, and Lancaster with his fae blood. Santorina, the Bounty with a power gifted to humans from the Warrior God, and Celissia as a sorcia, a bed of elthem flowers at their feet to tie to the God of Nature.

Finally, Tolek, who Damien said had stolen power from Thorn tonight.

And me, the connection to the Mystique Angel.

We were only missing one. Then, we'd have a representative of every god and Angel. Then, this could happen.

I exchanged a subtle nod with Damien that he reluctantly returned, confirming he would honor our deal, then I exchanged one with Lancaster. His stone-laced stare told me Damien had relayed my request. His expression was miserable, hardened, and I feared what had happened tonight to make him so agreeable.

The Mystique Prime Warrior moved among them all as I turned back to face Echnid. The defenseless god watched both me and the Angels with fury as their betrayal fully struck him.

Taking one last glance at Tol, I mouthed through trembling lips, *Infinitely*.

His eyes widened as if he realized the secret in my hunched shoulders. The sorrow in the tears I couldn't fight.

Tolek ripped the *L.V.* dagger from his waist, prepared to battle his way toward me, but Lancaster was ready. The fae whispered bargained words in Tol's ears that would not allow him to fight to reach me.

Lancaster might have been the only one who figured out exactly what I was going to do before this moment. The others were only just realizing, but I'd asked Damien to ensure the male called his bargain against Tolek when he inevitably fought to stop me.

I sent the fae a silent thank you.

The Angels swept down on each warrior, fae, or creature, and with their own ancient blades, made a cut over their collarbone to let the blood near their heart flow freely.

Blood blessed by every God and Angel. The sacrifice of a powerful bloodline at the hands of the Angels themselves had opened the door to Xenovia tonight. It would take an alliance of all of Ambrisk to kill Echnid, just not in the way we'd thought.

Now, with something freely given of each, I would seal the Warrior God's death for good.

The others raged—Jezebel and Santorina understanding now, too—but the Angels held them back.

And with my heart splintering, I dug up every last drop of seraph magic remaining in my tired body and exploded with it.

The force of the magic ricocheted around me, the capitol building crumbling to further ruin behind Echnid. I flew back from the force, tumbling across the stairs like I was no more than a rag doll. My lungs pinched, my skin slicing on rubble.

Tolek's desperate screams for me bounced off swords and shields across the city center, but I created a solid force to keep him at bay—a sixty-foot wall curving between where Echnid and I stood and the God-and-Angelblessed line waiting below.

As I hefted myself to my hands and knees, body bone tired, Jezebel pummeled my wall of light with her own myth magic, but she couldn't destroy the seraph power.

I was no longer a myth.

Her screams melted with Tolek's, shredding me apart.

I lifted my head, searching for the dagger to finish this with no distractions, and I made the same slice to my skin that the others now had. I knew their promises had been sealed—Vale, the final piece, included—because the cut didn't only sting, it burned with a bright white light. Purer than any star, more powerful than any god. One derived of ancient realms and restoring Balances.

I sighed in relief.

Only one more step now.

My gaze dropped to the steel of the Vincienzo dagger, pressed between my hand and the cracked stairs. The metal reflected the burning wall of Angellight, and within it, a wavering shadow emerged along the sharp edge.

My head snapped up, pain shooting through my lungs. I coughed over the dirt swirling in the air, squinting at the glimmering gold wall as shocks of light shot up to the deep purple clouds.

I was hallucinating. I had to be.

But no.

From within the light, a figure emerged. Her tall, willowy frame drank up the shimmering gold, a sapphire gown draping low between her breasts and gusting around her legs under the force of my magic.

And I wheezed, "Aimee?"

Chapter Eighty-Five
Malakai

Ophelia is going to sacrifice herself.

That's what Vale had told me as we raced around the edge of the square, speeding to a set of side steps leading up to the capitol building. The entire front of the building had been crowded with warriors and creatures alike.

"You have to stop her," Vale panted as we climbed. We tried to have the khrysaor fly us in, but Vale insisted we had to be on this side, and there was too much smoke and debris to navigate the narrow alleys on Dynaxtar's back.

"How the fuck am I supposed to stop her? Do you *know* how fucking stubborn Ophelia is?" I asked as I scaled what used to be a pillar but now formed a waist-high wall of rubble across our path, then turned to help Vale.

"The Fates didn't tell me *how*." Vale jumped down, her short sword clanging against the rock. "Tackle her if you have to, I don't care. But get that dagger away from her before she—"

Golden light exploded at our backs. I ducked against it, and when I stood, the air burning, Vale was gone, swept up by Valyrie and flying around to the front of the capitol building.

As the Angel held a dagger to Vale's collarbone, she called, "Go, Malakai!"

I hurried up the rest of the stairs, trying to figure this out. When we were in Damenal, the book I found about other realms

583

said on Revarris, they'd fought off the gods by discovering their fatal flaw, taking them out with a weapon of their own trove. That was the weapon Ophelia had forged, but what if it wasn't only about the weapon.

What if she wasn't the only—

"Holy fucking Spirits," I swore as I emerged onto the wide landing in the center of the main flight leading to the capitol building.

A wall of Angellight stood at the foot of the stairs, separating Ophelia and Echnid from everyone else. With purple lightning feeding into it, the barrier towered over the city, but through the wavering gold, I could barely make out Mila fighting off Rozelyn with—were those *spirits?* By the fucking Angels, is that where she'd gone?

As I watched, Rozelyn's serpentine hair snapped out at Mila. Her vicious smile from earlier flashed back to me. She *wanted* Mila, wanted me.

A snaking tendril whipped out from Rozelyn's head and came within an inch of biting down on Mila's neck. It took every fucking ounce of strength not to run to her, to fight with her, as more of those deadly serpents flashed their fangs.

I looked between Mila and Ophelia, and I knew which way I had to choose if I wanted to end this for good. Not just save Mila for another few moments, but ensure she got the peace she sought after so many battles. That everyone did.

Ophelia was on her hands and knees, coughing as she squinted into the light. With her limp wings dragging through the dust, she looked so tired. Defeated. My Bind twisted in pain for her. I couldn't let her do this.

A figure emerged from the gold wall, parting it like it was nothing more than a waterfall. There was something so familiar but so out of place in her features, the cascading dark hair.

I'd seen her earlier tonight, leaving the room with Artale's mural. But also—

"What in the fucking realms is she doing here?"

CHAPTER EIGHTY-SIX
OPHELIA

I POURED EVERY LAST OUNCE OF POWER I RETAINED INTO keeping that wall stretching toward the heavens, draining myself. I wouldn't need it anymore.

My spine was shredded from the stairs; my arms, wings, and legs heavy and limp like they'd been weighted by boulders.

"Aimee?" I forced out again as my lungs seized, her name high and broken on my cracked lips. My aching head swam, gold blistering around the Storyteller's frame, around the entire square.

Violet lightning bolted from the sky, striking the top of the wall and melding with the pure gold light. The added power sent a wave of euphoria through me. The clouds continued to feed into my magic, to warp and twist the surface of the seraph power, until it appeared a veil was being torn right in the center.

And behind Aimee, four more forms wavered, too distorted within the light for me to make them out.

"Hello, Ophelia," Aimee said. The gold chain belt around her low hips and matching stacked necklaces gleamed as she bowed her head.

"We came looking for you," I coughed out over the dust in my throat. My fingers curled into the stairs, debris digging into my knees. "The other Storytellers—they didn't know you."

"I know, Chosen Child. I am sorry I was not there."

It was too late. Too late for apologies. Too late for her help. We'd needed answers before, but now...now, we were out of time.

Echnid paced liked a caged beast behind me, his mortality a curse now that he couldn't fight back.

"You woke the beasts," Aimee said, gazing across the square through the shimmering violet streaked wall of light. Awe shone in her eyes. "They are here to help." Her voice rained around me like a light mist, touching my skin and healing where it hurt.

With my fading strength, I looked around the square, too. At the wolves now baring warriors, as large as the *lupine daimons* that guarded the tundra during the Undertaking. At the human and warrior and spirit allies who had arrived at the last possible minute, full of the vigor our dying forces needed. At the phoenixes and sphinxes, the gryphons and khrysaor and Sapphire, whom I'd woken. Woken to get them here. All leading to this moment, when a girl had to die in order for everyone else to live.

"They'll be okay," I choked out, each word sharp with the tang of my blood.

"I am sorry it came to this," Aimee said.

But how could she say that, truly? It wasn't her doing. The gods had always planned to use me. At least this way, I'd be taking out the worst of them with me. From the Spirit Realm, I'd plot to do away with the rest. With my father, with Lyria, with all those who'd come to save us tonight, we'd keep going.

Softly, Aimee said, "When you are done, we will dispose of the god."

Digging my shredded palms into the step beneath me, I staggered upright. The Vincienzo dagger glimmered on the ground, the blade nicked but humming with magic. The kind that knew it had a task to complete. And like the dregs of magic within me, it *hungered* for it.

Echnid was mortal, I reminded myself as I wrapped my fingers around the hilt.

I can kill him, I encouraged as I lifted the Vincienzo dagger high, trying not to look at the sharpened point.

But right before I lowered the blade to my own heart, a scream tore through the air, "Ophelia, stop!"

And I met Malakai's eyes right as he shoved Lucidius's dagger into his chest, at the heart of his North Star Bind.

CHAPTER EIGHTY-SEVEN
OPHELIA

"NO!" THE SCREAM SHREDDED MY THROAT. MY ENTIRE body. I was being ripped apart as the wall of Angellight dissolved into a shower of sparks and roaring golden flames.

Echnid screamed as Malakai fell, and my shimmering, agonized fire swam over him. The god collapsed, blood gushing from his chest, and his body withered upon the steps.

Without my conscious direction, what was left of my magic rose. It was a tide ready to drown. A storm seeking to demolish. A captive monster devouring its dying master whole.

Leashes of light tied his limbs down as fire licked up Echnid's arms and legs, scorching every inch of his mortal body. It drove beneath his skin and boiled his blood. Raised a torrent in his bones and sent inky fingers to shred his veins. It pried his ribs open and ripped his lungs out his back, a set of glorious, bloody wings.

And I killed the god from the inside out.

This, I told him as he met my eyes, all of our screams drowning in the night. *This is who you wanted me to become.*

This was who he made me—a weapon, a defense of the gods, his unending salvation. But instead, I took that image, and I became his beautiful undoing, drenched in the light of the seraphs.

And though something within me was severing, a fate was sealed as I watched the god die beneath my seraph magic.

The Vincienzo dagger clattered to the stone stairs, light crackling and sparking around me, and I ran. Not toward Echnid—toward Malakai.

The tearing of my chest, my lungs, sent my knees buckling and the world spinning. Something vital was being severed, but I forced my feet to carry me—stumbling—to Malakai's side. Or maybe it was my broken heart that was doing it, the girl who loved the boy with the freckles and forest-green eyes like her life depended on it.

I collapsed beside him where he had propped himself against a chunk of a fallen pillar, both of us struggling to pull down air. Blood across his chest. Face so pale. My body went numb aside from the endless tearing behind my ribs.

"Malakai," I said through a rough breath. Tears poured over my cheeks, every word ragged. "Malakai, why in the Angels did you do this?"

Malakai's hand fumbled through the air, and I gripped it tight, meeting those forest-green eyes for the thousandth time in my life. "You don't deserve to die, Phel."

"Neither do you!" My voice cracked. I squeezed his hand tighter.

"Tired of us all fighting. Had to stop." He repeated the worries he'd confessed to me earlier tonight, but my argument still stood.

"*You fought, too*," I growled. "You never wanted to be a part of this. You shouldn't have had to."

Years ago, he'd signed the treaty willingly for the good of the Mystiques, but ever since the truth of that deceit was exposed, he'd been searching for a way out. He didn't want to be a Chosen Child or anything connected to it. But he always had been because of these tattoos we'd naively marked ourselves with at seventeen years old.

Teenagers who unknowingly had the power to change the tides of ancient wars.

Whose spirits weighed as much as a god's when it came to the fate of the realms.

Because I was the life that had to be given for Echnid's, but Malakai...Malakai had a piece of *my* soul within him, tied to his own. The Bind may have never worked properly—had never been meant to be—but that didn't mean it hadn't been so very real. A true born link between our spirits.

And when Malakai drove a dagger through the home of that connection, he didn't only give his own life. He killed the piece of mine that lived in him. He sacrificed himself so *I* could live.

I breathed over the pain of my soul dying, curling on the ground beside Malakai as my body trembled with sobs. He rolled his head to face me, and if there wasn't such destruction around us, tears pouring over my cheeks and blood staining his chest, I could have thought we were sixteen years old and back in our clearing.

For a moment, we were. The world fell away, tall grasses curving up to shield our shadowed frames and a star-flecked night overhead to protect us.

He'd never been tortured.

We'd never been ripped apart.

We were living out that beautiful future we thought we'd have, so full of innocence and hope.

Perhaps in another life, we'd get that.

My vision was going dark from the pain of the Bind severing and the strength the seraph magic took from me. As I saw myself reflected in those green eyes, I thought his were darkening, too.

People moved around us, the air growing warmer with their bodies. Tolek and Cypherion. Santorina and Jezebel. Vale. Mila.

Mila.

She threw herself at Malakai's other side, brushing his hair back from his face. Sobbing, she pressed her forehead to his, saying things I couldn't hear, but my heart broke even further for the both of them.

This wasn't *fucking fair*.

"Gorgons," Malakai croaked, still checking on her. Even now.

"All dead," Mila sobbed.

Malakai hissed, shifting. "I promised nothing but death would take me from you, General."

Mila shushed him, kissed him. "Tomorrow," she said. "Every tomorrow." Her words were acceptance, but the pain was in her trembling lips.

"Tomorrow," he said, and there was an embrace in that word, too.

"I love you, Warrior Prince."

"No," I wheezed as they said goodbye.

No, this couldn't be it. I'd been prepared to give up my life, but Malakai's? He didn't deserve this end. I forced myself to sit up and search around us. Pain from the Bind throbbed through me, every breath pressing on an open wound.

Malakai squeezed my hand.

My attention dropped down to him, and he whispered, "Peace."

Peace. The word filtered through me like an unexpected wind, unsettling and soothing all at once. That was all he wanted after years of pain. And it was what he deserved. So, with Tolek holding my limp body for support, I curved back toward Malakai.

"It's okay," I told him over the pain of our shredded Bind, my entire body trembling and revolting at the words. "It's okay, Malakai. You don't have to fight anymore if you want to go." I squeezed his hand, my soul aching. "You can go. We will be okay. You took care of us."

He'd been fighting for us all for years. Before any of us even knew it. Day after day, he threw himself before blades meant for *our* hearts. One of them finally struck true.

One was fatal.

"I love you, Malakai," I said.

His response was a wheezed whisper. "Until the stars stop shining."

"Until the stars stop shining," I agreed.

He had been those stars, had been the one that showed me what they looked like as a young girl. My North Star, even after everything we'd been through. I thought he'd be that for years to come once we fought our way out of this. After Echnid and the seraph magic, some reliance had sealed between us.

But Malakai and I never got our happy ending.

His gaze rolled back to Mila, searching her tear-streaked face like he was committing it to memory. His blood wasn't flowing as quickly anymore. His eyes were dull.

And I swore, time stopped in that moment. Everything froze, taking on this murky, detached feeling like the world moved through mud.

Aimee attended to Echnid's scorched, bloodied corpse behind us. The khrysaor and the phoenixes burned Echnid's remaining shadowed beasts. The cerberus and demigods were swallowed by the explosion of Angellight and violet lightning. But none of it mattered.

Because if we lived in a world where innocent warriors had to die for the life of a god, did any of this mean anything? If I was crying over Malakai's body with Tolek, Cypherion, Santorina, and Jezebel—with the friends who had defended each other and fought for each other at every turn only for one of us to not see the dawn—why had we fought in the first place?

What were we leaving behind? The Angels swore we were their legacy, but they'd offered us up readily, for reasons I still didn't know. What would remain now?

Malakai would leave behind a hole in our lives. A vast empty space, more permanent than it had been the first time we lost him because this time it would lack something vital: hope.

Tolek and Cypherion were on either side of me, tears streaming down both of their dust-strewn faces as they said good-bye. Rina choked off her own words as she tried to heal his wound, but it was no use. Somehow, that blade had been infallible. Answers we'd never get now.

Vale shook her head, muttering to Erista as her breathing sped. "I didn't know. This was only one fortune of thousands. I didn't know he'd choose this."

The pain ripping through me deepened as Malakai slipped away. My breaths came in seizing gasps. The world already felt so wrong without him.

So, with my own stubborn will, I clung to the slice of Malakai's soul that was connected to mine. Fed it all of those memories I had stored up over the past twenty-one years. Of us, of him and Tolek and Cypherion, images of the future he deserved. I gripped the thread tighter and *begged* someone to change this outcome.

Because though our Bind may be severed, I would never stop fighting for my North Star.

I'd told him it was okay to let go, but I didn't want him to choose that. I willed him to hang on, to keep the stars shining because his story was not done being written.

Shadows descended around us. The Angels. All but Thorn joined the vigil. My eyes locked with Damien's purple pair, pain bleeding through them. And anger emboldened me to rise onto my knees.

"*Fix this!*" I raged over the shredding pain in my chest. "Fix it, Damien! This is *all your fault!* You are the reason we are here—the reason he sacrificed himself! *Save him!*"

Across the city center, silence had fallen, making room for every one of my slicing, guttural words to land their desperate blows. Pain hummed in my ears, the Bind on fire as I clung feverishly to Malakai's life.

"SAVE HIM!" I screeched, one hand curling around Malakai's, the other locked to Tolek's arm around my waist as he held me up.

"There might not be time," Damien said. "It may not be what he wanted."

"He wants it!" Mila blurted. Malakai's eyes closed as his head rested in her lap. "He wanted another chance at our lives after this." She didn't look away from Malakai, but her words were cutting enough that even Damien would feel them. "He only did this because he wanted it all to *end* and because his heart is so bruised, he thought everyone deserved to see tomorrow more than he did. If there is a way, give him the *fucking* chance after what he did for you all."

Damien swallowed at the command, rarely having interacted with my friends beyond me. The other Angels were quiet behind him, deferring to the Mystique Prime Warrior.

And around Xenovia, no one said a word in defiance. Warriors kneeled in the city center, the injured cried out as healers transported them, and spirits continued to undo Thorn's mind manipulation. But the mythical creatures perched on rooftops. Soldiers placed their hands over their hearts. And everyone waited in tense silence for the Angels to act.

Damien exchanged a glance with Xenique, and she nodded. What that meant, I didn't know. Didn't care.

He turned back to us and said, "I will try."

Without more of an explanation, Damien lifted Malakai's limp body gently into his arms. I squeezed his hand, and Mila kissed the man she loved one more time, whispering to him though his chest didn't rise or fall.

Then, the Angel beat his wings and launched into the air.

I slumped back against Tolek, pulling Mila with me, her frame quivering more the further Malakai got.

And as Damien flew off toward the mountains, the night was pitch black.

Every star had stopped shining.

CHAPTER EIGHTY-EIGHT
DAMIEN

I HAD NOT IMAGINED VICTORY WOULD TASTE SO BITTER.

In all my existence, I had suffered hundreds of wars. And never once had surviving been so heavy. The loss of life was always sorrowful, but it was necessary.

This star-tied boy in my arms, though, was not. He was never the one meant to suffer. It had always been the Chosen. And for the first time, I considered perhaps she had not been treated fairly either.

My brothers, sisters, and I had one goal. To reclaim the power that had been unfairly taken from us so we could restore the Balance and find those lost to time. We had been willing to see anyone suffer for it because it was so much bigger than us. Than any warriors on Ambrisk. The power we once contained spread across realms, to those suppressed and held down, to the hands of the great mist herself.

I landed atop the rocky ridge. Heat I had not felt since prior to the Ascension burned across my wings and flesh. Ravenous lava sparked into the air, bubbling and wanting. It churned, more insistent than I ever recalled.

It hungered for a warrior. For a subject to take just as my brothers and sisters and I had taken. The body in my arms did not move, his life nearly faded away now. There was only one chance.

"We did not work so hard only for you to die today, Malakai Blastwood," I said.

The molten fire yearned to claim him, and one way or another it would. So, I lowered him into the heat and let him slip away. It was up to his spirit what happened next.

CHAPTER EIGHTY-NINE
MALAKAI

DEATH WAS LIGHTER THAN I EXPECTED.

It wasn't often that I considered what the Spirit Realm would be like. When I was imprisoned, the idea had hounded me, but I never came up with a clear picture of it.

Dark, though. Heavy. Weighed down by the things you carried on your spirit. That's what I had always expected in that cave within the Mystique Mountains. But now, I was weightless.

Air swished past me, and warmth cocooned me.

Warmth?

Why was it warm here?

I wrenched my eyes open, and an involuntary scream bellowed from me.

I wasn't in the Spirit Realm—or maybe I was. Either way, I was fucking falling, rocky walls streaking past in blurs woven with veins of orange and yellow. *Fire*.

My limbs wheeled around me, looking for anything to grab on to, but there was nothing in this endless descent, just the sky a pinprick so far above. Until finally, I flipped feet over head, and tumbled across a rocky cave floor. My teeth sliced into my tongue, my shoulder jarring against the ground.

"Pretty fucking rough for someone who just died to save the entire realm," I grumbled to myself as I braced my hands against the ground and struggled upright. The rock was warm beneath my palms, and while I definitely felt disoriented, like I was outside of my body in a way, I jumped a bit at the sensation.

"You aren't the first," a gruff voice said, and I shot to my feet, spinning toward it.

"Holy fucking Spirits," I gasped.

He sighed. "Always so disrespectful."

I guessed in a way he was right because this was no warrior before me. Not a living one at least. This was a *fucking Spirit*. His slender frame was sheer white, eerily similar to Echnid's mist, but with a smoky texture that shimmered as the man folded his arms where he floated.

And I was—

I pivoted, eyes flicking from the veins of flame running up the walls to the stalagmites rimming the perimeter of the circular space. The pool of fire that took up one edge bubbling and flickering blue as it shot sporadically into the air.

"I'm in the Spirit Volcano," I exhaled.

The Spirit grunted in confirmation, a frown carving his full lips.

"How in the fucking Spirits am I here?" I blurted out.

"Will you stop saying that?" he grumbled.

"Sorry," I said halfheartedly, sure I'd do it again. I wandered to the nearest wall, every step enhancing that weird, in-between feeling. The ground was solid, my boots echoing as they thumped across stone, but the weight of my feet against it didn't feel centered.

I dragged a hand across the rough wall, pressing my thumb onto a sharp point. It didn't cut me. And the fire didn't burn when I swept a finger through it.

"Stop touching that," the Spirit barked.

I shot to attention, turning back to him. "But I *died*. How in the realms am I *here*?" My head snapped down, and—"Fuck." I breathed as a wave of nausea rolled through me. The stab wound through my tattoo shone. It was clean, but not healed. Just a gaping hole in my fucking chest, the North Star beneath torn up.

"It appears someone has done you a favor" was all the Spirit said.

I narrowed my eyes at him. He clearly wasn't the helpful kind. Of fucking course. I sacrificed myself to save the realm and the Spirits see to it that I get the most ill-tempered of them all to greet me.

"What am I doing here?"

"Isn't it obvious," he drawled. "You are here to complete the Undertaking."

My heart thudded. Throat dry, I forced out, "What do you mean?"

"It will not be exactly as it is for living warriors, but you are going through the steps of the process just the same, should you choose to."

"I never wanted to complete the Undertaking," I blubbered like an absolute fool. I'd decided after Echnid had tried to turn me into a seraph while the Angels stood by that I wanted nothing to do with the rituals they'd passed down to us.

The Spirit lifted one thick, perfectly trimmed brow. "Then I suppose it is a good thing you cannot."

My hands fisted at my side. "What does that mean?"

"We will find out together," he said, adding on a low grumble, "if the others deign to show—"

As if summoned, a second Spirit materialized beside the first, the woman's form was the same white smoke as his, but where silver hair floated around his shoulders, hers was braided tightly down her back. I couldn't tell what either of their coloring would have been in life, and the monotony of it rose the hair on my arms. Angels, I wanted to get out of here.

"Apologies for my late arrival," she said, her voice much warmer than the first. "This was unprecedented. I had to work quickly to ensure he could make it."

Across the woman's bare arms, a patchwork shimmered— something I recognized even void of color.

Scars.

"Then we can begin," the man said.

"Aren't there supposed to be three of you?" I asked. I may not have planned to attempt the ritual, but I knew how the damn thing worked. Three Spirits to provide mental challenges, likely pointing out things you'd rather leave untouched. "And what about the physical feat?"

"You put a knife through your own chest," the man pointed out. "The physical task is more than fulfilled."

Avoiding looking at that gaping wound again, I supposed he was right. Still, I didn't want to do this.

"Can't I just go to the Spirit Realm like all others who die?" Other than the agony of leaving the people I loved behind, I thought it would be a quick and painless journey. Apparently not.

The woman's lips tipped into a soft, eerily familiar smile. "Humor us."

I supposed I truly had no other way out of this. "Fine," I agreed. "What are your names?"

I skipped right over the formalities of the ritual, wanting to get to the point. There was a lot that remained secret about the Undertaking, but these two had to have been assigned to me for a reason. There were countless Spirits in the Volcano; it wasn't random.

"I am Brenna," the woman said cordially. "Please to meet you Malakai Augustus Blastwood."

"You, too," I lied, turning toward the man.

"Hectatios."

Hectatios was a man of many words it appeared.

"Good to meet you," I said, and he—to no surprise—grunted. I fought off the agitation that pounded through my chest at the dismissal.

Hectatios said, "There is something that has persisted through ancient histories. It has painted every legend in crimson sorrows, yet it is the purest form of adoration. It is something you know intimately after tonight, Malakai Augustus Blastwood. A consequence and its driving force, things I once stood at the end of. A decision that warps the heart and stains the stones of existence for eternity."

This was his test, I realized. More of a general rambling than a riddle, but a lesson I was meant to unravel all the same.

And it was all too personal for me to pretend I didn't know exactly what Hectatios was speaking of.

"You mean sacrifice?" I asked. The wound on my chest stung.

"I do."

"What of it?" Because that could not be the only point to Hectatios's presence here. To acknowledge my sacrifice.

"You and I are not that different," Hectatios said.

"How?" I asked.

His silver hair waved around him as his shoulders rose and fell with a reluctant breath. "I once was tied to an Alabath cursed to defy the Angels."

"You loved...Annellius?" I asked.

"He was my closest confidant," Hectatios stated. "We were together since birth. And I, too, gave my life for this curse."

"You were..."

"I was you, many centuries ago," Hectatios clarified.

"What do you mean?" *How?*

"During the age of the first Angelcurse, I was the one by Annellius's side. I was the one whose life was lost in order for him to realize this curse was in fact a plague on Ambrisk, not a restoration of the Balance."

"But Annellius didn't free Echnid."

"No," he agreed. "My sacrifice came much sooner than yours. It was the wake-up call he needed, and I took it willingly, seeing much further ahead than he could, blinded as he was by greed."

Dammit, look at what this Angelcurse did to those who dared to love an Alabath.

Love. That was what he wanted from me here. To admit the connection between the two.

"Sacrifice," I repeated the first explanation to his rambling. "And the driving force of it: love."

It was such a simple answer, the two really worked hand in hand. When you were utterly devoted to someone, what lengths would you go to keep them?

Apparently, the ends of Angelblessed existence. And you would hold no regret in your spirit as you went.

Hectatios nodded. I'd reached the conclusion he'd hoped for and understood that final message.

"I will go next," Brenna said, a bit obviously given that it was only the two of them. The fires lining the cavern dimmed, but those scars across her arms still shimmered like freshly healed skin.

Brenna swept before Hectatios, her long braid swinging to her waist. Her square cheekbones pulled at her skin, as if she had been very thin when she lived.

"While you were trapped by bars and chains, I suffered from being slain. Not by blades or enemies, but unseen deadly maladies. An infirmary bed was my prison, but one bright day, I was risen. It was not what I hoped as fate, yet it was written on my death date. And when it came, I accepted it as true, in order to attend those needing a change of tune."

Her words skated along the walls with a trickling power, almost tangible. I ignored the fact that she broke the rhyme at the end, attempting to unravel what she'd stated.

She wasn't killed. An infirmary bed—so she'd been sick. That was likely what had taken her life, how she got the scars adorning her skin, and why she appeared so frail.

Why would a warrior who died of disease be one of my Spirits? I studied her as I considered, counting her scars to try to clear my mind.

If I was her, I would have questioned *why me*. Why was I dealt this fate when so many others weren't? But something in her words rang more positive. Like she'd made peace—

Peace.

That's what I had been searching for all these fucking years. But while Brenna's battle had been a physical ailment, I'd fought mine in my mind. The days of crushing darkness. The days I'd tried to run—run so fucking far and fast that no one would find me. That I could barricade myself within my own mind.

But someone had pushed through.

Someone fought for me. Someone helped me heal.

Heal.

I pressed a hand to the wound on my chest, barely feeling it.

Brenna hadn't healed physically, but she'd found acceptance in her fate. Enough to be one of the Spirits deeming warriors worthy or not in their own Undertaking. She had not healed her body...

My attention snapped from a scar twisting the skin of her wrist to her eyes. And as if she heard my reasoning, Brenna smiled.

"A healed spirit," I said confidently.

And when Brenna nodded, the empty cage in my chest inflated with pride. And it felt...good. Accomplished to have gotten a true riddle of the Spirits correct. *Right* to have tried.

"And do you feel you have that now?" Brenna asked.

I balked, a bit thrown off guard that she had more questions. I assumed I would just move from one to the next. But I answered honestly, "Yes."

"Do you truly?" Brenna challenged, her fingers drumming against her arm. "Do you feel that you have conquered your demons? That you could go on?"

If my heart could beat, it would have been thundering. I'd made progress toward overcoming my past. I understood a lot of the shit I experienced and why I reacted the way I did a lot better now. I could stand on a battlefield without running.

But was I healed?

"Do you ever fully heal?" I asked, and Brenna nodded for me to go on. "I have healed, yes. My spirit—well, it's a lot fucking stronger than it once was. It's being pieced back together after it was shredded. That's definitely healing. But from what I've experienced, healing is a process. One step, one hurdle at a time. One demon slain each day. But the healing never ends. You have to continue to work on it, to fight."

Brenna asked, "And is that something you are prepared to do?"

Yes. I was. I didn't take that blade for Ophelia because I didn't want to fight. I took it because *she* had fought enough.

I sought peace, yes, but I would always be fighting internally. Even if some days were good and quiet, one day, my mind would get loud again. The scars would ache. The deceit would resurface. I'd have to work.

And I could do that, but...

"How do you just carry on?" I asked. If I was being honest, the prospect was fucking daunting. "If I want to, how do I?"

And Brenna grinned. "Look up."

Look up. The words rang through my mind in another voice.

"If you are asking these questions, then I believe you are ready for your third Spirit," Brenna said, drifting back beside Hectatios.

"Third?" I asked, looking between them.

A voice I never wanted to hear again said, "Malakai."

Not him.

How—why? This was all such a fucking joke. Sacrificial love, healed spirits, and now...this. It made sense why the first two Spirits' challenges hadn't been that difficult. They had only been priming me for the third. Reminding me of how I got here and what I needed if I wanted to fight through what came next.

When I turned around, my father was there. Lucidius Blastwood, with the smoky-white form of the two Spirits behind me.

And when I met his eyes, my mind warred to retreat. Like a wounded creature who had been struck time and again, something within me cowered. It hid in the darkest parts of my chest, hoping the shadows would mask its presence before the man who had caused me so much pain.

But I would not shrink in the face of this man who'd sullied our name and began the chain of torture I'd endured. It took every ounce of strength I had left, but I pulled that damaged bit to the forefront and displayed it outright, let him see who he beat down time and again and who rose from it.

"What are you doing here?" I asked, voice lethal. "Forget it," I added as he opened his mouth. I faced the other two Spirits, careful not to turn my back entirely on Lucidius. "I don't want to talk to him."

"Malakai—" he said.

"Quiet!" I barked. "How do I get out of here?"

"The only way out is through," Brenna said, her voice still a melody.

"Not with him," I argued.

"I'm not trying to win you over," Lucidius said. "Stop being childish and listen."

"Ah, there's the loving father I remember."

He ignored the heavy sarcasm layering my voice. "I am here for an explanation and to provide something you desperately need, son."

I peeked at him. His voice was so much more level than when

I'd last seen him. So much saner. And his last words echoed through my head, spoken in a cavern not unlike this one. *There is so much you do not know.*

I took a deep, steadying breath, and searched for the *healed* part of me I'd just claimed I'd found. "Explain," I clipped.

"I have to go back far," Lucidius clarified.

"I am dead, *father*," I sneered. "I have nothing but time."

His tongue dragged across his teeth in a way I so often did. But I shook away the wrench that realization dug in my gut as he began, "I knew what was meant for the Alabath girl."

Surprise bolted through me. "How?"

"When I first became Revered, with my scheme with Queen Kakias to unite the warrior clans under one ruler"—Spirits, he still spoke of her with reverence—"I began studying Angel lore. I wanted to be as prepared as possible for what we were attempting, and history seemed like the best way. But Kakias always spoke like she knew more than me, and I know now that she did."

"Because of Bant's Spirit," I clarified.

He nodded. "I did not know that the Spirit of the Engrossian Angel was within her. That he was attempting to turn her into a Chosen Child, that she was aware of the emblems hidden across the continent or what Ophelia would be able to do with them." A touch of sadness entered his voice at that. "There were clues, and that was when I started piecing things together. Started visiting sacred sites and keeping track in the journals you and your brother have studied."

The journals that were no more than ramblings because the strength of the magic and the desperation to uncover Kakias's secrets drove him mad.

"I am sorry, son," Lucidius said, and those words shocked me to attention.

"For what?"

"For all of it. I never wanted you to be imprisoned or tortured."

Anger roared within me. "You were the one that ordered it done!"

"I was not in my right mind," he admitted. "I never was once the Angel magic touched me. I was not made to handle it, and I understand that now. And when you received that Bind with the Alabath girl, I knew it was a death sentence for you. I knew what I was doing in separating you from her—in forcing your hand to sign the treaty—but I was not in control of my mind when the torture began. Powers were stirring too deeply in the world. Echnid's magic was tampering with the Balance, and I was lost to it."

He'd been livid the night he found out about the Bind. It was the angriest I'd ever seen him. And that was why. He knew of pieces of the Angelcurse. He knew tying myself to Ophelia would ensure I was killed or at the very least suffered the loss of a soul bond. I supposed in one way, that had been a well-intentioned argument.

But not how he tried to *save* me from that fate.

"You think I will forgive you that easily?" I asked. "I was tortured for *two years*, father. People I love were tortured during that war."

"The general," Lucidius said, understanding. "She is so good, Malakai. Do not let her go."

"Not that I would ever take your advice on romance," I bit out, "but I have no intention of ever doing so."

"Good," he said, as if he was actually, in any forsaken realm, trying to give me fatherly guidance.

He hadn't been himself. I was trying to separate the way the Angel magic had warped him from the man who tried to save me, but it was so fucking hard. Could it even truly be two people? Even the man who tried to save me was still loyal to Kakias over the Mystiques.

I ran my hands through my hair, attempting to gather myself.

"I don't forgive you," I clarified, and a part of me was proud of myself for standing my ground. He looked like he didn't expect me to extend any sort of repentance anyway. "But I want to understand for my own sake. I want closure." It was something I'd been living without for years. Something I needed to really move on. "Beyond the Angel magic, what was your purpose in all of this?"

There is so much you do not know.

"In my travels, I learned of an almighty dagger. One that could kill the most powerful life sources if forged in a sacred source of magic from each of the seven clans." His eyes dropped to my waist. I hadn't realized the very dagger I'd stabbed myself with—his dagger—had found its way back to my belt.

And the pieces snapped together.

"This is the dagger?" I asked. "This one, that I took from your body when you died. This is the weapon Echnid was trying to destroy? It's the one he burned the trove to melt?"

"Yes," Lucidius said. "Though the one the Alabath sisters imbued is powerful, *that* is the weapon the god was after. It is the one that could have turned him mortal originally, and the magic within is what sealed your death tonight so none of your healer friends could help."

And I'd had it all this time.

Used it on myself so I would kill the piece of Ophelia's soul tied to mine. It was all I could think to do when I realized she was about to sacrifice herself.

"Of course, I didn't know what it was for when I made it. I simply wanted the power, and I never imagined the horror that would befall Ambrisk after my death. But I am happy I did it. Happy that you had it."

"So I could sacrifice myself?" I scoffed. "Right."

"No, Malakai. So you could rid the world of Echnid and return to a peaceful realm."

"Return?" I asked.

"You do not have to," he corrected. "You have survived horrors, and now you have a choice. You can stop fighting, remain in the Spirit Volcano, and finally rest. Or you can face the Spirit Fire and see if you'll make it back to your life."

I looked from the misty white frame of Lucidius's spirit to the swirling pool of fire rippling along the cavern's edge. The final step of the Undertaking. A melding of oranges and yellows and blues that was one of the most potent sources of magic on Ambrisk. A gate to the heart of the mountains. Even from here, the heat seared.

Why should I do it? Why should I go back? To keep fighting

battles we'd already lost, with my father's traitorous blood in my veins?

No. That wasn't all it meant, was it? It couldn't be.

Going back also meant living. Right? It meant feeling the love that made a sacrifice so easy and working to heal a broken spirit. It meant the victories and defeats of battles, the thrill of waking up every damn day to ice-blue eyes and a low laugh.

That's what the point of Hectatios's and Brenna's messages had been, right? They weren't the typical riddles of the ritual, but reminders of the path forward. A question of *how does one go on* and the promise that it would be hard but worth it. It had to be.

There had to be something on the other side of the Spirit Fire, or else what was the point of burning?

Or—my resolve faltered as the dagger at my waist heated— maybe the way to the quiet was staying here. Here within these cavernous walls. Becoming a blessed spirit, claimed by the dead. Going to the Spirit Realm.

You don't have to fight anymore if you want to go.

Look up.

The sky was a pinprick high above, smoke obscuring the stars. My chest tightened. I looked between my father and the Spirit Fire, decision made.

CHAPTER NINETY
OPHELIA

THE FIRST SENSATION I REGISTERED AFTER HOURS OF numb silence in the guest house was tearing. I screamed, crashing to the floor of the sitting room where we'd all gathered after Damien took Malakai.

"Alabath?" Tolek shouted as he caught me, pulling me back onto the settee to rest against his chest. My wings were limp over the soft velvet cushion, the agony extending to every part of my body. We'd been sitting here all day with our friends, barely anyone talking, no one daring to hope.

"Holy fucking Angels," I said through gritted teeth. "It hurts!"

It was ripping. Like threads were woven through my flesh, pulling fiercely against the skin, all the way down to my spirit. Tugging my bones and blood and self.

"What hurts?" Tolek asked, concern bleeding through his voice even as he fought to stay calm.

"My—Ahh!" I cried out, unable to form coherent words. They barely made sense as they floated through my mind.

"Is it the seraph power?" Jezebel asked. She must have been kneeling on the foot of the settee, but I couldn't pry my eyes open. Everything was heavy, like the exhaustion after a battle hard fought. Like I was being stuffed into a suffocating nothingness.

"I don't know." Tolek brushed my sweaty hair back from my brow.

"She's not feverish or bleeding," a steady voice said, near enough to be assessing me. Everyone was blending together beneath the sharp hum of my soul being ripped apart. "It could be an internal injury from the battle."

It's not, I wanted to say. *It is so much worse.*

"It's not seraph power," a knowing, bell-like voice said. Thank the fucking Angels. "And it's not an injury. It's the Bind. It's severing."

A cracking female voice—one ragged with tears—answered, "But soul bonds only sever if one party dies."

An emptiness settled over me, and I blinked open heavy eyes, meeting a crystal blue pair. Mila shook her head as if she was asking me to say it wasn't true.

But if my Bind was severing, that meant Malakai...

Malakai had truly died.

∾

THE HOLLOW SENSATION was a void in my spirit. I was compressed into this space of endless nothingness—nothing but pain and something severely lacking.

An emptiness where a sense of someone else belonged.

I sat before the sitting room window until the sun was setting over the desert. Setting on a day that marked a change in the entire realm, in all of us within this house.

Throughout Xenovia, warriors were mourning. They were beginning the long process of restoring their city after a barrage of godly and Angelic magical attacks.

A god was dead, scorched by my Angellight and the ashes disposed of. Ambrisk was free of his threat.

And in his place, an innocent soul had been claimed.

I tried to feel down the broken Bind, but nothing answered.

My knees were pulled to my chest. The dunes beyond the floor-to-ceiling windows wavered, their shapes indeterminable in my cloudy vision.

"Drink something, *apeagna*," Tolek whispered from his spot beside me. As he had every so often all day. He hadn't left. No one had, but he remained close enough for me to touch when I needed to.

Numbly, I did as I was told, then looked back over the dunes. At the way the gold light shimmered along their rounded tops. At the way—

Gold light.

I sat up straighter. At my sudden movement, everyone jumped.

"The sunsets in Xenovia are deeper," I muttered.

And then, I was out the door. Running. Hope inflating the empty void of the Bind severance.

I tore through the yard, footsteps hounding me because they all saw it now, too.

Damien had returned. He descended from the sky in the direction of the mountains, gold ether tumbling off his wings and dusting the sand.

And in his arms—

"Malakai," I gasped.

Alive and grinning to see us all sprinting for him. Alive and his heart beating strongly enough that I could hear it from feet away. Alive and with a ghastly scar distorting his North Star tattoo—

But *alive.*

And despite the pain of the severed Bind, pure bliss ignited in my chest as Mila launched herself at Malakai. As he sank to the ground with her sobbing in his arms, and Tolek and Cypherion piled on top of them. Then, Barrett and Jezebel, Santorina yelling at them all not to hurt him after what he went through.

And when he finally emerged and stood, pulling me in for a hug, my head fell right against that North Star scar. Tears streaked down my face, but the quiet kind. The kind that were relieved to hear his heart beating and couldn't quite believe this was happening.

"I thought the stars stopped shining," I said, barely more than a whisper as my voice cracked.

"Never, Phel," he promised, squeezing me tight. His leather and honeysuckle scent was achingly familiar, and a fresh wave of tears started anew when I considered I almost never smelled it again. "Those stars are never going to stop shining."

Never. Malakai had fought his way back to us.

Jezebel wedged herself between us, her arms tight around Malakai's waist. "How?" she asked, voice thick as he hugged her back.

"The Undertaking," Malakai said.

My eyes widened, flicking between him and Damien. "You completed it?"

Tolek and Cypherion cheered, Mila holding tight to Malakai's hand and gazing up at him. But Malakai shook his head. "I couldn't. Not being dead, but given what I sacrificed, the ritual could restore me back to life."

"So, you didn't ascend to become a full warrior?" Mila asked, squeezing his hand.

"No," Malakai answered and wrapped his arm around her. "I was too far gone for that. The Spirit Fire just restored *me*."

"How does that feel?" Cypherion asked warily.

Malakai dragged his tongue over his teeth, assessing all of us. "It feels right," he confirmed. "I didn't want to complete the Undertaking. I'm happy without it."

And it truly was the happiest he'd sounded in ages. That alone dulled the hollow ache in my soul. We may have lost that faulty bond, may have killed pieces of our souls in the process, but we were here. And we were happy.

As the others swarmed Malakai, I met Damien's stare behind him. I squeezed Tolek's hand, jerking my head at the Angel. Tol flashed Damien a glare but nodded to me.

My wings held strongly at my back, I crossed the dunes to the Angel, walking right past him toward the streams in the distance, surrounded by cyphers and palms. Damien followed, though I didn't look at him.

"Thank you," I said when I stopped.

"He deserved another chance," Damien answered.

"You owed it to him," I clipped. My breaths turned short at the next question. "Echnid is truly gone?"

It was a worry I hadn't dared voice to my friends. In the aftermath of losing Malakai, we'd let Aimee see to disposing of the ashes. Nerves twitched through my fingers as I waited for Damien's answer.

"Yes," he finally said. "He is truly gone."

"And Thorn?" Tolek had told me how he'd disappeared under Cypherion's scythe.

Damien's feathers ruffled. "It appears Xenique employed a few...unique sources of magic when she forged that weapon. Things that could cleave open bridges."

"*Realmspinner magic*," I breathed. Thorn has been sent...elsewhere.

The Angel didn't confirm or deny it. "Thorn will be found. He will be fine." Damien's throat bobbed. "The scythe is dangerous when combined with the right magic source. It was the key Echnid was searching for. One he didn't know existed until yesterday when Xenique revealed she thought it was in this city."

The first night Echnid ever manipulated me came flashing back. When he'd seemed so aggrieved over the loss of the Realmspinners. "That's why he came?"

Damien nodded. "And because when your friends sought to distract him while you recruited Mindshaper allies, Valyrie revealed that the stars showed her how to break through Artale's defense."

Two key facts I was certain Valyrie and Xenique held for much longer than the god knew. More ploys of the Angels to get Echnid to act only when they wanted him to.

With a foreboding dip of his chin, Damien added, "See that the scythe is guarded."

I nodded, swallowing that weight. "And the gorgons and demigods?"

"All dead or returned to where they belong with no way to break back into this world, save for the aid of a Realmspinner."

My attention whipped toward him. "How?" How had they left the realm?

"Your magic was a magnificent display in that battle, Ophelia," Damien began. "And combined with Xenique's potent Godsblood and the veil she opened using the Realmspinner scythe, it created a way for the enemies to be sent away."

The violet lightning and churning black clouds. Xenique was

not only an Angel but a demigoddess, and she'd used Cypherion's scythe to create that storm. She'd had it waiting on Ambrisk all these years for a time when she needed help from...

The beings I saw when Aimee appeared, wavering in the light behind her. My skin tingled as I realized with certainty exactly who the Soulguider Angel had called on.

"The gods were here," I whispered.

Again, Damien didn't confirm it, but he didn't need to.

They may have abandoned us to fight the Angelcurse, but in the end, the gods had come.

My eyes stung, and I wiped at them. We had not been entirely alone.

"Will the Angels stay on Ambrisk?" I asked.

Damien's jaw tightened. "For now. The full might of our raw power will return to us with Echnid gone. We will carry the weight of his death as your friend does Moirenna's, and I think we would all like to embrace it. We have unfinished business in this realm. Stories to complete and secrets we are seeking. For now, though... we will be here."

The nagging curiosity within me wanted to ask more. To know what he meant by stories and secrets. But a larger part of me was tired. I didn't have room for anyone else's fights. Not right now at least.

I glanced over my shoulder to where my friends had sprawled across the sand, Tolek watching us with a quirked brow, then back at the Angel beside me.

"Thank you for not choosing any of them as your sacrifice." It had been my greatest fear when I figured out what the Angels were doing. That Damien would take one of my friends for the offering. He'd chosen an older general who had won many battles, and while it was a horrible loss felt across our army, selfishly, I was grateful.

"We needed them." That was true—many of my friends had been needed in those final moments to tighten the knot of Echnid's demise—but based on the sorrow in his voice, I had a feeling Damien had partially done it for me.

"Good luck, Damien," I said, and though he'd caused me so much strife, it was sincere. "I hope we don't see each other soon."

"Farewell, Ophelia," he muttered. "And thank you."

And instead of pushing to learn more about the ongoing quests of Angels, I turned away from the Mystique Prime Warrior and returned home.

~

We sat on the dunes until the sun was fully set, basking in the truth that we were here. Tolek and me, Malakai and Mila. Cypherion and Vale, who had disappeared inside only a moment ago to gather drinks for all of us.

Santorina was curled in Lancaster's lap, the fae's grip on her achingly tight and his eyes distant as he reeled with the loss of his sister. He'd barely spoken to anyone besides Rina, and we were giving him—both of them—the space to figure out what came next, both with grieving and their bond.

Erista and Jezebel were laying on their backs, gazing at the stars, and the three Engrossians were here, too. Barrett had returned to his normal self, thank the Spirits, though his charismatic humor seemed dulled. Tolek's, too. Everyone whose mind had been touched by Thorn seemed to be working through that violation. I was sure they would for years to come.

There were great losses in every clan. Vale shed silent tears for Harlen, and Ezalia's last words floated through my mind.

You are...good leader.

Tell my daughter I'm sorry.

I would have to visit her family. And as I sat in the sand, head on Tolek's shoulder, I watched the stars and quietly vowed to support Ezalia's daughter in whatever that apology carried, however she'd allow.

Still, for the most part, my family was here. Bruised and scarred and haunted, but here. And that was a result I hadn't dared hope for.

Tomorrow. We would start restoring Xenovia tomorrow. When that was done, we'd return to Damenal and figure out what the world looked like in the wake of two gods dying and the Angels returning to Ambrisk.

For the rest of my days, I'd do my best to live up to the words Ezalia spoke with her dying breath. To be a good leader.

But tonight, we'd rest and remember those we lost.

"Congratulations, Chosen Child," a melodic voice said from behind us, and our entire group spun. Aimee nodded to me, a small smile growing on her lips as her gaze flitted across the group. "And thank you."

"Aimee," I greeted, standing. "Why did you come?"

"It was the place I needed to be" was all she offered. "I have taken care of the ashes of the god."

I swallowed the enormity of that truth. Damien had promised it, but every time someone said it, it all slammed back into me.

"Thank you," I said.

She nodded once more, then turned. "I will see you later, Chosen Child." The Storyteller walked barefoot across the night-bathed dunes. Her long skirts trailed behind her, swishing in the sand until she was no more than a speck.

And then she was gone. Malakai and Mila were whispering to each other, the latter shaking her head as they watched the Storyteller disappear.

"Who was that?" Vale asked, returning with Cypherion, a basket in her arms while Cyph carried a tray of drinks.

"Aimee," I breathed as I took a glass and sat in the sand beside Tol. "The Storyteller I first saw in the Wayward Inn. The one Tolek saw in Bodymelder Territory months later. Then again in the pleasure house in Lendelli."

"*That* was her?" Mila blurted. She looked up at Malakai, asking him, "You might be right. That was her, right?"

He nodded. "Like I said."

"What do you mean?" I asked.

"She was in Ritalia's palace," Mila explained. "When we went to meet the queen in the isles, and Malakai and I snuck off to the library, that woman was the librarian." Her brows pulled together.

Lancaster said dully, "She isn't a fae librarian."

"She pretended to be," Mila clarified. "Before the real librarian returned."

Malakai added, "And we saw her last night when we snuck away during the bonding festivities." Barrett let out a scoff at his brother's confession, but Malakai ignored him. "She led us to the room where the door opened to lead to the information about Cypherion's scythe." He wrapped his arms tighter around Mila. "I saw her during the battle, too. Right before…"

Right before he'd sacrificed himself. Aimee had emerged from the wall of Angellight with the gods wavering behind her.

"I was confused about it," Malakai added.

"Holy Cursed Spirits," Cypherion exclaimed, nearly dropping the tray he still balanced. "I thought she looked familiar. She was in Lumin, too. When Vale and I were trying to fix her magic." He nodded at Vale. "In the fighting rings when your session took over, *that* was the Starsearcher that gave us the reading."

Vale blinked at us all. "You've all seen that woman before?"

Apparently we had. The Storyteller had been following us around Gallantia for months. Vale's expression morphed into total shock.

"What is it?" I asked, eyes flicking to the dunes Aimee had disappeared across. My skin tingled, feathers ruffling.

"That wasn't a Storyteller," Vale said. "I've seen her before—in readings. And she appeared in Valyn when the gorgon shot Jezebel. She fought her off for us." Vale shook her head. "I thought I was confused from the hysteria. Seeing things…" She gazed across the dunes. "But I suppose not."

"If she isn't a Storyteller, who is she?" Tolek asked.

Vale's attention drew back to us, and she said, "That was Thallia."

Celissia gasped, jumping up. "Thallia as in the Witch Goddess of Sorcia?"

She was the one we'd been seeing for months. Who had pointed me in the direction of the Angel emblems. Who had dropped hints for Tolek about Annellius and shown Malakai and Mila where to find the sphinx books. Who told me where the warrior sisters in the *fel strella mythos* had come from and that we should go to the Gates of Angeldust.

The very same goddess who had forged the lock that sealed Echnid in the Stone Realm had reappeared—shadowed by the other four gods—to see the Warrior God's downfall and the resolution of the Angelcurse.

"How in the everlasting Angel fuck?" Barrett asked.

"I don't know," I said, head swiveling to where the goddess had disappeared.

But it seemed that the gods had been much closer than we'd ever thought.

And as we sat around a mystlight lantern, a part of me wondered whether that was a good thing or not, and where Thallia had gone now.

But just like I had with Damien, I set aside the curiosities. We'd survived this battle, gods be damned. We'd won with the strength of our own true warrior hearts, the magic woven in myths, and the ferocity of the last seraph.

And now, we earned the right to rest.

So, I leaned back against Tolek's shoulder and let the gentle sounds of the desert mesh with my friends' casual conversations, the laughter forcing itself through the darkness, and the warmth hovering among our cabal of damaged spirits.

And as I watched the stars sit contently in the sky, I didn't think about the legends they spun, the battles they oversaw, or the deities waiting between them.

I only took a deep breath and embraced the peace we'd earned.

EPILOGUE
MALAKAI

Four Months Later

"Stop fussing," Mila said, swatting my hand away from my collar.

"Sorry, but I've never done this before." I ran my palms down my thin tunic. The green fabric clung to my skin in the lingering summer heat. Here in northern Mystique Territory, it wasn't quite as warm as it got down in Palerman, but given how anxious I was, the air was heavier than normal.

Mila tracked the way my fingers ticked over the hilt of the dagger at my waist, absently counting the gems lining the handle. I hadn't even realized I was doing it.

"Don't be nervous," she assured.

I scoffed. "Easy for you to say!"

She turned toward me, tilting her face up. The streaks of sunlight through the cypher branches highlighted just how bright the blues of her eyes were. For a minute, I got lost in them as she ran her hands up my chest, batting away my own from continuing to fiddle. I settled on her hips instead, dragging her a step closer. The silk tunic she had tucked into her leathers was cool. Calming. And the leather corset she wore over it cinched her waist, leaving nothing to the imagination.

Maybe this was a bad idea. Maybe we should just go back to the cottage we were renting. Try again tomorrow—

"They're going to love you," Mila stated.

"How do you know that?" I challenged.

Her arms tightened behind my head, the smaller gold bracelets she swapped out for her usual cuffs clinking together, her scars visible. Spirits, I loved how open she was about them now.

She whispered, "Because I do."

Mila loved me. She told me every day, and still I didn't think I'd ever get used to it. A love I'd come back from the dead for. Her along with all my friends and family, but especially her. Those two words that had been the ones that pushed me to dive into the Spirit Fire during the Undertaking. *Look up*.

The scar over my former North Star tattoo throbbed.

It had been her voice I'd heard when I swam through the flames—when they'd pulled me apart and shredded my being to test if I was worthy of returning. A part of me still doubted I was. Thought they must have heard her words echoing in my mind and got confused, thinking it was my own internal strength.

Whatever it was, I didn't care. They brought me back to her, and I'd selfishly take it.

"I love you, too," I whispered, ducking to kiss her.

Her hands tightened behind my neck, digging into my hair, and Mila pressed onto her toes. I slipped my arms around her waist and lifted her off her feet, wanting her as close as possible so I could get lost in her cinnamon and vanilla taste.

Unfortunately, that meant neither of us heard the boots pounding down the path until someone cleared their throat, and a second voice cheered, "Look at little *Mila!*"

Fuck. I immediately set her down, my heart plummeting to my stomach.

Unfazed, Mila laughed and launched herself at who I could only assume was one of her brothers. His hair was sandier to her platinum, but he had the same lightly tanned skin and bright eyes that squinted as he met her laughter.

Catching her, he whispered, "Hey, little warrior."

"Not just warrior," another voice said from behind these two as he approached, arms slung with woven grocery bags. "Our little sister is a *general*."

He stopped beside the others, squeezing Mila to him despite the armful.

"It's good to see you, Cor," Mila whispered, tears in her eyes.

"Good to see you, too, little general." Cor, the second oldest brother with dark brunette hair and pale blue eyes, kissed the top of Mila's head. He exchanged a grin with the one who'd hugged her first, who I thought was Levi. The youngest of her older siblings, save the one whom they lost in the first war.

But it was the third brother—the one who hadn't spoken beyond clearing his throat—that I stepped up to, holding out my hand. "Malakai Blastwood."

This was Brennan. It had to be based on the platinum hair identical to his sister's and the firm, judgmental set of his features. The oldest of the Lovall children and the one who—according to Mila—tended to be protective and hard to win over. He would be my biggest challenge of the day.

Greater even than her father, who apparently was a ferocious warrior but as soft as any in his retired age, or her mother, who Mila compared to a kitten. She'd be guarded at first, but doting once she trusted me.

Brennan, though. He was the one to crack.

He uncrossed his arms, gripping my hand tightly. Almost too tightly, but I didn't grimace. I returned the strength and held eye contact as the other three Lovalls studied us, curiosity bustling between them.

The air on the street seemed to still. Other families walked to and from the nearby market, calling hello to Mila at her return. This street was crowded with family residences—simple two-story homes with painted shutters and fences, flower and vegetable beds in yards littered with wooden swords and rope swings hanging from trees. A subtle breeze wound between the cypher branches dipping low on either side of the street, but even the rustling leaves hummed quieter than usual as Brennan assessed me.

Finally, he let go and nodded to his siblings. "Come on. Mother will need the groceries."

"Yes, sir," Cor joked with a mock solute.

Brennan marched ahead, ignoring him. Kissing my cheek, Mila whispered, "I'm going to go speak with him," and took off after her eldest brother.

As Levi followed, he shook my hand, clapping my shoulder welcomingly. "Don't worry about Bren. If he didn't kick you out already, he likes you."

"Or he'll at least tolerate you," Cor added.

"Better than the alternative." I supposed, though I was determined to get to more than just *tolerates you*. "Can I help with those?" I gestured to the bags Cor carried.

He handed me one, beaming. "I knew I had a good feeling about you."

"I mean it," Levi assured me. "If Brennan didn't approve, he would have already said it. He's a grumpy fucker, but he's a great judge of character."

As we crossed through the gate onto their quaint property, Cor nodded, adding, "He's extra protective of Mila since..."

Since they lost their youngest brother.

Mila had explained that after that loss, all of the Lovall children grieved in their own ways. She'd gone off with Lyria, and each of her brothers had their own stories in the past few years. None of them joined the recent Engrossian-Mystique battles. She hadn't even told them she had until it was nearly over. They would have joined out of obligation, and she swore if it wasn't solely their choice, she couldn't be responsible.

So damn admirable, my General.

"I get it," I said, following Cor and Levi up the steps. "And I wouldn't want anyone to be less protective of her. Spirits know, I am."

Levi and Cor both laughed, the latter saying, "Yeah, you'll be fine here."

The front porch was crowded with mismatched wicker furniture, the paint chipping along the railing making the place feel lived in. Twin doors stood in the entrance, dark, shining wood with clouded glass in the center of each.

Mila pushed them open, the rest of us trailing after. Brennan,

Levi, and Cor headed through the sitting room and into the hall beyond.

The walls of the foyer were lined with expertly painted portraits and a few classic renditions of landscapes, but the ones that caught my eye were of the family. Five children at every stage of their lives.

Mila as a toddler with eager, angular blue eyes and two braids adorned with bows.

Mila and all of her brothers as children in formal wear they looked less than pleased about.

Mila in a gown that hugged her waist, skirts pooling around her like a waterfall and her short swords strapped across her back. Both beautiful and strong.

"That one is from after I completed my Undertaking." She tilted her head, and I realized four other portraits lined the hall, one of each brother. "My mother painted them."

"She *painted* these?" I blurted.

Mila smiled fondly. "She's very talented."

"Did they have reservations about you and your brothers completing the Undertaking after Brennan since you weren't the oldest?"

"No." She shook her head. "Mother never attempted hers, and I think she always regretted that. So, they encouraged us to chase our dreams."

My own experience within the Volcano flashed through my memory, the scar on my chest aching. Though my ritual wasn't traditional, it had been empowering. Made me feel like I could conquer anything. Every warrior deserved that feeling.

I studied the portrait of Mila. The sharp set of her gaze. The way the moon overhead reflected perfectly in her eyes and illuminated her features. How her hair and skirt fanned out behind her as if on a breeze. The entire thing tightened my chest.

"I wouldn't discourage our children either," I muttered absently.

Mila leaned into my side, her arms tight around my waist. She didn't respond, but her answer was clear in the soft smile. In the way her eyes lined with silver. One day, we'd have that future. And we'd help them claim whatever they dreamed of.

"Who's that?" I asked, nodding to a portrait on the opposite wall above the mantle. It was clearly done by a less practiced hand but had the same lighting effects as Mila's. The woman had a square face and strong stature, but something about her seemed familiar.

Mila looked over her shoulder. "That's my great grandmother. She died before I was born, but she practically raised my mother. That was how she envisioned her after her Undertaking. It was the portrait that started the tradition actually."

I studied the woman's expression, the hair on my arms standing up. "How did she die?"

"Disease," Mila said, and as she went on, my stomach sank. "It was slow moving—not hereditary—but something that plagued her her entire life. It left her body scarred."

"What was her name?" I asked.

"Brenna. My oldest brother is named after her."

Brenna. It *was* her then. The Spirit from my Undertaking who died of illness, who encouraged me to carry on and work toward healing. Emotion clogged my throat as I looked at her and saw how similar she was to Mila. The long platinum braid and steely, angular blue eyes.

Had she known then that those words would push me to come back from the dead for her great-granddaughter? Had she somehow seen us here, months later, in the home of the woman she helped raise?

"Come on, Warrior Prince," Mila said, resting her head on my chest over where my Bind with Ophelia used to be. "Let's face our next adventure."

She pulled me through the sitting room, and as we left, I sent a silent *thank you* to her great-grandmother for giving me the tools to recognize I had the strength to return from the Spirit Volcano. For showing me I wasn't alone in my pain, even if everyone's looked different. For helping me be here today, where—assuming everything went well with her parents—I was going to ask Mila to receive the Bind with me.

And though I longed for quiet, a part of me hoped Mila and I never stopped having these small adventures. That she never lost the warrior heart that shone through the Undertaking portrait her mother had captured, even if our battles were the mundane, daily ones rather than the realm-altering.

As long as it was the two of us facing them together. For every damn tomorrow.

EPILOGUE
OPHELIA

Eight More Months Later

"ARE YOU SURE?" I ASKED FOR THE HUNDREDTH TIME. My heart was pattering in my chest, knees a bit weak at the idea that he may say no this time.

Tolek stopped walking so suddenly, I slammed into his back. Before I could even say sorry, he spun. His hand slipped from where it held mine, thumb tipping my chin up and fingers curving around the back of my neck. He kissed me, and though he'd been doing so for well over a year now, every time was like the first.

My heart somehow sped even quicker, and if I'd thought my knees were weak before, I was wrong. Chills spread along the place where my wings met my back, and I leaned all my weight into him.

Too soon, Tolek pulled back, smiling only an inch away, panting just like I was. The amber specks in his eyes shone brighter than the fire of the Spirit Volcano.

"Does that convince you how certain I am, *apeagna*?" he asked, and if the kiss hadn't sealed it, that rough tone of his voice would have.

I swallowed, nodding because my voice was still lost somewhere in the feel of his lips against mine. In the way my entire body woke and hungered for him. That feeling never went away.

"Good," he said, kissing my forehead. "Now stop asking."

Needing to be sure, I finally found my voice. "But the first time—"

"The first time was different. I promise."

I searched those eyes I knew so well. There was no chance in the Spirit Realm they'd be that bright if he was lying. Tolek may have hidden parts of himself he was embarrassed about for years, but he never lied to me.

And I finally allowed myself to accept the enormity of what we were about to do. It soared through me, my stomach dropping like I was diving through the air on my own wings.

"Okay," I finally said, biting my lip to fight my grin. "Let's go."

He didn't wait another second, spinning back toward the Merchant Quarter of Damenal.

Warriors crowded the streets on the calm, spring morning, waving hello as we passed by. The sun shone down, warming the cobblestones and calling flowers to tilt their faces up. The scents of fresh pastries baking wound through the markets, hammers hit steel in the distance, and shop owners of every variety threw their windows wide to welcome the day.

You'd never be able to tell that only a year ago, a god had plagued these streets. That there had been constant, thick gray clouds shrouding the glory of the city atop the peeks. That he'd been terrorizing me, too.

Now, the city was revelrous and open. We hosted festivals on palace grounds and tournaments in the local arenas. I wasn't a prisoner in my own home, but a part of its beating heart once again, knowing warriors on every block by name.

I squeezed Tol's hand as he pushed open the parlor door, his answering smirk over his shoulder banishing the lingering taint of Echnid that still lifted its head from time to time.

He was haunted, too. The nightmares of what Thorn had done to him were less frequent but still present. The way he seemed to buzz with a hum of the power he'd wrenched from the still-banished Mindshaper during those final moments made him more restless than ever. Not to mention how the strength of the Blackfyre still thrummed through his sword.

But today, that smirk was real.

Nothing would ruin this. Not a dead god or a missing Angel.

We hadn't seen much of the Prime Warriors since we'd done away with Echnid. Most resided in their own territories, doing Spirits knew what. Damien allowed us to retain Damenal. He came by from time to time, and we had a temporary truce despite how they'd used me, but it seemed they were all processing their existences in their own ways. Damien needed solitude in his mountains.

I let the Angels handle that. It was their mess to clean up, and I was done being their toy.

I wanted to be here.

"Ophelia! Tolek!" Marxian, the tattoo artist, greeted us as he emerged from the back room of his shop.

"It's good to see you," I said, hugging him.

Tolek shook his hand. "The parlor looks great. Are the window displays new?"

"They are." Marxian nodded. "Our latest apprentice drew them herself. She's trying to bring in some younger clientele."

The burly warrior shrugged, but a fond smile hid beneath his dark beard. I glanced at the displays hanging behind the fresh glass window—replaced after the Battle of Damenal tore through the city. Two long scrolls dangled from the ceiling, each baring a number of tattoo designs.

Marxian had always operated on word of mouth, not caring much to decorate the space, but it added a nice touch. That, plus the mural now taking up one wall, depicting a vibrant phoenix and gryphon tangled artistically, along with what I thought might have been a dragon. I sure as Spirits hadn't woken one of *those*, though, so I assumed the artist worked off a myth.

"They look wonderful," I added. "She must be talented."

"She is," he agreed, crossing his arms. "So, what can I do for you two, this time?"

Marxian had inked our Band tattoos along with those of our friends months ago, before the parlor had been redecorated. We each had a string of peonies and delicate vines around our upper arm now, declaring our high rank among the Mystique Warriors.

I looked up at Tolek, his broad smile forcing one out of me.

"We're ready for the Bind," I stated.

Just saying the words had my wings fluttering and Angellight curling around the feathers. I fidgeted, rising up and down on my toes. Tolek laughed, bringing my hand to his lips. Where he kissed, my entire body heated.

"You're sure?" Marxian asked, brows raised. His eyes dropped to the North Star on my arm.

"We've waited a year," I reminded him, "to see if there were any lingering effects. But there haven't been."

The North Star Bind Malakai and I had received as teenagers was well and truly severed, the strands of our souls ripping apart in his death.

Marxian's gaze flitted skeptically to Tolek, and I knew he was thinking of when he'd inked the Bonds on the back of our necks nearly two years ago. Tol's had been incredibly painful for him, and it was part of the reason I put off the Bind, but his Band had been easier.

"We're positive," Tolek confirmed, no hint of doubt in his voice.

Marxian nodded, and even he smiled. "Then by all means, show me the design."

As he prepared his supplies, Marxian asked, "If you're receiving the Bind, will there also be an official ceremony? Vows and name changing and all that?"

"Sure will," Tolek said proudly, holding my stare. "Call me Tolek Vincienzo Alabath until the Spirit Realm takes me, Marxian."

My cheeks heated with the intention in his voice. Warrior couples and their children took the last name of the most prominent, powerful family in the pair.

And Tolek Vincienzo, the boy who had been so spurned by his father but reclaimed his name for him and his sister, wanted *my* name attached to his. To make something our own. To be mine, infinitely.

Tol settled on the table first. His tattoo was going to be larger than mine, starting on the inside of his forearm and winding both down around his wrist and hand, but also up around his arm and torso.

The tips of the gold wing tattoo he got in Xenovia gleamed beneath the mystlight, waking something predatory and anticipatory within me.

I held tightly to his other hand as Marxian worked with the imbued ink, but Tolek didn't so much as flinch. He just watched me with that heated gaze that scorched all the way to my toes.

When I laid on the table, discarding my loosely fitting top and listening to the steady hum of the needle, I studied the way the ink wove across Tol's skin. And as the very same dark pattern was etched into mine, as the magic that built a Bind sank into my flesh, I gasped.

Not from pain, but from *rightness*.

The magic stretched deeply into me, through blood and bones and spirit. It was familiar in the sense that this was now my fourth time receiving one of the Mystique tattoos, but it was—

"It's *more*," I whispered to Tolek as my eyes stung.

This was so much more. It wasn't just a feeling of magic seeping into my body, it was a sense of true belonging as our souls merged into one. Destined and inevitable. As this man who had always understood me, protected me and cherished me, became tethered to me in a way beyond this earthly plane.

Two halves of broken spirits becoming one, two lives unceasingly bonded.

Tolek nodded at me, squeezing my hand. "It's so much more," he said.

We stayed in that awed silence for the majority of the time that Marxian worked on me, and with each passing second, Tolek infiltrated my being more. His warmth spread across the new bond, his gentle nature and heated passion caressing it. A slight hint of teasing edged along the slip of soul until I was practically squirming, sending the adoration and desire right back to him.

By the time Marxian was done, my breathing was nearly ragged.

This was how it was supposed to feel? Perhaps the Bind was different for every pair that received it. Where my first had been one full of innocence and hope, this was a preordained, destined need I'd never before experienced.

It had me stumbling out the door, pressing my lips to Tolek's and whispering, "Take me home."

∾

WE BARELY MADE it back to our suite in the palace before we were ripping each other's clothes off. We left a trail through the foyer, his tunic and my leathers falling among the combinations of our favorite artworks we'd purchased in Damenal this past year.

On the way here, I'd healed both of our fresh tattoos with seraph magic so they wouldn't be tender to the touch, because I didn't want soft from Tolek now. Not with this desire raging between us.

As we spun into the bedchamber, his lips feverish on mine, I pulled at the buckles of his leathers. Tol ran his hand down my spine, hovering over the joint of my wings so I arched against him, my bare skin hot and sensitive.

"I want to see it," Tolek whispered as he kissed down my neck.

I moaned in answer, my head tipping back, but I sent a feeling of utter compliance down the bond.

Tol scooped me up, laying me back on our grand bed, the cream silk comforter cool beneath me. He held my wrists in one hand above my head and with his other, he traced the fresh black ink adorning my body.

He started at the end, where the delicate rope design trailed between my breasts, curving beneath one. I gasped at his touch, my back arching and core aching for him. With a combination of hunger and disbelief shining in his eyes, his fingers followed the pattern to my ribs, where the rope curved into a perfect infinity knot.

He studied it for a long, silent moment as if committing it to memory.

I'd chosen the spot because it was intimate. Somewhere others might see part of the tattoo, but where only Tolek saw it fully on display. Where he could trace it night after night as we laid in this very bed together for the centuries to come. Where he could leave kisses as he whispered all those salacious promises and words of adoration he loved so much.

We'd given so much of ourselves to Ambrisk, I wanted this piece to be for us.

And Tolek...he'd chosen his because it was somewhere he could see at any moment. That he could use to remember where he was and what grounded him when memories and nightmares pushed into his mind.

Tugging one wrist from his grip, I lifted his hand, tracing the way the infinity knot painted the inside of his forearm. The rope curled up around his bicep and shoulder, weaving between the scars that littered his torso. On this end, it stretched all the way to the scar on his thigh—the one he'd received on our way to the Undertaking, when he'd pushed me out of the way of an Engrossian ax.

And on the other end, the rope wrapped around his wrist and hand, trailing down over his pinky. I thought of the time we'd fallen asleep in a dark cave, pinkies entwined, and tears rushed to my eyes at the memory.

This was a tattoo to ground him, but it also decorated the scars of his commitment to me. It was woven through *our* story.

Tolek linked his fingers through mine and ducked his head to kiss first the knot on my ribs, then along the rope until he stopped between my breasts. His eyes lifted to mine, and he whispered, "Infinitely."

"Infinitely," I repeated, cupping his cheek and pulling him up to me.

And it only took a moment of lips against lips, of his tongue pushing into my mouth, for both of us to become desperate. He was already hard against my center, my legs hitched tightly around his waist, and I ground against him, seeking relief.

"I need you," he groaned the words straight from my head.

"Please," I begged, even that one word cracking. I was so ready for him from just the wait.

The soul bond between us was strung tight, pulling on either end as we discarded the rest of our clothes. As he lined himself up with my entrance and hovered above me. As he slowly sank into me and never broke eye contact for a moment.

"Spirits, *apeanga*," he groaned as he pushed all the way in. "I didn't think it was possible for you to feel any better around my cock, but somehow you do now."

His hand gripped my ribs, just below the Bind, and I realized that at the angle they were inked, when he held me like that, where my tattoo ended, Tolek's began. One unbreakable bond. At the thought, I urged him on faster.

"I can feel you deeper than before," I gasped out. And I knew he understood from the way his hips jerked against me. It wasn't just physically deeper—it was in our souls.

As he pulled his hips back and snapped forward again, Tolek's insatiable hunger poured down the bond, a golden rope glimmering between us in my mind. I could practically hear the words of love and adoration chanting through his mind. That he didn't know how he got here, but he'd never do anything to let me go.

I sent a wave of appreciation back as I leaned up to kiss him, pressing as close as possible because Angels I couldn't get enough. Skin on skin, heartbeat against heartbeat.

Gratitude flooded down the bond. That he had always been my moonlight on a dark night, that he had fought unquestioningly by my side against Angels and curses and gods, that we had *survived*.

He clearly felt that word because he groaned, and a burst of anger shot down the bond, tempered by desperation. He paused, flipping us over so he was sitting on the bed, and I was straddling him. Gripping my waist, he slammed me down on his length, and I cried out.

Swiveling my hips, I dragged my nails across the Bind on his arm, the ink so fresh and dark. Then, I traced the tips of the gold feathers at his shoulders.

Mine.

Tol's lips closed around my breast as he rocked me forward so my clit ground against him, and I moaned his name, hands diving into his hair.

His teeth scraped across my nipple, and he slipped one hand around my back. I arched into him before the touch even came, in pure anticipation. But when he dragged a finger down the joint where my wing met my skin and pressed down, I fell apart.

I clenched tightly around him, and he exploded into me. And as we crashed apart, something in the Bind sparked to life. An acceptance and a belonging. A safety and cherishing that ignited that gold rope that was the tethered slips of our souls.

Love tunneled between them. Love and promises and desire, all with Tolek's dizzying charm and playful lust stamped upon them, just as it was on my spirit.

"I love you so much," I whispered as I came down.

"Infinitely, *apeagna*," he agreed, stroking a thumb absently across my Bind.

And I grinned against his shoulder. He was infinitely mine. And we had survived.

~

"*APEAGNA*," Tolek whispered in my ear as I dozed against his chest.

I groaned in response. My body was so heavy, sated. I couldn't wake up now. Not unless he wanted to get very clever about how he did so.

Tol laughed, and I had a feeling I'd unintentionally sent that thought right down our Bind. "I promise to wake you in a much more pleasurable way tomorrow," he said, kissing me softly. "But I have a surprise for you."

"What surprise?" I mumbled. My wings dragged against the comforter behind me as I leaned further into him. Based on the sun warming my feathers, it was still afternoon. I'd probably only been asleep for an hour or so.

"Come on," Tolek said, jostling me as he climbed off the bed, taking my favorite pillow—his chest—with him.

I squinted, catching him as he tugged on a pair of leathers. Sleeveless, they left his new Bind on display. The tips of the golden wing tattoo were visible around his shoulder, and something inside of me purred when I saw the two together. He laughed, striding to the dressing chamber to pull out clothes for me as well.

As I sat up, I took in the light slanting across the overflowing bookshelf. Full of Tol's favorite volumes, we'd move it in here a year ago now. The space had transformed not only into mine, but into both of ours. His clothes hung beside mine in the dressing chamber, his belongings lined shelves in the office, his journal—which made my heart ache every time I remembered reading his poems and letters—sat atop one of the bedside tables. He wrote me one of those letters every day now, and I tucked them all away in the top drawer of my nightstand.

Every inch of the palace was a home.

The insistent, eager smile Tol flashed me as he returned had the lingering sleep clearing, and I rose to dress and followed him.

"WHAT ARE we doing in the training arena?" I asked as we strolled down the open-air walkway the led to the stairs descending into the dirt training circuit on palace grounds.

"It's been exactly a year," Tol stated, and I froze. "I know you haven't wanted to speak about it."

I stopped walking, swallowing. "It still hasn't felt real."

Even exactly a year after we defeated the Warrior God—to the day—it hadn't felt real. I jolted out of bed this morning with my heart racing and repeated my mantra.

My body is my own.

My mind is my own.

Then, I'd insisted we received the Bind today. I had my reservations on the way there—worried Tolek would be in pain and that he was only agreeing because he could tell I needed it—but I'd wanted to make today about something other than Echnid's memory.

I'd wanted to stake a claim on our lives that shrouded what he'd done to us.

"It is real, *apeagna*." Tolek took a step closer so I had to look up to speak to him. "It's real and we deserve to remember that. Thinking of it won't bring him back to life."

How he knew that was my exact fear despite the fact that I hadn't dared speak it never failed to amaze me. Tolek never failed to amaze me.

I was about to say that when noise drifted up from the circuit. Not just noise. Bickering.

"What is that?" I asked, brows creased.

Tolek smirked. "Go look."

He stepped aside so I could take the lead on the last few steps. And when I stopped, looking down into the arena below, my jaw dropped.

"What are you all doing here?" I shouted, flying down the stairs.

I collided with my sister first, where she antagonized Cypherion and Malakai. She was now one of the Masters of Communications on my council, responsible for nurturing relations between clans, primarily our Soulguider contact.

Jezebel and Erista were supposed to be on a mission to Xenovia, aiding our allies in the ongoing restoration, but now, they both grinned at me. I held Jez tightly to chase away the memories of one year ago when I thought I wouldn't ever hold her again.

I hugged each of the boys next, letting their familiar presences chip away further at those fears and make me feel whole. Vale, Erista, and Mila, too. And finally—

"Rina!" I screeched, jumping on her. "I thought you wouldn't return for another month."

As I pulled back, she shrugged one shoulder and exchanged a look with Tolek. "We lied."

"How was Vercuella?" I burst, gripping her hands. She and Lancaster had been traveling the fae continent for the past five months. When they were on Gallantia, they stayed in Damenal with us, but they'd left to take some time to honor his sister's memory and learn more about an *aquealis* bond between a human and a fae.

"I'll tell you all about it over dinner tonight," Rina said, squeezing my hands. There was a healthy glow to her skin, and I was sure part of it was due to the male who stood over her shoulder dressed in all black.

Spirits, I even hugged him, giving him a nod that said I understood he was still mourning his sister, but I wouldn't make him speak of it.

"Truly, what are all of you doing here?" I repeated, turning to where Tolek was showing Cypherion and Malakai the new tattoo.

"We thought we should all be together today," Malakai said. Malakai, who one year ago today, had *died* for us all to stand here. Chills spread over my skin at the reminder, but a warm nudge came down the new Bind from Tolek, and I flushed.

"How's Cub's?" I asked Malakai.

He smiled fondly. "Thriving."

And that one word, paired with the softly content smile he gave me as he wrapped his arm around Mila and rested his chin on her head told me everything I needed to know.

They'd reopened the tavern back in Palerman with Rina's blessing. They were even talking about opening a second near Mila's parents' home in the north so they could travel between the two. In the past year, they'd barely been in Damenal, and although Tolek and I hated that—and flew to see them as often as we could —it had seemed like a necessary escape for Malakai.

"Good." I grinned at him, so fucking grateful that the stars hadn't stopped shining a year ago. "And Cyph? I thought you guys were in Starsearcher Territory."

While he and Vale primarily resided in Damenal since he was my Second—and they had their own grand house on the outskirts of the city—Cyren requested them in Valyn every so often to assist with magical coordination, since Vale was still the Fatecatcher. With Dynaxtar, the trips were quick, but they'd only left two days ago.

"It wasn't a long meeting." Cypherion shrugged.

"How long are you back for?"

Cyph looked to Vale, and she answered, "We'll be going back and forth between here and Valyn for a month or two while they finalize their candidates for chancellor. Cyren asked for my opinion. But once that's done, we shouldn't be needed in the capital except for extraordinary circumstances."

"Short trips might still be made," Cyph rushed to add, but from the look he gave Vale and the way her cheeks flushed in response, I had a feeling he wasn't referring to official business requirements.

I sighed mockingly. "I supposed I can approve of that as Revered."

"Happy to negotiate it," Cyph said confidently. Something had changed within him during the last battle against Echnid. Ever since then, he seemed to understand just how perfect he was as my Second. As the rest of us had known all along.

Cypherion watched his Fatesworn adoringly, and as Vale laughed at something Mila said, she seemed freer than ever. Happier.

Spirits, I was so happy for all of them. For us. For these lives we'd fought to build, and these loves we once thought we'd never save.

"Barrett, Dax, and Celissia were meant to come, too, but they got held up with their work with the orphanage," Malakai explained. "Barrett said to tell everyone that whatever bets Tolek wins during the reunion, he wants to play for double at Daminius this year."

I laughed, lighter with every word from my friends' lips. The Engrossian King had taken it upon himself to make caring for local orphans a priority of his reign. I had a feeling it was because he was dreaming of the day he and Dax would bring one of those children home themselves. Or a horde of them.

The general's scar from Kakias hadn't once plagued him since Echnid died. We weren't sure if Bant did something to dull the magic or if the god's death had siphoned it off, but he was healed, the pair enjoying their work with the children.

As if summoned by the thought of young warriors, three tiny forms raced into the yard, dressed for training with their tutors on their heels. Although, they weren't as tiny as they'd once been, especially the boys. Tolek's siblings were now nearly teenagers and had the attitudes for it.

After Echnid, Tolek and I had visited his father. It took every ounce of his self-control to not turn it into an argument. I had a feeling only Lyria's memory stopped him. Instead, he'd pitched the idea of bringing the triplets to Damenal with us to prepare them for future positions in government or armies.

We wouldn't force that on them, but Tol's dad didn't have to know that. Now, the three of them each had a grand suite in the west wing of the palace and the best schooling and training available in the city.

As I watched their innocent and carefree spirits soar, Tolek's arms wrapped around me, my head falling back against his chest. Sapphire, Zanox, and Dynaxtar soared overhead, the latter frolicking in circles among the clouds and drawing a loving smile from Vale.

And for a moment, with everyone here, I truly banished the fear of Echnid's memory.

"What do you say, sister?" Jezebel asked, breaking me from the reverie. She picked up a pair of spears and tossed one to me. It landed in my palm like it was made for me. "Care to spar?"

"You know," I said thoughtfully as I tested my grip, "I never used to like spears."

Tolek chuckled as he stepped back, allowing me and my sister the floor. "How do you feel about them now?" he asked.

My heart panged for the spear I'd lost, but I didn't want that one back. Angelborn had been a part of my past, but I had become so much more. And as I set my stance with this scratched training spear and my friends bickered behind me, a sense of fulfillment flowed through me.

"They're not so bad," I said, but in my other hand, I summoned a sword of pure gold seraph magic.

"Good," Jezebel agreed with her most mischievous grin. Silver-blue magic sparked along her weapon. "On your count then."

And just as we had all our lives—but now with both warrior steel and the magic of myths—my sister and I danced circles around a dusty training circuit, sparring with our friends antagonizing us and the power of the Gallantian Warriors beating through our hearts.

As it would for centuries to come.

THE END

~

Thank you so much for reading *The Legacy of Ophelia*. If you're so inclined, please consider leaving a review on Goodreads, Amazon, your favorite retailers, or social media.

~

Not ready to leave these characters yet? Scan below or click here for a bonus Santorina and Lancaster epilogue of their time on Vercuella!

~

Want to keep up with what's next from Nicole, including bonus chapters and first looks? Subscribe to the Gallantia Gazette today!

We aren't done in this realm yet. Coming 2026, a brand new **dark Romantasy series** set in the same world as the Curse of Ophelia!

Follow a brand new cast of characters in a tale of star-crossed and prophesied love, murder and mystery, and even more dangerous legends in **The Fatesworn Saga**.

Add book one on Goodreads now (expected Spring 2026) and subscribe to Nicole's newsletter to be sure you don't miss any announcements.

ACKNOWLEDGMENTS

Honestly, I've been procrastinating on writing these acknowledgements for quite a while. I don't know how you sum up an entire series, over 800,000 words, years of hard work, and all of the gratitude I feel in just a few paragraphs. I'm going to do my best, but know that whatever I say will never do it justice.

First, to my family. None of this would be possible without your support. I am so lucky to have parents and a brother who didn't blink twice when I said I wanted to pursue writing. Not only that, but you have all gone above and beyond to help out on the days I'm drowning, to listen to my endless ideas even though I'm a broken record, and to lighten the load whenever you can. Being an indie author is so hard, and so much of the work is done alone, but it's a little easier thanks to your eager help.

To my friends, the DDs, who are always there when I need you–thank you. You guys never fail to cheer me up when I'm extra stressed or celebrate the wins with me, even though this industry is so foreign to you. I have a tendency to downplay the hard days, but I couldn't get through them without you.

To the phenomenal editing team that shaped these books into what they are: Kelley, Friel, and Kay. I am so lucky to have editors who are so passionate about this series and who truly understand the characters and their story. Thank you from the bottom of my heart. And thank you to my agent, Ezra, and the EELA team for supporting my career and this series so fiercely. To Fran, my talented cover designer, who gave this series the most perfect, unique, and showstopping covers, and Meri for the unreal hardcover editions.

To the many authors I have been lucky to call friends, thank you for making this career more fun. To L.B. Divine, for being here since day one when I first started drafting The Curse of Ophelia. You have always been the biggest believer in this series–and of course the president of Tolek's Fan Club since 2021. And to Olivia Rose Darling, I am so grateful for your unwavering support and friendship. It's always a highlight when I wake up to daily voice memos. One day we'll be sitting on your porch writing instead of Facetiming. There are so many more authors I could name, but we'd be here for a while. This community is one of the most special things about self publishing. If our paths have crossed, know that I am grateful.

To the phenomenal team of Alpha/Beta readers who gave feedback on this book: Katie, Chiara, Madi, Jessica, Max, and Kaitlyn. Some of you have been here from the very start, and it's crazy to think about how much we've all been through over the years. I can confidently say this series wouldn't be what it was without your insight. Thank you so much for giving your time and minds to help.

To the many talented artists who have brought my characters to life, thank you so much for all the hard work you do. To my street team, Nicole's Angels, thank you for all of the excitement you've shown this series. It keeps me going more than you know. To the readers, bloggers, bookstagrammers, booktokers, and so many more, thank you.

To Ophelia. For walking into my head all those years ago with your friends and never leaving. For being my first published baby and taking on this journey with me. For letting me tell your story, I only hope I did it justice. I may write other books, but this series will always be beyond special to me.

Lastly, to you. Thank you for reading this and allowing me to chase this crazy dream. This isn't the end, warriors. We have plenty more stories to tell in Gallantia and other realms. I hope you found what you were searching for in these pages and know you always have a home to return to here. I'll see you back on Ambrisk in 2026 for The Fatesworn Saga.

Until then...Infinitely yours until the stars stop shining,
Nicole

Photo by Polich Company

Nicole Platania was born and raised in Los Angeles and completed her B.A. in Communications at the University of California, Santa Barbara. After two years of working in social media marketing, she traded Santa Barbara beaches for the rainy magic of London, where she completed her Masters in Creative Writing at Birkbeck, University of London. Nicole harbors a love for broken and twisty characters, stories that feel like puzzles, and all things romance. She can always be found with a cup of coffee or glass of wine in hand, ready to discuss everything from celebrity gossip to your latest book theories.

Connect with her on Instagram and TikTok as @bynicoleplatania or on www.nicoleplatania.com.